THE
ICE
MONSTER

selected places to visit are arranged in alphabetical
and French are the official languages used in Canada.
shown in the form normally used locally; the English
in those regions where English is the main language,
pellings in the French-speaking areas.

H 6

ish Columbia. Population: 106,000

hamber of Commerce, 2462 McCallum Rd, Abbotsford, BC
(604) 8599651.

nd Clearbrook, two parishes which have grown together
mber over 100,000 inhabitants, lie in the shadow of the
80 ft) high Mount Baker which forms part of the Cascade
ountains south of the state border. These two towns
tre of the Fraser Valley, where the mild climate has led to
ent as an agricultural region, which, for example, pro-
han 80 per cent of Canada's raspberry crop.

nt of the year is the Abbotsford Berry Festival held every
l as fields of fruit bushes and narcissi – the latter being a
sight in spring – large chicken farms also dominate the
me 80 per cent of British Columbia's eggs are produced in
very August the Abbotsford International Air Show, one of
f its kind in North America, is held here.

i-Sumas-Abbotsford Museum, housed in Tretheway
Ware St., which was built in 1919 and has recently been
ored, is rather out of the ordinary and offers the oppor-
dy exhibits of items used by the Red Indians who orig-
ited the country as well as memorabilia from the
eriod. Particularly interesting are the documents about
, which was drained in 1924, thus producing 12,140 ha
s) of fertile grazing and farmland which lie almost one
sea-level and are protected by means of a dyke from the
flooded by the Fraser River. Open Mon.–Sat. 10am–noon,

m of the Mennonite Historical Society of British Columbia
d in the Clearbrook Community Centre at 2825 Clearbrook
vides information about the history and life-style of the
in British Columbia. Open Mon.–Fri. 9am–4.30pm, Sat.

H 17/18

New Brunswick, Nova Scotia, Prince Edward Island,

rmation offices in the above provinces.

outh-east of the Lower St Lawrence River and on the Bay of
called New France, are now known as "Acadia". Many sec-
land which has been developed by man over the centuries now

er skyline

One of the more unusual railway experiences is provided by the 300 km
(186 mi.) journey on the Ontario Northland Railway from Cochrane to
Moosonee, a historic fur-trading station on James Bay (on the Hudson
Bay). Quite apart from the rugged, bog-ridden landscape, the passengers on the "Polar Bear Express" – Indians, trappers and adventurers –
are an experience in themselves.

Ontario Northland Railway, Polar Bear Express

From Skagway (Alaska), at the northern end of the Inside Passage, a
narrow-gauge railway climbs a historic stretch to White Pass and the
station at Fraser, the small town at the north-western extremity of British
Columbia. From here a bus can be taken to Whitehorse, capital of the
Yukon Territory.

White Pass & Yukon Railway

Railway enthusiasts can enjoy a wide range of journeys by steam. In
addition to the "Royal Hudson" (North Vancouver–Howe Sound–
Squamish; see above), steam trains operate in Calgary (Heritage Park),
Edmonton (Fort Edmonton), Winnipeg (Prairie Dog), Ottawa (Gatineau
Park) and around Stettler (Alberta).

Museum trains

The passenger services operated by VIA Rail and other rail companies
are restricted to more or less profitable routes. However buses extend
access to the hinterland from nearly all stations of any size. Bus timetables are co-ordinated with train arrival and departure times.

Bus–rail combinations

Coach Tours

Canada can be explored relatively inexpensively by coach. Many
companies offer packages, anything from short breaks of just a few days
to extended trips lasting several weeks. In addition so-called Inter City
Buses operate between Canada's main centres, allowing transcontinental travel in either direction (Inter City Bus departure points are usually
conveniently situated in city and town centres).
    Canadian coaches are generally comfortable, with air-conditioning
and onboard toilets. There is often more leg room than is usual on
European coaches.

Greyhound Canada offers the greatest range of services between
Ontario and the Canadian West, with offices in all the larger towns.
Other companies operate province to province or region to region.

Ontario–Western Canada

The Calgary area and the Rocky Mountain National Parks most popular
with tourists (Banff National Park, Jasper National Park, Yoho National
Park) are well served by coaches owned by the "Brewster" company.

Rocky Mountains

"Voyageur" coaches operate on all major routes in the adjacent
provinces of Ontario and Québec.

Ontario–Québec

"SMT Eastern" buses provide services in the provinces of New
Brunswick and Prince Edward Island. Acadian Lines serves Nova Scotia.

Atlantic Canada

Advice
The followir
order. Englis
Each place
name is use
and French

Abbotsford · **Clearbrook**

Province: Br

Information
Abbotsford
V2S 3P9; tel.

Location
Abbotsford
and now nu
3285 m (10,
Range of r
form the ce
its develop
duces more

Events
The high po
June. As we
magnificent
landscape; s
this region.
the largest

Matsqui-Sumas-
Museum
The Matsc
House, 231
lovingly re
tunity to s
inally inha
pioneering
Sumas Lak
(30,000 acr
metre belo
risk of bein
1pm–4pm.

Mennonite
Historical
Society Museum
The Museu
will be fou
Road. It pr
Mennonites
9am–noon.

Acadia

Provinces:
Québec

Information
Tourist info

Location
The areas
Fundy, onc
tions of thi

◀ Vancou

belong to the Canadian Atlantic Provinces of New Brunswick, Nova Scotia and Prince Edward Island – in some parts of which old French is still spoken – and to the French-speaking province of Québec and the US state of Maine.

In 1604 Samuel de Champlain (see Famous People) and his companions landed on Docher's Island, now Maine in the United States. They founded a colony here, which was moved the following year to a sheltered bay on the eastern side of the Bay of Fundy (now Annapolis in Nova Scotia). The new colony was named Port Royal.

This new, rapidly developing French colony was attacked as early as 1613 by British troops, and subsequently ownership alternated between France and England. In 1632 it was returned to France and remained so for some time. Civil war-like conditions provided the opportunity for the British to take it over again between 1654 and 1667. Under the Treaty of Breda Acadia was returned to France. In 1710 British and Scottish troops seized Port Royal and renamed it Annapolis, after the Scottish Queen Anne Stuart.

Under the Treaty of Utrecht in 1713 the larger part of Nova Scotia was ceded to England, while Cape Breton Island, New Brunswick and Prince Edward Island remained French. Shortly before the outbreak of the Seven Years' War the 10,000 or so French settlers were deported from Acadia by the English governor and scattered in small groups in other British possessions. Some made a new home for themselves in Louisiana or in the West Indies. Finally, under the terms of the Treaty of Paris in 1763, the whole of Canada came under the rule of the British monarchy.

The French-speaking descendants of the Acadian settlers are now scattered in pockets in Canada. Some still live in the Edmundston area and along the middle course of the St John River, as well as along the boundary with the USA, with many others scattered along the Atlantic coast between Moncton (see entry) and the Baie des Chaleurs and the Gaspésie (see entry). Small settlements are also to be found on the south-west coast of Cape Breton (see entry), on the Île Madame, near Chéticamp on the north-west coast of Nova Scotia, in the west of Prince Edward Island and on the Îles de la Madeleine.

Cajun music combines elements of American "hillbilly" and square dance tempos with music introduced by settlers from Normandy and Brittany. This music has become very popular in Canada and is now spreading to Europe as well. The main instruments used are the accordion and violin with suitable song accompaniment.

Cajun music is basically French-American folk-music which originated in Louisiana in the early 19th c. "Cajuns" is the name given to those French-Canadians who, after 1775, left their homeland of Acadia (the present Canadian provinces of Nova Scotia and New Brunswick) and moved to Louisiana.

Originally cajun music was purely French folk-music, but it has absorbed an increasing number of English and West African elements and is now strongly influenced by "blues" music from the southern states of the USA. For a long time the fiddle was the dominant instrument, but the accordion and triangle now play an increasingly important role. Modern cajun bands, influenced by commercial country and western trends, often add electric guitars and percussion instruments.

The first records were made in 1928, when the accordionist Joe Falcon played "Allons à Lafayette". With that title he paid tribute to one of the most important centres of cajun music in Louisiana, the town of Lafayette. Cajun music spread further afield mainly through the influence of Clifton Chenier (1925–87) who, in the opinion of the musical magazine "Rolling Stone", was the best Acadian accordionist in the world. At the end of the 1970s Chenier and his "Red Hot Louisiana Band" went to Europe and played at the Montreux Festival.

Elements of cajun music can be found today mainly in the mainstream country and western style.

★★Alaska Highway   E/F 1–6

Location

The Alaska Highway (Alaska–Canada Military Highway; Alcan), 2430 km (1500 mi.) long, is the main route from Dawson Creek in British Columbia through the Yukon Territory to Fairbanks in Alaska. The following distances are measured from the starting point at Dawson Creek.

Fort Nelson: 480 km (298 mi.)
Watson Lake: 1015 km (630 mi.)
Whitehorse: 1473 km (915 mi.)
Fairbanks: 2444 km (1515 mi.)

Although the highway is open to traffic all the year round, there is always the possibility, especially in the Canadian section, that weather conditions such as melting snow in spring and heavy rainfall in summer can lead to some stretches being blocked.

The speed limit is 80 kph (50 mph), and higher speeds are definitely not recommended. Filling stations will be found at regular intervals along the road, and they can also carry out running repairs. Also along the whole length, but particularly on the section between Watson Lake and Whitehorse, motels, service areas and camp-sites can be found close to the highway.

Importance

The main reason for building the Alaska Highway was the Japanese occupation of the Aleutian Islands off the coast of Alaska during the Second World War in 1941. In a record time of eight months between March and October 1942, equivalent to 10 km (6 mi.) a day, Canadian and American soldiers constructed a marked-out route in the extreme north of the states which provided safe transport for troops and provisions to Alaska, which until then had been almost unprotected in a military sense. Originally built solely to meet military needs, after the end of the war the Alaska Highway was opened to civilian traffic and since then has become the major access road and tourist route into the Yukon Territory and southern Alaska.

★★Suggested route

Dawson Creek

The Alaska Highway begins in the town of Dawson Creek, in the fertile corn-growing plain of Peace River (see entry), on the border with Alberta. Beyond Fort Nelson some 500 km (310 mi.) to the north the road approaches the Rocky Mountains. There are two notable nature parks along this stretch, Stone Mountain and Muncho Lake Provincial Park.

Watson Lake

The first community of any size in the Yukon Territory is Watson Lake, also known as the "Gateway to the Yukon", with some 1200 inhabitants. Founded in the 1890s, it developed into an economic and cultural centre during the building of the Alaska Highway, when up to 25,000 troops were stationed here. The newly-established information centre will provide the visitor with background information on the construction of this giant highway. The most famous landmarks in Watson Lake, the Watson Lake Signposts, are linked to the building of the road; following the example set by a homesick building worker, thousands of tourists have erected signs at the junction of the highway and Campbell Highway (see entry) showing the name of and distance to their own home town, producing a veritable "forest of signs" over the years.

Teslin Lake

For some miles between Watson Lake and Whitehorse the Alaska Highway hugs Teslin Lake which, although 125 km (78 mi.) long, is only some 3 km (2 mi.) wide on average. From the road there are magnificent views to be had of this uniquely-shaped lake and also of the heights of the Yukon Plateau (see Yukon Territory). In the George Johnston Museum in Teslin can be seen exhibits illustrating the period of the gold-diggers and the way of life and culture of the native Indians.

From Jakes Corner it is worthwhile branching off southward for some 100 km (60 mi.) to Atlin. This little township, a settlement dating from the time of the gold-rush, is charmingly situated on the shore of Lake Atlin. Between Jakes Corner and Whitehorse (see entry), the capital of the Yukon Territory, the highway stays parallel for some 15 km (9½ mi.) to Marsh Lake, with its shimmering turquoise waters framed by mountains beyond. Because of its proximity to Whitehorse larger crowds must be expected here than at other lakeside areas.

Haines Junction

Beyond Whitehorse the Alaska Highway turns westward towards the coastal range of the St Elias Mountains. Passing the little township of Haines Junction the road leads to Kluane National Park (see entry) in the western corner of the Yukon – a unique nature conservation area with Canada's highest peak, Mount Logan (5951 m (20,130 ft)), which should definitely be on the itinerary.

In Haines Junction will be found the National Park Visitors Center, which provides an informative multi-media show about the park. There is excellent fishing to be had at Kluane Lake, some 60 km (37 mi.) north of Haines Junction.

Beaver Creek

This little place, with about 100 inhabitants, was founded as a supply station when the highway was being built, and can claim to be the most westerly settlement in Canada; it has a few motels with bars and cafés.

A few miles beyond Beaver Creek, and about 1950 km (1210 mi.) after starting out from Dawson Creek, we leave Canadian territory. It is a further 500 km (300 mi.) or so to Fairbanks in Alaska.

Alberta   F–H 7/8

Geographical location: latitude 49°–60° north/longitude 110°–120° west
Area: 661,200 sq. km (255,290 sq. mi.)
Population: 2,850,000. Capital: Edmonton

Information

Travel Alberta, PO Box 2500, Edmonton, AB T5J 2Z4; tel. (403) 4274321, fax. (403) 4270867.

Alberta covers 6.6 per cent of Canada's total area, and is its fourth largest province. The longest distance north–south is an impressive 1206 km (750 mi.) at longitude 114° west, while the maximun east–west is 660 km (410 mi.) at latitude 55° north. The longitudinal and latitudinal borders are parallel, except in the Rocky Mountains where it follows the line of the watershed. Manitoba, Saskatchewan and Alberta together form what are known as the Prairie States of Canada, over 70 per cent of the total area being taken up by the Alberta Plain, a high-lying prairie mainly between 900 and 1000 m (2950 and 3300 ft) above sea-level. 570 million years ago this entire region formed part of a giant inland lake. 70 million years ago the folding of the Rockies began to take place in the west (see British Columbia) and on the main ridge, Mount Columbia at 3747 m (12,300 ft) being the highest mountain in Alberta. The prairies now consist largely of material released and deposited during the period of the structural deformation of the Rockies, with rich black and brown soil predominating, ideal for agriculture. Alberta can be divided into three sections: South Alberta, covering the southern third of the province and with a slightly hilly prairie landscape, the "rolling prairies"; the "parklands" of Central Alberta, with their wide valleys and mountain-chains, numerous rivers and lakes, and crisscrossed with forests; and Northern Alberta, covering almost a half of the whole, characterised by large areas of coniferous forest divided up by the Peace and Athabasca Rivers. Less than three percent of the total area is taken up by lakes and waterways, a relatively small amount compared to nearly nineteen per cent in Manitoba. The largest areas of water are Little Slave Lake (1150 sq. km (444 sq. mi.)) and Peace River (1916 km (1190 mi.)).

◀ *Alaska Highway: milepost "0"*

Alberta

© Baedeker

As the Rocky Mountains follow the meridian and consequently the western edge of the mountain ridge is protected from rain, Alberta by and large enjoys a continental climate. Where the mountains afford protection from wind and rain the average annual precipitation is only 400–500 mm (16–20 in). The lack of an east–west mountain barrier results in an interchange of Arctic and tropical air masses. This means that in winter dry polar air pushes far into southern Alberta, while in summer tropical air masses can result in heavy falls of rain. On the prairies this results in hot summers with frequent thunder storms and winters with little snow but low temperatures. Even as late as April the average minimum in Alberta is below freezing point, and there are signs of impending winter in October. As an example, Lethbridge in the south of the province enjoys an average maximum temperature in July of 26°C (79°F) and over ten hours sunshine each day. A unique feature of Alberta is the "chinook", a warm dry wind coming from the Rocky Mountains, which frequently brings about an early thaw in the south.

Climate

The dominant natural vegetation in the north of Alberta is coniferous forest, which becomes tundra especially in the higher regions bordering the Northwest Territories. In the north conifers such as spruce and larch predominate, while towards the south deciduous trees including beech, birch and maple come more into their own. In the south-east flourishes a form of natural grassland, so that the "short grass prairie" of the north becomes the "long grass prairie" of the south.

Vegetation

There is evidence of human settlement in Alberta going back more than 11,000 years. Cypress Hills, protected from the ravages of the Ice Age, were inhabited by aboriginals for over 7000 years. Present-day Alberta was entrusted to the Hudson's Bay Company after it was founded in 1670, with trade being mainly in furs. In 1754 Anthony Henday was the first white man to explore as far as the Rocky Mountains. Between 1792 and 1801 Peter Fidler pushed far south into Alberta and discovered rich coal deposits by the Red Deer River. In the south missionaries founded

History

schools and churches and made the first contacts with the Indians. Trading posts – such as that at Peter Pond Lake on the Athabasa River – began to be set up in 1778, and Fort Edmonton was built as a fur-trading centre in 1795. In the Oregon Border Treaty of 1846 it was laid down that the 49th parallel should be the southern border with the United States. In 1870 the area between Manitoba and the Rockies came under the administrative aegis of the Northwest Territories. In 1880 Father Albert Lacomte helped to negotiate a treaty with the Blackfoot Indians, with whose assistance the Canadian Pacific Railway was able to undertake the construction of the Trans-Canada Railroad, which was completed in 1886. In that same year John "Kootenia" Brown was the first to discover oil, and sold it as lubricating oil for one dollar a gallon. The gold-rush started in 1890 and Edmonton became the chief meeting-place of the gold-diggers. The Province of Alberta was founded in 1905 and joined the Confederation of Canadian States on September 1st of that year. The province was named after the fourth daughter of Queen Victoria, Princess Louise Caroline Alberta, the wife of the Governor General of Canada from 1878–83.

Drought

During the period of the great drought between 1931 and 1934 there were signs of widespread erosion leading to increased farm failures and death of livestock. In 1962 the TransCanada Highway was built through Alberta, guaranteeing a quicker link between the Atlantic and Pacific coasts. In 1968 a start was made on exploiting the Athabasca Tar Sands near Fort McMurray.

Population

Alberta's 2,469,000 inhabitants represent 9·2 per cent of the whole Canadian population, and is equivalent to 3·7 persons per square kilometre or 9·6 per square mile. This compares with the appreciably lower population densities found in Manitoba (1·7 per sq. km (4·4 per sq. mi.)) and Saskatchewan (1·5 per sq. km (3·9 per sq. mi.)). The reason for this is to be found mainly in the influx of people following the discovery of crude oil in the 1960s. Some 77 per cent of Alberta's population live in the towns and cities, concentrated on four large conurbations, especially Calgary with 671,000 inhabitants and Edmonton with 785,000. From 1869 onwards most of Alberta's settlers were white, a trend which was fostered still further by the Law of Pioneer Settlement passed in 1875. The development of the province was further assisted by the building of the railroad network by the Canadian Pacific Railway after 1885. 44 per cent of the present population have British roots, followed by Germans with 14 per cent and East Europeans with 11 per cent; as a result it is not surprising that the main religion is Protestant. The largest groups of native inhabitants are to be found at Athabasca in the North and Algonkin in the south-east; both are prairie Indians who used to make a living mainly from hunting bison. Today such Indians live on the edge of society, mainly outside the larger towns. 4.4 per cent of Alberta's population is made up of native Indians, which means that 14.6 per cent of all Canada's Indian population live here. An insight into the Indian way of life can be gleaned from a visit to the Indian Collection at the Glenbow Museum in Calgary.

Mention should also be made of the fact that for years Alberta has had the highest divorce rate in Canada, and that Calgary is the city with the most divorces per 100,000 couples.

Economy

The province of Alberta contributes annually more than ten per cent to the Canadian gross domestic product, even though its population is only 9.2 per cent of the country's total. The two main branches of Alberta's economy are mining (19.3 per cent of Alberta's G.D.P.) and agriculture and farming (although representing only 3.8 per cent of the G.D.P.). 62 per cent of the land is covered in forests, with only ten per cent under the plough. The forests are mainly state-owned, being leased out to private firms. More than 9000 people are employed in forestry itself, with a further 20,000 in allied industries, and this branch of the economy contributes more than 900 million dollars per annum to the gross domestic product.

Gigantic excavators dig out the oil-bearing sand

Wheat is the most important crop grown in Alberta. The first large ranch in the West, Cochrane Ranch, was built in 1878, and many other farms and mills followed. The wheat crop is mainly summer wheat and it has been found possible to reduce the growing period to between 100 and 110 days, so that it can now be grown even further north than before. The size of the farms which average some 354 ha (874 acres), has resulted in a high degree of mechanisation. Although Alberta covers only 6·6 per cent of Canada's total land area nearly twenty per cent of the country's farms are to be found here. In recent years farmers have diversified and broken away from the tradition of growing only wheat; in particular they now grow more forage cereals to provide food for cattle. Whereas in 1926 56 per cent of farm income evolved from wheat, today 60 per cent is derived from cattle rearing. In the south-east, with the assistance of improved irrigation systems, 4000 sq. km (1550 sq. mi.) of new useable land has been opened up. The problems of agriculture, made public in particular in the "Dirty Thirties", are mainly those arising from soil erosion. Drought, pests and acid soil also play a major part.

In the field of mineral resources Alberta also plays an important role, as it is here that 70 per cent of the country's coal stocks, 80 per cent of its crude oil and 68 per cent of its natural gas are to be found, with only comparatively small amounts being used within the province itself. Coal deposits are estimated at 48,000,000,000 tonnes, with about five-sixths thereof under the plains and one-sixth in the Rocky Mountains. In Alberta coal is utilised mainly in the generation of electricity, 91·6 per cent of all electricity being produced with coal as the fuel. Damage to the environment is nevertheless relatively small, as the coal contains only small amounts of sulphur. The remaining electricity needs are met by means of giant hydro-electric power stations.

Crude oil has been extracted in Alberta since 1886, and has increased more and more in importance during the present century. Today there are 17,000 oil-wells in Alberta and a pipeline network stretching more than 100,000 km (63,000 mi.). While most of the oil-storage sites are in the south, giant deposits of oil in sand have been found in the north (Fort McMurray), estimated at about one-third of the total world supply. Because of the difficult processes involved in separating the oil from the sand it has only recently – since 1967 – been found viable to exploit these resources. All the processes cause some environmental problems since – as well as causing damage to the earth's surface – 22 tonnes of water are required to extract one tonne of crude oil. All Canadian oil companies now have their headquarters in Calgary.

Leisure, sport, tourism

Alberta offers ideal leisure facilities throughout the year. As regards winter sports, there are five well-equipped skiing areas available from November to May, with plenty of ski-runs in the south-west of the province. A lot of ice-hockey is also played in Alberta. In summer 59 provincial parks and five national parks are open – especially Jasper National Park, covering 10,878 sq. km (4200 sq. mi.), and Banff National Park, 6642 sq. km (2565 sq. mi.). Leisure pursuits range from trekking along well-maintained paths to water-sports and riding. Outside the parks there are ideal opportunities for hunting, especially in the north. As well as shooting water-fowl the hunting of large wild animals, including bear and elk, could well prove an attractive proposition. Those who prefer more leisurely pursuits may like to indulge in a little fishing. The towns of Edmonton and Calgary have some unique attractions for visitors. Every July since 1912 the "Stampede" has been held in Calgary, a sort of world championship in rodeo skills. The town's attractions have increased even further since the Winter Olympics were held here in 1988. Edmonton can boast, by way of example, the West Edmonton Mall, the world's largest shopping and leisure complex, where it is quite possible to spend hours or even days without becoming bored. However, tourists from Europe will no doubt wish to concentrate on the natural beauties to be found in the south-western corner of the province, and perhaps not concern themselves with Alberta's other attractions. The Tourist Offices to be found everywhere in Alberta will be more than happy to provide up-to-date information on all manner of sights and facilities.

★Algonquin Provincial Park   H 15

Province: Ontario
Area: 7600 sq. km (2935 sq. mi.). Founded: 1893

Information

Angonquin Provincial Park Visitor Information, PO Box 219, Whitney, ON K0J 2M0; tel. (705) 6335572.

Access

From Toronto (see entry), northwards on Highways 400 and 11 to Huntsville, then eastwards on Highway 60 into the Park.

Facilities

In Algonquin Provincial Park there are eight camping sites and numerous picnic areas. In addition there are three lodges for anglers and hunters as well as some outfitters.

Algonquin Provincial Park, the second largest of its kind in Canada, stretches to the south-east of North Bay (see entry) and south of the upper reaches of the Ottawa River. This forest area, studded with more than 2,400 lakes, gets its name from the Algonquin Indian tribe who lived here and indeed still do.

A start was made on developing this vast area in the 19th c., when it was extensively cultivated. From time to time there have been catastrophic forest fires, and since 1893 continuous attempts have been made to safeguard the threatened forests.

Forest

The subsoil of the park is of granite. The forest itself is a mixture of deciduous and coniferous trees, with spruce, Scots pine and maple predominating. It is especially beautiful here in the "Indian summer", in early autumn when the leaves are changing colour. It is here that the artist Tom Thomson and his "Group of Seven" are said to have been particularly inspired.

A large variety of fauna inhabit Algonquin Provincial Park: bears, deer, wolves, otters and musk rats are only a few of the many mammals found here. In the rivers and lakes numerous fish are at play, including various species of salmon and trout. The banks of the lakes and brooks as well as many other areas are home to numerous kinds of birds.

Fauna

Originally the Algonquin lived in the region between the sources of the Mississipi and the St Lawrence River in enclosed villages with houses roofed with thatch and bark. As skilled gatherers, fishers and hunters they were able to exploit to the full the potential of the woodlands. They also knew how to clear the land and grow crops of maize.

Algonquin Indians

Their lives were shattered from the 17th c. onwards when the white man arrived in the forests of eastern Canada, as well as through increasing conflicts with the neighbouring Mic-Mac tribe, who had been driven from the lowlands of the St Lawrence by European colonists from the Atlantic coast. Nowadays the Algonquin barter furs for tools, alcohol and cheap knick-knacks from Europe.

The Pioneer Logging Museum stands near the Whitney entrance gate to the park. Here stands an old steam locomotive as a reminder of the times when the present nature reserve was the scene of much timber-felling. An old log-cabin gives an idea of the way in which the lumber-jacks used to live. Open mid-Jun.–early Sep., daily 9am–6pm (Sat. and Sun. only in spring and autumn).

Pioneer Logging Museum

Because of its many waterways Algonquin Provincial Park is very popular with canoeists. There are more than 1600 km (1000 mi.) of rivers and lakes marked out for those keen on this sport.

Canoeing

Some 20 km (13 mi.) from the east entrance to the park will be found the very informative Park Museum. It portrays in great detail the flora and fauna to be found in the Algonquin Provincial Park. Open mid-Jun.–mid-Oct. daily 9am–5pm; mid-May–mid-Jun. weekends only.

Park Museum

The village of Kiosk forms the northern entrance to the park. It is a favourite spot for anglers looking for trout.

Kiosk

On the far side of Highway 630 is the Eau Claire Gorge Conservation Area with a wild and romantic stretch of water.

In the Madawaska Valley on the southern edge of the park lies the busy little town of Bancroft, with 3000 inhabitants. In recent years Bancroft has developed into a popular holiday resort. Experts have found some beautiful minerals in the surrounding countryside, which geologically forms part of the Canadian Shield. In August every year a mineral exhibition is held in Bancroft, attended by many people interested in precious stones.

Bancroft

★★Annapolis Royal J 17

Province: Nova Scotia. Population: 600

Tourism Annapolis Royal, PO Box 2, Annapolis Royal, NS B0S 1A0; tel. (902) 5325769.

Information

The oldest permanent French settlement in Canada, known as the "Habitation Port-Royal", lies on the estuary of a small river which here enters the Bay of Fundy (see entry). The settlement was founded in 1605 by Sieur de Monts who had emigrated to North America with Samuel de Champlain (see Famous People) and – with the permission of the French

History

King Henry IV – founded the colony of Acadia (see entry). Thanks mainly to the rich agricultural soil the little colony quickly prospered, and trading links were established with the native Indians. In 1613 Port-Royal was destroyed by a British expeditionary force, and after that it found itself alternately under English/Scottish and French rule.

In 1629 a Scottish fort was built a little way from the French settlement. This Scottish settlement – named after Queen Anna Stuart – is considered to have been the nucleus of the present province of Nova Scotia. After the region had been handed back to France in 1632 the fortified settlement was destroyed by its inhabitants.

The colony was rebuilt by Seigneur d'Aulnay around 1636, and quickly prospered. After quarrels among the French ruling classes Port-Royal again became an English possession in 1654, but under the Treaty of Breda 1667 it was once more returned to France.

In 1710 the settlement was finally captured by the British and Annapolis Royal became the first capital of Nova Scotia.

Sights

Lower St George Street

Along Lower St George Street some buildings dating from the early period of this old French and later English/Scottish colony have recently been restored, and there are some interesting exhibitions to be viewed.

Dykes

The French dykes around the harbour basin have been preserved, and there is a fine view to be had from there.

McNamara House

The 18th c. McNamara House, together with some furniture and fittings from the same period, has been prettily restored.

O'Dell Inn

The Victorian period has been brought back to life in the well-restored O'Dell Inn.

★★Fort Anne

Fort Anne, the scene of so many battles in the past, is today classified as a historical monument. The old fortifications, the powder magazine and the ramparts are all open to visitors. Tall chimneys mark the officers' quarters. There are memorials to Sieur de Monts (see above), Samuel Vetch, Acadia's first governor, and Jean Paul Mascarene. On the fort flies the flag showing the English St George's Cross and the Scottish St Andrew's Cross.

There is also a museum depicting in detail the history of the town and that of Acadia and Nova Scotia, as well as the natural history of the region. Some Indian canoes and various other artifacts complete the exhibition. Open mid-May–mid-Oct. daily; at other times of the year Mon.–Fri. only, 10am–5pm – guided tours.

Gardens

To the south of Fort Anne lie some very well-tended gardens, including the Governor's Garden from the early 18th c., a Victorian Garden and a very pretty Rose Garden.

★Tidal power station

The tidal power station at Annapolis is the first of its kind in North America. It started up in 1985 and utilises the hydro-energy released by the tidal rise, which is the highest in the world. It is also a pilot scheme for a much larger power station based on the same principle, which is expected to produce 6000 megawatts of electricity. The information centre is open mid-May–mid-Jun. and early Sep.–mid-Oct. daily 9am–5pm; mid-Jun.–early Sep. 9am–8pm.

Surroundings

Granville Ferry

The North Hills Museum in Granville Ferry is worth a visit. This little half-timbered building is furnished in 18th c. style. Open mid-May to mid-Oct. Mon.–Sat. 9.30am–5.30pm, Sun. 1–5.30pm.

Outside Annapolis Royal, about 10 km (6 mi.) to the north on the north bank of the Annapolis River, stands the Habitation Port-Royal settlement of Sieur des Monts (see above), which has been faithfully restored. The whole complex is now an historic monument.

★★Habitation Port-Royal

The plain wooden buildings are in early 17th c. style. There is a Governor's Residence, a Priest's House, a smithy and a room in which the Indians used to barter their furs for European goods. Most interesting is the house of the apothecary Louis Hébert, the first European farmer in North America who later settled in Québec (see entry).

In the "Habitation" in 1606 Samuel de Champlain (see Famous People) founded "L'Ordre de Bon Temps", the first society in North America based on the doctrine of love for one's fellow man.

★★Annapolis Valley   J 17/18

Province: Nova Scotia

Nova Scotia Department of Tourism, PO Box 456, Halifax, NS B3J 2R5; tel. (902) 4245000, fax. (902) 4242668.

Information

Annapolis Valley, situated in charmingly landscaped countryside in Nova Scotia, stretches northward from Digby and Annapolis Royal and runs parallel to the coastline of the Bay of Fundy. The valley with its fertile soil is protected on both sides from cold and unfavourable winds by mountains over 200 m (650 ft) high, in the north by the North Range and in the south by the South Range. Being thus protected from the weather various kinds of fruit and vegetable can flourish. A lot of maize (Indian corn) is also grown here. In May, when the fruit trees are in blossom, the valley is a wonderful sight.

★★Suggested route

The best place to set out from on a drive through the Annapolis Valley is Digby or Annapolis Royal (see entry).

The little fishing village of Digby, famous for its mussels and with a population of 3000, lies by the link road between the Annapolis Valley and the Bay of Fundy. From Digby it is possible to take a boat trip across the Bay of Fundy to St Jean in New Brunswick.

Digby

See entry

Annapolis Royal

Beyond Annapolis Royal the road crosses the Annapolis River, lined with well-tilled fields and apple trees as far as the eye can see. The road passes through the pretty townships of Bridgetown, Lawrencetown and Middletown, where a number of neat little Loyalist houses can still be seen.

Loyalist houses

Then comes Greenwich, about 5 km (3 mi.) beyond which, on the 358, stands Prescott House, a very beautiful brick house in the Georgian style built by the business man and inspired amateur gardener Charles Prescott in the 19th c. Prescott specialised in producing new varieties of fruit, especially apples, pears and cherries, and the farmers in the region were glad to profit from his experiments. Prescott is renowned far and wide as the father of the Annapolis Valley fruit garden. Open mid-May–Oct. daily 9.30am–5.30pm, Sun. 1–5.30pm.

Prescott House Greenwich

The road from Greenwich next passes through the village of Wolfville, and 4 km (2½ mi.) east lies the "Grand-Pré" (Great Meadow), an historical site under a preservation order.

★Grand-Pré

Grand-Pré was one of the main Acadian settlements in the early 18th c. By means of an ingenious system of dams and canals the Acadians succeeded in reclaiming fertile land from the sea and laid out large and

Apple blossom in the Annapolis Valley

productive fields. In its heyday there were more than 200 farms here. However, in 1755 the Acadians were driven out, their homes destroyed and their cattle taken, and the land parcelled out to colonists from New England. After the American Declaration of Independence American Loyalists were also similarly rewarded.

The Grand Pré National Historic Site is mainly in memory of the Acadian settlers and the problems they had with the English and Scottish forces. In the gardens stands a memorial to Henry Longfellow, who in 1847 immortalised the tragic fate of the Acadians in his poem "Evangéline". There is also a statue of his heroine Evangéline. Both memorials were sculpted by the Acadian artist Philippe Hébert. There are "Living History" presentations.

The gardens are open daily, but the actual buildings are open only mid-May to mid-Oct. daily 9am–6pm.

Windsor

At the confluence of the Avon and Ste Croix rivers lies the little Nova Scotian port of Windsor (pop. 4000), on the spot where the Acadian settlement of Piziquid stood in the 18th c.

Today Windsor is important as a port from which wood and building materials, including plaster, are exported.

Museum of Nova Scotia

The Museum of Nova Scotia on Clifton Avenue is worth a visit. The buildings were constructed in 1833, and the writer and humorist Thomas Chandler Haliburton lived here and wrote his famous "Sam Slick", which tells the story of an American clockmaker who offered his wares to the good people of Nova Scotia.

The most impressive parts of the building are the tastefully furnished entrance hall, the dining room and the living room. There are guided tours each day mid-May to Oct.

Near the dyke stands Fort Edward, built in the mid-18th c. by the English ★Fort Edward
to defend the route from Halifax to the Bay of Fundy. It was here, too, that
the sad deportation of the French-speaking Acadians was organised. This
wooden fort is one of the oldest existing buildings of its kind in Canada.

From the earth-wall which surrounds the fort there is a beautiful view
of the valley of the Avon River and over the Bay of Fundy.

★★L'Anse aux Meadows National Historic Park   G 19

Province: Newfoundland. Founded: 1962

Roads 430 and 436 from the TransCanada Highway, Deer Lake turn-off,   Access
about 400 km (250 mi.) north of Corner Brook, Newfoundland.

L'Anse aux Meadows National Historic Park, PO Box 70, St Lunaire-   Information
Griquet, NF A0K 2X0; tel. (709) 6232608.

L'Anse aux Meadows National Historic Park, a green plain with some
moorland, lies at the northern tip of the Newfoundland Great Northern
Peninsula. Here were discovered six houses made of grass sods, probably built by the Vikings around the year 1000. Since 1978 it has been the
first of its kind to be included in the UNESCO World List of Protected
Cultural Monuments.

Back in 1962 a small Viking settlement dating from around AD 1000 was   History
discovered here. It is the oldest known European settlement in North
America and to date is the only authentic trace of Viking settlements in
the New World. Probably L'Anse aux Meadows is the "Vinland" discovered by Leif Erikson.

The oldest known European settlement in North America

Ashcroft

In the excavations carried out by the Norwegian Helge Ingstad between 1961 and 1968 at least six houses made of turves were discovered, including a smithy of the kind built by the Norwegians in Iceland. Iron relics, various kinds of artefacts clearly of Norwegian origin, as well as bones, peat and charcoal all came to light. Three reconstructed houses are open to visitors; a long-house, a workshop and a stable. The finds unearthed here are on display in the Visitors' Centre.

Open all the year round; Visitors' Centre mid-Jun.–Labour Day daily 9am–8pm or 9am–4pm.

Ashcroft   G 6

Province: British Columbia
Population: 3000. Altitude: 335–460 m (1100–1510 ft)

Information

Tourism British Columbia, 802–865 Hornby St., Vancouver, BC V6Z 2G3; tel. (604) 6602861, fax. (604) 6603383.

Ashcroft lies almost 470 km (292 mi.) north-east of Vancouver, on the far side of the TransCanada Highway on the eastern bank of the Thompson River where the Cascade Mountains fall away to the east. When the railroad link was completed in 1856 it replaced Yale as the main trade centre for the Cariboo Road. Rainfall here is a mere 180 mm (7 in.) per annum, making Ashcroft one of the driest regions in British Columbia.

Ashcroft Museum

In the Ashcroft Museum at 404 Brink St., from Victoria Day to Labour Day, numerous photographs, slide shows, etc. illustrate the town's glorious history. Open 10am–7pm daily.

Ashcroft Manor

The Ashcroft Manor estate was laid out in 1862 by two brothers from Cornwall. For many years it was a famous resting-place on the Cariboo Waggon Road. The owners lived here in the style of landed gentry, complete with horse-racing and fox-hunting. When post and freight were carried by stage coach the estate served as the first court and post office in the region. Today Ashcroft Manor, lying in the shade of two hundred year-old elm trees, is a museum with two craft and antique shops and a charming tea-room.

Cominco

In summer the Travel InfoCentre arranges visits to Highland Valley Copper (Cominco), one of the largest open copper mines in the world, and situated amid the charming scenery of the Highland Valley (in the direction of Logan Lake).

Cache Creek

In Cache Creek, which exists mainly on income from through traffic and tourism, the Cariboo Highway 97 (see entry) branches off to the north. This road then enters truly unspoilt regions of territory, providing relatively quick access to the Yellowhead region and to Alaska. In Ashcroft-Cache Creek there is much that is reminscent of the old west of Canada. Many cattle farms in the region take in paying guests. The barren hills nearby are becoming increasingly popular with hang-gliders.

Spences Bridge

The little township of Spences Bridge (pop. 300) lies about 30 minutes by car down the valley by a bridge over the Thompson River built by Thomas Spence in 1864. This is where Highway 8 turns south-east and follows the valley of the Nicola River, with its cattle-rearing and fruit growing, to Merritt 65 km (40 mi.) away by the new Coquila Highway. Farmers offer their seasonal produce for sale at roadside stalls. In 1905 there was a powerful landslide, the scars of which can still be seen today, which claimed the lives of eighteen people. An Indian village was destroyed and the Thompson River blocked for several hours.

Athabasca River

Province: Alberta

The Athabasca River (Indian for "where reeds grow") rises in the Rocky Mountains near the Columbia Icefield (see Icefields Parkway) at about 2200 m (7220 ft) above sea-level. It runs through Jasper National Park (see entry), plunges down on to a shelf some 150 km (90 mi.) above the Grand Rapids and after a further 1225 km (760 mi.) flows into Lake Athabasca in the North-east of Alberta; this lake covers an area of some 8000 sq. km 3100 sq. mi.) and is 320 km (200 mi.) long and up to 60 m (200 ft) deep. Above it, where the Peace River and Stone River also enter the lake, stands Fort Chipewyan, built in 1788 and one of the oldest fur-trading posts in the whole of Canada.

   Along the Athabasca, between the settlement of the same name and the town of Fort McMurray, rich deposits of crude oil and oil-sands were discovered and eventually exploited at great expense.

Course

The Athabasca was an important trade route in the past, used to transport not only furs but also seed and corn.

Means of transport

The Athabasca River, over 1200 km (745 mi.) in length, is one of the few rivers in North America to remain clean and it therefore attracts anglers and canoeists in particular.

Sport and leisure

Athabasca

Province: Alberta. Population: 2000

See Alberta

Information

Oil-bearing sands on the Athabasca

West   East

Athabasca

© Baedeker

|0   20 Km|

Exaggerated drawing (after Seifried)

Ice-Age strata	Oil sand (Devon)	Dolomite (Devon)
Clay (chalk)	Chalk, Karst (Devon)	Sand (Devon)
Salt (chalk)	Sand (Devon)	Granite

The rural township of Athabasca lies some 150 km (90 mi.) north of Edmonton (see entry). It is the seat of an Open University. Known until 1926 as Athabasca's Landing, it was the main trading centre for the Hudson's Bay Company in northern Canada. The Athabasca, most of which is navigable, offered good access upstream via Little Slave Lake to the Peace River region, and downstream by way of Fort McMurray to the Mackenzie River and thence to Alaska. In 1887 the first steamship to be built here was launched. In 1912 the railroad ceased transporting freight along the troublesome 150 km (90 mi.) long Athabasca Landing Trail from Fort Edmonton. For more than 40 years – until the Northern Alberta Railroad to Waterways and Fort McMurray was completed – steamships on the river were the very life-blood of the town.

Today the townscape is dominated by the corn warehouses so typical of the Canadian prairies. Athabasca is also a favourite point from which to set out on tours and excursions into the largely undeveloped forest and lake regions of Northern Alberta.

Baffin Island   C–E 13–17

Administrative Unit: Northwest Territories, District of Franklin
Population: 8,000

Information

Nunavut Tourism,
PO Box 1450, Iqaluit, NU X0A 0H0.
Tel. (867) 9796551, fax. (867) 9791261.
Internet: www.nunatour.nt.ca

Air travel

There are direct flights to Iqaluit from Ottawa and Montréal which take about three hours. From Iqaluit there are scheduled flights to Baffin Island: Cape Dorset (1¼ hours), Lake Harbour (¾ hour), Pangnirtung (1 hour), Broughton Island (1½ hours), Clyde River (3 hours), Pond Inlet (4½ hours), Nanisvik (2 hours). Considerable savings can often be made if the connecting flight is booked together with the main translatlantic flight; a travel agent can provide up-to-date details.

Baffin Island, the most south-easterly and the largest on the Canadian archipelago, with its breathtaking landscape, the hospitality of the Inuit people and the numerous opportunities for an unusual holiday ("Baffin has adventure for every taste"), is clearly doing all it can to attract tourists. Nevertheless – some might say fortunately – it can hardly be said that it suffers from invasions of visitors. The only way to get to it is by air, and that is rather expensive, the cost of living is high and the climate very "unfriendly", not to mention the hordes of insects which descend on the unfortunate traveller in summer; all in all, perhaps somewhere for the specialist.

Baffin Island forms part of the Franklin District of the Northwest Territories; it covers an area of 507,451 sq. km (195,930 sq. mi.), making it the fifth largest island in the world (Spain, for example, is 497,500 sq. km (192,085 sq. mi.)). In the east it is separated from Greenland by Baffin Bay and Davis Strait, to the south lies the Hudson Strait and to the west Foxe Basin. The coastline and land surface varies considerably: on the eastern coast, very similar to Norway with its steep fiords and small off-shore islands, lies a long, narrow Alpine-like mountainous zone which reaches a height of 2591 m (8504 ft) in the Auyuittuq National Park on the Cumberland peninsula. The southern foothills form highlands, while to the west lie flat lowlands.

Climate

In the east of the Northwest Territories the Canadian Arctic extends as far as St James' Bay in the south of Hudson Bay; as a result Baffin Island lies in the permafrost region with a summer lasting from early June to the end of August with temperatures above 0°C (32°F). As the distance North to South

On Baffin Island

measures some 1300 km (800 mi.) between latitudes 73° 30′ and 61° 30′ and extends beyond the Arctic Circle, there are marked climatic differences; while in Lake Harbour the average temperature in March does not fall below −22°C (8°F), this is the maximum in Arctic Bay. All in all the climate is High Arctic; even Frobisher Bay, situated 230 km (143 mi.) south of the Arctic Circle, is free of ice only in July and August, and Iqaluit has an annual average of −9°C (16°F) (July average min. 2·5°C (36°F), max. 9°C/48°F).

People of the Dorset culture came to the Cumberland Peninsula around 1500 BC, and in the 12th–13th c. the Thule culture spread to Baffin Island. It is possible that Vikings came here in the 10th–11th c.; the "Helluland" of Viking legend could be Baffin Island. Baffin Island got its name from the English seafarer William Baffin, but it was "discovered" by Martin Frobisher (1539–94) who landed in Frobisher Bay in 1567 when searching for the North West Passage. He brought back to England from the Meta Incognita Peninsula some ore which he thought to be gold, but it turned out to be iron pyrites, or "fools' gold". The first permanent settlements here were those of whale-catchers, pursuing a trade which prospered until early in the 20th c. The first mission stations were set up by Anglicans on Cumberland Sound. The Hudson's Bay Company first came here to Lake Harbour in 1911, and ten years later the first police station was built. | History

About 1000 people live permanently on Baffin Island, a quarter of whom are white and three-quarters Inuits, who have given up their nomadic existence and settled along the coast. The main administrative town is Iqaluit on Frobisher Bay; mention should also be made of Cape Dorset, Lake Harbour, Pangnirtung, Clyde River, Pond Inlet, Nanisivik and Arctic Bay. | Settlements

Cape Dorset, pop. 1000, is well-known as a place where many finds have been made relating to the Dorset culture, which flourished roughly between | **Cape Dorset**

1000 BC and AD 1100 and was replaced by the Thule culture, as well as for its outstanding Inuit artists (lithographs, sculptures). At the end of July the Baffin Summer Games, contests in traditional Inuit sports, are held here.

Pangnirtung

Pangnirtung (Pangniqtuuq in the Inuktitut language, meaning "where there are a lot of caribou bulls"), with a population of 1000, lies in some superb countryside – "Arctic Switzerland" – and is important as a setting-out point to Kekerten Historic Park 50 km (30 mi.) away with an open-air museum of the history of whaling, and to Auyuittuq National Park (see below). The town is also associated with Franz Boa, a German linguist and founder of modern American ethnology, who carried out research here in 1883 and 1884.

Nanisivik

The mining settlement of Nanisivik, on the north coast, was founded in 1974. Lead, zinc, silver and cadmium are mined here, but there are only eight weeks in the year when the harbour is free of ice and the ores can be shipped away. At the time of the summer solstice the Midnight Sun Marathon is held here, with participants from the whole of North America. Nanisivik can be reached by taxi from Arctic Bay (pop. 550) on Admiralty Inlet, which was founded by the Hudson's Bay Company in the 1920s and can be used as a base for tours.

Iqaluit

For many years the gateway to Baffin Island at the end of Frobisher Bay was frequented by whalers, scientists, traders and missionaries, but only in 1942, when it was a US military airfield, did it grow in size. In the years 1955–58 Frobisher Bay was extended as part of the "Distant Early Warning Line". In 1986 the Inuit name of Iqaluit – meaning "many fish" – was again made official.

Now the service and administrative centre of the Baffin Region, Iqaluit is a modern town with a complete infrastructure of hotels, schools, hospital, weather and radio station and camping-site, and a population of 3200. The tourist will find all he needs in the way of equipment and guides, etc., while the range of goods available, such as jewellery, carvings, parkas, is excellent. No. 212 near the beach, a restored Hudson's Bay Company building, contains the local museum known as Nunatta Sunaqutangit ("Things of the Country").

The most important event held here is Toonik Tyme in the third week in April, a festival with competitions and entertainment, such as beard-growing competitions, igloo-building, dog and snowmobile races, tea-making, traditional singing and dancing. This event celebrates the end of winter and is in honour of the Tooniks, the legendary strong little ancestors of the Inuit. The culmination is the "coronation" of Mr Toonik, who arrives on a dog-sleigh to open the festivities.

Surroundings of Iqaluit

Interesting places in the vicinity include Sylvia Grinnell River, with kayaks and raft-races, and Qaummaarviit Historic Park, an island some 12 km (7 mi.) away, taking about 30 minutes by boat. It has relics of the settlement's 2500-year history, including winter dwellings from the Thule culture, c. AD 1000–1700.

Auyuittuq National Park

Founded: 1972
Area: 21,470 sq. km (8290 sq. mi.)

Information

Superintendent, Auyuittuq National Park Reserve, Pangnirtung, NU X0A 0R0; tel. (819) 4738962
Nunavut Tourism, PO Box 1450, Iqaluit, NU X0A 0H0; tel. (867) 9796551, fax. (867) 9791261.

Location

Auyuittuq National Park lies in the south-east of Baffin Island, on the Cumberland Peninsula, just north of the Arctic Circle, and extends about

200 km (125 mi.) to the north. A large part is taken up by the Penny Ice Cap, remains of the Ice Age glaciation of eastern Canada; it is described by the Inuit word Auyuittuq, "land where it never thaws". This landscape of primitive rocks on the edge of the Canadian continent is characterised by broad glaciated valleys and rugged mountains with vertical walls rising up to 1200 m (4000 ft) in height and typical flat-topped peaks, that of Mount Asgard being particularly impressive.

The preferred route through the National Park leads diagonally across the peninsula to a point about 100 km (63 mi.) from Overlord at the end of the Pangnirtung Fiord. Although it is possible to cover the whole stretch, this would take some ten to fourteen days, and the connection to Broughton Island is fraught with problems. Therefore most people prefer to make round trips of varying length from Overlord, the longest one being to Summit Lake or Glacier Lake. This "great" route is 103 km (65 mi.) and takes about 48 hours actual walking time. The only camping site is in Overlord; it is about 31 km (19 mi.) from Pangnirtung and can be reached on foot, by snowmobile or – in summer – by boat ("canoe-taxi"). However, attempting it on foot is not recommended, as it takes considerably longer – about three days – and is unattractive. To undertake such a trek lasting several days in the uninhabited Arctic requires a high degree of fitness and experience as well as very careful preparation; the walker must be equipped so as to be completely self-sufficient and be prepared for the worst of weather – such as rainstorms in summer lasting several days – and for crossing rivers and other watercourses.

Pangnirtung Pass

Baie James   G 14/15

Province: Quebec

Tourisme Baie-James, 166 Bvd. Springer, Chapais, PQ G0W 1H0; tel. (418) 7453979, fax. (418) 7453970
Association touristique du Nunavik, C.P. 218, Kuujjuaq, PQ J0M 1C0; tel. (819) 9642876, fax. (819) 9642002
Société de Dévelopement de la Baie James, Matagami, PQ; tel. (819) 7628181
Hydro-Québec, Chantier de la Grande 2A, Radisson, PQ; tel. (819) 6386870

Information

Baie James (James Bay) is the flat southern part of Hudson Bay. It was discovered in 1610 by the English seafarer Henry Hudson and explored by Thomas James in 1631. From 1663 onwards the French adventurers Radisson and Chouart des Groseilliers traded here in furs. In 1671 Father Charles Albanel and Paul Deys de Saint-Simon discovered the region to the east of James Bay. One of the places they passed was Lake Mistassini, the largest lake in the province of Québec.
  Between 1930 and 1935 lay brothers from the settlements at Wasganish (Fort Rupert) set out for Chisasibi (Fort George), where they tilled the land and reared cattle. This satisfied the needs of the Cris Indians living there.

History

The few villages are scattered along the coast, the main one, Chisasibi (Fort George) being at the mouth of the Grande Rivière.

Settlements

"La Grande" is the name given to a huge energy generation project designed to produce vast quantities of hydro-electricity by harnessing and diverting some of the rivers on the east side of Baie James some 1200 km (750 mi.) or so north of Montréal. The massive generating plants constructed here by Hydro-Québec will supply electricity not only to the industrial centres of Québec province but also for export to the USA. During the planning phase in the 1960s and 1970s, the project aroused furious controversy throughout the province. The scheme had the support of influential political circles surrounding the former Prime Minister Robert Bourassa.

La Grande Project

Ranged against it were conservationists who stressed the environmental risks, and representatives of the Indian population of the affected area who feared for their way of life and culture. Opposition parties and economists doubted the financial viability of the scheme. The issue finally came to a head when the Fédération des Travailleurs du Québec came out in support of starting work on the vast construction site. Following a long and turbulent debate in the provincial parliament, the vote went in favour of the project. Hydro-Québec emphasised the value of the hydro-energy potential of the region, while the Baie James Development Company pointed to the possible dangers to nature on this 350,000 sq. km (135,000 sq. mi.) area.

From the various alternative programmes it was decided for a number of reasons to go ahead with the Grande Rivière project. The granite and gneiss stone found on this fairly high plateau behind the coastal strip was well-suited to the construction of a complex of this kind. Other points in its favour were the many Ice Age lakes and moraines, the 800 km (500 mi.) long Grande Rivière with its tributaries and the other waterways in the region. There are frequent floods, but for the purposes of the current project the rivers Nottaway, Broadback and Rupert have been brought under control. Weather conditions are extreme: on average, temperatures range between −23°C (9°F) to +20°C (68°F) in summer and in winter the dry cold can take temperatures down to as low as −50°C (58°F).

The Inuit and Cris Indians who lived there presented a further problem. Controversy ranged and in December 1972 work was postponed. In 1975 a contract was signed agreeing on a compensation payment and a change in the way the project was to be carried out.

Among other things this project includes the construction of three giant power stations along the Grande Rivière and the diversion of the Eastmain, Opinaca and Caniapiscau rivers. About 1600 km (1000 mi.) of roads will have to be built, as well as five airports, five villages and seven camps for the 17,000 or more workers. Ultimately the hydro-electric output will be in the region of 16 million kilowatts.

The building programme is in two phases: the first, already completed, embraced the construction of three power stations between 1972 and 1985, a power grid of 5000 km (3100 mi.) with cables carrying some 740 kV and two river diversions. The cost was about 15 billion dollars, with European – especially French – shareholders.

The second phase includes the Grande Rivière, Grande Baleine and Mattaway-Broadback-Rupert projects. Estimated cost: 55 billion dollars. It appears, however, that this will not proceed unless the USA guarantees that it will buy some of the electricity produced.

While building work is going on the highway from Matagami to Radisson is closed to private traffic.

The Baie James Energy Company (SEBJ) will allow groups of at least fifteen people to visit its building sites between April 15th and October 15th. Access is by aircraft, but there are no overnight facilities. Because of the large distances involved only one site can be visited on any one day. Information: Bureau de Tourisme, km 6, Route Matagami-Radisson; tel. (819) 6388486.

Chisasibi

In days gone by this town was an outpost of the Hudson's Bay Company, and today has a population of 2000, mostly Indians. About 200 km (125 mi.) further south lies Fort Eastmain, which also used to be a Hudson's Bay Company outpost. Quite a number of descendants of the original inhabitants still live here.

Waskaganish

Waskaganish is the oldest settlement in this inhospitable region.

Nouveau Québec

The Nouveau Québec region in the north of Québec Province extends to the 62nd degree of latitude. This vast area has only the occasional settlement. North of Chisasibi a few small settlements can be found along the coast of Hudson Bay (see entry), and a few people live by the Baie d'Ungava.

Poste de la Baleine

At the mouth of the Grande Rivière lies the Indian settlement of Poste de la Baleine.

Off the Hudson Bay coast lie the barren Belcher Islands.

The Inuit village of Povungnituk consists of about 100 buildings, including a mission station. More recently it has become well-known as a port, fishing-village and handicraft centre producing among other things stone sculptures and decorated textiles.

Sulluk, some 300 km (190 mi.) further north, a mission station since 1947, lies in the Perpetual Ice by the Hudson Waterway. For three hundred years ships have passed by here as they entered Hudson Bay from the Atlantic looking, for example, for the port of Churchill in the southwest of Hudson Bay.

★★Banff National Park   G 7

Province: Alberta. Area: 6641 sq. km (2564 sq. mi.)

Superintendent, Banff National Park, P.O. Box 900, Banff, AB T0C 0C0; Banff Information Centre, 224 Banff Ave., Banff, AB; tel. (403) 7621550 Lake Louise Information Centre, Village Rd., Lake Louise, AB; tel. (403) 5223833

Information

Road: TransCanada Highway 1 (Calgary–Banff–Lake Louise); Banff–Windemere Highway (Highway 93 South); Icefields Parkway (Highway 93 North); David Thompson Highway (Highway 11; Saskatchewan Crossing–Rocky Mountain House).

Access

Rail (tour): "The Rocky Mountaineer" (Vancouver–Banff–Calgary).

Coach: Excursions from Calgary, Banff (Townsite) and Jasper.

Banff National Park lies in the region of the glaciated Rocky Mountain ridge east of the continental watershed and about 130 km (80 mi.) west of Calgary.
     In the north it adjoins Jasper National Park (see entry), with which it is linked by the unique Icefields Parkway (see entry), and in the west it runs into the Yoho and Kootenay National Park (see entries).

Location

Banff National Park is one of Canada's greatest tourist attractions. Together with its three neighbouring parks it has been included since 1985 in UNESCO's list of protected natural and cultural monuments. Banff National Park forms part of the main Rocky Mountain ridge east of the continental watershed and the Front Range which falls away steeply to the Great Plain, and in this park alone there are two dozen peaks of more than 3000 m (9850 ft). More than three million visitors a year are fascinated by the picturesque turquoise mountain lakes mirroring the snow-covered peaks, glaciers and mountain forests, by the luxuriant mountain meadows in early summer and the impressive waterfalls, charming streams, lonely highland valleys and areas of quiet and untamed natural scenery only a few hundred metres from the main roads.
     The health resort of Banff, with its hot springs, is the only township in the park. The Icefields Parkway, which winds for 230 km (143 mi.) through the 3000–4000 m (10,000–13,000 ft) high mountains, connects Banff with the numerous sights and Jasper National Park to the north. The highlights of this impressive journey along the Parkway are the world-famous Lake Louise, in whose ice-cold waters under a deep-blue sky are reflected the surrounding mountains, the aristocratic-looking Canadian Pacific Hotel "Château Lake Louise", and the huge Columbia Icefield.
     At any time of the year this national park offers good facilities for sport and leisure: there are mountain tours on foot and on horseback, "back-

Topography

Mountain scenery in Banff National Park ▶

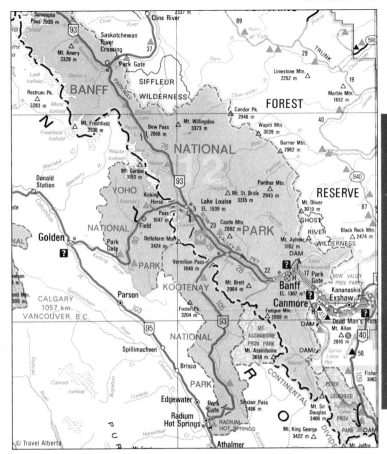

© Travel Alberta

packing" (a licence being required for trips lasting several days), golf courses and tennis courts, "river rafting" on the Bow River or peaceful canoe trips on one of the beautiful lakes.

Typical of this section of the Rocky Mountains, there are marked seasonal differences depending on the height. The town of Banff itself, one of the lowest places in the national park, lies about 1400 m (4600 ft) above sea-level.

Climate

Winters are generally long and minimum temperatures below −30°C (22°F) are not uncommon. In January the average maximum temperatures are −7°C (19°F), the minima being −16°C (3°F). The relatively cool summers are short, although brief periods when the temperature rises as high as 30°C (86°F) are not unknown. In July and August average daily maxima of more than 20°C (68°F) and minima of some 7°C (45°F) are attained.

In the long valleys in the lee of the high mountain chains annual rainfall amounts are very small, being only 380 mm (15 in.), while in the continental water-shed region they may measure more than 1250 mm

(50 in.). The best months for travelling are July and August, but in view of the crowds of tourists at that time it may be better to go earlier in the year or in September.

History

Man settled in the great valleys 11,000 years ago, as is shown by excavations made at Vermilion Lakes near Banff. When the first Europeans arrived Stoney and Kootenay Indians as well as members of the Blackfoot tribes already lived and hunted here.

Banff's first "tourist" was undoubtedly Sir George Simpson who in 1841, when Governor of the Hudson's Bay Company, accompanied by an Indian guide on one of his inspection trips crossed the Bow River to what is now the town of Banff and passed over the Rocky Mountains along a pass since named after him. After that fur-hunters roved through the present national park.

In 1883 the Canadian Pacific Railway reached Banff, then prosaically known simply as "Siding 29", and Lake Louise. In the same year railroad workers seeking minerals stumbled across the hot sulphur springs at Cave & Basin Springs, where initially the railroad workers and subsequently rheumatism sufferers from all over the world came to seek relief. Disputes as to ownership of the springs led in 1885 to the establishment of the Hot Springs Reserve at the foot of Sulphur Mountain. Two years later Rocky Mountains Park was laid out, from which sprang the Banff National Park in 1930.

The opening of the railroad brought settlers and tourists to the mountain valley. In 1888 the Canadian Pacific Railway (CPR) opened the Banff Springs Hotel, followed by the Château Lake Louise in 1890. In 1899 the CPR hired Swiss mountain guides to take tourists up the peaks in the park. By the turn of the century Banff was able to boast more than eight luxury hotels.

As the CPR had a monopoly of entrance to the park it was 1911 before the increasingly popular motor car could bring people in. Then from 1920 until 1940, roads were built to Lake Louise, Radium Hot Springs and Jasper. Around 1930 a start was made on building the first ski huts. Today there are excellent ski slopes to be found on Mount Norquay in Banff, in Sunshine Village 17 km (11 mi.) west of Banff and on the slopes of Mount Whitehorn near Lake Louise.

Finds of minerals – copper, coal, zinc and lead – in Bow River Valley led to the establishment, albeit short-lived, of mining camps. From 1881 to 1886 the mining town of Silver City existed at the foot of Castle Mountain, but when the copper supply became exhausted it quickly disappeared. Then coal was found 6 km (4 mi.) east of Banff, but the mine closed down around the turn of the century. A further example of a short-lived coal town is Bankhead 6 km (4 mi.) north of Banff. Coal was mined here for a few years after 1905; the remains of the settlement can still be seen today.

In the 1930s the authorities put a stop to the mining of minerals and commercial tree-felling in the park. Up to 1915 railroad workers and at times more than 10,000 miners seriously decimated the original giant herds of wild animals, including elk, mountain sheep, caribou and mountain goats, so hunting was banned and rangers employed. Today, however, the authorities try to interfere as little as possible in the natural way of things.

Geology

The folding and lifting of the Rocky Mountains took place over a period lasting from the Mesozoic into the Tertiary (roughly 60 million years ago). Under intense pressure from the west the massive layers of sediment, several thousand metres deep in places, were broken up and folded. Several parallel fractures occurred, whole strata were forced eastwards and semi-vertical layers of chalk and sandstone were formed. The main ridge of the mountains which form the western part of the National Park are made up of such layers of sediment which had been forced up and distorted; however, this region is only slightly folded compared with the

Front Range which breaks off steeply to the east. The formation of the surfaces as seen today occurred mainly during the Ice Ages, the last push ending about 10,000 years ago. At that time great masses of ice filled the valleys, creating wide valley-floors, slopes, passes and sharp ridges. Wind, water, frost and ice still continue the work of the Ice Age glaciers.

The broad valleys and lower mountain slopes up to about 1500 m (5000 ft) display typical montane vegetation consisting of open forest – studded with grassy areas – of Douglas pine, silver fir, lodgepole pine and the aspen trees which turn such a beautiful gold in autumn. Steep, dry southern slopes are often carpeted with grass. Above this and up as far as the tree line at about 2200 m (7200 ft) is the sub-Alpine zone. No aspen trees will be found there. Characteristic of the lower slopes are self-contained coniferous forests of spruce and lodgepole pine. In the lower regions where there is considerable snowfall and a vegetation period of one to three months the pine trees gradually disappear. In summer the sub-Alpine mountain meadows are covered with carpets of flowers. The area of bent and distorted trees near the tree line is followed by the Alpine zone. Typical of the vegetation here, reminiscent of the Arctic tundra, are the shrubland, small bushes, heather, mountain flowers and grass, gradually to be replaced in the extreme environmental conditions by the well-suited mosses and lichens before naked rock, rubble and ice finally take over.

Vegetation zones

There are still more than fifty species of mammals to be found in the national parks of this rocky region. Large wild animals are most likely to be spotted in the early morning and the evening. Elk predominate in the damp meadows of the valleys, while forest caribou, roe-deer, wapiti deer and mule deer frequent the thicker woods and meadows. Mountain goats and thick-horned sheep are found on the higher mountain slopes.

Animal kingdom

Based on estimates made by the park authorities there are still about 200 grizzly bears in the four national parks. Normally they do not come near roads and towns. When walking in the "backcountry", however, it is wise to keep an eye open for them and for the more common black bear. The latter prefer wooded areas and thick undergrowth on the flat valley floors and sunny south-facing slopes, while grizzlies keep to the Alpine regions in summer but seek food lower down in spring and autumn. Under normal circumstances there is little likelihood of meeting a bear face to face. These animals have poor sight but can smell or hear approaching humans long before they see them. Bears can be surprisingly quick, so on no account approach one. The park administration offices have leaflets on correct behaviour in "bearland". Feeding the bears is strictly prohibited, as this can spoil their natural way of life and make them less shy of people. During long walks and at camp sites, therefore, a close watch should be kept on foodstuffs and cosmetics, and they should be kept either in special bear-proof containers or securely packed in air-tight boxes in the boot of the car. For waste extra bear-proof rubbish-bins are provided. Scratch marks clearly caused by bears' claws should be a warning to take due care. For their own protection, bears found begging or looking for scraps in the vicinity of human habitation are taken into custody.

Bears

Banff or Banff Townsite, lying in a charming valley in the south of Banff National Park and dominated by high mountains, has a permanent population of some 4200 and ample accommodation makes it the tourist centre of the park. During the summer months its broad main street, Banff Avenue, is crammed with visitors, and it is almost as busy as a city. Between Wolf Street and Bow River will be found row upon row of shopping streets. Here, too, is the Parks Canada Information Centre at 224 Banff Avenue, open mid-Jun.–Sep. 8am–10pm; at other times 10am–6pm; where information about events, "backcountry permits", and maps and guides for excursions and tours can be obtained.

In summer there are pleasant excursions available by horse-driven coaches around Banff and the surrounding countryside. On Banff Avenue

★Banff

A grizzly bear on the prowl

– between Rocky Mountains Resort Avenue and the Banff Springs Hotel – runs a tram or trolleybus line constructed in early 20th c. style.

Natural History Museum

It is worth paying a visit to the Natural History Museum at 112 Banff Avenue, on the first floor of the Clock Tower Village Mall. Exhibits explain the formation of the Rocky Mountains and the topography of the region. Open May–Jun. 10am–8pm; Jul.–Aug. 10am–10pm; at other times 10am–6pm.

Banff Park Museum

Banff Park Museum (93 Banff Ave. is housed in a building dating from 1903, which used to be the park administration offices. The very instructive exhibition provides information mainly about the animal life of the park. Open 10am–6pm.

Whyte Museum of the Canadian Rockies

Banff has the artists Catherine and Peter Whyte to thank for the Whyte Museum of the Canadian Rockies. Situated at 111 Bear St., it is open daily in summer 10am–6pm, at other times by arrangement; concerts on Sun. afternoons. The museum houses the archives of the Canadian Rocky Mountains as well as art exhibitions and some interesting material on the history of Banff. Adjoining it are the "Heritage Homes". Guided tours show what life was like in Banff in the 1920s.

Cascade Gardens

To the south Banff Avenue ends on the far side of Bow River in Cascade Gardens; these are laid out in terrace fashion, and this is where the park administration buildings can be found.

Luxton Museum

Luxton Museum (1 Birch Ave.) stands on the far side of Bow River. Open daily 10am–5pm.

Sundry scenes from the life of the plains Indians before the Europeans arrived are depicted in a reconstructed fur-trading station.

★Banff Springs Hotel

Banff Springs Hotel at Spray Ave. (guided tours) was built in 1888 and is today the emblem of Banff. Once planned to be the largest hotel complex in the world this traditionally-designed, castle-like Grand Hotel still preserves much of the glamour of the early days of railway tourism, when only very well-to-do travellers could afford to make the journey into the then still remote region of the Canadian Rocky Mountains.

Below the Banff Springs Hotel the Bow River tumbles over a cliff-like rise formed from sloping layers of limestone. In pre-glacial times Bow River initially flowed north of Tunnel Mountain through Cascade Valley and Lake Minnewanka; later the valley became cut off by retrograde erosion, causing the river to flow between Fairholme Range and Tunnel Mountain. Massive moraines of Ice Age glaciers then blocked the original course and probably formed a lake until such time as the river was able to burst through between Mount Rundle and Tunnel Mountain.

★ Bow Falls

The Cave & Basin Centennial Centre (Cave Ave) grew up around the hot sulphur springs discovered in 1883. The Canadian National Park system developed here, based on the US model. Exhibitions, slide-shows and computer games provide information on the national parks, two short instructive walks provide a key to the geology and the history of the hot springs which issue forth from a cave and to the specific ecological system linked thereto. Open: mid-Jun.–Sep. 10am–8pm, at other times 10am–5pm.

Cave & Basin Centennial Centre

On the occasion of its centenary the historical buildings around the public swimming pool were restored. The swimming bath built in 1887 is a most imposing building. Open: mid-Jun.–Sep.

From the Cave & Basin Centennial Centre a charming walkway and cycle path leads along Bow River and past some flat marshland – formed by beaver dams! – to Sundance Canyon.

A 2 km (1¼ mi.) long instructive path adjoins this. Marsh Loop, almost 3 km (2 mi.) long, is another way round, leading to beaver dams and lodges. In these marshy surroundings some rare species of birds can be observed.

Marsh Loop

Some 4 km (2½ mi.) from Banff Townsite, 1600 m (5250 ft) up on Sulphur Mountain, is the hottest of the five hot sulphur springs. In summer its water temperature is 42°C (107°F), in winter 29°C (84°F).

Sulphur Mountain

Open mid-Jun.–mid-Oct. daily 8.30am–10.30pm, at other times of the year Mon.–Thu. 2.30–8.30pm, Fri., Sat., Sun 8.30am–10.30pm.

From the lower station of the Sulphur Mountain Gondola cable railway, opposite (in use all the year round, but at varying times) it is an eight minute trip to the upper station at 2270 m (7450 ft) above sea-level. On a clear day there a splendid panoramic view from the three terrace decks and the mountain-top restaurant. The mountain walk known as the Vista Trail leads to the nearby Samson Peak.

After travelling for 6½ km (4 mi.) along Mount Norquay Road, with its many hairpin bends, we come to the lower station of the chairlift, which goes up to Mount Norquay, 2135 m (7007 ft). There is a superb panoramic view to be had from the Cliffhouses Restaurant. Skiers enjoy themselves here in winter.

Mount Norquay

A road 11 km (7 mi.) long leads to the three Vermilion Lakes west of the town. They lie in the floodplain of the Bow River and are a refuge for numerous waterfowl. Ornithologists come here to observe bald eagles, osprey and Canadian geese. With a little luck beavers and elk may also be spotted.

Vermilion Lakes

North of the town – about 1 km (½ mi.) west of the junction of Banff Ave. and the TransCanada Highway – it is possible to drive through Buffalo Paddocks, an area of some 40ha/100 acres where bison graze between May and October.

Buffalo Paddocks

Banff National Park

Horse-riding	The impressive mountain country around Banff can also be explored on horseback. Guided tours lasting one or more days are also available.
Tunnel Mountain	It is also worthwhile climbing Tunnel Mountain where hoodoos, or pictures formed in the rock by erosion, can be seen and from where there is a breathtaking view.
River-rafting	From June to the end of September a number of firms offer trips by rubber dinghy or raft on the Bow, Kootenay and Kicking Horse rivers.
Helicopter flights	Banff Heli Sports offers sightseeing trips by helicopter and will also take walkers to the more remote valleys or skiers to regions where they can be sure of snow.
Bankhead	About 7 km (4½ mi.) north-east of Banff Townsite, on the narrow bending road to Lake Minnewanka, can be found the remains of the old coal-mining town of Bankhead, which enjoyed its heyday in the first half of this century. An instructive footpath – with boards displaying old photographs and explanatory notes – helps give an idea of what this ghost town was like.
Lake Minnewanka	Lake Minnewanka ("Devil's Lake" in the Indian language), 11 km (7 mi.) north-east of Banff, is now the largest lake within the national park. Simpson, the Governor of Hudson's Bay Company, rested here in 1841. Along the banks of the lake an old Indian path leads by the edge of the rocky mountain range. Around the turn of the century a small health resort grew up here, but it was not until 1912 that the first dam was built which raised the level of the lake by three metres. When the mines at Bankhead closed the government decided to build a power station here to provide electricity for Banff. Then, in 1941, a further dam was built below the lake on Cascade River, which raised the water level of Lake Minnewanka by a further 25 m (82 ft). The lake became 8 km (5 mi.) longer, sinking the holiday resort, forests and all traces of the old trail. Now, between May and September, there are trips lasting two hours round the charmingly situated lake which is now some 20 km (13 mi.) long. On the trip it is often possible to spot thick-horned sheep, deer and black bear.

Lake Minnewanka is the only lake in the park on which motor-boats are allowed. It is worthwhile going on to Two Jack Lake – where canoes can be hired – and Johnson Lake. Swimming is possible in summer in the relatively calm lake. A fairly easy path leads round the lake.

Sunshine Region	9 km (5½ mi.) west of Banff Sunshine Road branches south off the Trans-Canada Highway. A further 10 km (6 mi.) brings visitors to the lower station of the longest cable railway – about 5000 m (16,400 ft) – in the Canadian Rockies (winter operation only). A twenty-minute ride takes them up to Sunshine Meadows, a very inviting mountain region where some beautiful hill-walks can be enjoyed, such as that to Rock Isle Lake. This region is particularly magnificent in summer, when the mountain flora is in full splendour. In winter the Sunshine Region is a favourite skiing area. A small Interpretive Centre provides information about the topography, and nature walks start from here. A chair-lift goes up to Standish Peak on the continental watershed, which here forms the boundary with British Columbia. From the end of June to early September the Sunshine Inn guesthouse offers food and lodging.
★Bow Valley Parkway	The 48 km (30 mi.) long Bow Valley Parkway to Lake Louise offers an alternative to the busy TransCanada Highway. Viewing points, camping and picnic sites as well as stopping-places with information boards make it possible to get to know the charming countryside of Bow Valley and to learn more about its geology and topography. Towering above it all is Castle Mountain, whose Eisenhower Peak is 2728 m (8950 ft) high.
Johnston Canyon	26 km (16 mi.) along the road sees the start of a favourite path through Johnston Canyon with its two waterfalls. Some 6 km (4 mi.) on the far

side of the canyon are the Ink Pots, a group of springs of which two basins are particularly striking because of the bluish-green colour of the water.

The only remnants of the old mining settlement of Silver City, 27 km (17 mi.) west of Banff, are a meadow and a sign.

The main attraction in Banff National Park is Lake Louise in its delightful setting 1731 m (5680 ft) above sea-level and 60 km (37 mi.) north-west of Banff. Its shimmering waters are mainly turquoise to dark green in colour, and it is about 2 km (1¼ mi.) long, up to 600 m (1970 ft) wide and 69 m (230 ft) deep and surrounded by glacial mountains up to 3000 m (9850 ft) in height. The Victoria Glacier reaches right down almost to the shores of the lake. Although the water is too cold for bathing it is ideal for canoeing. At the western end of Lake Louise Mount Victoria, 3469 m (11,385 ft) in height, rises in majestic splendour. A breathtaking view can be had from the famous Grand Hotel Château Lake which stands in beautifully tended gardens.

The Stoney Indians named Lake Louise "Lake of the Little Fishes". This "Jewel of the Rocky Mountains" was discovered in 1882 when the Pacific Railroad was being laid. Tom Wilson, survey packer of the CPR, named it Emerald Lake. However, in honour of Princess Louise, the daughter of Queen Victoria and wife of the Governor-General of Canada, the name was soon changed to Lake Louise.

In 1890 the CPR built the first Château Lake Louise on the moraine at the end of the lake. Easily accessible by rail, Lake Louise and the surrounding countryside soon developed into a tourist centre. From here expeditions started out to explore the rocky region on horseback. Mountaineers from England and the United States scaled the as yet unknown peaks. The present massive hotel was built in 1924 after a fire had destroyed its smaller wooden predecessor. In the early days horse-driven coaches – later to be superseded by trams – transported guests from the rail station down in the valley to the hotel 6 km (4 mi.) away.

Lake Louise

In the 1920s a road was built from Banff to Lake Louise. In the Bow River Valley the holiday village of Lake Louise developed, with nearly 400 permanent inhabitants.

Plain of Six Glaciers

Well-known from many picture postcards, Lake Louise is a starting point for some rewarding walks, the best of which perhaps being that to the Plain of Six Glaciers, which will take a total of some five hours. First follow the tarred and even road along the north-west shore of the lake as far as the river mouth, then climb up 360 m (1180 ft) to the travellers' rest, where food and drink can be purchased in summer, below the Victoria Glacier. A further 6 km (4 mi.) brings the walker to a good viewing-point.

Lake Agnes

Another very popular walk is that to Lake Agnes (difference in altitude 365 m (1200 ft)) picturesquely situated between the two round hills known as the Bee Hives. The strenuous climb to the top of one of the Bee Hives will be rewarded by a superb view. In summer the restaurant supplies food and refreshing drinks.

Mount Whitehorn

On the far side of the Bow River Valley a chair-lift provides access to Mount Whitehorn and the Lake Louise ski-slopes. This chair-lift operates mid-Jun.–mid-Sep. daily 8am–6pm. The viewing platform at 2034 m (6675 ft) – with restaurant and terrace – offers a magnificent view of Lake Louise, the Victoria Glacier and the glaciated ridges and peaks of the Bow Range. There is skiing from mid-Nov.–mid-May, with ski-school, ski hire and cafeteria.

★★Moraine Lake

Pictured on the reverse of the Canadian twenty dollar note, Moraine Lake in the Valley of the Ten Peaks is just as beautiful as Lake Louise but seems to attract fewer visitors. One charming view after another is revealed along the 13 km (8 mi.) approach road, which soon comes to a lake formed as a result of a landslide (not by a moraine, as Walter Wilcox wrongly assumed). This picturesque lake in a mountain valley, often a shimmering turquoise in colour, is overshadowed by ten peaks each over 3000 m (10,000 ft) high, forming the Wenckchema Glacier. In the distance the thundering of falling glaciers or landslides can be heard. Accommodation, provisions and canoe-hire are available at the rustic Moraine Lake Lodge.

A path 1½ km (1 mi.) long runs along the north-west shore. The short climb up the Rockpile Trail is very worthwhile; from this hill formed as the result of a landslide there is the best view of the lake. The walk into Larch Valley and to Sentinel Pass, one of the highest mountain passes in the national park, is somewhat exhausting, but from this mountain valley some 300 m (1000 ft) up there is another superb view. The tour is particularly charming in autumn (fall), when the larches are changing colour. After climbing a total of 6 km (4 mi.) and ascending 520 m (1700 ft) the Sentinel Pass (2611 m (8570 ft)) is reached.

Banks Island   C 5–7

Administrative Unit: Northwest Territories

Information

Northwest Territories Arctic Tourism, Box 610, Suite 400, Yellowknife, NT X1A 2N5; tel. (867) 8737200, fax. (867) 8734059.

Location

This, the most westerly island of the Canadian archipelago, covers an area of 70,028 sq. km (27,038 sq. mi.), somewhat less than the Republic of Ireland. North to south it measures about 400 km (250 mi.) between latitudes 71° and 74° 30′ north. Its coasts other than the north are free of ice in summer. In contrast to most islands on the archipelago there are very few fiords along its coastline, and the interior is not boldly formed, the landscape being in the main gently undulating with broad river valleys.

Banks Island possesses rich tundra vegetation, home to many animals, especially 25,000 musk-oxen (*Ovibus moschatus*), the largest population of these all together anywhere in the world. The south-western part of Banks Island, equal to about one-third of the whole, is a bird sanctuary. About 100 km (60 mi.) of the Thomsen River can be navigated by raft.

Although it had been used for hunting for perhaps 3500 years it was not until 1929 that Banks Island had a permanent settlement, when three Inuit families put down roots in Ikaahuk on the north-western tip of the island. Its "European" name derives from the Canadian Arctic expedition of 1913–15 led by Vilhjalmur Stefansson, whose ship was called "Mary Sachs". Ikaahuk, with a population of about 160, is a starting point for excursions. Banks Island Museum provides information on the history and archaeology of the island. There are flights to Ikaahuk from Inuvik.

Ikaahuk
Sachs Harbour

Since 1970 an archaeological institute from Tübingen in Germany has been carrying out digs on Banks Island. In the region around Umingmak ("musk-oxen") by Shoran Lake stone tools and weapons as well as bones from the Pre-Dorset culture *c.* 2000–1500 BC were found, some of them decorated with cult and mythological scratch-drawings. It has also been shown how, for the Inuit, the arrival of the Europeans in the 19th c. marked the start of their own "Iron Age". Having hitherto led a completely self-sufficient life, they integrated the new material with their traditional tools.

Archaeological
digs

Situated in the north of the island, Aulavik, with its numerous musk-oxen, was only designated a National Park in 1994. During the summer months is home to a large proportion of Canada's snow geese. A completely intact tundra flora is still to be found here.

Aulavik National
Park

★★Barkerville

G 6

Province: British Columbia

Highway 26 (about 100 km (62 mi.) east of Quesnel).

Access

The township of Barkerville, once the centre of the Cariboo gold-rush, is picturesquely situated surrounded by mountains in the valley of William Creek. It is the oldest remaining historic settlement in British Columbia.

Location

When the news spread in 1858 that gold had been found in the fluvial sand of the Fraser River there were soon thousands of men panning for gold all along the river and its tributaries. When in the summer of 1862 Billy Barker made his sensational find here at Williams Creek a typical gold-digging town of simple wooden huts, tents, saloons and shops sprang up almost overnight.

★★Barkerville
Historic Park

Until it burned down in 1868 Barkerville was the "largest town west of Chicago and north of San Francisco". Although it was immediately rebuilt to a high standard the end of the gold boom was already apparent. The introduction of machinery meant there was a need for fewer men but more capital. Chinese coolies worked longer hours for less pay and Chinese dealers began to monopolise the market. A marked social regrouping took place in the new Barkerville.

Following the end of the gold-rush Barkerville continued to fulfil the function of the centre of a region which was now inhabited by settlers and lumberjacks. so that the old gold-digging metropolis was saved from becoming just a ghost town.

Today the tourist will find a restored gold-digging town with about 75 historic buildings. When employees dressed in the fashions of the period act out "living history" in summer it is possible to visit a printing-works or smithy, a typical general store, the "Wellington Moses Barbershop" or the

"Barkerville Hotel" and feel completely transported back to the times of the gold-rush. The music-hall tradition is continued in the "Theatre Royal", and in the "Eldorado Mine" visitors can try their luck at panning for gold.

The Barkerville open-air museum is open daily from the end of June to early Sept. 8am–7pm.

Richfield
Courthouse

About 2 km (1¼ mi.) uphill from Williams Creek, in the historic Richfield Courthouse, lives the ghost of the famous Judge Begbie, remembered for a number of episodes in his colourful career.

★Bas St-Laurent H 16/17

Province: Québec

Information

Le Québec Maritime, 84 rue St. Germain Est, Rimouski, PQ G5L 8M1; tel. (418) 7247889, fax. (418) 7247278.

Access

From the city of Québec or Lévis on Highway 20 along the south coast of the St Lawrence River.

Location

"Bas St-Laurent" is the name given to that stretch of gently undulating countryside to the south of the St Lawrence River with a number of impressive agricultural estates. Further south the natural border is formed by the foothills of the Appalachians. A few rocky ridges and sandy plateaux protrude into this intensively cultivated region.

Immigrants from Europe settled on the southern shores of the St Lawrence many years ago.

Close to the river – alongside which the main road also winds – fishing villages nudge each other like pearls in a necklace. Cod, mackerel, lobsters and shrimps are here in abundance, and everywhere tourists are tempted to stay and watch fish being smoked in little huts.

Pretty villages and industrious towns with woodworking and textile factories and the like bear witness to the prosperity of this stretch of country.

★Drive to Rimouski from Québec (city) or Lévis (about 300 km/190 miles)

Lévis

The city of Québec (see entry) lies opposite the industrialised suburb of Lévis (pop. 20,000), from where there is a fine view to be had of the silhouette of the provincial capital with such a colourful past.

St-Jean-Port-Joli

St-Jean-Port-Joli (pop. 4000) is the handicraft centre of Québec province, where dozens of boutiques rub shoulders with one another.

In the centre of the little town stands the pleasing 18th c. church with its two bell-towers. Also worth a visit is the Musée des Anciens Canadiens exhibiting some outstanding work by native artists, including some Bougault sculptures. Open daily 10am–6pm.

St-Roch-des-
Aulnaies

St-Roch-des-Aulnaies (pop. 1200) belongs to the "Siegneurie des Aulnaies", an imposing estate bearing the street number 132, the castle-like main building of which dates from the middle of the 19th c. A guided tour gives an insight into the way the upper classes lived.

It is possible to visit the 19th c. corn-mill which is still in working order.

La Pocatière

The little town of La Pocatière (pop. 5000) lies on a terrace above the St Lawrence coastal plain. It is an important centre of rural education.

A visit to the Musée Franáois Pilote at the rear of the Collège Ste-Anne is worthwhile. This collection of regional studies provides information on the production of maple syrup and on the history of the local woodworking industry. There is also an interesting exhibition of horse-drawn carriages and carts. Open Mon.–Sat. 9am–6pm.

Kamouraska (pop. 500), with its picturesque little houses, is a typical small fishing-village.
    From this side of the St Lawrence River on a fine day there is a beautiful view over towards Charlevoix (see entry), the wild and rugged coastal band opposite and to the north.

Kamouraska

The busy industrial town of Rivière-du-Loup, with a population of 15,000, is also an important traffic junction, as it is here that the main road branches off southwards to the neighbouring province of New Brunswick. The town has a marina, beautifully laid-out places for bathing and a camp-site. Popular with visitors is the waterfall, which plunges down from a ledge 30 m (100 ft) high.

Rivière-du-Loup

Completely charming in every respect, the end of 18th c. town of Bic (pop. 4000) on the St Lawrence River lies in a "hunchback world" of wooded hills. This has been declared a protected area, with the aim of allowing the marine life to become re-established.

★Bic

Rimouski (pop. 31,000) is the administrative, economic and cultural centre of the region along the lower reaches of the St Lawrence River. It has a high school and is an important port serving a wider area.
    The Musée de la Mer is open daily 9am–6pm and houses exhibitions on marine studies.
    To the west of the town the waters of the Rivière Rimouski plunge through a wild gorge. Some 5 km (3 mi.) further west a pretty lake for bathing has been constructed.

Rimouski

North-east of Rimouski lies the town of Ste-Flavie, the entrance gate to the Gaspésie peninsula (see entry).

Ste-Flavie

Bathurst

H 17

Province: New Brunswick. Population: 14,000

Tourism Bathurst, 256 St Andrew's St., Bathurst, NB E2A 3Z1; tel. (506) 5480410.

Information

New Brunswick Highways 11 & 34.

Access

The very busy little town of Bathurst lies on Baie Nepsiguit, a cove at the south of Baie des Chaleurs, into which the Nepsiguit River flows.
    The town was founded in the 17th c. by French-speaking Acadians led by Governor Nicholas Denys.

Location

Today Bathurst is an important industrial town and business centre for an extensive area. One of the world's largest zinc mines is worked near here. In the town centre will be found more than 80 different shops and service industries, with a further 50 shops, boutiques, etc. in the modern Centre Chaleur.

Importance

Sights

Bathurst has a small sheltered harbour used by fishermen and with a marina enjoyed by spare-time sailors.

Harbour

The Farmers Market is held in Main Street every Saturday from 9am to 1pm.

Farmers Market

There is a Museum of Military History in St Pierre Avenue.

Military museum

The well-tended Youghall Provincial Park extends along the north side of Bathurst harbour bay. There are some fine spots for bathing and a marina. Not far away is an interesting bird-sanctuary.

Youghall Provincial Park

Surroundings

★Zinc mine

20 km (13 mi.) south-west of Bathurst is one of the world's most productive zinc mines. The production plant can be visited by prior arrangement with the Chamber of Commerce (see Information above).

Waterfalls

Tetagouche, to the south-west of Bathurst, and Pabineau Falls to the south, are two most impressive waterfalls.

New Brunswick Mining & Mineral Interpretation Centre

To the north of Bathurst, near Petit-Rocher (see Campbellton) the New Brunswick Mining & Mineral Interpretation Centre is open to visitors. A mining shaft gives an idea of what working underground is like. Visitors can look into caverns and see how an actual subterranean road network is laid out to enable the valuable minerals to be extracted.

★★Batoche National Historic Park   G 9

Province: Saskatchewan

History

Batoche, the stronghold of the Métis people (the offspring of a white person and a Canadian Indian) on the Saskatchewan River, was the headquarters of their ringleader Louis Riel during the North West Rebellion in 1885. This is where the decisive battle took place between the insurgents under Riel and Gabriel Dumont and General Middleton with his troops from the North West Mounted Police; this marked the end of the rebellion.

Batoche

The village of Batoche was founded in the early 1870s, when Xavier Letendre, also known as "Batoche", constructed a ferry, a shop and a storehouse on the spot where the Carlton Trail crossed the river. It soon grew into a trade centre for the growing number of Métis settlers along the river. In 1883 a presbytery was built, and in the following year the Church of St Antoine de Padoue.

Near the river bank lies East Village, the original village, of which foundations and cellars still remain. This is where the Batoche ferry crossed the South Saskatchewan River.

Visitor Reception Centre

In the Visitor Reception Centre are displays illustrating the way of life of the Métis, the events which led up to the rebellion and the battle of May 1885. Dioramas portray such scenes as a buffalo-hunt, the Métis digging defensive ditches such as those used in the Battle of Batoche, and Middleton's troops using a nine-pounder field-gun. Among the numerous exhibits are Louis Riel's writing-case, his bridle and stirrups.

St Antoine de Padoue

The presbytery, where shell and bullet-holes suffered in the battle can still be seen, and the Church of St Antoine de Padoue (1883–84) are now excellent museums, displaying photographs and other memorabilia of the battle and of the earlier Métis culture. The Gothic church still contains some of the original pews as well as the harmonium and stove.

The graves of Dumont and Letendre and a mass-grave of fallen Métis can be seen in the churchyard. There is also a memorial to the Métis and Indians who died during the conflict.

Nearby stands a fenced-in store, the "zareba", built by the military. By day it served as a point from which attacks were directed and by night as a defensive post.

Hollows along the river bank mark the position of the trenches from which Middleton's soldiers fired on the Métis. Nearby stands a farmhouse which was rebuilt in 1895 after having been destroyed by the army. From the other side of the road there is a superb view of the South Saskatchewan River. From the presbytery a path leads across the prairie to a defensive trench which has been opened up. These trenches were marked with tree-trunks and cleverly camouflaged with rows of trees.

In Fish Creek, south of Batoche, the first clash between Riel's troops and the military took place. Markings show the way to the field where the battle was fought, Middleton's troops camped and the dead were buried.

Fish Creek

May, June, Sept. 9am–5pm; July, Aug. 10am–6pm.

Opening times

★Battleford

G 9

Province: Saskatchewan

Battleford Chamber of Commerce, PO Box 1000, North Battleford, SK S9A 3E6; tel. (306) 445–62 26.

Information

The towns of North Battleford (pop. 14,000) and Battleford, linked by the longest bridge over the North Saskatchewan River, lie in the centre of the province of Saskatchewan, an area steeped in history.

Location

Battleford (pop. 4000) was the first seat of government in the Northwest Territories (see entry) and an important Mounted Police post.

Importance

Tourists are recommended to visit the historic Western Development Museum–Heritage Farm & Village which illustrates the history of agriculture. The exhibition of agricultural equipment and tools is supplemented in summer by demonstrations of farming techniques from before the 1920s. In addition a small 1925 town has been built incorporating many original buildings from surrounding places. It includes houses built in the style of Ukranian and French- Canadian settlers, a railway station, a barber's shop and a school. Open May 1st–Oct. 31st 9am–6pm,

★Western Development Museum

The Allen Sapp Gallery in 100th St. houses the "Gonor Collection" of pictures by the Cree artist Allen Sapp, one of the leading contemporary Canadian artists. His art gives a rare insight into the lives of the Cree people. Open Tue.–Sun. 1–5pm.

Allen Sapp Gallery

The George Hooey Wildlife Exhibit, housed in Battleford's Wildlife Federation Building displays over 400 preserved specimens of animals, including fishes and birds, some of which date back as far as 1890. Open by prior arrangement Jun. 1st–Aug. 31st.

George Hooey Wildlife Exhibit

In Fort Battleford National Historic Park the rich and varied pattern of Battleford's history is brought to life. The Fort was the seat of government of the Northwest Territories between 1876 and 1882.

★Fort Battleford

The Canadian Northern Railway Station, built in 1908 at the corner of 22nd St. and 1st. Ave., and which marked Battleford's link-up with the railway, was converted into a restaurant in 1976.

Station

The Fred Light Museum is a reproduction of a shop, a class-room and an armoury with a fine collection of weapons. In addition many utensils are exhibited, such as shaving mugs and lamps, which were in use at the turn of the century.
  Other departments are devoted to the history of the military and the Mounted Police. Open daily May 14th.–Sep. 10th 10am–6pm.

Fred Light Museum

Nearly 5 km (3 mi.) south-east of Battleford lies Battleford National Historic Park. This clearly explains the role played by the North West Mounted Police (the "Mounties") in the development of Western Canada. For example, on display is their base established in 1876, as well as five buildings, four furnished in the style of the time, and reconstructed ramparts. The 1886 barracks house some informative exhibitions. Open May 1st–Oct. 10th, Mon.–Sat. 9am–5pm, Sun. 10am–6pm; July, Aug. daily 10am–6pm.

★Battleford National Historic Park

Bonavista Peninsula

★Cut Knife National Historic Site

16 km (10 mi.) to the north the Cut Knife National Historic Site overlooks Battle River Valley. This is another important arena depicting the North West Rebellion, as it was here that the battle took place in 1885 between the Canadian troops under Colonel Otter and the Indians under Chief Poundmaker. Otter thought the Indians had been responsible for plundering Battleford and burning it to the ground. The natives were victorious in this battle. Chief Poundmaker was convicted of treason, imprisoned, died a year later and was buried up on the hill.

Cut Knife

The Clayton McLain Memorial Museum (open Jun. 1st–Aug. 31st 9am–8pm, at other times by arrangement) displays articles used by the combatants in the Battle of Cut Knife. In addition, the following restored and furnished buildings are open to visitors: school (1908), railway station (1912), shop (1920), village church (1925) and a log-cabin (1930). Items on display include objects used by the Indians and the pioneers, machines, antiques, shotguns, archive material, etc.

Hanging near the museum in Tomahawk Park is the biggest tomahawk in the world, nearly 12 m (39 ft) tall and weighing 8 tonnes. This remarkable architectural feat is a symbol of the public-spiritedness and friendship exisiting between the good people of Cut Knife.

Battlefords Provincial Park

Some 40 km (25 mi.) further north Battlefords Provincial Park spans an area alongside Jackfish Lake, a favourite spot with anglers. The park offers the following attractions: camping, picnicking, a golf-course, minigolf, hire of boats and bicycles, a nature path and an excellent sandy beach.

★★Bonavista Peninsula   H 20

Province: Newfoundland

Information

See Newfoundland

Location

The best-known peninsula in Newfoundland is Bonavista, where John Cabot is thought to have sighted the "New World" for the first time in 1497.

One of the most impressive pieces of scenery on this peninsula so rich in forests and waterways and with its rugged coastline is to be found by turning off Road 230 onto the 235. The beautiful smaller places should also not be missed; these include Plate Cove and King's Cove, one of the oldest settlements here and founded by fishermen from Bonavista in the middle of the 18th c.

Bonavista

The fishing-town of Bonavista with its population of 5000 is one of the main towns on the peninsula. Its port was used by European fishing fleets back in the 16th c. Around 1600 Bonavista was a British settlement and remained so in spite of attempts by the French to take it in the 18th c.

Bonavista Museum in Church Street is open in summer and in winter by prior arrangement. It explains the history of the area by means of exhibits collected by the inhabitants.

The Mockbeggar Property (open daily in summer) is made up of a number of buildings which reflect various aspects of the traditional Newfoundland life-style.

★★Cape Bonavista

A very beautiful 5 km (3 mi.) stretch leads from here to the cape which is probably that sighted by John Cabot in 1497 and which he named Bonavista, or "beautiful view". The cape is quite magnificent with its breakers, clear blue sea and interesting rock formations. Here stands a statue of Cabot in memory of the first man to discover North America, although more recent research throws doubt on the authenticity of his claim.

The old lighthouse, a Provincial Historic Site, dates from 1843 and was restored about 1870; it is open daily in Jul. and Aug.; guides wear historical costume.

Bonavista Bay

Port Union

Port Union is named after the first Newfoundland fishermen's union. Here will be found an impressive memorial to William Coaker, the organiser of the union and founder of the town.

The old railway station now houses the Port Union Museum with maritime exhibits.

Campers can spend the night in Lockston Path Provincial Park on Route 236. From the view-point above the lake there is a spectacular panorama of the surrounding countryside.

★ Trinity

Picturesque Trinity, from which the offshore bay gets its name, is an old fishing and trading town which still has its wharves. The historical charac- ter of the town has been well preserved. Ryan Premises, which are privately owned but may be visited on request, The Society of Fishermen's Hall and other 19th c. buildings have remained almost unchanged in appearance. Trinity is one of Newfoundland's oldest settlements, having been founded in 1615 as the seat of the first maritime court.

Trinity Museum

Over 1000 items are on display in the historical little Trinity Museum and Archives, built in 1880 and open every day in summer; these include models of ships and items connected with whale-catching and with handicrafts such as shoe-making and barrel-making.

Hiscock House

Hiscock House – renovated in 1910 – is also a Provincial Historic Site; guides in contemporary dress explain how life was in a typical local household in the early 20th c. Open daily in Jul. and Aug.

Battery

Above the marina can be seen the remains of the Battery at Admiral's Point, which was destroyed by the French in 1762. It had been surrendered by the British garrison in the middle of the 18th c.

★Brandon H 11

Province: Manitoba. Population: 40,000

Location

The "wheat town" of Brandon, with the Assiniboine River flowing through it, lies in the Pembina Valley, surrounded by blue hills. Brandon, the central terminal for the shipping of corn, is Manitoba's second largest town and a booming tourist centre, in spite of the fact that it is somewhat spoiled by the presence of dairies, packing industry and even oil refineries.

Paterson/Matheson House

Paterson/Matheson House in Louise Ave. was built in 1893. It is a very good example of the East Lake Style of building.

Daly House

Daly House was the residence of the town's first mayor, Thomas Mayne Daly (1882). The historical furniture and fittings are much to be admired. Open daily 10am–noon, 1pm–5pm.

★B. J. Hales Museum of Natural History

Also worth a visit is the B.J. Hales Museum of Natural History in Brandon University on 18th St. On exhibition here are items which belonged to the Sioux and Plains Indians, such as pipes, ceramics, arrowheads and tools. There are also 250 stuffed specimens of local birds in models of their natural habitat. The exhibition is completed by a collection of mammals, such as animals from the North in their "icy" surroundings. Jack Lane was curator of the museum for many years. The legendary "Bluebird Man" saved many species of birds from extinction, such as the American Robin. In the 1930s the number of those birds had reduced to a few dozen. With children's help Lane set up nests around the town and the number of birds increased to 15,000. Open daily Apr.–Sep. 1.30pm–4.30pm; Oct.–Mar. Mon.–Sat. 1.30pm–4.30pm.

Allied Arts Centre

Every year there are temporary exhibitions and displays of handicraft and painting to be seen in the Brandon Allied Arts Centre on Princess Ave.

Agriculture Canada Station

The Agriculture Canada Station does research into plant-foods, herbicides and fodder, the genetics of barley and the breeding and feeding of cattle, pigs and poultry. Two-thirds of the total area of corn grown in Western Canada is planted with varieties developed here. Open Mon.–Fri. 8am–4.30pm.

University

At Brandon University, where there are guided tours available, the Administration Building, built in 1901, the 1906 School of Music and the J.R. Brodie Science Building are of interest.

Commonwealth Air Training Plan Museum

The Commonwealth Air Training Plan Museum (No. 1 Hangar, McGill Field restores and exhibits aircraft and training equipment. Open May–Sep. daily 9am–4.30pm; Oct.–Apr. Mon.–Fri. 9am–4.30pm.

Artillery Museum

The 26th Field Artillery Regiment Museum displays military equipment, uniforms and memorabilia. A library adjoins it. Open Sun. 2–4.30pm and by arrangement.

Keystone Sports

The Keystone Sports Complex, covering some 34 ha (85 acres) will be of interest to sports enthusiasts. It was built in 1979 as a venue for the Canadian Winter Games.

Surroundings

★Grand Valley Provincial Recreation Park

In the Grand Valley Provincial Recreation Park 10 km (6 mi.) west of the town lies Stott Site. In this archaeologically important region where bison were once hunted bones and objects at least 1200 years old have been found.

★Brantford

Province: Ontario. Population: 85,000

Tourism Brantford, 1 Sherwood Dr., Brantford, 0N N3T 1N3; tel. (519) 7519900.

Information

Brantford, the main town in Brant Country, lies on the Grant River about 100 km (60 mi.) south-west of Toronto. In the American War of Indepen- dence the Six Nations Indians, under their leader Joseph Brant, fought on the side of Britain. When they fled from the USA they founded this settlement in 1784. In 1830 white settlers came here and acquired the area where the town now stands. Economic prosperity came with the railroad; Brantford is situated at the junction of some important rail routes. Alexander Graham Bell (see Famous People) also contributed in no small measure to the fame of the town; he solved the problem of passing sound waves along cables and so discovered the telephone, which made him a rich man.

Location

This chapel stands at the junction of Mohawk St. and Greenwich St. King George II donated the money to the town to build a church in return for its assistance during the American Revolution. This, the oldest Protestant church in Ontario, soon made Brantfort the religious centre of the region.

★Her Majesty's Chapel of the Mohawks

This museum at 184 Mohawk St. displays an impressive collection of Indian artefacts portraying the everyday life of the Indians of the eastern forests. Naturally, the emphasis is on the Six Nations Indians, who are a part of these ethnic groups.

★Museum of the Woodland Indian

The Bell Homestead estate at 94 Tutela Heights Road is a large and invit- ing house with period furniture and containing some original memora- bilia from the life of Alexander Graham Bell (see Famous People).

Bell Homestead

British Columbia

Geographical location: latitude 49°–60° north/longitude 118°–130° west
Area: 947,800 sq. km (365,851 sq. mi.)
Population: 4 million. Capital: Victoria

Tourism British Columbia,
802–865 Horny St., Vancouver, BC V6Z 2G3; tel. (604) 6602861, fax. (604) 6603383.

Information

British Columbia covers 9·4 per cent of the total area of Canada, making it the third largest province. The province is characterised mainly by the two mountain chains of the Canadian Cordilleras and the geologically deposited plateau. The Coast Range Mountains are very rugged and carved up by fiords. The offshore islands, including Vancouver Island, are remains of another mountain chain, the Insular Mountains, and provide a unique form of landscape. Mount Waddington, at 4016 m (13,180 ft), is the highest in the Coast Range Mountains and indeed in the whole of British Columbia. The plateaux are 800–1200 m (2600–4000 ft) high, composed of Tertiary lava, ashes and freshwater deposits. The Rocky Mountains, forming the eastern border of the province of Alberta, are relatively young mountains, having folded in the Tertiary period, and based on sediment from the Triassic and Jurassic periods. During the Pleistocene Age British Columbia, like North and Central Europe, was completely covered in ice. Traces of the four Ice Ages can still be seen in the shape of numerous glaciers, for example in the Columbia Icefield near the border with Alberta, which covers an area of 389 sq. km (150 sq. mi.) and is still 1000 m (3300 ft) thick. The main ridge of the Rockies also forms the water-shed of Canada. Thus British Columbia is the only province which drains into the Pacific Ocean; by comparison, 66 per cent of Canada's land surface drains into the Arctic Ocean. The highest

Location

mountain in the Rockies is Mount Robson, 3954 m (12,977 ft) high. As a result of the mountain structure the river network is very ramified. The Fraser River is 1360 km (845 mi.) long and the Columbia 1840 km (1143 mi.).

Climate

The individual mountain chains which make up the Canadian Cordilleras have a marked influence on the climate of British Columbia. On the western sides the rainfall is generally very heavy; for example, Prince Rupert has 2330 mm (91·7in.) per annum, Vancouver 1460 mm (57·5 in.). In the lee of the mountains, on the other hand, there are some very dry pockets, such as Kamloops with 268 mm (10·5 in.) per annum and Penticton with 300 mm (11·8 in.). Winters generally mean a lot of snow, up to 5 m (17 ft), although there are some valleys which see very little in the way of snow. In the interior of British Columbia, shielded by the mountains, the climate is quite continental, with short, very hot summers and long, extremely cold winters; Kamloops, for example, has an average January minimum of −10°C (14°F), and an average maximum in July of 29°C (83°F). The coast is blessed with the Kuro Schio, a warm ocean current producing really mild temperatures; Vancouver, for instance, has an average January minimum of 0°C (32°F) and an average maximum of 24°C (74°F) in July, while Prince Rupert's average January minimum is −1°C (31°F), July maximum 17°C (62°F).

Vegetation

British Columbia's natural vegetation is determined largely by the high mountains. Coniferous forest predominates, changing to tundra and glaciated regions as one goes higher. The offshore islands, like the whole of the Pacific coast, are heavily wooded, mainly with coniferous trees. Here are still found large expanses of temperate coastal rain forest harbouring some of the oldest and largest fir trees in the world. These primeval woodlands, exceptionally valuable not only in resource terms but also from an ecological point of view, are today under threat from Canada's profit-orientated timber industry (see Baedeker Special p. 502).The hot summers in the valleys and the low rainfall result in steppe-like vegetation where – with adequate irrigation (see The Okanagan) – even fruit such as peaches and apricots can be grown.

History

In the 17th c. Spanish mariners sailed northwards up the Pacific coast and discovered British Columbia, which until then had for thousands of years been inhabited only by native Indians. In 1778 James Cook was the first white man to set foot on Vancouver Island. In that same year Capt. John Meares founded the first English settlement of Nootka, but this had to be ceded to Spain on the grounds of old claims held by the latter. In 1790 the Spaniards renounced their claims, however, and Capt. George Vancouver was able to take possession of the island for Great Britain. Alexander Mackenzie was the first white man to reach the Pacific by the land route in 1793, to be followed by Simon Fraser and David Thompson, after whom the largest rivers in the province are named.

In British Columbia too the "49th parallel" was made the border between Canada and the United States, in accordance with the terms of the Oregon Treaty. In 1849 Vancouver Island was declared a Crown Colony. Seven years later important gold finds attracted large numbers of adventurers and settlers to Fraser Valley and Barkerville. In 1886 the mainland of British Columbia and Vancouver Island off the coast were merged and joined the Canadian Confederation in 1871. Victoria was made the capital of this new province. Between 1923 and 1926 organised immigration from Europe led to further settlements being established in the province. Following the Japanese occupation of the Aleutians during the Second World War the United States decided in 1942 to build a land route to Alaska, the present Alaskan Highway (see entry), which runs from Dawson Creek B.C. to Fairbanks, Alaska. The east-west link was improved in 1962 by the completion of the TransCanada Highway. In 1986 the World Exhibition was held in Vancouver.

Population

British Columbia has a relatively high population density of 4·2 per square kilometre (10·9 per square mile). However, there is a marked fall

British Columbia

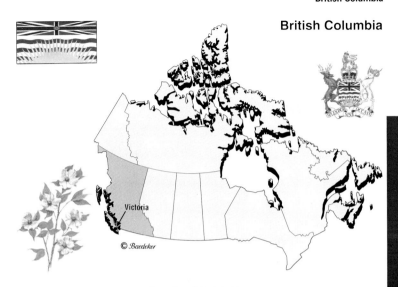

© Baedeker

Victoria

in population as one moves northward, and the inhabitants are concentrated in a very few towns and centres, with half the population in the Vancouver conurbation alone. The original native inhabitants were basically of two types, the Salish and the Kutenai, who lived mainly from hunting in the interior. In contrast to the Indians in the north-west of British Columbia they are nomads. Those living on the coast – including the Tlingits and the Wakashans – rely mainly on the resources of the sea and live in permanent settlements. 4·4 per cent of the population of British Columbia are the original native Indians, i.e. about a sixth of the total Canadian native population. While almost 80 per cent of the white population live in towns and cities only 40 per cent of the Indians do so, mainly as a result of the fact that their small settlements are well organised and are almost urban in character. Naturally the British constitute the largest group of immigrants in British Columbia (60 per cent), as can be clearly seen in Victoria, the provincial capital. As Vancouver is an important trading centre with Asia it is not surprising to find a large Asian minority in British Columbia, especially in Vancouver itself.

British Columbia is one of Canada's richest provinces. The main branches of its economy are forestry, fishing, mining and tourism. About 60 per cent of Canada's utilisable timber comes from British Columbia. The province provides 30 per cent of the needs of the newspaper industry, making it the largest timber-producer in Canada, with 45 per cent of the net product and 45 per cent of the total workers employed in the timber industry. Timber is exported mainly to the United States (42·9 per cent), Japan (19·0 per cent) and to EU countries (22·3 per cent). As in Alberta, the forests are given over to private firms who are allowed to cut down trees on a quota system in line with the reforesting programme. State politics incline towards localised wood-working, thus guaranteeing a balanced sharing. The main difficulties encountered by the timber industry result from many factories being out-of-date and excessive energy requirements compared with its competitors, such as Sweden. Pests and forest fires are natural obstacles which cannot readily be legislated for. Views have changed on the subject of establishing

Economy

139

A gold-washing site

new forests, and in the 1980s 110,000 ha (275,000 acres) of trees were planted.

In addition to the lumber industry, fishing is also of great importance. 95 per cent of the Canadian salmon industry is in British Columbia. As well as five different species of salmon there is also herring, 95 per cent of which is exported to Japan. Sales of herring alone total $85,000,000 per annum. Together with traditional forms of fishing aquaculture is gaining in importance, breeding mainly salmon, but also trout, prawns and mussels. 22,000 people are directly employed in the fishing industry and 25,000 in allied processing trades.

In contrast to the "prairie states", agriculture plays only a minor role. A small amount of corn is grown in the north-east near Peace River, and fruit and vine cultivation plays is quite important in the valleys to the south. The main mines are those producing coal, stretching from the south-east to the north-west of Alberta across British Columbia to the Yukon Territory. In addition lead, zinc and asbestos is mined, and the copper stocks equal 50 per cent of Canada's total copper resources. Hydro-electric power and natural gas provide the bulk of energy requirements, while crude oil has to be imported from Alberta. Its position on the Pacific means that British Columbia is ideally situated to trade with Asia and Australia. Alberta markets its giant coal and crude oil deposits via the trade centres of British Columbia. The varied leisure facilities make tourism an important economic factor for British Columbia. Most European tourists chose this province for their holiday.

Tourism

Its unspoiled mountains, extensive forests and numerous lakes make British Columbia a paradise for sports lovers of every ilk. Those keen on water-sports are catered for by numerous lakes and charming rivers, with paddling on lonely lakes to rafting on the rivers. The unique fiord-like coastline is ideal for sailing, while swimming in the Pacific is a question of taste, in spite of the warm ocean currents. In contrast, the hot sun raises the temperatures of the lakes further inland almost to those of a swimming-pool.

For fishermen the salmon spawning season in August and September offers fantastic sport. Every conceivable variety of fish can be caught in the many lakes and rivers.

The varied nature of the countryside makes British Columbia an ideal place for walking, especially in the national and provincial parks where North America's natural charms are there to be enjoyed. Hunting is forbidden in these parks, but elsewhere there are plenty of opportunities to hunt black and brown bear, mink, beaver and varities of duck. After a tiring day it is so refreshing to relax in a hot spring. For horse-lovers there are wonderful opportunities to hire a horse on a ranch. For anyone wishing to try their hand at golf Canada is the place, because equipment can be hired at any golf-club. In winter thousands of sports are available. Mount Whistler, 125 km (76 mi.) from Vancouver, offers ski-runs of varying degrees of difficulty. There are ample sports opportunities for visitors from Europe to enjoy, and the numerous tourist bureaux scattered throughout the province will be glad to assist in all matters relating to leisure pursuits.

Burin Peninsula   H 19

Province: Newfoundland

See Newfoundland   Information

Route 210 to the Burin Peninsula leaves the TransCanada Highway near   Access
Goobies. The greater part of this stretch runs inland with short side-
roads branching off to some pretty little coastal towns.
    The countryside here is hilly and rather barren moorland.

The peninsula has a rich history linked to fishing in Grand Banks. From   History
about the 15th c. onwards it became a European fishing ground, when
French, British and Portuguese came here in summer to fish. After
people began to settle permanently it still remained important from a
fishing point of view, and even today the inhabitants depend almost
completely on the fishing industry for their living.

Mention should be made of Swift Current, situated 24 km (15 mi.) past the   Swift Current
turn-off, because of its magnificent beaches and its beautiful river,
Piper's Hole in Provincial Park. There is a stretch of heathland below the
town.

Route 212 leads off right to Bay l'Argent and Little Bay East, two places   Coastline
of lasting beauty. Bay l'Argent has some long beaches of silvery
rocks.

Baine Harbour and Rushoon on the opposite side of the peninsula are
also worth a visit. Further south lie the loveliest spots, John the Bay,
Little Bay and Beau Bois, known worldwide for its beauty.

Further along Route 210 lie:

The shipyard port of Marystown (pop. 6700), beautifully situated on   **Marystown**
Little Bay, is the largest town in the province. This is where the mainly
large fishing-boats are built.

Nearby Mortier Bay is both picturesque and tranquil.   **Mortier Bay**
    From Marystown the 210 and 220 roads lead round the "boot" of the
peninsula, with stops in Burin, St Lawrence, Fortune and Grand Bank. A
large part of this 159 km (99 mi.) stretch passes through barren and
wind-lashed countryside.

At Golden Sands Resort, near Salt Pond, will be found huts and camp-   **Golden Sands**
ing-sites and a lovely beach suitable for bathing.   **Resort**

Cabano

Route 221 leads to an entrancing piece of coast with hundreds of islands and projecting rock formations.

Burin

Burin, which developed as a result of the fishing industry, consists of a collection of villages dating back to the 18th c. and scattered between small bays and inlets.

The 220 leads you to Freshwater Pond Provincial Park, a good place at which to learn more about the island.

Not only is this place a centre of ship-building, it also has large fleets of fishing-steamers and some of the largest fish-production plants on the island. Huge quantities are brought here for processing every year from the towns at the southern tip.

St Lawrence

St Lawrence, surrounded by pretty towns and villages, was at one time one of the world's largest producers of the mineral fluorite (fluorspar). Miner's Museum, open daily in summer, documents the history of the local mining industry and the lives of the miners.

The breakers off the south coast at Allan Island, High Beach and Point au Gaul can be very spectacular.

Just before reaching Grand Bank there is a beautiful view of the south coast, Brunette Island and Miquelon Island.

Grand Bank

Grand Bank is the largest and most varied of the "banks" in the south and east, shallow waterways with large stocks of fish which have attracted fishermen for centuries and still continue to do so. Grand Bank is where the Labrador current and the Gulf Stream meet, causing the colder stream to sink below the warmer, thus churning up plankton from the sea-bed. The plankton then rises to the surface and attracts great shoals of fish. Traditionally mainly fish of the cod group are caught, together with some herring. The fishing-boats used to be known as "bankers".

Oil and gas are also drilled for on Grand Bank.

Grand Bank

The beautifully situated town of Grand Bank is an important fishing centre. It has some attractive houses with "widow-walks", small open galleries on the roof from which the women could watch for the return of their menfolk from the sea.

In the Southern Newfoundland Seamen's Museum, built in triangular blocks to imitate sails, will be found some interesting exhibits illustrating the history of fishing on the "banks" and the lives of the fisherfolk; it is open every day. Of special interest are photographs of ships and fish, as well as models of the ships which were used.

★Cabano   H 17

Province: Québec. Population: 3000

Information

Tourisme Québec, PO Box 979, Montréal, PQ H3C 2W3; tel. (514) 8732015, fax. (514) 8643838

Location

Cabano, the centre of the timber industry, lies in the far south of Québec Province near its border with New Brunswick and the US state of Maine on the TransCanada Highway.

Situated in some most charming countryside nearby is Lake Témiscouta, once an important staging-post in the transport of timber between the St Lawrence and the St John River catchment area.

In the past, especially in the 19th c., there were constant disputes between the owners of land belonging to Québec and New Brunswick on the one hand and their US neighbours on the other.

★Fort Ingall

Some 2 km (1¼ mi.) out of Cabano on Route 232 lies Fort Ingall, built of wood in 1839 and which at one time housed 200 soldiers. The fort was lovingly restored a few years ago. A small museum explains how the officers and men lived here and what disputes and clashes they were faced with. From the terrace of the fort surrounded with stout palisades there is a lovely view over Lake Témiscouata. There is also a beautiful picnic site here.

Cabot Trail

See Cape Breton Island

Cache Creek

See Ashcroft · Cache Creek

★★Calgary   G 8

Province: Alberta
Altitude: 1049 m (3443 ft). Population: 768,000

Calgary Convention & Visitors Bureau, 237 8th Avenue, S.E., Calgary, AB   Information
T2G 0K8; tel. (800) 6611678 (Service Centre in foyer of Calgary Tower,
Centre Street & 9th Avenue, S.E.)

By air:
Calgary International Airport (12 km (7½ mi.) north-east of the city centre)   Access
is well integrated into the North American airline network. Buses operate shuttle services between the airport and Downtown Calgary, also all
the major hotels.

By rail:
From mid-April until mid-October, and during the Christmas period, the
"Rocky Mountaineer" runs several times a week between Calgary and
Vancouver (see Facts and Figures, Canada by Rail). There are currently
no VIA Rail services to Calgary.

By bus:
Greyhound: daily coach services from Calgary to Vancouver, Regina,
Saskatchewan and Winnipeg.
Red Arrow Express: from Calgary several times a day to Red Deer and
Edmonton.
Brewster Buses: daily high season service from Calgary via Banff and
the Icefields Parkway to Jasper and return.

Calgary Transit buses cover most parts of the city.   City buses

Since 1987 the suburban railway system known as "LRT" (Light Rail   LRT
Transit; called "C" Train) has been in operation, latterly with services to
some outlying districts. From the city centre three lines run south as far
as Anderson Road, north-east as far as Whitehorn Station (44 Ave., N. E.)
and north-west to the University. Between Downtown Mall (10th St.
S. W.) and City Hall transport is free.

The present city of Calgary lies on the western edge of the Canadian   Location
prairie where Elbow River enters Bow River, about 250 km (155 mi.) north
of the Canada-USA border.

Particularly on days when the chinook, a dry warm fall wind, blows over   Climate
the Rocky Mountains less than 100 km (60 mi.) away, the glaciated
mountain peaks on the western horizon appear like an insurmountable
barrier rising from the plain. In winter this west wind, related to the föhn
of Alpine countries, sometimes causes temperatures rapidly to rise by
over 30°C (90°F) and the snows to melt. Lying as it does in the lee of the
Rockies Calgary has little rainfall; summer days are mostly dry, sunny
and warm, the nights refreshingly cool.

Calgary

Calgary Stampede

★★Stampede

Calgary, the city lying between the wilderness and the wheat-fields and ever since its foundation in competition with its sister city to the north, Edmonton, justifies its reputation as a "cowboy town" only once in the year, when the ten-day "stampede" is held. Then the population seems to feel obliged to dress accordingly, and blue jeans and brightly-coloured stetsons become the order of the day. Calgary becomes the centre of attraction for all Wild West fans; rodeos and wagon-racing teams, an authentic Indian camp of wigwams and traditional Indian dances, as well as agricultural shows all contribute to this great outdoor event.

Economy

On the occasion of the Winter Olympics in 1988 Calgary showed that today it is more than just an agricultural arena, a chamber of commerce for the Alberta wheat trade or a trans-shipment centre for cattle. In that year visitors from all over the world found a welcome in the city.

Calgary can thank the oil being extracted from nearby for its dramatic development during the last 40 years from a provincial town to a modern metropolis, to a veritable "Manhattan of the prairies". In the busy city centre the glittering office buildings belonging to oil companies, banks and insurance companies tower 30 floors or more up into the sky. Around them stretch more than 527 sq. km (204 sq. mi.) of suburbs laid out in strict chess-board fashion, making Calgary Canada's third largest city.

Calgary boasts one of the most modern high-speed railway systems in Canada and the unique, mainly covered-in pedestrian street network known as the "Plus 15" Walkway System. Most of the office buildings, department stores, hotels and multi-storey car parks in the city are linked to one another by a system of footbridges totalling some 30 km (20 mi.) in length. A pedestrian zone in the city centre with trees and street cafés is a very pleasant place in which to stroll.

The city's emblem and a useful guide for those who lose their bearings is the 191 m (627 ft) high Calgary Tower, with a superb panorama to be seen from its viewing platform. As the Rocky Mountains with their well-known national parks are relatively near the city is an excellent choice for a holiday stay. The popular skiing and walking regions in the mountains or the unspoilt wilderness can be reached in one or two hours. Fast-water canoeing, more leisurely canoe or cycle trips and excursions into the interesting countryside round about make Calgary a good starting-out point for trips into western Canada.

The city developed from a North West Mounted Police (now the RCMP) post which was set up here on Bow River in 1875, with orders to put an end to the smuggling of whisky across the American border.The commandant, named MacLeod and of Scottish extraction, gave this first camp the name of Calgary, which in Gaelic means "quickly-flowing clear water".

History

Even before the first fur-hunters arrived here in the 19th c. this confluence of two rivers was a favourite camping place for the Indians. After the Blackfoot Indians had obtained horses and weapons from the white man they became the dominant tribe. The increasing influx of white fur-traders and settlers into their tribal territories resulted in a number of conflicts, however, but these were finally largely settled under the terms of a treaty signed in 1877. Today the one-time proud rulers of the prairie live in a number of reservations south of Calgary.

The relatively favourable natural conditions persuaded an increasing number of American cattle breeders to leave their over-grazed ranches and settle north of the border. Soon giant herds of cattle were grazing around Calgary, to be followed by large concerns dealing in meat and foodstuffs.

When the Canadian Pacific Railway reached Calgary in 1883 the little police post rapidly began to develop. By the end of that year it boasted a population of 600. More and more settlers came to the Calgary region, and by 1891 it had its own power and water supplies. In 1893 the town was granted its charter.

Since the turn of the century prospectors have dug for oil in and around Calgary. Finally, in 1914, oil was found in Turner Valley 61 km (38 mi.) to the south-west, resulting in enormous development of the area. Today Calgary is an important centre of the Canadian petro-chemical industry; four-fifths of all the firms engaged in the crude oil and natural gas business in Canada have their head offices in Calgary. The city is also the financial centre of the province of Alberta.

Development has slowed somewhat since oil prices started to fall in the 1980s. Many ambitious city development projects came to grief and unemployment – previously well below the Canadian average – increased enormously. Commercial firms, restaurants and the entertainment industry all felt the effect of the reduced spending power of the workers employed in the petro-chemical industry.

To a certain extent this was offset by the building boom which accompanied the preparations for the XV Winter Olympics in 1988.

The place from which to set out on a tour of the relatively small inner city of Calgary is Calgary Tower on 9th Ave./Centre St., which is open daily 7.30am–midnight. It has a viewing platform and revolving restaurant and being 191 m (627 ft) high it is the city's landmark and was, until 1985, its tallest building. In 1988 a giant torch on the tower bore witness to the spirit of the Olympics.

★ Calgary Tower

Stephen Avenue, Calgary's main shopping street, is a pedestrian zone between 1st. St. S. E. and 4th St. S. W. Here still stand a large number of old buildings built in a variety of styles from local sandstone. In the former Imperial Bank of Canada at 102–8th Ave. the Alberta Historical Resources Foundation has its headquarters; this foundation dedicated to preserving the history and monuments of the province of Alberta is open Mon.–Fri. 8.30am–4.30pm. An informative brochure entitled "Stephen Avenue Mall Walking Tour" can be obtained here.

Stephen Avenue

From Lancaster Building (304–8th Ave.) opposite the Royal Bank building the "Plus 15' Walkway System" (look for the blue and white sign)

Calgary

.... LRT (Straßenbahn)

leads to Toronto Dominion Square and the Scotia Centre, two sizeable shopping centres on 7th Avenue.

Devonian Gardens

On the third floor (4th level) of Toronto Dominion Square at 2nd/3rd St. the visitor will come somewhat unexpectedly upon the Devonian Gardens, a floral paradise covering about one hectare/two and a half acres with ponds, fountains and a small waterfall. 20,000 tropical, sub-tropical and native plants thrive here under glass. Open daily 9am–9pm.

"C" Train

In 7th Ave, the best way to get about is by using the "C" Train, which is free in this inner city area. By this means the City Hall is reached in a few minutes (two stops).

City Hall

The historical old sandstone town hall built in 1911 had become too small, so in 1986 a triangular and highly modern office complex was built; its glass front is visible from a long way off. The City Council meets here.

Olympic Plaza

In front of the City Hall lies the Olympic Plaza, where medal award ceremonies were held every evening during the 1988 Winter Olympics. It is now a popular meeting-place in summer, and various events, such as open-air concerts, cabarets, firework displays and laser shows, are held here.

★Sarcee People's Museum

South-west of Glenmore Reservoir lies the reservation of the Sarcee (Sarsi) Indians, a tribe which once was linked with the Blackfeet Indians,

146

and now forms part of the Athabask tribe. In 1983, to mark the occasion of the century of its written history, the tribe furnished a small museum at 3700 Anderson Rd. S. W. Open Mon.–Fri. 8am–4pm.

In the foothills of the mountains to the west of the city rise the strange-looking towers of the Olympic ski-slopes. The bob-sleigh run and tobog-gan-run are also here. Guided tours take place every day 9am–5pm, when a panoramic view of the Calgary skyline can be enjoyed from the top of the 90 m (295 ft) ski-slope.

★ Canada Olympic Park

Memories of the Olympic Games are provided by means of documents and films in the Olympic Hall of Fame. Open daily 10am–5pm, to 8pm in high summer.

Olympic Hall of Fame

About 10 km (6 mi.) west of the city – take the TransCanada Highway and then the Springbank exit – lies the largest adventure park in the whole of south-west Canada. Coach-loads of visitors come to enjoy the numer-ous attractions, including roller coasters and an artificial watercourse, as well as colourful evening entertainment programmes. From the Terrace Garden Restaurant there is a good view of the Rocky Mountains. Open mid-May–mid-Oct., but opening times vary.

Calaway Park

On the campus of Calgary University (15,000 students) in the west of the city is the Olympic Oval, the first covered 400 m speed-skating rink. Open daily 7am–11pm.

University of Calgary, Olympic Oval

The McMahon Stadium on University Drive, mainly used for football, is where the opening and closing ceremonies for the 1988 Winter Olympics took place.

McMahon Stadium

Also on the campus will be found the Nickle Arts Museum containing a large coin collection as well as ancient European exhibits. Temporary exhibitions are also held here.

Nickle Arts Museum

In the Alberta Science Centre at 701–11th St./7th Ave. there is the oppor-tunity to enjoy a "hands-on" experience of the natural sciences. There are some three dozen themes of popular interest with which the visitor can himself experiment. The Centennial Planetarium – with laser-astro-shows among other things – also attracts a lot of interest. Open Wed.–Sun. 1.30pm–9pm, daily in summer.

Alberta Science Centre, Centennial Planetarium

In the neighbouring Pleiades Theatre modern as well as more traditional plays are performed.

Pleiades Theatre

The little museum in the main office buildings of the West Canadian Gas Company at 909–1th Ave. S. W. illustrates the development of the gas industry from July 17th 1912, when Calgary was first provided with natural gas. Open Mon.–Fri. 8am–4pm.

Canadian Western Natural Gas Museum

The first outpost of the North West Mounted Police was set up in 1875 at the confluence of the Elbow and Bow Rivers. The foundations of the original fort can still be seen. The history of the city of Calgary is illus-trated in the Visitors' Centre on 750–9th Ave. S. E. Open May–late Oct., late Oct.–Apr., Wed.-Sun. daily 10am–6pm.
    On the other side of the bridge stands Deane House, built in 1906 for the commandant of the outpost, which is now a tea-room.

Fort Calgary

On St George's Island in Bow River, at 1300 Zoo Rd. N. E., lies Calgary Zoo, founded in 1912. The owners are particularly proud of their 388 examples of rare and threatened species of animals as well as of the adjoining botanical gardens. In a prehistoric theme park stand numer-ous replicas of animals which lived in south-western Canada millions of years ago. Open daily 9am–dusk.

Calgary Zoo & Prehistoric Park

In the Aerospace Museum at 64 McTavish Ave. can be seen Second World War aviation equipment and military aircraft supplemented by

Aerospace Museum

Olympic Saddledome

documents from the period. Open Mon.–Fri. 9am–4pm, Sat. and Sun. noon–4pm.

Calgary Centre for Performing Arts

The "Plus 15' System", linked to the Municipal Building, provides access to the modern 1985-built Calgary centre for Performing Arts on the south side of the square at 205–8th Ave. S. E. Comprising three stages and the John Singer Concert Hall, this impressive city theatre is connected to two older buildings, Calgary Public Building (1930) and Burns Building (1913), which is the information centre of the Calgary Tourist & Convention Bureau.

★Glenbow Museum

A further footbridge leads from the municipal theatre to the Calgary Convention Centre and to the Glenbow Museum on 130–9th Ave./1st St. S. E. In the museum can be seen some rare exhibits illustrating the historical development of western Canada., covering the time of the early fur-hunters and the arrival of the North West Mounted Police, as well as the Métis uprising under Louis Riel. The development of the oil industry is also catered for. As well as personal effects belonging to the pioneers who came here from all over the world there are artistic and everyday items left by the Indians, including the Ojibwa, the Cree and some prairie tribes and the Inuit. Particularly impressive is the leather tepee of the Blackfoot tribe. Open Tue.–Sun. 10am–6pm.

Palliser Square

Another footbridge leads to Palliser Square. At the foot of the lofty CN Tower lies Calgary's main railway station.

Stampede Park

In the south-east of the city, by Elbow River at 14th Ave./4th St., Stampede Park extends over 24 ha (60 acres). Every year since 1912 the Calgary Exhibition and the Stampede have been held here. In the month of July the Wild West lives again. In the world's biggest and wildest rodeo cowboys compete to be the "best of the bunch". Prizes are awarded for the best breed of animal and neck-breaking chuckwagon races are held. Spectacular shows are also put on for the public. During the rest of the year fairs and exhibitions of all kinds are held here, and there are horse races in the Grand Stand.

Near the Stampede Buildings is the Olympic Saddledome, probably one of the most beautiful ice-arenas in the world. This giant hall, built in the shape of a saddle, reflects the spirit of the Wild West. In 1988 the Olympic ice-skating competitions were held here. Built in 1983, the Saddledome holds 20,000 spectators and is the home of the world-famous ice-hockey team "Calgary Flames".

★Olympic Saddledome

The "Grain Academy" of the Alberta Wheat Pool is also situated in Stampede Park. Linked to it is an exhibition – situated at 17th Ave./2nd St, open Apr.–Sep., Mon.–Fri. 10am–4pm, Sat. noon–4pm – with a model of a railway which brought the grain from the prairies over the Rocky Mountains to Vancouver Harbour, as well as a functioning granary. There are also films and explanatory documents giving information about the production and importance of various types of grain.

Grain Academy

Glenmore reservoir in the south-west of the city is very popular with water-sports enthusiasts, who can sail, canoe and row here.

Glenmore Reservoir

A typical village from the pioneering period consisting of more than 100 historical buildings has been reconstructed near the reservoir. Heritage Park is at 1900 Heritage Park Drive/14th St. S. W. An old steam engine provides transport to it. There is also a paddle-steamer such as was used years ago on the rivers of western Canada which is available for trips round the reservoir. In addition there are nostalgic ferries operating, an historic bakery and the Wainwright Hotel. Open Jul.-Labour Day, daily 10am–6pm, and at limited times during the year.

Heritage Park

After leaving Calgary and travelling about 80 km (50 mi.) west along the four-lane TransCanada Highway 1, there is a turn-off south on Highway 40 into some most charming countryside and to the unspoiled Kananaskis Valley, a favourite spot for walkers in summer. A short way from the junction is the Alberta Centre, which provides information and maps.
    Some 8 km (5 mi.) further on lies "Colonel's Cabin", a Second World War prisoner-of-war camp, with a watch-tower and the commandant's hut still preserved. Historical photographs may be seen. The dam across Barrier Lake was also constructed by German prisoners-of-war.

Kananaskis Valley

As the tour continues a fine view opens up of Mt Allan, more than 2800 m (9200 ft) high, on the side of which can be seen the ski-slope laid down for the Alpine competitions. In only two years an international skiing region was created from a veritable wilderness; at the foot was built "Nakiska" (Indian for "meeting-point"), with lift-stations, a ski-school and ski-hire, a cafeteria and a bar.
    Some 22 km (14 mi.) south of the TransCanada Highway and by Ribbon Creek 4 km (2½ mi.) away stretches the holiday resort of Kananaskis Village comprising a number of hotel and apartment buildings.
    A rather special kind of attraction is the Kananaskis Country Golf Course, laid out almost 1500 m (4900 ft) above sea-level; it is Alberta's only golf-course and has 36 holes.

★**Nakiska Mt Allan**

23 km (14 mi.) further south there is another ski-region on Fortress Mountain, with lifts, ski-school, ski-hire, restaurant and bar.

Fortress Mountain

After 136 km (85 mi.) the tour reaches the Peter Lougheed Provincial Park – known as Kananaskis Provincial Park until 1985 – which forms the very heart of the Kananaskis region and where elk, Wapiti deer, thick-horned sheep, mountain-goats, beaver, grizzly and black bears, pumas and wolves may all be encountered. It covers 508 sq. km (196 sq. mi.), which makes it the largest provincial park in Alberta. In summer especially many adventurous holiday-makers are attracted here by the superb mountain scenery, traversed by various trails and dotted with numerous high lakes. Well worthwhile is the detour to the Park Visitor

★**Peter Lougheed Provincial Park**

Centre at the northern end of Lower Kananaskis Lake, which is open end of Jun.–Sep. 9.30am–5pm, Thu., Fri., Sat. to 8pm. Various exhibitions and slide-shows give an insight into the geography and history of the Kananaskis region. Board and lodging is available in nearby William Watson Lodge. A number of interesting trails and instructional paths start from here, including Boulton Creek Trail, Kananaskis Canyon Trail and Rock Wall Trail. The road leading to the park ends at Upper Kananaskis Lake.

★Badlands

This tour starts from Calgary city centre on the TransCanada Highway 1, branching off after 30 km (19 mi.) on to Highway 9 to the north. Passing through rich, partly irrigated arable and pasture land with flat hills it arrives at Drumheller in the valley of the Red Deer River. Some 25 km (16 mi.) west of the town, in the deeply-slashed Horseshoe Canyon, can be seen for the first time the erosion forms so typical of this part of the Red Deer River and known as the "Badlands"; the complete lack of vegetation makes a lasting impression. It is wise to obtain brochures about the various tours on offer from the Tourist Information Office when arriving in the town.

Drumheller

After covering 142 km (88 mi.) the tour reaches Drumheller, a town of scarcely 7000 inhabitants which proudly calls itself the Town of the Dinosaurs. 75 million years ago, in the Upper Cretaceous Period, various species of dinosaurs roamed this region. Some remains of this life form have been preserved in the sedimentary strata.

From 1910 to the 1940s Drumheller depended on coal-mining. Then oil and natural gas largely took over from coal as energy sources so that today the little town is mainly a commercial centre for the farmers of the region. The very dry Badlands, quite unsuitable for agriculture, have long attracted numbers of tourists.

★Drumheller
Dinosaur & Fossil
Museum

The Drumheller Dinosaur & Fossil Museum at 335–1st St. E. is open Apr.–Oct. daily 9am–8pm, Jul.–Sep. to 6pm only. In addition to a collection of minerals and some Indian exhibits the main emphasis is on bones and skeletons of dinosaurs and other prehistoric animals.

★Dinosaur Trail

The Dinosaur Trail along Highway 838, a tour 48 km (30 mi.) long to the west of the town along Red Deer River which cuts its way more than 120 m (400 ft) deep into the prairie, takes in the area of steep and barren rocky slopes, from which wind and rain have carved the mushroom-shaped pillars known as "hoodoos" and revealed whole dinosaur skeletons. Ancient river-courses have carved up the prairie here into rocky tablelands on which grass struggles to grow where the soil has not been completely eroded. In the Badlands will be found sagebrush and greasewood bushes, so typical of arid regions in America, as well as cacti. At the bridge where Highway 9 crosses Red Deer River tyrannosaurus rex, a much photographed replica of a mighty dinosaur, greets the passer-by.

Homestead
Antique Museum

The Homestead Antique Museum will be found about 1 km (⅔ mi.) north-west of the town. In the grounds of the museum can be seen different pieces of farming equipment and machinery from the pioneering period. Open May–Oct. daily 10am–5pm, Jul.–Sep. 9am–9pm.

★★Tyrell
Museum
of Palaeontology

The Tyrell Museum of Palaeontology, on the north bank of the Red Deer River, was opened in 1985. It lies 6 km (4 mi.) to the north-west on the western edge of Midland Provincial Park. This most interesting museum has earned a worldwide reputation. Open Apr.–mid-Oct. daily 9am–9pm, at other times of the year Tue.–Sun. and public holidays 10am–5pm.

The most modern museum techniques have brought millions of years of the earth's history back to life. 800 fossils, including 35 dinosaur skeletons, films and – last but not least – twenty easy to use computer terminals, provide the visitor with an insight into the fascinating evolution of life on earth. A primeval garden shows tropical and subtropical plant

A dinosaur in the Tyrell Museum of Palaeontology

species and their descendants as they were 350 million years ago, at the start of the Carbonaceous Period.

The museum also provides information on the genesis and geology of the region and on the history of discovery.

In 1884, by sheer chance, the geologist J. B. Tyrell happened to stumble across some dinosaur bones lying among the cacti and stones of the Badlands. Quite unwittingly he started the "great Canadian dinosaur-rush": palaentologists and collectors from all over the world streamed into the Badlands in their horse-drawn wagons and dug up many of the skeletons which can today be seen in numerous museums, including some outside Canada.

During the transition to the Tertiary Period Alberta as we know it today was one vast inland lake. The climate was tropical and the vegetation very lush, ideal living conditions for dinosaurs. When these conditions changed within a relatively short period, however, the coast became one giant dinosaur cemetery.

After a small chapel built in 1957 had collapsed the Horsethief Canyon Viewpoint was constructed, from where there is a good view of the various sedimentary layers in the canyon. Footpaths lead down to fossilised oyster-beds.

Horsethief Canyon Viewpoint

The Bleriot Ferry is in operation from early Apr.-early Nov. daily 7am–11pm. It embarks from the little township of.Munson 8 km (5 mi.) to the west and carries passengers across the Red Deer River. This ferry, which has been in operation since 1913, is one of the last sailing-ferries still used in Canada.

Bleriot Ferry

From the western bank of the river the tour returns to Drumheller.

1 km (⅔ mi.) west of the town centre lies the Dinosaur Park. Situated on South Railroad Ave. it displays twenty giant dinosaurs made of concrete. Open Apr.–mid-Oct. from 9am.

Dinosaur Park

Calgary

★Hoodoo Drive

Another charming tour takes in the 60 km (37 mi.) long Hoodoo Drive and starts from Drumheller on Highway 10 to the east. After about 10 km (6 mi.) the route passes the Rosedale Swinging Suspension Bridge, originally built by the workers of the Old Star Coal Mine and which leads across to a now unused coal-mine.

Hoodoos

The actual Hoodoo region, west of East Coulee, is 18 km (11 mi.) further on. Most of these bizarre rock-columns, so typical of the Red Deer River Badlands, are topped with a "bonnet" of hard rock which protects them from erosion.

East Coulee

23 km (14 mi.): when coal-mining flourished and there were 34 mines in the valley East Coulee was a lively little town with a population of 4000. Today only some 200 still live here. The schoolhouse built in 1930 today houses a School Museum. Open Jul.–Aug. daily 9am–9pm, rest of the year 8.30am–4.30pm.

The return trip to Drumheller can be either along Highway 10 or roads 569 and 56.

The tour then continues along Highway 56 to the north initially, and then on Highway 9 eastwards towards Hanna. After some 50 km (30 mi.) the Handhills rise out of the prairie to heights approaching 185 m (607 ft); these are some of the highest points between the Rockies and the east coast.

Hanna

224 km (140 mi.): at the entrance to the township of Hanna (pop. 3000) a picture of a grey goose underlines the good hunting to be had around here. A reconstructed village illustrating the lives of the 19th c. pioneers can be seen in the Pioneer Museum on E. Municipal Rd./4th. St. Open mid-May–Sep. daily 10am–7pm or other times by prior arrangement.

Now turning south on Highway 36 – where some stretches of bad road can be encountered – carry on for about 105 km (65 mi.) and then turn off east to the Dinosaur Provincial Park (about 40 km (25 mi.)).

Typical "Hoodoos"

380 km (236 mi.): The Dinosaur Provincial Park, covering 6039 ha (14,920 acres), is a unique palaeontological site which was declared a World Heritage Site by UNESCO in 1979. The remains of more than 35 species of dinosaurs and other saurians were found here.

⋆**Dinosaur Provincial Park**

In the vicinity of this park the Red Deer River has cut its way more than 100 m (330 ft) deep into the valley floor. Annual rainfalls of 300 to 400 mm (12 to 16 in.) have produced what must be the most spectacular Badlands in Canada, with fascinating hoodoos, rock-needles, gorges and mesas. The slopes, devoid of any vegetation, shimmer in shades of reddish-black and greyish-green. This barren moonscape-like region forms the bulk of the park; beyond it the Badland spreads relatively fast and devours about 1 cm (½ in.) more land and loose material every year.

T. C. Weston discovered these superb fossil deposits in 1889, and by the turn of the century the Canadian Geological Society has carried out extensive digs. The Badlands and the archaeological sites, including a dinosaur skeleton left "in situ", can be seen on a circular tour of 3½ km (2 mi.). However, most of the park can be seen only on a guided tour led by a park ranger or on a coach trip. Early reservation for these tours is essential; write to PO Box 60, Patricia, Alta. T0J 2K0 or tel. (403) 3784587.

Fossil deposits

The Tyrell Museum of Palaeontology maintains a field station here. Palaeontologists can also be watched as they prepare finds.

430 km (267 mi.): Brooks (pop. 10,000) lies 48 km (30 mi.) further south in the middle of irrigated farmland and meadows. Brooks Aqueduct was hailed as a brilliant technical achievement when it was built in 1913.

⋆**Brooks**

The importance of irrigation is illustrated in the Brooks & District Museum, consisting of several restored buildings and situated at Sutherland Drive. Some well-chosen exhibits depict the culture of the Indians and describe the lives of the early settlers, ranchers and railroad pioneers. There is also some Royal Canadian Mounted Police memorabilia. Open May–Oct. daily 10am–5pm.

From Brooks there is an interesting detour of 78 km (48 mi.) into the Badlands of the Red Deer River to the Dinosaur Provincial Park.

13 km (8 mi.) south of Brooks Kinbrook Island, Provincial Park lies on the east bank of Lake Newell, a 65 km (40 mi.) long reservoir formed by the Bassano Dam built in 1909. Bathing can be enjoyed here, and there are colonies of cormorants, white pelicans and Californian seagulls, as well as Canadian geese, to be seen. Lake Newell forms part of an extensive irrigation project which was begun early in this century in south-eastern Alberta.

Lake Newell

The return route to Calgary from Brooks – 185 km (115 mi.) – is along TransCanada Highway 1.

Campbell Highway

E 3–5

Administrative Unit: Yukon Territory

Tourism Yukon, PO Box 2703, Whitehorse, YT Y1A 2C6; tel. (867) 6675340, fax. (867) 6675346

Information

In the south-east of the Yukon Territory, near Watson Lake, Campbell Highway No. 4 (573 km (356 mil.) in length in all) branches off to the north from the Alaska Highway (see entry) and after some 356 km (220 mi.) passes through the township of Ross River, then after a further 60 km (37 mi.) reaches the town of Faro and finally joins up with the Klondike Highway (see Klondike) near Carmacks by the Yukon River.

Campbell Highway follows the trail of the Scotsman Robert Campbell who in the 19th c. crossed rivers and passes and pushed forward into the very centre of the Yukon Territory in order to set up trading posts for the Hudson's Bay Company.

Robert Campbell

Suggested route

Watson Lake	Watson Lake (see Alaska Highway), the "Gateway to the Yukon", with its 1200 inhabitants, is the point at the junction of Alaska and Campbell where the highway starts.
Simpson Lake	For many people the first stop is Simpson Lake, 80 km (50 mi.) away. This lake, nowadays so popular with anglers, was named by Campbell after Sir George Simpson, the general manager of the Hudson's Bay Company.
Miner's Junction	After a further 30 km (19 mi.) or so the road reaches Miner's Junction, named after a jade mine; jade jewellery is on sale in a small shop. To the east of Miner's Junction Nahanni Range Road provides the link with the Northwest Territories (see entry).
Fort Pelly Banks	At the 268 kilometre point, and at 167 m (550 ft) above sea-level, stands the trading post known as Fort Pelly Banks which was set up by Campbell in 1844, but has been unused for many years.
Ross River	After 360 km (224 mi.) the highway arrives in Ross River on the south bank of the Pelly River. Ross River lies at the junction of Campbell Highway and Canol Road, the latter providing the link between Whitehorse (see entry) via Ross River to the Selwyn and Mackenzie Mountains in the adjoining Northwest Territories (see entry). North of Watson Lake the town of Ross River is the nearest tourist centre and place where anglers and hunters can obtain supplies and provisions. Most of the 400 inhabitants are Kaska Indians. Its convenient situation at the mouth of the river of the same name has meant that Pelly River has grown in importance as a point from which to explore for minerals and other natural resources in the central Yukon. Tours in the unspoilt mountains and flights – such as those offered by Flying Service Ross River, tel. (403) 9692547 – over the scenically charming valleys of Ross and Pelly River are much to be recommended.
Faro	Campbell Highway now follows the Pelly River until, after covering a total of 415 km (258 mi.) from the start, a road branches off to Faro 6 km (4 mi.) to the north. This mining village, with a population of 1700, grew up in 1968 with the mining of nearby stocks of lead and zinc. After the mines had to be shut down in 1982 because they proved unprofitable Faro threatened to become a ghost town, but early in 1986 a further area was discovered and mined with the aid of new methods of exploration. Between 1986 and 1990 production amounted to some 5 million tonnes per annum; the lead and zinc mines at Faro belonging to Curragh Resources Inc. are now the largest in Canada.

★Campbellton   H 17

Province: New Brunswick. Population: 9000

Access	By car, Highways 11 and 17
Information	Campbellton Chamber of Commerce, 18 Water Street, Campbellton, NB E3N 3G4; tel. (506) 7597856

The little harbour town of Campbellton lies at the foot of the Pain de Sucre mountain on the narrow estuary of the Restigouche River and at the western end of the Baie des Chaleurs, quite near the border with the province of Québec. It is an important trade centre for the Gaspésie Peninsula (see entry). Timber and timber products are also shipped from here. Salmon-fishing plays an important role in the town's economy, as is underlined by the "Festival du Saumon/Salmon Festival" which takes place every year in the first week of July.

Campbellton was founded in the 17th c. by French-speaking Acadians, but they left in 1760. In that same year the last North American battle of the Seven Years' War between France and England took place in the waters off Campbellton.

A few years later the Scots settled here, and the town was named after the governor of the province, Sir Archibald Campbell.

Sights

In the Restigouche Gallery can be seen works by local artists as well as various temporary exhibitions.

Restigouche Gallery

A steep path leads up to the peak of the towering mountain known as Pain de Sucre/Sugarloaf. It is 283 m (930 ft) high and there are impressive views.
    At the bottom of the mountain a provincial park has been laid out, with sporting and leisure facilities, including bathing in the lake, tennis, camping and picnic-sites. In the Visitor Centre there is much to be learned about Campbellton and its environs.

Sugarloaf Provincial Park

Surroundings

20 km (13 mi.) north-east of Campbellton the pretty little town of Dalhousie nestles by the Baie des Chaleurs. Today it is an important centre of the New Brunswick woodworking industry.
    A visit is recommended to the Restigouche Regional Museum with its exhibits covering the pioneering period, development of fishing and agriculture in the region.
    In Inch Arran Park there is bathing and tennis. The coastline is impressive, especially the Bon Ami Rocks eroded by the surf.

Dalhousie

The prettily situated Chaleur Bay Provincial Park attracts many holiday-makers, especially in summer. It is also a pleasant place to bathe when water temperatures allow.

★**Chaleur Bay Provincial Park**

A boat trip from Dalhousie along the charming Gaspésie (see entry) coast in the province of Québec is a memorable experience.

Boat excursion

Nearly 30 km (19 mi.) east of Campbellton lies the holiday resort of Charlo on the Baie des Chaleurs.

Charlo

From Charlo Route 134 winds south-eastward along the Baie des Chaleurs to Bathurst (see entry) on Baie Nepisguit. Along the coast beautiful stretches of beach rub shoulders with impressive rock formations. There are pretty bathing places in Jacquet River, Belledune (the largest strawberry market in the world), Petit-Rocher, Nigado, Beresford and Bathurst.
    Between Pointe-Verte and Petit-Rocher the New Brunswick Mining & Mineral Interpretation Center, which illustrates the history of mining in eastern Canada (see Bathurst) is well worth a visit.

Route 134

Canmore   G 7

Province: Alberta. Population: 9000

Canmore & Kananaskis Chamber of Commerce, PO Box 1178, Canmore, AB T0L 0M0; tel. (403) 6784094

Information

The now famous winter-sports resort of Canmore, only 3 km (2 mi.) east of the boundary of the Banff National Park (see entry) by the TransCanada Highway and in the Bow River valley, lies under the shadow of the majestic Three Sisters. During the 1988 Winter Olympics the cross-country and biathlon skiing events were held here. Now the 60 km (40 mi.) or so of ski-runs along the Smith-Dorrien Highway and the Nordic Centre on Mount Rundle are open to serious and amateur sportsmen alike.

In summer Canmore, framed by snow-covered mountain peaks, is a starting point for tours of the Rocky Mountains lasting one or several days. Other leisure activities are mountain climbing, cycling, horse-riding, fast-water and other canoeing, fishing, golf and helicopter flights.

History

The town of Canmore grew up in 1883 when coal was discovered in the area and mining started. Now the coal mines are closed and Canmore survives mainly as a year-round tourist resort, a base for some fantastic excursions to the Kananaskis area (see Calgary, Surroundings) and into the Banff National Park.

Winter Carnival

A "Winter Carnival" , with dog sleigh races in which some of the best husky drivers in North America participate, is held here every year in January.

Smith-Dorrien
Spray Trail

The unmade-up road known as the Smith-Dorrien Trail leads southwards through magnificent and wild mountain country to Spray Lake Reservoir and to Highway 40 in the Peter Lougheed Provincial Park (see Calgary).

★★Cape Breton Island   H 18

Province: Nova Scotia

Information

See Nova Scotia

Cape Breton Island is actually the north-eastern part of the province of Nova Scotia, separated from it by the Strait of Canso and linked by a dam, to cross which a toll is charged.

A charming blend of sea and land is the hallmark of this island, so rich in stocks of coal and at the same time boasting the highest mountains in Nova Scotia.

Lac Bras d'Or

Port Hawkesbury

Port Hawkesbury is a small industrial town with oil refineries; the three main link-roads on the island fan out from here.

Whycocomagh

The village of Whycocomagh nestles enchantingly in a bay on the west bank of a lake. In the old church for many years the first part of the services used to be held in Gaelic and the second half in English.

Nearby is an Indian reserve where wooden sculptures and baskets are made.

**★Whycocomagh
Provincial Park**

6 km (4 mi.) north of Whycocomagh in the Baddeck direction lies this charmingly landscaped provincial park with numerous Norwegian spruce, pine, beech and maple trees. A beautiful view can be enjoyed from the 300 m (980 ft) high Mount Salt.

★Baddeck

Baddeck is one of the most beautiful villages in Nova Scotia. Its name means "where an island is nearby". Alexander Graham Bell (see Famous People), the inventor of the telephone, had a summer residence here.

**Alexander
Graham
Bell National
Historic Site**

In the Alexander Graham Bell National Historic Site can be seen personal effects and documents belonging to the inventor, as well as parts

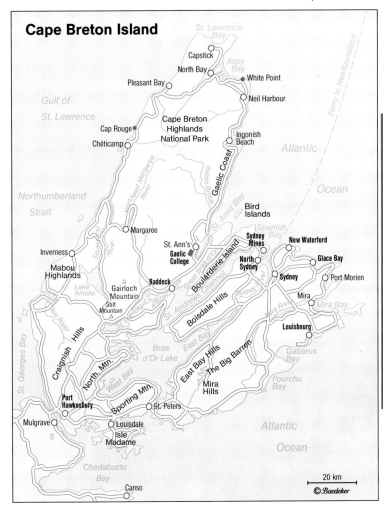

Cape Breton Island

(Map labels:) St. Lawrence Bay, Capstick, North Bay, White Point, Pleasant Bay, Aspy Bay, Neil Harbour, Gulf of St. Lawrence, Cape Breton Highlands National Park, Cap Rouge, Chéticamp, Ingonish Beach, Gaelic Coast, Atlantic Ocean, Ferry to Newfoundland, Northwest Margaree River, Indian Brook, Northumberland Strait, Bird Islands, St. Anns Bay, Margaree, Spanish Bay, St. Ann's Gaelic College, Sydney Mines, New Waterford, North Sydney, Glace Bay, Inverness, Boularderie Island, Sydney, Port Morien, Mabou Highlands, Great Bras d'Or Channel, Baddeck, Southwest Margaree River, Lake Ainslie, Gairloch Mountain, Salt Mountain, St. Andrews Channel, Boisdale Hills, Sydney River, Mira, Mira Bay, Mira River, Louisbourg, Bras d'Or Lake, East Bay, Gabarus Bay, Craignish Hills, North Mtn., West Bay, East Bay Hills, The Big Barren, Fourchu Bay, Mira Hills, St. Georges Bay, Mabou River, Sporting Mtn., Port Hawkesbury, St. Peters, Mulgrave, Louisdale, Isle Madame, Atlantic Ocean, Chedabucto Bay, Canso

20 km

© Baedeker

of two hydroplanes made by Bell and powered by aircraft engines. Open Jul. 1st–Sep. 30th daily 9am–9pm, Oct. 1st–Jun. 30th daily 9am–5pm.

From this busy harbour ships sail to Newfoundland. North Sydney is also the eastern terminus of the continental railway network.

North Sydney

Sydney is the largest town on the island. Sydney harbour was used from the 16th c. initially by European fishermen and then frequently by English and Scottish fleets. Between 1830 and 1870 the town enjoyed an enormous boost through the ironworking industry, and iron ore from Newfoundland is still processed here today.

Sydney

Cape Breton Island

St Peters	St Peters is one of the oldest villages on the island. The restored fortified trading post set up by Nicolas Denis, a 17th c. French colonist, is worth a visit. Open Jun.–Sep. daily 9am–5pm.
Île Madame	Île Madame was colonised by Acadians after their flight from Louisburg from the English in 1758, and French is still spoken here today.
Arichat	A visit is recommended to the Lenoir Museum in Arichat; this is a reconstruction of an early 19th c. smithy.

★★Cabot Trail

The Cabot Trail is a 300 km (190 mi.) stretch in the north-west of the island, starting from Baddeck. It got its name from the Italian seafarer Giovanni Caboto (John Cabot, see Famous People), who is thought to have been the first to land in North America in 1497.

The enchanting combination of prairieland, hills and forests together with the proximity of the sea must make the Cabot Trail one of the most beautiful scenic stretches in the whole of North America.

Sights

Margaree Harbour	Margaree Harbour is a small fishing hamlet opposite the Île Margaree, an island which is home to numerous species of birds, such as cormorants and seagulls.
Chéticamp	Chéticamp is a little Acadian fishing village on the edge of Highlands National Park, with many craft workshops. A visit is recommended to the Acadian Museum and to the prettily decorated Church of St-Pierre built in 1893.

Scottish folklore on the Cabot Trail

★★Cape Breton Highlands National Park

This national park with numerous footpaths extends over 985 sq. km (380 sq. mi.) in the north of the island between the St Lawrence River and the Atlantic. The varied animal life is particularly impressive and includes beaver, deer, wild-cats, parrots, wild duck and eagles. | Location

The Information Offices in this park are to be found near Chéticamp and Igonish on the Cabot Trail, They are open in summer daily 8am–9pm, late spring and autumn daily 9am–5pm; during the remainder of the year information can be obtained from the offices in Ingonish which are open every day. | Information

The little fishing village of Ingonish with its picturesque harbour is a favourite place for outings both in summer and winter on account of its sporting attractions which include fishing, golf, tennis and swimming. | **Ingonish**

12 km (8 mi.) south of Ingonish lies Cape Smoky, 365 m (1200 ft) high, with a chair-lift to the top. On clear days there is a fantastic view of the surrounding countryside. | **Cape Smoky**

★★Caraquet   H 17/18

Province: New Brunswick. Population: 7000

Office de Tourisme de la Ville de Caraquet | Information

Highway 11 (Campbellton–Bathurst–Chatham–Moncton). | Access

The little town of Caraquet lies on the Côte Acadienne (Acadian Coast) which forms the southern border of the Baie des Chaleurs, that is to say, on the Acadian Peninsula about 65 km (40 mi.) north-east of Bathurst (see entry).

Caraquet was founded in 1758 and now forms the cultural centre of Acadia. Every summer a large-scale Acadian Festival is held here, the highlight of which is August 15th, National Acadian Festival Day. | History

Caraquet is also the home port of New Brunswick's largest fishing fleet, together with a school for fishermen and a very busy fish-market. | Fishing port

Caraquet's picturesque fishing harbour will delight the eye and the palate. It will illustrate how hard the fisherman's life is, while the many harbour bars and smart restaurants all offer a fine selection of speciality fish dishes. | ★Port

The Acadian Museum in Caraquet, near the wharf and school of fishing, provides detailed information about the history of the Acadian culture and the first French-speaking pioneers in this region.
   There are also exhibits dealing with the unfortunate disputes with the English, Scottish and Irish. | ★Musée Acadian

To the south-east of Caraquet, near Bertrand on Road 11, lies the "Village Historique Acadien" open-air museum, one of New Brunswick's main attractions. | ★★Village Historique Acadien

In this "living visual workshop" visitors can see how Acadians lived between 1780 and 1890. Museum staff dressed in the original costumes of the period perform old crafts, such as spinning wool, weaving cloth and making clothes, forging iron, making furniture and wagons, printing books and posters, making soap, drying fish, and preserving vegetables and meats. | Old crafts

A system of dykes and sluices laid out as it was shows how land used to be reclaimed and made into fertile soil for corn and vegetables. | Aboiteaux

Fishing village on the Côte Acadienne   *Village Historique Acadian*

Other buildings	In recent years some valuable old Acadian buildings of considerable historical significance have been moved and re-erected here, including the mill known as "Moulin Riordin", "Maison Thériault" and a restaurant where patrons can sample food prepared from old Acadian recipes.
Opening times	Early Jun.–early Sep. daily 10am–6pm.
★Grande-Anse	From the Grand-Anse west of Caraquet there is a breathtaking view over the Baie des Chaleurs, with its amalgam of quiet bays and dramatic rock formations. Nearby is a newly laid-out park with a beautiful bathing beach. In the town of Grand Anse, founded in 1810, the "Pope Museum", with a model of St Peter's in Rome and portraits of all the popes, warrants a visit.

Cariboo Highway   G 6

Province: British Columbia

Information   See British Columbia

The Cariboo Highway (Highway 97) largely follows the route of the Cariboo Trail and Cariboo Waggon Road, which led from Lillooet (see Vancouver) to the gold-rush regions in the Cariboo Mountains. However, the present Cariboo Highway 97 begins at the TransCanada Highway (see entry) near Cache Creek and connects the latter with Yellowhead Highway (see entry) further to the north near Prince George, a distance of 445 km (276 mi.). From there it is known as the "John Hart Highway" and continues further north to create a link between the TransCanada Highway and Vancouver and Dawson Creek, where the Alaska Highway begins. In a southerly direction the Highway initially follows the TransCanada Highway eastwards, then turns off with three alternative routes into Okanagan Valley (see entry) and links up with the east-west link road, Crowsnest Highway (Highway 3; see entry), which runs near to the USA–Canadian border.

The first gold-seekers, on hearing news of great finds of gold in the interior of British Columbia, came north from California, initially following the rocky Cariboo Trail along the Fraser River. In 1862 the governor of the province, Sir James Douglas, had a road 6 m (20 ft) wide and 640 km (400 mi.) long laid into the interior to take wagons and ox-carts; by 1865 it was completed as far as the Barkerville goldfields. Several travellers' rests were built along the way; names such as "100 Mile House" or "150 Mile House" still remind us of these mainly modest stations which have long since disappeared.

Although the new Waggon Road actually started in Yale, skirted Lillooet and did not meet the old Cariboo Trail until it reached Clinton, for some curious reason the miles were counted starting from Lillooet which, following the boom period in the early 1860s, had lost much of its importance. In Lillooet, which today lies 75 km (47 mi.) west of Highway 97, there is a tablet recalling the "0" miles mark of the old Cariboo Waggon Road.

Cache Creek, lying 670 m (2200 ft) above sea-level and with a population of 1000, was at one time a busy centre for freight going north or east. From here "Bernard's Express", a stage-coach service, ran for 50 years; it could reach Barkerville in four days.

40 km (25 mi.): Clinton (pop. 800; 887 m (2912 ft)), originally called "47 Mile House", was an important traffic junction during the Cariboo gold-rush. In 1861 a road led from here via Pavilion Mountain to Lillooet; today it is a gravel road usable only in summer. Clinton has so far retained the atmosphere of a pionering town, and a number of the "19th c.-type" ranches take in paying guests.

At 1419 Cariboo Highway stands the old brick-built schoolhouse dating from 1892; today it houses the South Cariboo Historical Museum.

Winter on the Cariboo Highway

Its exhibits reflect the pioneering period and the old Waggon Road. The many lakes in the vicinity are very popular with anglers. Open Jul.–Aug. daily 10am–8pm.

100 Mile House

116 km (72 mi.): 100 Mile House (pop. 2000; 930 m (3052 ft)), a centre for the remote ranches round about and the site of two modern saw-mills, gets its name from the old Cariboo Waggon Road. This is where the "100 Mile Roadhouse" was opened in 1862. One of the original red Bernard's Express mail coaches stands in front of the Red Coach Inn as a reminder of the past. In 1912 the Marquess of Exeter purchased more than 6000 ha (15,000 acres) of land around here for his extensive Bridge Creek Ranch, which the family still owns.

The historical 108 Mile House, 13 km (8 mi.) north of here, is currently a Heritage Site Museum.

Clearwater

11 km (7 mi.) south of the town is the turn-off to Highway 24. This winds through some charming countryside to Little Fort 110 km (68 mi.) away on Highway 5 (Yellowhead Highway, South). A few miles further north is the township of Clearwater and the approach road through Clearwater Valley to Wells Gray Provincial Park.

Lakes

Access to the western part of Wells Gray Provincial Park is by way of an 88 km (55 mi.) long approach road. The 35 km (22 mi.) long Canim Lake, charmingly situated in the mountains, and Mahood Lake – which is 19 km (12 mi.) long, with a camp site at its western end, and forms part of the provincial park – are very popular with canoeing enthusiasts.

Mahood and Canim River Falls, together with Deception Falls, are favourites with walkers.

★**Lac La Hache**

140 km (87 mi.): in recent years tourist facilities (including boat-hire) have sprung up along the 19 km (12 mi.) long Lac La Hache with its beautiful bathing beaches.

Williams Lake

204 km (127 mi.): Williams Lake (pop. 10,000; 586 m (1923 ft)) lies in the centre of the Cariboo region. As well as the timber industry, cattle-rearing and mining of copper molybdenum, tourism – with the attractions of fishing and hunting for wild animals – plays an ever more important role.

In the vicinity can be found numerous traces of the gold-rush period and the William Lake Museum at 1148 Broadway provides information about this. A special attraction is a small reactivated gold-mine. Open May–Sep. daily 9am–6pm.

Each year, on the first week-end in July, one of Canada's larger rodeos, the Williams Lake Stampede, takes place here.

Highway 20

There is a detour from Williams Lake to Highway 20 – a gravel road usually suitable for driving in summer – which leads through some charming countryside and for 480 km (300 mi.) west through the sparsely inhabited Chilcotin or Fraser Plateau with its huge ranches, an area which is reasonably dry because it lies in the rain shadow of the glaciated coastal mountain range. The route then continues via the coastal range of mountains to Bella Coola, the only port on the Pacific coast between Prince Rupert and Lake Powell which has a road-link.

Highway 20 – only the first 113 km (70 mi.) as far as Alexis Creek and the last 60 km (37 mi.) or so in the Bella Coola Valley are made-up – links the few remote settlements along the frontier with the still largely undeveloped wilderness and opens up some really unspoiled and original hunting and fishing grounds. Several ranches will take in paying guests for riding holidays. Alexis Creek, with a population of about 100, provides supplies and provisions to the 1000 or so people who live by the Chilcotin River.

Tatla Lake

In Tatla Lake, a small township 69 km (43 mi.) further west with a restaurant, school, shop, post-office and medical station, a road branches off to the Coastal Mountains. The shimmering turquoise waters of Tatlayoko Lake are highly attractive; here visitors can enjoy Alpine Wilderness

Adventures, ranch holidays, treks with pack-horses in the Coast Mountains and fishing. A few miles further west rises British Columbia's highest mountain peak, Mount Waddington, which is 4016 m (13,180 ft) high.

Anahim Lake (142 km (88 mi.)), at the western end of the Chilcotin Plateau and a westerly provisions centre, is a starting-out point for wilderness tours. A certain degree of "outdoor experience" and a locally knowledgeable guide are recommended.

Anahim Lake

From here the road climbs up to Heckman Pass (1524 m (5060 ft)) in Tweedsmuir Provincial Park, which covers an area of 9810 sq. km (3788 sq. mi.), making it the largest such park in British Columbia. The road then zigzags its way down to Bella Coola Valley, surrounded by snow and ice-capped peaks.

Tweedsmuir Provincial Park

The southern part of the park, better reached along Highway 20 (for the northern part see Yellowhead Highway), is an undeveloped wilderness. In the east, in the Rainbow Nature Conservancy Area, the Rainbow Range – including Tsitsutl Peak 2478 m (8133 ft) – protrudes sharply up from the plateau which itself is some 1350 m (4430 ft) above sea-level at its centre. This mountain range resembles a massive cathedral of volcanic origin and unusual coloration. In the west tower the glaciated peaks of the rugged Coastal Mountains.

Rainbow National Conservation Area

The spectacular Hunlen Falls at the northern end of Turner Lake are an outstanding sight. The water plunges down from a height of 260 m (853 ft), making them the highest waterfalls in the whole of Canada. It takes a day's trek to reach them; there is a primitive tent-site by Turner Lake. During the autumn salmon season large numbers of grizzly and black bear find their way to the Atnarko River (visitors should exercise caution). There is limited basic accommodation to be had in Tweedsmir Lodge by the Atnarko River and in Tweedsmuir Wilderness Centre.

★Hunlen Falls

This exhausting trek through wild country takes at least three weeks and follows in the footsteps of Alexander Mackenzie in 1793. The path leads from West Road (Blackwater) River – between Quesnel and Prince George – to Burnt Bridge Creek on Highway 20, and has become well-known even outside Canada. After covering about 80km/50 miles the road passes through an extremely charming part of Tweedsmuir Provincial Park; information and a trail guide can be obtained from The Alexander Mackenzie Trail Association, PO Box 425, Kelowna, B.C. V1Y 1Y1.

Alexander Mackenzie Heritage Trail

The little Indian fishing village of Bella Coola (pop. 2000) at the end of Highway 20 lies in a protected spot on North Bentinck Arm, a fiord which reaches far inland. On the northern shore of Dean Channel west of Bella Coola there is a plaque on "Mackenzie's Rock" in memory of Alexander Mackenzie, who in 1793 became the first European to cross the whole of the North American continent. He and his Indian guide followed the Indian "Grease Trail", an old trade route along which the coastal Indians transported fish-oil, dried fish, berries or cedar-bark far into the interior in order to barter them for elk and buffalo hides, beaver-fur and obsidian. When he reached the western end of his journey Mackenzie inscribed on a rock the words "Alex Mackenzie, from Canada, by Land, the 22nd day of July 1793". This rock now stands in the Sir Alexander Mackenzie Provincial Park and can be reached only by boat or seaplane from Bella Coola.

Bella Coola

From 1869 onwards the Hudson's Bay Company had an outpost here for thirteen years, but it was not until 1894 that some 90 or so Norwegian settlers and fishermen established a colony here. The little museum in the town centre (open: June–Sept. Mon.–Fri. 10am–4pm) includes in its exhibits some items which these settlers from Norway brought with them.

325 km (200 mi.): The town of Quesnel, 545 m (1790 ft) above sea-level and with a population of 9000, lies at the confluence of the Quesnel and Fraser Rivers. It is the centre of the northern Cariboo region and proudly

Quesnel

calls itself "Gold Pan City" in memory of the 1860 gold-rush. Various old buildings have been restored, such as the Hudson's Bay Company Trading Post of 1867, the Cornish Wheel, a giant water-wheel used at the time of the gold-rush, and Bohanon House, a lovingly restored dwelling.

The Quesnel & District Museum at 707 Carson Ave./Highway 97 documents the history of settlers in the region, including gold-diggers, farmers, lumberjacks and ranchers as well as Indians and Chinese. Open May–Sep. Tue.–Sun. 10am–5pm.

Billy Barker Days are held every July as a reminder of the gold-rush period.

★**Bowron Lake Provincial Park**

33 km (20 mi.) east of Wells along a gravel road brings the visitor to Bowron Lake Provincial Park. This magnificent region, mainly an untamed wilderness, covers an area of 1231 sq. km (475 sq. mi.). Ever popular are canoe tours on the eleven lakes in the park covering a total of 116 km (72 mi.) and lasting eight to ten days; linked one with the other by five rivers, these lakes are surrounded by the massive peaks of the Cariboo Mountains rising to heights of up to 2530 m (8300 ft). There are only seven occasions when the pleasure of canoeing has to be interrupted by the need to convey the canoe to the next stretch of water, the maximum length to carry it being 3 km (2 mi.); mosquitoes can be a nuisance.

Most of the time is spent paddling along still or gently flowing waters. There are 45 places where overnight stays can be made in small tents equipped with bear-proof platforms in order to keep food stocks safe, simple toilet facilities and some with cooking shelters. Canoes can be hired at two lodges at the park entrance; information and maps can be obtained from the Nature House at the northern end of Bowron Lake, where those going on a canoe tour must sign themselves in and out. Outward-bound experience, physical fitness and suitable equipment are essential.

In summer the number of permits issued for the total round trip is limited to 50 canoeists per day. Bowron Lake and the straggling Spectacle Lakes are suitable for shorter boat trips – without the need to carry the boat across land.

Information: Ministry of Environment & Parks, District Manager, Parks and Outdoor Recreation Division, RR1, Dunsmuir Road, Lac La Hache, B.C. V0K 1T0; tel. (604) 3967225.

Charlevoix H 16/17

Province: Québec

Location

Charlevoix is the name given to the stretch of country along the left bank of the St Lawrence River, from Côte de Beaupré as far as Saquenay. It gets its name from the Jesuit François Xavier De-Charlevoix (1682–1761), who published the first historical record of Canada in 1744. Extensive forests, mountains and the St Lawrence give Charlevoix its charm.

History

The first settlers arrived in Charlevoix early in the 18th c., when farmers, hunters and lumberjacks began to put down roots here in small numbers, at first in Petite-Rivière-St-François, then in Baie-St-Paul and on the Île aux Coudres.

After 1760 many Scottish Highlanders emigrated to Charlevoix. The Scottish ancestry of their descendants is still to be found in the names commonly met in this area, such as Warren, Harvey or Blackburn.

Before the first road was built in 1824 the St Lawrence River provided the only means of access. As a result professions linked with sea-faring continued to dominate here into the 20th c. Today the woodworking industry, with giant resources at its command, still plays an important role

Sights

Île aux Coudres

From St-Joseph-de-la-Rive boats ply to Île aux Coudres, which lies in the

Baie-St-Paul, about 3 km (2 mi.) off the bank of the St Lawrence. Jacques Cartier was the first to land here on September 6th 1535 and gave it its present name because of the large number of hazelnut bushes he found growing on the island.

With its many stone houses and windmills the Île aux Coudres must be one of the most idyllic regions of Québec province.

On September 7th 1535 the famous Guillaume le Breton, one of the two priests who had accompanied Cartier on his expedition, celebrated the first mass to be held in the new French colony. There is a memorial to this event in St-Bernard. In St-Louis visitors can explore the interior of one of the many ships which have run aground here. The schooner "Mont-St-Louis" today houses the "Musée des voitures d'eau", which is open daily in summer, and provides background on the history of seafaring in this area. Also worth a visit are the two 18th c. Desgagné windmills and Maison Leclerc in La Baleine which contains some old Québec furniture; the latter is open daily in summer 10am–6pm.

In the upper-class villa district of Pointe-au-Pic can be found one of the oldest hotels in Canada, the luxury Manoir Richelieu. | Pointe-au-Pic

The name of this little industrial town, which translates into English as "Bad Bay", is attributed to Samuel de Champlain, whose ship ran aground here in 1608. | **La Malbaie**

From the enchanting hamlet of Port-au-Persil there is a wonderful view of the Île aux Lièvres. | **Port-au-Persil**

★Charlottetown H 18

Province: Prince Edward Island · Île Prince Edouard
Population: 33,000

Greater Charlottetown Area Chamber of Commerce, 127 Kent Street, Charlottetown, PEI C1A 7K2; tel. (902) 6282000 | Information

Charlottetown, capital of Prince Edward Island, is centrally situated, on sheltered Hillsborough Bay. Smallest of the country's provincial capitals, historically speaking it is perhaps the most significant. Despite having grown considerably in the past two decades, it remains essentially a quiet rural town, hub of the island's administration and schools. In the little town centre, easily explored on foot, there are some pretty Victorian buildings. Most of the old buildings have been painstakingly restored down to the last detail. The old harbour quarter has also been nicely restored and is particularly popular with visitors. | Location

Jacques Cartier took possession of the island for the French in 1534, when it was called the Île-St-Jean. The harbour settlement of Port la Joye grew up on the site now covered by Charlottetown. In the first half of the 18th c. the French–Arcadian influence still held sway on the island. In 1758 however the British took over and the Arcadians were deported. A few years later Charlottetown was founded, named after the wife of King George III. In September 1864 Charlottetown was the venue of the famous conference which led to the unification of Canada. | History

The ultra-modern Confederation Centre of Arts on the corner of Grafton Street and Queen Street was opened in 1964 as Canada's national monument to the Confederation. Every Canadian citizen paid fifteen cents towards the cost of the building and continues to pay towards its maintenance. Inside will be found an art gallery, a museum, a provincial library, a memorial hall, two theatres and a restaurant. | ★Confederation Centre of the Arts

The museum is on the ground floor, the entrance being on the side opposite Province House. Open Jul.–Aug. daily 10am–8pm; other times of the year daily except Mon. 10am–5pm.

Charlottetown

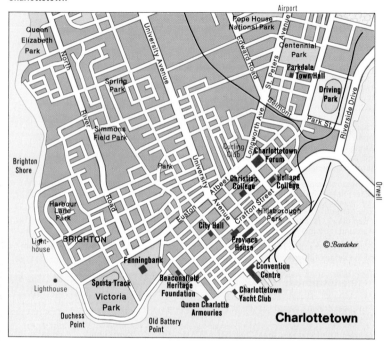

In the foyer stands a very beautiful sculpture in chrome and crystal decorated with the coats-of-arms of each Canadian province; it was a gift from the USA to mark the centenary of the Confederation of Canada.

In the art gallery on the third floor some magnificent works by modern Canadian artists are on display. One room is devoted to Robert Harris, one of Canada's most renowned painters from the turn of the century. Also well worth seeing is the soapstone sculpture of Mother and Child by Inukpuk, a master of Inuit art.

The Charlotte Town Festival, held in the Confederation Centre from June to September, offers excellent entertainment; The highlights are visits by guest stars with shows and musical performances, including the annually performed musical version of the successful play "Anne of Green Gables".

★Province House National Historic Site

Near the Confederation Centre stands Province House, the "Birthplace of Canada". This three-storey sandstone building was constructed as the colonial government building in 1843–47. Other buildings were pulled down in 1963 to make room for the Confederation Centre. Today Province House is the seat of the Parliament of Prince Edward Island. Open Jun.–Sep. daily 9am–8pm; otherwise weekdays 9am–5pm.

The Confederation Chamber, where in 1864 representatives from the British possessions in North America met to launch the modern state of Canada, was restored some years ago. Photographs and documents of this historic event are also on display. The parliamentary rooms are also open to visitors.

St Paul's Anglican Church

Standing to the east of Province House, St Paul's Anglican Church (18th c.) is the island's oldest Protestant church.

St James Presbyterian Church, better known as simply "The Kirk", has some impressive stained glass windows and old relics from the island of Iona, the first part of Scotland to become converted to Christianity. A granite block standing on a marble slab in the north wall comes from St Mary's Cathedral on Iona.

St James Presbyterian Church,

To the south of Province House on the corner of Great George Street and Richmond Street stands St Dunstan's Basilica, built at the end of the 19th c. in the Neo-Gothic style, the seat of the Roman Catholic diocese of the province. It is one of the largest buildings of its kind in eastern Canada and famed for its altar with its beautiful Italian carving and a superb rose window.

St Dunstan's Basilica

A walk along Richmond Street and Kent Street to its north with their gabled houses and extensive parks and gardens provides an impressive reminder of Charlottetown's Victorian heritage.

St Peter's Cathedral in the north-west corner of Rochford Square was built in 1879. The 1888 chapel was designed by W. C. Harris and is decorated with murals by his famous brother Robert Harris.

St Peter's Cathedral

At the beginning of Kent Street stands Beaconsfield, a villa designed by W. C. Harris and built in 1877, with lace-like wooden decoration, a mansard roof and a graceful dome – a prime example of Victorian architecture. It now houses the Prince Edward Island Museum, the offices of the Heritage Foundation, the Centre for Genealogical Research and a bookshop which specialises in publications relating to the island. From time to time exhibitions of local history are held here, and the interior design of this lovely old house itself makes a visit well worthwhile. Admission is free; open: Mon.–Fri. 10am–4pm.

Beaconsfield

The white edifice of Government House built in Colonial style on the top of a hill, can still be seen. After 1835 it became the official seat of the Governor of the island.

Government House

Also in Victoria Park and looking down on the harbour stands Fort Edward, built in 1805. It is one of the fortifications along the harbour entrance and from it there is a view over the said entrance to Fort Amherst.

Fort Edward

Chilliwack

H 6

Province: British Columbia
Population: 42,000. Altitude: 10 m (33 ft)

Chilliwack Chamber of Commerce, 44150 Luckakuck Avenue, Chilliwack, BC V2R 4A7; tel. (604) 8588121

Information

70 km (43 mi.) east of Vancouver lies Chillawack, a striving rural town which proudly calls itself the "Green Heart" of British Columbia. Yale Road, the old meandering road to Rosedale, passes through fields of hops and vegetables and pastureland. Farmers offer their produce for sale at the roadside. Chilliwack – its name comes from the Indian word meaning "valley of many rivers" – dates from 1858, when Volker Vedder settled here. He had crossed the continent in an ox-wagon and was the first settler in this fertile valley.

Location

Chilliwack Museum is devoted to the culture of the Salish Indians and of the pioneering period. It is situated at Evergreen Hall, 9291 Corbould St. Open Mon.–Fri. 9am–4.30pm, Sat. 10am–4pm. The Canadian Military Engineers Museum is to be found at Canadian Forces Base Chilliwack, Vedder Crossing. On display are weapons and militaria collected since 1815, together with a diorama of the Battle of Waterloo. Open Sun. 1–4pm, and in summer also on Tue.–Fri. 10am–4pm.

Museum

14 km (8¾ mi.) south-west of Chilliwack in the midst of wooded hills lies Cultus Lake, 5 km (3 mi.) long. It is one of the most popular lakeside leisure resorts in the south of the province, with a park and recreational

Cultus Lake

area. In the north on Cultus Lake Waterpark there are water-chutes and a go-cart track.

Chilliwack Lake

Near Vedder Crossing Chilliwack Lake Road branches off into the charming mountain landscape by the USA border north of the Cascade Mountain Range. For the most part the road follows the enchanting valley of the Chilliwach River, where there are opportunities for white-water canoeing and rafting as well as fishing.

After a further 64 km (40 mi.), the last 15 km (9 mi.) of which are gravel, the road comes to Chilliwack Lake, a beautiful lake surrounded by mountains over 2000 m (6600 ft) high and very popular with water-sports enthusiasts and anglers alike. Canoes can be hired from Western Canoeing in Abbotsford.

Bridal Falls
Tourist Area

250 km (155 mi.): Here, at the junction with Highway 9, a number of tourist attractions have grown up in recent years.

Flintstone
Bedrock
City

Flintstone Bedrock City is a leisure park with themes and figures from the animated cartoon film of the Flintstone family. Life-sized figures of Wilma and Fred Flintstone, Barney Rubble and Dino greet the visitors. Open May and Sep. Sat. and Sun. only; mid-Jun.–beginning Sep. daily, 9am–8pm.

Minter Gardens

Between April and October the 10 ha (25 acres) of Minter Gardens offer lavish displays and charming gardens and open areas divided into ten different theme parks. Open Apr.–Oct. daily from 9am.

Trans-Canada
Waterslides

Open from the end of May, the Trans-Canada Waterslides offer five swimming-pools with water-chutes. A mini-golf course adjoins.

Bridal Veil Falls
Provincial Park

From the rest-area it is a three-quarters of an hour walk through a forest of spruce and cedar to the impressive 60 m (200 ft) high Bridal Veil Falls.

★Churchill   F 12

Province: Manitoba
Population: 1500. Altitude: 30 m (99 ft)

Informaton

Churchill Chamber of Commerce, 211 Kelsey Bvd., Churchill, MB R0B 0E0; tel. (204) 6752022

Access

From Winnipeg by air or rail

History

Inuits or aboriginals lived in the Churchill region at least as long ago as 1700 BC. The first European settlers arrived when the Danish seafarer Jens Munck spent the winter of 1619–20 here during his unsuccessful search for the Northwest Passage. Of his original crew of 65 only Munck and two sailors survived the winter to return to Denmark. In 1717 the Hudson's Bay Company built a trading-post in Churchill. Between 1731 and 1771 Fort Prince of Wales was built.

Churchill, popularly known as the "Polar Bear Capital of the World" and an important corn transporting centre, lies on the harsh rocky coast of Hudson Bay. It is the terminus of the Hudson Bay Railway which was completed in 1929 by 3000 men who had to struggle through freezing conditions and bogs.

The spectacular aurora borealis lights up the long sub-arctic nights.

Fauna and flora

In and around the town there is a thriving animal kingdom, including some species not found anywhere else in the world. It is a paradise for bird-lovers. Countless geese, cranes and 200 other species of birds pass along the coast of Hudson's Bay and through the town on their way to their nesting sites in the Arctic. For a number of years now even the rare and beautiful Ross gull, which originates from Siberia, has been nesting here.

Various kinds of seals surface in the harbour, and the protected beluga whales frolic in the waters between June and early September. Caribou can also be spotted along the coast at that time of year.

In autumn polar bears wander onto the ice-floes in the bay to hunt seals. The visitors who come here every year can go on tours in tundra-buggies – giant large-wheeled vehicles – of the places where the bears collect.

Along the harsh coast trees have been lashed by the wind and withered away. In spring – which starts in the middle of June – and autumn the Arctic flora, lichen and miniature bushes present a marvellously colourful scene.

In the Visitor Reception centre at Bayport Plaza, films are shown on various subjects, such as polar bears, the construction of the railroad and the Arctic landscape, and furs, muskets and trade goods used by the Hudson's Bay Company in the 18th and 19th c. are also on display. Open Jun. to mid-Sep. daily 9am–6pm.

Visitor Reception Centre

The excellent Inuit Museum in Vérendrye St. is open Mon. 1–5pm, Tue.–Sat. 9am–noon and 1–5pm. Its exhibits include Inuit works of art and tools dating from the Pre-Dorset (1700 BC) through the Dorset and Thule cultures to the present day, and information is also provided on the fauna of the North.

★★Inuit Museum

The large and partly restored Fort Prince of Wales, a National Historic Park accessible by boat and open in July and August, lies on the other side of the river. It was built by the Hudson's Bay Company in the 18th c. in order to defend the interests of the English fur trade in the New World. A start was made on its construction in 1732, with workers, horses and oxen shipped over from England. Forty years later this outstanding building with its extremely beautiful masonry was finally finished. In 1782 the fort, its garrison led by Samuel Hearne, fell without a struggle into the hands of the French, who then destroyed it.

★Fort Prince of Wales

At each corner stands a lozenge-shaped bulwark; one was a storehouse, the second a carpenter's workshop, the third a stable and the fourth a powder magazine. Inside the walls is a gallery for cannon. On the ground floor can be seen the remains of the commandant's quarters, the provisions store and barracks.

On the Cape Merry coast on the eastern side of the river mouth, 3 km (2 mi.) from the town, stand heaps of giant grey blocks of quarzite, which were smoothed and rounded by retreating glaciers. On the soft tundra grass between the rocks grows a magnificent plethora of plants, including willow, dwarf cranberries, bear-berries and crowberries.

Cape Merry

Here stood a stone bastion which was supposed to protect the fort. One of the six original cannon and a part of the powder magazine can still be seen. A mound of stones is in memory of the Danish Captain Jens Munk who landed here in 1619 with two ships. There is also a tablet here in honour of Thomas Button; in 1612 he became the first European to reach the mouth of the Churchill River.

Cochrane

H 14

Province: Ontario Population: 5000

Cochrane Timiskaming Travel Association, PO Box 1162, Timmins, Ontario, P4N 7H9; tel. (705) 2649589.

Information

From North Bay (see entry) about 370 km (230 mi.) north on the Trans-Canada Highway.

Access

This little mining and industrial town situated in the district of the same name in north-eastern Ontario grew up early in the 20th c. as a result of the legendary finds of gold. Its own iron and steel industries combined with its location at the rail junction of the Ontario Northland Railway linking it to the north and the east-west line of the Canadian Pacific Railway made it an important loading and transportation centre for the minerals mined throughout the region. As a gateway to the as yet unde-

Location

veloped hinterland south of James Bay the town is now a valued and busy place where trappers, outfitters and those in search of adventure meet and set out on their journeys.

Railway & Pioneer Museum	A locomotive with four wagons, reconstructed interiors, historical implements and photographs from the pioneering period provide the visitor with a vivid picture of the history of the James Bay frontier. The museum is open daily mid-Jun.–Labour Day.
Greenwater Provincial Park	This nature park near Cochrane is ideal for walks, camping and fishing.
★Polar Bear Express	The 300 km (190 mi.) stretch of railway between Cochrane and Moosonee was built in 1932 and for a long time thereafter remained the only link with the region at the mouth of the Moose River. A one-day excursion from Cochrane involves a five and a half hour journey on the legendary Polar Bear Express through the untamed wilderness. In the summer months the train travels each way every day except Fridays, and three days a week in winter. Anyone with more time to spend and who wants to get a genuine feel of the hunting and trapping atmosphere should take the slower train which stops at all stations on the way.

More detailed information available from Ontario Northland Railway, Passenger Service Department, North Bay, Ontario, P1B 8L3. Tel. (705) 4724500.

Moosonee	See entry

Columbia River   G/H 7

Province: British Columbia

Information	See British Columbia
Course	The Columbia River rises in the Kootenay District, in the south-east of British Columbia at the foot of the Kootenays (see Kootenay National Park) a part of the western edge of the Rocky Mountains. First it flows north along a deeply slashed valley – known as the Rocky Mountains Trench – which was formed as the result of tectonic folding of the earth's crust. As these geological deformations were accompanied by strong volcanic activity many places with hot springs were formed on the edge of the valley, such as Fairmont Hot Springs and Radium Hot Spring.

Initially the Columbia River flows round the Columbia Mountain ranges, which consist of several chains – the Purcell, Selkirk, Cariboo and Monashee Mountains – rising to more than 3000 m (9850 ft) In Glacier National Park (see entry) they reach heights of 3390 m (11,125 ft). Rogers Pass, 1327 m (4355 ft) up, was an ideal route for the TransCanada Railway and the TransCanada Highway to wind its way over the Columbia Mountains.

South of the Cariboo Mountains – which extend as far as the Fraser River, another important river system in British Columbia -the Columbia River is diverted southwards. The Mica Dam blocks off the river for the production of hydro-electric power. The Columbia now flows southward along the Monashee Mountains. Numerous dams have been built in this wide canyon in order to provide water-power, including the Revelstoke Dam, Whatshany Dam and others, forming elongated lakes, such as Revelstoke Lake and Upper Arrow Lake. Numerous tributaries flowing down from the adjoining mountain chains and often fed by melting glaciers provide the Columbia with ample supplies of water. In spring, when snow melts in Canada's most snowy regions, the water level can be too high.

After passing the USA border the Columbia is again frequently dammed and now flows along the Columbia Plateau, the northernmost of the three great intermontane highlands of the USA, where flat tertiary layers of basalt lava are frequently found.

After 1840 km (1150 mi.) the Columbia reaches the Pacific in Oregon. Its delta is about 56 km (35 mi.) long and 11 km (7 mi.) wide. In all the

Valley of the Columbia River

Columbia has a catchment area of 775,000 sq. km (300,000 sq. mi.). Only parts of it are fully navigable, however; smallish ships can sail as far as 250 km (150 mi.) inland.

Côte Nord   G/H 17–19

Province: Québec

See Québec   Information

The Côte Nord stretches along the left bank of the St Lawrence River   Location
between Saguenay and the Belle-Île Straits. Because of its relatively
unspoiled hinterland with extensive coniferous forests and numerous
rivers North Shore – especially Sept-Îles – is an ideal setting-out point for
walkers, anglers and hunters.

The road for vehicular traffic ends in Havre-St-Pierre, the region further   Blanc-Sablon
north being accessible by ferry. The firm of Relais Nordik provides a
ferry-service from Rimouski, Sept-Îles, Port-Menier and Havre-St-Pierre
between early April and the end of September.

Founded in 1958, the fast-expanding town of Port-Cartier has the second   Port-Cartier
most important harbour, after that of Sept-Îles, for the export of the iron-
ore mined in Nouveau Québec and Labrador.

Sept-Îles, the largest town on the North Shore, lies at the entrance to   Sept-Îles
Sept-Îles Bay. It was given its name by Jacques Cartier, who discovered
this bay with its seven islands in 1535. In 1650 Father Jean Dequen
founded a mission here. Following colonisation in the middle of the 19th
c., mainly fishermen and lumberjacks settled here.

On the Côte Nord

★★**Mingan National Park**

Mingan is a little fishing port on the Détroit Jacques Cartier (Jacques Cartier Strait). In Ste-Geneviève Bay, near the coast between Mingan and Havre-St-Pierre, lies a string of forty islands, the Îles de Mingan. This archipelago is a National Park and a paradise for birds.

Île d'Anticosti

Since 1975 the Île d'Anticosti has been under the control of the Ministry of Tourism, Hunting and Fishing in Québec. Discovered by Jacques Cartier in 1534, the island has a population of only 300 or so. The climate is damp and cold and the island often disappears under a mantle of thick fog.

Advice

Anyone wishing to wander on the island needs a permit from the above-mentioned ministry.

★★Crowsnest Highway H 6–8

Province: British Columbia, Alberta

Information

Tourism British Columbia, 802–865 Hornby St., Vancouver, BC V6Z 2G3; tel. (604) 6602861, fax. (604) 6603383.
Travel Alberta, PO Box 2500, Edmonton, AB T5J 2Z4; tel. (403) 4274321, fax. (403) 4270867.

History

Crowsnest Highway (Highway 3: Dewdney Trail) is the scenic and, in parts, quite charming south-lying road in Western Canada which provides the east-west link via Crowsnest Pass (1396 m (4581 ft)). Near Hope (see entry), 154 km (96 mi.) east of Vancouver, this less busy highway branches off from the TransCanada Highway and passes close to the USA border through the south-east of British Columbia and over the Rocky Mountains into southern Alberta. After nearly 2000 km (1240 mi.) it again meets up with TransCanada Highway 1 in Medicine Hat near the Saskatchewan border. It then continues in the shape of the "Red Coat Trail", a tourist route consisting mainly of by-roads through unspoilt rural countryside in the south of Saskatchewan and Manitoba as far as Winnipeg; to a large extent this is the route taken in 1874 by the men of the North West Mounted Police when they came West to restore law and order. After the Oregon treaty of 1846 had decreed that the lower reaches of the Columbia River south of the 49th Parallel should belong to the USA the Hudson's Bay Company was obliged to find new routes along which to transport their goods into the interior of British Columbia. In the middle of the 19th c. they built a trading post in Hope. In 1859 gold was discovered by the Kettle and Similkameen Rivers, whereupon the governor, James Douglas, appointed two young British engineers, E. Dewdney and W. Moberly, to construct the first "mule-track" along the 120 km (75 mi.) stretch between Hope and Vermilion Forks, now Princetown. Further discoveries of gold in the Kootenay region persuaded his successor Seymour to build a 480 km (300 mi.) extension of the road through the wilderness to Wild Horse Creek in the Rocky Mountains, so that gold being found would not be lost to the United States simply because of a lack of an adequate road link with Vancouver. At that time it took at least three weeks to travel from the Okanagan Valley to Wild Horse Creek in the Rockies. Today long stretches of the modern Crowsnest Highway 3 follow the route chosen by Dewdney.

The Crowsnest Highway crosses five massive mountain chains, the Cascade, Monashee, Selkirk, Purcell and Rocky Mountains, winding through passes up to 1774 m (5822 ft) high and sampling almost all British Columbia's varied scenery, from the rain-forests of the Pacific Coast through the fruit plantations of the climatically-favoured Okanagan valley (see entry), the green farmlands around Creston to the snow and ice-covered Rocky Mountains and the gently undulating prairies of southern Alberta.

Between Princetown and Keremeos there is good wild-water canoeing on the Similkameen River. In Princetown Highway 5A branches off to the north to Merritt and Kamloops (see entry).

An old mill near Keremeos

Crowsnest Highway

Hope

The Crowsnest Highway starts in the west at Hope (see entry), about two hours drive from Vancouver (see entry), 18 km (11 mi.) from Hope the road passes Hope Slide, a massive landslip; 8 km (5 mi.) further on lies Manning Provincial Park.

Keremeos

204 km (127 mi.): Keremeos (pop. 1000; 413 m (1355 ft)), the fruit-growing centre situated in the middle of the fertile Simikameen valley, a protected area, boasts that it has more fruit-stalls per inhabitant than any other town in Canada. During the harvest season the roadside is littered with stalls set up by the farmers and fruit-growers.

In the first half of the 19th c. the Hudson's Bay Company ran a ranch in Keremeos, and in the 1860s the first settlers came to the warm valley, a Mexican built the first and for a long time the only corn-mill, great herds of cattle spent the winter on the wide valley floor and in spring were driven along the Dewdney Trail to Hope. In 1897 F. X. Richter, an immigrant from Bohemia, planted the first fruit plantation. After the introduction of artificial irrigation meadows gave way to fields of vegetables and fruit plantations. In 1907 the first canning factory was built.

What was once the prison cell in the court building on 6th Ave. and 6th St. today houses the little Keremeos Museum. Open Jun.–Aug. 9am–5pm.

On Upper Bench Road, 3 km (2 mi.) north via Highway 3, will be found Price's Grist Mill, a corn-mill with a water-wheel, built in 1876. The mill, together with a small historical museum in the former general store, is open to visitors May–Sep. Wed.–Sun. 9am–5pm.

Highway 3 leads from Keremeos direct into the Okanagan Valley (see entry) at Penedicton, 50 km (30 mi.) north.

Cathedral Provincial Park

5 km (3 mi.) before it reaches Keremeos the 24 km (15 mi.) approach road turns off along the Ashnola River to the Cathedral Provincial Park. This untamed mountain wilderness on the border with Washington USA, with its deep-blue lakes, steep peaks more than 2000 m (6600 ft) high, imposing rock formations and Alpine-like meadows is particularly attractive to those keen on "the great outdoors".

This park in the Okanagan Mountain Range, covering some 330 sq. km (205 sq. mi.), is the area between the thick, damp forests of the Cascade Mountains and the arid Okanagan Valley. When walking through it the visitor can observe deer, mountain-goats or Californian thick-horned sheep, as well as marmot. The centre of the park is the area surrounding the charming Cathedral Lakes; note, however, that it is not accessible by private car – only all-wheel drive vehicles can cope with the rough road, and walkers and guests of the Cathedral Lakes Resort by Quiniscoe Lake, which is not run by the parks authority, will be collected and driven there.

There is a walk lasting several hours from Quiniscoe Lake and by way of Glacier Lake to Stone City, a group of huge granite blocks, and to Giant Cleft. This great cleft was left after the removal of the geomorphologically softer volcanic materials that had been forced into the granite. Other interesting geological formations along the way are Devil's Woodpile, a group of basalt columns so named because they are thought to resemble a pile of wood gathered by the Devil for his fires in Hell, as well as "Smokey the Bear", a prominent rock overhang which looks very much like the figure of a bear which is used by the Forestry Commission in their campaign to prevent forest fires.

On clear days there is a magnificent view from the crest of the Cathedral Range as far as Mount Rainier 290 km (180 mi.) to the south-west which, being 4392 m (14,415 ft) high, is the fifth highest peak in the USA, or of the snow-capped peak of Mount Baker (3285 m (10,781ft)) to the west.

Crowsnest Highway 3 now continues southward for 30 km (19 mi.) along the winding Simikameen Valley and then by way of the Richter Pass (682 m (2238 ft)) into the lower Okanagan Valley.

Osoyoos

252 km (156 mi.): Osoyoos (pop. 3000; 277 m (909 ft)), only 6 km (3¾ mi.)

from the US frontier, lies at the southern end of the "Canadian Desert". From here as far as Okanagan Falls, some 43 km (27 mi.) to the north, stretches a northern outcrop of the semi-desert region which extends from Mexico and Arizona as far as Montana and Washington. The average annual rainfall is less than 200 mm (8 in.), and summer temperatures between 40°C and 50°C (104°F and 122°F) are not uncommon. Keep an eye open for rattlesnakes when walking in this region.

This sandy tongue of land, known since 1811 and extending through almost the whole of Osoyoos Lake, was favoured as a storage place by the Indians and fur-hunters. The first ranch was built here more than 50 years later. Around 1890 more than 20,000 cattle grazed between Keremeos and Osoyoos.

Since the early 20th c., however, intensive fruit and vegetable cultivation has formed the basis of the life of the region, aided by between 120 and 180 frost-free days each year. From March to May thousand of apricot, cherry, peach and apple trees transform the valley into a sea of blossom. The "Cherry Festival" is held every year. In summer Osoyoos Lake, with its sandy beaches and water temperatures of 24°C (75°F), is a favourite place for bathers.

This region resembles the dry areas of southern California and is also reminiscent of parts of the Iberian Peninsula; to give the place a unique appearance it was decided in 1975 to introduce a Spanish style of building. Since then the main street has been dominated by whitewashed buildings with gleaming red roofs and wrought-iron grilles.

In Community Park there is a small museum that provides details of the town's history and of the methods of artificial irrigation and cultivation of fruit in the region. Works of art and utensils produced by Okanagan Indians can also be purchased here, and tourist information is available. Open Jul.–Sep. 10am–5.30pm.

335 km (208 mi.): (pop. 1000; 750 m (2461 ft)). Evidence of the wealth for-   **Greenwood**

Fruit for sale on the Crowsnest Highway

merly enjoyed by this once flourishing mining town is provided by the magnificent buildings in the town centre, such as Greenwood Inn (1899), Sacred Heart Catholic Church (1900), the vicarage (1906), the court buildings (1902) and the post-office built in 1915. In the 1880s ore deposits were discovered in the mountains. In the town's heyday more than 2000 people lived here. Of the smelting works set up in 1901 by the B. C. Copper Co., which once employed 400 men, only the ruins of the 37 m (121 ft) high chimney in the Lotzgar Memorial Park and the slag-heaps still remain. As early as 1918 the fall in copper prices after the end of the First World War led to the closure of this and of the two other plants in the vicinity. Greenwood was on the way to becoming a ghost town when in 1942 some 1200 Japanese living in western Canada were interned here and some remained when the war ended.

In the new Greenwood Museum and Tourist Information Centre at Copper St./Highway 3 the history of mining in this region is illustrated. Open mid-May–mid-Sep. daily 9am–6pm.

In Phoenix 8 km (5 mi.) away, which for twenty years was one of the richest mining towns in Boundary Country, only two graveyards and a memorial remain. In 1919 Granby Consolidated Mining closed down its copper mine and the people left. When mining was resumed in 1955 the remains of the town disappeared under a giant open-cast mine which was itself closed down in 1978.

Grand Forks   378 km (235 mi.): From the top of Phoenix Mountain (1105 m (3627 ft)) there is a fine view to be had of Grand Forks (pop. 3000; 516 m (1693 ft)) situated in the broad and sunny Sunshine Valley at the confluence of Kettle River and Granby River. The first cattle-breeders settled here at the end of the 19th c., and in 1894 the little town of Grand Forks was founded. During the mining boom three smelting plants were built in the town, and dark slag-heaps remain as a reminder. Granby Mine ran one of the largest of such plants in the British Empire here, with a daily capacity of up to 5000 tonnes.

Together with fruit and vegetable growing, the paper factories and slag-processing plants today constitute the main industries, and modern Grand Forks boasts excellent potato crops. A large number of wooden buildings in the Victorian style bear witness to the former wealth of this little town; for example, various buildings at "Golden Heights" can be visited in the course of the Heritage Home Tour. In the charming Grand Forks Boundary Museum & Tourist Information Centre at 7370 5th St./Highway 3 the brief but highly varied history of Boundary Country is documented. Open mid-May–mid-Oct. daily 9am–5pm, to 8pm in summer.

Conspicuous in the townscape and surounding countryside are several sizeable dwelling-houses. They were built early in the 20th c. by the Doukhobors, members of a spiritualist sect formed in Russia in the 18th c. under the influence of the Quakers. After suffering persecution in Russia they came to Canada in 1898 and to Grand Forks in 1909. About one thousand of them lived in large communal dwellings each housing up to 35 or 40 people, built a saw-mill and began to irrigate the land and plant fruit trees.

Mountain View Doukhobor Museum on Hardy Road, 5 km (3 mi.) to the north-west gives an insight into the beliefs and lives of this group of people, whose influence can still be felt in the town's restaurants. On the first week-end in August each year the "Sunshine & Borschtsch Festival" is celebrated. Open Jun.–Sep. daily 9am–7pm.

20 km (13 mi.) further east Highway 3 crosses the US 395; 207 km (129 mi.) down the latter road lies the town of Spokane in the US state of Washington.

Christina Lake   400 km (250 mi.): Christina Lake (pop. 2000; 600 m (1969 ft)) lies by the lake of the same name 20 km (13 mi.) long but at the most 1½ km (1 mi.) wide, which is very popular with water sports enthusiasts because of its clear warm water and sandy banks, and with anglers because of its abundance of fish.

36 km (22 mi.) of the historic Dewdney trail across the mountains have been reconstructed between Christina Lake and Rossland. The present Highway 3, laid down in 1962, deviates from this old road and now climbs up to the 1535 m (5038 ft) high Bonanza Pass. This mountain area

marks the beginning of the Kootenay Region with its chain of mountains running north to south and the deeply-slashed valleys and lakes, earning it its familiar name of the "Switzerland of North America".

473 km (294 mi.): Castlegar (pop. 7000; 610 m (2000 ft)), at the confluence of the Kootenay and Columbia Rivers, was for many years an important traffic junction in the Kootenay region. Today the main employment is in the timber industry and the sawmill, while the CanCel cellulose factory has 750 workers.

Castlegar

North of the town the 51 m (167 ft) high Hugh Keenleyside Dam controls the flow of the Columbia from Arrow Lake, providing electric power and guarding against flooding. There is a lock for small boats. Boats can be chartered or rented, cycles rented and there are sightseeing flights available.

Doukhobor Historic Village near the airport off Highway 3 provides an insight into the way of life of the Russian Doukhobors who emigrated here around the turn of the century and lived here from 1908 until the 1930s (see also Grand Forks p. 173). Typical of the settlements of the "Christian Community of Universal Brotherhood", as they called themselves, were their brick-built communal houses surrounded by working quarters. Open May–Sep. 9am–5pm. The nearby "Doukhobor Restaurant" specialises in Russian food.

★Doukhobor Historic Village

Difficulties with their Canadian neighbours arose mainly with the members of a fanatical Doukhobor sect who settled in Krestova, the "Sons of Freedom" who – like almost all Doukhobors – refused to register births and deaths and rejected the state educational system as being an intrusion into their pacifist and secluded ways. They set fire to schools and protested naked in the streets against government ordinances. Time and again they threw home-made bombs on the grave in Robson Rd/Highway 3 of the founder of the settlement, Pjotr Verigin, who was killed in 1926 during an attack on a train. Today all has quietened down and most of the Doukhobors have become farmers and adjusted to the Canadian way of life. Only a few of the typical Doukhobor villages are still inhabited.

From 7th Ave in the town centre a suspension bridge leads to an island at the mouth of the Kootenay River, on which will be found Zuckerberg Island Heritage Park. In this park lies Chapel House, erected in the style of a Russian church and the house and studio of the Russian emigré mathematics teacher, engineer and sculptor Alexander F. Zuckerberg, who came to Castlegar to teach in 1931 at the request of the then leader of the Doukhobors, Pjotr Verigin II. Zuckerberg died in 1961 and the island started to become overgrown. However, the town council took it over in the early 1980s and the buildings were restored. Today walkways lead through the sparse woods along the river bank. Traces of Indian mud-huts and a small reconstruction serve as a reminder that for at least 3500 years the island served as winter quarters for Salish Indians living in the Kootenay region. It is thought that they built a sort of weir or dyke out of large stones from the river in order to catch salmon as they swam upstream. However, since the first dam was built across the Columbia in 1934 there have been no more salmon in the river.

Zuckerberg Island Heritage Park

A car-ferry runs from Castlegar across the Columbia River, which is not very wide here, to Robson Trail – there are Trail Rides to be had at Dry Creek Ranch – and further to the Syringa Creek Provincial Park 19 km (12 mi.) north of Castlegar on the eastern shores of Arrow Lake. The park offers a beach, windsurfing and fishing, and there are guided natural history tours from mid-June to Labour Day.

43 km (27 mi.): Nelson (pop. 10,000; 543 m (1782 ft)) lies in a beautiful spot on the western arm of the long and charmingly situated Kootenay Lake, surrounded by the snow and ice-covered peaks, some as high as 2000 m (6500 ft), of the Selkirk Mountains. This mining town which grew up at the end of the 19th c. quickly developed into a tourist centre. There are skiing regions in the surrounding area, such as the "Wild Water Ski Area", 20 km (13 mi.) to

★Nelson

the south on Mount Ymir which is 2585 m (8484 ft) high; there are chair-lifts and a ski-tow, and the top of the ski-slope is 400 m (1300 ft) from the bottom.

Its many carefully preserved Victorian buildings give Nelson a charm all of its own, and it proudly calls itself the "Heritage Capital of the Kootenays".

Kokanee Creek Provincial Park

63 km (39 mi.): Kokanee Creek Provincial Park by Kootenay Lake covers 260 ha (642 acres) and lies in the delta of Kokanee Creek at the foot of the Slocan Range which forms part of the Selkirk Mountains. There are sandy beaches, a camp-site, a visitors' centre and an office providing information on tours in Kokanee Glacier Provincial Park and various walks through sparse deciduous forests of alder and cottonwood-poplar and through mixed and coniferous forest higher up. The name Kokanee, which is Indian for "red fish", refers to the Kokanee salmon which spawns in Kokanee Creek and is a species of salmon which lives only in inland waters; during the spawning season in August and September there are guided explanatory tours and informative events.

Archaeologists have found signs of two seasonal Indian storage sites in the park as well as remains of settlements from the pioneering period.

West Kootenay Visitor Centre provides information on the history of the region, mining, the Kootenay (Kutenai) Indians as well as about the paddle-steamer with its paddle-wheel at the stern which used to ply on the lake. Open Jul.–Aug. daily 11am–9pm; other times of the year Sun. only 1–4pm.

Kokanee Glacier Provincial Park

A gravel road some 16 km (10 mi.) long winds alongside the deeply slashed Kokanee Creek to Gibson Lake and provides access to a magnificent area of wild country in the Slocan Range of the Selkirk Mountains. In Kokanee Glacier Provincial Park, covering almost 260 sq. km (100 sq. mi.), are numerous picturesque mountain lakes as well as snow and ice-capped peaks. Most of this unspoilt mountain region lies at a height of more than 2100 m (6900 ft) above sea-level. Kokanee Peak, 2774 m (9100 ft) high, towers majestically above the rest. This is a splendid spot for mountain walks and climbs.

Salmo

512 km (318 mi.): Near Salmo (pop. 1000; 663 m (2176 ft)) Crowsnest Highway 3 crosses Highway No. 6 which runs from Nelson to the US frontier.

15 km (9 mi.) to the south is the beginning of the new "Kootenay Skyway" across the southern part of the Selkirk Mountains, which winds its way up over a distance of 23 km (14 mi.) to Kootenay Pass, 1774 m (5822 ft) above sea-level. All along this stretch of 70 km (43 mi.) in total the traveller will keep coming across tower-like huts from which, when there is a threat of avalanches in winter, action can be taken in good time to avoid them.

Stagleap Provincial Park

550 km (342 mi.): Along the pass lies Stagleap Provincial Park, named after the mountain caribou which pass through here during the short summer. At present there exists only a small herd of less than two dozen animals which, in the course of their annual wanderings, also pass through the north-eastern part of the US state of Washington and north Idaho. At the western end of Bridal Lake – which is often frozen over until June – at the foot of the 2393 m (7854 ft) high Riddle Mountain a small visitors' centre provides information on the flora and fauna, especially about this rare species of caribou now threatened with extinction and which the American and Canadian authorities are co-operating closely to try and save.

Creston

596 km (370 mi.): Creston (pop. 4000; 611 m (2005 ft)) in the broad Kootenay Valley, surrounded by long snow-covered peaks, lies in the midst of fields of corn, strawberries and vegetables as well as fruit plantations. This land, once swamps and damp meadows, was dyked and drained at the end of the last century. Every year prior to this the untamed Kootenay River had flooded wide expanses of the fertile valley floor. By 1930 80 km (50 mi.) of dams had been thrown up and 10,000 ha (250,000 acres) of arable land reclaimed. Today the town proudly calls itself the "Fruit-basket of the Kootenays" and boasts its own corn warehouses in the south of British Columbia just like those of the Canadian prairie regions.

For more than forty years the four-day "Blossom Festival" has been celebrated every May.

The dams are now a favourite spot for walks and strolls.

Creston Valley Museum at 219 Devon Rd./Highway 3 North is built of local stone and contains relics from the pioneering period as well as numerous works of art and everyday utensils of the Kootenay (Kutenai) Indians, including reproduction of a canoe such as was used by that tribe. Life-sized speaking dolls give information about life in the times of the early pioneers. Open in summer daily 9am–5pm at other times by arrangement.

Creston Valley Museum

10 km (6 mi.) north-west of the town, on Highway 3, in a nature reserve covering 6½ sq. km (2½ sq. mi.), which preserves a part of the typically swampy areas of the Kootenay River delta. It has become a refuge for more than 240 species of birds – such as osprey, blue heron and countless migratory birds including "whistling swans" – as well as for elk, beaver, bears, coyotes and deer. An insight into the flora and fauna of the region is given by means of instructive nature walks, guided treks and canoe-tours, an observation tower with telescopes, and an Interpretation Centre. Open May–Oct. 9am–5pm; Mar.–Apr. restricted opening times.

Creston Valley Wildlife Management Area

From Summit Creek Recreation Area there is access to a reconstructed section of the 1865 Dewdney Trail along the south-western shores of Leach Lake.

From Creston Highway 21 leads southwards into "Panhandle", the name given to the northern extremity of the US state of Idaho.

42 km (26 mi.) further east Highway 95 turns off to the state frontier and continues in the USA as US 95.

Crowsnest Highway 3 now winds for the next 60 km (37 mi.) through the sparsely inhabitated Purcell Mountains and, at the 653 km (406 mi.) point on the journey, crosses from the Pacific to the Mountain Time Zone.

703 km (437 mi.): Cranbrook (pop. 16,000; 921 m (3023 ft)), lying in the valley between the Purcell Mountains and the Rockies, is the largest town in the south-east of British Columbia. Sheltered from the rains by the Purcell Mountains Cranbrook enjoys a dry climate with plenty of sunshine and there are some excellent excursions to be made into the charming countryside surrounding it.

Cranbrook

In addition to tourism, the town's economy is nowadays based mainly on the timber industry, mining, cattle-rearing and service industries for the region's 70,000 or so inhabitants.

In the mid-1880s, a time of great tension between the settlers who streamed here across the Rockies when the Canadian Pacific Railway was completed and the native Kootenay Indians who feared for their traditional way of life. Colonel James Baker built a ranch here on Joseph's Prairie and fenced in grazing land. From this modest beginning the township of Cranbrook gradually grew. Later Colonel Baker became a partner in the Crowsnest Coal and Mineral Company, which won the contract to build a railway line for the CPR from Lethbridge in Alberta over Crowsnest Pass to Kootenay Lake, thus running across Baker's land. The line was completed in 1898, Baker's ranch had a link to the main line and he was able to set up a small township here.

Fort Steele 16 km (10 mi.) away, at the time a booming mining town and provision centre for the region, was by-passed by this rail route and gradually surrendered its importance to the new town.

In the old town centre, at 10th–13th Ave. and 1st–4th St. South, a number of stately buildings from the turn of the century have been preserved; these include the City Hall, Fire Hall, Mount Baker Hotel, Tudor House Hotel (1900), the old Freemasons' Lodge and the 1902 Imperial Bank Building. "Baker's House" at 1st. St./Baker Park, the residence of the founder of the town and built in 1889, today houses some offices and also a small museum displaying some historic photographs. Open Mon.–Fri. 9am–5pm.

St Eugene Mission Church – at St Mary's Reserve, between Cranbrook and

Kimberley was built in the 1890s for the Kootenay Indians. It is a good example of a typical Victorian wooden church. Open Mon.–Fri. 9am–4.30pm.

★Cranbrook Railway Museum

Cranbrook Railway Museum at 1 Van Horne St. North has on exhibition some restored carriages dated 1929 of TransCanada Limited, the legendary train belonging to the Canadian Pacific Railway. Sleeping-cars, dining and saloon cars have been refitted with their original furnishings and show the luxurious standards enjoyed by the rail-travellers of the 1930s. Open Jun.–Aug. daily 9am–8pm; at other times of the year Sun.–Thu. noon–5pm.

Since the 1960s, as a reminder of the pioneering days, Cranbrook has been holding "Sam Steele Days", a week-long celebration with numerous events and a procession.

Highway 95A

A few miles beyond Cranbrook Highway 95A turns off to Kimberley; Fort Steele and Highway 3 can be reached by means of a detour of some 70 km (43 mi.).

Kimberley

30 km (19 mi.): Kimberley (pop. 7000; 1113 m (3653 ft)) promotes itself as the "Bavarian City". A start was made in 1972 to change the appearance of this old highland mining town to a tourist resort in the Bavarian style. A "Bavarian Platzl" (square) was built in the town centre, and a pedestrian zone laid out with a small stream, flower-tubs, seats and benches, street-cafés and buskers. It also boasts what is said to be the biggest cuckoo-clock in the world. The houses are decorated with Alpine façades or are half-timbered, and the "Bavarian atmosphere" is further emphasised by the wearing of "lederhosen" and "dirndl" (Alpine dress with bodice and full skirt) by assistants in shops and bars. At the end of the square, in the library building, is the Kimberley Heritage Museum with exhibits from Kimberley's mining past and some minerals. Open Jul.–Aug. Mon.–Sat. 9am–4.30pm, at other times of the year 1–4pm.

Further attractions are the Bavarian City Mining Railway, a narrow-gauge railway at Gerry Sorenson Way (open Jul.–Aug. 11am–7.30pm), a guided tour through Sullivan Mine belonging to Cominco Ltd. (meeting point at Travel Infocentre, "The Hut", 255 Walinger Ave.; Jul.–Aug. Mon.–Fri. 9am), a functioning lead and zinc mine, one of the largest of its kind, as well as the Alpine Slide and Chairlift in the Kimberley Ski and Summer Resort, 3 km (2 mi.) from the town centre.

North Star Mountain

A charming skiing area has developed here on North Star Mountain. The distance from top to bottom is 700 m (2300 ft), and there are 34 descents, a chair-lift and ski-tows. In summer the chair-lift and the 800 m (2625 ft) long summer chute are in use. From the upper station there is a magnificent view over the wide valley to the distant Rocky Mountain chain, a part of the Rocky Mountains Trench, a tectonic rift valley zone almost 1500 km (930 mi.) long and 3 to 16 km (2 to 10 mi.) wide running parallel to the Rockies.

A Winter Festival is held on the second week-end in February, and later in the year there is the "July Festival" when beer is consumed by the gallon! After 55 km (34 mi.) Highway 95 joins Highway 95/93, which leads southwards to Fort Steele, a journey of 33 km (20 mi.).

To the north is a scenically charming route by way of Fairmont Hot Springs (pop. 200; 800 m (2625 ft)). Here there is a bathing centre, opened in 1922, with four thermal pools with temperatures of up 42°C (108°F) (open daily 8am–10pm). More than 750,000 visitors come here every year. There are helicopter flights and flights over the glaciers, trail riding Jun.–Sep. and an 18-hole golf course.

Invermere

The town of Invermere (pop. 2000; 859 m (2820 ft)) lies by Lake Windermere which is drained by the Columbia River; here windsurfing, trail riding and hang-gliding can be enjoyed. Windermere Valley Pioneer Museum at 622 3rd. St. is an historical museum built round the old Canadian Pacific Railway station. Open Jun.–Aug. daily 10am–4.30pm.

In a nearby mountain valley lies Panorama Resort in the middle of a large skiing area where snow is assured. The slopes are 1156 m (3794 ft) from top to bottom, with 33 descents, four chair-lifts and a ski-tow. This was used for skiing races in the World Cup Competition. After Radium Hot Springs the route continues to Kootenay National Park – 74 km (46 mi.) in all – or further on Highway 95 downstream by the Columbia River to Golden (see entry) by the TransCanada Highway 1 (180 km (112 mi.)).

720 km (447 mi.): see Fort Steele Provincial Park **Fort Steele**

812 km (505 mi.): Fernie (pop. 6000; 1009 m (3312 ft)), a small mining **Fernie** township at the foot of Trinity Mountain, lies in the middle of the Rocky Mountains and in recent years has developed into an all-the-year-round holiday centre. In winter Fernie Snow Holiday Resport offers excellent winter sports facilities, especially for families. The slopes are 640 m (2100 ft), with 34 descents, three chair-lifts and three ski-tows.

Fernie and District Museum was opened in 1979 in the old vicarage of the 1905 church at 502–5th Ave. and its exhibits illustrate the lives of the early pioneers in this region as well as coal-mining at the turn of the century. Open Jul.–Aug. daily 1.30–5pm.

In 1908 a catastrophic fire devastated this young mining town. When it was rebuilt many of the typical wooden houses were replaced by sturdier brick and tile buildings, some of which still remain. The Court Building and Leroux Mansion are fine examples of this style of building.

During working hours Weststar Mining Ltd. and Fording Coal Ltd. offer guided tours through their large open-cast coal-mines; information is obtainable from Travel Info Centre, Rotary Park.

From Sparwood Crowsnest Highway 3 turns south-east and after 18km ★Crowsnest Pass (11 mi.) at Crowsnest Pass it crosses the border into Alberta.

To the east of the pass, in Crowsnest Valley, sprawls the parish of **Crowsnest** Crowsnest (pop. 8000), formed from the mining settlements of Blairmore, Coleman, Frank, Bellevue and Hillcrest Mines.

When the Canadian Pacific Railway line was laid across the pass in 1897–98 conditions improved for mining the rich coal deposits in the region, and settlers and miners flocked here from all over the world.

Some 50 km (31 mi.) east of the border the Crowsnest River plunges **Lundbreck Falls** down 12 m (40 ft) into a gorge.

923 km (⅚ mi.): Highway 6 turn-off to the south leads to the Waterton **Pincher Creek** Glacier International Peace Park (see entry) and to the US frontier. The township of Pincher Creek (pop. 4000) lies a few miles to the south in the midst of the gently undulating foothills. It is the gateway to the Rocky Mountains and the already mentioned National Park 48 km (30 mi.) further south. Summer activities here include trail riding, walking in the charming countryside, water-sports and fishing. In winter Westcastle Park, 47 km (29 mi.) south-west on Highway 507/744, is a popular ski resort, with slopes measuring 520 m (1700 ft) and three ski-tows.

In 1875 the North West Mounted Police built a stud-farm here in the wide grasslands on the eastern edge of the Rockies for the troops stationed in Fort MacLeod. At the end of the 18th c. the first cattle-breeders and settlers followed their example. In the Pincher Creek Museum and Kootenay (kutenai) Brown Historical Park at James Ave./Grove St. the history of the region is depicted. Several buildings and log cabins built true to the originals, including that of Kootenay (kutenai) Brown, an Irishman who was the first man to settle here in 1889, are open to visitors. Open daily in summer 10am–8pm, 1–4pm at other times of the year.

★★Cypress Hills Provincial Park H 8

Provinces: Alberta, Saskatchewan
Area: 200 sq. km (77 sq. mi.)

Cypress Hills Provincial Park

Information

Travel Alberta, PO Box 2500, Edmonton, AB T5J 2Z4; tel. (403) 4274321, fax. (403) 4270867.
Tourism Saskatchewan, 500–1900 Albert Street, Regina, SK S4P 4L9; tel. (306) 7872300, fax. (306) 7875744

Topography

Cypress Hills Provincial Park – access to which is by way of the Buffalo Trail (Highway 40) – lies about 60 km (37 mi.) south-east of Medicine Hat by the TransCanada Highway. This impressive piece of countryside extends into the neighbouring province of Saskatchewan. The plateaux are covered with rich forests in the midst of a flat, dry prairie. Scientists assume that about 30 million years ago a river running westwards deposited both coarse and fine sediment over an area which thus gradually became higher and was then shaped by the forces of erosion.

In the middle of the prairie wooded mountainous country rises to as high as 1462 m (4800 ft) above sea-level. During the last Ice Age this region was not covered by glaciers. When John Palliser arrived here in 1859 when on an expedition he described it as a green oasis in the middle of the dry prairies he had spent weeks in crossing. The hills rising 500 m (1640 ft) above the flat surrounding countryside represent an eco-system which is unusual for this part of Canada, and the vegetation is somewhat reminiscent of Alpine regions. Until the early 20th c. these hills provided a refuge for many species of animals threatened by the increasing numbers of settlers on the plains; the last bison was shot here in 1882, the last puma in 1912 and the last wolf in 1925. Today only a few wild turkeys still live here.

For more than 7000 years the Indians came to Cypress Hills and its sheltered valleys abounding in water. In the 1870s the hills provided hide-outs for American traders selling illegal whisky to the Indians.

Being 1392 m (4568 high), the Cypress Hills are the highest in Saskatchewan. The region has pine forests and rare wild flowers and animals such as the wapiti and the endangered trumpet-swan. In many areas prairie falcons, some rare species of song-birds and elk can be seen. The park has some very instructive walks – that to Bald Butte being particularly picturesque – and also contains an artificial lake. Its main attractions include the Conglomerate Cliffs as well as a swimming-pool, beach, golf-course, riding stables, camp sites and tennis courts. In winter cross-country skiing and rides on snowmobiles are possible.

★★Fort Walsh
National Historic
Park

Fort Walsh was one of the most important posts set up by the North West Mounted Police in western Canada in the 19th c. It was built in 1875 under the leadership of James Walsh in order to put an end to the illegal whisky trade, and was in use for eight years. During that time the troops fought for law and order and negotiated with the whisky traders, the native Indians and the thousands of Sioux warriors who sought refuge in Canada after clashes with the US cavalry. Following the building of the railway and the return of the Sioux people to the USA the fort was dismantled and left. For many years after that the area was used privately for cattle-rearing. In 1942 the Royal Canadian Mounted Police acquired the land and built a ranch on which to breed horses for the army. When the RCMP were transferred to Ontario the estate became a National Park. Since then extensive historical and archaeological research has been carried out, being the first stage in a comprehensive reconstruction programme for the fort. This reconstruction, which will include the still existing ranch buildings, will give an idea of what Fort Walsh looked like during its heyday in 1880.

The first thing to do on arriving in the park is to call at the Visitor Reception Centre. Here in the large gallery an exhibition illustrates the highlights of the region's rich history, such as the Mounted Police, the people of the plains, the fur and whisky traders, government expeditions and the town of Fort Walsh.

The fort buildings are made of whitewashed tree-trunks, one with a roof of turfs, the others with pointed roofs to keep out the damp. Open May–Sep. 9am–6pm.

The Royal Canadian Mounted Police in action

In 1877 an important meeting was held in the officers' mess, attended by Chief Sitting Bull and other Sioux chiefs as well as representatives of an American commission. The aim was to persuade the Sioux to return to the USA.

Sitting Bull

Other buildings of interest are the police commissioner's house, the smithy, a carpenter's shop, stables, the guard-room as well as arms and goods stores.

Other buildings

Near the fort lies the North West Mounted Police and civilian cemetery.

Cemetery

Some 3 km (2 mi.) further south will be found Salomon's Post (not open to visitors) and Farewell's Trading Post (open daily 9am–5.30pm) furnished with items used by the American traders who crossed the border and sold whisky illegally to the Indians. In the 1870s rifles and furs were the most important commodity. The present-day posts are reconstructions built on the site of the original buildings which were burnt down in 1873.

Trading Posts

Farewell's Trading Post consists of four buildings, namely, the shop containing brightly-coloured clothing, pearls, furs, blankets and canned goods, the barrack dormitories, Farewell's house and that of his assistant.

Near Fort Walsh a flourishing town grew up, which in its heyday had several hundred inhabitants. Embankments and cellars are all that remain.

★Dawson City

E 3

Administrative unit: Yukon Territory
Population: 1300

Visitor Reception Centre, Front & King Streets, Dawson City, YT; tel. (867) 9935566

Information

Dawson City

Dawson City lies in the west of the Yukon Territory (see entry), roughly 100 km (60 mi.) from the Canadian frontier at the confluence of the Klondike and Yukon Rivers.

Dawson City was founded and flourished during the time of the gold-rush along the Klondike (see entry) and Yukon Rivers (see Yukon Territory). A few months after George Washington Carmack found gold-nuggets the size of his fist in Bonanza Creek in 1896 thousands of gold-seekers streamed into the Yukon and Klondike region hoping to stumble on equally rich veins. Dawson City grew up in the middle of it all.

Most of the early gold-seekers came ill-equipped with provisions. Later Canada did pass a law making it a rule that every person had to bring with him clothing and food for at least one year, but at the end of 1897 Dawson City already had 3500 inhabitants who were not adequately provided for. When ships were unable to get through with stocks of provisions before the onset of winter a large proportion of the towns-people were evacuated to an outpost 350 miles away, but in spite of these measures many did not live to see the spring, when the longed-for wagons finally got through with supplies. A number of traders were then able to make their fortune selling food on Dawson City market.

Gold-seekers arriving in the summer of 1898 soon realised that all the profitable claims had been staked long before. The uncrowned "Kings of the Klondike" subsequently turned the town into the "San Francisco of the North" and used their gold to finance the building of luxurious albeit dubious hotels, saloons, dance-halls and casinos and acquired a number of shipping companies. The ships brought in the finest Paris fashions, Persian carpets, expensive furniture and delicacies to Dawson City; and the French can-can took the saloons and dance-halls by storm the theatre built by Arizona Charlie Meadows, saw the appearance of the legendary Kitty Rockwell alias Klondike Kate. One of the Klondike's best-known adventurers was "Big Alex" McDonald, owner of numerous claims to gold and who at one time made 5500 dollars a day and amassed a fortune of seven million dollars. "Big Alex" became so famous that he even earned a private audience with the Pope in Rome. For most of the gold-seekers however Dawson City meant a daily struggle for survival with only very faint hopes of stumbling on a rich find, and many ended up working in the large mines for men like Big Alex. No sooner were gold nuggets found or wages earned than they were spent in the saloons, and it was not uncommon for hundreds of thousands of dollars to change hands in one night at the gaming tables. After an initial "Wild West" era posts of the North West Mounted Police were set up to guarantee law and order and to control the border with Alaska. When new gold finds were reported near Nome in Alaska in August 1899 the first 8000 gold-seekers returned west, soon to be followed by further people from Dawson City, so that by the 1930s the town had a population of only about 4000. Dawson City retained its position as capital of the Yukon Territory until 1953, when it had to cede it to the up-and-coming Whitehorse (see entry).

Today Dawson City has the appearance of a Wild West scene from a Hollywood film, the only difference being that here everything is genuine. Since the 1960s over thirty buildings have been restored by the Canadian Office for the Preservation of Historical Monuments and more wooden houses have been built in the style of the turn of the century. In the early 1980s the whole town was declared an historical area and is now visited every summer by more than 17,000 tourists wishing to see can-can shows, visit the old goldfields and savour the atmosphere of days gone by, when the glamour and the misery of the gold-rush left their stamp on the town.

One of the most impressive reminders of the past is Palace Grand Theatre in King Street, built in 1899 by the American Arizona Charlie Meadows and restored in 1962 by order of the Canadian Government. During the day visitors can inspect the theatre, and in the evening

Winter 1899 in Dawson City

Can-can girls, as in the time of the Gold Rush

Dawson City

(except Tuesdays) "Gaslight Follies" present an authentic 1898 vaudeville show with songs, can-can dancers and cabaret.

★ Diamond Tooth Gertie's Gambling Hall

Canada's only legalised casino is Diamond Tooth Gertie's Gambling Hall on Fourth Avenue at the corner of Queen Street, which has been faithfully restored. It owes its name to one of the "Queens of the Dance Halls" of 1898. As well as blackjack, roulette and poker there are also can-can shows.

Municipal museum

Dawson City Museum on 5th Avenue gives an insight into the town's history as well as that of the Klondike (see entry) from the start of the gold-rush to the present day. A slide show about Dempster Highway (see entry) gives a good impression of the only highway in Canada to cross the polar circle.

Jack London's Cabin

In the wooden cabin where the American writer Jack London (actually John Griffith London, 1876–1916) lived in 1897 readings are given daily from his novels, such as "Call of the Wild" (1903), "The Sea Wolf" (1904) and "The Lure of Gold" (1910).

Robert Service's Cabin

In 8th Avenue stands the log-cabin built in 1898 by Robert Service, known as the "Bard of the Yukon" and who around the turn of the century composed numerous poems and ballads, including "The Funeral of Sam McGee" and "The Shooting of Dan McGrew".

Front Street

Along Front Street several buildings dating from the time of the gold-rush are still standing. The most notable are the Federal Building, once the seat of government before it was moved to Whitehorse (see entry), the Old Post Office of 1901, Madame Tremblay's shop complete with articles of clothing like those worn by the gold-seekers, the Canadian Bank of Commerce, where gold was once melted down, and the 1922 paddle-steamer S.S. "Keno" – now a museum – the last of over 200 "sternwheelers" which plied on the Yukon between Dawson City and Whitehorse (see entry) until the end of the 1850s.

★ Midnight Dome

A favourite outing, usually combined with a visit to the theatre, is the trip to the hill known as Midnight Dome, about 7 km (5 mi.) south-east of the town, from where a fantastic panoramic view of Dawson City and the Yukon River, the Klondike Valley and the surrounding Ogilvie Mountains can be enjoyed. Many of the gold-seekers found their last resting-place in the cemetery on the side of the hill.

Trips on the Yukon

A trip along the Yukon River on the "Yukon Lou" miniature steamer or the luxury catamaran, the M.V. "Klondike", will be found most rewarding. These trips take in the "cemetery" of the old paddle-steamers.

Search for gold

All around the town are many sites where prospectors used to sift and pan for gold. Anyone wishing to follow in the footsteps of George Carmack can visit the spot by Bonanza Creek where he made his discovery claim. The Visitor Reception Centre in Dawson City will provide information about tours to the gold-fields and mines in Bonanza Creek and Guggieville as well as in Bear Creek Complex 13 km (8 mi.) to the south, the massive machines of which were still being used to quarry gold deposits until 1966.

★ Top of the World Highway

The Top of the World Highway owes its name to the many plateaux and ranges of hills – mainly above the tree-line – over which it runs on its route between Dawson and then westwards to Alaska. The border is passed after covering a 107 km (66 mi.) stretch of road with some of the most impressive panoramic views imaginable. From the border it is a further 181 km (112 mi.) to Tetlin Junction, where the Alaska Highway is reached.

★ Klondike Highway

Southwards from Dawson the Klondike Highway (see Klondike) provides the link with Whitehorse (see entry).

Dempster Highway

Administrative Units: Yukon Territory/Northwest Territories

See Yukon, Northwest Territories · Information

The only public road in North America which actually extends beyond the Arctic Circle starts 40 km (25 mi.) south of Dawson City in the Yukon Territory and ends some 740 km (460 mi.) further north in Inuvik in the Mackenzie Delta (Northwest Territories) on the Arctic coast.

This largely untarred road threads its way through a mainly untamed wilderness with areas of varying vegetation and marked variations in climate, temperatures ranging from 35°C (95°F) in summer to −45°C (−49°F) in winter.

As early as the beginning of this century a trail, following an old Indian trade route, led from Dawson to Fort McPherson and was patrolled by the Northwest Mounted Police. This path received sad notoriety in the winter of 1911 when a police patrol strayed from the route and were later found dead. The present highway is named after the leader of search party which found them, Corporal W.D. Dempster. When, in the 1950s, a start was made on searching for raw materials in this largely unexplored region the first few miles of the rough road were made up. Oil and gas exploration in the Beaufort Sea speeded up work on the road – necessary to provide a link and transport provisions to the sites – as far as the mouth of Mackenzie River (see entry) and this was completed in 1979.

A thorough servicing of the car is strongly recommended before setting off along this highway. Petrol stations with repair facilities will be found only in Eagle Plains, Fort McPherson and Inuvik. · Note

Suggested route

The highway begins on the southern slopes of the Ogilvie Mountains some 40 km (25 mi.) south of Dawson (see entry). After about 70 km (44 mi.), just before North Fork Pass (1290 m (4234 ft)) it reaches the timber line. From the pass can be seen the wedge-shaped Tombstone Mountain standing out against the background of hills. · **Ogilvie Mountains**

The Blackstone Highlands on the far side of the pass are home to several species of birds and dall sheep. · **Blackstone Highlands**

Eagle Plains Hotel, one of the few places on the edge of the Highlands which offer accommodation, lies about halfway between Dawson and Inuvik and offers the only opportunity of enjoying a restaurant meal and sleeping in a hotel bed instead of a tent.

After travelling a further 403 km (250 mi.) the Arctic Circle is reached. The highway climbs up the slopes of the Richardson Mountains, almost bare of trees and covered in detritus and boulders. After crossing the high land of the Peel Plateau the road descends gradually to the plains of the Mackenzie Delta. · Arctic Circle

Peel River, crossed by a ferry, is one of the longest tributaries of the Mackenzie River (see entry). · **Peel River**

On the east bank of the Peel River lies Fort McPherson an old fur-trading station, like most of the settlements near the Mackenzie River. Today it is home to about 820 Dene Indians. The highway then threads its way through a forest region rich in lakes to the Arctic Red River (see Mackenzie River, Arctic Red River), where the ferry crosses the Mackenzie. · **Fort McPherson**

See entry. · Inuvik

★★Edmonton   G 8

Province: Alberta. Altitude: 668 m (2192 ft)
Population: 620,000 (Metropolitan Area: 870,000)

Information
Edmonton Tourism, Shaw Conference Centre, 9797 Jasper Avenue NW, Edmonton, AB T5J 1N9; tel; (403) 4968400 and (800) 4634667
Edmonton Tourism Visitor Centre, Spruce Grove, Yellowhead Highway 16; tel. (403) 4968400
Travel Alberta; tel. (403) 4274321 and (800) 6618888

Access
By air:
Edmonton International Airport, 29 km (18 mi.) south; fully integrated into the North American airline network. Most European arrivals are via Toronto. Edmonton Municipal Airport, north-west of the town centre; regional flights.
Coach shuttle-services between the town centre and the two airports.

By rail:
VIA Rail (10004–104 Ave.). Routes: Edmonton–Jasper–Vancouver; Edmonton–Prince George/Prince Rupert; Edmonton–Saskatoon–Winnipeg.

By coach;
Greyhound Bus Lines (Depot 10324 103 ST.); Red Arrow Express between Edmonton–Calgary, Edmonton–Fort McMurray.

City buses
Edmonton Transit; bus routes to all parts of the city and its suburbs.

LRT
Light Rail Transit (LRT); underground and suburban lines between Corona Station (city centre, Jasper Ave./108 St.) and the north-eastern suburb of Clareview.

Edmonton, the capital of Alberta, stretches along both banks of North Saskatchewan River in roughly the centre of the province. This dynamic and rapidly growing metropolis is the fifth largest and most northerly city in Canada. Edmonton lies in the northern extremities of the great Canadian prairies and is the centre of the wheat-growing region which extends to the north and to the east but soon changes to vast expanses of forest and lakes. Since its very beginnings the city has been the gateway to the north and an important communications centre.

Economy
Edmonton competes with Calgary – only 300 km (190 mi.) to the south – for the title of "oil capital of Canada". More than ten per cent of Canada's total crude oil is produced from fewer than 2300 boreholes within a radius of 40 km (25 mi.). Giant refineries and petro-chemical works have sprung up in the south-eastern part of the city.
During the last twenty years whole streets in the inner city have had to be sacrificed to make way for hyper-modern high-rise buildings, side by side with congress halls, leisure facilities and large shopping centres. The West Edmonton Mall is the largest leisure and shopping centre in the world, where even during the long cold winters, when temperatures average −15°C (5°F), shoppers are still enticed to linger.
In the mainly dry and warm summers many people are attracted by the various charmingly laid-out squares, the parks along both sides of the North Saskatchewan River and the numerous lakes around the city.
The city has also invested in art and culture and built theatres and museums. A start has also been made on cleaning and restoring the older parts and buildings. In spite of the oil and construction boom of the 1970s and 1980s something of the typical West Canadian atmosphere can still be detected in Edmonton.

The skyline of Edmonton

The greatest event in Edmonton's calendar is the ten-day festival known   ★★Klondike Days
as the "Klondike Days", held every year at the end of July. The wild days
of the Klondike Gold-rush of 1890 come to life once more. The citizens
act out the pioneer period and don the clothes of the late 1890s. Street-
parties, dancing, parades, gold-panning competitions liven up the whole
city. The highlight, however, is the "World Championship Sourdough
Raft Race" on the North Saskatchewan River.

Edmonton was founded on the fur trade. Back in the 17th c. hunters from   History
the two rival fur companies made their way through the fur-rich region of
Northern Alberta. In 1795 both the North West Company (Fort Augustus)
and the Hudson's Bay Company (Edmonton House) set up trading posts
along the North Saskatchewan River for the Cree and Blackfoot Indians
living there. The two posts were protected by a common wooden palisade
almost 5 m (16 ft) high, and soon developed into the chief administrative
and supply centres for the whole of the Saskatchewan Basin. Almost
everyone travelling north or to the Pacific stopped off in Edmonton.
In the 1870s the first settlers came to the region and in 1874 a base for
the Royal Canadian Mounted Police was set up. The timber industry gradually began to oust the fur-trade and river traffic on the North Saskatchewan
became more and more important. Initially the town's development was
hampered by the decision of the Canadian Pacific Railway to build the
transcontinental line through the more southerly town of Calgary, and it
was not until 1891 that the railway age started in earnest for Edmonton.
When in 1897/1898 the rush for gold in the Klondike (Yukon) began the
town became the chief maintenance centre. Within a short time its population sextupled, and so there was no question that Edmonton would be
chosen as the capital when the province of Alberta was founded in 1905.
Two new railway lines were built, and from 1915 onwards Edmonton
quickly developed into the main western rail junction. More and more

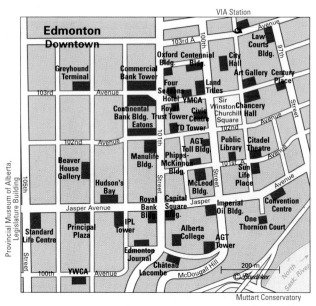

VIA Station

Edmonton Downtown

Muttart Conservatory

European immigrants settled here and in the area around. In the 1930s bush-pilots began to take provisions to the remote settlements in the north. The building of the Alaska Highway in 1941 brought a new upturn in economic fortunes and the discovery of rich oil deposits in 1947 in Leduc 40 km (25 mi.) to the south-west was the start of the transformation of the western provincial town into a modern industrial city.

★Edmonton Convention Centre

It is suggested that a tour of the relatively small city centre should begin with a visit to the modern Congress Centre, built in 1983 at 9797 Jasper Ave., which is constructed in the form of terraces on the steep northern bank of the North Saskatchewan River.

Canada Place

Opposite stands "Canada Place", an impressive post-modern skyscraper accommodating shops, business premises and some Alberta government offices.

Sir Winston Churchill Square

A few blocks to the north the new Civic Centre has gone up in the last few years on 100th Street and around Sir Winston Churchill Square which itself takes up a whole block. The City Hall, the Court Buildings, the impressive Citadel Theatre of glass, comprising several theatres and a charming Winter Garden, the 1924 Art Gallery (open Mon.–Wed. 10.30am–5pm, Thu., Fri. 10.30am–8pm, Sat., Sun. 11am–5pm) and the Centennial Library all form one urban development unit. To the north it adjoins the railway station built in 1966 and the CN Tower.

Manulife Place

To the west of the square towers Manulife Place, a new glass-built landmark. Like the neighbouring 40-storied Eaton Centre it houses shopping arcades and large businesses on several levels.

Alberta Government Telephone Tower

A fine panoramic view of the city can be enjoyed from the 33rd floor (118 m (387 ft) high) of the Alberta Government Telephone Tower, 10020 100 St. which was built in 1971 and houses the administrative offices of AGT. Open daily in summer 10am–8pm.

Athabasca

Kingsway
Garden
Mall

SPRUCE

AVENUE

Edmonton

500 m

106th Street
101st

Kingsway

Avenue

Commonwealth
Stadium

St. Albert

Edmonton Space & Science Centre

111th

109th

105th

Avenue

CHURCHILL

Clarke
Stadium

111th

97th Street

Stadium Road

MC CAULEY

Avenue

107th A

107th

Avenue

Avenue

Street

101st Street

96th Street

Avenue

Rowland Road

Street

Avenue

Street

104th

Avenue

109th

Street

104th Avenue

VIA Station

103rd A

Greyhound
Terminal

CITY CENTRE

City
Hall

Court
House

YMCA

Art Gallery

Chancery Hall

Jasper

RIVERDALE

Beaver
House
Gallery

Civic
Centre

Citadel
Theatre

Provincial Museum of Alberta,
West Edmonton Mall

Jasper

Avenue

Alberta
College

Convention
Centre

River

Strathcona
Science Park

YWCA

103rd

AGT
Tower

Chateau
Lacombe

Low Level
Bridge

98th Avenue

Street

James
McDonald
Bridge

Muttart
Conservatory

97th Avenue

Street

Legislature
Building

Conners Road

High Level
Bridge

Renfrew
Stadium

North

105th
Street
Bridge

City Power
Plant

BONNIE

DOON

Saskatchewan

Dr. Scona Road

Mill Creek

Mill Creek Ravine

© Baedeker

University

Walterdale Hill

Queen Elizabeth
Park

Saskatchewan Road

Fort Edmonton Park

Old Strathcona,
Airport

Dr. Scona Road

Provincial Museum of Alberta
Edmonton

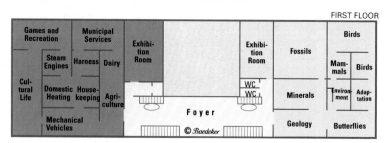

FIRST FLOOR

Games and Recreation	Municipal Services	Exhibition Room		Exhibition Room	Fossils		Birds
Steam Engines	Harness	Dairy				Mammals	Birds
Cultural Life	Domestic Heating	House-keeping	Agriculture		Minerals	Environment	Adaptation
	Mechanical Vehicles			Foyer	Geology	Butterflies	

WC
WC
© Baedeker

GROUND FLOOR

Transport
Religion | Provision for Life | Exhibition Room | Museum Courtyard | Prairie | Park-land | Wood-land | Moun-tains
Fur Trade
Games and Sport | Pre-and Early History

WC
Lecture Room | Dining Room | Cafeteria | Museum Shop | WC | WC | Cloaks | Lecture Hall
© Baedeker

Library

■ Cultural History   ▨ Indians, Fur trade

□ Natural History   ▨ Bio-spheres

The small exhibition entitled "Man and Communications" provides information about historical and modern news techniques.

Legislature Building

In the midst of a park-like garden high above the North Saskatchewan River where the last Fort Edmonton once stood, is today the site of the Government Centre together with the Legislature Building constructed in 1911/1912 (109 St./97 Ave. From the terrace there is a beautiful view across the river. In the basement is the Exhibition Hall with exhibits illustrating the history, art and culture of Alberta Province.

The Centennial Carillon can often be heard in the 13 ha (32 acre) park with its music pavilion and hothouses. Open Mon.–Fri. 9am–8.30pm and Sat., Sun. 9am–4.30pm.

★Provincial Museum of Alberta

The Provincial Museum of Alberta is to be found at 12845–102 Ave. and is open daily 10am–8pm. Its four main departments provide information about the varying topography and the fauna, geology and paleontology of

Downtown Edmonton   Aviation Hall of Fame, Wetaskiwin

the province. Particularly impressive are the life-size models of dinosaurs found in Alberta. In the cultural history departments the culture and lives of the Indians, fur-traders, trappers and early settlers are all vividly displayed. There are also touring exhibitions and special events and programmes.

All kinds of handicraft techniques are demonstrated on Sundays.

Linked to the museum are the Alberta Archives with an exceptional collection of historical photographs.

Alberta Archives

High above the river near the museum stands Government House, built in 1912. Until 1938 it was the seat of the Lieutenant Governor of Alberta. Today it is used for official receptions and conferences; there are guided tours on Sundays.

Government House

Nearby stands the charming Carriage House, where the Lieutenant Governor's staff once lived and the state coach was housed.

In the surrounding parkland will be found some excellent sculptures by Canadian artists. Also worthy of note are the totem-pole erected here in 1983 and a massive fossilised tree-trunk.

Other historical buildings have been preserved to the east of the Provincial Museum.

Carriage House

A few street blocks further north at Coronation Park, 142 St./111 Ave. stands the impressive modern white building of the Edmonton Space Science Museum. In the IMAX Theatre fascinating films from all over the world are shown. Adjoining is an excellent planetarium. Laser shows and sundry exhibitions are given. Open daily 10am–10pm. Sat., Sun to 10.30pm.

Edmonton Space Science Centre

West Edmonton Mall at 8770–170 St. on the western edge of the city is the third largest covered shopping and leisure centre in the world, and

★★West Edmonton Mall

193

West Edmonton Mall: World Water Park

was completed in1986. The Perso-Armenian family clan of Germesian amassed 1·1 billion Canadian dollars to pay for the project and also intends to build similar centres elsewhere in the world.

Within a year from opening West Edmonton Mall became a top tourist attraction, and now has some six million visitors every year! Open Mon.–Sat. 10am–10pm, Sun. 10am–8pm.

Mall

West Edmonton Mall with its many and varied attractions has already appeared three times in the Guiness Book of Records. Over an area the size of more than 100 football pitches there are more than 830 shops and branches of large departmental stores, over 110 restaurants, about twenty cinemas and the twelve-storied "Fantasyland Hotel". In Europa Boulevard many of the shops have European-style fronts and carry the names of international fashion designers, and in Bourbon Street, a copy of the famous street in New York, the tourist will find restaurants serving Creole food and bars serving up jazz. Among other major attractions are the very popular "Ice Palace" which hosts top quality ice-hockey matches, and the highly impressive "World Water Park" boasting an exciting range of water chutes as well as several temperate aquaria with sharks, tropical fish and penguins. There are also animal enclosures.

Canada Fantasyland

Canada Fantasyland, a large covered amusement park, offers 25 different sorts of rides. The main attraction is a roller coaster with three "loop the loops", the "Deep Sea Adventure", a real lake with four submarines, a full-scale replica of Christopher Columbus' ship, the "Santa Maria" (marriage services are conducted in the captain's cabin), and a dolphinarium.

World Water Park

The World Water Park covers 2 ha (5 acres) and is the world's largest indoor swimming-pool. Covered by a glass dome this giant leisure pool with artificially-induced waves has no less than 22 water-chutes!

Valley Zoo

Opened in 1959, Edmonton's Valley Zoo is at 134 St./Buena Vista Road.

Its main object is research into threatened animal species and keeping them for breeding. Open May–Sep. 10am–6pm.

In the valley pastures of the North Saskatchewan River extends a 16 km (10 mi.) long leisure area consisting of several parks linked one with the other; here there are excellent opportunities for long walks and cycle tours. Cycles can be rented Apr.–Sep. from River Valley Cycle Tours, 9701 100 A St.

River Valley

A little way outside the city, on the south bank of the river on Whitemud Drive/Fox Drive, lies Fort Edmonton Park. In this open-air museum, with old buildings faithfully reconstructed and staff dressed in contemporary costume, a successful attempt has been made to reflect Edmonton's historical development. The buildings include a typical 1846 fort belonging to the Hudson's Bay Company, a street from a pioneer town of 1885 and the up-and-coming provincial capital in 1905, as well as buildings from the 1920s. Among the different forms of old transport displayed in the extensive grounds are an historic mail coach and horse-drawn wagon as well as an old tram and a steam train. Open mid-May–early Sep. daily 10am–6pm, Sep.–Oct. Sat., Sun. only 1–5pm.

★**Fort Edmonton Park**

Near Fort Edmonton Park will be found an interesting Nature Centre covering various aspects of the geology and ecology of Alberta. The rich and varied programme of events includes nature walks. Open Victoria Day–Labour Day daily 10am–6pm, otherwise Mon.–Fri. 9am–4pm, Sat., Sun. 1–4pm.

John Jantzen Nature Centre

Strathcona, also on the south bank of the North Saskatchewan River, was a separate town until 1912. It grew up in 1899 by the railway line to Calgary. In the former town centre, about ten blocks between Saskatchewan Drive and Whyte Avenue, some of the original buildings still remain, and restoration work has been going on since the 1970s.

Old Strathcona

In recent years traders have been moving back into Main Street (104 St.) and those running parallel to it. Here the visitor can stroll and shop among souvenir and speciality goods shops, booksellers, boutiques and art galleries, natural food shops, European-style bistros and restaurants. Special events are held throughout the year, such as theatre festivals, jazz concerts, street parties, markets and art exhibitions.

A short walk through the historic quarter, armed with a brochure obtainable from the Old Strathcona Foundation at 8331–104 St., 2nd floor, or from the Information Centre, will enable the visitor to enjoy a number of renovated old buildings.

Main Street

Further west sprawls the campus of the University of Alberta. This educational site is the second largest and the oldest of the four such colleges in the province of Alberta.

★University of Alberta

At 11153 Saskatchewan Drive stands historical Rutherford House, open Victoria Day–Labour Day daily 10am–6pm, at other times of the year Sat., Sun. noon–5pm. Built in 1911, it was for a long time the residence of A.C. Rutherford, Alberta's first prime minister. The building has now been refurnished in the 1915 style and gives a good idea of the urban lifestyle enjoyed in Alberta at that time.

Staff in contemporary dress busy themselves in the house, and the programme of events is extremely varied.

Rutherford House

On the south bank, at 98 Ave./96A St. will be found four hothouses built in a most unusual pyramidal shape. They are open daily 11am–9pm during the summer months, with restricted opening times during the rest of the year. In the Tropical Pavilion a study can be made of plants native to Burma and the Fiji Islands. In the Temperate Pavilion the visitor can see American Redwood, Australian eucalyptus and magnificent magno-

★Muttart Conservatory

Muttart Conservatory

lias, while in the Arid Pavilion plants from various desert regions of the world are displayed. There is a Show Pavilion for special exhibitions.

From the high ground above the river there is a beautiful view of the gleaming pyramids against the skyline of Edmonton city centre.

Strathcona Science Park

In the east of the city, also on the south bank of the river and on the edge of the industrial zone, Strathcona Science Park has been constructed on the site of an abandoned coal-mine. Adjoining it is the Alberta Natural Resources Science Centre, at 17th St., between Highway 16 and 16A East (open Victoria Day–Labour Day daily 10am–6pm; other times of the year Sun. only 11am–5pm). These centres are concerned with mineral and raw material deposits in Alberta, and displays and sundry exhibits seek to explain how minerals are discovered and mined. The Energy Department, providing information about the way oil is obtained from Edmonton's sub-soil, is particulary interesting.

Strathcona Archaeological Centre

Nearby, at 17th St. in Strathconal Science Park West, lies Strathcona Archaeological Centre. This park was constructed on the excavated site of a 5000 year-old Indian settlement. In the course of a walk through the 1.6 ha (4 acre) site and the archaeological laboratory scientists can be observed as they work. Open Victoria Day–Labour Day daily 10am–6pm; closed in winter.

Archaeological Pavilion

Ample informative material about the history of Indian settlements can be obtained from the Archaeological Pavilion.

★Ukrainian Canadian Archives & Museum of Alberta

North of the city centre, at 9543–110 Ave., will be found the institute known as the Ukrainian Canadian Archives & Museum of Alberta. This building houses a collection of documents relating to numerous Ukrainian pioneers who laboured under the harshest of conditions to contribute in no small degree to the opening up of the prairies of

Alberta. Typical dress and traditional musical instruments are on display in the adjoining museum. Further exhibits bear witness to the rich religious and cultural customs of this ethnic group. Open Mon.–Sat. 1–5pm, Sun. 2–5pm.

Surroundings

The town of St Albert is a drive of only minutes north-west from Downtown Edmonton. Situated on the Sturgeon River, it is today all but continuous with the Albertan capital. The original settlement of St Albert evolved from a mission station founded in 1861 by Father Albert Lacombe, around which swiftly grew up the largest Métis community in the Canadian west. It acquired civic status in 1904, and until 1912 was the seat of a Catholic bishop. The best views of the town are from the simple whitewashed wooden chapel built by Father Lacombe (open Victoria Day–Labour Day daily l0am–6pm). The former cathedral stands next to it, and the history of the town is documented in the St Albert Heritage Museum, a few paces downhill.

St Albert

About 45 km (28 mi.) north, Highway 28 reaches Biggson, a rapidly expanding settlement on the Sturgeon River. This was the starting point of the Athabasca Landing Trail, an overland route linking the Sturgeon to the North Saskatchewan River. Up until the early 20th c. the trail was the principal communications route for opening up the Canadian north.

Biggson

About half an hour's drive east of Edmonton, the Yellowhead Highway 16 traverses the park-like landscape of the Beaver Hills, an area once teeming with game. Today this oasis of unspoilt countryside with its sparsely wooded hills, hidden lakes, beaver dams, grassland and moose has become Elk Island National Park.
    The Beaver Hills area was originally the tribal home of the Scarcee Indians. They were driven out by the Crees who came hunting beaver and buffalo pelts for sale to the large fur-trading companies. By the close of the 19th c. these animals had been hunted virtually to extinction in the region. The Cree Indians were followed by white settlers who had to toil hard to survive here. In 1913 Elk Island was declared a Dominion Park, and later – after being extended several times – acquired National Park status.

★Elk Island National Park

The main attraction of the park is the large herd of buffalo (bison) which graze over a special enclosure. Anyone driving slowly along the road through the Park cannot fail to catch sight of one of these massive shaggy beasts. A second herd of the somewhat smaller wood buffalo is kept in another enclosure south of the Yellowhead Highway. Many of the wood buffalo seen in zoos throughout the world have been bred from this herd.
    Although almost wiped out by the start of the 20th c., some Beaver Hills buffalo, having escaped the hunters, are thought to have been captured in 1909 and placed in a reserve of their own. These are the forebears of the animals now living in Elk Island National Park.

Buffalo

At Astontin Lake, 23 km (14 mi.) north of the Park entrance on the Yellowhead Highway, there are various leisure facilities (e.g. bathing beach, campsite, golf course, canoe hire). The Interpretive Center here has a great deal of information about the flora and fauna of the Park (open: Victoria Day–Labour Day Mon.–Fri. noon–4pm, Sat. and Sun. until 5pm, otherwise weekends only 11am–4pm).

Astontin Lake

There are several waymarked walks, in the course of which, with any luck, buffalo, mule deer and moose will be spotted. More patience is

Round walks

needed to catch a glimpse of a beaver by its dam or lodge. Rare bird species can be observed at the lakes hidden away in clearings in the forest.

★★Ukrainian Cultural Heritage Village

A few minutes drive east of Elk Island National Park along the Yellowhead Highway is the Ukrainian Heritage Village. Established in the 1970s, this open-air museum preserves the cultural heritage of the many immigrants from Bukovina and the Ukraine who settled in what is now Alberta in the 1890s. An interesting display in the Visitor Centre provides information about the reasons behind these migrations and the years of hardship experienced in the new homeland. The latest Ukrainian settlements in Alberta are also featured.

Various historic buildings have been reconstructed on the site, the pale onion dome of a Ukrainian church being visible from afar. "Living History' is presented in an old school, a traditional farmstead, an old smithy and an old-fashioned general store. Museum staff in traditional costume people the houses and demonstrate old crafts. Folk-dances from back home are also sometimes performed. Museum open Victoria Day–Labour Day daily 10am–6pm, otherwise Mon.–Fri. 10am–4pm.

Wetaskiwin

One hour by car south of Downtown Edmonton is the friendly little town of Wetaskiwin. Here the main attraction is the Reynolds Alberta Museum, dedicated to everything to do with aircraft and vehicle construction. There are open-air displays of old agricultural machinery and tools, including some real dinosaurs – steam tractors, threshing machines, caterpillar tractors and trucks, also veteran aircraft. In the new main hall the history of vehicle production is presented in all its facets. Machinery and tools now long out of service can be seen in use in old films on various topics such as cereal harvesting. A second large hall reveals the glorious history of Canadian military and civil aviation, with the opportunity to inspect at close quarters some historic planes.

Ellesmere Island A/B 13–17

Administrative Unit: Nunavut

Information

Nunavut Tourism, PO Box 1450, Iqaluit, NV X0A 0H0; tel. (867) 9796551, fax. (867) 9791261

Location

Ellesmere Island lies in the extreme north of Canada. Measuring 800 km (500 mi.) from north to south between latitudes 76° and 83°N, it covers an area of 212,000 sq. km (81,850 sq. mi.), making it the second largest island – after Baffin Island (see entry) – on the Canadian archipelago. William Baffin had reached the south-east of the island as early as 1616, and in the second half of the 19th c. attempts were made to explore even further north by way of the narrow Smith Sound, which separates Ellesmere Island from Greenland. It was from Cape Columbia that Peary set out in 1909 to walk to the North Pole.

Ausuittuq

Traces of prehistoric settlements have been found on the south coast of Ellesmere Island, and there is also evidence of Thule culture. The "recent" history of Ausuittuq (Grise Fiord), the northernmost Canadian Inuit community, began in 1953 when the Canadian government moved four Inuit families from the east coast of Hudson Bay to the south-east of Ellesmere Island, without taking account of the fact that these people were accustomed to quite different living conditions. Here, only 1500 km (930 mi.) from the North Pole, average temperatures in March lie between −35°C and −25°C (−31°F and −13°F), and in July between 0°C and 6°C (32°F and 43°F), and winter is spent in total darkness, making the climate even more inhospitable to man than Labrador; to make matters worse, while on Hudson Bay rivers and lakes provide drinking water all the year round, on Ellesmere drift ice has to be melted down for this purpose, and only an expert can tell which is freshwater ice. The reasons behind the move were a certain colonialist attitude on the part of the government linked with a growing unfavourable situation in the Hudson Bay region brought about by increases in population and a resultant strain on resources. After the Québec Inuit had spent a winter under very difficult conditions a family from Pond Inlet on Baffin Island who were familiar with the conditions was sent to help them. In spite of the good conditions for hunting – the "Northwest Territories Explorer's Guide" for 1986 stated "Inuit families moved here to settle because of the rich stocks of animals to hunt ..." – the Inuits never felt at home here and after nearly forty years many considered leaving. The two Inuit groups have failed to integrate and have retained their separate languages and customs; even as late as 1962, when Grise Fiord was founded as a settlement, their houses were kept separate. In spite of Grise Fjord being a show-piece settlement with a number of advantages – relatively well provided with the benefits of "civilisation" – these are more than offset by the disadvantages of a small, still somewhat "artificial" settlement with a number of social problems, not the least of which is finding a suitable spouse.

At present Ausuittuq ("place where it never thaws") has rather more than one hundred inhabitants and is trying to share in the benefits of Arctic tourism; again in the words of the "Explorer's Guide" it offers "the most beautiful landscape in the NWT" and tours by canoe and snowmobile to view Arctic birds and polar bears! Ausuittuq can be reached by air from Yellowknife and Iqaluit via Resolute Bay.

Eureka

The Eureka Radio and Weather Station, run by the USA and Canada since 1948, lies at latitude 80°N on the west coast, separated from Axel Heiberg Island only by a narrow strait. Eureka became known for the fossilised forests from the Eocene Period, approximately 35–60 million years ago, which were discovered on Eureka Sound and Hot Weather Creek in the Remus Basin. In the cold, dry Arctic climate tree-stumps, covered in sand, remained almost unchanged and – together with fossils of turtles and lizards – are evidence of a former much warmer climate.

Alert

The most northerly and permanently inhabited settlement in the world is Alert, a radio and weather station set up by the Canadian army in 1950 on the north coast at 82° 30'N and 700 km (435 mi.) from the North Pole. Alert was the name of the flagship of a British marine expedition under Captain Nares which spent the winter here in 1875. Being a military station, Alert is not open to tourists.

Ellesmere Island National Park Reserve

In the extreme north of the island, in mountainous and glaciated country rising to some 2600 m (8500 ft), an area of about 40,000 sq. km (15,500 sq. mi.) has been designated a National Park. In this predominantly dry Arctic waste there are pockets which are warm and moist enough to enable plants to grow and animals to exist, such as in the area around Lake Hazen – a large lake north of the Arctic Circle – which enjoys a surprisingly long and warm summer. Here can be found musk-ox, Peary caribou, arctic foxes and wolves, lemmings, and over thirty species of birds have been counted. The flora is made up of over 130 kinds of plants. It is hoped that the National Park will serve to safeguard these sensitive forms of animal and plant life.

★Estrie

H 16

Province: Québec

Tourisme Cantons-de-l'Est, 20 rue Don-Bosco Sud, Sherbrooke, J1L 1W4; tel. (819) 8202020, fax. (819) 5664445   Information

Estrie

Location

The Estrie region – also known as "Cantons de l'Est" or "Eastern Townships" – covers an area of more than 13,000 sq. km (5000 sq. mi.) east of Montréal, and is one of the most varied regions of Québec province. Large uninhabited areas mingle with picturesque little towns. The hilly and wooded stretches are the most charming. At the feet of Mont Sutton and Mont Orford some of the province's major winter sports centres have sprung up.

History

People began to populate Estrie at the end of the 18th c. when many Americans and British fled there in the confusion of the American War of Independence 1776–83. It was they who chose the best places for their rich towns surrounded by parkland. After 1850 more and more French-speaking people settled in the area, and since 1950 they have dominated the entire Estrie region.

Granby

The little industrial town of Granby, the "Princess of Estrie", was founded in 1842. It owes its name to John Manners, the margrave of Granby, and is today the gastronomic capital of Estrie. Particularly charming are the open spaces such as Parc Pelletier. Also worth a visit is the Zoological Garden at 347 Avenue Bourget (open May–Oct. daily 10am–5pm; in July 10am–6pm).

Parc du Mont-Orford

Parc du Mont-Orford covers an area of almost 40 sq. km (16 sq. mi.) at the foot of the 793 m (2602 ft) high Mont-Orford. This mountain is very popular with skiers in winter, and from its peak – accessible by means of a chair-lift – there is a wonderful view of Estrie, Lac Memphremagog and the Vermont heights.

Magog

The industrial town of Magog, also known as the "Jewel of Estrie", was founded by Loyalists in 1799. Because of its charming position on the north bank of Lac Memphremagog is popular with tourists. The green sheen of Lac Memphremagog, 52 km (32 mi.) long and 3–6 km (2–4 mi.) wide, a fifth of which forms part of the US state of Vermont, is an ideal spot for quiet boat trips in summer.

★St-Benoît-du-Lac

About 20 km (13 mi.) south of Magog stands the Benedictine abbey of St-Benoît-du-Lac. This imposing Neo-Gothic building was consecrated by Paul Vannier in 1912. Some 60 monks live here today. Visitors are welcome to join in morning mass, held daily at 11am, and vespers each evening at 5pm.

Sherbrooke

Sherbrooke, the chief town in Estrie, lies surrounded by hills at the confluence of the Magog and St-François Rivers. The town owes its name to Lord Sherbrooke who was Governor of Canada from 1816 to 1818.

Pin Solitaire

The rock in the town centre known as "Pin Solitaire" is a reminder of the time when the Iroquois and Abenaqui Indians lived in the area. In February 1592 the two tribes were unable to agree on the outcome of a battle, so a curious competition was held at this spot. One Iroquois and one Abenaqui had to run round and round a pine tree until one dropped from exhaustion. The Abenaqui lasted the better and so won the right to kill the Iroquois.

Musée des Sciences naturelles

A visit is recommended to the Musée des Sciences Naturelles du Séminaire, one of the oldest museums in Québec province (195 Rue Marquette. Open Tue.–Thu. and Sun. 12.30–7.30pm.

Drummondville

The important industrial town of Drummondville is Estrie's second largest town. It was founded in 1816 by the Scottish General Heriot.

★Village québécois

The "Village québécois d'antan" is well worth a visit. Reconstructed in the style of the pioneering period, staff dressed in period costume describe everyday life between the years 1840 and 1910. Open daily Jun. 1st–Labour Day.

6 km (4 mi.) east of the neighbouring town of Victoriaville lies the little township of Arthabaska. Canada's first Prime Minister, Wilfred Laurier, had a house built here in 1877; situated at 16, Rue Laurier Quest, it today houses the Musée Laurier. Open Jun.–Aug. daily, 9am–noon and 1.30–7pm; Sep.–May closed on Mon. and public holidays.

Arthabaska

Flin Flon
G 10

Province: Manitoba. Population: 8000

See Manitoba

Information

Flin Flon lies in the middle of mountainous and very wooded country, marked by steep rocky slopes. All round the town are stores of ore and raw materials, including gold, copper, zinc and silver, so it will come as no surprise to learn that mining is the dominant industry, the main mines being those belonging to Flin Flon Mines and the Hudson Bay Mining and Smelting Company.
    The town's second most important source of income is the timber industry.

Economy

In 1915 gold-seekers found a tattered copy of a penny novel about Josiah Flintabbatey Flonatin who discovered a gold-town. They named the place after this fictional character, and the name soon became shortened to "Flin Flon".

Name

In the town centre stands a 7½ m (25 ft) tall statue of the legendary Mr Flonatin, designed by the caricaturist Al Capp.

Flonatin statue

The Flin Flon Museum near Highway 10A. exhibits items from the pioneering period as well as tools and impressive minerals belonging to the Hudson Bay Mining & Smelting Company. Open May–mid-Sep. daily 10am–6pm.

Museum

At the junction of Highways 10 and 10A lies Many Mine, Manitoba's first copper mine.

Many Mine

In addition to gold the Hudson Bay Mining & Smelting Co. mines copper, zinc and silver. Visitors can watch the above-ground workers between June and August. There are guided tours.

Hudson Bay Mining & Smelting Co.

★★Forestry Trunk Road
G/H 7/8

Province: Alberta

See Alberta

Information

Eastern slopes of the Rocky Mountains.

Route

Forestry Trunk Road (Highway 940) in Alberta, parts of which are well surfaced, threads its way for some 1000 km (620 mi.) along the eastern slopes of the Rockies in Alberta. It was initially laid to make it easier to fight the forest fires which are a frequent feature of this region. This route, so far known to only few tourists, covers some scenically spectacular parts of the country. There are magnificent views to be had from Plateau Mountain, and many visitors are particularly impressed by the rushing waters of the Oldman River.
    Kananaskis Provincial Park (see Calgary) is also very beautiful.

Topography

Highway 940 starts in Hinton, 250 km (155 mi.) west of Edmonton. It can also be joined near Nordegg (Highway 11), Ghost Lake (TransCanada

Location

Highway 1a), Seebe Highway (the 541 from High River onwards) or Crowsnest Pass.
See Calgary, Surroundings.

★Fort Carlton   G 9

Province: Saskatchewan

Information | See Saskatchewan

History

Fort Carlton, in the Historic Park of the same name (open mid-May–early Sep. daily 10am–6pm) was built in 1820 at the bottom of a valley by a natural ford of the North Saskatchewan River.

For 75 years it was an important outpost, lying as it did at the junction of a main waterway, the North Saskatchewan River, with an important overland route – the Carlton Trail – which linked Winnipeg with Fort Edmonton (see entries).

In its early years the fort's main task was to provide the river patrols and other posts of the Hudson's Bay Company with supplies. It obtained meat, lard, furs and skins from the Indians and other traders, in exchange for rifles, tobacco, clothing, blankets, pearls and metal goods such as cooking utensils, axes, knives and traps.

Even when canoe patrols, York boats and steamships came west the fort remained an important trading centre and continued to look after the settlers who arrived in the 1870s.

Officers of the Northwest Mounted Police were sent to the fort to negotiate with the Indians.

East of the fort a stone pyramid marks the spot where a treaty was signed under the terms of which the Cree Indians renounced their claim to 320,000 sq. km (123,500 sq. mi.) of land.

Using the fort as a base Commander Crozier of Battleford first led his troops into battle near Duck Lake against the insurgents in the Northwest Rebellion in 1885. The police troops suffered heavy losses and retreated to the fort. As they were unable to defend it the post was surrendered and the troops withdrew to Prince Albert. During the hastily organised evacuation fire broke out and destroyed large parts of the fort.

Reconstructed buildings

Earlier this century archaeologists examined the site and as a result it has been possible to carry out a partial reconstruction of Fort Carlton as it once was. In 1967 the historical provincial park was opened.

Store

The period around 1860 is also reflected in the rebuilt wooden houses and stockade fences. At one end stands the largest building, a Hudson's Bay Company store, equipped with the type of goods needed in those days, such as blankets, rifles, pearls, pipes and snowshoes. Also displayed here are agricultural products, dried meat and lard which formed the basis of the fur-traders' diet.

Dwelling

Another wooden shack, fitted out with old furniture, gives a good idea of how the Hudson's Bay Company's employees lived in the late 19th c.

Press

A press has also been installed, such as was used to press skins and hides into compact bundles.

Exhibition of furs

Various kinds of furs are exhibited in another wooden shack, together with information about the fur trade.

Canoe landing

A short path leads to the river where the fur-traders tied up their boats and stored goods and provisions.

★Carlton Trail

The Carlton Trail starts behind the picnic site and threads its way over hills and through woods, where the old trappers' path can still be seen.

★Fort Langley

Province: British Columbia. Population: 16,000

See British Columbia

Information

Fort Langley, strategically well-placed near the mouth of the Fraser River, was built in 1827 as the first permanent outpost of the Hudson's Bay Company. George Simpson, the then Governor of British Columbia, thought the Fraser would become an important connecting link with the countryside beyond, but in fact this was not to be so, mainly because of the sheer and insurmountable Fraser Canyon. As a result the trading post lost importance, and even the Cariboo gold-rush passed it silently by. In 1839 it was burned down, but was rebuilt in the following year. In 1886 the Hudson's Bay Company closed down this outpost.

History

After a very quiet period, however, the settlement developed to become the centre of the "Langley prairie", where agriculture and farming, particularly dairy-farming, now predominate.

Renovation of the fort began in 1955 when laying out the Fort Langley National Historic Park (see below) was begun.

In the British Columbia Farm Machinery Museum at 9131 King St. visitors can view numerous examples of old engines and equipment that were once used in agriculture, forestry and fishing in the Fraser region. Open Mar.–Nov. Mon.–Sat. 11am–5pm, Sun. 1–5pm.

Farm Machinery Museum

The neighbouring Langley Centennial Museum & National Exhibition Centre at 9135 King St. display objets d'art and everyday articles used by the coastal Salian tribes as well as relics of the pioneer age. Open daily in summer 10am–5pm, in winter Tue.–Sat. 10am–5pm, Sun. 1–5pm.

Centennial Museum & National Exhibition Centre

5 km (3 mi.) north of the TransCanada Highway can be found the partially reconstructed old Hudson's Bay Company trading post on the banks of the Fraser River, at 23433 Mavis St. Now accessible to the public it is known as Fort Langley National Historic Park. Open Jun.–Labour Day 10am–7pm, at other times of the year 10am–4.30pm).

★Fort Langley National Historic Park

4 km (2½ mi.) further downstream is Fort Langley (see above). The only preserved building is the former general store, which still reflects the style of the 19th c. It was in the "Big House" (officers' mess) here that British Columbia was declared a British Crown Colony in 1858. James Douglas was its first governor.

Inside the renovated fort it is possible to get a good idea of how the fur-traders and trappers lived along the Canadian west coast in the mid-19th c.

Employees of Parks Canada enthusiastically act out "Living History", portraying typical scenes from everyday life as it was in this Hudson's Bay Company fort.

★★Fort MacLeod

Province: Alberta. Population: 3000

Fort MacLeod & District Chamber of Commerce, P.O. Box 178, Fort MacLeod, AB T0L 0Z0; tel. (403) 553–49 55

Information

It was the whisky-smuggling trade which led to the founding of the town of Fort MacLeod by the Crowsnest Highway (see entry) in southern Alberta. In the 1870s American smugglers traded extensively with the prairie Indians, especially with the Blackfoot, bartering cheap whisky for buffalo hides.

History

In 1874, after their famous march through wild country, the Northwest

Fort MacLeod

Mounted Police set up their new headquarters here with the aim of putting an end to this illegal trade and restoring peace and order to this frontier region. The "Old West" is remembered in various historical buildings in the town centre.

★Fort MacLeod Museum

Built in 1957 at 25 St./3rd Ave., the Fort MacLeod Museum sets out to portray the Northwest Mounted Police fort built in 1874 and southern Alberta's first outpost; this is achieved by means of some original buildings, Indian tepees made of buffalo hide, exhibitions about the police, the lifestyle and history of the Blackfoot Indians and pioneers, and the story behind the fortifications. Open May–mid-Oct. daily 9am–5pm; in summer to 7pm.

In July and August a police patrol wearing the 1878 scarlet uniforms rides through the streets four times a day.

★★Head-Smashed-In Buffalo Jump

Some 16 km (10 mi.) west of Highway 2 North, by the unmade-up Highway 785, lies the area known as Head-Smashed-In Buffalo Jump, declared a World Heritage Site by UNESCO in 1981. A band of rock some 300 m (984 ft) long in the lush, undulating grassland ends in a steep precipice, and for more than 5000 years the prairie Indians in the course of their organised buffalo hunts used to drive the panic-stricken beasts over the precipice to their death. It was not until the Indians obtained horses and firearms from the white man in the 18th c. that they finally gave up this traditional method of hunting.

The name "Head-Smashed-in Buffalo Jump" originates from a hunting accident in the 18th c. A man watching the hunt from below the cliff was killed when the Indians drove some fleeing animals over the precipice on top of him. In 1987 a modern Interpretive Centre was established. As well as displaying archaeological finds, the Centre gives an insight into the way of life and traditional hunting methods of the region's indigenous Blackfoot Indians and demonstrates how rapidly Indian life changed after contact was made with the white man. Open May–Labour Day 9am–8pm; other times of the year 9am–6pm.

Northwest Mounted Police in Ford MacLeod (Alberta)

In the interesting museum local topography is described, and the life of the prairie Indians and their hunting techniques are explained. Emphasis is also laid on the rapid changes in the lives of the Indians after they came into contact with the white man.

★★Fort McMurray

F 8

Province: Alberta. Population: 37,000

Fort McMurray Visitors Bureau, 400 Sakitawaw Tr., Fort McMurray, AB T9H 4Z3; tel. (403) 7914336

Information

The town of Fort McMurray lies at the confluence of Clearwater River and Athabasca River (see entry). Its somewhat stormy development since the 1960s is due in no small measure to the existence of giant stocks of oil for many miles around. It is anticipated that more than 700 billion barrels of this valuable form of energy can be brought to the surface.
    In 1971 the population of this remote town was only 7000; now it has increased five-fold. A third of the inhabitants are between 20 and 40 years of age.

Location

The history of Fort McMurray begins in the last quarter of the 18th c., when the North West Company set up a trading post here in the fur-rich north of Alberta. In the 19th c. it developed into the main supply centre along the fur-route from the northern Saskatchewan River to Lake Athabasca. In 1883 regular steamship services were extended as far as this, and a start could be made in exploiting the rich natural resources of this vast region. The railroad connection laid in 1925 was an important factor in its continued development; it was now possible to transport timber and mineral resources at an economic cost.

History

The presence of oil beneath the sand was mentioned in reports by the explorers Peter Pond and Alexander Mackenzie back in the 18th c. Indians and fur-hunters were in the habit of mixing the crude tar with resin to caulk their canoes. In the early 20th c. a start was made on using the sand for surfacing Alberta's roads. Attempts to extract crude oil were initially unsuccessful, but during the Second World War the Abasand Oils Project, 8 km (5 mi.) north of Fort McMurray, succeeded in producing about 200 barrels a day. It was not until the 1960s that resources were really tapped to an economic degree, leading finally to an oil-boom in Fort McMurray.
    Today the oil is extracted by means of very sophisticated processes, e.g. by the firms of Suncor and Syncrude, 34 km (21 mi.) north of Fort McMurray. Obtained by means of the hot-water process – at present some 180,000 barrels a day – the oil is pumped to Edmonton through a pipeline.

Extracting oil

The Fort McMurray Oil Sands Interpretive Centre (Highway 63/Mackenzie Blvd.) is worth a visit. Models, drawings, films and experiments spread over more than 2300 sq. m (2750 sq. yd) provide information about the development of the extraction of crude oil from the sand, with the emphasis on the highly modern technology now used. Equally impressive are the huge machines used to extract the valuable raw material. Open from Victoria Day–Labour Day daily 10am–6pm, at other times of the year noon–5pm.

★★Fort McMurray Oil Sands Interpretive Centre

By prior arrangement during the summer months visitors can join in guided tours of the Syncrude Works at 400 Sakitawaw Trail. The tours commence at 9.15 am Tue.–Thu. and at 11.15 am Sat.

Syncrude Tours (extracting oil)

Some buildings which formed part of the old Fort McMurray have been restored. Situated at King St./Tolen Drive on the bank of Haningstone River, they are open end of Jun.–end of Aug. daily 10am–6pm. They

Heritage Park

Bulldozer Fort McMurray

include a church, the Hill Drugstore Museum and, last but not least, the former posts of the Royal Canadian Mounted Police.

★Fort Providence   E 7

	Territory: Northwest Territories Population: 700
Information	Northwest Territories Arctic Tourism, PO Box 610, Suite 400, Yellowknife, NT X1A 2N5; tel. (867) 8737200, fax. (867) 8734059
Access	**By air:** From Edmonton via Hay River or Yellowknife
	By road: From Edmonton north to near Peace River, then via the Mackenzie Highway (AB Highway 35, NT Highway 1) to Fort Providence
Location	The little town of Fort Providence lies on the Mackenzie River where it flows into the south-western corner of Great Slave Lake, on Highway 3 going towards Rae-Ezdo. The town is known for the wide selection of Indian arts and crafts and handmade anoraks and parkas in the shops. Boats can be rented at the filling stations in the town.
History	The famous American Arctic explorer Sir John Franklin (1786–1847) chose Fort Providence as the starting point for his journeys of discovery to the Barren Grounds in 1819–22. At the western end of town stands a memorial to the American explorer Sir Alexander Mackenzie (see Famous People), who stopped off in Fort Providence in 1789 in the course of his putative trek to the Pacific Ocean which he hoped would take him to the Arctic Ocean.

The Mackenzie Bison sanctuary lies north of Fort Providence on Highway 3 in the direction of Rae-Edzo. In 1963 the Canadian Government transferred here nineteen wood buffalo, a species threatened with extinction. This, the only herd of these buffalo still in existence in North America, has since grown to many hundred. Anyone driving along Highway 3 in the early morning or evening is almost certain to see one or two wood buffalo at the roadside. Mostly, though, they stay near the shores of the Great Slave Lake (see entry).

★Mackenzie Bison sanctuary

★★Fort St James

G 6

Province: British Columbia. Population: 2000

Fort St James Chamber of Commerce, 115 Douglas Avenue, Fort St James, BC V0J 1P0; tel. (250) 9967063

Information

Fort St James on Stuart Lake is the capital of the historic district of New Caledonia and the second oldest town in British Columbia. As long ago as 1806 Simon Fraser and John Stuart of the North West Company set up a trading post here near an Indian settlement at the eastern end of the over 100 km (62 mi.) long Stuart Lake. This lake actually forms part of a system of lakes and rivers more than 400 km (250 mi.) in length. In 1821, when the two rival fur companies, North West and Hudson's Bay, amalgamated, Fort St James became the administrative and supply centre of the fur hunting teams which operated from here throughout western Canada. In 1843 a Catholic mission was built near the fort.

History

In 1869 gold was found in the Omineca Region further north. A veritable gold-rush resulted which had its effects on Fort St James as well.

Today Fort St James is a modern township on the northern edge of the old settlement. Four large timber concerns, mining and tourism form the backbone of its economy.

Fort St James National Historic Park

Fort St John

★★Fort St James National Historic Park

In 1971, at great expense, the old fort was reconstructed to resemble its appearance in 1896. During the summer months park staff dressed in contemporary costume, employing much enthusiasm and imagination, act out typical everyday situations portraying the hard lives led by the fur-traders. Visitors can look over the somewhat more comfortable administrator's residence, various storehouses, men's quarters, shops and offices. Exhibitions and film-shows in the Visitor Centre provide background on the history of this remote trading post in the "Canadian Siberia".

There are guided tours May–Oct. 9am–6pm, at other times of the year Mon.–Fri. 9am–noon and 1–4pm.

Our Lady of Good Hope

Nearby stands the Catholic Church of Our Lady of Good Hope, a pretty wooden church built in 1873, where mass is still celebrated in summer.

Fort St John   F 6

Province: British Columbia. Population: 15,000

Information

Fort St John Chamber of Commerce, 9323 100th Street, Fort St John, BC V1J 4N4; tel. (250) 7853033

History

Fort St John, standing 693 m (2275 ft) above sea-level and situated about 80 km (50 mi.) north-west of Dawson Creek, grew from a fort built in 1806 by the North West Company at the nearby mouth of the Beatton River.

However, archaeologists have established that as long ago as 1794 there was already a fort at the mouth of the smaller Peace River 8 km (5 mi.) south of the present town centre, thus making the town one of the oldest Euro-Canadian settlements on the mainland of British Columbia.

Back in 1793, when he became acquainted with this region during his voyage to the Pacific, Alexander Mackenzie (see Famous People) recognised how suitable this spot was for a settlement. When, in 1821, five men from the trading post since set up by the Hudson's Bay Company were killed by Indians the company decided to close the outpost down.

It was not until 1860 that a new fort was built on the banks of Peace River; this was moved several times in the years that followed. In the 1890s a Catholic mission station was attached to the Hudson's Bay Company fort.

Gold-rush

During the Klondike gold-rush Fort St John lay on the route taken by the gold-diggers. Around the turn of the century the first settlers also came north to Peace River (see entry) and realised the agricultural potential of the region. Gradually Fort St John became an important rural centre.

During the Second World War an airport and the Alaksa Highway were built, resulting in an economic upturn for Fort St John.

In 1952 the John Hart Highway was completed, and for the first time in its history Fort St John had road links with the other major centres in British Columbia.

Economy

In the 1950s deposits of oil and natural gas were discovered in the countryside around Fort St John. A large refinery was built in the neighbouring town of Taylor. In addition to agriculture and forestry, the petro-chemical industry developed into an important branch of industry. Furthermore, new coal deposits were found to the south and west of the town.

North Peace Museum

Built in 1983, the exhibits vividly portray the history of the region, the lives of the Indians and trappers and first settlers, the construction of the Alaska Highway and the development of the oil industry. The 40 m (130 ft) high derrick was constructed by the museum in 1982. Open daily in summer 8am–8pm; other times of the year Mon.–Fri. 11am–4pm.

★★Fort Steele   H 7

Province: British Columbia

On the Crowsnest Highway (TransCanada Highway 3) running through southern Alberta and British Columbia. Alternatively take TransCanada Highway 1 to Golden, then head south on Highway 95 towards the US frontier.

Fort Steele Heritage Town; tel. (250) 426–73 52

In 1864 gold was discovered by three American gold-diggers at Wild Horse Creek, in country which until then had been penetrated only by the Kootenay Indians. Within a few weeks a gold-rush town had grown up, most of the inhabitants having come from the USA, since getting here from the west across the high mountain chains was too difficult. So the first politicians in Victoria heard about the finds of gold in the remote south-west of their territory was when they read about it in the American newspapers. Even before the completion of the Dewdney Trail the gold-boom at Wild Horse Creek reached its peak in 1865, when more than 5000 gold-diggers were at work, some even digging out deposits from under the very town itself.

A new town grew up on the Kootenay River near Galbraith's Ferry, the present-day Fort Steele. Galbraith had soon realised the need for a ferry over the Kootenay and operated such a service until the first bridge was built in 1888.

Around 1880, after the gold-rush, farmers and ranchers settled here in increasing numbers. There were the inevitable conflicts with the original owners of the land, the Kootenay Indians. Chief Isadore and his warriors declined to enter the Indian reserve that was quickly set up and there continued to be many battles with the white settlers who refused to entertain the Indians' claims to ownership of land. There were fears of a new uprising only a few years after the Riel uprising had been quelled. In 1887 a unit of the Northwest Mounted Police was sent from Fort MacLeod to the Kootenay River with instructions to arbitrate. Only a year later this first troop of "Redcoats" to come west of the Rocky Mountains was able to withdraw, its task successfully accomplished, and the grateful settlers re-named the place Fort Steele, after Samuel Steele, the superintendent in charge of this troop of only a few dozen but nevertheless highly effective men.

The discovery of rich silver deposits in eastern Kootenay in the 1890s resulted in a fresh mining boom. Ore and supplies were transported by steamer along the Kootenay River between Fort Steele and Jennings in Montana, where there was a link with the Great Northern Railway to Seattle. Fort Steele became the region's administrative and supply centre and following the boom there was strong speculation about a rail link. The town was hard hit therefore when, contrary to all expectations, it was the neighbouring town of Cranbrook which was in fact connected to the railway. As early as 1910 Fort Steele had become a ghost town, and by 1945 only 50 people still lived there.

The decision taken some years ago by the provincial government to build an open-air museum breathed fresh life into the town. Since then a growing stream of tourists has created further jobs and brought a new sense of optimism to the local employment scene. Now several hundred people are again resident in and around Fort Steele.

Fort Steele Provincial Park was built in the 1960s on Highway 95/93, a few miles after Crowsnest Highway 3 turns off south-east. It is laid out in the form of a typical town from the turn of the century, complete with a Northwest Mounted Police post. Many visitors are attracted every year to the open-air museum with four dozen buildings, either restored, reconstructed from historical records or moved here from other parts of the Kootenay (see entry) region. Staff and volunteers dressed in contemporary costume act out "living history" in the houses, most of which are furnished in Victorian style, and demonstrate old crafts and perform household tasks in the manner of the pioneering period. Open May–Oct. daily 10am–5pm, in summer 9am–8pm.

Wild Horse Theatre	Musicals, drama and comedies from that period can be watched in the Wild Horse Theatre.
Wasa Hotel	The region's varied history is portrayed in a building constructed on the lines of the old Wasa Hotel.
Kershaw General Store	In the Kershaw General Store the visitor can purchase goods such as were bought in the early 19th c.
Other attractions	There are horse-rides with guides, coach drives, and special trips in an old steam train, covering a distance of 4½ km (2¾ mi.).

★★Fraser Valley   G/H 6/7

	Province: British Columbia
Information	See British Columbia
Access	TransCanada Highway, eastwards from Vancouver (see entry).
Course	The Fraser, or Frazer River, 1368 km (850 mi.) long, is one of the major rivers in North America. It rises in the Rocky Mountains near Jasper National Park (see entry), flows north for 440 km (275 mi.) through the Rocky Mountain Trench and then turns south near Prince George (see entry). On its path southwards of some 660 km (410 mi.) it cuts through the Fraser Plateau, 1200–1500 m (4000–5000 ft) above sea-level, and then flows along the eastern slopes of the Coast Mountains.

Near Hope (see entry) it turns west and bursts through the Coast Mountains walled by a magnificent, deeply-slashed canyon.

Finally the Fraser River enters the Pacific Ocean in the Strait of Georgia near Vancouver (see entry).

View of Fraser Valley

Fish Ladder on Fraser River

The most generously watered tributaries of the Fraser are the North Thompson River (340 km (212 mi.) long), the South Thompson (330 km (205 mi.)), the Nechako (460 km (286 mi.)) and the Stuart (410 km (255 mi.)).

Important tributaries

Profitable agricultural and horticultural businesses flourish in the wide southern valleys and the river delta. A number of sizeable industrial firms have also become established in the delta region.

Economy

As salmon fishing remains of paramount importance it has not been possible to utilise to the full the water-power potential of the Fraser River. The only high-performance power-stations belonging to the B. C. Electric Co. are those installed on the two small tributaries, Bridge River and Stave River.

Hydro-electric power

The important contribution that the Fraser Valley could make to the opening-up of the mainland of western Canada was realised by Alexander Mackenzie (see Famous People) in 1793. From 1808 onwards the legendary adventurer explored the course of the river; fifty years later huge numbers of gold-seekers settled on its banks.

History of discovery

Around 1886 a new communications centre grew up near Ashcroft, and the old Cariboo Waggon Road through the canyon was no longer used. Until 1915, when a start was made on building the Canadian National Railway, the Canadian Pacific Railway line was the only traffic route through the Fraser Canyon.

In the 1920s the authorities realised the need for a road link, but there was little room for this, because the railway lines already took up the narrow space available along both river banks. In 1926, however, the road to Lytton was completed and in the 1950s, at great expense, this was extended to become the TransCanada Highway as we know it today.

The little town of Yale (76 m (249 ft); pop. 500) lies at the southern entrance to the Fraser Canyon. It was here that Simon Fraser once camped after his famous trek through the canyon, aided by Indians who for centuries had roamed through it and scaled its semi-vertical walls with the aid of ladders. In 1848 the Hudson's Bay Company set up a small trading-post here, which developed within ten years – as a direct result of the gold-rush – into a wild gold-diggers' town. Yale, the terminus of all river traffic, remained until the 1880s the main trade centre for all goods passing through deeper into British Columbia and to the goldfields. Until the Cariboo Waggon Road was built in 1861–63 all goods being transported to Kamloops (see entry) had to be transferred to the backs of mules. A number of historic buildings still remain as a reminder of the times when Yale was such an important trading centre.

Yale

Nearby, in an 1880 building at 31179 Douglas St., stands the historic little Yale Museum (open: Jun.–Sep. daily 10am–5pm). In front of the museum there is a memorial stone to the Chinese workers employed in the building of the Canadian Pacific Railway. About three quarters of all the workers came from China; they were paid only half the wages of the white workers, and hundreds died in accidents or from sickness. The route taken by the railroad followed in the main the Cariboo Waggon Road. Parts had to be detonated through the Fraser Canyon. With the completion of the railway line as far as Kamloops the setting-out point for mail-coaches and freight wagons was moved further upstream.

Yale Museum

The wild Fraser Canyon, a drive of no more than three hours east of Vancouver, is one of Canada's most impressive gorges. Here the raging torrents of the Fraser force their way through a narrow pass between rocky walls towering almost vertically above the river. In days gone by the Indians found a perilous way across by using ladders. The first things to take the eye are the narrowness and rough-hewn walls of the Fraser Canyon and the difficulties involved in laying a road at the narrowest spot, known as Hell's Gate. A funicular railway, giving a view of the wild gorge below, leads down to the other bank which is 150 m (490 ft) lower. Down here the tourist will find souvenir shops, a restaurant

★★**Fraser Canyon**

and a small centre providing information, by means of films, models of the "fish-ladders" (see below), etc., about the four-yearly migration cycle of the salmon. It is a climb of a few minutes down a reasonable path to the white, foaming river below. The opposite bank can be reached by means of a swaying suspension bridge.

On average, 900 million litres (200 gallons) (British) or 240 gallons (American) of water per minute shoot through the canyon which is only 34 m (112 ft) wide at this point. Normally the river here is about 40 m (130 ft) deep, but when the snow thaws it can rise by more than 20 m (65 ft) within a very short time.

When dynamite was used to provide a way through for the railroad in 1914 a massive rock-fall resulted, thus narrowing the river-bed still further. The estimated 5 million salmon swimming upstream were now no longer able to battle against a river flowing at 37 kmph (23 mph) and so found themselves cut off from their spawning grounds. This resulted in a catastrophic reduction in the numbers of salmon caught in the Fraser River. Therefore from 1944 "fish-ladders" were built, long stepped concrete tunnels through which the water flows comparatively slowly, thus enabling the salmon to pass through Hell's Gate once again. Today more than two million salmon a year successfully negotiate the canyon.

The tourist facilities near Hell's Gate are open Mar.–Oct. daily 9am–4.30pm, Jun.–Aug. daily 8am–8pm.

The town of Lytton (171 m (561 ft); pop. 400) lies about 400 km (250 mi.) upstream from Vancouver along the TransCanada Highway. Before the gold-rush and the building of the Canadian Pacific Railway there was an Indian village here at the confluence of the Fraser and Thompson Rivers. Named Cumchin, meaning "fork in the river", it lived mainly from salmon-fishing.	Lytton
Lytton, lying in the rain shadow of the Coastal Mountains, is known for its hot, dry summers and proudly calls itself the "Rafting Capital of Canada". Kumasheen Raft Adventures, of 281 Main Street, P.O. Box 339, Lytton B.C. V0K 1Z0; tel. (604) 455–22 96, are one of the largest organisers of raft trips in British Columbia; they offer half to five-day "white-water rafting" trips between May and September on the Fraser, Thompson, Chilko and Chilcotin Rivers, as well as through the raging rapids at Hell's Gate.

In Lytton Highway 12, following the old Cariboo Waggon Road, branches off to Lillooet 70 km (44 mi.) north on the Fraser River (see Vancouver, Nugget Route). | White-water rafting |
| From Lytton the TransCanada Highway follows the Thompson River. As a result of the dry conditions the rocky slopes are relatively devoid of vegetation. The main trees found here are Ponderosa pine or the "sage-brush" so typical of the arid regions of America and cacti which, of course, also thrive in relatively dry conditions. For the most part, crops can be grown only with the aid of artificial irrigation. | Thompson River |

In the narrow river-valley between Lytton and Spences Bridge there was often scarcely sufficient room for the modern highway to be built by the side of the railway lines, so frequently the road was constructed on steel girders directly above the river.

★Fredericton   H 17

Province: New Brunswick. Population: 47,000

Fredericton Visitor Information Centre, City Hall, Queen & York Streets, Fredericton, NB E3B 4Y7; tel. (506) 4529616	Information

◀ Hell's Gate

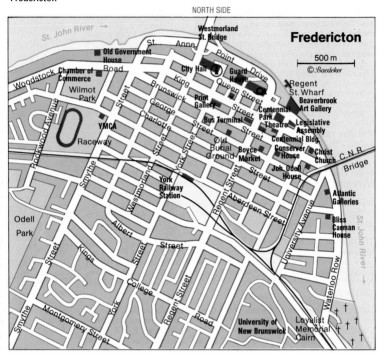

Fredericton, the capital of the east Canadian province of New Brunswick, is charmingly situated on the lower reaches of the St John's River. It is home to a university and the seat of an Anglican bishop. Although, in comparison with other Canadian cities, it is quite small it boasts an active cultural scene.

Fredericton, originally limited to administrative and educational establishments, has developed in recent years into a commercial and service centre for a wide area around. In addition a number of industrial firms, including a leather manufacturer, have set up here.

History

The capital of New Brunswick grew out of a small Acadian settlement named Pointe Ste-Anne, founded by French-speaking immigrants around 1732. In subsequent years the new settlement suffered as a result of civil war-like disputes among the Acadians themselves as well as from attacks by the British and by the native Micmac Indians who refused to tolerate the settlement.

From 1768 onwards American loyalists settled here. They named the colony after the second son of King George III of England, and this received the blessing of Queen Victoria in 1845. From then onwards it developed into a prosperous garrison and residential town.

★Christ Church
Cathedral

Christ Church Cathedral, an Anglican diocesan church, is a remarkable building. It was built in the Neo-Gothic style in the middle of the 19th c. The stained glass and the wooden interior are true works of art. The visitor's attention is also drawn to the gravestone of the first Anglican bishop of Fredericton, constructed in a form not usually found in North America.

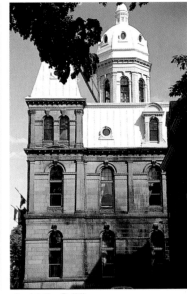

Fredericton: Christchurch Cathedral   *Legislative Building*

The venerable building occupied by the New Brunswick legislative assembly was built in the 1880s. The high conference chamber is very beautiful; here visitors can admire portraits of King George III and Queen Charlotte by the famous artist Joshua Reynolds.

Legislative Building

The parliamentary library owns a complete set of copper-plate engravings of the famous "Birds of America" by the Haiti-born American artist John James Audubon (1785–1851).
    There are guided tours of the parliamentary buildings mid-June–early Sept. daily by prior arrangement at the entrance door.

★Birds of America

Opposite the Legislative Building, at the north end of "The Green" by St John River, stands the Beaverbrook Art Gallery, opened in 1959.
    The gallery is named after Lord Beaverbrook (1879–1964), who was raised in Newcastle, New Brunswick, settled in England in 1910 and built up a giant newspaper empire there. During the Second World War he was a very influential member of Sir Winston Churchill's cabinet. Lord Beaverbrook first came to the fore as a great patron of the cultural life of New Brunswick. His collection of paintings forms the basis of the gallery's exhibits. He also financed the local playhouse and several of the buildings of New Brunswick University.
    Resplendent in the entrance hall hangs the giant work by Salvador Dali, "Santiago el Grande". Other magnificent paintings include Botticelli's "Resurrection", a portrait of Lord Beaverbrook by Graham Sutherland, Krieghoff's "Merrymaking" and a number of works by the British painters Gainsborough, Hogarth, Reynolds and Turner as well as some by Corneille, Lukas Cranach and Delacroix. Outstanding, too, is the collection of works by Canadian painters, including Cornelius Krieghoff (see above), Paul Kane, the Group of Seven and Emily Carr. Also on display are some fine works by Inuit artists. Open daily 9am–6pm, except Sun. and Mon. mornings.

★★Beaverbrook Art Gallery

Frederiction

Playhouse

The neighbouring playhouse in St John Street also owes its existence to the town's great patron, Lord Beaverbrook. He also financed the first theatrical troupe in the province.

Military Compound

The park-like area known as the Military Compound lies in the town centre between Queen Street and the river. At one time the British garrison was stationed here. In more recent years the trappings and equipment of the Canadian army have been moved to a site out of town.

The Guard House on Carleton Street, between Queen Street and the bridge, has been reconstructed in the style of the 19th c. It contains quarters for officers and other ranks. Uniforms and military equipment are also on display. Open Jun.–early Sep. Mon.–Sat. 10am–4pm.

★York-Sunbury Museum

The York-Sunbury Museum with its comprehensive collections is housed in an extension to the officers' mess and provides background information on the history of the region. Of particular interest are the exhibitions dealing with the Indian aboriginals, as well as those collections covering the Victorian period and the story of Fredericton as a garrison town up to and including the First World War.

Craft School

The New Brunswick Craft School is also housed in the Military Compound. Here the artists and craftsmen can be watched as they work and examples of their work can be purchased.

"Pioneer Princess III"

Daily in the high season the paddle-steamer "Pioneer Princess III" leaves from Regent Street Wharf for trips on the river.

University of New Brunswick

The University was built in 1785, making it the third oldest in Canada. It stands southwest of the St John River on a hill from which there are excellent views. The library and the provincial archives it houses include a number of first editions donated by Lord Beaverbrook, including works by V. Bennett, Charles Dickens and H.G. Wells.

Oromocto

Access to the picturesque town of Oromocto is by Route 102. It lies at the confluence of the Oromocto and St John Rivers, and its history of the place goes back to the times of the Micmac and Malecit Indians. A reconstructed log-cabin is reminiscent of the Canadian Revolution of 1777. Near Oromocto is one of the largest military academies in the British Commonwealth.

In the Canadian army base at Gagetown there is an interesting military museum.

Scottish Highland Games are held every summer in Oromocto. It also has a popular golf-course.

Sunbury-Oromocto Provincial Park

In the nearby Sunbury-Oromocto Provincial Park there are facilities for cycling, bathing and horse-riding excursions, together with a camp-site and several picnic areas.

Gagetown

In the picturesque old town of Gagetown, wonderfully situated by the river, time seems to have stood still. Numbers of craftsmen, especially weavers, have come here to live and work. The Queen's County Museum can be found in the house which belonged to Sir Leonard Tilley, one of the co-founders of the Canadian Confederation.

During the summer months Gagetown boasts a very popular marina, where amateur sailors from all over the world can feel at home.

★Route 102

Route 102 winds along through the charming countryside at the mouth of the St John River, which is here strongly influenced by the marked variations in tide levels in the Bay of Fundy. There are ample opportunities to cross to the other side of the river by ferry. Also along the road the visitor will obtain a good impression of the land as developed and cultivated by man. There are also opportunities for bird-watching.

See entry.

★★**Fundy Bay**

Provinces: New Brunswick/Nova Scotia

See New Brunswick, Nova Scotia

Measuring up to 80 km (50 mi.) wide at its mouth, Fundy Bay (Bay of
Fundy) is a delta-shaped bay in the Atlantic Ocean, almost 300 km (190
mi.) deep and penetrating the North American mainland between the
Canadian provinces of New Brunswick and Nova Scotia.

Fundy Bay is neither the largest nor the deepest in the world, but its
maximum tidal flow between low and high of 19 m (10 fathoms) in the
extreme north of the bay at Moncton and Truro (see entries) is not
exceeded anywhere else. Its average tidal flow is about 9 m (30 ft), but
during the spring tides 13 m (43 ft) can easily be exceeded. Ebb and
flow, brought about by the gravitational pull of the sun and the moon,
occur when waves in the ocean are stationary. As a result of the earth's
rotation, or coriolis power, and the shape of the oceanic basin the tidal
waves revolve around a central point, or amphidrom. The determinant
amphidrom in the North Atlantic revolves anti-clockwise once every 13
hours, producing a complete tidal change. The extended delta-like shape
of the Bay of Fundy has an intensifying effect on the tides which are a
mere 80 cm (32 in.) (!) high out in the open sea. The relative rise in the
sea-level about 6000 years ago resulted in Fundy Bay being joined to the
Atlantic, and from then onwards the tides were high. Since then the
average tidal flow has continually increased, so that now during the
spring tides it reaches up to 16 m (53 ft) in the furthermost corner of
Fundy Bay. If in the future either man – by, for example, building giant
tidal power-stations – or Mother Nature herself brings about marked
changes in the shape of the bay that will almost certainly put an end to
this fascinating natural spectacle.

Sights

The small industrial town of St Stephen lies on the little St Croix River
where it enters Fundy Bay. Founded in the 17th c., St Stephen did not
really develop until one hundred years later, when American loyalists
settled here. It is now home to the woodworking, paper and textile industries. The bridge over the river leads to Calais, in the US state of Maine.

In the far south of New Brunswick and close to the border with Maine
the pretty little fishing-port of St Andrews (pop. 2000) lies on the
"appendix" of the Bay of Fundy known as Passamaquoddy Bay. Its typical New England-type houses are very pretty. Twice daily between mid-
May and October boats leave St Andrews for trips around Fundy Bay.

On little Deer Island off the coast live some 1000 descendants of
American loyalists who settled here in 1784. The island is best known for
the large numbers of lobsters which breed on the giant lobster-banks.

On the island of Campobello further offshore to the south lies the spacious country seat of the Roosevelt family. Until 1921 the US President
often stayed here, but his visits became less frequent in the 1930s.
   At one time Campobello was named "Port-aux-Coquilles" by the
French colonists because of the abundance of mussels to be found here.

The fishing port of Black's Harbour is the home of Canada's largest can-

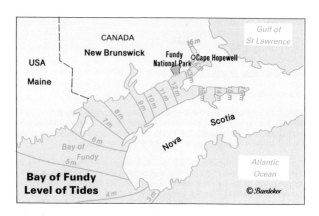

Bay of Fundy
Level of Tides
© Baedeker

ning factory, where sardines are processed. There is a ferry service across to Grand Manan Island.

★ **Grand Manan Island**

Grand Manan Island lies at the south-western entrance to the Bay of Fundy. Barely 3000 people live on the island, which is about 35 km (22 mi.) long and up to 10 km (6 mi.) wide. The marshlands interspersed with rocky ridges make it a favourite resting place for numerous species of birds – more than 300 different kinds have been spotted. The Ornithological Museum in the town of Grand Harbour is worth a visit.

Mineral-hunters will be attracted to the north-western part of the island near Dark Harbour, shaped by volcanic activity. Here semiprecious stones such as amethysts, jasper and agate can be found.

★★Fundy National Park

Area: 206 sq. km (80 sq. mi.). Established: 1948

Information

The Superintendent, Fundy National Park, PO Box 40, Alma N.B., E0A 1B0; tel. (506) 8876000.

Access

From the TransCanada Highway, turn off on to Route 114 near Sussex/Moncton.

Accommodation

There are four camp sites with a total of 660 places, a motel and holidayhomes in the park, and bed and breakfast is available in Alma and the surrounding villages.

Geography

This park on the steep south coast of New Brunswick includes a 13 km (8 mi.) strip of the wild coast on the Bay of Fundy. Cliffs rise steeply up from the shore and the otherwise slightly hilly landscape is slashed here and there by deep gorges.

The strong influence exerted by the bay means that two quite different climatic regions are to be found within the comparatively small National Park. That on the coast is characterised by cool summers with frequent mist and mild winters. On the higher land the summers are warmer, with no mist, and the winters colder. When the wind comes off the sea in summer the temperature on the coast can differ by as much as 6°C (11°F) from that inland.

The arrival of European settlers had an adverse effect on the eco-system of Fundy National Park. In the 19th c. the developing timber industry meant that large areas of trees were cut down for ship-building. When the timber industry declined in the early years of this century the land was deserted. Attempts to mine ore failed, and only very few mines – which are now open to visitors – proved profitable. The topsoil was not deep enough to be properly cultivated, although a few farmers managed to scrape a living by diversifying. When the region was declared a National Park in 1948 the few remaining inhabitants received small sums in compensation and their houses were pulled down. Salmon, peregrine falcons and ermine, once frequent denizens of the park, had died out, and had to be laboriously imported over the last forty years or so and gradually familiarised with their new surroundings. The natural Arcadian Forest too, with its mixture of ash, elm, spruce, pine and fir, was severely affected by having trees cut down. Caterpillars of a certain species of moth which feed on pine and spruce-needles have seriously decimated the young trees planted in the place of the old. A new type of forest with a higher proportion of birch and small clearings has grown up. In spring in particular a brilliant display of flowers can be seen under the shade of the trees. Large ferns and rare orchids are a sight to behold.

The fascinating spectacle of the tides – low and high tides every 6¼ hours – can best be experienced near Alma where the beach is about a mile long at ebb tide. A walk along the beach at low tide provides an insight into an unsuspected world of theatre with crabs, shrimps, sea-anemones and sand-fleas as the main performers.

★★ The Edge of the Tide

In 1852 a surveyor wrote thus about this strip of land: "The land is stony, rough and littered with fallen trees, is known as the Devil's Half Acre and is as full of holes as a piece of Swiss cheese". Even though geologists can explain the curious natural phenomena as being the result of erosion by water and unstable stone strata, anyone walking through here is more likely to be reminded of the local legend which says that these strange hollows and holes are the work of the very Devil himself. On a foggy day or after a shower of rain the inhospitable trail takes on a most eerie atmosphere. At the end, however, the rambler is rewarded with a superb view over the bay. It takes about 30 minutes to cover the 2 km (1¼ mi.) stretch.

★ Devil's Half Acre Trail

From the main offices a single path 9 km (5½ mi.) long leads up onto a mountain ridge and past deep, moss-covered crevices to a viewing place with a protective fence by the beach in Herring Cove, from where a telescope can be used to view the cove. The walk takes about four and a half hours. The path then continues up through the coastal forest which is often heavy with mist, along the cliffs and ending in Pointe Wolfe.

★ Coastal Trail

The rambler will soon come to a waterfall in a narrow ravine below the wooden bridge. In 1826 a sawmill was built near the dam and a small village grew up around it. Much of the sawn wood was sent to the USA or to St John for building sailing ships.

The dam, like those in most rivers in the bay, cuts off the upper reaches from the lower, resulting in a drastic reduction in fishing. Salmon, smelt and Canadian herring could no longer swim upstream to spawn. From the dam the trail leads to a viewing platform overlooking the "fiord"; distance 1 km (⅔ mi.), time required about 30 minutes.

Pointe Wolfe Gorge

This trail is 3½ km (2 mi.) in length and takes about 1–1½ hours to cover. The vegetation along the edge is typical of that in the National Park; passing by evergreen bracken and through dark deciduous forests and rivulets lined with alder trees it finally reaches a lowland moor. Near the two moorland lakes the visitor can observe some rare plants as well as snakes, beaver and elk.

Information boards give details of the origin and the inhabitants of the moors.

Caribou Plain Trail

This river, quiet in its upper reaches, wild and spectacular in the middle and flat and stony lower down its course, is typical of the park. Situated in the north-east, the river is pleasantly situated off the main tourist

Upper Salmon River

track. Being so quiet it is a good place to visit in the high season, and deep pools and small waterfalls make it a bathing paradise for dedicated walkers. However, the water temperature rarely exceeds 18°C (65°F). In late summer Atlantic salmon can often be observed resting in certain pools at the bottom of waterfalls. The distance to be covered is between 10–20 km (6–12 mi.), depending on the trail chosen.

★★Gaspésie　H 17/18

Province: Québec

Information	Office de Tourisme de Gaspé, 39 rue York Est, Gaspé PQ G0C 1R0; tel. (418) 3686335 Office de Tourisme de Percé, 142 Route 132 Ouest, Percé, PQ G0C 2L0; tel. (418) 7825448
Location	The Gaspé Peninsula (250 km (155 mi.) long and 100–140 km (62–87 mi.) across), on the Gulf of St Lawrence, is more or less cut off from the rest of Québec Province by Lake Matapédia and the Matapédia River. Inland, Gaspésie is a mountainous, wooded wilderness, and the only sizeable settlement has grown up around the copper mine at Murdochville. The highest point on the peninsula is Mont Jacques-Cartier (1268 m (5162 ft)), part of the Schickshock Mountains, geologically the northern terminal of the Appalachians.
Economy	The peninsula has a wild and rugged north coast, where the people live in small villages and depend partly on fishing for their livelihood. The south coast, on the other hand, is gentler and not so steep, and has some farmland as well as the usual timber. Tourism plays a role too, with arts and crafts such as weaving, wood-carving, and making model ships providing another source of income. Not least of Gaspé's attractions is its excellent cuisine, which is in the best French tradition, especially the game and fish (including trout, Atlantic salmon, lobster and other seafood).
★Parc de Métis	The Parc de Métis extends from Ste-Flavie to Matane, below Lake Matapédia, and is notable for its great variety of vegetation. The climate means that most plants flower two months later than elsewhere, so spring does not start until June. The Parc de Métis was the work of Elsie Reford, niece of Canadian railway tycoon Lord George Stephen. She transformed the area, originally used for salmon fishing, into magnificent English-style gardens. The Stephen mansion and the Reford Apartments are well worth visiting for the glimpses they afford of life here at the turn of the century.
Matane River	The small industrial centre of Matane lies on the Matane River, famous for its salmon. Between mid-June and October a nearby path around a dam is a good viewpoint for watching the salmon on migration.
Parc de la Gaspésie	The road from Matane to de la Gaspésie Park leads up into a hilly, wooded area before the park gives way to the broad valley of the Ste-Anne River. This area contains the highest points in the Shickshocks, including Mont Jacques-Cartier, Mont Richardson and Mont Albert, with, between them, spacious valleys, while, around Gîte du Mont Albert, the proportions are postively alpine. The trails here include one to Mont Cartier, and a Nature Interpretation Centre for the Gaspésie area.
Ste-Anne-des-Monts	The road to Ste-Anne-des-Monts is typical of the rocky coast, running through impenetrable terrain, either at the water's edge or along the clifftops, and passing through many little fishing villages with relatively large churches, and nothing but waves, white horses and seagulls as far as the eye can see.

The slate cliffs surrounding Mont-St-Pierre Bay are particularly spectacular.   **Mont-St-Pierre**

The village of Grande-Vallée still has a covered wooden bridge, dating   **Grande-Vallée**
from 1923.

The road also leads through Gaspésie's most important fishing centre,   **Rivière-au-Renard**
Rivière-au-Renard, before circling round the Forillon Peninsula where
the land is highly cultivated.

At the tip of the Gaspé Peninsula, this scenic park extends into the Gulf   ★★**Parc National**
of St Lawrence. Its northern coast is wild and rugged, with mostly lime-   **de Forillon**
stone cliffs. The southern coastal strip is less grand, but just as impressive, with opportunities for birdwatching and for whalewatching trips by
boat. For anyone wanting to know more about the wildlife of the area
there is an information centre at Cap des Rosiers.
  Further on, at Cap Bon-Ami, a narrow path leads down to the beach
and there is a magnificent view of the cape and the cliffs.

A road on the south side of the peninsula leads to Anse-aux-Sauvages,   **Anse-aux-**
from where a path goes to Cap Gaspé, the eastern tip of the national park.   **Sauvages**

Gaspé, the main town of the peninsula and the administrative and com-   ★**Gaspé**
mercial centre, is on a hillside overlooking the York Rivière, which runs into
Gaspé Bay. The town owes its fame to Jacques Cartier (see Famous
People), since it was here that he first set foot on the continent of North
America in July 1534, fashioned a wooden cross under the gaze of the local
settlers and took possession of the land "in the name of the King of France".
  Nowadays Gaspé has a population of over 17,000, earning their living
from fishing and the fishing industry. It is the see of a Catholic bishop.

The modern cathedral, built almost entirely of wood and containing   Cathedral
beautiful stained-glass, is well worth a visit.

The legendary wooden cross was replaced in 1934 by the stone cross   Croix de Gaspé
near the city hall.

The local museum tells of Jacques Cartier's voyages. It also gives an   Musée
account of the Anglo-French struggle for power over this region, and
depicts the lives of those early settlers.

Formerly a remote fishing village, its wonderful setting has made Percé a   **Percé**
great attraction for visitors, especially in the summer months. It has plenty
of good restaurants and cafés, and there is even an open-air theatre.
  The town gets its name from a heavily eroded rock, which is pierced
(percé in French) by a large hole at one end.
  All the natural beauties of the Gaspé Peninsula are to be found in and
around Percé within a very small area, and it is a good place to see the
effects of the forces that have shaped the landscape (the rising and
falling in geological periods, erosion).

The whole of the coast around Percé is a magnificent natural spectacle,   Percé coast
providing many opportunities for photography, with rocky outcrops, and
towering cliffs, often bare, or only sparsely covered with turf.

From the "Belvédère" there is a good view of the Pic de l'Aurore, look-   ★★Pic de
ing like a giant tooth, and of the Grande-Coupe range of hills.   l'Aurore

Cap Barré has a view of the offshore rocks known as the "Three Sisters",   Cap Barré
the Trois Söurs.   Trois Sœurs

From Mont-Joli there is a view of the Trois Söurs, Cap Barré and, inland,   ★★Mont-Joli
the red cliffs of Mont Ste-Anne and a sculpture-like block of limestone

The coast of Percé

which resembles a ship at anchor. The rock has meanwhile has broken up, the remains forming a kind of obelisk joined to Mont-Joli by a sandy spit.

Île Bonaventure

This island is a bird sanctuary, and its about 4 sq. km (1½ sq. mi.) is North America's largest gannetry, with about 50,000 birds here in summer. The eastern side of the island is an ideal nesting site with rocky clefts and ledges. Besides the gannets, there are cormorants and other seabirds, with a nature trail so that visitors can see them better.

★★View

From the top (320 m (1050 ft)) of this gleaming redrock mountain there is a magnificent view of Percé and the surrounding region.

★Grande Crevasse

A path from the Gîte de Gargantua along the western slope of the 426 m (1398 ft) Mont-Blanc leads to a precipitous chasm known as "Grande Crevasse", although this is a walk for experienced ramblers only!

Centre d'Interpretation

The interpretive centre above Percé to the south gives an account of Percé's wildlife, heritage and local history.

South Coast

Gaspé's south coast has a considerably less rugged landscape than the north, much of it farmland but there is also all kinds of economic activity. Each small bay has its fishing village. On a clear day it is possible from many observation points to see Acadia (see entry) over the other side of the Baie des Chaleurs.

Bonaventura

This little holiday place is on a bay, and was founded by Acadians fleeing here to escape deportation.

Carleton

Carleton is on a bay with an offshore sandbank. The scenery here is dominated by Mont St-Joseph, which is just under 600 m (197 ft). From Carleton a small road leads up to the top from where there is a magnificent view over the Baie des Chaleurs.

This peninsula marks the beginning of the Baie des Chaleurs, or the end of the estuary of the Restigouche River (see Campbellton).

Miguasha Peninsula

This museum of palaeontology provides an introduction to petrology and helps with the identification of the many kinds of fossils that can be found in the local rock formations.

Musée de Miguasha

This little village is in a lovely setting amidst green hills between famous salmon rivers.

Matapédia

★★Georgian Bay

H/J 14/15

Province: Ontario

Midland Chamber of Commerce, 208 King St, Midland, ON L4R 3L9; tel. (705) 5267884
Georgian Bay Islands National Park, PO Box 28, Honey Harbour, ON P0E 1E0; tel. (705) 7562415

Information

Highways 400 and 93 from Toronto (see entry).

Access

A large bay, so cut off it is almost a lake, Georgian Bay is part of Lake Huron, and was named after George IV. In the north, with its wild, rocky shoreline, it has an atmosphere all its own, dotted with small islands, some no more than a big, bare rock, others with a couple of crooked pine trees. The bay shore in the west and in parts of the south has the high limestone cliffs of the Niagara Escarpment, which, together with the long, sandy beaches on the southern shore and the Midland Peninsula, help to make Georgian Bay the ideal place for anyone who enjoys spending time on, in, or around the water.
    Owen Sound, Penetanguishene, Washaga Beach, Midland, Parry Sound and Collingwood are all popular holiday resorts on the bay's shores, rich in history and atmosphere.

Natural features

In the early 17th c., Georgian Bay, home to the Huron Indians, was where the Jesuit missions first set out to convert the Indians, starting with Etienne Brulé in 1610. He was followed by trappers and Jesuit missionaries from Québec, who established their first station here in 1639. Weakened by disease introduced by the new settlers, and under constant threat of attack from the Iroquois to the south, the Huron eventually succumbed, but when several of the Jesuits were tortured to death in 1649, the Ste-Marie mission station was abandoned.

Huronia

Sights

The resorts on the southern shores of Georgian Bay are very popular at weekends and in the summer, and can become just as crowded as any European holiday playground.

The little port of Midland (population: 13,000), on the southern side of the Bay, is the centre for a fairly large surrounding area, and a considerable amount of grain passes through it every year. It is also a good base for visiting several nearby historical sites.

Midland

The replica of an Indian village in Little Lake Park (King St.) shows what life was like for the Huron. It includes the big longhouses that a large family would have lived in, a medicine man's house, store-rooms, etc., plus demonstrations of how canoes were made.
    Huronia Museum, nearby, holds an interesting collection of Indian utensils and artefacts.

Huron Indian village

St. Mary among the Hurons

© Baedeker

Exit
Museum

Entrance
Museum

1 Tannery	7 Chapel	14 Herb Garden	20 Cemetery
2 Timber store	8 Recreation room	15 "En Columbage"	21 Pharmacy
Huts	9 Jesuits' quarters	16 Sawhorse	22 Sick quarters
3 Grain store	10 Kitchen building	17 Tailoring	23 Well
4 Stonemasonry	11 Stables	Shoemaking	
5 Smithy	12 Farmhouse	18 "En Pilier"	B Bastion
6 Carpentry	13 Bolvin House	19 St Joseph's Church	L Nave

★★St Mary among the Hurons

Open late May–Oct. 10am–6pm

The reconstruction of the mission station of St Mary among the Hurons is about 5 km (3 mi.) east of Midland on the Wye River. Founded by the Jesuits in 1639, for a decade the mission served as the mainstay for Europeans in "Wendat", the land of the Huron – in 1648 about 20 per cent of the Europeans living in New France were probably in Ste-Marie. The fortified mission station, which was organised along the lines of a European monastery, was divided into three parts.

The northern section was where the Europeans and the priests lived. They also had a chapel, the mission kitchen and a few workshops.

Next came some more workshops to the south, while the rest of the southern section was where the Indian converts lived. Here there was a longhouse, the Indians' own church, an infirmary and a vegetable garden. In front of a palisade, but still within the confines of the station, Indians who had yet to be fully converted could live in a longhouse or wigwams.

As time went on there was constant conflict with the Indians. The Huron (Wendat) were decimated by diseases imported by the Europeans. Several Indian tribes fought each other and occasionally there were attacks by the Iroquois in which not only Christians and Hurons but even European priests were killed. In 1649 the Jesuits abandoned their settlement and returned to Québec.

Reconstructed between 1964 and 1967, the mission is also the final resting place of Jean de Brébeuf and Gabriel Lalement who were tortured to death and are now venerated as martyrs.

Designated a national monument in May 1989, the station also has a museum dealing with its history and showing a documentary film on the subject, as well as putting on occasional "Living History" shows in which amateurs portray life in the mission station as it was in the 17th century.

★Martyrs' Shrine

Across Highway 12, the massive church built in 1926 serves as a memorial to eight French Jesuit priests from the first mission station, who were murdered and are commemorated in its Martyrs' Shrine, consecrated in 1926. This shrine to René Goupil, Isaac Jogues, Jean de la Lande, Antoine Daniel, Jean de Brébeuf, Gabriel Lalement, Charles Garnier and Noël Chabanel is visited by thousands of pilgrims every year. Pope John Paul II celebrated mass here a few years ago. Inside the church, which is almost entirely wood-panelled, the sandalwood canoe-shaped vault is particularly impressive. A small lookout tower in front of the church affords a splendid view of the surrounding area.

Nature lovers, and birdwatchers in particular, should be sure to visit the Wye Marsh Wildlife Centre, a marshland area by the Wye River, with boardwalks and a tower hide where many kinds of flora and fauna can be seen.

Penetanguishene is a former garrison town, a few miles northwest of Midland, in a scenic setting on Georgian Bay. A large hospital has been established here. To symbolise Anglo-French harmony, the French-Canadians, who are in the majority here, have put up two angels at the south entrance to the town.

In 1812 the war with the Americans forced the British to set up a naval base on Lake Huron. After two garrisons in the area fell to the Americans in 1818 Penetanguishene became a garrison town as well. Some buildings on the harbour have recently been restored, and visitors can see recreations of the officers' quarters, crew rooms, stores, and ships' repair shops.

The busy holiday resort of Wasaga Beach (pop. 6000) lies on a sandy spur of land between Georgian Bay and the Nottawasaga River. Its main attraction is its beach of fine, white sand, stretching for about 14 km (8½ mi.).

The Schooner "Nancy" was a British supply vessel, and the only ship to survive the naval battle on Lake Erie which the British lost in 1812, but the Americans discovered the "Nancy" hidden away on the Nattawasaga River and subsequently sank her. The hull was salvaged in 1927 and today stands in front of the museum which tells the story of the War of 1812 and the three hundred years of navigation on Lake Superior. There is also a reconstruction of the engine room of a Great Lakes steamer.

Wasaga Provincial Park (140 ha (346 acres)) is open all year round and has beautiful beaches, picnic areas, tennis courts, cycle tracks and, in the winter, ice rinks, and snowmobile and cross-country skiing trails.

"Wasaga Waterworld" and "Wasaga Landing", two immensely popular water theme parks, are open from mid-June to the beginning of September.

The delightful islands of Georgian Bay are from a natural point of view part of the Canadian shield, their topography shaped by the last Ice Age. This paradise of some 30,000 islets and small islands has long been a magnet for outdoor enthusiasts and artists such as Tom Thomsen and the "Group of Seven". In 1929 some 59 of the archipelago's islands were designated a National Park. Still virtually unspoilt, they can only be visited by boat, trips being run from mid-May to October from Honey Harbour, Penetanguishene and Midland. They follow much the same routes as were taken by the French surveyors Brulé, Champlain and LaSalle when setting out to explore the North American interior.

Owen Sound, a friendly town (pop. 20,000) in a delightful setting at the south end of Georgian Bay, is surrounded by limestone hills forming part of the Niagara Escarpment, and has good sailing and fishing.

This museum (975 6th St. E.), housed in three galleries and five restored old buildings, is the local history museum providing a survey of events from 1815 to 1920. Open Tue.–Sun. 9am to 6pm.

This well-kept park (46 ha (114 acres)) is especially worth visiting in spring for the blossom and in the autumn "Indian Summer". There are picnic areas, campsites, and waterfalls, etc.

The Tom Thomson Memorial Art Gallery (840 1st Ave. W.) is worth a visit to see a small cross-section of the work of probably Canada's best-known landscape artist, along with works by the "Group of Seven" and several other artists. Open Tue.–Sun. 9am–6pm.

Story Book Park is about 3 km (2 mi.) south of the town beyond Highways 6 and 10, and is aimed at families with children. Open end-May–beginning Oct. daily 10am to 6pm.

Glace Bay

Waterfalls	These three lovely waterfalls, hidden away outside Owen Sound, are top favourites with photographers.
★Bruce Trail	The breathtakingly beautiful Bruce Trail leads up along the Niagara Escarpment, with its great views, and is the main trail in a whole network of paths, opening up one of Ontario's finest areas for hiking and walking.
Blue Mountain	The scenic road along the southern shore of Georgian Bay from Collingwood to Meaford – 35 km (22 mi.) on Route 26 – leads to the Blue Mountain Chairlift, 11 km (7 mi.) west of Collingwood. On a clear day the view from the highest part of the escarpment over the Bay and surrounding cliffs is an exceptional experience.
★**Tobermory**	Tobermory is a picturesque little fishing village (pop. 600) with half-timbered houses and secluded coves at the northern tip of the Bruce Peninsula – geologically speaking a foothill of the Niagara Escarpment – which separates Georgian Bay from Lake Huron itself. The crystal-clear water also make it very popular with scuba-divers.
Peninsula & St Edmunds Museum	The Peninsula & St Edmunds Museum, about 3 km (2 mi.) south of Tobermory, on Highway 6 has mementoes from the pioneering days and displays on the natural history of Georgian Bay. Open Victoria Day to Thanksgiving Day at weekends and in Jul. and Aug. daily.
★★Bruce Island National Park	The northern tip of the Bruce Peninsula, recently designated a National Park, has bizarre limestone formations and eroded rock pillars, very rare orchids and all kinds of wildlife, but especially amphibians. It is accessible from a network of footpaths
★Fathom Five National Marine Park	Fathom Five National Marine Park north of Tobermory is the site of more than a dozen shipwrecks, of which some are heavily overgrown. These, together with the extraordinarily clear waters, make the Marine Park a Mecca for divers and underwater photography. Another most unusual attraction is the so-called Flowerpot, a rock pillar in the shape of a huge vase (excursion boats from Tobermory).
Manitoulin Island	Between the beginning of May and mid-October a ferry runs twice daily from Tobermory to nearby Manitoulin Island, close north. The island is a popular holiday destination with attractive beaches, a golf course and excellent canoeing.
	Among sights worth visiting are the Assiginack Museum (of regional history), St Paul's Anglican Church (1845), the Manitoulin Roller Mills (built in 1883 but now a memorial to technology), and the steam ship S.S. "Norisle", a freight and passenger vessel in service from 1946 to 1974. Burns Wharf Theatre, likewise built in 1883, puts on a programme of entertaining plays during the summer months.

★Glace Bay

Province: Nova Scotia. Population: 20,000

History	The busy town of Glace Bay is situated on a north-east facing promontory of Cap Breton Island. In earlier times soldiers from the nearby French Fort Louisbourg mined coal here and the name probably comes from the ice (Fr. "glace") that the Louisbourg soldiers found in the bay in winter. The hill on which the town was built contained vast coal deposits, mined by the French since 1720. In the 19th c. when iron was discovered in neighbouring Newfoundland further north, heavy industry quickly became established. Glace Bay flourished and many European emigrants arrived in the area. Nor did the town's growth grind to a halt

when the coal ran out in the 1950s. A State programme helped to set up new industries, and rising oil prices could make the liquefaction of coal a profitable proposition here also.

The Museum at Quarry Point (follow the signs!) shows how coal orig-inated, as well as demonstrating old and new coal mining methods. A tour of a mine is particularly impressive. Old miners graphically illus-trate life at the coal seams.

★Cape Breton
Miners Museum

Next to the museum is a reconstruction of miners' quarters in the second half of the 19th c. The coal company's shop impressively illus-trates how dependent the miners were.

★Glacier National Park

G 7

Province: British Columbia
Area:Glacier National Park 1350 sq. km (521 sq. mi.), Mount Revelstoke National Park 263 sq. km (102 sq. mi.)

The Superintendent, Glacier & Mount Revelstoke National Parks, PO Box 350, Revelstoke, BC V0E 2S0; tel. (250) 8377500. Information Centre at Rogers Pass (open Jul.–Labour Day only, 8am–8pm)

Information

Road:
TransCanada Highway 1 (Golden–Rogers Pass–Revelstoke) passes through Glacier National Park and skirts the edge of Mount Revelstoke National Park.

Access

Rail:
"The Canadian", VIA Rail's transcontinental express (Toronto–Edmonton–Vancouver); or "The Rocky Mountaineer" tourist train (Vancouver–Kamloops–Jasper, stopping at Revelstoke).

Glacier National Park, very scenic and a great favourite with climbers, and Mount Revelstoke National Park, a few miles further west, lie in one of Canada's most inhospitable mountainous regions, the almost inac-cessible northern Selkirk Range of the Columbia Mountains. These run parallel to the Rockies, with lots of jagged peaks, steep descents and narrow valleys cut deep into the rock, to the west of the Rocky Mountain rift valley. The wet west winds from the Pacific result in high levels of precipitation on the western flank of the Columbia Mountains which are over 3,000 m (9846 ft) high. It rains almost every day, even in summer, and snows almost every day in winter – the weather station on Mount Fidelity has in fact measured 23 m (75 ft) of snow in a year. These con-siderable snows feed more than 400 glaciers in and around Glacier National Park. Over 12½ per cent of the park is permanently covered in ice and snow and the roads are very prone to avalanches. At lower levels, up to about 1300 m (4267 ft), there are real "Columbia type" rain forests with some enormous old trees – western red cedars, hemlock firs – with groundcover of ferns and the densest of undergrowth.

The eastern flank, on the other hand, starved of rain, has a dry, conti-nental climate.

Both parks are home to mountain goat, caribou, and golden eagle, and the scrub in the wake of avalanches is the haunt of black and grizzly bear.

Even the Indians fought shy of the Selkirk mountains, on account of their terrain, climate, avalanches, lack of game and almost impenetrable veg-etation, and they were only really explored when the need to build the railway became apparent. It was not until 1881, when Major A. B. Rogers discovered the 1327 m (4355 ft) high pass that bears his name, that the barrier of the Selkirk Mountains could finally be overcome.

History

When the Canadian Pacific Railway went through the pass in 1885, the first Canadian trans-continental railway line was complete, and tourists

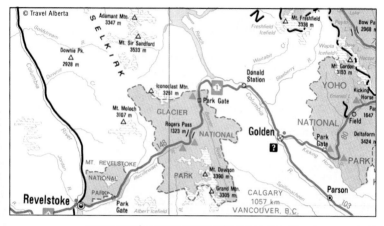

came to see the remote mountain landscape. The railroad company built four hotels along the line.

One of these was Glacier House, on the Illecillewaet Glacier, a Grand Hotel that by 1900 was attracting guests and climbers from all over the world – two Swiss mountain guides had been taken on in 1899 for visitors to the "Canadian Alps".

Avalanches

When, despite avalanche barriers and galleries, 62 railway workers lost their lives in an avalanche in 1910, it was decided to cut the 8 km (5 mi.)-long Connaught Tunnel through Mount MacDonald, thus cutting off the world-famous Glacier House from the railway. Since few guests were prepared to undertake the long journey in horse-drawn carriages, the hotel was closed in 1925 and demolished soon afterwards. Today this elegant establishment is commemorated by a memorial tablet at the Illecillewaet campsite.

In 1962 part of the new TransCanada Highway was built on the old railway route over the Rogers Pass – too late for Glacier House.

The Canadian government made 76 sq. km (29 sq. mi.) of this spectacular alpine landscape a national park as early as 1886 and Glacier National Park in 1930. The beauties of Mount Revelstoke's scenery inspired the creation of Mount Revelstoke National Park in 1912, and in 1927 the Prince of Wales opened the Summit Road, leading to the top of Mount Revelstoke, with its breathtaking views.

★Glacier National Park

A 50 km (31 mi.) section of the TransCanada Highway runs through Glacier National Park, providing easy access to trails such as the Loop Brook Interpretive Trail (round trail 6 km (3½ mi.) west of Rogers Pass, 1 hour's walking) with several good views and interpretive panels about the old railway route over the pass. The Illecillewaet campsite also serves as a starting point for the Avalanche Crest Trail (steep climb, 3 hours; magnificent view from the ridge), the Great Glacier Trail (2–3 hours, climb to the head of the Illecillewaet Glacier) or the Glacier Crest Trail (several hours' climb, 800–1000 m (2600–3300 ft) difference in height; good view of the Illecillewaet and Asuikan Glaciers).

As the Glacier National Park is "bear country", many walkers fix small bells to their rucksacks to warn the bears of their approach.

Rogers Pass

The visitors' centre at Rogers Pass (1327 m (4355 ft)) is in a building like the old avalanche galleries (also accommodation, restaurant and filling station). The centre has models showing the history of the railway as well as maps and information about the national park. Open Jun./Oct. daily

8am–8pm; Apr./May daily 9am–4pm, and at other times Mon.–Fri. only 9am–4pm.

Anyone wishing to hike or climb in the mountains, explore caves, or walk on glaciers, must register with the Ranger Station opposite.

The Abandoned Rails Interpretive Trail is about an hour's walk along a small section of the old railway line to several old avalanche galleries. Interpretive panels with historic photographs provide information.

From Revelstoke (435 m (1428 ft); pop. 9000), the scenic Summit Road, 26 km (16 mi.) long and passable only in summer, winds its way to the summit of Mount Revelstoke (1936 m (6354 ft)). The alpine-like plateau on the western edge of the Selkirk Mountains is especially worth visiting for its wild flowers in summer.

★Mount Revelstoke National Park

From the summit there is a breathtaking view across the broad Columbia River valley and the mountain peaks of the Monashee Range in the west, some of them still unnamed.

Various trails branch off from the road, leading to the three mountain lakes, Eva Lake, Miller Lake and Upper Jade Lake – several hours of very strenuous hiking. Apart from Mount Revelstoke itself, the rest of the National Park, with the Clachnacudainn Icefield, is not easy to reach. The TransCanada Highway, which follows the Illecillewaet River valley, only skirts its southern edge.

The Giant Cedars Interpretive Trail in the Revelstoke National Park, is a boardwalk through what is still a well-preserved section of typical "Columbia Forest," cool-temperate rain forest, with giant red cedars (highly recommended).

Giant Cedars

Golden

G 7

Province: British Columbia
Population: 4000

Golden Chamber of Commerce, 500 10th Avenue N, Golden, BC V0A 1H0; tel. (250) 3447125

Information

Golden (790 m (2593 ft)), the famous holiday and winter-sports resort at the confluence of the Columbia and Kicking Horse rivers, is the gateway to the magnificent National Parks of the Canadian Rocky Mountains.

Amid the jagged peaks of the Selkirk Mountains and the Rockies, Golden is the starting point for tours into largely unspoilt wild mountain regions, where visitors can go hiking, mountain-climbing and tour the Mummery Icefield glacier. There is whitewater rafting on the Kicking Horse River and canoeing on the Columbia and Blackberry rivers, as well as golf, riding (several guest ranches), fishing and big-game hunting, plus "Flightseeing" tours, which can also be booked.

Activities

The "Golden Triangle" cycling tour is very popular, from Golden, through Radium Hot Springs into Banff National Park, and back through Lake Louise to Golden again (320 km (199 mi.)).

The Rodeo on Labour Day every year is a great attraction.

The new Whitetooth Ski Area, on the slopes of the Purcell Mountains southwest of the town, was opened in 1987. With a descent of 526 m (1726 ft), it has eight ski-runs, ski lifts (usually weekends only), heliskiing and snow-mobiles.

Golden, which dates from the building of the railroad, now mainly lives from tourism, but also has a timber industry and a Canadian Pacific Railway repair shop.

History

The old town centre south of the Kicking Horse River has been made more attractive by the restoration of stores and houses in the early 1980s.

Grasslands National Park

Museum	The small Golden & District Museum in the old schoolhouse (11th Ave./14th St, gives the history of the town and tells how the first Swiss mountain guides helped to open up the surrounding mountain areas. Open Jul.–Labour Day, daily 9am–5pm.
Edelweiss	Edelweiss, above Golden to the north, has houses built by the Swiss guides at the turn of the century.
TransCanada Highway	From Golden, the TransCanada Highway follows the Kicking Horse River into the Rocky Mountains to Kicking Horse Pass (72 km (45 mi.)) passing through Yoho National Park (see entry).

★Grasslands National Park   H 9

	Province: Saskatchewan Area: 907 sq. km (350 sq. mi.)
Information	Grasslands National Park PO Box 150, Val Marie, SK S0N 2T0; tel. (306) 2982257
Access	Grasslands National Park is best reached from Swift Current, at the intersection of Saskatchewan Highway 4 and TransCanada Highway 1. Head south from Swift Current to arrive eventually at the western edge of the reserve.
Natural features	The beauty, grandeur and solitude of the Great Plains is to be found in the recently designated Grasslands National Park between Val Marie and Killdeer. Open all year, this virtually untouched landscape is unique in its wild beauty.
Climate	Its harsh climate has helped to preserve this part of the plains. A few

In Grasslands National Park (Saskatchewan)

people came here in the early days of prairie settlement, but were unable to bear the conditions for long, since when Grasslands has been used for virtually nothing but grazing.

This area has a history to it, despite its poor climate. Prairie Indians roamed here in search of buffalo, as the rock drawings and tepee rings show. It was also a favourite hunting-ground of the Métis from the early Red River settlements.

The Grasslands are home to many different creatures. Frenchman River Valley has antelope, hawks, eagles, reptiles (including many rattlesnakes) and packs of prairie dogs.

South of Val Marie is the Prairie Dog Town Nature Reserve, set up by the Saskatchewan Natural History Society.

Other attractions include the Killdeer Badlands, Sinking Hill and historical trails from the pre-settlement period.
    As the park is still being developed, permits are issued by the Administration Office in Val Marie, which is also still quite short of recreational facilities.

Great Bear Lake

D 6/7

Administrative Unit: Northwest Territories
Altitude: 156 m (512 ft). Area: 31,153 sq. km (12,025 sq. mi.)

Northern Frontier Regional Visitor Centre, 4807 49th Street, Yellowknife, NT X1A 3T5; tel. (867) 8733131

The eighth largest lake in the world, Great Bear Lake is 240 km (149 mi.) long and 400 km (249 mi.) across. It is covered with ice for eight months of the year, often as late as July. It has an outflow via the 120 km (75 mi.) Great Bear River to the Mackenzie River (see entry). It has an all-year-round population of only 500 inhabitants, most of them around Fort Franklin.

The shores of Great Bear Lake are rich in wildlife, martens are particularly numerous. The shores are roamed by grizzly bears in summer, and the pinewoods are the haunt of elk in winter.
    Great Bear Lake has achieved more angling records than any other lake in North America. It is especially famous for its trout, and the world's biggest trout, weighing up to 65 pounds, have been caught here, as well as the top-weight grayling and whitefish. Arctic char can be found in the nearby Tree River which can be reached from Plummers Great Bear Lodge.
    For a fishing tour of Great Bear Lake, hire a guide in Fort Franklin.

The waters of Great Bear Lake are ecologically extremely sensitive. Its lake trout take at least 15 years, and in some cases as many as 26 years, to reach sexual maturity, and they also only spawn once every 2 to 3 years. This means that stocks can soon become endangered, as has happened several times in the past. Today, however, strict regulations are in force, applying to anglers as well, in order to conserve this incomparable resource.

Most of the 500 permanent population of Great Bear Lake live in Fort Franklin, depending mainly on fishing.

★Great Slave Lake

E 7–9

Administrative Unit: Northwest Territories
Altitude: 156 m (512 ft)
Area: 28,570 sq. km (11,028 sq. mi.)

Northern Frontier Regional Visitor Centre, 4807 49th Street, Yellowknife, NT X1A 3T5; tel. (867) 8733131

★Natural features	Great Slave Lake gets its name from the Slave Indians who used to live on its shores. Part of the Mackenzie river system (see entry), it is in the district of the same name and the fifth largest lake in North America, with a number of tributary lakes to the north-east and the south. The lake is more than 600 m (1970 ft) deep in places, reaching a length of up to 480 km (298 mi.) east to west, and 110 km (68 mi.) across at its widest part.
	It is covered with ice for eight months of the year. Its main source is the Slave River and it flows out into the Mackenzie River (see entry).
Settlement	Most settlement is at the mouths of the tributaries. Lead and zinc are also mined on the southern shore.
Recreation	Great Slave Lake is famous amongst anglers for its excellent trout and pike, while there are plenty of Arctic grayling in the tributaries.
	Spectacular sailing races are held on the lake, which also has some sandy beaches.
History	Great Slave Lake was discovered by Samuel Hearne in 1771. He was followed by Alexander Mackenzie (see Famous People) heading for the mouth of the river named after him, and by John Franklin. The gold prospectors who passed here on the way to Klondike in 1896–99 reported on the region's beauty, but nobody wanted to come here. It was not until 1930, when pitchblende was discovered on the lakeshore, that people got more interested in the area. The discovery of gold on Yellowknife Bay four years later led to a boom in Yellowknife (see entry).
	Fishing has gained in importance since the Second World War.

Sights

Fort Providence	See entry.
Mackenzie Bison Sanctuary	See Fort Providence.
Fort Resolution	Fort Resolution was built by the Hudson's Bay Company on Moose Deer Island in 1819, and transferred to its present site around 1822. It was an important centre, with lighters bringing goods from Fort McMurray up the Slave River. The trading post lies 5 km (3 mi.) south-west of the main estuary of Slave River. The large mission house and the school are no longer used.
Hay River	See entry

★★Gros Morne National Park   H 19

Province: Newfoundland
Area: about 1,800 sq. km (695 sq. mi.)

Information	Gros Morne National Park, PO Box 130, Rocky Harbour, NF A0K 4N0; tel. (709) 4582996
Natural features	Gros Morne National Park is undoubtedly one of the most impressive natural features in eastern Canada, a magnificent landscape of fiords and mountains, partly covered with dense forest, and with wildlife and plantlife adapted to cold conditions which are found scarcely anywhere else so far south.
	The slopes of the Gros Morne (French for "big bleak hill") end in a plateau at about 600 m (1970 ft), with cliffs dropping down to the deep fiords (750 m (2460 ft)) of the Gulf of St Lawrence.
Geology	The park clearly shows the results of 400 million years of continental

In the Gros Morne National Park

drift followed by successive ice ages which ended 12,000 years ago. The Long Range Mountains are amongst the oldest mountains on earth and have been shaped by advancing ice and the forces of erosion.

The difficult, 4 km (2½ mi.) rocky ascent to the summit of the Gros Morne Mountain (806 m (2645 ft)) by the James Callaghan Trail is worth making for the breathtaking view over the whole park and coastal towns below. This is a place to see caribou and snow hares. — **Trail**

The park offers rock-climbing, boating, swimming, camping and fishing. — **Leisure**

Route No. 431 from the park entrance at Wiltondale follows the south shore of the delightfully scenic Bonne Bay, alongside a deep fiord enclosed by the peaks of the Long Range Mountains. — **★Bonne Bay**

Route 431 runs through a hilly lake district to Glenburnie, from where there is a pleasant trip along the South Arm. — **Glenburnie**

It is worth making the detour to Trout River for the wonderful view over the coast and the plateau. — **Trout River**

Woody Point, one of the picturesque places on the west coast, is a good place to visit on the way back, since the scenery here is truly beautiful. — **★★Woody Point**

From here it is possible to take a 15-minute ferry trip to Norris Point, and return to Route No. 430 in Rocky Harbour by a different route. This was where the Dorset Culture of the Inuit once flourished, and their artefacts, along with those of other pre-European cultures dating back to 2500 BC, have been found in the coastal regions of the National Park. — **Norris Point**

The drive from Norris Point to Rocky Harbour affords splendid views over Bonne Bay. Like its neighbour Neddy Harbour, Rocky Harbour was — Harbours named after one of the earliest pioneers. It is in a scenic setting at the entrance to the bay, surrounded by cliffs.

★East Arm Fiord
Route No. 430 from Wiltondale to Rocky Harbour on East Arm Fiord is another beautiful road. After Baker's Brook there is a lovely stretch along the coast, with views of the mountains around Bonne Bay to the south.

Lobster Cove Head
The sealife exhibition in the restored lighthouse-keeper's house at nearby Lobster Cove Head is worth seeing. Below the lighthouse, there are seawater pools full of sea urchins, starfish and sea snails.

Sally's Cove
Route 430 now crosses the higher western coastal plain to Green Point campsite, a few miles from Sally's Cove.

★★Western Brook
The Western Brook gorge, cutting through the Long Range Mountains, is one of the most spectacular sights in North America. It is 200 m (656 ft) deep, with steep faces towering as high as 600 m (197 ft) on either side, and an 8 km (5 mi.) circular trail on a wooden walk-way leads through magnificent forests and marshy meadows to the edge of the "Pond" the central part of which can only be reached by boat. Along the 14 km (8½ mi.) trail to the end of the pond there are waterfalls plummeting 600 m (1970 ft) from the plateau. (Tours can be booked in the park information centre.)

St Paul's
The road continues along the coast through St Paul's, a fishing village huddled around the entrance to a very impressive deep fiord.
   Swimming in the Gulf of St Lawrence is not to be recommended, since the temperatures off the beaches of Shallow Bay (campsite) and Western Brook scarcely rise above 15°C (47°F).
   Black bear, moose, otter, beaver, caribou, bald eagles, sea eagles, ospreys, snow grouse, and snow hares can all be seen along the local trails.

Cow Head
The Tête de Vache Museum at Cow Head is worth a visit. It is a local museum illustrating daily life in the early 20th c.

★★Halifax   J 18

Province: Nova Scotia
Population: 114,000 (Metropolitan Area: 330,000)

Information
Nova Scotia Department of Tourism & Culture, PO Box 456, Halifax, NS B3J 2R5; tel. (902) 4245000, fax. (902) 4242668

Natural features
Halifax, the capital of Nova Scotia (New Scotland), is on a bay cut deeply into the Atlantic coastline, and has one of the most beautiful natural harbours in the world, with docks and piers starting at the point where the 7 km (4½ mi.)-long outer bay narrows. The 5 × 2½ km (3 × 1½ mi.) inner harbour, known as the Bedford Basin, is very deep and sheltered by the peninsula on which the city is built. Despite the skyscrapers of more recent times, the peninsula is still dominated by a hill topped by a star-shaped citadel. Halifax owes its existence to these two factors – its natural harbour and its citadel.

History
Halifax was founded in July 1749 when Edward Cornwallis and a number of settlers built a garrison here. The idea of a stronghold on this natural harbour was not new, and the French had considered it after they lost the mainland of Nova Scotia in 1713 before opting for Louisbourg on Cape Breton instead. Louisbourg was the real reason for the building of Halifax, which was intended to act as its strategic counterpoint after the French fortress had been returned to the French following capture by the British in 1744.

Military base
Halifax was a thus a garrison from the outset, full of soldiers in the citadel and other military buildings, and of British sailors from the naval

The famous clock-tower of Halifax

vessels always in the harbour. This military presence made its mark on the city – from the balls and assemblies held by the naval and army officers, to the countless brothels round the harbour and below the citadel. Even justice was meted out according to martial law, and it was more than a hundred years before the civilians in Halifax had a say in how their community was run.

Royal princes

Halifax offered a home to two unruly sons of King George III when he more or less banished them from England. The future King William IV celebrated his 21st birthday with a wild party in the port, and passed many a night in the arms of Frances Wentworth, later to become the wife of the Governor.

His brother, Prince Edward, the Duke of Kent and future father of Queen Victoria, lived for six years in Halifax as Commander of the Nova Scotia forces. During that time he spent a fortune on fortifying the city, and made Halifax part of the famous British defensive square – Britain, Gibraltar, Bermuda and now Halifax. He was a strict disciplinarian, and would have his men whipped or even hanged for minor offences. But he also created the first telegraph system in North America, making it possible for him to issue orders to his men from Annapolis Royal (on the other side of the peninsula) or from his love-nest on the Bedford Basin, where his mistress, the beautiful Julie St Laurent, lived.

Halifax explosion

The history of Halifax was not always so colourful. However, periods of prosperity often coincided with times of war, while peacetime often brought economic depression. The Napoleonic Wars, the American Civil War and, finally, the First and Second World Wars were times of major military activity in Halifax, and of burgeoning wealth as well as great tragedy. During both World Wars Halifax was a collection point for convoys which were supposed to enable shipping to cross the Atlantic in greater safety, and protect themselves against attack from German U-

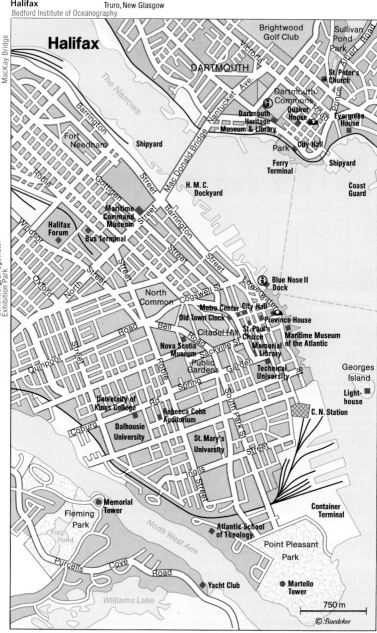

Halifax
Bedford Institute of Oceanography

Truro, New Glasgow

Halifax

MacKay Bridge

The Narrows

Brightwood
Golf Club

Sullivan
Pond
Park

Victoria

DARTMOUTH

St. Peter's
Church

Barrington

Prince

Albert Road

Fort
Needham

Gottingen

Shipyard

Nantucket Ave.

Dartmouth
Commons

Quaker
House

Evergreen
House

Robie

Street

MacDonald Bridge

Dartmouth
Heritage
Museum & Library

City Hall

Park

Barrington

Ferry
Terminal

Shipyard

H. M. C.
Dockyard

Coast
Guard

Windsor

Halifax
Forum

Maritime
Command
Museum

Street

Bus Terminal

Street

Barrington

Street

Lowerwater

Blue Nose II
Dock

Oxford

North

Street

Street

North
Common

Cogswell St.

Metro Center

City Hall

Province House

Lunenburg, Bridgewater
Exhibition Park

Quinpool

Road

Bell

Road

Robie

Old Town Clock

Citadel Hill

Nova Scotia
Museum

Sackville St.

St. Paul's
Church

Memorial
Library

Maritime Museum
of the Atlantic

Georges
Island

University of
Kings College

Rd.

Public
Gardens

Spring

Garden

Technical
University

Light-
house

Coburg

Rebecca Cohn
Auditorium

South Park St.

C. N. Station

Dalhousie
University

St. Mary's
University

Street

Inglis

Street

Container
Terminal

Memorial
Tower

Fleming
Park

Frag
Pond

North West Arm

Atlantic School
of Theology

Point Pleasant
Park

Purcells

Cove

Road

Yacht Club

Martello
Tower

Williams Lake

750 m

©Baedeker

236

boats. In 1917 the French munition ship "Mont-Blanc", which had arrived to join one such convoy, collided with the Belgian "Imo", causing the world's worst explosion prior to the dropping of the atom bomb on Hiroshima in 1945. The whole of the northern end of Halifax was razed to the ground, and port and rail installations were destroyed. The casualties included 1400 people killed outright, several hundred more who died later, about 9000 injured and 200 blinded. Windows were shattered as far away as Truro, some 100 km (62 mi.) distant. The explosion was heard within a radius of 160 km (100 mi.). All that was left of the "Mont-Blanc" was a cannon in Albro Lake behind Dartmouth and a fragment of the anchor, which landed in the forest over 3 km (2 mi.) away (the ship's crew survived, however, having left the ship in good time). There are still people in Halifax today drawing pensions for the injuries they sustained at the time.

Halifax is not just the capital of Nova Scotia, it is also the commercial hub of Canada's Maritime provinces, as well as being an important centre for research with no fewer than six universities and colleges. It continues to have a strong military presence, although the soldiers are no longer in the citadel. Halifax is the Atlantic base of the Canadian navy, with large dockyards and a research centre (the latter in Dartmouth, Halifax's twin town on the other side of the bay, connected to it by two bridges). | Importance

The port of Halifax can turn around more than 16 million tonnes a year, and is particularly busy in winter when the St Lawrence Seaway is closed. It has an enormous container port and auto-port, as well as ship-building and repair dockyards. | Port

Important dates in Halifax's annual calendar of events are July 24th, or Natal Day, when Halifax celebrates its birthday, mid-August, when the Nova Scotia Festival of the Arts takes place, and the end of September, date of the Joseph Howe Festival. | Events

Sights

The Old Town Clock, which has become the symbol of Halifax, was originally commissioned by Prince Edward in 1803. It has four clock-faces and chimes, and is an enduring memorial to the punctuality of that strict disciplinarian. Open: daily 9am to 5pm, and until 8pm in summer. There are guided tours and a snack bar. | ★★Old Town Clock

The hill on which the citadel stands (National Historic Park) is in downtown Halifax, rather like Mont-Royal in Montréal. The top of what was a precipitous, tree-covered hill was levelled off to build the garrison which has been part of the townscape since the 18th c. | ★★Halifax Citadel

Easily reached by car from the city centre along Citadel Road, the Citadel has excellent views of the city, the harbour, Dartmouth, little George Island and the Angus McDonald suspension bridge. | Citadel Road

Three citadels stood here before the foundation stone for the present star-shaped construction was laid in 1828 on the order of the Duke of Wellington. The entrance is by a bridge over a wide, dry moat. Infantry and artillery drills are re-enacted in summer on the parade ground in the centre. Visitors can walk along the top of the earthworks and see the cannons that were the citadel's main means of defence. They can also go through a tunnel under the moat, marvel at the mighty walls, and look at the cannon-proof outer defences. This outer wall also contains a musketeers' gallery for shooting at anyone who managed to get as far as the moat. | History

This is an excellent audio-visual account of the turbulent history of Halifax and its fortifications. | "Tides of History"

237

Halifax

Army museum

Housed in the casements this museum has a number of interesting models from the Halifax region and a collection of weapons, uniforms and decorations.

Other exhibitions

There is an exhibition in the old Powder magazine, with exhibits about communication methods and the construction of the Citadel. A replica of the defence casement and a garrison cell can also be seen.

Harbourfront

The harbourfront area on either side of Lower Water Street between Duke Street and the Cogswell intersection has been refurbished as "Historic Properties", an attractive pedestrian precinct containing restored 19th c. stone warehouses and old wharf buildings made into bright shops and artists' studios, restaurants and taverns with terraces overlooking the harbour. The roads are closed to normal traffic. The square between two warehouses has been roofed over to make an equally attractive mall; there are sightseeing cruises round the harbour, some of them on sailing ships.

Harbour cruises

Depart from Privateers' Wharf, daily from June to mid-October (duration: 2 hours).

"Haligonian III"

The best cruise of the harbour and the North West Arm is on the "Haligonian III". An interesting commentary describes such features as the Halifax shipyards, where 7000 ships were repaired during the Second World War, the vast naval docks, with destroyers, submarines, etc., the National Harbour Board's loading station with a gigantic grain-conveyor (busiest in winter when the St Lawrence Seaway is closed to shipping), and the container terminal, where immense cranes are at work, loading and unloading the container vessels.

This cruise also takes in Mount Pleasant and the North West Arm, a beautiful inlet, lined with yacht clubs and the waterfront homes of the rich – a contrast to the dockyards.

★Maritime Museum of the Atlantic

The nearby Maritime Museum of the Atlantic has a view over Halifax harbour. It contains a selection of small craft, model ships, photographs and exhibits of maritime history. The restored ship's cabin housed in one of the warehouses, is of particular interest, giving a survey of the tools used by sailors. Other exhibitions are devoted to the age of large sailing ships and to steamships. Open daily, except in the winter holidays.

CSS "Acadia"

The survey vessel "Acadia", berthed at the museum wharf, was built for the Canadian hydrographic service in 1913. It is open to visitors in the summer.

"Bluenose II"

The "Bluenose II" is sometimes here as well. This was the winner of the International Fishing Trophy in 1921, which it held for the whole of its career, before being taken out of service in 1963 to act as a good will ambassador for Nova Scotia. In summer, when not on a visit to foreign ports, it does duty as a harbour sight-seeing schooner (2-hour cruises three times daily except for Monday, July/August).

★Province House

This Georgian sandstone building (main entrance on Hollis Street), completed in 1819, is the seat of Nova Scotia's Parliament, in existence since 1758. The guided tour includes the "Red Chamber" where the Council used to meet. The two portraits are of Caroline von Anspach, wife of King George II, and of her father-in-law, King George I, whose portrait was sent over from England in 1820 in mistake for that of his son. The tour also takes in the parliament chamber and the library which, with its two grand staircases, was once the Supreme Court of Nova Scotia. This is where, in 1835, Joseph Howe defended himself against the charge of defamation. His acquittal is regarded as the beginning of a free press in Nova Scotia. He later went into politics and led the campaign against confederation, but ultimately joined the dominion government in Ottawa.

The last room on the tour has two sculptures of headless hawks. They were beheaded at the height of anti-American feeling in the 1840s because they looked too much like the American eagle! Tours last half an hour and take place daily except Saturdays and Sundays and winter holidays.

This lovely square, bordered by the City Hall at one end and by St Paul's Anglican Church – a half-timbered building dating back to 1750 and the oldest Protestant church in Canada – at the other, was the centre of Halifax from the very beginning. This was where military drills and parades took place.

★Grand Parade

This museum, with its entrance on Summer Street, gives a full account of the natural history of the province, including particularly impressive natural history and sealife dioramas (including whales and sharks). The museum also has exhibits about past history and social life.

★Nova Scotia Museum

The first sight to greet the visitor is a restored mail-coach, used on the Yarmouth–Tusket line in the late 19th c. There are also exhibits about the Micmac Indians and furnishings of the first European immigrants. The museum also maintains various historic buildings scattered over the entire province. Open daily except Mon. and winter holidays.

Point Pleasant Park is closed to vehicles; these can be parked on Point Pleasant Drive, Tower Road, and near the container station.

★Point Pleasant Park

There are magnificent views from this beautiful park, situated on the southernmost point of the Halifax peninsula, over Halifax harbour and the North West Arm. This is also the best place to watch "Bluenose II" cruising in the harbour under full sail.

There are plenty of footpaths and trails, as well as excellent picnic sites. Intrepid bathers can also take the plunge here.

For a long time this was a military no-go area, full of dugouts and fortifications, some of which can still be seen.

This round stone tower was built by Prince Edward in 1796. It was the first of its kind in North America, the prototype "Martello Tower". Prince Edward adapted the shape of a similar structure on the island of Corsica which had proved virtually impregnable. The basic idea was to combine soldiers' accommodation, a store-house and cannon mountings in a unit capable of defending itself, surrounded by immensely thick stone walls, with access only by a retractable ladder to the first floor. Canada subsequently had a great many of these towers which became redundant from about 1870 with the advent of steam engines, metal hulls and improved ship's artillery.

Prince of Wales Martello Tower

The Prince of Wales Tower, named by Edward after his brother who was to become King George IV, was built to keep guard over Halifax harbour – a fact not immediately obvious today, because of the tall trees that have grown up around it. Visitors can look at the powder magazines and the gun emplacements on the roof. Open mid-Jun. to Labour Day daily.

This 7 ha (17 acre) park was opened to the public in 1867, and is a good example of Victorian horticulture, with an ornamental bandstand, fountains, statues and formal flower-beds. Open May to Oct., daily 8am till dusk.

Public gardens

About 40 km (25 mi.) to the northwest, on Mt Uniacke, in a beautiful setting in a park near a lake, stands this fine example of colonial architecture with a portico over two storeys high. It was built between 1813 and 1815 by Richard Uniacke, Nova Scotia's Public Prosecutor from 1797 to 1830.

★**Uniacke House**

Inside it looks exactly as it did in 1815 when furnished by the Uniacke family. Open mid-May to mid-Oct. daily 9am to 5pm.

The first defence works outside Halifax are about 10 km (6 mi.) away at Sandwich Point. They were built in 1793 and substantially reinforced on the orders of Prince Edward, who had a tower built as part of his telegraph signalling system. The fort was later extensively renovated and

★**York Redoubt**

named after Edward's brother, the Duke of York. It remained in military use until the Second World War, when it was the centre for co-ordinating defence of the harbour and city against possible German attack.

This command post, a labyrinth of underground passages below the tower, is open to visitors. The tower itself, with displays on Halifax's fortifications, has a splendid view of the harbour on a clear day.

Along the walls of the redoubt there are 250 mm (10 inch) front-loader cannons, and the adjoining buildings have such items on show as a furnace for heating up cannon-balls, and transport to take the hot cannon-balls to the cannons (cannon-balls were only heated for smooth-bore cannons). Open mid-Jun. to Labour Day 9am to 6pm; park open all year round.

★**Peggy's Cove** 43 km (27 mi.) south-west of Halifax lies Peggy's Cove, a particularly delightful little bay on the rugged Atlantic coast. Colourful houses and an old lighthouse give the pretty spot a special atmosphere. Peggy's Cove achieved sad notoriety in September 1998, when a Swissair plane crashed into the sea killing 229 people.

★★Hamilton J 15

Province: Ontario. Population: 323,000

Information Greater Hamilton Visitor Information, 127 King Street E., Hamilton, ON L8L 1B1; tel. (905) 5462666

Location Located at the westernmost point of Lake Ontario, Hamilton is the third largest city in the province of Ontario and the main centre of the Canadian steel industry (Hamilton Steel Co., etc.). It owes its importance to its harbour, which lies on the shipping route from the Great Lakes to the Atlantic via the St Lawrence (see entry). Industries include engineering, instrument-making and chemicals. Hamilton has a technical university (with the first Canadian atomic-research reactor) and is the seat of a Catholic and an Anglican bishop. Its pleasant climate also makes it famous for its vineyards and its apricots.

History Hamilton is known to have been settled since the 1660s, but the city's foundation was actually in 1812. The modernisation of navigation and the completion of the Welland canal (see entry) meant that Hamilton became much more important, as raw materials from around the Great Lakes could be processed here at low cost. This was particularly true of iron and steel, which became a major industry very early on.

Sights

★**Hess Village** Hess Village, between Hess Street, George Street and Main Street, is the 19th c. quarter, with pretty restaurants, boutiques and some commercial art galleries.

Whitehern House Whitehern House (Jackson Street) is a Georgian mansion with a small garden that was the home of the McQuestern family (1840–1959), and has its original furnishings. The well-to-do McQuesterns were steel tycoons who lived in Hamilton from the early 19th c. Open daily 2pm–5pm (guided tours).

★**Hamilton Place** The city centre's main attraction is the ultra-modern cultural centre Hamilton Place, built in the 1970s, with a large auditorium seating 2200, and a studio theatre seating 400. This is home to the Hamilton Philharmonic Orchestra, and a venue for major dance and drama companies.

Art Gallery Hamilton's Art Gallery contains collections of 19th and 20th c. Canadian art, while showing temporary exhibitions as well. Open Tue.–Sun., 10am–6pm; tel. 5276610.

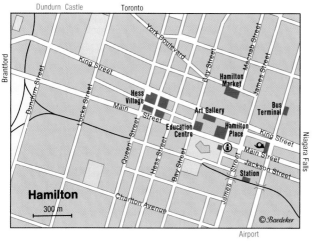

On York Boulevard there is one of the largest market halls in Ontario, selling local produce on Tuesdays and Thursdays.

Market

Dundurn Castle, the 25-room mansion of Sir Allan Napier MacNab, Prime Minister of Canada from 1854 to 1856, was built between 1832 and 1835 overlooking the harbour. Today it is a museum of military history and has a collection of 19th c. furniture.

★Dundurn Castle

The Canadian Football Hall of Fame, near the cultural centre portrays various aspects of this typical Canadian sport. Open Mon.–Fri., 11am–5pm, and Sun. also 11am–5pm in summer.

Canadian Football Hall of Fame

New City Hall has a mural by artist Franklin Arbuckle on the theme "A City and its People".

New City Hall

Outskirts

The Botanical Gardens (Plains Road) extends up over 1000 ha (2500 acres) on the western side of Lake Ontario, with an alpine garden, an arboretum, rose and lily gardens and gardening exhibitions and flower shows according to season. There is a garden centre and a cafeteria. Open daily 9am to sunset (information in visitors' centre; tel. 527–1158).

★★Botanical Gardens

A Victorian pumping station (900 Woodward Ave.) still equipped as it was in 1859 is furnished as a technical museum. Open Jun.–Sep. noon–5pm; Oct.–May 11am–4pm.

Technical museum

Surroundings

Some 32 km (20 mi.) west of Hamilton, at Rockton, there is a drive-through safari park with African and North American animals (including lions, tigers and elephants) plus, of course, some North American bison. Open mid-Apr.–mid-Oct., 9am–6pm.

Rockton

Burlington (population 117,000), a few miles north of Hamilton is in a delightful setting on the western shore of Lake Ontario. Places worth seeing include the Cultural Centre (425 Brock Ave.; open Tue.–Sun.), the

Burlington

Joseph Brant Museum (1240 N.Shore Blvd. E; open daily) with mementoes of the Mohawk leaders and other Indian artefacts, and the Village Square with its attractively restored old houses.

★Hay River   E 7

Administrative unit: Northwest Territories
Population: 4000

Information

Hay River Chamber of Commerce, PO Box 4291, Hay River, NT X0E 0R0; tel. (867) 8742565

Location

Hay River is one of the largest places in the Mackenzie District. On the southern bank of Great Slave Lake (see entry), it is the southernmost port on the Mackenzie river system (see entry). Hay River's strategic position earned it the title of "Centre of the North". Here freight (mainly building materials and fuel) destined for settlements along the Mackenzie River and in the Arctic was and continues to be transferred to barges. During the four to five-month summer season, the port is choc-a-bloc with barges, fishing boats and coastguard launches. Fish processing – white fish from the Great Slave Lake, also trout, pike etc. – is a long-established industry.

History

For thousands of years this was the home of the Slave and Dene Indians. The Hudson's Bay Company built the first trading post here in 1868, which rapidly became the main trans-shipment point for the north. But it wasn't until the Mackenzie region began to be opened up by road that the population really started to expand. A railway, the Eine Railroad, built for transporting ore, was only completed in 1964. Road building in the Mackenzie region also pushed ahead from Hay River. The discovery of oil and natural gas in the far north, a region in the opening up of which Hay River played an important role, brought further new development.

★Old town

The little wooden houses of the old town lie at the mouth of the Hay River, where the quays are piled high with supplies for despatch to distant settlements. This is also where the fishermen live, often returning home with rich catches from the Great Slave Lake or Hay and Mackenzie rivers.

New town

Devastating floods led to the building of a new town centre on higher ground, dominated by a 14-storey tower block awaiting a gas pipeline in the Mackenzie Valley.

Coast guard

Anyone wanting to find out more about the kind of situation that can arise on Great Slave Lake and along the MacKenzie River should arrange to visit the Hay River Coast Guard station.

Diamond Jenness School

The Diamond Jenness School, opposite the tower block, is an outstanding example of northern architecture. Named after an anthropologist who, around 1910, was the first to study northern native culture, its colour purple makes it the landmark of Hay River.

Hay River Indian Reserve

Hay River Indian Reserve, a few miles outside the town, centres on the old Hudson's Bay Company's trading post, where there are still a few old buildings, including a church.

★Hope   H 6

Information

Province: British Columbia. Population: 6500

Hope Chamber of Commerce, 919 Water Ave., Hope, BC V0X 1L0; tel. (604) 8692021

The township of Hope (42 m (138 ft)), amidst the often snowcapped Coastal Mountains, was originally a fort erected there in 1848/49 by the Hudson's Bay Company at the mouth of the Coquihalla River. The territory of the lower reaches of the Columbia River, the old route for the fur traders, was transferred to the USA with the Treaty of Oregon in 1846, and the Hudson's Bay Company was forced to find new ways into the interior. When gold was discovered on the Fraser River in 1858, a new town grew up next to the old trading post, which could now be reached by river steamers from Fort Langley (see entry). The first sawmills appeared, then in the 1870s silver deposits were found nearby and the first Waggon Road to New Westminster was built. The building of the railroad which started in the 1880s also acted as a boost to the whole region.

History

Nowadays the TransCanada Highway runs north from Hope through the Fraser River Canyon (see entry), and the wonderfully scenic Crowsnest Highway 3 (see entry) goes east. A 134 km (83 mi.) stretch of mountain and valley road takes in several mountain ranges, from Hope to the 1352 m (4437 ft) Allison Pass in Manning Provincial Park. Coquihalla Highway 5, opened in 1986/87, also starts here. This new, four-lane highway which provides a 90 km (56 mi.) shortcut to Kamloops (toll road), goes round the Fraser Canyon and acts as a relief road to the TransCanada Highway, taking much of the through traffic. Surrounded by lakes, rivers and mountains, Hope is a great place for outdoor pursuits as well as being the gateway to Manning Provincial Park, the Canadian continuation of the North Cascades National Park in the USA.

Road routes

Sights

Hope Museum, on the TransCanada Highway (919 Water St., with items from the days of the fur traders and the Cariboo gold-rush, is also where the Tourist Information Centre is located. Open May–Sep. daily 9am–5pm.

Hope Museum & Hope Travel InfoCentre

Christ Church, a few blocks down the street, is a wooden Anglican church dating from 1861 and one of the oldest churches in British Columbia; services are still held here.

Christ Church

Surroundings

The Hope Slide, just under 20 km (12 mi.) away, is where a landslide caused by an earthquake in 1965 buried a 3 km (2 mi.) stretch of the highway, filling in a lake in the Nicolum River valley as well. There is a plaque commemorating this natural disaster in a lay-by 55 m (180 ft) above the original road level.

Hope Slide

Manning Provincial Park, about 25 km (16 mi.) from Hope, was opened in 1941, and covers more than 714 sq. km (276 sq. mi.) of magnificent mountain scenery. It is characterised by jagged mountain peaks over 2000 m (6500 ft) high, deep valleys, and thickly wooded slopes, making it the northern continuation of the North Cascades National Park in the USA.

★Manning Provincial Park

To the west of the park, in the Cascades, lies the 326 sq. km (126 sq. mi.) Skagit Valley Provincial Recreation Area (drive to Ross Lake but from the TransCanada Highway). There are canoe trips on the Skagit River, and good hiking on the Skagit River Trail (30 km (19 mi.)), as well as horseback riding, fishing, hunting and, in winter, skiing.
  From the western park entrance, the highway first crosses the "Rhododendron Flats", which are at their best in mid-June when the wild rhododendrons are in bloom (20-minute round trip).

Skagit Valley

Manning Park Resort, 32 km (20 mi.) beyond the Allison Pass, has a

Manning Park Resort

motel, restaurant, riding stables, 190 km (118 mi.) of Wilderness Trails, and is relatively sure of snow in winter, with more than 30 km (19 mi.) of cross-country skiing trails, downhill skiing around the Gibson Pass, ski-lifts, snow-mobiles, etc. Information about the area can be obtained from the visitors' centre.

★Cascade Lookout

It is well worth driving up to Cascade Lookout with its magnificent view of the Similkameen Valley and the surrounding 2000 m (6500 ft) mountain peaks.

Hudson Bay   E/F 12–15

Hudson Bay, in north-east Canada, is the world's largest inland sea, extending between 63° and 51° latitude north. 1350 km (839 mi.) from north to south, and 830 km (516 mi.) across, it covers an area of 637,000 sq. km (395,830 sq. mi.) and has an average depth of 128 m (420 ft) and a maximum depth of 259 m (850 ft). Partly within the Arctic Circle, it connects with the Atlantic to the east by the Hudson Strait (60–240 km (37–150 mi.) across and about 800 km (500 mi.) long) and the Sea of Labrador, and with the Arctic Ocean to the north, by the Foxe Channel (150–300 km (93–186 mi.) across, about 300 km (186 mi.) long), the Foxe Basin and the Gulf of Boothia.

Landscape

Hudson Bay, around it the glacial elevations of the Canadian Shield with Pre-Cambrian gneiss and granite, has a hinterland with the typical, flat ground-moraine landscape of Arctic tundra, stretching to the northern timber line far to the south in the James Bay area. Baffin Island, a remainder of the crystalline mountains of the Canadian Shield, rises to heights of 2000 m (6500 ft) in the north.

The harshness of the terrain has so far made it difficult to produce accurate maps.

Climate

The climate is subpolar-continental. During the long winter, with temperatures as low as 60°C (76°F), Hudson Bay is covered with ice 1–2 m (3–6½ ft) thick. When there are strong north-westerly winds, the pack-ice can tower as high as 8 m (26 ft). During the brief summer, when temperatures can reach 20°C (52°F), the permafrost on land thaws down to depths of 60 m (197 ft), transforming the landscape into a broad, impassable bog.

The constant process of freezing then thawing has led to the formation of special phenomena such as pingos, mounds of earth formed through pressure from a layer of water trapped between newly frozen ice and underlying permafrost.

Wildlife

Although the growing season is generally less than five months, there is still an astounding variety of Arctic vegetation. In fact, more than 800 plant species have been identified, including mosses, lichens, ferns, and flowers such as polar poppies, purple saxifrage, arctic campanulas and arctic lupins. However, the harsh climate also means there is less wildlife, although there are plenty of migratory birds and seals, as well as the polar bears that occasionally venture into the settlements in search of food. In summer the marshy landscape swarms with midges and flies. Hudson Bay has vast fish stocks, as yet largely untapped, and the occasional school of white Beluga whales.

History

Hudson Bay was discovered in 1610 by Henry Hudson (see Famous People) and later named after him. The first European to reach Hudson Bay overland was Pierre Esprit Radisson, in 1662, and the first trading post followed, at the mouth of the Rupert River, in 1668.

Population

The area around Hudson Bay is very sparsely populated. The biggest sector of the population is the Inuit, who have largely given up their traditional way of life as hunters, living from fishing and handicrafts in the few small trading posts along the coast.

The Hudson Bay region is rich in natural resources, but their exploitation and transport have been so seriously curtailed by the nature of the terrain and the harsh living conditions as to make their extraction uneconomical. The fact that this potentially good waterway freezes over brings shipping to a standstill from October to June. It was 1929 before what is still the only railway line was opened between Winnipeg (see entry) and Churchill (see entry), a newly created port for getting wheat out of the Canadian prairie provinces. There are no roads that are passable all year round. The most important means of transport is currently by plane. The fur trade, and cod and salmon fishing are still of economic importance.

Economy

The oldest company still trading in North America, the Hudson's Bay Company can look back over a 300-year history. On May 2nd 1670, King Charles II granted a team of Englishmen led by his cousin, Prince Rupert of Bohemia, full mining and trading rights for the territories draining into Hudson Bay. The company thus acquired control of a territory of around 8 million sq. km (5 million sq. mi.), or 1/12 of the earth's surface, with rich mineral resources and fabulous fur-hunting grounds. The fur of the beaver, widespread here, was a sought-after luxury in Europe at that time, used for making beaver hats and other articles of clothing. The Hudson's Bay Company established a network of trading posts over the largely unexplored north of Canada, bases for the later settlement and development of the country. The English traders' almost total monopoly of the fur trade did not run into any serious competition until a century later, when the North West Company was founded in 1779. After a bitter struggle however, this new rival was forced into a merger in 1821. Nevertheless the changed technical, political and social circumstances meant the powerful company could no longer maintain its hegemony and, in 1870, it had to sell its land to the Canadian government. Other holdings, including the fur trading company, have been disposed of in recent decades. Nowadays the former fur traders own many big department stores throughout Canada and still employ over 38,000 people.

Hudson's Bay Company

See entry

Baie James

★★Hull

H 15

Province: Québec. Population: 63,000

Tourisme Ottawa – Hull, 103 rue Laurier, Hull, PQ J8X 3V8; tel. (819) 7782222

Information

Hull, which is a French-speaking city, stands on the banks of the Gatineau and Ottawa Rivers on the edge of the Outaouais (see entry), across the river from Ottawa. An important centre for the timber and paper industry, it also has a number of federal government departments, their buildings dominating the landscape, especially La Chaudière and the Place du Portage.

In recent years Hull city centre has been restructured into two core areas, linked by the Promenade de Portage, an ultra-modern administrative complex of six buildings for approximately 19,000 federal and provincial government officials.

Location

From Jacques-Cartier Park, there is a fine view over the Ottawa River to the Parliament building, the Rideau slopes and other major features of Ottawa.

View

The Gatineau area was traversed by the Indians long before the first European settlement. The first French explorers, such as Champlain, came here in 1613 and 1615, to be followed by woodsmen and other

History

adventurers in search of furs and engaged in setting up trading posts. Around 1800 the American Philemon Wright began farming here, using the slopes of the Chaudière, and founded a colony which he named Hull after his parents' birthplace in England. In 1806 he sent a consignment of timber by raft to Québec, and thus became the founder of a major industry. Some time later another American, Ezra Butler Eddy, made the town famous throughout the world with the matches he produced here.

★★Musée
Canadien des
Civilisations

This magnificent museum stands on the river bank opposite Ottawa's Parliament buildings. Its architect, Douglas Cardinal, wanted its flowing lines to call to mind the immensity and diversity of the Canadian landscape.

Open July–Labour
Day Tue.–Sun.
9am–6pm (Sun. to
5pm,Thu. to 9pm)

The Pavillon du Bouclier Canadien, to the left of the main entrance, holds the museum's offices, laboratories and storage for about 3,500,000 items. The exhibition rooms of the Pavillon du Glacier (total area 16,500 sq. m (6369 sq. ft)) are to the right of the entrance. There are also audio-visual displays illustrating the more than 240 different cultures found in Canada.

Grande Galerie

In the Grande Galerie, six wooden longhouses and their totem poles symbolise the culture of six Indian tribes on the Pacific.

Salle de la
Histoire

Here a thousand years of Canada's past history is brought to life in a succession of scenes of costumed figures from the period in question before a magnificent natural backdrop.

Musée des
Enfants

In this enchanting museum, children can play at discovering the world's remotest corners.

Ciné-Plus

The vast IMAX screen is seven stories high under an enormous dome, and shows special films that provide an unforgettable experience.

★★Gatineau

Gatineau Park, administered by the federal government, is a woodland and lakeland district in the hills of this part of the Canadian Shield alongside the River Gatineau, large areas of which are still primeval forest. Some places are set aside for outdoor activities such as camping, jogging, walking, riding, swimming, fishing, cycling and downhill and cross-country skiing.

Lac Mousseau

The official summer residence of the prime minister of Canada is on Lac Mousseau in the centre of the park.

Parc de Gatineau

© Baedeker

1 Amphitheatre
2 Mackenzie-King Estate
3 Mulvilhill Picnic Place
4 Dunlop Picnic Place
5 Etienne Brûlé Viewpoint
6 Champlain Viewpoint
7 Luskville Waterfalls
8 Fire tower
9 Lusk Cave
10 Viewpoint
11 Camping site
12 Landing-stage
13 Graham's Hill Picnic Place
14 Camping site
15 Church Hill Picnic Place
16 Boat rental; snack-bar
M Toll

The footpaths through the southern part of the park are an especially beautiful walk in the autumn, as the leaves change colours.

Autumn colours

The Belvédère Champlain, about 26 km (16 mi.) from the park entrance, provides a wonderful view over the Gatineau hills, a sharp contrast with the farmland in the Ottawa and Gatineau river valley.

★Belvédère Champlain

The country estate of former premier William Mackenzie-King can be found in the heart of the Gatineau mountains on the way to Kingsmere. The estate includes several small homes on a lakeshore, with period settings, and audio-visual aids to take the visitor back to the early years of this century.

Domaine Mackenzie-King

The main house is Moorside, where the visitor can have tea or a meal in the dining room, and see items from the Mackenzie-King days. The ruins in the park are from the Canadian Parliament building in Ottawa which burned down in 1916, and were put there by MacKenzie-King. Open mid-May–mid-Oct. daily 11am–6pm.

Moorside

The Moulin de Wakefield stands about 40 km (25 mi.) north of Hull (Highway 105) above the River Pêche just before it joins the Gatineau. Built in 1838 to grind corn, it has been restored to working order. Guided tours end of May–mid-Oct.).

Moulin de Wakefield

★★Icefields Parkway

G 7

Provinces: Alberta/British Columbia
Length: 230 km (143 mi.)
Driving time: at least 4 hours

Jasper National Park, PO Box 10, Jasper, AB T0E 1E0; tel. (403) 8526161
Banff National Park, PO Box 900, Banff, AB T0L 0C0; tel. (403) 7621550

Information

Icefields Parkway (Highway 93) crosses the northern part of Banff National Park and southern part of Jasper National Park, and forms a link between TransCanada Highway 1 and Yellowhead Highway 16. Unlike the busy TransCanada Highway, the Icefields Parkway is purely and simply a sightseeing route through magnificent high mountain scenery.

Tourist route

Between Lake Louise and Jasper the road follows a narrow valley running north–south for 230 km (143 mi.) between the glaciated peaks of the main range of the Rocky Mountains. Originally built as a project to create work during the Depression, the highway was extended and completed in 1960. It passes first along upper Bow Valley, and winds over Bow Pass (2068 m (6787 ft)) to the Mistaya and North Saskatchewan River valley, then over the Sunwapta Pass, only marginally lower at 2035 m (6679 ft), and close to the Columbia Icefield it reaches the Sunwapta/Athabasca River and Jasper. Frequent lay-bys and parking places provide opportunities to enjoy the breathtaking views and there are interpretive panels to fill in the background about the landscape and local history.

Bighorn sheep and mountain goats – down at the roadside or on the mountain tops – romantic waterfalls, the shimmering turquoise waters of mountain lakes, looming icefields and snowclad mountain peaks all make for a journey of infinite variety.

Bow Lake, 34 km (21 mi.) north of Lake Louise (see Banff), lies below the Crowfoot Glacier (shaped like a crow's foot and clearly visible from the road) and Bow Glacier. The lake's still, clear waters mirror the towering, snow-covered peaks of the continental divide. These glaciers form part of the great Waputik Icefield. Num-ti-jah Lodge, a little hotel on the shore of Bow Lake, built in 1939 by Jimmy Simpson, an early pioneer of mountain tourism, was the setting for many a Nelson Eddy movie in the 1950s. There are lovely walks along the lake to a waterfall at the foot of

Bow Lake

Angel Glacier

Athabasca Glacier

the Bow Glacier (half a day) or to Helen Lake and Catherine Lake at the Dolomite Pass to the east (whole day).

Bow Pass

At 2068 m (6787 ft) Bow Pass is the highest pass in the Banff National Park (see entry), and the watershed between the river systems of the North and South Saskatchewan River. A short branch road leads to the magnificent Peyto Lake viewpoint and there is another superb lookout point that can be reached on foot about a third of a mile further on. This is especially lovely in summer, when Bow Summit's mountain meadows are carpeted with wild flowers.

Peyto Lake

A longer and steeper path leads down for 2½ km (1½ mi.) to Peyto Lake, named after the mountain guide Bill Peyto, who began exploring the area in 1894 and took packhorses of supplies north over Bow Summit.

Mistaya Canyon

About 70 km (43 mi.) north of Lake Louise, a short path leads down from the car-park to the narrow, winding Mistaya Canyon ("mistaya" is Indian for "grizzly bear"), with its virtually vertical rockfaces and characteristic "pot-holes".

David Thompson Highway

After another 6 km (3½ mi.), the David Thompson Highway branches off towards the east where the North Saskatchewan River cuts north/south through the Rocky Mountains.

★Panther Falls

About 120 km (75 mi.) north of Lake Louise there is a path leading from the far end of the car park down to Nigel Creek and the awesome Panther Falls. These can be seen from above by taking the footpath from the top end of the car park.

Parker Ridge

About 4 km (2½ mi.) further north a winding path climbs 275 m (903 ft) from the car park up to Parker Ridge. From the top there is a magnificent view of the 11 km (7 mi.)-long Saskatchewan Glacier, the longest glacier

Picturesque Peyto Lake

tongue of the Columbia Icefield. Mountain goats can often be seen on the ridge. This is a particularly attractive area in summer when the wild flowers are in bloom.

The Sunwapta Pass (2035 m (6679 ft)) forms the watershed between the North Saskatchewan River which flows into the Hudson Bay and the Athabasca River which flows into the Beaufort Sea. It is also the border-line between Banff and Jasper National Park (see entries). **Sunwapta Pass**

The Columbia Icefield, the most important of the icefields from which the parkway gets its name, is close on 130 km (80 mi.) north of Lake Louise. Covering a total area of 389 sq. km (150 sq. mi.), with the sur-rounding glaciers, it is the biggest continuous icefield in the Rockies. On the main field, the ice is 600 m to 900 m (2000 to 3000 ft) thick in places. **★★Columbia Icefield**

From the Columbia Icefield, which lies on the continental divide, sev-eral hanging glaciers flow down the mountain, their tongues stretching deep into the valleys.

Mount Snowdome (3520 m (11,553 ft)) is the very apex of Canada, from where the melted snow and ice flow into three different oceans, the Pacific to the west, the Beaufort Sea to the north through the Athabasca River and Mackenzie River, and hence the Arctic, and through the Saskatchewan River into Hudson Bay, and thence the Atlantic. The enormous icefield – its size can only be appreciated from the air – is a relic of the immense glaciation in the Rocky Mountains during the ice age which shaped the present topography of the area. Over the last 300 years the individual tongues of the Columbia Icefield glaciers have retreated considerably.

In the Icefield Centre can be seen a model of the Columbia Icefield and a multi-vision slide show explains the development of the icefield and its individual glaciers. Open end of May–mid-Oct. daily 9am–5pm, and till 7pm in high summer. Icefield Centre

249

The world-famous Columbia Icefield

From the Icefield Centre there is an excellent view of the tongue of the 7 km (4½ mi.)-long Athabasca Glacier and the glaciated north wall of Mount Athabasca (3491 m (11,457 ft)). There is an even better view from the meadows above the Icefield Chalet (overnight accommodation), which is also a good starting point for several hikes in the mountains.

Snow Coach tours May–Sep. daily 9am–5pm

The guided tours by Snow Coach onto the surface of the Athabasca Glacier are a memorable experience. These robust coaches with four-wheel drive travel on part of the glacier. Guided walks on the glacier lasting several hours can also be booked (tel. 762–2241), but these chances to walk on ice which is about 400 years old are very popular, so it is necessary to book early.

Athabasca Glacier

Early in this century the tongue of the Athabasca Glacier still covered the whole valley, including where the highway runs today, so explorers and early travellers went over the nearby Wilcox Pass to reach Jasper.

After parking at Sunwapta Lake and climbing up to the debris-strewn tongue of the glacier, it is possible to see from the date-posts just how fast the ice has retreated, leaving clearly identifiable moraine deposits in its wake.

Sunwapta Falls

Just 180 km (112 mi.) north of Lake Louise, and 60 km (37 mi.) south of Jasper, a side-road leads to the Sunwapta Falls ("sunwapta" = rushing water) where the Sunwapta River abruptly changes course and cascades down into a ravine.

★Athabasca Falls

About 200 km (125 mi.) north of Lake Louise (and 33 km (20 mi.) south of Jasper) the Athabasca River plunges down over a solid rock of Pre-Cambrian quartz sandstone. By retrograde erosion the waterfall is steadily retreating leaving a narrow gorge which funnels masses of water into a seething maelstrom, especially when the snow melts in early summer.

A path with a bridge and various lookout points circles around the 22 m (72 ft) waterfalls and the gorge with its precipitous rockfaces.

Highway 93A, which used to be the main road to Jasper, branches off near the waterfalls and serves as an alternative route. It can be used to reach the approach roads to Mount Edith in the Cavell district (see Jasper), with the Angel Glacier and the Marmot Basin, very popular for skiing in winter.

Highway 93A

★Îles de la Madeleine

H 18

Province: Québec

Tourisme Îles de la Madeleine, PO Box 1028, Cap-aux-Meules, PQ G0B 1B0; tel. (418) 9862245
Internet: www.ilesdelamadeleine.com

Information

By air:
Flights from Charlottetown (PEI), Moncton (NB), Ville de Québec (PQ) and Montréal (PQ)

Access

By ferry:
Car ferries daily (except Thursdays) in summer from Souris (Prince Edward Island). Also two-day cruises from Montréal (likewise in summer).

The Îles de la Madeleine archipelago lies in the Gulf of St Lawrence, close on 300 km (186 mi.) from Gaspé and 120 km (75 mi.) from Prince Edward Island (see entry) and consists of twelve islands and a few small reefs. Their name goes back to Samuel de Champlain (see Famous People), who in 1629 entered "La Magdeleine" on his chart. Of the seven inhabited islands, six are joined together by a road running along a 90 km (56-mi.) strip of dunes.

★Topography

Coast of the Îles de la Madeleine

251

The Îles de la Madeleine are typically grayish-red sandstone, gypsum and other volcanic rock. The cliffs and rocks have been carved into fascinating shapes by erosion, and have disintegrated in parts to form broad, long sandy beaches.

The inhabitants of the Îles de la Madeleine, or the "Madelinots", are mainly descendants of the Acadians who settled here after 1755. About 14,000 people – French, Scottish, English and Irish – live here throughout the year, fishing and farming, and seal-hunting in March and April.

Sport and leisure

The islands are ideal for water-sports enthusiasts, birdwatchers and anyone who enjoys long walks in the dunes.

The best time for a visit is in August. Spring is less to be recommended because of the thick fogs.

Île du Havre aux Maisons

The Île du Havre aux Maisons, with its gentle, green hills, its winding paths and scattered houses is one of the archipelago's most beautiful islands. In the south of the island the Hydro-Québec Generating Company has set up a windmill park.

Cap Alrith

Cap Alrith is noted for its impressive offshore rock formations.

Île du Cap aux Meules

Half the people of the archipelago live on Île du Cap aux Meules, the source of all the islands' supplies. There is a wonderful view from the Butte du Vent over the surrounding islands and on a clear day it is possible to see as far as Cape Breton Island (see entry), nearly 100 km (62 mi.) away.

Near Etang-du-Nord the sea has created some particularly bizarre rock shapes.

From Cap-aux-Meules, a ferry crosses to Île d'Entrée, the only inhabited island not connected to the others.

Île du Havre-Albert

Île du Havre-Albert is the southernmost island in the archipelago and its little town has a Musée de la Mer. Open Mon.–Fri. 9am–6pm, Sat. and Sun. 10am–6pm.

★Inside Passage

F–H 3–6

Province: British Columbia
Ferry between Port Hardy (Vancouver Island) and Prince Rupert
Distance: 274 nautical miles (about 507 km (315 mi.))
Time taken: 15 hours

Information

BC Ferries, 1112 Fort Street, Victoria, BC V8V 4V2; tel. (250) 3863431, fax. (250) 3815452
Internet: www.bcferries.bc.ca

★Coastal waterway

The Inside Passage, a shipping route off the Canadian Pacific coast, in the lee of countless small islands, extends from Puget Sound in the south, near Seattle (Washington), through the Georgia and Queen Charlotte Straits, up towards the "Alaska Panhandle" (about 1500 km (930 mi.)).

There are cruises to Alaska, lasting about a week, from Seattle and Vancouver. The best time to go is from July to September, when according to the statistics there should be a greater number of sunny days. In fact the climate on the Canadian Pacific coast is relatively mild all year round, although the mainly westerly winds bring plenty of rain, because of the warm Japanese current.

"Queen of the North"

The best known cruise, and a particularly impressive one in fine weather, is the 15-hour voyage on the M.V. "Queen of the North", a ferry which takes about 750 passengers and 150 vehicles along the Inside Passage from Port Hardy, on the north-east tip of Vancouver Island, to Prince Rupert through a labyrinth of thickly wooded, hilly and virtually uninhabited islands, narrow channels and fiords, a lonely, almost untouched landscape. Only occasionally do slopes devoid of trees bear witness to human activity. With luck the ship will be accompanied part of the way

Inside Passage: on the M.V. "Queen of the North"

by dolphins or killer whales, sea-lions will be sunning themselves on the rocks, and eagles will be circling above, while on the mainland the snow-capped coastal mountain ranges can be seen looming against the sky.

During the six months of summer, the ferry runs north one day and south the next. Once a week it also calls at Bella Bella a fishing and lumbering settlement on Campbell Island, where most of the population are Indians (Waglisla Indian Village).

At Prince Rupert passengers can join the Alaska Marine Highway ferries and continue on through Ketchikan (a busy little fishing harbour, with impressive totem poles and historic Creek Street built on stilts), Wrangell, Petersburg, Juneau (capital of Alaska in the USA with excursions to Glacier Bay National Park) and Haines (for the Chilkat Indian Dancers and Chilkat State Park), to Skagway, the "Gateway to the Yukon", and Klondike Goldrush National Historical Park, the road to the Alaska Highway. The whole trip takes about 36 hours. — Detour

Information and reservations: Alaska Marine Highway, P.O. Box R, Juneau, Alaska 99811, USA; tel. (907) 4653941, or within the USA 18006420066. — Alaska Marine Highway

★Inuvik

D 4

Territory: Northwest Territories
Population: 4000

Western Arctic Tourism Association, PO Box 2600, Inuvik, NT X0E 0P0; tel. (867) 7774321 — Information

By air: — Access

Inuvik

Flights several times a week from Edmonton (AB) and Yellowknife (NT), also Whitehorse (NT).

By road:
Via the Alaska Highway, Klondike Highway and Demptster Highway (see entries).

Location

"Place of Man" is the Inuit meaning of the name for this modern settlement in the Arctic circle on the Mackenzie River delta (see entry). Built between 1955 and 1961, during the oil and gas exploration, it replaced Aklavik, which was badly located and prone to flooding. Today Inuvik is the trading, administrative and supply centre for the western Arctic. It has an airfield, several schools and a hospital. From here the supply planes set off for the exploration bases in the far north (Mackenzie delta, Beaufort Sea). Sightseeing flights over the Arctic also take off from here.

Permafrost

Since the earth is permanently frozen, any form of building poses considerable technical problems. All utility supply lines have to be laid above the ground and the houses built on stilts to prevent the melting of the permafrost, which would result in subsidence.

Events

A famous curling tournament is held here at the end of March, followed a month later by the Top of the World skiing championship.
There are many street parties during June and July when the sun barely sets.

Sights

★Roman Catholic church

Inuvik's Catholic church, a modern, igloo-shaped building, is very impressive and contains a tabernacle which is also igloo-shaped, and a remarkable "Way of the Cross" by Inuit artist Mona Trasher.

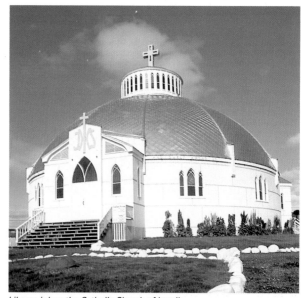

Like an igloo: the Catholic Church of Inuvik

Surroundings

Aklavik, Inuit for "home of the polar bears", is west of Inuvik and has a population of 800. It was founded by the Hudson's Bay Company in 1912 in the middle of the Mackenzie delta, an area prone to flooding.

    Aklavik was the main town in the western Arctic until the building of Inuvik. The Anglican episcopal church with its highly original stained-glass is well worth a visit. Scenes from the life of Christ are set in local conditions, so the Holy Family are depicted with a polar bear, the Adoration of the Magi takes place in the snow, and the Virgin and Child are wrapped in furs.

Aklavik

Tuktut Nogait National Park to the east of Inuvik was established in 1996. A vast and hitherto largely unspoilt tract of 16,340 sq. km (6307 sq. mi.), the Park boasts some truly overwhelming arctic rock scenery with spectacular canyons and cliffs. Finds made at literally dozens of archaeological sites within the conservation area show that this now inhospitable region was inhabited thousands of years ago.

★Tuktut Nogait National Park

★★Jasper National Park   G 7

Province: Alberta. Situation: Rocky Mountains
Area: 10,878 sq.km/4199 sq.miles

The Superintendent, Jasper National Park, PO Box 10, Jasper, AB T0E 1E0; tel. (403) 8526161
Jasper National Park Visitor Centre, 500 Connaught Dr. (near the station), Jasper, AB
Jasper Park Chamber of Commerce, 632 Connaught Dr. (by the station), PO Box 98, Jasper, AB T0E 1E0; tel. (403) 8523858

Information

By road
Yellowhead Highway 16, Prince George–Jasper–Edmonton; Icefields Parkway (see entry; Highway 93 Jasper–Lake Louise)

Access

By rail
"The Canadian" (VIA Rail: Toronto–Edmonton–Jasper–Vancouver); "The Rocky Mountaineer" (Vancouver–Jasper)

By bus
Brewster Transportation & Tours, from Calgary via Banff and the Icefields Parkway (see entry) to Jasper

Jasper National Park, with an area of 10,878 sq. km (4,199 sq. mi.), is the biggest National Park in Canada's Rocky Mountains, a continuation of magnificent mountain scenery, with majestic mountains, glaciers, crystal-clear lakes, waterfalls and narrow gorges, pine woods and, in summer, lovely mountain meadows covered with flowers. Here on the border of British Columbia the snowcapped pyramid of Mount Columbia peaks at 3747 m (12,298 ft) on the edge of the Columbia Icefield (see Icefields Parkway). Some tourist roads to particularly lovely areas also give the motorist easy access to the most spectacular scenery. However large sections of the National Park are being kept in their original state, and can only be reached on foot, by canoe or on horseback.

Location

The town of Jasper dates from 1911 when the Grand Trunk Pacific Railway was built along the Athabasca River to the Yellowhead Pass, although David Thompson had already established a modest little settlement here a hundred years earlier for the North West Company when he was looking for a northern route over the Rocky Mountains in 1811. For fifty years the fur trappers' main route was to lead over the Athabasca Pass. A little monument near Beauvert Lake commemorates "Henry House" (Old Fort Point), a refuge for trappers and the place where they got their supplies.

    Jasper House, named after Jasper Hawes who lived here for a long

History

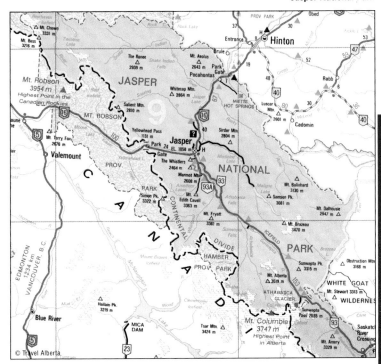

time, was built in what is now the eastern section of Jasper Park in 1813.
In the second half of the 19th c. the number of travellers here dwindled
until Jasper was visited only by a few adventurers and gold-prospectors,
explorers and particular enthusiasts such as the painter Paul Kane or the
extraordinary Mary Schäffer, who followed old Indian trails and in 1908
reached Maligne Lake, hitherto unknown.

By 1907 several thousand square miles of wilderness had been designated the Jasper National Park.

When the railroad reached Jasper in 1911, the settlement which grew up on **Jasper**
the Athabasca River was initially called Fitzhugh, and this remained its
name until it was changed to Jasper in 1913. The Brewster brothers set up
a small tent city for tourists on Beauvert Lake, which was replaced by Jasper
Park Lodge in 1920. Mountaineers climbed the previously unknown peaks,
and outfitters took enterprising tourists to remote regions on horseback.

Jasper townsite, somewhat less crowded than its sister resort of Banff, Present
has a permanent population of about 3300. It is the tourist centre for importance
Jasper Park, with plenty of accommodation, stores, etc.

Connaught Drive is Jasper's main street. The Canada Parks offices are Connaught Drive
opposite the station where, from late summer onwards, long goods
trains, often numbering more than a hundred freightcars, laden with
grain from the prairies, are assembled in the vast marshalling yards
before going on to Vancouver through Yellowhead Pass.

◀ *Jasper National Park: Maligne Lake*

Jasper National Park

★Jasper Park Lodge
Jasper Park Lodge, about 7 km (4½ mi.) east of Jasper townsite and in a beautiful setting on Beauvert Lake, is a vacation resort open from mid-May to October and dating back to the 1920s. It has excellent facilities, including a golf course, riding stables, boat-hire, etc.

★Whistlers Mountain
The Jasper Tramway station is about 7 km (4½ mi.) south of the town, near a large campsite. This mountain tramway, which runs from 8am to 6pm, April to October, goes up Whistlers Mountain, named after the whistling of the marmots which run around here in the summer. There is a good view of Jasper from the mountain station (restaurant) at 2277 m (7473 ft), but it is also well worth walking all the way up to the summit (2464 m (8087 ft)) to take in the magnificent panoramic view.

Jasper raft tours
Half-day raft tours on the lovely Athabasca River, the one-time highway of the furtrappers, operate from the Brewster Bus Depot on Connaught Drive from June to September.

Lakes
About 7 km (4½ mi.) north of Jasper, Pyramid Lake and Patricia Lake are reached by a winding road. These two attractive mountain lakes below the impressive 2768 m (9085 ft) Pyramid Mountain have good windsurfing, canoeing and boating as well as sailing.
  A 5 km (3 mi.) circular trail past Patricia Lake leaves from the Pyramid riding stables.

Cottonwood Creek
Moose, deer and beaver can be seen in the Cottonwood Creek area, in the early morning or in the evening.

★Maligne Canyon
Scenic Maligne Lake is a good destination for a day out, reached by taking the Maligne Road, which branches off from the Yellowhead Highway 3 km (2 mi.) beyond Jasper. The Maligne Canyon, 11 km (7 mi.) east of Jasper, is one of the most beautiful canyons in the Rockies. It has several waterfalls and a 4 km (2½ mi.) nature trail, starting at the lodge (open in

Cordilleras: Medicine Lake in Jasper National Park

summer) and leading along the Maligne Canyon, its chalky sandstone walls as high as 50 m (164 ft), with interpretive panels explaining the geo-morphological features. The canyon is very narrow in places and spanned by several bridges. Its lower section carries far more water than the upper part since water from Medicine Lake enters the canyon at various places, flowing through subterranean clefts and gushing out of karst hollows.

Medicine Lake, a few miles further south, is 6 km (3½ mi.) long, and appears to have no outflow to speak of at its northern end, yet the water-level varies greatly during the course of the year. In late autumn the lake is almost empty, with only a trickle of water meandering between the mud banks on the lake bed, to seep away at the north-east side of the basin. This phenomenon was a mystery to the local Indians, and their medicine men took advantage of it, hence the name.

Medicine Lake

Maligne Lake, 11 km (7 mi.) further on, is the largest glacial lake in North America. At a height of 1673 m (5491 ft) in the beautifully scenic Maligne Valley, the lake, which is surrounded by majestic ice and snow-covered peaks, is about 22 km (14 mi.) long and just under 2 km (1¼ mi.) across at its widest part. It is well worth taking the boat trip (June–Sept., 10am–4pm) to the southern end of the lake, past the world famous pic-ture postcard views of the Narrows and Spirit Island.

★★Maligne Lake

There are also very lovely walks along the lakeside to Schäffer Viewpoint (about 1.5 km (1 mi.)) or up to the Opal Hills. The climb of about 8 km (5 mi.), taking 3 hours brings the walker 305 m (1001 ft) higher up and is rewarded by a splendid view.

From June to September, visitors can join in white-water rafting for 11 km (7 mi.) downriver on Maligne River. For information contact Maligne Tours, 626 Connaught Dr., Jasper, or The Chalet, Lake Maligne.

White-water rafting

Just 50 km (31 mi.) north of Jasper, the Miette Hot Springs road branches off the Yellowhead Highway at Pocahontas, a few miles before the east-ern entrance to the park. Coal deposits were discovered here in 1908 and mined for about ten years after the railway line was completed in 1911. All that now remains of the Pocahontas mine are a few foundations.

Pocahontas

The Punchbowl Falls, cascading down a narrow crevasse, are a few miles further on.

Punchbowl Falls

From here there is still a drive of 15 km (9½ mi.) to Miette Hot Springs, at 54°C (129°F) the hottest springs in the Canadian Rockies. The thermal baths (39°C (102°F); open 8.30am–10.30pm, May to Labour Day) are part of a larger leisure complex with accommodation, restaurants and riding stables. There are also some lovely walks in the vicinity.

Miette Hot Springs

From Jasper, it is well worth making the trip 30 km (19 mi.) further south to Mount Cavell (3363 m (11,0374 ft); approach on Highway 93 A) named after the British nurse who was a First World War heroine. A winding mountain road, about 15 km (9½ mi.) long (open Jun.–Oct.) twists and turns up to Cavell Lake and a car park at the foot of the impressive north face. The Angel Glacier moves downwards from a saddle. A short footpath leads through the moraine to a little lake below the tongue of the glacier. There is a very pleasant 3 to 4-hour walk up to the Cavell Meadows, from where there is a particularly good view of the Angel Glacier.

★Mount Cavell

Marmot Basin, just 20 km (13 mi.) south of Jasper, on the other side of the Whistler massif, is a popular new ski resort with a restaurant, cafe-teria, ski school, ski hire, etc.

Marmot Basin

★John Hart–Peace River Highway

F/G 6

Province: British Columbia
Prince George–Fort St John/Dawson Creek

John Hart–Peace River Highway

Information	See British Columbia
Route	The John Hart–Peace River Highway (Hwy 97) is the northern continuation of the Cariboo Highway (see entry). It starts at Prince George on the Yellowhead Highway (Hwy 16; see entry), the northernmost of Canada's three east-west routes across the Rockies. The highway then runs north for 412 km (256 mi.) through timberland to join the Alaska Highway at Dawson Creek. There is an alternative route to the west on Highway 29 which follows the Peace River for 465 km (289 mi.) to Fort St John (see entry) and the Alaska Highway (see entry). At Summit Lake, a few kilometres beyond Prince George, the road almost imperceptibly crosses the Great Divide, the continental watershed, which is quite flat here.
★Carp Lake Provincial Park	After 143 km (90 mi.), at MacLeod Lake, a narrow, winding metalled road branches off westwards to Carp Lake Provincial Park on the Nechako Plateau (32 km (20 mi.)). The lake, full of islands, is very popular with anglers and open-air enthusiasts. In the days of Simon Fraser and the North West Company, the major route connecting Fort St James and Fort MacLeod passed through here, and parts of this have been retained at the northern and western ends of the lake. As yet unrestored ruins of the historic Fort MacLeod (Fort MacLeod Provincial Historic Park), in 1805 the first of Simon Fraser's trading posts west of the Rockies, are near the present-day settlement of McLeod Lake, but can only be reached on foot.
Mackenzie	After 160 km (100 mi.), Highway 39 branches off to Mackenzie (30 km (19 mi.); 701 m (2300 ft)) at the south end of Lake Williston, an artificial lake which has scarcely been opened up to tourism. Until 1965 the area around the northern Rocky Mountain Trench was still just a wilderness. Since then a town has grown up, its population of 6000 here to work in the sawmills and paper factories of the local economic mainstay, the timber industry, although ore deposits have now also been found in the vicinity. At the entrance to the town stands the huge "tree crusher", an enormous, 175-tonne machine, which, when Lake Williston was created, was used to crush the trees which were of no commercial value. Morfee Lake, a nearby resort, has a hydroplane base and swimming, water sports and fishing.
Pine Pass	190 km (118 mi.): Highway 97 crosses Pine Pass, at 935 m (3069 ft), the lowest pass in the Canadian Rockies. Not far from the pass there is Powder King Ski Village, a popular ski resort (640 m (2100 ft) descent, 23 ski runs, 1 chairlift, 2 ski tows), and the Bijoux Falls (about 40 m (131 ft)-high waterfall).
Chetwynd	310 km (193 mi.): Chetwynd (pop. 3000, 615 m (2018 ft)), already in the foothills of the Rockies, is another young settlement on the northern frontier, on the edge of the untamed wilderness and the starting point for wilderness tours (hiking, canoeing, hunting, fishing).
Gwillim Lake	From here, Highway 23 leads southwards to Gwillim Lake (56 km (35 mi.)), a beautiful, deep-blue lake in largely untouched surroundings (splendid view of the bare mountain ridges to the northwest of the lake), and to Tumbler Ridge (105 km (65 mi.)), a new mining town, part of the Northeast Coal Project, and currently home to about 2000 workers and their families. There are sightseeing tours from mid-June to mid-September round the mining areas, and the enormous computerised conveyor systems of Quintette Coal Ltd., plus excursions to Monkman Provincial Park with the impressive 70 m (230 ft) Kinuseo Falls (accessible only on foot or by hydroplane).
Dawson Creek	412 km (256 mi.): Dawson Creek (pop. 11,000, 666 m (2186 ft)), at the end of the John Hart Highway, is already in the predominantly flat lands of the Peace River Region, Canada's northernmost farming area (grain, oilseed rape, dairy farming). The "0" milepost, 3 m (10 ft) high and decorated with flags, marks the start of the famous Alaska Highway (see entry) built by the US Army

between 1942 and 1944. The town first came into being in the 1930s, when a railhead was built here to serve Peace River's wheatlands, but its rapid growth only took off with the construction of the Alaska Highway. The town landmarks are the big grain silos of Alberta Pool Elevators Ltd. at the station.

Nowadays the railroad is freight only; the old Northern Alberta Railway station at 900 Alaska Avenue, built in 1931, houses the Dawson Creek Station Museum with displays about the local wildlife, the culture of the Cree Indians, pioneer days, historic grain silos from the 1930s, and a small art gallery and tourist information centre. Open Jun.–Aug. daily 8am–8pm; at other times Mon.–Fri. 9am–5pm.

Walter Wright Pioneer Village is about 3 km (2 mi.) east of Dawson Creek on Hwy 2 to Edmonton. It is an open-air museum with 14 typical historical buildings that have been moved here. These include an old smithy, grocery store, school-house, two churches and a trapper's log cabin. Open Jun.–Sep. daily 10.30am–6.30pm.

Walter Wright Pioneer Village

The beautifully scenic Highway 29 branches off at Chetwynd (310 km (193 mi.)) and follows Peace River to Fort St John.

Highway 29

376 km (234 mi.): Hudson's Hope (pop. 1000, 520 m (1707 ft)) is one of the oldest settlements in British Columbia. A small trapper post was established here on Peace River as long ago as 1805. Whether it got its name from a hopeful prospector by the name of Hudson, or because the Hudson's Bay Company was trying to steal a march on its rival the North West Company, it is too late to tell. Nowadays most of the people living here on the edge of the wilderness work for the two power stations at the Bennett and Peace Canyon dams. These produce just under 40 per cent of British Columbia's hydro-electric power.

Hudson's Hope

From the highway it is possible to see black bears (often scavenging on the local rubbish tip), white-headed sea-eagles, moose and deer.

The little museum on the north bank of the Peace River vividly conveys the history of the region, and tells of the dinosaurs whose bones and footprints have been found in the sedimentary rocks of the Peace River Canyon, now flooded. Visitors can obtain pans in the museum to try their luck at panning for gold in the Peace River. Open Victoria Day to Labour Day daily 9.30am–5.30pm; and Labour Day to Thanksgiving, Sat. and Sun. only.

Next to the museum stands St Peter's Church, built in a simple log-cabin style.

About 5 km (3 mi.) south of Hudson's Hope, Peace Canyon Dam, 50 m (164 ft) high, and 533 m (1749 ft) long, dams up Peace River for a second time, where it leaves the canyon, 23 km (14 mi.) below Bennett Dam. In the Visitor Centre next to the power station more exhibitions tell of the natural history of the region and the history of its settlement. These include life-size models of dinosaurs, a reconstructed stern-wheel steamer, that used to ply on the Peace River, and a model of a dam and power station. The power station can be visited by arrangement. Open Victoria Day–Labour Day daily 8am–4pm; Mon.–Fri. at other times.

★Peace Canyon Dam

The W.A.C. Bennett Dam, one of the world's biggest earth-filled dams, is 24 km (15 mi.) west of the town and reached via a scenic side-road. This dam, which is 2 km (1¼ mi.) long, 183 m (601 ft) high, and up to 830 m (2724 ft) thick at its base, was completed in 1967 and holds back the 362 km (225 mi.)-long Williston Lake in the Rocky Mountain Trench. Until recently, the 1646sq.km/635sq.mile artificial lake had hardly been opened up for tourism, but more and more water-sports enthusiasts are now making their way here. Anglers can charter boats as well. The Visitor Centre gives information about hydro-electric power generation and the construction of the enormous dam, and on working days there are guided tours of the power station. Open Victoria Day–Labour Day daily 8am–4pm; Mon.–Fri. 8am–4pm at other times. From May to September there is a good view of it from a lookout point on the west side of the dam.

★W.A.C. Bennett Dam

From Hudson's Hope the highway follows the Peace River north

The Bennett Dam on Williston Lake

wards, mostly high above the steep banks, and after 76 km (47 mi.) reaches the Alaska Highway 13 km (8 mi.) north of Fort St John.
465 km (289 mi.): Fort St John (see entry)

Joliette   H 16

Province: Québec. Population: 18,000

Information   Tourisme Joliette, 500 rue Dollard, Joliette, PQ; tel. (450) 7595013

This charming little town is at the centre of a region of beautiful scenery, known as Lanaudière. It was founded in 1841 by Barthélemi Joliette, a descendent of Louis Joliette, discoverer of Mississippi.

Musée d'Art   Joliette's art museum (Wilfrid-Corbeil 145; open Tue.–Sun. end of Jun.–beginning of Sep.; Wed.–Sun. at other times) provides a complete overview of Canadian art, with special emphasis on Québec artists such as d'Ozias Leduc, along with church art from Québec and Europe.

★Kamloops   G 6

Province: British Columbia. Population: 77,000

Information   Kamloops Visitor Information Centre, 1290 W. TransCanada Highway 1, Kamloops, BC V2C 6R3; tel. (250) 3743377

History   Since the time of the trappers, Kamloops has been at the heart of the dry, high country of south-central British Columbia. First settled in 1811 at the confluence of the North and South Thompson Rivers, which here form the narrow Kamloops Lake, by the North West Company under the name of Fort Thompson, the town was later renamed "Kamloops" from the local Indian dialect for "meeting of the waters".

In the 1860s this little settlement found itself in the throes of the gold-rush as the "Overlanders", a group of gold-seekers and pioneers, arrived here in 1862, who, embarking on a dangerous and exhausting three-month journey, crossed the Yellowhead Pass, hitherto virtually unknown, and followed the North Thompson River southwards into the heart of British Columbia.

In the 1880s there were also steamboats on the Thompson River at Kamloops and on the Sushwap Lake, but this came to an end when the Canadian Pacific Railway reached Kamloops in 1885.

Today Kamloops is an important junction. It is the meeting point for several road and rail routes – the Canadian Pacific Railway, Canadian National Railway, TransCanada Highway, Yellowhead Highway 5 north, Coquihalla Highway and Highway 5 south into the Nicola Valley and to Merritt, and Highway 97 south-eastwards into the Okanagan Valley – as well as being the local capital for the 130,000 people living in what is mainly a rural region, farming sheep and cattle, while sawmills and paper factories exploit the timber from the hinterland. The firm of Wayerhaeuser Canada provides guided tours through their paper factory where 700,000 tonnes of timber and wood shaving are processed annually.

Economy

Tourism is also starting to play an increasingly important part in this lake district setting (fishing, windsurfing, sailing and mountain tours) with its favourable climate – Kamloops has only about 160 mm (6½ in.) of rainfall and more than 2000 hours of sunshine a year. There is also horseracing as an added attraction.

Tourism

The Travel InfoCentre has leaflets for a tour of the town centre which still has many of its old buildings (courthouse, St Joseph's Church (1887), Chinese cemetery, reconstruction of Fort Kamloops in McArthur Island Park, and an old Canadian steam loco 2141 in Riverside Park).

★Heritage Walking Tour

The historic Kamloops Museum (207 Seymour St., open Jun.–Aug. daily 10am–9pm, at other times Mon.–Sat. 10am–5pm, Sun. 1–5pm) has exhibitions on how the Indians lived, the days of the pioneers and fur trappers, and life in Kamloops at the turn of the century.

Kamloops Museum and Archives

From May to September the paddlewheeler "Wanda Sue" takes people on 2-hour trips on the Thompson River.

"Wanda Sue"

The Secwepemc Museum (345 Yellowhead Hwy. 5; open Mon.–Fri. 8.30am–noon and 1–4.30pm) is primarily an Indian museum, concentrating on the culture of the local Sushwap, and the Salish Indians.

★Secwepemc Museum

Kamloops' famous Indian Band Days take place in August.

Indian Band Days

The Kamloops Wildlife Park with its small zoo and leisure pool is another attraction. It has about 100 different species, including many native to Canada (e.g. bear, puma, moose, Wapiti, eagle and buffalo). The miniature railway is also very popular.

Kamloops Wildlife Park

Kamloops Waterslide & Vacation Land, with waterchutes, whirlpools, etc., is about 20 km (13 mi.) from the town centre, on the TransCanada Highway, and is a good place for a swim to cool off during the relatively dry, hot summer. It also has a miniature golf course.

Kamloops Waterslide & Vacation Land

Harper Mountain, 23 km (14 mi.) northeast of Kamloops, is a popular ski area in winter (425 m (1395 ft), difference in altitude, 13 pistes, ski lifts).

Harper Mountain

Tod Mountain winter sports resort is 53 km (33 mi.) north of Kamloops. It has a difference in altitude of 945 m (3101 ft), and boasts 42 pistes with chairlifts and ski tows.

Tod Mountain

The Lac Le Jeune Resort, 25 km (16 mi.) further south, has 100 km (62

Lac Le Jeune Resort

mi.) of cross-country skiing courses, and a further 130 km (80 mi.) of marked ski trails on a high plateau.

★Shuswap Lakes Chase (457 m (1500 ft); pop. 3000), at the western end of the Little Shuswap Lake, is the western gateway to the Shuswap Lakes. There are more than 1600 km (994 mi.) of banks and a relatively hot, dry climate make these ideal for those who enjoy water sports. They are best explored from a houseboat.

Rodeo Its Rodeo in the autumn provides a real touch of the Wild West.

Squilax Pow Wow The Squilax Pow Wow in the nearby Squilax Reserve, where Indian dance groups from all over North America come to take part, attracts thousands of visitors every year.

Adams Lake At Squilax the road branches off to the south end of Adams Lake, which is 70 km (43 mi.) long (houseboats), and to the resorts, campsites and bathing beaches on the north shore of Shuswap Lake. Scotch Creek (boat rental) is very pleasant, as is Shuswap Lake Provincial Park (open from May to September; visitor centre with wildlife and cultural exhibits). The reconstruction of a Kekuli pit-house is worth seeing. Shuswap Indians lived in these during the winter until about 1908. Other beauty spots include Magna Bay and Anglemont (houseboats).

Sorrento The town of Sorrento (350 m (1149 ft); pop. 3000) was given its name by J.R. Kinghorn, a pioneer who, seeing Copper Island in the distance, was reminded of the Isle of Capri and the Gulf of Naples. Houseboats can be taken out on the Shuswap Lake, where there is a fine beach for swimming. A popular summer resort, especially with senior citizens, Sorrento owes its growth primarily to the construction of the railroad in 1885 when a rail station and a little settlement were built because of the additional steam locomotives (in use until 1958) that were needed for the steep haul up Notch Hill. Farmers settled in the fertile surroundings.

Interior White Water Expeditions offer whitewater rafting on the nearby Adams River or on the Clearwater River in Wells Gray Provincial Park (Yellowhead Highway 5 South).

East of Sorrento the TransCanada Highway turns south.

Salmon Arm Salmon Arm (358 m (1175 ft); pop. 12,000), on the southern arm of Shuswap Lake, is the centre of the Shuswap Region, and grew up when the railroad was built in the 1890s. The moderate, dry climate (1800 hours of sunshine, 140 mm (5½ in.) of rainfall a year) has made Salmon Arm popular as a retirement haven.

Houseboat rental; day trips on Shuswap Lake on the little paddlewheel boat M.S. "Rockwood"; sailing, wind-surfing. Also Salmon Arm Waterslide, local market (Tues. and Fri. 8am–1pm; farm produce, handicrafts), Salmon Arm Museum (51 3rd St; open May–Aug. Tue.–Sun. noon–5pm), and horseback riding.

Sicamous Sicamous (352 m (1155 ft); pop. 4000), between Shuswap Lake and Mara Lake, proudly proclaims itself Canada's "Houseboat Capital". It also has golf, hang-gliding, water sports, and fishing, and the "Phoebe Ann" takes people for cruises on the lake (Jun.–Sep. Mon., Wed., Fri.; Jul. and Aug. daily except Sat. 8am).

Highway 97A branches off towards the south here, past scenic Mara Lake (16 km (10 mi.)) to Vernon in the Okanagan Valley (see entry).

Craigellachie From Sicamous the TransCanada Highway follows the route of the Canadian Pacific Railway, built in the 1880s, over Eagle Pass (discovered in 1865) through the rugged 2500–3000 m (8200–9850 ft) Monashee Mountains, where the road can be blocked at times by heavy snowfalls in winter. After 26 km (16 mi.), at Craigellachie, the place is reached where in 1885 the last spike was driven into place in the Canadian Pacific

Railroad, completing the country's first trans-continental railway. Six months later the first passenger train left Montréal to arrive after six days in Port Moody, near Vancouver, making what was then the longest scheduled railway connection in the world, and the monument here commemorates the importance of this event.

The "Enchanted Forest", 13 km (8 mi.) further east, and open from 8.30am May to September, is a fairy-tale theme park beneath gigantic cedars hundreds of years old, with a pseudo medieval castle and populated by about 300 fairy-tale characters – fairies, witches and mermaids – with, of course, a wishing well.

Enchanted Forest

Three Valley Gap, situated in a valley in the Monashee Mountains at the eastern end of Three Valleys Lake, with its inviting little sandy beach, is a recreation of the old Wild West, built here in the 1960s near the 19th c. gold-rush ghost town and lumbering settlement. Open: May–Sept. from 8am. It has old buildings that were moved here from all over the region, trappers' log cabins, Sicamous' historic Bellevue Hotel, and old barns, complete with a few donkeys and other animals in the stables. There is also a motel, restaurant and miniature railway.

Three Valley Gap

★★Kingston   J 15

Province: Ontario. Population: 44,000

Kingston Tourist Information Bureau, 209 Ontario Street, Kingston, ON K7L 2Z1; tel. (613) 5484415

Information

The city of Kingston lies at the northern end of Lake Ontario, where it becomes the St Lawrence River. It attracts many visitors and is the starting point for cruises to enjoy the beautiful scenery of Thousand Islands (see below).

Location

Fort Catasaqui, or Fort Frontenac as it was also called, was established here in 1673 to oversee the fur trade, and for a short time was itself an important fur-trading post.

In 1788 the place was resettled by the English who christened it Kingston. Its strategic location soon made it an important naval base, especially during the 1812 war with the Americans.

After the war the English built the Rideau Canal, linking Montréal with the Great Lakes, via the valley of the Ottawa River.

Kingston rapidly expanded between 1841 and 1844 when it was the capital of Upper Canada.

History

City Hall, opposite the harbour, dates from 1844 and its sandstone architecture is indicative of the hopes once cherished by the people of Kingston that their city might become the capital of all Canada.

The Law Courts and the University also date from the 19th century.

City Hall

Fort Henry was built on the river between 1812 and 1837 to defend Kingston and to bar the way to the St Lawrence, but it never came under attack.

Nowadays the fort houses a museum of British-Canadian military history which is open from mid–May to mid–Oct. from 9am to 6pm. In summer students from Kingston's Royal Military College re-enact the 19th c. ceremonial retreat at sunset on Mondays, Wednesdays and at weekends if the weather is fine.

★Fort Henry

The Villa Bellevue, built in 1840 near the university, is modelled on an Italian Palazzo. Open daily except for winter holidays, it belonged to Sir John MacDonald, Prime Minister from 1867 to 1873, and is furnished as it was at that period.

Villa Bellevue

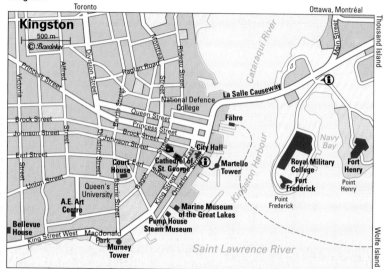

Steam pump museum

This museum is in a former pumping station which was built in 1849. The two pumps also date from this period. All the machines on display have been restored to full working order. Open mid-Jun.–Sep. daily except Fridays (technical demonstrations) and mid-Mar.–mid-Nov., but without guided tours.

Shipping museum

The shipping museum in a former shipyard on Lake Ontario (open Apr.–mid-Dec. daily 9am–6pm; closed Mon. in Nov. and Dec.) has various types of steam and sailing ship on display, a reminder that Kingston was at one time important for its shipyards.

★★Thousand Islands National Park

Dotted all over an 80 km (50 mi.) stretch of the St Lawrence are thousands of little islands.

They are on a granite shelf extending from the Canadian Shield to the Adirondack Mountains in the United States – the boundary actually runs between the islands. It is an area of great scenic beauty, and one of the oldest and best-known holiday venues in North America, particularly for holidays on and around the water.

Cruises

A cruise in this maze of islands is highly recommended. Operating between mid-May and mid-October; lasting about 3 hours, and the ever-changing vistas will include glimpses of holiday homes that range from the plainest of log cabins to the most luxurious of summer villas.

Heart Island

Some cruises call at Heart Island to enable passengers to look round Boldt Castle (NB: US formalities), which is well worth a visit. It was built by the wealthy owner of New York's Waldorf Astoria, but was never completed.

The scenic road along the St Lawrence, between motorway exits 107 and 110A, has many lovely views over the water.

Hill Island Skydeck

Another good view is to be had from the outlook tower of Hill Island Skydeck (120 m (400 ft) high; open May–Oct.). From here a whole range of islands can be seen.

Hill Island Skydeck can be reached over a bridge near Ivy Led.

Thousand Islands National Park

The road alongside the St Lawrence leads to Mallorytown Landing and the official entrance to Thousand Islands National Park (open mid-May–mid-Oct.). From here it is possible to get to several islands which can only be reached by boat, and to see the wreck of an early 19th c. gunboat.

★**Mallorytown Landing National Park**

Kitchener-Waterloo

J 14

Province: Ontario. Population: 178,000

Kitchener–Waterloo Conventions and Visitors Bureau, 2848 King Street E., Kitchener, ON N2A 1H3; tel. (800) 2656959

Information

The twin cities of Kitchener and Waterloo are situated about 100 km (60 mi.) west of Toronto (see entry).
    Kitchener, known as "Berlin" until the First World War, and renamed after General Lord Kitchener, is Canada's biggest centre of German immigration. It derives most of its income from the food and drink industry.

Location

Kitchener's special attraction is its annual October festival complete with Bavarian brass bands, beer, sausage and sauerkraut, the second largest in the world after Munich. It attracts visitors from all over North America.

★★**October festival**

The twin cities of Kitchener and Waterloo were founded in the late 18th c. by the Mennonites, originally a German sect and named after its Friesian founder, Menno Simons (1492–1559). Some of its members emigrated straight to Canada, while others came here from Pennsylvania in 1783 during the American War of Independence. Like the Amish – named after their founder Jakob Ammann – the Mennonites are Anabaptists, a sect founded in Zurich in 1525 and persecuted from

History

Mennonites on the road

the outset because of their beliefs in adult baptism and pacifism, who finally found a new homeland on the North American continent. Today the orthodox Mennonites still speak an old German dialect and wear plain, unadorned dress with no buttons, collars or pockets.

Buggies

They ride in horse-drawn buggies as they are not allowed to own cars; neither can they own telephones or other such products of modern technology, and live by farming without machinery, as they did 150 years ago. They still sell their produce on local markets in Kitchener and Waterloo. The Mennonites in Canada now number around 100,000.

Sights

★Joseph Schneider House

Joseph Schneider House (466 Queen St S.) is a Mennonite home with original 19th c. furnishings. As "living history" the "inhabitants" of the house, in traditional costumes, offer visitors biscuits baked in the old German manner, and re-enact life as it was lived in the 19th c. (open daily 10am–5pm in summer; Wed.–Sat. 10am–5pm and Sun. 1–5pm in winter).

★Doon Heritage Crossroads

Doon Heritage Crossroads, on Houmer Watson Boulevard, is an open-air museum showing life in the town in the days of the pioneers. Its thirty or so buildings on a site of 23 ha (57 acres) provide an insight into what life was like here in the 19th century (open May–Sep. 10am–4.30pm; end of Sep.–Christmas 1–4.30pm).

★Seagram Museum

Seagram Museum, at 57 Erb Street West, provides a wealth of information on the history of the wine and spirits industry. In the old storage rooms of the first Seagram distillery, now extended with a modern wing, it illustrates the various stages of the distillation process with exhibits and film shows (open Tue.–Sat. noon–6pm; for information tel. 8851857).

★Woodside House

Woodside House, built in 1853 and open daily from 10am to 5pm, was the parental home of Mackenzie King, Prime Minister of Canada from 1921 to 1930 and from 1935 to 1948, and is furnished as it was in the late 19th c.

Markets

Kitchener Market: since 1839; Duke St/Fredrick St; open Wed. and Sat. mornings. Waterloo Market: Webber St; open Wed. all day and Sat. morning. St Jacob's Farmers Market: north of Waterloo; open daily 10am–5pm.
　　Besides selling farm produce and such specialities as maple syrup and maple syrup products, these markets also sell Mennonite handicrafts and their home-produced remedies and cosmetics.

Surroundings

Around Kitchener and Waterloo there are still a few Mennonite villages, such as Elmira and Elora.

St Jacobs seems like an open-air museum in itself, but has a museum of its own, "The Meeting Place" at 33 King Street, which tells the story of the Anabaptists and how they were driven out of Europe in general and Switzerland in particular.

This scenic park, along the course of a pretty river, is particularly lovely in the spring and in the autumn, when it attracts many visitors. It has a campsite, picnic areas, footpaths, and an information centre, and there is canoeing on the river.

The river valley above Elmira has lovely scenery and is a favourite recreational area for people living around Hamilton and London. There are also designated recreational areas around the artificial lakes created by the damming of the river.

★Klondike

Administrative unit: Yukon Territory

Tourism Yukon, PO Box 2703, Whitehorse, YT Y1A 2C6; tel. (867) 6675340, fax. (867) 6673546

The Klondike is a tributary of the Yukon River, and flows for 150 km (93 mi.) from its source in the Tintina, east of the Klondike Highway, into the Yukon at Dawson City (see entry).

The legendary gold-rush in the Klondike began when George Washington Carmack and his two Indian brothers-in-law, Tagish Charlie and Shookum Jim, registered their first claim which they had made in Bonanza Creek, a branch of the Klondike River, on August 17th 1896 in Fortymile. News of the gold nuggets – as big as a fist – which Carmack had found on the bed of Bonanza Creek spread like wildfire in the Yukon and neighbouring Alaska. When the largest shipment of gold which had ever been made in the States was loaded in Seattle it triggered a gold-rush, and in a short time more than 100,000 people from all over the world came pouring into the Klondike. The worldwide depression meant that the lure of the gold, so vividly described by Jack London, proved irresistible, although less than half those who hoped to make their fortune in the Yukon probably never actually got there. Many of them who came from the Pacific died trying to get over White Pass or even Chilkoot Pass to Bennett Lake and to the boats in Carcross which would take them down the Yukon to Whitehorse (see entry); as many again suffered the unspeakable hardships of the long trek from the east through Edmonton (see entry) to the Yukon. Dawson City (see entry), the gold-rush's famous capital city of tents and log cabins, sprang up overnight at the confluence of the Klondike and the Yukon, and by 1898 had a population of about 25,000. By 1903 the rivers and creeks of the Klondike had yielded gold worth about 96 million dollars, at an average price of 20 dollars per ounce (31g), but there were very few whose dreams of great riches came true.

When gold was found in August 1899 at Nome, near the mouth of the Yukon, the prospectors moved on to Alaska. The Klondike gold-rush eventually ended ten years after it began, leaving the valley to sink back into obscurity.

The search for gold continued, but the individual gold-panners were replaced by big corporations using industrial machinery. The damage they caused to the environment is still visible, as gold continues to be mined, and more extensive operations are under discussion.

The 717 km (445 mi.) Klondike Highway, completed in the late 1970s, leads from Skagway (Alaska) through Whitehorse (see entry) to Dawson City (see entry) and the Klondike goldfields.

Klondike

It follows the route taken by the prospectors in 1898, a gruelling and perilous journey from Skagway over White Pass to Carcross, from where they continued by boat, raft and later by sternwheeler through Whitehorse (see entry) to Dawson City (see entry).

Tourists can now travel this legendary stretch by boat, an unforgettable experience and far less harrowing than it was 100 years ago. Information is available from the Visitor Centres in Whitehorse and Dawson (see entries).

Skagway

Today Skagway (pop. 1000) lives from tourism and its many renovated buildings and boardwalks have the feeling of the gold-rush days. Its name comes from the Tlingit dialect and means "home of the north wind".

Carcross

The road from Skagway to Carcross, 106 km (66 mi.) away, is passable all year round. Situated 40 km (25 mi.) south of Whitehorse (see entry) on Bennett Lake, Carcross, where time seems to stand still, was such an important place at the turn of the century, but now has a population of only 150. The first people to live there were Indians who hunted around this area. They named the place "Caribou Crossing" and the abbreviated version of this was later adopted by the gold-prospectors.

The Caribou Hotel, built in 1898 and renovated in 1909 is the oldest hotel still trading in the Yukon. Visitors can see S.S. "Tutsi", an old paddlesteamer, and the "Duchess", a tiny locomotive that travelled the line from Taku to Atlin Lake early this century. Matthew Watson's General Store was built in 1911, and the Watson family still ran it until quite recently.

Whitehorse

See entry

Alaska Highway

The Klondike Highway crosses the Alaska Highway (see entry) at the 158 km mark (98 mi.).

Takhini Hot Springs, at the 198 km mark (123 mi.), is a good place for a swim, with temperatures of 36°C (97°F).

Takhini Hot Springs

Braeburn Lodge, famous for its food, at 281 km (189 mi.), is worth making the next stop.

Braeburn Lodge

Carmacks, after 357 km (222 mi.), named after George Washington Carmack one of the three discoverers of the Klondike gold, is a place to stop for services. Most of the 400 people living here are descendants of the original Indian inhabitants.

Carmacks

Just north of Carmacks the Campbell Highway (see entry) forks east to Watson Lake on the Alaska Highway (see entry), passing through Faro and Ross River.

Campbell Highway

Five Finger Rapids, where the prospectors had to haul their boats through on ropes, are at 381 km (237 mi.).

Five Finger Rapids

At Minto (431 km (268 mi.)), another trading post set up by Robert Campbell for the Hudson's Bay Company, the Klondike Highway leaves the Yukon River to cross the central Yukon Plateau and the valleys of the Pelly and Steward rivers.

Minto

At Stewart Crossing (538 km (334 mi.)), the last services for 140 km (87 mi.), the Silver Trail branches north-east to Mayo, Elsa and Keno in the silver-mining territory around the upper Stewart River.

Stewart Crossing

Today most of the silver is mined in the United Keno Hill Mine at Elsa, and the ore shipped to Mayo, an Indian township about 46 km (29 mi.) south. Keno City, in a lovely setting at the foot of the Keno Mountain (1889 m (6170 ft)) is pretty much a ghost town, since mining here has long since been abandoned.

Silver mining

Soon after reaching the Klondike Valley, the Klondike River Lodge services come up at the 678 km mark (421 mi.). Here the Dempster Highway (see entry) turns off into the Canadian north, eventually reaching to Inuvik in the Mackenzie River delta (see entry) after about 750 km (466 mi.) of magnificent scenery.

★Dempster Highway

See entry

Dawson City

★★Kluane National Park

E/F 2/3

Administrative unit: Yukon Territory

Kluane National Park, PO Box 5495, Haines Junction, YT Y0B 1L0; tel. (867) 6342251

Information

Kluane National Park, in the south-west corner of Yukon Territory (see entry) and bordering on Alaska and British Columbia (see entry) extends over an area of 2,2015 sq. km (8498 sq. mi.). Part of the Haines Road (Highway 3) and the Alaska Highway (see entry) run along its eastern edge.

Location

The snowcapped mountains of the Kluane (pronounced Klu-ah-nay), Canada's largest park of its kind, which has the world's most massive icefields outside the polar region, was designated a Mountain Park in 1976, and recognised as a United Nations World Heritage site in 1979. Great glaciers at the edges of the ice – up to 1.6 km (1 mi.) thick in places – have swept over the mountain valleys. Many of the close on 4000 glaciers are more than 10 km (6 mi.) across and up to 100 km (60 mi.) long.

Topography

The most common conifer in the park's river valleys is white spruce (picea glauca), and the most common deciduous trees are birch (betula) and poplar (populus). The colourful alpine and arctic flora beyond the tree line extend to stunted shrubs, flowers and grasses, whilst on islands

Flora and fauna

Mount Logan, Canada's highest mountain

in the everlasting ice mosses and lichens defy the harsh winters, forming a vital link in the food chain. The park is rich in wildlife such as grizzly and black bear, moose, caribou, wolf, mountain goat, Dall sheep, beaver, marten, fox, musk rat, and eagle, and has many kinds of fish, including salmon, trout and pike.

★★**Mount Logan**   Dominating Kluane National Park, the peaks of the St Elias Mountains, traverse it in a south-easterly direction. Mount Logan, Canada's highest mountain peak (6050 m (19,856 ft)) soars above the vast icefields, the highest mountain in North America after Alaska's Mount McKinley (6193 m (20,325 ft)).

★★**St Elias**   The ice-covered peaks of the St Elias Mountains can be seen from the
Mountains   Alaska Highway (see entry), almost 160 km (100 mi.) away, beyond the Kluane Range (up to 2500 m (8205 ft)).

Tourism   Climbers and naturalists from all over the world come here every year to explore this fantastic mountain world. The first of the St Elias peaks to be conquered was Mount St Elias (5498 m (18044 ft)), climbed by the Duke of Abruzzi in 1897. Mount Logan was first climbed in 1925. Trekking tours in the park and around Mount Logan require physical fitness and careful planning. For further information, including details of such facilities as winter camping, contact the Visitor Centre and park headquarters at Haines Junction (tel. (403) 6342251).

★★Kootenay National Park   G 7

Province: British Columbia
Area: 1406 sq. km (543 sq. mi.)

Kootenay National Park, PO Box 220, Radium Hot Springs, B.C. V0A 1M0; tel. (250) 3479615

The Banff-Windermere Parkway (Highway 93) runs through Kootenay National Park. It is at least a 3-hour drive.

Access

Kootenay National Park ("kootemik" is Indian for "places of hot water") is in the Rocky Mountains, in south-east British Columbia. It adjoins the more famous Banff National Park (see entry) and Yoho National Park (see entry), and takes in the magnificent western flank of the Canadian Rockies.

Landscape

Banff–Windermere Highway, 105 km (65 mi.) long, runs south from the TransCanada Highway at Castle Junction, 28 km (17 mi.) north-west of Banff, down to Radium Hot Springs, passing through spectacular mountain scenery west of the continental divide and following the valleys of the Vermilion and Kootenay rivers. These two valleys form the core of Kootenay National Park. There are plenty of parking places along the way so that visitors can explore the virtually untouched hinterland.

Banff–Windermere Highway

The main mountain range reaches heights of over 3,000 m (9846 ft), and is predominantly closely packed layers of stratification. The younger sedimentary layers of the western ranges show much more folding and erosion, and such typical features as rugged rocky ridges and sawtooth peaks, snow and ice-covered massifs, cirques, glaciers, hanging valleys and narrow gorges cut deep into marbled limestone, make the drive through the Kootenay National Park quite a unique experience. With any luck, it will be possible to see moose, Wapiti and mountain goat as well.
  Unlike the towering mountains of the north, the less rugged uplands in the south of the park get less snow and rain, and have a milder climate that enables many of different creatures to spend the winter in the lower Kootenay valley.

Geology

Archaeological evidence shows that for thousands of years the valleys and passes of what is now Kootenay National Park served as important trade routes for the Indians. The rock drawings at Radium Hot Springs are an indication of how significant a place this was for the Indians of the Plains as well as those of the mountains.
  In the 19th c. the Hudson's Bay Company explorers followed the old Indian trails into the Kootenay area in search of furs and a suitable route to get to the Columbia River and the Pacific. They were followed by settlers, prospectors and mountaineers. Resourceful entrepreneurs soon discovered the value of the hot springs, and Radium Hot Springs got its first spa hotel in 1911. The area was declared a national park in 1920 when the province of British Columbia transferred the land to the Canadian government. The Banff-Windermere Parkway, the first major highway through the central Rockies, was built without delay and subsequently much improved in the 1950s. It now has plenty of parking places and lookout points where visitors can stop to admire the magnificent scenery.

History

The Vermilion Pass (summit 1651 m (5382 ft)), only 38 km (24 mi.) north-west of Banff (see entry), is where the Parkway crosses the Continental Divide, and where Alberta meets British Columbia and Banff National Park (see entry) meets the Kootenay National Park.
  Here in 1968, a forest fire, started by lightning, raged for four days, and devastated 2440 ha (6029 acres); the results are still clearly visible.

Vermilion Pass

The scenery around Vermilion Pass is reminiscent of the Swiss Alps: the famous Stanley Glacier, on the slopes of Stanley Peak (3155 m (10,355 ft)) to the south, can be reached by a lovely if rather strenuous hike in one day through the Stanley Creek hanging valley.

Stanley Glacier

The Banff–Windermere Highway in the Kootenay National Park ▶

Mount Whymper (2844 m (9334 ft)) to the west of Vermilion Pass also has its glacier. It is named after the conqueror of the Matterhorn, who also climbed many of Canada's mountains.

Mount Whymper

45 km (28 mi.): Marble Canyon is a deep narrow gorge, formed by Tokumm Creek, which owes its name to its pale marbled limestone and dolomite walls. An interpretive trail of about a mile circles the canyon to a waterfall. Marble Canyon is spanned by several bridges, and has a small information centre open to visitors in summer.

★**Marble Canyon**

48 km (30 mi.): a little trail of about 1 km (⅔ mi.) leads from the next parking area over the Vermilion River to the "Ochre Beds", and the three small pools known as the "Paint Pots". These are fed by mineral springs with a high iron content, hence the colour. The Indians came here from far afield to get the ochre-coloured clay for their war-paint and for dyeing their clothes and tepees. The Europeans took advantage of the red clay, too, using it to produce dyes in Calgary.

Paint Pots

The Banff/Windermere Highway Exhibit at Kootenay Crossing is worth seeing, particularly for its account of how this part of the Rockies was opened up by the highway, and how the national park was set up.

Kootenay Crossing

Further south the highway passes by Crooks Meadow, Dolly Varden, and McLeod Meadow, all pretty resorts where campsites should be booked in advance.

Resorts

There is a wonderful view from Kootenay Viewpoint over the Kootenay River valley to the Mitchell and Stanford mountain ranges.

View

120 km (75 mi.): from the Kootenay Valley the route crosses Sinclair Pass (1486 m (4877 ft)) to get into the lovely high-mountain valley of fast-running Sinclair Creek. After the Iron Gates Tunnel steep limestone and dolomite walls, coloured red by iron oxide form a kind of gateway. In spring and in August big-horn sheep congregate here.

Sinclair Pass

Redwall Fault is the site of mineral springs with a high iron content.

Redwall Fault

Still within the national park, Radium Hot Springs (pop. 1000) was a place prized by the Indians for its hot springs, and these continue to be the source of its fame. Its Aquacourt (open daily in summer, 8.30am–11pm, otherwise Mon.–Fri. 2–10pm, Sat./Sun. 10am–10pm) has two swimming pools (39°C (102°F) and 28°C (82°F)), thermal baths, and a restaurant. Radium Hot Springs Lodge, above the springs, also has beautiful views. Whitewater rafting is possible as well.

★**Radium Hot Springs**

Near the Radium Hot Springs Sinclair Canyon forces its way through a stupendous defile.

Sinclair Canyon

★★'Ksan

F 5

Province: British Columbia

North by Northwest Tourism Association, PO Box 1030, Smithers, BC V0J 2N0; tel. (604) 8475227, fax. (604) 8477585

Information

The fact that there are three Hazeltons – Hazelton, New Hazelton (306 m (1004 ft)) and South Hazelton – with a total population of about 400, is due to a dispute about the station for the Grand Turk Pacific Railway. Nowadays the trains stop at New Hazelton, at the foot of the impressive, partially glaciated Rocher-Déboulé massif. In 1914, when the railway was being built, this was the scene of a spectacular bank holdup, when

Hazeltons

'Ksan Indian Village

five of the gang were gunned down and the sixth escaped with the loot of just 1400 dollars.

Hazelton old town is 8 km (5 mi.) north of Yellowhead Highway and the railroad, on the north bank of the Bulkley River, near where it flows into the Skeena River.

Hagwilget

The deep canyon here is spanned by a 76 m (250 ft)-high suspension bridge. Below it there used to be a rock that formed a kind of natural weir in the rushing river, used to their advantage by the Indians who lived mainly from salmon fishing. The remains of Hagwilget, "the home of the quiet people", where the Indians lived, are to be found below the bridge. This was a Carrier Indian Village used only in summer, and archaeologists have found traces of settlements here dating back to 3000 BC. When the fishing authorities removed the rock in 1959, the Indians, who fished only with wooden fish traps and harpoons, found that their catches were drastically reduced, and the village was abandoned. As early as the 19th c. the Indians had skilfully constructed a wooden suspension bridge over the canyon.

★★'Ksan Indian Village

'Ksan Indian Village, near Hazelton, is an open-air museum near a traditional Gitksan Indian settlement (open mid-May–Oct. 9am–6pm, limited opening in winter). In summer there are also film shows and traditional dances. Various aspects of Gitskan culture are on display in seven tribal longhouses, each guarded by their ancient totem pole.

Three houses can only be viewed as part of a guided tour. This is an opportunity to learn about these people's daily lives and the potlatch ceremony, as well as the symbolism of the carving on the totem poles. A number of Indian carvers have their workshops in the village, and their work is on sale in the Gift Shop together with other Indian books and artefacts.

The North Western National Exhibition Centre and Museum (open daily in summer 10.30am–4.30pm; at other times closed Tue./Wed.) houses valuable carvings and ritual objects.

★Labrador

Provinces: Québec, Newfoundland

Québec Province, Newfoundland (see entries)

The Labrador Peninsula, an area of 1,560,000 sq. km (602,160 sq. mi.) between Hudson Bay and the Atlantic, is the eastern flank of the Canadian Shield, and contains a wealth of mineral deposits in its Pre-Cambrian plutonic rocks. Labrador's central uplands range between 200 m (650 ft) and 500 m (1650 ft), reaching heights in the north-east of between 800 m (2625 ft) and 1800 m (5907 ft). The peninsula was the final resting place of the glaciers of the last continental Ice Age, until they too melted about 6000–7000 years ago. The landscape has many clearly glacial features, especially in the north. Countless rivers have carved deep valleys across the face of Labrador, which has deep fiords as well, particularly along the Atlantic coast, also typically glaciated. The hummock-covered pristine wilderness of the interior has broad basins that have been filled with lakes, moraine spoil or sand. The lowlands around Hudson Bay and Ungava Bay were under water when times got warmer.

★Natural features

The Labrador Peninsula lies between 50° and 60° latitude north, and has a sub-arctic climate that counts as extreme in European terms. This is intensified by the cold Labrador current that swirls around the edge of this land mass. Temperatures in central Labrador can fall to −50°C (−58°F), and they can even get as low as −40°C (−40°F) on the coast. Average summer temperatures are between 5°C (41°F) and 10°C (50°F), and higher in places. Average precipitation is between 500 mm (20 in.) and 1000 mm (40 in.), depending on the lie of the land, and rather less on the Ungava peninsula, with a quarter to a third falling as snow.

Climate

Traces of the Ice-Age: a fiord in Labrador

Labrador

Vegetation

Most of northern Labrador is in the permafrost, and has the typical tundra vegetation of sparse, sub-arctic pine and birch. The south, on the Gulf of St Lawrence and around Goose Bay, mostly has boreal timber.

Labrador dog

The Labrador is a breed of dog native to eastern Canada, and probably related to the Newfoundland, although not as large. Labradors have a short, thick coat, ranging in colour from pure white to black, occasionally with a tinge of brown. Here in Canada they are mainly used for pulling sledges.

Resources

The waters off Labrador are among the world's best fishing grounds, so there is a long fishing tradition. In the past furs also played an important role in the local economy. Timber felling and processing are also of economic importance, mostly concentrated on the Gulf of St Lawrence seaboard.

Eastern Labrador is among the world's major mining regions, and the vast iron ore reserves between the Churchill and Koksoak rivers yield over 10 million tonnes a year.

Its enormous hydro-electric potential has made Labrador a major supplier of energy to the industries of south-eastern Canada and the United States eastern seaboard.

History

Labrador was probably discovered by the Vikings in about 986. John Cabot reached the peninsula in 1498, then later came immigrants from the British Isles. Trappers, fur-traders and lumbermen were roaming the territory up until 1900, when the population numbered about 5000, most of them Inuit and Indian.

Vast reserves of iron ore were discovered in the late 19th c. and as they came to be mined, particularly after the Second World War, the population grew. By 1950 it had already risen to 18,000, about a third being Inuit or Indian.

Most of Labrador is in Québec Province, but the east coast and part of the hinterland come under Newfoundland, although these boundaries have shifted several times since 1763.

Schefferville

Schefferville (Québec Province) is a young town at the end of the Québec Shore & Labrador Railway, founded in 1950 as a mining settlement when vast iron ore reserves – estimated at four billion tonnes – were discovered at Knob Lake, as the place was then called. Only ten years later there were 4000 people living in what is now Schefferville. It is linked to the port of Sept-Îles by rail, and by occasional flights, which also go to Québec and Montréal.

Sept-Îles

Sept-Îles (Seven Islands) (Québec Province, pop. 30,000) is a booming French-Canadian port on the Gulf of St Lawrence, about 600 km (373 mi.) north of Québec City (see entry).

At the entrance to a fiord, in the lee of seven rocky islands, its site was discovered by Jacques Cartier (see Famous People) in 1535. A mission station was founded here in the 17th c. but the place only appears to have been permanently settled from the mid-19th century. In 1950 Sept-Îles was a sleepy fishing village of a few hundred people.

Since then, the port of Sept-Îles, which also has the regional airport, has become the administrative and supply centre for the entire north shore, due largely to being the terminal for the 575 km (357-mi.) rail line bringing mineral raw materials from such parts of Labrador as Labrador City and Wabush, and above all the iron ore from Schefferville for shipment to the USA, Japan and Europe in the giant freighters operating out of the sheltered, deepwater fiord harbour, with the second highest volume of shipping tonnage in Canada.

Fort

The reconstructed fort (open Jun.–Aug. daily 10am–5pm) on the Vieux-Poste River was originally founded by Louis Jolliet in 1661, but burned down in 1695.

The north coast regional museum on Laure Boulevard is open Mon.–Fri. 9am–noon; and weekends 1–5pm.

Musée Régional

Sept-Îles is a good base for hunting and fishing trips in the locality, and particularly for salmon at Moisie, about 12 km (7½ mi.) to the east.

Moisie

Ungava Bay, covering 621,000 sq. km (239,700 sq. mi.) and only ice-free in summer, is in the north-east of the Labrador peninsula, opening onto the Hudson Strait. The many large rivers flowing into the bay include the George, Koksoak, Leaf, Payne and Whale. Large iron ore deposits were found around the bay in the 1950s and these are now being mined on a grand scale.

Ungava Bay

Fort Chimo is an Inuit settlement on the Koksoak River, about 50 km (30 mi.) inland from the bay.

Fort Chimo

Labrador current

The Labrador current is an ocean current that flows along the north-east and east coast of North America southwards from Baffin Bay. It is basically a coldwater current that flows from the Arctic, and is joined off the coast of Labrador by the waters from Hudson Bay off the Labrador coast. Up to 200 m (656 ft) deep, the current flows south over the coastal shelf of Labrador and Newfoundland. Its salt content, at 3.3 per cent, is 0.2–0.3 per cent lower than normal. The temperature of the water in the deeper layers gets close to the freezing mark. On the surface the current moves at a rate of 0.5 km (¼ mi.)–1.5 km (1 mi.) an hour. The intensity of the current varies considerably from year to year and according to the time of year.

These variations can also have a considerable influence on Europe's weather. When it meets the Gulf Stream (west of Newfoundland) the intensity of the current determines whether the Gulf Stream turns north or south. The cooler and therefore denser waters of the Labrador current sink below the warmer, less dense waters of the Gulf Stream. The Labrador current therefore helps to determine whether spring will be late in Europe, or whether it will be very wet. The icebergs that accompany the current also present a considerable danger to shipping when the Gulf Stream carries them eastward into the North Atlantic sea lanes.

The meeting of the ocean currents with their different temperatures and carrying their different nutrients provides good conditions for a whole host of marine creatures.

For centuries, the waters off the Canadian coast have been known for their rich stocks of fish, and their cod, salmon, herring and mackerel have provided catches for fishing vessels from all over the world. In more recent times it has been possible precisely to chart and plot the size and direction of the ocean currents by satellite, and then relay the information to the fishing fleets to direct them to their fishing grounds.

Labrador Straits

The icy-cold Labrador current flows through the 17 km (11 mi.)-wide Strait of Belle Isle which separates Labrador from Newfoundland (see entry), into the Gulf of St Lawrence. Southern Labrador was traditionally the summer fishing grounds for centuries of fishermen heading here from Newfoundland (see entry).

At L'Anse Amour archaeologists have uncovered an ancient burial site with finds over 7500 years old. The people who originally lived here on the south coast of Labrador almost 9000 years ago, at the end of the ice age, were the ancestors of the primitive caribou-hunters of eastern

L'Anse Amour

North America. They lived in small settlements and were later to become the fishing and whaling tribes of the Belle Isle Strait.

Red Bay   Red Bay is the oldest industrial archaeological site in the New World, with the remains of a 16th c. Basque whaling station and shipwrecked Basque vessels. The Basque Whaling Archaeological Site can be visited in summer by arrangement.

Goose Bay

Goose Bay can be reached by a 34-hour ferry trip from Lewisporte in Newfoundland, passing through Lake Melville, the "Markland" (woodland) discovered by the Vikings.

Along the shores of Lake Melville between Rigolet and Goose Bay there are a number of smallish but major settlements, where conditions are ideal for trapping, fishing and felling timber. One of the most important is North West River, or Sheshatshui ("narrow place in the river" in the Naskapi language) home to the Naskapi and the descendants of the English, French and Scottish settlers who originally worked here as hunters and trappers. The whole area has undergone considerable change since the Second World War, especially Happy Valley and Goose Bay.

Region   The Goose Bay region – part of Newfoundland – is in eastern Labrador. The Allies built a big military base here during the Second World War, and the area is still used for military purposes, such as NATO training and low-level flying.

The Goose Bay area has a population of over 10,000. Close on 1200 are from the original Indian peoples, but their lives are seriously affected by the military presence.

Town   The town of Goose Bay (pop. 7000) is on an ice-age sandy site on the shore of Lake Melville. Its Labrador Heritage and Culture Centre Museum, in the north of the town, is open daily in summer, and its exhibits telling the story of Labrador and its people include a trapper's tilt, a kind of tarpaulin tent that provided shelter in the wilderness, trappers' tools and some beautiful furs. The items from Wallace Hubbard's ill-fated expeditions into the interior are of particular interest.

From Goose Bay the route continues on the Trans-Labrador Highway, to Churchill Falls.

Churchill Falls   Churchill Falls has what is considered to be the world's greatest hydroelectric power site. The main reservoir, covering an area of 3520 sq. km (1359 sq. mi.), is as big as Sicily, and the water drops 300 m (985 ft) over a distance of about 32 km (20 mi.). The largely automated power station generates 5,225,000 kW of electricity, serving over 3,500,000 Canadians and exporting the rest to the USA.

Travel around this area requires a special permit, but the scenery and the sight of partridges, beavers, caribou and even black bears compensate the visitor for the difficult drive.

Wabush
Labrador City   The twin towns of Wabush and Labrador City are in the middle of the wilderness, about 25 km (16 mi.) from the Québec border. They were constructed in the 1960s in an iron ore area. Ore to the value of about 1 billion Canadian dollars is mined here annually.

From Labrador City it is possible to cover the 400 km (250 mi.) to Sept-Îles by rail, a journey that takes six hours.

North Labrador

To get from Goose Bay to Nain it is best to take the ferry that sails along the coast once a week between late June and late November. Anyone wanting to travel further north will have to charter a boat or plane, always allowing for the harshness of the terrain and the changes in the weather.

In 1782 the British Government allowed the Moravian Brethren to set up a mission station in Labrador. This little complex is made up of a church, a grocery store, the minister's house, stores and little log-cabins for the native Indians. | **Hopedale**

Founded in 1771 by a group of Moravian Brethren, Nain's population of 1000 are Inuit, who live either from welfare or by the traditional ways of taking shellfish and salmon, and hunting caribou. The interesting little Nain School Museum illustrates the life of the Inuit and the Moravian Brethren, with kayaks and other items from northern Labrador, as well as telling the story of the Moravian mission. | **Nain**

Hebron, the northernmost of the Moravian Brethren's Labrador missions, is on the remote shore of Kangershutsoak Bay. Established in 1829, it was abandoned in 1959 but the buildings remain, having been declared a national monument in 1970. | **Hebron**

Lac La Biche   G 8

Province: Alberta. Area: 230 sq. km (89 sq. mi.).

See Alberta | Information

Lac La Biche (230 sq. km (89 sq. mi.)), about 200 km 125 mi.) north-east of Edmonton, has miles of sandy beaches, plus boat slipways.

The settlement of Lac La Biche (pop. 6000), at the south-east end of the lake, dates from the trading post set up by David Thompson for the North West Company in 1798. It lies on a well-trodden route for the fur trappers, who could use a 2 km (1 mi.) portage between Beaver Lake (the route into Hudson Bay through Churchill River) and Lac La Biche. | Settlement

A mission station was built here in the mid-19th c., and Alberta's first wheat was grown in its fields. It had relatively more comfortable wooden houses, instead of the usual log cabins, and even ran to its own library. | Mission station

Lac La Biche Pow Wow and Blue Feather Fish Derby every year at the beginning of August provide a good opportunity to find out more about the culture of the Métis. | Pow Wow, Blue Feather Fish Derby

On an island about 10 km (6 mi.) north of the town, where farmland meets the northern pine forest, this provincial park is a great place for watching waterfowl and migrant birds. There are nature trails through the dense woodland of conifers, some of them over 140 years old and as tall as 23 m (75 ft). | Sir Winston Churchill Provincial Park

Lac Megantic   H 16

Province: Québec

Tourisme Cantons-de-l'Est, La Route de Sud, 20 rue Don-Bosco Sud, Sherbrooke, PQ J1L 1W4; tel. (819) 8202020, fax. (819) 5664445 | Information

Lac Megantic, in Frontenac County, was and continues to be the homeland of the Abnaki Indians, and has good hunting and fishing. | Settlement

The principal town of the locality, also called Lac Megantic (pop. 10,000), is on the Chaudière River, and has several lumber companies, as well as some farming.

★★Lac St-Jean   H 16

Province: Québec. Area: 1002 sq. km (387 sq. mi.)

Information

Association Touristique du Saguenay – Lac St-Jean, 198 rue Racine Est, Chicoutimi, PQ G7H 1R9; tel. (543) 9778, fax. (543) 1805

Scenery

Lac St-Jean, a former glacial basin, is the source of the Saguenay River that flows out through the scenic cliff-lined Saguenay Fiord (see entry) to the northern shore of the St Lawrence. The fertile plains and forests around the lake are part of the Canadian Shield, and its mountain setting gives Lac St-Jean some of the most beautiful scenery in the Province of Québec.

In August large quantities of blueberries are harvested here and the district is also well-known for its cheese.

Trans-lake swim

Every year there is an international marathon swim on the last Sunday in July across the lake from Péribonca to Robertval.

Desbiens

In May every year the "Festival de la Ouananiche" (Indian for freshwater salmon) is held in Desbiens, a little village at the mouth of the Métabetchouane.

Trou de la Fée

The "Trou de la Fée", or "Fairy Hole", is a cave about 8 km (5 mi.) south of Desbiens, which can be seen on a very steep trail.

★Val-Jalbert

Val-Jalbert is a deserted village standing in the centre of the provincial park of that name (established 1960; open end of May–beginning of Sep. daily 9am–7pm) near the mouth of the Ouitchouane. Here, close to a spectacular 72 m (236 ft)-high waterfall capable of providing almost unlimited water power, the industrialist Damas Jalbert built, in 1901, a sawmill and paper and cardboard factory, together with a village to accommodate the workforce which was 1000 strong. By 1927 the factory had closed down and the settlement became a ghost town. Part of the factory and the machinery survive and can be seen. A number of buildings including the school, butcher's shop and grocer's shop, have recently been restored and there is also an interesting little museum documenting the history of the project.

St-Félicien

In the island zoo north-west of St-Félicien (open mid-May–end Sep. daily 9am–5pm, 7pm in Jul.), caribou, black bear and many of Canada's other wild creatures can be seen at very close quarters. An Indian village and a lumberjack camp are also among its attractions.

Péribonca

Writer Louis Hémon (1880–1913) lived for several months in Péribonca, and made it the setting for his novel "Maria Chapdelaine" (1916), a major work of Canadian literature, and a glorification of the settler ethos.

The Louis Hémon Museum, dedicated to the life of the author, is open Jun.–Sep. daily 9am–6pm; Sep.–Jun. Mon.–Fri. 9.30am–4pm.

★Lake of the Woods   H 11/12

Provinces: Ontario and Manitoba
Area: 4860 sq. km (1876 sq. mi.)

Information

See Ontario, Manitoba

Access

TransCanada Highway 1; VIA-Rail

Setting

On the borders of the Canadian provinces of Manitoba and Ontario, Lake of the Woods (Lac des Bois) is half in Canada and half in the US State of

Minnesota. In a very scenic setting, its waters, fed by the Rainy River and draining into Lake Winnipeg through the Winnipeg River, are between 25 and 27 m (82 and 87 ft) deep, and full of fish. Islands and islets fringe the heavily indented Canadian north shore, while the south shore is flat, sandy and very marshy in places.

Lake of the Woods was discovered in 1688, providing trappers and "voyageurs" with a passage westwards. Nowadays it is a popular holiday hideaway.

Kenora on the north-east shore of Lake of the Woods is in Ontario Province and the centre for the many hydroplanes and other light aircraft that ferry adventurous holidaymakers around on their fishing and hunting trips out of the many lodges.

Kenora

Rushing River Provincial Park is a park of over 160 ha (395 acres) around a series of cascades in the Rushing River about 40 km (25 mi.) below the lake.

Rushing River Provincial Park

The village of Sioux Narrows is on the narrows between fingers of Lake of the Woods on Whitefish Bay, at one time the scene of skirmishes between the Sioux and the Ojibwa.

Sioux Narrows

★★Laurentians

G/H 16–17

Province: Québec

See Québec (Province)

Information

The Laurentian (Les Laurentides) uplands extend from Ottawa in the west to the Saguenay River in the east, with the St Lawrence (see entry) as their southern boundary. They also form part of the southern Pre-Cambrian Canadian Shield. Throughout the year this rolling mountain range, with its maple woods, plentiful game – including the mighty moose – secret lakes, romantic waterfalls and lovely valleys, is a favourite playground not just for the city folk from Ottawa, Montréal and Québec, but for the whole of the densely populated St Lawrence seaboard (see entries).

Topography

Generally speaking the Laurentians are understood to mean the whole of the upland area of the Laurentine massif between the Ottawa and Saguenay rivers north of the St Lawrence, and more specifically the resort area northwest of Montréal. They were opened up between 1870 and 1891 through Antoine Labelle, a priest of St-Jérome, who founded twenty homesteads here since he feared many of his fellow countrymen would otherwise be tempted to emigrate to New England in search of better farming land.

However, it was not until the development of tourism after the Second World War that the Laurentians became less the kind of recreation area they are today, offering countless lakes and rivers, about 30 golf courses, over 20 winter sports resorts (including Mont-Tremblant, Morin Heights, Mont-Olympia), and facilities for riding, hunting and fishing. One of North America's most attractive and popular recreational areas, enjoying a reputation as Québec Province's "Switzerland", the Laurentians boast the greatest concentration of hotels, restaurants and holiday homes in North America.

★Montréal Laurentians

By road
Laurentian Autoroute 15 (toll-road), then Highway 117; frequent buses from Montréal at peak holiday times, i.e. July/August, Christmas and February/March.

Access

The Laurentians north of Montréal are the setting for some of Canada's most famous resorts, such as Ste-Adèle, Ste-Agathe, St-Donat,

Laurentians

St-Sauveur, Estérel and Val Morin. On a par with the best in Europe, they attract visitors throughout the year, offering top hotels, plenty of entertainment, including Canadian folksong bars, a good network of walks and trails, water sports on the lakes, horseback riding, golf and tennis, and full winter sports facilities such as ski-lifts, cross-country routes, etc.

Mirabel

Built in 1975, Montréal's international airport at Mirabel is one of the largest in America.

St-Jérome

The gateway to the Laurentians is the town of St-Jérome. A statue opposite the Cathedral commemorates its famous priest, Antoine Labelle.

St-Sauveur-des-Monts

One of Québec's finest resorts, St-Sauveur-des-Monts is well-known for winter sports with its 30 ski-lifts.

Laurentides

The little township of Laurentides, with a population of 2000, just 30 km (19 mi.) north of Montréal, is the birthplace of Sir Wilfred Laurier (see Famous People). Maison Laurier, the pretty house where Canada's first French-Canadian Prime Minister spent his childhood, is now a national monument, with guided tours daily between May and September.

Mont Gabriel

Mont Gabriel, a summer and winter resort, boasts one of the biggest and highest priced hotels in the Laurentians.

Ste-Adèle

Founded in 1852, the little town of Ste-Adèle (pop. 5000) on the slopes of Mont Ste-Adèle, is picturesquely located by Lac Rond and has long been a favourite haunt of writers and artists.

Séraphin

Ste-Adèle's Village de Séraphin, famous as the setting for a television series, recaptures the life and times of the Laurentians in the 19th c. (open mid-May–mid-Oct.; admission fee). Séraphin Bastien, the inspiration of Claude-Henri Grignon's 1933 novel "Un homme et son péché", lived in the Jos Malterre inn from 1832.

Ste-Agathe-des-Monts

Ste-Agathe-des-Monts (pop. 7000), the lively and scenic resort on Lac des Sables in the Laurentians near Montréal, is full of town dwellers holiday homes. There are boat cruises around the lake between May and October and a music and folk festival in July.

Mont Tremblant

Mont Tremblant, the highest peak in the Laurentians (960 m (3151 ft)) and about 150 km (93 mi.) north of Montréal, is at the heart of the Mont Tremblant Provincial Park, a particular favourite with visitors in the Indian Summer when the leaves change colour and for its skiing in winter.

Established in 1894, the park and nature reserve covers about 3200 sq. km (1235 sq. mi.). It has two well-signed trails, and camping and canoeing is allowed.

The mountain owes its name to the roar of the rushing streams, sounding like the boom of an earthquake to the Indians. The park's wildlife includes deer, black bear, moose, lynx, otter, mink and beaver.

St-Jovite

Close to Mont Tremblant is St-Jovite and the Weir Satellite Reception Station which has public guided tours from mid-June to September.

Joliette

See entry

★Laurentides

Parc du Mont Ste-Anne

Half an hour by car north-east of Québec City is the glorious scenery of the Mont Ste-Anne Park, a favourite recreation area summer and winter for the people of Québec, with its wildly romantic river valleys, Black Forest type mountains, and its uplands and mountain valleys with good grazing for dairy cattle and for raising livestock.

Mont Ste-Anne is also good for winter sports, and has numbers of chalets and holiday homes, plus a reputation for gourmet eating.

The vast Laurentides wildlife conservation area lies about 60 km (37 mi.) north of Québec City and takes in the Parc de Conservation Jacques-Cartier, the Parc de Conservation des Grands-Jardins, Lac Beauséjour and Lac Jacques-Cartier at the foot of Montagne Camille-Pouliot. The highway passing through this section of the Laurentians, drained by the Montmorency River, is Route 175, with plenty of roadside accommodation where the traveller can stay overnight or stop for a meal.

Réserve faunique des Laurentides

Extending over 10514 sq. km (4058 sq. mi.) of lakes and forests, with some peaks above 900 m (3000 ft), this park in the Canadian Shield was designated a protected area as early as 1895. It was originally intended as an enormous reserve for the conservation of the caribou, and after they became extinct here in 1930 some were reintroduced in the western half of the park in 1969.

The park is also home to black bear, lynx, deer, wolf and many other smaller creatures. Although hunting is forbidden fishing in its lakes and rivers is permitted. There is also kayaking on Lac Jacques-Cartier, and over 50 km (31 mi.) of cross-country skiing trails around Mercier in winter. The reception centres at Jacques-Cartier, Mercier and Grands-Jardins can all provide plenty of information and literature.

See entry

Lac St-Jean

★Lesser Slave Lake   F 7

Province: Alberta. Area: 1150 sq. km (444 sq. mi.)

See Alberta

Information

About 90 km (56 mi.) long and up to 20 km (12 mi.) wide, Lesser Slave Lake covers an area of 1150 sq. km (444 sq. mi.), its waters filling a great Pre-Ice Age valley that became the catchment area for the Ice-Age glacier. The dunes and broad sandy beaches around the lake – where stormy weather can bring 9ft high waves at times – are indicative of considerable fluctuations in the water level.

Setting

Lesser Slave Lake Provincial Park lies on the flat east shore of the lake, about 5 km (3 mi.) north of the town of Slave Lake. It has a campsite, with swimming, fishing, surfing and canoeing in summer. Keen anglers can take part in the Golden Pike Fish Derby between May and September.

★Lesser Slave Lake Provincial Park

Birdwatchers can see over 170 species, while osprey and bald eagle breed on Dog Island.

Other park wildlife includes moose, black bear and beaver, together with grizzlies and wolves when the year is at its coldest.

Marten Mountain is the highest point (1030 m (3380 ft)) of the Pelican Mountain Uplands adjoining the park, with a panoramic view over the surrounding countryside from the firetower on the top.

Marten Mountain

The little village of Grouard (pop. 200) at the west end of the lake is named after an earlier Catholic Bishop of Athabasca. Its population was in thousands rather than hundreds at the start of this century until the decision was taken not to route the railroad to the north through the town.

Grouard

It is possible to see round the Indian Museum and the mission that Bishop Grouard founded in 1884 and to visit his grave in the mission cemetery.

Hillard's Bay Provincial Park on the lake shore about 13 km (8 mi.) east of Grouard dates from 1978. A lovely recreation area, it has campsites and good sandy beaches, with a nature trail of just over a mile outlining the ecology of the northern pinewoods.

Hillard's Bay Provincial Park

Lesser Slave Lake

Lesser Slave Lake

Shaw's Point

Shaw's Point, the ½-mile spit of land where the lake's old paddle-steamers used to come alongside, was once the start of the Grouard Trail, an alternative route from Edmonton to the goldfields of the Yukon. The old wagon trail, which early settlers also travelled to reach Peace River territory, can still be seen today.

Swan Hills

For lovers of the great outdoors the forested uplands of the Swan Hills, south of Lesser Slave Lake and over 1200 m (3928 ft) at their highest point, are something of a promised land, to which access can only be gained via the tracks laid down for hauling out the oil and timber.

The expanding township of Swan Hills (pop. 2500) is capitalising on the five oil companies that operate nearby.

Fort Assiniboine

Fort Assiniboine (pop. 200), on the Athabasca River, dates from 1824 when the Hudson's Bay Company founded it as a trading post on the Beaver Route. It boasts a reconstruction of the old fort, which holds a small local history museum. Open mid-May–Oct. daily 1–4pm; at other times Wed. and Sun. only.

Barrhead

Barrhead (pop. 4000) is a township serving an area of farming and forestry.

From here Highway 33 runs south for 72 km (45 mi.) through undulating farmland to the Yellowhead Highway (see entry).

★Slave Lake

In the past Slave Lake (pop. 6000), at the south-east end of Lesser Slave Lake, lived primarily from the timber trade, but owes its rapid expansion since the 1960s to the petroleum and natural gas industry.

David Thompson, in 1799, was the first European to reach Lesser Slave Lake and realise the territory's potential for the fur trade. The North West Company's first trading post on Lesser Slave Lake went up that same year, followed by the Hudson's Bay Company in 1815. The trading posts developed into a general centre for servicing the north, known until 1923 as Sawridge, with landing stages for the paddle-steamers that plied the lake. Many prospectors passed through here during the Klondike Goldrush, and the paddle-steamers carried on until 1915, when the railroad first reached Slave Lake. The town is still the point of departure for trekking northwards today, as hunters take off from here after bear and moose in the hunting season. The lake gets its name from the Slave Indians who lived here when the first Europeans arrived. Like the Beaver Indians further north, they were among the Athabascan tribes, but subservient to the Cree Indians, part of the Algonquin nation. The 18th c. was a time of intertribal strife, particularly once the Cree became the first to obtain guns from the White Man, and a peace treaty only came when the Cree had been decimated by smallpox. Descendants of the original local peoples, along with the more recently arrived Métis, live on in Lesser Slave Lake territory today.

The Slave Lake Native Friendship Centre (408 5th Ave. NE, open 8.30am to 4.30pm), with its own management structure and leisure facilities, helps with integration, and also has handmade moccasins, jewellery and Indian garments for sale.

★Lethbridge   H 8

Province: Alberta. Population: 63,000

Lethbridge Chamber of Commerce, 529 6th St S., Lethbridge, AB T1J 2E1; tel. (403) 3271586 — Information

The fast-growing city of Lethbridge on the Oldman River mainly owes its prosperity to the oil and gas industry. Other important local industries are tourism and farming (livestock, corn, sugarbeet and vegetables). — Economy

Lethbridge was founded in the 1870s when it was called Coalbank, a reference to the coal found nearby. It soon became a centre for farming and, at the turn of the century, was the site of Canada's first large-scale irrigation system. — History

Nearby townships like Coaldale and Coalhurst are reminders of the fact that up until 1965 coal was still being mined in the region's deep valleys where previously there had been only outposts set up in 1869 for the benefit of the unscrupulous liquor runners.

The Nikka Yuko Japanese Gardens (8th Ave.S/Mayor Magrath Drive, open mid-May–mid-Oct. daily 9am–7pm) are the pride of Lethbridge. The beautiful, carefully tended gardens are a symbol of Canadian-Japanese friendship. — ★Nikka Yuko Gardens

Indian Battle Park on the Oldman River commemorates the great Indian battle in 1870 between the Blackfoot Confederation and the Cree Indians, when an attack by the Cree with their allies the Assiniboine on the camp of the Blackfoot, already weakened by an outbreak of smallpox, was repulsed but at the cost of almost 400 lives. — ★Indian Battle Park

Writing-on-Stone Provincial Park is reached by first going to Milk River (pop. 1000) 85 km (53 mi.) south of Lethbridge, then travelling east on Highway 501 for 32 km (20 mi.) and turning south down a tarmac road for another 10 km (6 mi.). — ★**Writing-on-Stone Provincial Park**

The Park gets its name from the many Indian drawings on the sandstone rocks, eroded into bizarre shapes, that form the steep gulch of the Milk River.

These lands were of great spiritual significance for the Plains Indians who believed the spirits of the departed would "write" messages on the rock walls. Warrior braves came here to try and discover what might happen if they went on the warpath, but they never stayed long since it was too dangerous to linger near the spirits of the dead.

In 1908 the graves of five men, a woman and a child were found here, together with items from the US Cavalry. It is thought they could have been survivors of the Nez-Percé who were almost wiped out in 1877 by the US Cavalry near the Canadian border, or they could have been from the tribe of Sitting Bull who fled into southern Canada after their victory over General Custer in 1876 at the Battle of the Little Bighorn.

The bare rocks and hoodoos on the valley edge and the semi-arid prairie contrast starkly with the lush vegetation in the valley itself, where the Milk River lends itself well to canoeing. The Indian petroglyphs can only be seen on guided tours.

US border | Highway 4 runs south-east from Lethbridge to the only frontier crossing into the States from Alberta which is open 24 hours a day.

★Lloydminster   G 8/9

Province: Saskatchewan. Population: 19,000

Information | Lloydminster Chamber of Commerce, 4420 50th Avenue, Lloydminster, AB T9V 0W2; tel. (403) 8759013

Location | Founded in 1903 by British colonists headed by the cleric Isaac Barr, Lloydminster is on the Yellowhead Highway close to the border with Alberta, and the centre of a thriving region that owes much of its prosperity to oil and farming.

Barr Heritage Cultural Centre | The Barr Heritage Cultural Centre (open end May–beginning Sep. daily 10am–8pm; in winter Mon.–Fri. 10am–8pm, Sat., Sun. 1–5pm) contains several kinds of cultural displays and function rooms.

The Barr Colony Antique Museum | The Barr Colony Antique Museum, has exhibits from the founding of the town, including a completely furnished schoolroom and a model oil refinery.

The Fuchs' Wildlife Display | In the Fuchs' Wildlife Display can be seen dioramas with about 1000 mounted birds and other animals.

The Imhoff Art Gallery | The Imhoff Art Gallery shows the works of Berthold von Imhoff, an artist well-known for his religious pictures and his landscapes.

★Weaver Park | It is worth paying a visit to Weaver Park (Hwy. 16E, 44th & 45th St., open mid-May–mid-Sep. 9am–9pm) where the restored buildings show the place as lived in by the first settlers.

★Petroleum industry sightseeing tours | The local Chamber of Commerce runs trips to some of the petroleum plants in and around Lloydminster, taking in a visit to the Char-Mil model drilling rig on 46th Street.

★London   J 14

Province: Ontario. Population: 326,000

Information | Tourism London, 300 Dufferin Avenue, London, ON N6B 1Z2; tel. (519) 6615000

Location | London – on the Canadian River Thames – is the centre for Ontario's prosperous agricultural and industrial south-west, the seat of a Catholic and an Anglican Bishop, and the cultural focus, with its university, symphony orchestra, theatre and museums, for a large area.

History | The city was founded in 1792 by John Graves Simcoe who named it after London, England. This was because Niagara-on-the-Lake, the provincial capital at that time, was right on the American frontier and he wanted his London – as in London, the capital of England, and also as a city deeper into Canada – to become the province's new capital.

London's main attraction is its art gallery, completed in 1980 and designed by Raymond Moriyama. Open Tue.–Sun. afternoons. This unusual building on Ridout Street shows the work of 18th and 19th c. Canadian artists, together with temporary exhibitions covering the whole range of old and new North American art.

★Art Gallery

Also on Ridout Street, just north of the gallery, Eldon House was the elegant home of an English naval captain, who moved here in 1834. It is now a museum (open Mar.–Nov. Tue.–Sun. afternoons).

Eldon House

Close by Eldon House Ridout Street also has several beautifully restored Georgian buildings.

Ridout Street

The Labatt Pioneer Brewery is a charming replica of the wooden brewery built here in 1828. Demonstrations inside the brewery, which is open on weekday afternoons from June to September, show how beer was brewed over 100 years ago, when they produced 300 barrels a year. Today's modern brewery next door, which can also be visited weekdays from June to September, between noon and 5pm by appointment (tel. 673–5211), turns out more than 1.2 million barrels of beer a year.

Labatt Pioneer Brewery

Springbank Park, on the western edge of the city, has a small zoo, fairy tale garden and flower beds, also boat trips by little paddle-steamers on the Thames in summer.

Springbank Park

The museum holds Canada's oldest infantry regiment's notable collection of weapons. These can be viewed Tuesday to Saturday, but not on public holidays.

Royal Canadian Regiment Museum

Located near a prehistoric Indian burial ground, the museum, at 1600 Attawarndaron Road, has 40,000 exhibits and tells the story of the 11,000 years of Indian settlement in Ontario. (Open Apr.–Nov. Wed.–Sun. 10am–5pm; and from 1 to 4pm for the rest of the year.)

★Museum of Indian Archaeology

Fanshawe Pioneer Village, about 16 km (10 mi.) north-east of London (open: May–Sept. daily 10am–4pm; by arrangement at other times) is the reconstruction of a settlement showing what life was like here before the coming of the railroad. It is on the shore of Fanshawe Lake, and its buildings include a Presbyterian church, grocery store, smithy, fire brigade storeroom and an assembly room recalling the influence in Ontario of the Orange Order founded in Ireland at the end of the 18th c. This is open between 10am and 4.30pm weekdays from October to December and daily from May to September.

Fanshawe Pioneer Village

Ska Nah Doht Indian Village (open Mon.–Fri. 9am to 6pm), about 30 km (19 mi.) south-west of London, is the palisaded replica of a 10th–12th c. Iroquois village, with three longhouses, a steam-room, areas for drying meat and fish, storage, etc., and patches of Indian crops such as squash, maize and beans.

★Ska Nah Doht Indian Village

St Thomas, a railroad junction and industrial town also some 30 km (19 mi.) south-west of London, shows clear signs of the influence of Belgian and Hungarian immigrants. Elgin County Pioneer Museum of regional history and Pinafore Park, with its flowerbeds, miniature railway and children's zoo, are worth a visit.

St Thomas

Just 60 km (39 mi.) north-east of London, Stratford (pop. 25,000) is inter-

★Stratford

nationally famous for its Festival. Named after the Bard's birthplace by 19th c. immigrants from Stratford, England, it sprang to fame in 1950 when a local newspaper editor organised the first festival. The 2250-seater Festival Theatre has been staging plays between May and October since 1953, with pride of place going to Shakespeare, but also, by public demand, putting on Molière, Brecht, and the like, not to mention the occasional Mozart opera.

★★Louisbourg   H 18

Province: Nova Scotia. Population: 1500

Location

Louisbourg (Forteresse de Louisbourg), once an important French military base and now one of the most visited historical sites in Canada, lies on the eastern side of Cape Breton Island about 40 km (25 mi.) south of the town of Sydney.

Information

Visitor Reception Centre (about 1 km (½ mi.) from the fortress, and where the bus leaves for the the park). The address for information on special events is: Forteresse de Louisbourg, National Historic Park, P.O. Box 160, Louisbourg.

Visiting

Louisbourg Fortress, which has been reconstructed, is open to visitors from the end of May until September daily 9am–6pm.

History

Under the terms of the Treaty of Utrecht which ended the War of the Spanish Succession, France was forced to cede Newfoundland and large tracts of Acadia to Britain, retaining only the Île Royale (now Cape Breton Island) and the Île St-Jean (now Prince Edward Island). These two islands became the hub of the exceptionally lucrative French cod fishing industry centred on the waters of the Grand Banks off Newfoundland. The port of Louisbourg

Fortress of Louisbourg

was established by the French on the east side of the Île Royale in 1719, at which time the substantial fortifications were also built. All around Louisbourg long rows of wooden racks were constructed on which the cod were salted and dried before being exported as "klipfish". Trade with France, Québec, the islands of the Caribbean and parts of Newfoundland flourished. In 1745, the French having declared war on Britain, Louisbourg came under attack. Being difficult to defend on the landward side, it fell to the British after seven weeks. The 1748 Treaty of Aachen however returned Louisbourg to France. Ten years later the British again laid seige to the port, this time with a force of 16,000 men and 150 ships. On this occasion too Louisbourg held out for seven weeks. Afterwards the British razed the fortress walls to prevent the town from being fortified anew.

In 1961 Canada's federal government undertook the reconstruction of part of the Forteresse de Louisbourg. The result is that fortifications, the harbour, buildings, courtyards and gardens can today be seen very much as they appeared in 1740. In the course of the rebuilding archaeologists excavated the old foundation walls.

Reconstruction

Louisbourg Fortress, or "la Forteresse de Louisbourg", is Canada's most famous historical reconstruction, the prototype of a "Living History Museum" offering visitors an opportunity to experience at first hand the rigours of mid 18th c. life on the far from hospitable, frequently mist-shrouded, east coast of Canada. Throughout the main tourist season appropriately costumed "townspeople" – servants, soldiers, merchants, maids and fishermen – re-enact the arduous daily round of those times. Two restaurants serve speciality dishes prepared from old recipes.

★★ Louisbourg Fortress

The Forteresse de Louisbourg, modelled on those built by Vauban, is surrounded by a wall with towers and bastions, and encompasses more than forty buildings. The town, of which seven blocks of houses were rebuilt, was right on the water, so that ships could moor there. The most luxurious buildings are in the "Bastion du Roi", and these were occupied by the French King's representative who was both Governor and Commandant. The ordinary soldiers' barracks, in which several had to share a room, were simply furnished. Among the numerous service facilities were a bakery, stores, a smithy, etc. The entrance to the fort is via the Porte Dauphine, close to the Armoury, and there is a museum by the Bastion du Roi.

★★Lunenburg

J 18

Province: Nova Scotia. Population: 3000

Lunenburg Visitor Information, PO Box 1300, Lunenburg, NS B0J 2C0; tel. (902) 6348100

Information

From Halifax (see entry) south on NS Highway 3.

Access

Lunenburg, is a little fishing port on a peninsula on the Nova Scotia coast between the town of Mahone Bay and the mouth of the La Have River. Because of its geographical position the town has two harbours, Back Harbour in the North and Lunenburg Harbour on the bay of the same name.

Location

Lunenburg got its name from the many settlers from Lüneburg in northern Germany who came here when the British colonial government founded it in 1753 as a settlement for Protestants in Nova Scotia, and the social and cultural life of Lunenburg, as well as its traditions and townscape, still bear the imprint of those early northern European settlers.

History

Lunenburg's main claim to fame is its harbour and the shipyard that make it the home port of the famous "Bluenose" schooner, built here in 1921 when it was the world's best racing schooner, and the winner of

Harbour

Fisheries Museum
of the Atlantic
Lunenburg
(Nova Scotia)

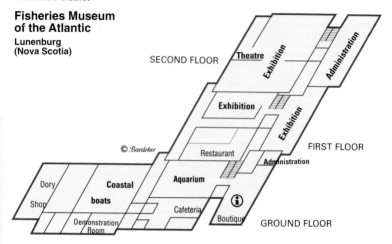

many an international race. It can still be seen today on one side of Canada's ten-cent coin. The sailing ship used in the "Mutiny on the Bounty" was also built in the Lunenburg shipyard.

The town's position as the centre of Canada's east coast fishing is reinforced every September when the Nova Scotia Fisheries Exhibition is held here. Besides the latest developments in shipping there is plenty of entertainment, on and off the water.

★★ Fisheries Museum of the Atlantic

The Fisheries Museum of the Atlantic, in a former fish factory on the waterfront at Duke Street, is well worth a visit (open mid-May to Oct., 9am–6pm, tel. 6344794).

Spread over three floors, it also has an aquarium, souvenir shop and restaurant, and tells the history of sailing and fishing along eastern Canada's coasts, enlivened by old prints, photographs, illustrations of fishing methods and equipment old and new, audiovisuals, etc. to make a visit here a memorable experience.

The museum's star attractions, moored in the port, are the "Cape Sable" trawler, and the "Theresa E. Connor", a 1938 schooner, where the museum staff vividly demonstrate the traditional methods of cod fishing and what life was like on board.

"Timberwind"

Between mid-June and mid-September there are two-hourly harbour trips, starting at 10.30am, from Lunenburg Harbour on the historic schooner "Timberwind".

Mackenzie District   D/E 3–7

Administrative unit: Northwest Territories

Information

Northwest Territories Arctic Tourism, Box 610, Suite 400, Yellowknife, NT X1A 2N5; tel. (867) 8737200, fax. (867) 8734059.

Location

Mackenzie District forms the western section of Canada's Northwest Territories, a vast expanse covering 1.5 million sq. km (579,000 sq. mi.) and bounded by Yukon Territory in the west, the continental coastline in the north, 120° longitude W in the east, and 60° latitude N in the south, with a population numbered only in several tens of thousands. Just on half of it is in the Arctic, and the forested sub-Arctic section of the district is home to a few thousand Indians.

The Mackenzie Mountains in the north-west of the district are a spur of the Cordilleras (see below), while the eastern section of this vast District is part of the Pre-Cambrian Canadian Shield. At its heart, however, is the alluvial valley of the Mackenzie River and the delta of this mighty north American river (see below).

Economy

In the 19th c. trade came from the few trappers and fishermen who lived here from time to time but in the first half of the 20th c. the forests in the Mackenzie Valley attracted the attention of the paper industry. This was followed by the discovery of oil at Norman Wells in the 1920s, pitch-blende at Port Radium and gold at Yellowknife (see entry) in the 1930s, with mining becoming a thriving industry after the Second World War.

Mackenzie
Mountains

The Mackenzie Mountains extend north-west into the Canadian Arctic as a spur of the North American Cordilleras, forming the frontier between Yukon Territory and the Mackenzie lowlands. Largely unexplored and relatively dry, with only sparse vegetation, the Mackenzies consist of two mountain chains, with the eastern one also known as Canyon Range. They cover about 800 km (497 mi.) and have peaks as high as 2900 m (9518 ft) in the west.

Mackenzie
Highway

The Mackenzie Highway was built shortly after the Second World War and is an all-weather road covering the 600 km (373 mi.) from Peace River in Alberta to Great Slave Lake and the territorial capital Yellowknife (see entry), serving to open up the mining district around Pine Point.

★★Mackenzie River   D/E 3–7

Administrative unit: Northwest Territories

Information

Northwest Territories Arctic Tourism, Box 610, Suite 400, Yellowknife, NT X1A 2N5; tel. (867) 8737200, fax. (867) 8734059.

Access

By air (Fort Simpson, Inuvik) or by road via the Mackenzie Highway

Course

With a length of 4250 km (2641 mi.), the Mackenzie is the second largest river in North America, one of the longest in the world (from the mouth to the source of the Finlay River, its longest tributary) and has a catchment area of 1.8 million sq. km (69,480 sq. mi.). The main sources of the Mackenzie are the Peace River and the Athabasca which merge to form the Slave River. On leaving Great Slave Lake this becomes the river bearing the name of the Scottish explorer Sir Alexander Mackenzie (see Famous People).

The river was already an important artery for the canoes of the fur trade in the 18th c. and is navigable today in summer by steamers as far upriver as Fort Smith, about 2000 km (1243 mi.).

Big oil and natural gas reserves have been discovered in the Mackenzie Delta and the Beaufort Sea, which opens out into the Arctic Ocean.

Most of the towns along the Mackenzie River were North West or Hudson's Bay Company trading posts, used for storing and trans-shipping skins and furs.

★★Mackenzie
Delta

The Mackenzie Delta can be reached by road along the Dempster Highway (see entry) or by air from Edmonton, Yellowknife and Whitehorse (see entries). Sightseeing charter flights can be booked in Inuvik.

The Mackenzie River Delta extends over about 12,000 sq. km (4632 sq. mi.) between the Richardson Mountains in the west and the Caribou Hills in the east, and its origins are partly interglacial, possibly pre-glacial.

Mackenzie River

In the Mackenzie Delta

About 200 km (124 mi.) before the river enters the Beaufort Sea its broad stream meanders and breaks up into countless smaller rivers and lakes.

Flora and Fauna

The vegetation of this delta landscape is mostly low bushes and shrubs, junipers, lichens and mosses, with magnificent displays of colour from flowers and mosses during the brief but intensive summer (from June to late July this is the land of the midnight sun). To complete the picture, this very special environment also has a great variety of wildlife on water as well as on land (see Facts and Figures, Flora and Fauna).

Population and economy

There are no more than about 7000 people in the delta. Their homes are in Aklavik, Tukoyaktuk, Inuvik (see entry), Fort McPherson and Arctic Red River, and they still live mostly from hunting and fishing.

The discovery of enormous gas and oilfields in the Mackenzie Delta and offshore in the Beaufort Sea is likely to alter the structure of the whole region and have a lasting impact on life in this remote landscape.

Fort Simpson

Fort Simpson is a community of about 1000 people where the Liard runs into the Mackenzie River west of Great Slave Lake about some 480 km (298 mi.) from the Northwest Territories' southern boundary with Alberta.

It is the oldest settlement on the Mackenzie River and was founded by the North West Company in 1804 for the trans-shipment of skins and furs at this strategic junction.

The town got its name from the Governor of the Hudson's Bay Company, Sir George Simpson, after the two companies merged in 1821. In the decades that followed Fort Simpson was vital as a staging post for the vessels carrying furs, food and raw materials up the Mackenzie River.

"Mackenzie Garden"

The fur traders, gold and oil prospectors were followed here by Christian missionaries who began tilling the fertile soil which has since earned the region the nickname of "Mackenzie Garden" on account of the vegetables and cereals grown in the area. Besides having a Roman Catholic mission, Fort Simpson has since 1858 also been a base for the Anglican Church.

★Manitoba   F–H 10–12

Geographical situation: 88°–102° longitude W, 48°–60° latitude N
Area: 650,000 sq. km (250,900 sq. mi.)
Population: 1.15 million
Languages: English, French, many Indian and Inuit languages
Capital: Winnipeg

Travel Manitoba, 155 Carlton Street, Winnipeg, MB R3C 3H8; tel. (204) 9453777, fax. (204) 9482517.   Information

By air: Flights to Winnipeg from many places in Canada   Access

By road: TransCanada Highway 1 from Ontario in the east and Saskatchewan in the west

By rail: By VIA Rail ("The Canadian", Toronto–Winnipeg–Edmonton–Vancouver)

Manitoba gets it name from "manito waba", an Ojibwan phrase used for the narrows on Lake Manitoba where the sound from the pebbles being ground against the shore by the storm-tossed waves seemed to the early Indians to have come from Manitou, the great spirit.   Name

Manitoba is bordered by the US State of North Dakota in the south, Saskatchewan in the west, Ontario in the east and the Northwest Territories in the north. Lakes and rivers cover just on a sixth of its surface area. It is 1225 km (761 mi.) from north to south and 793 km (493 mi.) from east to west. Manitoba's coastline, on Hudson Bay, runs for 645 km (401 mi.), and its port there is Churchill (see entry).   Location

Manitoba

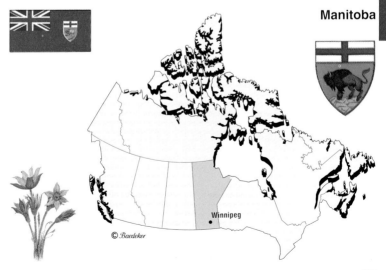

Winnipeg

© Baedeker

Manitoba

Geology

Manitoba's landscape bears the mark of the Ice Age, with its grassy prairie, uplands, dune wildernesses and craggy pine-covered hills, and criss-crossed by rivers flowing into Hudson's Bay.

The Hudson lowlands, with their layers of clayey topsoil, fringe the bay and stretch as far as 150 km (93 mi.) inland, before gently rising to the uplands south and west, the highest point being Baldy Mountain, at 831 m (2727 ft), in the Duck Mountains.

The biggest lakes in this "land of many thousand lakes" are those left from Lake Agassiz, the vast post-glacial lake that covered most of the province.

In the east and, above all, the north the Canadian Shield, consisting mostly of Pre-Cambrian granite, gneiss, quarzite, etc., covers over half the province.

Eastern Manitoba's highlands and plateaux were covered by glaciers. These massive moving icesheets carved deep clefts and depressions that eventually filled with water, and laid bare quartz and granite strata that were smoothed down to gentle hills. The thin covering of soil that these acquired was sufficient to support shallow-rooted dense evergreen vegetation.

Climate

The summers are hot, with average temperatures of between 17° and 24°C (62 and 75°F), and as much as 30°C (86°F) in high summer, although it can be quite cool at night, especially on the lakes.

Winters are long and very cold, getting as low as −40°C (−40°F).

In the intensively farmed south-west the frost-free period is about 100 days, but in the far north it is only 60 to 80 days.

Precipitation is comparatively low. Winnipeg, for example, only has about 120 days with significant precipitation a year.

Vegetation

Because of the differences in climate vegetation follows a particular sequence with the prairieland of the south bordered by a belt of parkland – open country dotted with trees, especially poplars – to the north. The dense forests begin around the southern lakes, starting with mixed woodland of poplar, birch, fir and pine, then becoming entirely coniferous before gradually giving way to tundra on Hudson Bay.

History

The ancestors of the native peoples of Manitoba got there from Asia over 12,000 years before the first Europeans. Around 1600 there were four Indian tribes in what is now Manitoba. The Chippewa lived in the bleak tundra around Hudson Bay, the Cree and Salteaux moved around the great forests of the Canadian Shield further south, while the Assiniboine, famous as buffalo-hunters, followed the herds on the prairies in the south-west along today's Canadian border with the USA.

The first European to explore the territory was Thomas Button, who sailed along the west coast of Hudson Bay in 1612 on a voyage of discovery, and spent the winter in Port Nelson, claiming the land for England. Like other later European explorers he was looking for the fabled Northwest Passage to India and instead of finding a sea route to the riches of the Orient had stumbled upon Hudson Bay and a land rich in game and wildfowl. The day of the lucrative fur trade had dawned.

A year earlier Henry Hudson and his son John, along with seven loyal seamen, had been cast adrift in an open boat in James Bay after a mutiny by the crew of his ship "Discovery". They were never seen again. Hudson had sailed along the east coast of Hudson Bay in 1610, also in search of the Northwest Passage. The harsh winter came on and along with it the mutiny, just as he had planned to head west again.

In 1631 and 1633 two English seafarers, Luke Fox and Thomas James – who gave his name to James Bay – explored the west coast of Hudson Bay and its southern inlet, James Bay, again in search of the Northwest Passage.

In 1670 King Charles II granted the Hudson's Bay Company the trading rights to all territories draining into Hudson Bay. They were named

Rupert's Land after the king's cousin, who was also titular head of the company which now had control of an area of about 8 million sq. km (3.08 million sq. mi.), one-twelfth of the land on earth! Thus the foundations were laid for the world's oldest company still active today, and its most far-flung. The company established trading posts and forts along the coast, then penetrated to the south and inland. Henry Kelsey set out a few years later from York Factory, at the mouth of the Nelson River, in search of yet more fur animals and lived for two years with the Plains Indians, travelling as far as what is today the boundary between Saskatchewan and Alberta.

The British and French were constantly at loggerheads over the fur trade and in 1731 Sieur de la Vérendrye began building a line of forts between Lake Superior and the lower Saskatchewan River. These included Fort Rouge, now Winnipeg, in 1738, as he sought to extend France's North American sphere of influence.

The rivalry lapsed with the defeat of the French in 1763 until the founding of the North West Company in 1779 to compete with the Hudson's Bay Company. The two companies were eventually merged in 1821, and the Hudson's Bay Company that emerged is still one of Canada's leading store chains, although it abandoned the fur trade in 1991.

While the fur-trading companies were still competing with one another the first farming settlement was planned, and in 1811 Lord Selkirk received over 260,000 sq. km (100,360 sq. mi.) from the Hudson's Bay Company, taking in parts of what is now Manitoba, the States of North Dakota and Minnesota, and north-west Ontario. The company wanted to get down the cost of importing foodstuffs, and thus gain a competitive advantage over its North West rival. Scottish and Irish settlers arrived a year later, to be joined by colonists from French Canada and a great many Métis. The North West Company tried in vain to destroy the settlement, and in 1816 Commander Robert Semple and 20 other men were killed at the battle of Seven Oaks near Winnipeg. But the settlement carried on and farming began to prosper, attracting more and more people to come and settle to farming out on the prairie.

When the Dominion of Canada came into being in 1867 it wanted to buy Rupert's Land from the Hudson's Bay Company and in 1870, in the biggest land deal in history, it bought this enormous territory, which then had a population of 170,000, from the company for 1.5 million dollars.

However, the settlers, led by Louis Riel, were opposed to this union by acquisition, in which they had had no say. Métis descendants of Indians and French fur traders, they feared for their special lifestyle, their language and their culture, as well as for their land rights. The threat to these led to an armed struggle at the Red River before the land purchase was finalised. Louis Riel, their leader, set up a provisional government and tried through negotiation to dictate the conditions for the territory's entry into the Dominion. Although his government collapsed and Riel was executed, the Bill of Rights he had negotiated, guaranteeing equal French and English language rights in school and church, was upheld and incorporated in the Manitoba Act that established the territory as the fifth Province. Those rights were to be the source of further conflict later on.

When Manitoba entered the confederation on July 15th 1870 it was known as the "postage stamp province", since it only covered 215 × 170 km (134 × 106 mi.), with Winnipeg its centre. Large parts of the province were not settled until late in the 19th c. Manitoba was extended west to its present boundary with Saskatchewan in 1881 and north to Hudson Bay and its present boundary with the Northwest Territories in 1912.

The railroad from the east reached Winnipeg in 1881, making it possible to export its grain. The influx of settlers that followed included many Mennonites, Icelanders and Ukrainians. The population soared from 62,000 in 1881, to 153,000 in 1891, 255,000 in 1901 and 461,000 in 1911. Winnipeg became a melting pot as immigrants of many nationalities – German, Scandinavian, Polish, Hungarian, Ukrainian and Jewish – stopped off in the city on their way west.

Manitoba

The policies enacted between 1890 and 1900 were to have a negative impact that is still making itself felt today. In 1890 the government of Manitoba passed the Public Schools Act, discontinuing public funding of Catholic schools and teaching in the French language. Manitoba's Official Language Act of the same year forbad the use of French in the courts and Parliament. These laws were condemned as a denial of equal rights by the French-speaking minority, and Catholic parents feared they would have to send their children to church schools. Both groups campaigned for almost a hundred years to get these statutes reversed until Canada's Supreme Court repealed the Language Act on the grounds that the Provincial Act could not take precedence over the Federal Act which proclaimed Manitoba a French-English province in 1870.

Province

The Provincial Parliament has 57 deputies. In Ottawa it is represented by 14 members in the House of Commons and 6 in the Senate.

Economy

Manitoba's economy gradually recovered from the 1982 recession and has been experiencing above-average growth over the past few years. More than 300,000 of its 490,000 workforce are employed in the services sector, mostly in banking, insurance, retailing, hotels and restaurants, schools, universities and government.

Minerals

Although not as rich in raw materials and renewable resources as its neighbours Alberta and Saskatchewan, Manitoba does have significant mineral deposits in the north. Its nickel, copper and zinc mines are working as normal again after closing down during the 1982/1983 recession, but the price fluctuations have caused limits to be set on how much can be mined. Mining companies have been moving into the Lynn Lake area in the north in recent years prospecting for gold.

In 1987 mining earned around 400 million dollars, the major minerals being nickel and copper.

Manitoba does not have much oil. For thirty years Virden in the southwest had a small-scale oil industry but output fell sharply in the 1890s.

Manitoba's energy reserves are in hydro-electric power. A billion dollar hydro-electric project is under way on the Nelson River. Work was begun in 1985 on the fourth of seven power stations on this river which is the Province's last exploitable watercourse.

Timber

Manitoba's timber trade brings in over 35 million dollars a year.

Agriculture

The importance of agriculture to the province's economy is demonstrated by the fact that it employs 40,000 people and is responsible for 20 per cent of the productive sector. Although the low grain prices of the 1980s meant that many of the 20,000 farms struggled to survive, returns in recent years have regularly exceeded one billion Canadian dollars.

Wheat is the main crop, followed by barley, oilseed rape, flax and rye. The short growing period in the north, where there are fewer than 90 days without frost, and the quality of the soil mean that further expansion of agricultural output is virtually impossible. Cattle rearing is becoming increasingly important, having almost caught up with grain cultivation from the point of view of income.

Fisheries

Manitoba's fisheries bring in about 15 million Canadian dollars. Two-thirds of the total catch comes from its three large lakes, and 90 per cent is exported to America's northern cities.

Industry

There are many different sides to Manitoba's economy. Manufacturing is the biggest sector, followed by farming, mining and hydro-electric power. The primary sector accounts for two-fifths of producing industry, including energy generation. The remaining three-fifths is spread over the secondary sector, such as building and construction.

The range of products extends from foodstuffs and farm equipment through vehicles and aircraft to energy plant and fibre-optics.

Tourism is growing in importance, with about 3 million visitors to the province every year.

English-speaking settlers from eastern Canada and the USA formed the first great wave of newcomers. These were followed by the Mennonites in 1874, then a great many Icelanders and French-speaking families from France and Québec in 1875. There was another big wave of English immigrants in 1891 and the first of a large number of Ukrainians. The fast- growing population went up from 62,000 in 1881 to 1.1 million in 1991, with about half of them living in and around Winnipeg.

Manitoba is a multicultural society, composed of many different ethnic groups. Almost 400,000 Manitobans are of English descent. Other important ethnic groups include Germans, Ukrainians, French, Dene Indians, Inuit, Poles, Dutch, Scandinavians, Hungarians, Jews and Italians. In recent years they have been joined by many Asians, especially Philippinos and Vietnamese, as well as South Americans. They have all managed to retain their cultural identity, so that in Winnipeg's Folklorama, Canada's National Ukrainian Festival, etc. Manitoba now hosts several of North America's biggest folk festivals.

According to the 1986 census, 758,310 of the population were English-speaking, 45,600 spoke French and 259,105 other languages. In terms of religion, 57 per cent of the population is Protestant, 31 per cent Catholic and 12 per cent of other faiths.

Suggested routes

From Winnipeg the Whiteshell Route passes through the Mennonite village of Steinbach, then on to Whiteshall Provincial Park, Falcon Lake, Winnipeg River and Pinawa.

Leaving Winnipeg on the TransCanada Highway the route enters the region of the Canadian Shield, its hills, lakes, valleys, forests and rivers abounding with opportunities for hunting and fishing or just relaxing. At Steinbach it is possible to visit an authentic Mennonite village. The resorts of Falcon Lake and West Hawk Lake further east offer fine beaches, sailing and waterskiing. Most of the route winds through the Whiteshell Provincial Park, along the Winnipeg River, criss-crossed by trails through forests that are home to moose, deer and black bear. Anglers can fish for pike and perch in the deep lakes but inside the park there are also shallow, marshy lakes, left by the Ice Age, and the haunt of wildfowl. Rocky crags to the north are covered with spruce and evergreens.

The Cornbelt route runs west out of Winnipeg on the TransCanada Highway across Whitehorse Plain to Brandon and south through the Turtle Mountain Provincial Park to the International Peace Garden.

It passes through the heart of the cornbelt, thousands of acres of wheat, barley and oats, the "breadbasket of the world", but also important for its livestock farming.

Many farmers and ranchers take in visitors as guests who can help with such farm chores as haymaking or sample the milking, or sample the pleasures of the lakes, rivers and streams. Spring is the best time for a farm visit since summer temperatures can be as high as 38°C (100°F).

The Interlake route follows the western shore of Lake Winnipeg north through Netley March and Gimli to the Hecla Provincial Park.

When in 1875 Iceland suffered intense and destruction volcanic eruptions many of its people chose to leave their beautiful but bleak homeland in search of a similar but more hospitable country where they could carry on with their farming and fishing. Liking what they saw of Manitoba, with its broad fertile prairie and many lakes they settled around Lake Winnipeg and Lake Manitoba.

La Mauricie

The first stretch of the route along the western shore of Lake Winnipeg takes in what was once New Iceland, an independent territory where lived and ruled the descendants of those first Icelandic settlers, and where their Icelandic traditions still live on today.

It is worth making a stopover in one of the Icelandic-style vacation resorts that have sprung up amidst the forests of spruce, aspen and Scotch pine. The lakes provide excellent swimming and sailing, and there are small car-free islands where moose and bear can be encountered, while in spring the skeins of geese and duck fly in to breed. The landscape is at its most scenic in the autumn, when the woods become a riot of colour and the ripe corn stands high in the fields.

North

The North Route takes the TransCanada Highway west out of Winnipeg to Portage La Prairie then north-west to the old fur-trading post of Neepawa and further through the Minnedosa River Valley to the Riding Mountain National Park and The Pas and Flin Flon.

It goes from the cornbelt towns deep in the interior to the lowlands around Hudson Bay, Riding Mountain National Park with its nature reserves and the timber and mining towns of Flin Flon and The Pas, where it is possible to get a flight to visit Churchill, Canada's only sub-Arctic seaport (see entry).

★★La Mauricie   H 16

Province: Québec

Information   See Québec Province

Location   La Mauricie refers to the very scenic area along both sides of the Saint Maurice River, a mighty river used for carrying timber, with Route 156 following the twists and turns of the narrow valley. This is also a good way of getting to Lac Saint-Jean (see entry).

★Suggested route (170 km (106 mi.))

Trois-Rivières   See entry

Forges de St-Maurice
The Forges de St-Maurice, 13 km (8 mi.) from Trois Rivières, leaving by the Blvd. des Forges, were Canada's first ironworks. They date back to 1730, and produced a whole range of items such as boilers and stoves until 1883 when the nearby stocks of iron ore and timber ran out and the works closed.

A pretty road leads to the river and the Fontaine du Diable, where there is an escape of natural gas that can be set alight.

Shawinigan
Shawinigan, 31 km (19 mi.) further on, owes its rapid development since early this century to the hydro-electric potential of its 50 m (164 ft) waterfalls. The two power plants are open to visitors from June to Dec. on weekdays; guided tours at 10am, 1.30 and 3pm (reservations tel. 372–3801).

The Centre Culturel (2100 Rue Dessaules, open 5–9pm) has a collection of contemporary art and sculpture, and puts on exhibitions of work by Québec artists.

Grand-Mère
An industrial town with a population of 16,000 41 km (25 mi.) along the road, Grand-Mère is another place that owes its existence to the power generated by the Mauricie River. Its name came from a nearby black rock with the craggy profile of an old grandmother, subsequently removed to the town park to make way for the power plant.

★★Mauricie National Park
A road leads from Grand-Mère via Saint-Jean-des-Piles to the south-east entrance to the Mauricie National Park.

The Parc de la Mauricie covers 544 sq. km (210 sq. mi.) and extends into the Laurentians that are part of the Canadian Shield. Its many kinds of tree range from maple, ash, cherry, lime and birch to a variety of conifers such as Scotch pine and cedar.

It is a reserve rich in wildlife, with black bear, wolf, fox, beaver, otter, mink, lynx and musk rat, and such birds as bittern, geese, snipe, osprey, hazelhen, etc. For the wildfowl there are close on fifty lakes, the finest being Lac Wapizagonke, 8 km (5 mi.) long, in the park's south-eastern section.

Saint-Tite (pop. 4000), reached after 44 km (27 mi.), and important for its leather industry, was founded in 1859 at the start of La Mauricie's timber trading, and in early September hosts a grand Western-style festival complete with rodeo, horse-races and processions.

Saint-Tite

The Musée du Bûcheron in Grand Piles, on the steep bank overlooking the river, provides a glimpse of the life of Canada's first lumberjacks.

Grand Piles

Route 155, which runs from here along the Parc National de la Mauricie, is reached by a road which turns off about half a mile beyond Mattawin. Near Rivière-aux-Rats a roads leads off to the Saint-Mauricie Nature Reserve. Both roads are passable from mid-April to mid-November.

167 km (104 mi.) further on, La Tuque (pop. 12,000), which was founded to exploit La Mauricie's timber, owes its industrial development to the building of a hydro-electric plant (216,000 kW). When the French first arrived here it was a major trading post.

La Tuque

The town owes its name to a rock by the river that looks like a "tuque", the knitted cap worn by the early Canadians.

Hydro-Québec's hydro-electric complex about 30 km (19 mi.) north of La Tuque is also associated with a big Compagnie International du Papier papermill which can be visited between 9 and 11am and 2 to 4pm.

Hydro-Québec paper factory

From La Tuque the railroad to Senneterre (449 km (278 mi.)) passes through the indescribably lonely terrain of Haute-Mauricie.

★Medicine Hat

G 8

Province: Alberta. Population: 47,000

Medicine Hat Chamber of Commerce, 413 6th Avenue S.E., Medicine Hat, AB T1A 2S7; tel. (403) 5275214

Information

Medicine Hat, on the South Saskatchewan River, is Alberta's fifth largest city. It gets its name from an Indian legend. During a battle between the Cree and the Blackfoot the Cree medicine man's headdress was blown off into the river. This was taken to be a bad omen by the Cree braves, who fled, and over time "the place where the medicine man lost his hat" became just plain "Medicine Hat". Rudyard Kipling described it as the place "with the whole of Hell as its cellar" when he visited the town in 1907, because enormous natural gas deposits had already been found when drilling for water in 1883.

Name

This natural gas today forms the basis for Medicine Hat's thriving petrochemical industry. Underground rivers also contribute to its intensive horticulture, the growing of flowers and vegetables in enormous greenhouses and highly irrigated fields.

Economy

South-eastern Alberta's ranching tradition is reflected in July's annual Agricultural Show and especially its rodeo and stampede.

Sights

There is a downtown walking tour which takes in buildings still left in the city centre from the turn of the century.

City centre

Mission

Medicine Hat Mall   The Medicine Hat Mall (Dunmore Rd. S.E.) includes over 60 different
                      stores and boutiques.

★City Hall   Medicine Hat's award-winning City Hall, supremely modern in its archi-
                      tecture and completed in 1986, is the pride of this mid-Western city.

Historical   The Historical Museum, which tells the story of the Canadian West – the
Museum   Plains Indians, pioneering days, etc. – also serves as the National Exhibition
                      Centre (1302 Bomford Crescent S.W., Hwy. 1/Hwy. 3; open Mon.–Fri.
                      10.30am–noon and 1–5pm, Sat., Sun. and public holidays 1–5pm).

Riverside   The Riverside Waterslide, with a variety of waterchutes, offers a chance
Waterslide   to cool off in summer.

★Rodeo and   Medicine Hat's annual three-day Rodeo and Stampede takes place in July.
Stampede

Mission   H 6

Province: British Columbia. Population: 31,000

Information   Mission Chamber of Commerce, 34033 Lougheed Highway, Mission, BC
                      V2V 5X8; tel. (604) 8266914

Location   About 70 km (43 mi.) west of Vancouver, the township of Mission in the
                      Fraser Valley gets its name from the mission station founded here in
                      1861 which soon became a staging post for trappers and "voyageurs"
                      on the Fraser River. The annual Mission Pow Wow in June still serves as
                      a reminder of its Indian missionary past.
                          The intensively farmed land around it is famous as having the longest
                      growing period in Canada, thanks to the protection afforded it in the lee of
                      the mountains. The Dutch who settled around the lower reaches of the
                      Fraser after 1848 built dykes to create a polder like their landscape back
                      home, and black and white cows can still be seen grazing the meadows here.
                          From Mission Highway 11 proceeds to the southern bank of the Fraser
                      River and the TransCanada Highway.

★Westminster   Westminster Abbey, a Benedictine abbey and seminary overlooking the
Abbey   town, is an impressive modern cathedral (reached via Dewdney Trunk
                      Road; viewing Mon.–Sat. 1.30–4pm, Sun. 2–4pm).

Mission Museum   The region's first bank, built in 1907, now contains the local museum
& Archives   (33201 2nd Ave., open Mon.–Fri. 10am–4pm, Sat., Sun. 2–4pm) with
                      exhibits of life among the pioneers and the Indians.

★★Moncton   H 18

Province: New Brunswick. Population: 60,000

Information   Greater Moncton Chamber of Commerce, 910 Main St, Moncton, NB E1C
                      1G6; tel. (506) 8572883

Location   An Acadian city in the south-east of the Province of New Brunswick,
                      Moncton is at the end of the narrow estuary of the Petitcodiac, one of the
                      tips of the Bay of Fundy, famed for having the world's highest tides.
                          Often hailed as the capital of Acadia, Moncton is an important east
                      Canadian road and rail junction, as well as having a French-speaking
                      university.

History   The French settled in the northern end of the Bay of Fundy in 1638, but the English destroyed their settlement a few years later and the inhabitants were abducted.

German settlers, previously from Pennsylvania, arrived here in the second half of the 18th c.

The east Canadian city owes its name to Robert Moncton, the British commander who took the nearby Fort Beauséjour in 1755.

Moncton University has a very interesting collection of works of art by modern Acadians. It also maintains a small museum on Acadian history. Both are open from June to September Tuesday to Friday 10am to 5pm, Saturday and Sunday 1 to 5pm; the rest of the year they are open Tuesday to Friday noon to 4pm and 2 to 4pm at weekends.

Galerie d'Art Musée de l'Acadie

Moncton Coliseum is one of the biggest venues of its kind in eastern Canada, staging big sporting events as well as gala balls, rock concerts and regional fairs.

Coliseum

Magnetic Hill, north-west of the city, is one of Canada's most visited natural wonders. It owes its fascination to the fact that a driver can put a car in neutral, release the brake and feel that it is being drawn uphill as though by some ghostly hand!

★Magnetic Hill

The giant waterchutes of Magic Mountain Water Park and its many other attractions make it very popular with visitors, especially in the summer.

Magic Mountain Water Park

Twice a day the high tide of the Atlantic Ocean flows through Fundy Bay and sweeps into the Petitcodiac estuary, swelling its trickle into a broad lake and covering the mudflats and salt-marsh all around.

★Tidal flow

Hillsborough, which is about 32 km (20 mi.) south of Moncton on the east side of the Petitcodiac estuary, has a historic steam train, of the Salem & Hillsborough Railroad (operating Jul., Aug. daily; mid-May–Jun. and Sep.–mid-Oct. Sat and Sun.; tel. (506) 734–31 95 for information).

Hillsborough

Hopewell Cape juts out into the Bay of Fundy's Shepody Bay and is just on 43 km (27 mi.) south of Moncton on Highway 114. Here the world's highest tides have sculpted an incredible coastal landscape, carving away at the soft rock to form the "flowerpots", strange pillars of granite topped with fir and spruce, apparently standing offshore but, as can be seen at low tide, still connected to the mainland.

★★**Hopewell Cape**

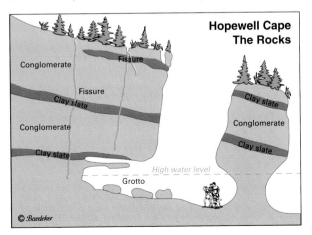

Hopewell Cape
The Rocks

Conglomerate
Fissure
Fissure
Clay slate
Conglomerate
Clay slate
Conglomerate
Clay slate
Clay slate
High water level
Grotto
© Baedeker

Moncton

★ Tidal Trail

The Tidal Trail leads from Moncton south on Highway 114, along the Petitcodiac estuary to Hopewell Cape (see above), where it turns south-west along Shepody Bay and Chignecto Bay. At Riverside-Albert a slight detour along the 915, a very narrow and fairly basic little road, leads to Cape Enrage, with its lighthouse, jutting out into Chignecto Bay, part of the Bay of Fundy (see entry). Bathing from the steep, stony beach below the cape is highly dangerous. Next come Waterside, a little resort, and Alma, the delightful fishing port at the entrance to the Fundy National Park (see Bay of Fundy).

★ Fort Beauséjour

Fort Beauséjour is a national park about 60 km (37 mi.) south-east of Moncton where Nova Scotia and New Brunswick meet (see entries). From the earthworks which are all that is left of the fort there is a fine view over the Cumberland Basin and Chignecto Bay. The fertile fen below the fort was farmed by French settlers as early as the 18th c.

History

The French settled here in the second half of the 17th c., calling the land around "Beau Bassin", but it passed to the Scots and English under the Treaty of Utrecht in 1713. The frontier between British Novia Scotia (New Scotland) and French Acadia ran then, as it does today, along the narrow land-bridge between New Brunswick and Nova Scotia. The British built Fort Lawrence on their side and the French built Fort Beauséjour on theirs. Fort Beauséjour was captured in 1755 by the British who then proceeded to drive out or deport the French-speaking Acadians who lived there.

Since 1926 Fort Beauséjour has been a protected national historic monument.

Information

The information centre at Fort Beauséjour recounts this place's turbulent history using various exhibitions and other visual aids.

New Brunswick's South-east Shore

New Brunswick's South-east Shore stretches north-east of Moncton along the Northumberland Strait, part of the Gulf of St Lawrence, and strung out along it are Canadian Atlantic seaside resorts where the bold actually venture into the water, mainly when summer is at its height.

Shediac

Shediac, on the Acadian "Costa del Sol" about 18 km (11 mi.) north-east of Moncton, is very popular with visitors in the summer months, priding itself on being the lobster capital of the world.

St Martin in the Wood, Shediac's Anglican church, built of Canadian red fir in 1821, is worth seeing.

★ Parlee Beach Provincial Park

Shediac's Parlee Beach Provincial Park is reckoned to have the finest sandy beach on Canada's Atlantic coast, and in summer the relatively shallow water here can get as warm as 20°C (68°F).

Cap-Pelé

Cap-Pelé, 60 km (37 mi.) north-east of Moncton, is a picturesque Acadian fishing village dating from 1780. It also has a lovely beach and the well-stocked fish market is particularly worth a visit.

Bouctouche

Bouctouche, about 50 km (31 mi.) north of Moncton, is another traditional Acadian fishing place, and the birthplace of K.C. Irving, the industrialist reputed to be one of the richest men in the world.

The Sacred Heart Chapel contains work by the Acadian artist Léon Léger (1848–1918).

Cogagne

An international hydroplane regatta takes place off the mouth of the Cogagne River, south of Bouctouche, every year. This is also a place for deepsea fishing expeditions.

★★ Kouchibouguac National Park

Kouchibouguac National Park is two hours' drive north of Moncton, along the Gulf of St Lawrence, where inland once lived the Micmac Indians.

The National Park of 238 sq. km (92 sq. mi.) has a unique ecosystem, with all kinds of coastal vegetation, including around 25 species of orchid, saltmarsh, high dunes, long sandbars and tidal lagoons stretching for close on 30 km (19 mi.), its coastline different after every storm.

The marshes and lagoons are breeding grounds for a whole world of waterloving creatures. It is a birdwatcher's paradise, with thousands of duck, geese, and other wildfowl, while seals love to bask on the sandbanks offshore.
    Further inland the park supports black bear, beaver, moose, deer, fox and coyote.

Wildlife

The park has its own campsites and trails, and can be explored by bike or canoe. There are obviously plenty of picnic sites, as well as a number of good beaches for bathing in summer, and skiing trails in winter.

Recreational facilities

A visitor centre of generous proportions provides plenty of information about the plants and creatures of the National Park. There are also audiovisual shows and guided nature trails.

Visitor centre

Kouchibouguac National Park, Kent County, New Brunswick, E0A 2A0; tel. (506) 8762443.

Information

★★Montréal

H 16

Province: Québec
Population: 1,017,000. Altitude: 233 m (765 ft)

Tourisme Montréal, 1555 rue Peel, bureau 600, Montréal, PQ H3A 3L8; tel. (514) 8445400, fax. (514) 8440541

Information

Montréal, in the south-west corner of Québec Province (see entry), is situated on the largest of the 234 islands that form the Hochelaga archipelago in the St Lawrence River. The heart of the city is the Île de Montréal (158 sq. km (61 sq. mi.)) at the confluence of the Ottawa River and the St Lawrence, which also takes in the slopes of the ancient volcano of Mont-Royal, or Mount Royal (238 m (260 ft)), the mountain park in the city centre.
    There are eight hills in and around Montréal, peaking as high as 527 m (1730 ft), the remnants of Ice-Age Devonian volcanoes.

Location

The city actually gets its name from one of the hills, the Mont-Royal, and nowadays a very popular park with a view. Jacques Cartier (see Famous People) landed here in 1535 and took the territory for his King, François I of France. Officially founded in 1642, Montréal is one of North America's most important cities. Not only is it the second biggest city in Canada, it is also the second largest French-speaking city in the world.
    Located as it is on the St Lawrence Seaway, the city has prospered since the 18th c. as a hub of communications and trade, a port of call for seagoing vessels from the Atlantic and the waterborne traffic along the St Lawrence and westward to the Great Lakes. It also has its share of administration and academic life, and is the seat of the bishopric.
    Having also won itself a high international profile with the Expo in 1967 and the Olympic Games in 1976, in 1992 Montréal celebrated the 350th anniversary of its foundation.

City

An impressive view of the city is to be had from Mount Royal or one of the skyscraper viewing platforms. Another way of enjoying the city skyline is from a boat trip on the St Lawrence.

View

Montréal's climate swings between the extremes of high humid heat in summer and heavy snowfalls in winter. The average temperature in January is −10°C (14°F), and −20°C (−4°F) is not unusual. In July the

Climate

thermometer hovers around 22°C (72°F), occasionally reaching 30°C (86°F). Mean precipitation over the year is around 750 mm (30 in.).

Montréal's population growth has always tended to be dominated by immigration, whether from overseas or elsewhere in North America. This was at its highest between 1851 and 1861, and 1951 to 1961. The city's population in the 19th c. was 82 per cent British and French in origin, but since the second half of the 19th c. it has been overwhelmingly French-Canadian. At the turn of the century there was an influx of Jews from Eastern Europe, followed by Southern Europeans. In 1971 the city had 64 per cent French Canadians, 11 per cent English Canadians, with 25 per cent ethnic minorities including Jews and Italians as the largest groupings, followed by German, Poles, Ukrainians and Dutch, Greeks and Portuguese, as well as Asians and Afro-Caribbeans. The number of inner-city dwellers has fallen sharply in recent years as many have moved out into the suburbs, and this exodus from downtown Montréal, and from elsewhere in Québec Province to suburbia for that matter, is continuing. While many small ethnic minorities get along with one another in the everyday way of city life, this is not the case with the French and English Canadians, for whom the gulf between their cultures seems as wide as ever, and the demands for autonomy of Canada's French-speaking population have intensified considerably in the recent past.

When Jacques Cartier (see Famous People), on his 1535/1536 voyage of discovery, was the first European to set foot in what is now Montréal, he found an Indian village of some thousand souls, called "Hochelaga" by the Huron, just below a hill (where McGill University stands today), which he named "Mont Réal", the royal mount, in honour of his French king. It was almost three-quarters of a century before the territory was visited again, this time by Samuel de Champlain (see Famous People), the founder of Québec, who came here in 1603. He found no trace of the Indian village, and in 1611 established a short-lived trading post called "Place Royale".

Another 30 years later Paul de Chomeday, the godfearing Sieur de Maisonneuve, founded a small mission station here in 1642. Called Ville Marie de Mont-Réal this was the original settlement that today is Montréal. He had accommodation built including a chapel and a hospital, run by Jeanne Mance, and built a palisade around it as protection against the Indians. Their conversion to Christianity was the object of the missionaries, foremost among them the Congrégation Notre-Dame and its Mother Superior Marguerite Bourgeoys, and the Compagnie de Saint-Sulpice, who had been given the Seigneurie of the Île Montréal in 1663 by the French king. By 1672 Montréal's population had grown to about 1500, the figure it remained at till the end of the 18th c.

In the comparatively calmer times following the peace treaty with the Iroquois in 1701 Montréal profited from its role as a centre of the fur trade, and farming began in the country round about. The burgeoning disputes between the British and the French finally erupted into war in the mid- 18th c. when the British succeeded in taking the city without a fight in 1760. During the American War of Independence the American revolutionary troops besieged the city briefly in the winter of 1775/76, but withdrew when its people sided with the British, refusing to take part in the Americans' fight for freedom.

In the time that followed Montréal benefited from an influx of Loyalists, fleeing from an America no longer loyal to the king, and from growing numbers of British traders, mainly Scots and Irish, who together formed the North West Company, stepped up the fur trade, and set Montréal up as an important trading post and rival to the Hudson's Bay Company. By 1792 Montréal's population, at about 6000, was enough to give it township status.

A further boost came with the opening of the St Lawrence to steamer traffic in 1809 and completion of the Lachine Canal in 1825, allowing shipping to get from the Atlantic to the Great Lakes. Population numbers

◀ *The City Hall in Montréal*

soared from 22,500 in 1825 to 44,000 in 1844 as immigrants flooded in from Great Britain. A dynamic business community invested heavily in timber and shipbuilding, then in import/export, and, after 1836, in railways and all the ancillary trades. Montréal became the most important centre of commerce, as well as an arena for social tensions, not only as between capitalism and the workers, but also between French-speaking and English-speaking factions as they struggled for political supremacy.

The Anglophile middleclass gained the upper hand with the defeat inflicted on the French patriots during the 1837 uprisings only to see their privileges swept away after 1867 as the French-speakers came to dominate the population. For a time, between 1844 and 1849 during the Canadian struggle for unification, Montréal became the capital, only to lose this status after the Parliament building fire during the unrest of 1849. Growing immigration from eastern and southern Europe meant that after 1900 the city became an even richer ethnic mix, its population soaring to close on 470,000 in 1922.

The boom for industry, trade, transport and financial institutions that followed the First World War gave way to the deep depression of the Thirties, when three-quarters of the million working population were forced on the dole, causing the collapse of the city budget.

The recovery, when it did come, was after the Second World War, when it was due to high demand from abroad and cheap immigrant labour, together with an army of refugees from rural life streaming into the cities. Montréal's economy received another boost from the joint venture with the USA to build the St Lawrence Seaway. The post-industrial era began in the Sixties with the demolition of much of the old centre of Montréal in order to construct the subway system, and massive expansion of the services sector. Giant multi-purpose building complexes sprang up while, below ground, a whole new town was built as a shopper's paradise, away from the harsh extremes of the Canadian winter. In fact there was virtually nothing that needed doing to improve on the already ideal business conditions. But all this actually had the opposite effect. The enormous infrastructure costs drove up prices, and this, together with political decisions to go for an independent French-speaking Québec, had industries and corporations in the 1970s moving away in droves to set up their headquarters in Toronto, where the business climate was better.

Since then the two cities, Toronto and Montréal, have been vying for the position of Canada's business capital. Montréal's staging of high-profile international events – Expo in 1967, the Olympics in 1976, Floralies Internationales 1980 – have taken a heavy toll of the city's finances to an extent well beyond the power of any short-term world-wide publicity to offset. In 1989 Montréal also played host to a major international conference on the hole in the ozone layer. The 350th anniversary of the city's foundation was celebrated in 1992 with a wide-ranging programme of cultural and other events, as well as in more permanent fashion by the opening of several fine new museums.

Economy

After the city's fortunes had been founded for a century and a half on the fur trade, the mid-19th c. brought a great shift towards industrialisation, followed on in the 20th c. by an expanding services and high-tech sector. In 1971 only 15 per cent of the active population worked in industry as compared with almost 25 per cent in management and administration and 24 per cent in services.

The availability of cheap electrical power has always been an important factor underpinning the city's industrial development. The major manufacturing industries are the construction of aircraft and rolling stock, electronics, textiles, petro-chemicals (oil refineries in east Montréal), food and drink (including breweries) and leather goods.

Montréal is the headquarters of a great many financial corporations, including Canada's oldest bank, the Bank of Montréal, founded in 1817, and other trading and money market concerns.

From its earliest days, Montréal's favourable location has made it a hub of communications. Its port caters for vessels engaged on both maritime and inland waterway trade, and is the second largest, after New York, on North America's Atlantic coast, covering 24 sq. km (9sq. mi.) and with berths for well over 120 ships. Thousands of freighters can be unloaded here during the ten ice-free months. There are enormous silos for handling the grain, and container terminals numbered amongst the most advanced of their kind in the world. All of Canada's main shipping lines are based in Montréal which has continued to gain in international importance for shipping since the opening of the St Lawrence Seaway.

The city is also traditionally the hub of Canadian rail traffic, astride all the transcontinental connections both east and west, and with the USA as well. It is the headquarters of Canadian National Railways, a conglomerate formed from a number of mergers, and of VIA Rail, Canada's rail passenger carrier. Canadian Pacific has also been duly represented since 1881.

Air traffic also figures prominently in Montréal, home to the national airline, Air Canada, and with two major international airports, Dorval for Canadian and US domestic flights, and Mirabel for all other international flights. Both IATA, the International Air Transport Association, and ICAO, the International Civil Aviation Organisation, with over 800 employees, have their headquarters here as well.

Road traffic is a big problem for the inner city, where it impinges on the quality of people's lives by wasting space or acting as a pollutant. There is an extensive network of urban motorways such as the six-lane Boule- vard Metropolitain, crossing Montréal from east to west, and there are many bridges – 15 road and 5 rail – linking the suburbs with the Île de Montréal.

The city has a good public transport system, with a modern underground and plenty of local buses. The "Metro", a subway named after its Parisian counterpart, and opened in 1966, has 65 stations (1988), each

The Olympia site in Montréal

Montréal

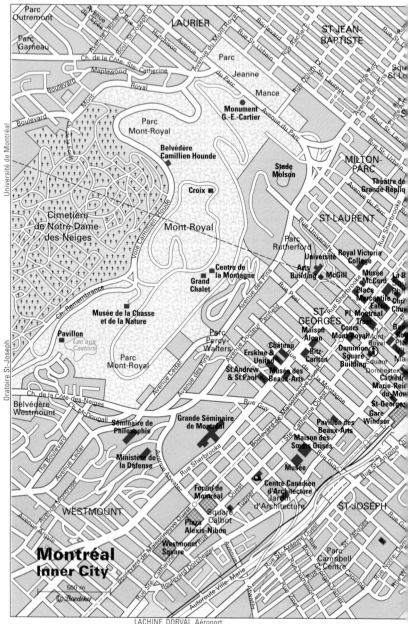

LACHINE, DORVAL, Aéroport
Ottawa, Toronto

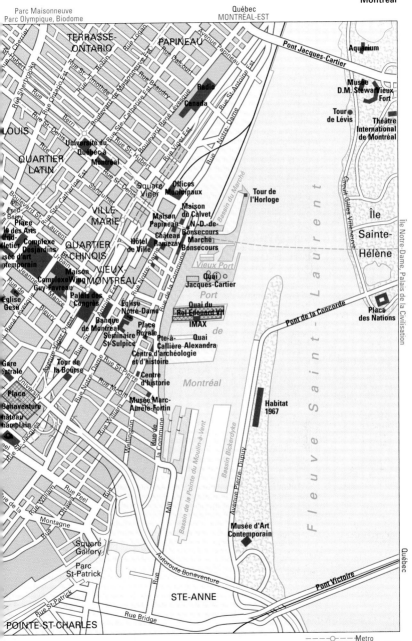

Montréal

Parc Maisonneuve
Parc Olympique, Biodôme

Québec
MONTRÉAL-EST

TERRASSE-ONTARIO

PAPINEAU

Pont Jacques-Cartier

Aquarium

Musée
D.M. Stewart Vieux-
Fort

Radio
Canada

Tour
de Lévis

Théâtre
International
de Montréal

LOUIS

Université du
Québec à
Montréal

QUARTIER
LATIN

Île

Square
Viger

Offices
Municipaux

Tour de
l'Horloge

Sainte-

VILLE-
MARIE

Maison
Papineau

Maison
du Calvet
N.-D.-de-
Bonsecours
Marché
Bonsecours

Hélène

Place
des Arts

Complexe
Desjardins

Hôtel
de Ville

Château
Ramezay

Place
des Arts

Musée d'art
contemporain

QUARTIER
CHINOIS

VIEUX-
MONTRÉAL

Vieux Port

Maison
Complexe Wing
Guy-Favreau

Quai
Jacques-Cartier

Port

Pont de la Concorde

Place
des Nations

Église
Gesù

Palais des
Congrès

Église
Notre-Dame

Quai du
Roi Édouard VII

IMAX

de

Banque
de Montréal

Place
Royale

Seminaire
St-Sulpice

Quai
Alexandra

Gare
centrale

Tour de
la Bourse

Pte-à-
Callière
Centre d'archéologie
et d'histoire

Montréal

Place
Bonaventure

Château
Champlain

Centre
d'histoire

Musée Marc-
Aurèle-Fortin

Habitat
1967

Rue William

Square
Gallery

Parc
St-Patrick

Musée d'Art
Contemporain

Autoroute Bonaventure

STE-ANNE

Pont Victoire

Rue Bridge

POINTE-ST-CHARLES

- - - -O- - - Metro

311

one different in its art and design, and about 60 km (37 mi.) of line running between all the important points in "Montréal Suburbain".

Sights

Vieux-Montréal	Said to be North America's most remarkable concentration of 17th, 18th and 19th c. buildings, "old Montréal" is the delightful Parisian-style quarter between the harbour and the banking district. Lovingly restored over the past thirty years, and very popular with visitors, it is best explored on foot, starting from the Metro for the Champ de Mars, just south of the station. A one-time drillground, then a promenade for the bourgeoisie, and now a square on the Rue Notre-Dame, this is overlooked by the two imposing 19th c. buildings of City Hall and the Palace of Justice.
★Hôtel de Ville	The City Hall was designed by Perrault with an eye to the French Empire style of Napoleon III. Built between 1872 and 1878 it had to be restored following a fire in 1922.
	Its hall of honour, which can be viewed daily between 9am and 4.30pm, is resplendent with marble and bronze, and has a bust of Jacques Viger, Montréal's first mayor in 1833.
"Vive le Québec libre" (see Baedeker Special p. 393)	It was from the balcony of City Hall that, during his visit to Canada in the summer of 1967, the French President Charles de Gaulle uttered his clarion call "vive le Québec libre!" – long live free Québec – meeting with an enthusiastic response from the crowds on the Place Cartier below but considerably upsetting Canada's Federal Government.
Vieux Palais de Justice	The old palace of justice, opened in 1856, is modelled on classical Greek lines and was completed in 1891 with the construction of the dome.
Place Vauquelin	Place Vauquelin is a square between the two public buildings, with a fountain and a statue of Jean Vauquelin (by Eugène Bénet, 1930), the officer who tried in vain to defend New France against the British in 1759/60.
Musée du Château Ramezay	Not far east along the Rue Notre-Dame, the Musée du Château Ramezay, which is open 10am to 4.30pm, Tuesday to Sunday, is an elegant mansion dating from 1705. It was the residence of Claude de Ramezay, Governor of Montréal from 1703 to 1724 and his successors, and provides a period setting for a collection of 18th and early 19th c. costume, furniture, and paintings.
Maison de George-Etienne Cartier	The nearby Maison de George-Etienne Cartier is a Gothic revival building, originally two stone dwellings which were the home of the first Canadian Prime Minister from 1841 to 1871. It is open daily from 9am to 5pm, mid-May to September, and from 10am to 5pm Wednesday to Sunday for the rest of the year. Part of the building has an exhibition of the life and work of Jacques Cartier (see Famous People).
Rue Bonsecours	The delightful Rue Bonsecours, off the Rue Notre-Dame, is one of Vieux-Montréal's oldest streets, with a whole range of the French architectural styles that went to make up the townscape of New France right through from the 17th to the 19th c.
Maison Pierre du Calvet	By the Rue Saint Paul is the Maison Pierre du Calvet, dating from 1770, with a rustic façade, asymmetric windows and a pointed roof, and containing a little museum with exhibits from the pioneer days.
Les Filles du Roi	Les Filles du Roi, now a restaurant, has an interesting history, being where the young women lived who were brought to Montréal by the King of France to become wives for the settlers whom he had heard were taking up with prostitutes and Indian women because of a shortage of females.
★Notre-Dame-de-Bonsecours	The city's oldest church, the Chapel of Our Lady de Bonsecours, at the

Maison "Les Filles du Roi"   *Notre-Dame-de-Bonsecours*

end of the street, was rebuilt in its present form in 1772 after a number of fires. It replaced the original wooden building (1657) put up by the founder of the Congrégation-de-Notre-Dame, Margeurite Bourgeoys, canonised in 1982. The church long contained a miraculous little madonna made of oak and given by the Baron de Fancamp in 1672. It was much venerated by the Congrégation de Notre Dame, and by seafarers, many of whom left offerings to the Virgin. Although today's madonna is a copy, the offerings, including some model ships, can still be seen.

The adjoining museum to Marguerite Bourgeoys tells of her Christian works.

Musée Margeurite Bourgeoys

The Marché Bonsecours nearby was built between 1845 and 1852 as a multi-purpose building in the Neo-Renaissance style by William Fortner. The Parliament of the unified Canada met here for a time in 1849 then it served as the town hall before becoming Montréal's vegetable market from 1878 to 1963 when, following restoration work in 1964, it became the offices of the City Administration.

★Marché Bonsecours

Extending along the river close to the Marché is the site of the old port, restored at great cost in recent years and today enjoying a new role as an entertainment and leisure centre. Special attractions include an ultra-modern IMAX cinema, a large junk market, and the Quai Jacques Cartier where, every July, the Festival of Laughter is held ("Juste pour rire"; festival office in the Rue St-Denis). From the old port a magnificent view is obtained of the impressive Montréal skyline. Boat tours run from the Quai Victoria.

★Vieux-Port

Festival of Laughter

Immediately to the north-west and stretching as far as the Rue Notre-Dame are the gardens of Place Jacques Cartier, where, under its Nelson's Column, there is a popular market of arts, crafts and souvenirs,

★Place Jacques Cartier

surrounded by inviting street cafés and fine 19th c. townhouses and mansions.

★Place d'Armes

The Place d'Armes is another square reached by taking the Rue Notre-Dame west out of the Place Jacques Cartier. The statue in the centre is by Philippe Hébert (1895) of Paul de Chomedey who in 1642 founded the mission Ville-Marie de Montréal from which the city is regarded as having developed.

Palais des Congrès

The Palais des Congrès, the futuristic conference centre at 201, avenue Viger Ouest (main entrance opposite the Complexe Guy-Fatreau), was built in 1983 on the Place d'Armes, over the Ville-Marie expressway. It is linked underground with the Place d'Armes and Place des Arts Metro stations, and has a unique five levels of the very latest in convention facilities on the grand scale, where 10,000 people at once could all take part in conferences, exhibitions and other events. One hall can seat 6,000 delegates. This is where the world climate conference was held in 1990, using its state of the art technology (e.g. satellite communications).

★★Notre-Dame Basilica

Also on the Place d'Armes, the Neo-Gothic façade of the Basilica of Our Lady, built in 1829, with its twin towers (69 m (226 ft)) fronts Montréal's oldest Catholic parish church (founded 1656). The amazing interior is the work of Victor Bourgeau, resplendent with woodcarving and stained glass illustrating the history of the city.

The Sacré Cœur altar (1982), in the chapel of the same name, consists of 32 bronze panels by Charles Daudelin.

The great organ is a Casavant and the recitals held in the church throughout the year are very popular.

Vieux Séminaire Saint-Sulpice

The Old Seminary of Saint Sulpice adjoining the Basilica dates from 1685. The foundation still belongs to the order of Saint Sulpice, a non-ordained priestly order. It began in Paris in 1642 with Abbé Dollier de Casson at its head, and much of the land of Montréal was gifted to it by the king in the 17th c. The seminary is the oldest stone dwelling in a city where originally most buildings were constructed more cheaply and simply in timber.

The building, which is not open to the public, is of a refined simplicity, with some late-Renaissance style embellishment. Through the grille can be glimpsed the oldest clocktower in North America, dating from 1710.

★Rue Saint-Paul

The Rue Saint Sulpice, as it runs down to the waterfront, is crossed by Montréal's oldest street, the Rue Saint-Paul, nowadays lined with all kinds of shops, but originally completed in March 1672 as the road between the fort and the Hôtel Dieu, the old hospital. It gets its name as much from Paul de Chomedey, the city's devout founder, as from St Paul the Apostle.

Place Royale

The Place Royale, a short distance to the west of the Rue Saint-Paul, was the heart of French colonial life, its market and its parade ground until transformed in the 19th c. with various government buildings.

The Neo-Classical customs house (1837) stands at the northern end.

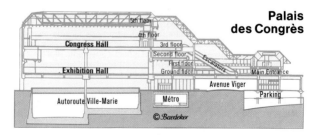

Palais des Congrès

To the south-east lies the Pointe-à-Callière, the "cradle of Montréal city". Two plaques and an obelisk, the work of Québécois artists, unveiled in 1894, commemorate the founding of the French settlement of Ville-Marie here in the late spring of 1642. The Musée d'archéologie et d'histoire (open Tue.–Sun. 9am–5pm), in buildings which are themselves of architectural interest, documents the city's beginnings. Remains of 17th and 18th c. foundations can be seen in the basement.

★Musée d'archéologie et d'histoire

Place d'Youville nearby was where in the 17th/18th c. canoes plied the waters of the Saint-Pierre River, now underground, as it flowed into the St Lawrence. Today the square is surrounded by 19th and 20th c. buildings. The courtyard of the Écuries d'Youville, close by, has some interesting old warehouses dating from about 1825.

Place d'Youville

The Centre d'Histoire de Montréal is in the old redbrick fire station (1903), and recounts Montréal's 350 year history (Open mid-May–mid-Sep. daily except Mon. and public holidays 10am–6pm; mid-Sep.–mid-May 11am–4.30pm.)

Centre d'Histoire de Montréal

East of the Place Youville stands the massive obelisk, the work of Québec artists, which was erected in 1894 to commemorate the 250th anniversary of the founding of the city.
The nearby Youville Stables, the Ecuries de Youville, were actually warehouses from around 1825 and are well worth seeing.

Obelisk

The Hopital général des Sœurs Grises is a short distance down the Rue Saint-Pierre. Montréal's second hospital dating from 1694, it was where Margeurite d'Youville founded the Congrégation des Sœurs Grises in 1753, the charitable order of the Grey Sisters. The wing of the building that the Mother Superior lived in was restored in 1980 and can be visited by prior appointment (tel. (514) 842–9411).

Hopital général des Sœurs Grises

Also in the Rue Saint-Pierre the Musée Marc-Aurèle-Fortin concentrates on works by this Canadian painter, but also shows pictures by artists from Québec Province. (Open Tue.–Sun. 11am to 5pm.)

Musée Marc-Aurèle-Fortin

Downtown Montréal · Ville-Marie

Ville-Marie Square is a good starting point for a look round the ultra-modern buildings of downtown Montréal, whose revitalisation began in 1962 with the cross-shaped towers of the Royal Bank of Canada building, 223 m (732 ft) and 49 floors high, its shops and offices providing employment for 15,000 people. The sculpture in the square is "Female Landscape" by Gerald Gladstone, a profound statement on modern architecture. Although there are plenty of stores at groundfloor level, the real shopper's paradise is below ground in the vast "Ville Souterraine", Montréal's subterranean city.

★Place Ville-Marie

Other downtown sights include the spacious Place du Canada, with a statue (1895) to Sir John Macdonald, the country's first Prime Minister (1867), in a group representing Canada and her seven children, or the seven provinces as they were then.

★Place du Canada

The church of Mary, Queen of the World, east of the square is the Catholic cathedral which was built in 1894 as a smaller version of St Peter's in Rome. The massive statues represent the patron saints of the Archbishopric of Montréal in the 19th c.

★Cathédrale Marie-Reine-du-Monde

Dorchester Square is reached by crossing Boulevard René-Lévesque. In its green gardens stands a statue by Emile Brunnet (1953) honouring Wilfrid Laurier, the French-Canadian statesman and Prime Minister of Canada

★Dorchester Square

from 1896 to 1911. Buildings around the square, which is also graced by Henry Moore's sculpture "Reclining Figure" (1962), include the Victorian bulk of the former Hotel Windsor (1878, renovated in 1985), the Neo-Classic Sun Life skyscraper, the city's oldest and put up between 1918 and 1933, and the towering Banque de Commerce Canadienne Impériale (1962), its 45 floors an example of a very fine architectural style that stands out from the often monotonous functionalism of many modern structures.

★Rue Ste-Cathérine

Rue Ste-Cathérine, which can be reached from Dorchester Square, is Montréal's main shopping thoroughfare, bustling with life and lined with department stores and shops of all kinds, as well as a host of eating places, ranging widely in the type of food on offer, as well as price.

It also leads to such other commercial centres as Cours Mont-Royal and the Promenade de la Cathédrale.

Place Montréal Trust

This futuristic marble and glass "megastructure", the creation of César Pelli and Mario Botta, has become one of the city's most popular meeting places. In addition to expensive shops the complex houses a number of service enterprises.

Cathédrale Christ Church

Christ Church Cathedral stands at the junction of Rue Ste-Cathérine and Rue University. The Gothic revival Anglican Cathedral dates from 1859. The statue in front of the cathedral (1870) is of Francis Fulford, the city's first Anglican Archbishop.

Maison des Coopérants

The Maison des Coopérants further along the Rue University is a massive glass and concrete tower, its own twin spires more or less a counterpoint to those on the façade of the cathedral.

★Musée McCord d'histoire canadienne

Also further along the Rue University, heading towards McGill University, the McCord Museum of Canadian History houses an outstanding collection of exhibits on Canada's social history, featuring the country's native peoples such as the Inuit and Pacific Coast Indians, and colonial life in the 18th c. Re-opened in 1992 following major restoration the museum also possesses an extensive pictorial archive comprising both contemporary and historical material. Open Tue.–Fri. 10am–6pm (Thu. until 9pm), Sat., Sun. 10am–5pm.

★McGill University

Not far from the museum is the extensive campus of McGill University, its student body currently numbering about 30,000. This major university was founded in 1821 thanks to the generosity of one James McGill, politician and fur trader, whose statue (1875) stands on what was once the site of Hochelaga, the Indian village. Also on the campus is the

Musée Redpath

Redpath Museum of Natural History. (Open Oct.–May Mon.–Fri. 9am–5pm; Jun.–Sep. Mon.–Thu. 9am–5pm.)

Place-des-Arts

The Place-des-Arts metro station, on the northern edge of downtown Montréal, gives access to the city's modern centre for the performing arts, the Place-des-Arts, built in 1964. It contains four venues – the Salle Wilfried-Pelletier (capacity about 3,000), home to the Orchestre Symphonique de Montréal and where Canada's top ballet companies take the stage, the Théâtre Maisonneuve, seating about 1300, the Théâtre Port-Royal, seating 755, and the recital room, the Café de la Place, with seating for 138.

Musée d'art contemporain

The Musée d'art contemporain (MAC; exhibitions of contemporary art; open Tue.–Sun. 11am–6pm), on the south side of the square, is particularly worth a visit. Young French-Canadian artists are accorded special prominence.

★Complexe Desjardins

To the south-east, between Rue Sainte-Cathérine and Boulevard René-Lévesque, stands the huge imposing Complexe Desjardins, 1976, with numerous shops, cinemas, banks and a post office.

There are more shopping arcades in the nearby Complexe Guy-Fabreau.

Montréal's Chinatown is centred around the Rue de la Gauchetière, with two Chinese arches marking the heart of the quarter. This dates from the late 1860s when many of the Chinese labourers who had come to work in the mines and on building the railroad moved into the cities in search of a better life. Today's Chinatown is no longer exclusively Chinese but a place where anyone can relax and enjoy a good meal.

The Musée des Beaux Arts (open Tue.–Sun. 11am–6pm, Sat. until 9pm), situated on the western edge of downtown Montréal, is the oldest museum in Canada, having been founded in 1860. Several dozen rooms house the city's public art collection comprising paintings, sculpture and items of applied art of all periods from Europe and Canada. For some years now the museum has also mounted major exhibitions of modern art. Equally noteworthy, this time from an architectural point of view, is the museum's annexe by Moshe Safdie (see Famous People).

Further to the south-west, in the Rue Baile, is an attraction of a rather special kind – the Centre Canadien d'Architecture. This quite exceptional museum, housed in an elegant post-modern building by Phyllis Lambert and Peter Ross, boasts an unusually comprehensive collection of architectural drawings and photographs, together with a library and archive.

Named after Sir John Sherbrooke, Governor General of Canada from 1816 to 1818, Rue Sherbrooke is probably the city's most elegant main shopping thoroughfare, still retaining in the downtown section something of its 19th c. charm as it cuts across the Île de Montréal from east to west. At the turn of the century the few thousand people living in this quarter on the slopes of Mont-Royal owned about 70 per cent of Canada's wealth, earning it the title of the "Golden Square Mile".

Around downtown Montréal, and easily reached by metro, there are several other places worth seeing between Mont-Royal in the west, Parc Maisonneuve and Parc Olympique in the north, Île Sainte-Hélène in the east and Parc Agrignon and the Jardin zoologique in the south.

Mont-Royal rises 233 km (765 ft) above the city and is the green lung near the city centre. A stroll through this lovely park enables the visitor to see monuments from Jacques Cartier to King George VI, to spend some time by the Lac-aux-Castors and to have a look at the cemeteries on the western slope where the city's different ethnic groups have rested in peace together for centuries. From the summit, or rather from a platform below the cross, there unfolds a magnificent panorama of the whole of the 51 km (32 mi.) length of the Île de Montréal and the St Lawrence. On clear days the view extends to the Adirondack Mountains in the USA.

The Oratoire Saint-Joseph (metro: Côte-des-Neiges), near the western exit from the park, is dedicated to Canada's patron saint, and is a mecca for pilgrims. A huge Renaissance-style domed basilica was built in 1924, at the instigation of Brother André of the Congrégation de Sainte-Croix who had already built a small chapel here in 1904, where he performed miraculous acts of healing for which he was canonised in 1982. His tomb is in one part of the sanctuary in the original chapel. Votive gifts are displayed in a second chapel. A cloister behind the church leads up to Mont-Royal. Brother André's monument is by Emile Brunnet and that for St Joseph by Alfred Laliberté. A small museum exhibits religious art. There is a good view from the observatory over north-west Montréal and Lac Saint-Louis.

Close by is the campus of the Catholic, French-speaking University of Montréal, founded in 1876 and with 17 faculties, plus a polytechnic and a business school. The University buildings are chiefly by Ernest Cormier and date from between 1924 and 1943.

Complexe Guy-Fabreau
★Chinatown

★Musée des Beaux Arts

★Centre Canadien d'Architecture

★Rue Sherbrooke

Île de Montéal

★★Mont-Royal

★Oratoire Saint-Joseph

Université de Montréal

Oratoire St-Joseph

Cross on the Mont-Royal

★ Westmount Square

Montréal's Anglo-Canadian Westmount district south-east of Mount Royal centres around the square of the same name (metro Atwater). Its steel and glass office buildings are by Mies van der Rohe and were completed in 1966, typifying the highrise international architecture of the mid-20th century.

It forms quite a contrast with the late 19th c. mansions and villas still very much a feature of the surrounding streets.

★★Jardin botanique

Across on the other side of the city is another oasis of greenery, the Parc Maisonneuve (metro Pie IX), incorporating North America's leading botanical garden, the lay-out of which is wonderfully imaginative. Visitors are drawn in particular to the Japanese Garden. The glasshouses too are exceptional, especially the displays of orchids and bonzai. The gardens contain in all some 26,000 species of plant. Open mid May to mid Oct., gardens 8am–8pm, glasshouses 9am–6pm.

★★Parc Olympique (map page 319)

The Olympic Park, to the east, was the site of the 1976 Summer Olympics.

The Olympic Stadium, at its centre, takes between 60,000 and 80,000 spectators and is nowadays used for baseball, festivals, fairs and shows. Looking like a great seashell, the bowl can be covered over against the elements by a roof attached by cables to the mast looming above it. A platform at the top of the mast reached by a lift affords a magnificent view, in fine weather, over the city and its surroundings.

The Olympic Stadium, one of the most visited sports arenas in North America, is the home of Montréal's famous baseball team, the "Montréal Expos".

★Biodome

In 1992 the former Olympic Velodrome, another of the Parc's architecturally eye-catching structures, was officially renamed the "Biodome", marking its transformation from sports arena to covered botanic-zoological garden. Visitors to this absorbing exposition are taken on an

Parc Olympique

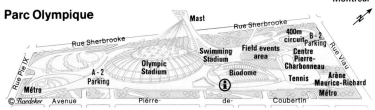

ecological journey through four different habitats – tropical rain forest, the St Lawrence River, the northern coniferous forest, and the arctic – travelling in effect from the equator to the pole. Every attempt has been made to reconstruct as accurately as possible the conditions typical of each environment, so providing a natural setting for the characteristic flora and fauna.

To the west of the Parc Olympique, on the other side of the Rue Pie IX, stands the palatial villa built in 1918 for the shoe manufacturer Thomas Dufresne. Modelled on the Petit Trianon at Versailles it today houses the Musée des Arts décoratifs (open Wed.–Sun. 11am–5pm), an exhibition of international design from 1940 onwards.

★Chateau Dufresne

It is worth paying a visit to the "Village" on the way back downtown. Between the Rues Saint-Denis and Papineau, it is a lively, colourful quarter comparable with New York's Greenwich Village. The restoration of the old houses has been going on for years, as its developing social and cultural life has unfolded around them.

Le Village

Square Saint-Louis, reached by taking the metro to Sherbrooke Station, is one of Montréal's prettiest old squares, set in a turn-of-the-century French-Canadian residential quarter. In the little streets around the tree-shaded square there are still a few of the attractive Victorian houses, some of them now pleasant restaurants. Part of the Rue Saint-Denis and the pedestrian mall along the Rue Prince-Arthur at the western end of the square are given over in summer to outdoor cafés, etc., in fact all the lively streetlife of a modern bohemian quarter.

★★Square Saint-Louis

The Boulevard Saint-Laurent close by, one of Montréal's main shopping streets, marks the dividing line between the French-Canadians on one side and the Anglo-Canadians on the other, but in fact is highly cosmopolitan along its length, especially around the Rue Laurier where newcomers tended to first settle down in the 18th c. Between 1900 and 1930 the district was predominantly Jewish, then Greek, followed by Eastern Europeans and most recently Hispanics. As all the different cultures mix and mingle in a welter of languages, the many small stores selling specialities from all over the world give parts of the street quite a bazaar-like atmosphere.

Boulevard Saint-Laurent

There are two islands in the St Lawrence: Sainte-Hélène, which is named after the wife of Samuel Champlain (see Famous People), and Notre-Dame which is artificial. Both have several features worth seeing (metro: Île Sainte-Hélène).

Île Sainte-Hélène, Île Notre-Dame

The two islands were the site of Expo '67, the theme of which was "Terre des Hommes" (Man and his World). Many of the national pavilions, in varying states of repair, still remain to give a flavour of the 1967 world fair, its architecture and the progressive spirit that marked the Sixties.

Expo '67

This monumental work by Alexander Calder, created for Expo, is 22 m (72 ft) high and weighs 60 tonnes. It symbolises Man's vigour, strength and progress.

★L'Homme

Montréal

La Ronde Amusement Park	Every year at the end of May/beginning of June, La Ronde, Île Sainte-Hélène's big amusement park (open mid May to Sep., daily 11am–midnight) is the venue for a huge firework spectacular.
Vieux-Fort, Musée David M. Stewart	Of historical interest is a visit to the Vieux-Fort, the old fort built as an arsenal by the British in 1820 and restored to hold the D.M. Stewart Museum (open May–Aug. Wed.–Mon. 10am–6pm, Sep.–Apr. until 5pm), a collection of firearms, maps, navigational instruments, etc. In the summer uniformed soldiers recreate the military drill of the 18th c. (daily 10am–6pm).
Île Notre-Dame	Being so close to the city this man-made island with its lake of the same name and Bassin Olympique (where the Olympic rowing events were held) is an immensely popular recreation area.
Les Floralies	In 1980 Île Notre-Dame played host to "Les Floralies", the world-famous International Garden Festival. Flower lovers can still enjoy the splendour of the displays adorning the lovely gardens.
Circuit Gilles Villeneuve	At least once a year – in June – Île Notre-Dame again becomes the focus of world attention when the Molson Grand Prix du Canada, a Formula 1 World Championship event, is staged on the Circuit Gilles Villeneuve, named after Canada's best known racing driver. The lap record for the 4.43 km (2¾ mi.) track, still one of the more challenging despite having been "made easier" in 1994, is at present held by Michael Schumacher with a time of 1min 21.5 secs (195.68 kmph (121.59 mph)).
Palais de la Civilisation	Renamed the "Palais de la Civilisation", the French pavilion for Expo '67, an impressive ultra-modern building by Jean Faugeron, is today used for a wide range of cultural events.
★★ Habitat '67	The principal attraction of the Cité du Havre (across the Pont de la Concorde from Île Sainte-Hélène) is the housing project known as Habitat '67. It was designed by the Israeli-born architect Moshe Safdie as one of the grandiose schemes of Expo '67 to provide low-cost futuristic inner-city housing, but was never actually completed in its entirety. Now rather past their prime, these precast concrete uniform building blocks with their terraces and in their great variety of combinations do provide a far from standard alternative to municipal housing in boring tower blocks or monotonous estates.
Maison Saint-Gabriel	The Maison Saint-Gabriel, a charming old stone farmhouse in the Saint-Gabriel district (metro Lasalle), dates from 1698. It was restored in 1960 and turned into a museum of colonial life, with exhibits from the 17th to 19th centuries (guided tours mid Apr. to mid Dec. Tue.–Sat. 1.30 and 3pm, Sun. 1.30, 2.30 and 3.30pm). Originally the farmhouse was where the "filles du Roy" lived, the unmarried young women sent over by the King of France to provide Nouvelle France with plenty of offspring to carry on the French line.

Surroundings

★Lachine	Lachine, with a population of 45,000 on the south-east bank of Montréal Island (in Lac St-Louis), got its name from the first pioneers who in the 17th c. made their way up the St Lawrence looking for a route to China (in French "la Chine"). It became an important staging post for conveying goods round the famous Lachine Rapids. Today it is an important industrial base. It offers plenty of opportunities for charming trips along the banks of the St Lawrence. The Lachine Canal, which was first begun as a way of getting round the rapids in the 17th c., was eventually dug in 1825. It is twenty years, however, since it was last used for shipping and nowadays forms

part of a park which includes an Interpretation Centre, telling the story of the canal and providing guided tours. (Pavillion Monk, 7e Ave./Blvd. Saint-Joseph; open mid May–mid Sep. Mon. 1–6pm, Tue.–Sun. 10am-noon and 1-6pm.) In summer it is possible to ride along the park's 11 km (7 mi.) of cycletracks, while in winter there is cross-country skiing.

Daily between the end of April and middle of October powerful motor-boats specially designed for the purpose run exciting – and usually very wet – trips through the rapids from the Vieux Port (Quai Victoria), departing 10am, noon, 2pm, 4pm and 6pm.

★Boat trips

The Musée de Lachine (open mid Mar.–Dec. Tue.–Sun. 11.30am–4.30pm) is in a restored building dating from 1669, and contains many of the items used in everyday life in the colonial days of la Nouvelle France.

Musée de Lachine

The Musée du Commerce de la Fourrure in an old fur warehouse (1803) illustrates impressively, various aspects of the fur trade in the 17th/18th c., long the mainstay of Montréal's existence.

Musée du Commerce de la Fourrure

On the south-west tip of Montréal Island, Sainte-Anne-de-Bellevue is the pleasant home to the Macdonald Agricultural College, founded in 1906. Much of its acreage is used for research, and there is an experimental farm that can be visited. The Morgan Arboretum, covering 24 ha (59 acres), has woodland trails, walks and ski-runs that are popular with visitors from much further afield as well.
    Buildings of historic interest in the early 18th c. Rue Sainte-Anne in the township centre include the house of Simon Fraser (1793), one of the heads of the North West Company of fur traders, the Victorian town hall and Saint Anne's Church (1853). A pleasant hour or so can also be whiled away in the cafés and restaurants along the waterfront promenade.

Sainte-Anne-de-Bellevue

From Saint Anne's Sluice – l'Ecluse de Sainte-Anne – dating from 1840, below the old iron railway bridge that linked the Île Montréal with the Île Perrot, there are boat trips on Lac Saint-Louis or Lac des Deux-Montagnes.

Boat trips

The Église de la Visitation in this part of town, on the Rivière des Prairies, is worth a visit. Built between 1749 and 1752, it is one of Montréal's oldest Catholic parish churches and has an interior covered with wood carvings by local artists. The monuments (1903) in front of the church are to Père Nicolas Vill and Ahuntsic, the Indian chief who lost his life during the Iroquois wars.
    The riverside park is a lovely place for a walk or a picnic.

Sault-au-Récollet

Moose Jaw   G 9

Province: Saskatchewan. Population: 33,000

Moose Jaw Chamber of Commerce, 88 Saskatchewan Street E., Moose Jaw, SK S6H 4R3; tel. (306) 6926414

Information

Moose Jaw, the "friendly city", is in the heart of the grain country, at the confluence of the Moose Jaw River and Thunder Creek. It is an industrial town and has a turbulent history; there are at least three versions of how it got its name, the most popular being that it comes from "moosegaw", the Cree word for warm breezes, since it is warmer here in winter than elsewhere in the vicinity.

Location

Moose Jaw has Canada's busiest airfield (at the Canadian military base, south of the town) which is also home to the famous Snowbirds aerial acrobatic group.

Airfield

In 1881 two land surveyors from Canadian Pacific decided that the point

History

where the railroads met should be where the Moose Jaw River met Thunder Creek. The fertile soil soon meant that people settled here permanently once the railroad was finished and Moose Jaw became a town in 1903 after it had grown to be an major junction. It also became important for its grainstores and meat-processing.

In the Roaring Twenties Moose Jaw, at the end of a direct line from Chicago, was from where Al Capone and his fellow gangsters ran their liquor empires during Prohibition. A few of the old buildings are still to be seen on Main Street.

Sights

Western Development Museum

The Western Development Museum (open Apr.–mid-Jun. daily 10am–5pm; mid-Jun.–beginning Sep. 9am–8pm) on Diefenbaker Drive, which was opened in 1976, is worth a visit since it is the only museum documenting the history of transport on the prairies. It gives an account of transport by road, rail, water and air, and includes automobiles, horse-drawn ambulance (1907), trucks, steamers and locomotives, even a ferry, as well as a railway station complete with telegraph office.

Art Museum & National Exhibition Centre

This museum and exhibition centre in Crescent Park puts on touring exhibitions of art, history and science. Among the 3000 items are clothing, Sioux and Cree beadwork, farming tools, etc. There is also a permanent exhibition of Canadian art. (Open Jun.–Sep. Tue.–Sun. noon–5pm and 7–9pm; Oct.–May Tue.–Sun. noon–5pm, Thu., Fri. also 7–9.30pm.)

Wild Animal Park

The Wild Animal Park, established in 1929, covers about 203 ha (502 acres) in the river valley south of Moose Jaw (open: May–Oct. daily 10am till dusk); it has about 300 native and exotic creatures, as well as a children's zoo and amusement centre.

Wakamow Valley

Open all year round, Wakamow Valley is a scenic new park on the Moose Jaw River east of the town. Its name is Cree for loop and alludes to the spot where the Moose Jaw River loops abruptly from north to east.

Plaxton's Lake

At Plaxton's Lake there are footpaths and cycletracks and opportunities for picnicking, canoeing and skating in winter.

★Moosonee   G 14

Province: Ontario. Population: 1400

Information

Northern Developments Office, Ferguson Road & 1st Street, Moosonee, ON P0L 1Y0; tel. (705) 3362991

Moosonee is the seat of administration for the north-east region of Ontario. It is at the mouth of the Moose River on James Bay (see Baie James) and there are no roads to it, so it can only be reached by rail (see Cochrane, Ontario, "Polar Bear Express") or plane.

★Moose Factory

In 1673 the Hudson's Bay Company built a fortified trading post on an island in the Moose River near where Moosonee is today. It was destroyed by French troops a few years later, but what remains can be seen in a little museum (open mid-Jun.–beginning of Sep. 9am–6pm). The smithy, about 200 years old, is the oldest wooden building in Ontario Province.

Révillon Frères Museum

The Révillon Frères Museum sets out to throw some light on the rivalry between the English Hudson's Bay Company and their French competitor which dogged Moosonee's history as they each sought to win the upper hand, both militarily and economically, in the territory around the mouth of the Moose River.

★★Muskoka   H 15

Province: Ontario
Area: over 650 sq. km (250 sq. mi.)

Georgian Lakelands Travel Association – Orillia Chamber of Commerce, | Information
150 Front Street S., Orillia, ON L3V 4S7; tel. (705) 3264424

Take Highway 400 north out of Toronto to Coldwater, then continue on | Access
Highway 69; the roads around Muskoka are Highways 118 (Glen
Orchard–Port Carling–Muskoka Falls) and 169 (Foot's Bay–Gravenhurst).

Muskoka, about two or three hours' drive north of Toronto (see entry), is | Landscape
one of North America's prettiest lake districts, bounded by Georgian Bay
(see entry) in the west and the Severn River in the south.
   Geologically, Muskoka is part of the Pre-Cambrian Canadian Shield, its
granite and gneiss shaped by the last Ice-Age, which left behind hundreds of lakes as the glaciers receded. This allowed a slight rise in
ground levels as the weight of the ice was removed.
   This lake district is very reminiscent of parts of central Sweden, with
a landscape of lakes and islands, rocky outcrops and crags amidst pine
forests with occasional groves of mixed woodland.

Thanks to its relative closeness to the cities on Lake Ontario and Toronto | Recreational
Muskoka has become a place for holidaymakers and weekenders, with | area
many marinas and holiday homes to prove it. Its waters are full of fish
and ideal for angling, canoeing and in many cases even sailing. There
are some beautiful trails that can be followed on foot or mountain bike.
It is a landscape that is particularly attractive in winter as well.

For visitors the main centre is little Port Carling (pop. 700), on the site of | ★Port Carling
an Indian settlement where sluices regulate the turbulent waters of the
river running from the upper lakes (such as Lake Rousseau and Lake
Joseph) into the much bigger Lake Muskoka. This is very busy especially
in the summer. The town's Pioneer Museum is worth a visit. Open daily
from Jun.–mid-Oct., it gives an account of the history of the area, including its long tradition of boat-building.

The township of Huntsville (pop.12,000) in the north of the Muskoka dis- | Huntsville
trict is also the western entrance to the Algonquin Provincial Park (see
entry). Lion's Lookout Park has a fine view over the town and the district.
For a good idea of the history of settlement locally visit the Muskoka
Pioneer Village on the Brunel Road (open from Jun. to mid-Oct.).
   Nearby Williams Port has a botanical garden around the Dyer
Memorial, commemorating a lawyer from Detroit.

★★Nahanni National Park   E 5/6

Administrative unit: Northwest Territories
Area: about 4784 sq. km (1847 sq. mi.)

Nahanni National Park, PO Bag 300, Fort Simpson, NT X0E 0N0; tel. (867) | Information
6953151

By air: From Fort Simpson (NT), Fort Liard (NT) and Fort Nelson (BC). | Access

By road: Access by canoe or expedition from Nahanni Butte, about 30 km (20
mi.) west off the Liard Highway connecting Fort Nelson and Fort Simpson.

Situated in the Mackenzie Mountains, Nahanni National Park covers a | Landscape
large portion of the lovely valley carved out by the South Nahanni River.
The magnificent scenery is of a wild beauty which the Canadian authorities have deliberately kept unspoilt, allowing neither roads nor tourist
accommodation within the conservation area.

Nahanni National Park

Designated a National Park in 1974, Nahanni was added to UNESCO's World Heritage List in 1978.

Geology

The labyrinthine karst ridges of the South Mackenzie Mountains are full of caves and gorges, hollowed out by water as softer minerals were dissolved from the limestone. The region's complex landforms are the result of its having been free from ice cover for some 250,000 years.

History

Nahanni means "people from over there" and is supposed to refer to a vanished Indian tribe.

Stories about the region began with the gold prospectors who travelled up the Liard River on their way to the Klondike. They were also drawn to the valley early this century when the three McLeod brothers came here and word got around that gold nuggets the size of grapes had been found. Three years later the headless bodies of two McLeods were found in the valley where their cabins stood, henceforth to be known as Headless Valley. The vein of gold was sought long but in vain. Albert Faille spent a lifetime trying to find out about the brothers, but what exactly befell them remains a mystery. Other people also disappeared, by 1969 as many as 44 of them. Tall tales and legends grew up and South Nahanni became somewhere to be avoided.

Flora and fauna

There are unusual plants to be found there such as orchids, and the wildlife includes bear, moose and caribou.

South Nahanni River

The Nahanni River flows through the Selwyn, Mackenzie and Franklin Mountains before running into the Liard River, a tributary of the Mackenzie, at Nahanni Butte. On its way it passes through awe inspiring gorges, over wonderful waterfalls and hot mineral springs, their heat producing vegetation unusual for these climes.

The South Nahanni's rapid changes in gradient and speed of current

The Virginia Falls in the Nahanni National Park

make canoeing suitable only for those with whitewater experience. A permit must be obtained from the park authorities. Anyone planning a trip should for safety's sake inform the park authorities in Fort Simpson or the Nahanni Butte station at the entrance to the park.

The 200 km (124 mi.) trip up the Nahanni River from Nahanni Butte to the Virginia Falls is an unforgettable experience of the great outdoors, taking in a change in level of 200 m (656 ft).

White-water trip

From Nahanni Butte the first stretch is to about 80 km (50 mi.) upstream, where the river divides itself into a number of "splits" and there are sulphurous hot springs (about 37°C (99°F)). Since the ground never freezes such exceptional plants grow there as ferns, roses, and wild cherries.

Soon the river passes through the towering walls of the first canyon, some around 1200 m (3950 ft) high, then after 27 km (17 mi.) Deadmen Valley opens up before, after 34 km (21 mi.) the second, dizzyingly high, canyon rears up, only to be followed by a third, where the river makes a turn of 90° through what is known as "the Gate", guarded by the mighty Pulpit Rock.

Beyond the canyons come the foaming torrents of Hell's Gate then, finally, after the fourth canyon the river rounds a bend to give a sudden breathtaking confrontation with the famous Virginia Falls.

In a magnificent setting, and twice as high as Niagara, the Virginia Falls plunge 90 m (295 ft) into a cauldron of foam encircled by rocks. From the Albert Faille Portage around the waterfall a road takes the canoeist to the rim of the cataract, where there is a beautiful view of this great natural spectacle.

Virginia Falls

New Brunswick

H 17/18

Maritime Province in eastern Canada
Area: 73,440 sq. km (28,348 sq. mi.)
Population: 762,000.

New Brunswick Tourism, PO Box 12345, Woodstock, NB E0J 2B0; tel. (506) 7892050, fax. (506) 7892044

Information

The name New Brunswick (Nouveau Brunswick) comes from the German Duchy of Braunschweig ruled by George III of England in the late 18th c. Virtually rectangular in shape, it borders on the Province of Québec and the St Lawrence in the north, and the US State of Maine to the west, with the Bay of Fundy and Nova Scotia to the south, and the Gulf of St Lawrence and Prince Edward Island to the north-east.

Location

The province has three kinds of landscape. In the south, along the Bay of Fundy, stretch the Southern Uplands, their highest point, Mount Pleasant, barely 400 m (1,312 ft). These are joined to the north by the Central Uplands, through which flows the Saint John River. The fertile lowlands in the south-east form the border with Nova Scotia. Like the eastern part of Québec Province, New Brunswick has the low relief of the paleolithic spur of the Appalachians – the undulating plateau rises from around 250 m (820 ft) to 820 m (2700 ft) at Mount Carleton in the north. A number of rivers – Saint John, Saint Croix, Petitcodiac, Miramichi, Nepisiguit and Restigouche – divide the province up into lots of shallow valleys that make good farmland, the most important being the valley of the Saint John River.

Topography

Along the coast New Brunswick has a relatively mild maritime climate. Inland, on the other hand, there are mostly continental extremes of temperature with hot dry summers and cold snowy winters, when the average temperature is around −10°C (14°F). In July the average is 19°C (66°F), although it has been known to soar to a record 38°C (100°F).

Climate

About four-fifths of the province is wooded, with only about 7 per cent used for farming, mainly potatoes.

Vegetation

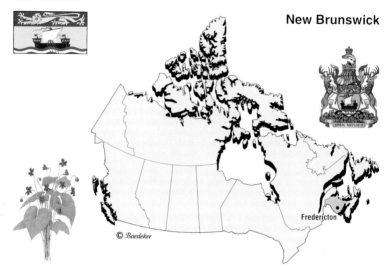

New Brunswick

© Baedeker

Fredericton

History

The Indians, who were here long before the arrival of the Europeans, were mainly Micmac, one of the Algonquin tribes. They lived mainly by hunting and fishing, using the rivers to make their way far inland. Many of the place names still show their Indian origin. Miramichi Bay (Miramichi means "Micmac country") was also presumably where the first contact was made with Europeans when Jacques Cartier (see Famous People) landed here with his French expedition in 1534. Early in the 17th c. his fellow countryman, Samuel de Champlain (see Famous People), began the systematic colonisation of Canada, claiming the territory for France as part of "la Nouvelle France".

Few French settlers came here to begin with, preferring other parts of Canada such as the Saint Lawrence lowlands. However, the Treaty of Utrecht in 1713 gave "Acadia" – the pseudo-Classical name for original French lands on the Atlantic coast, now Maine, New Brunswick and Nova Scotia – to the British, and the following years saw the population growing, with the French contingent mostly in the north and east, many of them Acadians driven out of nearby parts of Nova Scotia.

The southern part of the province was settled by about 14,000 English Loyalists after the American War of Independence in 1776, mainly around the lower reaches of the Saint John River. This led to New Brunswick becoming a separate province from Nova Scotia in 1784. The colony became internally self-governing in 1847 and in 1867 it was one of the four provinces to found the Canadian Confederation.

Population

New Brunswick can rightly claim to be Canada's only truly dual-language member of the Confederation. Its French-speaking minority of 35 per cent lives in close contact with the English-speaking majority. The official languages are French and English. All the road signs, for example, are in both languages, while ability to speak and write in both is a precondition of employment in the civil service. The province is officially called New/Nouveau Brunswick. The rest of the population are mostly of German, Dutch and Scandinavian origin.

Where people live depends on the lie of the land, so that while very few live in the forested interior, the river valleys, lowlands and coastal strip are relatively densely populated. The larger towns are Saint John, Moncton and the provincial capital, Fredericton (see entries).

Traditionally the economic mainstay of New Brunswick is the felling and processing of timber. Forests still cover over three quarters of the province, and about 25,000 people are employed in forestry and allied industries such as paper and pulp.

Tourism is coming to play an increasingly important part in the economy, centred mainly on the Baie des Chaleurs and in Restigouche. New Brunswick's fisheries have long been another important part of the economy, albeit not to the extent of the other Maritime Provinces, providing over 15,000 jobs in various branches of the industry.

Forestry

Intensive arable farming is mainly on the higher ground of the Saint John Valley, with potatoes the main crop, but some grain, fruit and vegetables as well. Between Saint John and Sussex agriculture predominantly takes the form of livestock and dairy farming.

Agriculture

Mining in New Brunswick did not get under way until after the Second World War. Besides coal there is zinc (at Bathurst), lead and copper.

Mining

★Newfoundland

G/H 19/20

Situation: latitude 46°30′–60°30′N and longitude 52°30′–67°30′W
Population: 563,000
Area: 405,720 sq. km (156,608 sq. mi.)
Capital: St John's

Tourism Newfoundland & Labrador, PO Box 8730, St John's, NF A1B 4K2; tel. (709) 7292830, fax. (709) 7290057

Information

The main airports on the island of Newfoundland are St John's, Gander, Stephenville and Deer Lake, which also take flights from Europe. Those worth mentioning in Labrador are Goose Bay, Churchill Falls and

Access

Newfoundland

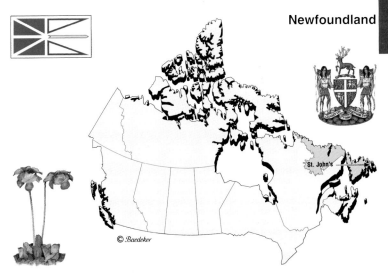

© Baedeker

St. John's

327

Newfoundland

Wabush, all of which, apart from Churchill Falls, can be reached from the larger Canadian airports.

There are ferry services to Newfoundland from North Sydney (Nova Scotia) to Port-aux-Basques (all year round) or Argentia (mid-June–mid-September), and to Labrador from St Barbe (Newfoundland) and Blanc Sablon (May–December) and Lewisporte and Goose Bay.

A partly tarmacked road runs between Baie Comeau (Québec) and Labrador City.

The old narrow-gauge railway on Newfoundland which linked Port-aux-Basques with St John's was closed in the 1960s. The line from Schefferville to Sept-Îles carries iron ore.

Location

Newfoundland, Canada's youngest province, consists of the island of that name together with countless other small islands and an area of some 300,000 sq. km (115,800 sq. mi.). Newfoundland Island, the tenth largest island in the world (roughly 110,000 sq. km (42,460 sq. mi.)) is in the Atlantic off Canada's north-east coast, separated from Nova Scotia by the Cabot Strait and from Labrador by the narrow Strait of Belle Isle, and measures 525 km (326 mi.) from north to south and 515 km (320 mi.) from east to west. Labrador, the peninsula called by Jacques Cartier "the land that God gave Cain", is bordered on the west and south by the Province of Québec and is 1046 km (650 mi.) north to south and 724 km (450 mi.) east to west.

Topography

Newfoundland Island is part of the Appalachian system and sits on the Continental Shelf. The famous "Grand Banks" offshore to the east and south of the island, which are only 200 m (656 ft) deep, are the world's richest fishing grounds. Newfoundland's varied landscape was shaped by the ice ages, leaving big fiords, moorland, lakes and gentle valleys. The highest point is Lewis Hill (814 m (2,672 ft)) in the Long Range Mountains on the west coast. These are wooded, as are the river valleys, with the rest a rocky wasteland.

From the Long Range Mountains the land falls away to the east and north-east. The Central Newfoundland plateau is one of North America's oldest geological formations, going back 400 million years to when it was part of the old Afro-European continent. The landscape in east Newfoundland, with the Bonavista, Burin and Avalon peninsulas, is pleasantly hilly.

Labrador is part of the east wing of the Canadian Shield surrounding the vastness of Hudson Bay. The undulating plateau of Pre-Cambrian granite and gneiss is 200–500 m (656–1,641 ft) above sea level, rising up to 1800 m (5908 ft) in the north-east. The coast is a typical fiord landscape.

Climate

Newfoundland's island climate is characterised by the fogs which occur all year round, caused in summer by the cold air from the Labrador current meeting the warmer air from the landmass, with the process reversed in winter. There are no great swings in temperature, the weather tends mainly to be rainy and cool. Average winter temperatures are between −2°C (28°F) and −9°C (16°F), often accompanied by violent storms, and in the middle of the island the thermometer can fall to −20°C (4°F) and below. Summer is fairly hot and wet on the coast and warmer further inland: the average July temperature is 15.3°C (59.5°F). The island has plenty of rain or snow all year round, especially in the east and on the coast (St John's 1346 mm (53 in.) a year).

Labrador has a much more severe climate, with greater extremes of temperature, but less rain. Its northern climate is arctic, with winter temperatures of below −40°C (−40°F) for six months of the year. In the three months of summer the average temperatures are around 10°C (50°F). The southern coastal areas are distinctly warmer. Goose Bay averages −14°C (7°F) in January and 21°C (70°F) in July, with an annual rainfall of 737 mm (29 in.).

Vegetation

The northern part of Newfoundland Island is largely covered with fir and spruce, while the south is moor and marsh, with a few stunted trees growing on the barren podzol.

Labrador's vegetation is predominantly conifers in the south giving way to sparser subarctic birch and small conifers and then the tundra of the far north.

Excavations at Port-au-Choix show that Indians were living in Newfoundland, the "cradle of the New World", at least 6,000 years ago. The Beothuk, the original North American Red Indians, were first known to Europeans as "redskins" because of the red ochre they used to decorate their bodies, and hence the name for them brought back to Europe by John Cabot.

The sensational diggings at L'Anse aux Meadows between 1961 and 1967 revealed traces of a Viking settlement from around 1000 AD, possibly making the legendary Leif Erikson, one of their number, the first discoverer of Newfoundland and hence North America. The island was rediscovered in 1497 by John Cabot, an Italian whose real name was Giovanni Caboto, but who was in the service of England, although Basque fishermen were already fishing the rich waters of the Grand Banks as early as the 14th c., but keeping the existence of those waters to themselves. Soon the seas off the "new found land" were keeping the whole of Europe supplied with fish. This contact with Europe had fatal consequences for the native peoples, and the last Beothuk died in St John's in 1829. Labrador's Montaignais and Inuit only managed to avoid the same fate because their lands were of no interest to the colonialists.

Newfoundland effectively became Britain's first colony when Elizabeth I was declared its Queen in St John's in 1583. For a century the island was in practice ruled by the "Fishing Admirals", the British West Country merchants who made rules to prevent any permanent settlement that would provide them with competition. Some small English fishing communities managed to establish themselves nevertheless, although they never actually succeeded in getting colonial status. The French, however,

Newfoundland: Bay of Quidi Vidi

did set up a colony, with a Governor, in Plaisance (Placentia) in 1662, and conflict between the French and the British over the island only ended in 1713 with the Treaty of Utrecht when the British got Newfoundland and the French ended up with just St-Pierre and Miquelon.

In the years that followed Newfoundland was settled by the Irish, Basques and English West Countrymen. Newfoundland became a self-governing dominion within the British Commonwealth in 1855. During the Second World War an economic boom was created by the Allied military bases. Although Newfoundland took part in the Québec Conference in 1867 it did not become the tenth province of the Canadian Confederation until March 31st 1949, following a 52 per cent vote in favour at a referendum.

Labrador has known human habitation for about 8,000 years (L'Anse Amour), and the Inuit in the north and the Naskapi Indians in the south long resisted French and English attempts to settle the coastline. John McLean began exploring the interior on behalf of the Hudson's Bay Company in 1839. The railway line between Sept-Îles (Québec) and Schefferville in central Labrador, completed in 1954, enabled exploitation of iron ore deposits discovered at the end of the 19th c. Goose Bay, an important Allied base during the Second World War, is now used by NATO.

"Titanic"

During the night of the 14th to 15th April 1912 the SS Titanic, on her maiden voyage from Southampton to New York, struck an iceberg over the Newfoundland Bank and sank within three hours in the waters of the Atlantic. Only 703 of the 1308 passengers and 898 crew of the supposedly unsinkable ship survived. The wreck now lies on the sea floor at a depth of 3797 m (12, 462 ft).

Population

Newfoundland is unusual for Canada in having a very homogenous population: 99 per cent of the "Newfies" are English-speaking and more than 95 per cent were born on the island. About 2700 speak French, and they live mainly in the north-east and south-west of Newfoundland (St George's, Port-au-Port) and in Labrador. The only native peoples to have survived are the Micmac Indians.

About 95 per cent of the population of the province live on Newfoundland, although at 5.1 persons per sq. km (2 per sq. mi.) it is still very thinly populated. About a fifth of the population live in the St John's commuter area, while the rest are in the fishing villages along the coast. Originally people lived along the whole length of the coast but in the 1970s they were grouped into small communities of one to two hundred as part of a resettlement campaign.

With a population of only 0.1 per sq. km (0.03 per sq. mi.), Labrador is virtually uninhabited, apart from the coast and the iron ore workings. Two Indian tribes live in the north-east and south-west of Labrador, the Naskapi and Montagnais. The Inuit community numbers about 2600, and they get their living from the sea.

Newfoundland dog

The Newfoundlander is an unusually large and heavy breed of dog, bear-like in appearance, with a flat coarse coat. The first settlers told of a breed of dog, around 1500, which lived on the island and was black, black and white, brown and grey in colour. These wild dogs had thick waterproof coats, and were used by the native Beothuk Indians to help haul in the fishing boats or pull sledges. Their appearance and their use in fishing caused speculation that they could be descendants of the Norwegian boarhound, since become extinct, and possibly brought to the island by the Vikings around the year ten hundred. Another theory is that the Vikings first brought the Newfoundland to Europe and inter-bred their dogs with the North American races to make the boarhound.

The Newfoundland was first brought to England and the North American mainland in the 17th c. where the massive, friendly dog was so popular it was much in demand, leading to such a drain on the native stock that systematic breeding of the strain was begun in Europe and North America towards the end of the 18th c. However to maintain the purity of the breed it was constantly necessary to import original native

Molly Mill's Beppo, a typical Newfoundland thoroughbred

dogs from Newfoundland. By 1907 all the Newfoundlands living in the wild in Canada were extinct. Recently consideration has been given to creating a new race of dog in Newfoundland by re-importing from Europe and America. Nowadays Newfoundlands are used as guide dogs for the blind and for rescue at sea.

The fishing for which Newfoundland was famed in the 15th c. is still its main industry, providing about half the island's jobs. Most of Newfoundland's 32,000 fishermen are in co-operatives, fishing mainly for cod but also taking herring, halibut and salmon. Increasing demand, penetration by Japanese and Russians fleets, and the building of enormous factory ships had such a devastating impact on the seemingly inexhaustible fish stocks after the Second World War that strict quotas and a 200 mile limit had to be imposed. Despite considerable subsidy, the industry is still in recession, its difficulties compounded by distribution problems and high interest rates, with many fishermen having to work as lumberjacks at times in order to survive. Since Newfoundland's earliest history seals have also been hunted for their meat and their skins, and this still contributes to many families' livelihoods. The seal pups are particularly prized for their valuable furs. There have been protests about the hunting of seals since the mid-Fifties due not so much to the numbers that are taken as to the method of killing, when they are clubbed to death. *Economy*

Farming is not important since very little land is suitable, and it employs only about 4,000 out of Newfoundland's workforce of 200,000. The farms on the Avalon Peninsula and in the Codroy Valley only supply the local markets. *Farming*

In recent years mining and forestry have outstripped fishing in terms of production. Iron ore has been mined in the province since the turn of the century, principally in the Labrador Trough in western Labrador; Labrador City, where there is one of the biggest opencast iron mines in the world, *Mining* and Wabush produce almost half of Canada's iron ore. Other minerals mined include lead, copper, gold, silver and gypsum. In the late 1970s large offshore oil and gas reserves were found off the coasts of Labrador and Newfoundland. There is estimated to be at least 1.85 billion barrels of oil in the Hibernia Field about 300 km (186 mi.) east of St John's, and deposits of the same order are believed to lie under the Grand Banks, although icefloes and pack ice will make extracting it very difficult.

The completion of the TransCanada Highway in 1962 gave a substantial boost to Newfoundland's paper industry (Grand Falls, Corner Brook), kept supplied by the province's timber on a sustainable basis thanks to the reforestation programme. Labrador's hydro-electric reserves are put at 7500 to 10,500 MW, and the hydro-electric power station at Churchill Falls supplies Québec with an output of 5600 MW.

Unemployment in Newfoundland is a major problem, touching on almost every sector of the economy and reaching record levels for Canada in May 1988 at 17.2 per cent.

Suggested routes

North Avalon

This short route round the Avalon peninsula can be covered in one or two days, starting at St John's and following the north coast, with its picturesque fishing villages.

Marine Drive

Marine Drive, one of the oldest roads in Newfoundland, begins in St John's on Highway 30 and meets Highway 20 in Torbay. There are good views of the Atlantic from several points.

Logy Bay

Logy, in North America, means slow or listless, and is also the name given to the big, slow fish caught in this bay.

The Marine Sciences Laboratory located here carries out oceanic research, and has guided tours on Mondays and Fridays in summer at 3pm.

A difficult landing in Pouch Cove, Newfoundland (see p. 333)

Flat Rock has a history going back at least to 1689. The village, where the sea has a very heavy swell, has indeed a huge flat rock forming a natural jetty and beach.

Flat Rock

Flat Rock is also known for its cave containing an altar to the Virgin which brings many pilgrims to the village every year.

There is proof of the existence of Pouch Cove, one of Newfoundland's oldest settlements, as far back as 1611. Its rather perilous harbour offered sanctuary to illegal immigrants in the 17th and 18th c. when permanent settlement was banned.

Pouch Cove

The Community Museum (open 9am–5pm) recounts the history of this little place which, like Flat Rock, has a very impressive swell, so that boats have to be hauled out of the water on sledges since there is nowhere for them to anchor with safety.

Close on 30 km (19 mi.) south of Pouch Cove lies one of the very oldest villages in Newfoundland, Portugal Cove, where the inhabitants still mainly rely for a living on fishing (cod and salmon in particular).

Portugal Cove

Highways 72 and 70 lead onto the Port-de-Grace Peninsula, with its lovely coast and scenic fishing settlements, chief among them being Harbour Grace (population 3,100). This flourishing little town on Conception Bay gets its name from "Havre de Grace", as it was christened by the French in the early 16th c. At one time the second biggest town on Newfoundland, a series of massive fires between 1814 and 1944 slowed down development of this "harbour of grace".

Harbour Grace

It is probably the only place in Canada to have a monument to a pirate. Captain Peter Easton based himself here in 1610 and pressed hundreds of Newfoundlanders into his buccaneer fleet, beating a French squadron in 1611. Eventually, having amassed an immense fortune from plundering the ships of all nations, he retired to Savoie in France as a Marquis. His pirate fort was in the east part of town where the old Customs House (1790) stands today. Now an excellent local museum, open every day in summer and with a beautiful view of Conception Bay, it has a large local history collection, including model ships, 19th c. furniture, photographs, etc. Harbour Grace also has the oldest stone church in Newfoundland, St Paul's Anglican Church, which was built in 1835.

A number of transatlantic flights set out from here, such as the Wiley Post world trip of 1931.

Heart's Content, in its lovely setting, was founded in 1650, making it one of the oldest places on the coast.

Heart's Content

In 1866 the first transatlantic cable reached here, covering a distance of about 4440 km (2760 mi.) from Ireland, and for a century it remained North America's most important relay station, taking 3000 messages a day, until automation led to its closure in 1965.

The cable station has been declared a provincial historical site and has been converted into an interesting museum which is open daily in July and August. It tells the story of communications from earliest times to the present, with a separate section dedicated to the transatlantic cable and the role that Heart's Content played in it, plus a replica of the cable station's first office.

The 81 km (50 mi.) journey south back to St John's via Highway 80 passes through scenic fishing villages such as Heart's Delight, Cavendish, Whiteway (strange rock formations) and Green's Harbour, picking up the TransCanada Highway at the end of Trinity Bay.

This tour follows the eastern and southern coastline of the Avalon Peninsula from St John's to Argentina, taking in two of the world's most important reserves for seabirds at Bay Bulls and Cape St Mary's and starting out on Highway 10 south out of St John's.

South Avalon

Open all year round, Cape Spear National Historic Park, on Highway 11 11 km (7 mi.) south of St John's, is the most easterly point in North

Cape Spear National Historic Park

America, and has Newfoundland's oldest lighthouse. Dating from 1835 it was in operation until 1955 and is now an interesting museum. In addition there are massive half-ruined gun emplacements from the Second World War, including the barrels of two guns each weighing 30 tonnes and having a range of 13 km (8 mi.).

★Castle Hill National Historic Park

Castle Hill National Historic Park is between Placentia and Highway 100. Open mid-Jun.–beginning of Sep. Mon.–Fri. 9am–8pm, and until 5pm for the rest of the year. It is the site of English and French fortifications, whose history is told in the Interpretive Centre. Fort Royal was built by the French in 1693 then handed over 20 years later to the British, who renamed it Castle Hill. There is a magnificent view from here over Placentia Bay, and from Le Gaillardin, 10 minutes' walk away, a redoute built by the French in 1692.

Central Newfoundland

Central Newfoundland is still largely untouched wilderness. Mostly marsh and moorland, it is covered with typical northern vegetation such as sheep laurel, caribou moss and Labrador tea, from which the Indians used to make a brew when they travelled.

This route covers 676 km (420 mi.) and traverses the island almost to the Avalon isthmus before turning south to the Burin Peninsula. The main stretch of the route is along the TransCanada Highway, Newfoundland's only east/west road, which at Springdale touches on Notre Dame Bay, where there are many picturesque little fishing villages.

From the Burin Peninsula it is possible to make a trip to enjoy the French atmosphere of St-Pierre and Miquelon.

Highway 1 runs along the north shore of Grand Lake and Sandy Lake between the two ranges of the Long Range Mountains. Lobster House and Mount Sheffield stand out on the other side of the lakes.

Western Newfoundland

Western Newfoundland is a land of rugged grandeur, with fast-flowing rivers, pine forests and rich and unusual flora and fauna.

The route down the west coast again mainly follows the TransCanada Highway, starting at Port aux Basques, where the ferry berths from North Sydney, Nova Scotia. Taking the highway northwards the Gulf of St Lawrence is on the left and the barren Long Range Mountains are on the right.

Halfway between Port aux Basques and Corner Brook is the Port au Port peninsula. Corner Brook is a popular starting point for trips into the centre of the island and for getting to Labrador. Gros Morne National Park, the next stop, is about 1000 sq. km (386 sq. mi.) and has the most spectacular fiords in North America.

From the park Highway 430 runs close to the west coast of the Great Northern peninsula.

★★Niagara   J 15

Province: Ontario

Information

Niagara Falls Canada Conventions & Visitors Bureau, 5433 Victoria Avenue, Niagara Falls, ON L2G 3L1; tel. (905) 3566061
The Niagara Parks Commission, PO Box 150, Niagara Falls, ON L2E 6T2; tel. (905) 3562241

Niagara Falls

The Niagara Falls are in the extreme south of the province of Ontario where the waters of Lake Erie plummet down almost 60 m (197 ft) into Lake Ontario below. Niagara Falls are amongst the largest, most beautiful and certainly most famous waterfalls in the world. They were first chronicled in 1678 by Jesuit missionary Louis Hennepin, who followed the sound of the rushing waters upstream along Lake Ontario to dis-

"Lady of the Mist"

Spanish Aerocar

cover this great body of falling water, nowadays seen by over 12 million visitors a year.

The falls are in two parts, the concave Horseshoe Falls, 640 m (2100 ft) across, which are Canadian, and in the Province of Ontario, and the American Falls, about 330 m (1083 ft) across, in the State of New York, so the national boundary between Canada and the States runs through the middle.
Horseshoe Falls/American Falls

Before the waters were used for hydro-electric power almost six million litres of water a second hurtled over the rocky rim. A Canadian/American agreement in 1951 for joint use guaranteed close on 3 million litres a second in summer and 1.4 million in winter. The spray rising from the foaming cauldron at the foot of the falls has beautiful rainbows when the sun shines.

Below the falls the Niagara River flows through the deep walls of the gorge, between 80 and 300 m (263 and 985 ft) across, forming the Whirlpool Rapids as the gorge narrows to the north-west.
Gorge

Just 6 km (4 mi.) below the Horseshoe Falls the river changes course and turns north-east, and at that point swirls around in another seething cauldron, this time known as the Whirlpool, before plunging down through the Lower Rapids into Lake Ontario.
Whirlpool

The falls came into being during the last Ice Age, when the river ran over a chalk plateau, part of the Niagara Escarpment, before dropping to the level of Lake Ontario where the city of Lewiston stands today. As the water undercut and wore away its rim, the falls moved upstream relatively quickly, and in the last 3000 years have moved from the point of Rainbow Bridge to where they are today. The pace of erosion depends on the volume of water rushing over the crest. At present the cut-back in the area of the Horseshoe Falls is from 6–10 cm (2–4 in.) a year. It can
Erosion

The American and Canadian Falls

thus be estimated that in a few hundred thousand years they will be level with the American city of Buffalo.

Energy potential

At present hydro-electric stations with a total capacity of 3 million kw are installed at the Niagara Falls. Plans for extension have been strongly opposed.

Views

There are wonderful views of Niagara from the viewing platforms on the Canadian side. There are also a number of towers, open day and night, such as the Skylon and the Minolta Tower, which are amongst the best points for night viewing, since the falls are floodlit at night.

Helicopter flights

Helicopters fly continuously from Niagara Falls station, taking passengers down to the Whirlpool, up the Gorge and then over the lip of the Falls.

Table Rock Scenic Tunnels

A walk along the river front from Rainbow Bridge, through Queen Victoria Park, gives a good view of the American Falls, while it is even possible to take a trip under the falls, through the Table Rock Scenic Tunnels, starting beneath Table Rock House, near the lip of the Horseshoe Falls.

"Maid of the Mist"

The "Maid of the Mist" sightseeing boats take visitors, duly provided with waterproofs, right to the foot of the Horseshoe Falls and past the American Falls, really the best way to get an idea of the amazing force of the waters.

Niagara Parkway

The Niagara Parkway from the falls to Niagara-on-the-Lake, where the river enters Lake Ontario, is administered by the Niagara Park Commission, who are responsible for the gardens and viewing points along the way. From the waterfalls the path leads under the Rainbow Bridge through an attractive residential area.

Gorge Trail

A lift down to the bottom of the Niagara Gorge gives access to a breathtaking walk past the foaming rapids along the Gorge Trail.

Niagara: the Canadian Horseshoe Falls, seen from a helicopter

The Spanish Aerocar is a cablecar that slowly makes its way over the face of the swirling waters of the Giant Whirlpool.

Spanish Aerocar

Students of this technical school raise flowers, bushes and trees. In June the rose garden is particularly attractive. About 1.5 km (1 mi.) further on the Canadian side of the river is the Robert Moses and Sir Adam Becket Generator Stations and nearby can be seen a large floral clock.

Niagara Parks Commission School of Horticulture

These heights are part of the Niagara escarpment where the falls once plunged into the river. Nowadays there is a park with a view over the river, with a statue in the middle to General Sir Isaac Brock, a hero of the 1812 war.

Queenston Heights

This cluster of lovely homes and gardens at the foot of the escarpment contains the Laura Secord homesteads. Laura Secord was responsible for the British winning the Battle of Beaver Dam, since she warned them of the Americans' planned attack.

Queenston

The Canadian Niagara Falls (pop. 73,000) is a clean and pleasant city on the more attractive west side of the Niagara Gorge. Its views of the falls make it a leading tourist centre, in fact there's no other place on earth quite like it. It has attractions to suit all tastes, honeymoon hotels to Monster Show.

Niagara Falls, Canada

There are three bridges linking the city of Niagara Falls with its American counterpart, all of them with fine views into the gorge that divides the two.
The view of the falls from Rainbow Bridge is particularly impressive.

Bridges

The American Niagara Falls (pop. 70,000) on the east side of the gorge also does well from the falls, and the accompanying tourism.
It is also an industrial area with unattractive factory sites.

Niagara Falls, USA

Niagara-on-the-Lake (pop.13,000) is a delightful small picture-book town

★★**Niagara-on-the-Lake**

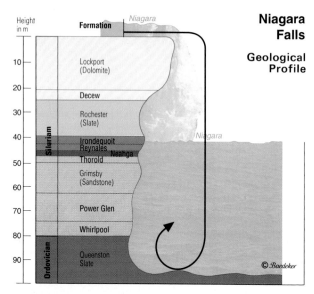

Niagara Falls

Geological Profile

© Baedeker

at the northern end of the falls and on the shores of Lake Ontario. The first capital of Upper Canada, it was razed to the ground by American troops during the War of 1812 against the British, but rebuilt with all due speed.

The town is full of pretty 19th c. houses set in their lovely gardens. Queen Street, its main street, has a clock tower in the middle and many little boutiques, eating places and hotels. The Niagara Apothecary, built in 1866, is especially quaint.

Theatre

The little town has three theatres and is especially famous for its annual George Bernard Shaw Festival.

Viticulture

The fertile hinterland of Niagara-on-the-Lake has a favourable climate for vine-growing and large vineyards have been established here. Some vintners and cellar-masters of German descent have settled here.

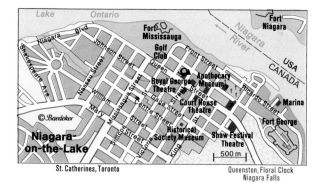

Lake Ontario
Queenston, Fort George, Floral Clock, Niagara Glen   Fort Niagara

Niagara Falls
(Ontario)

KANADA
USA

Whirl-
pool

Niagara University

Buscaglia-Castellani Art Gallery

Niagara Falls
(New York)

Helicopters

Spanish Aero Car

Niagara

Parkway

River

Whirlpool Rapids

Lewiston Road

Victoria

Palmer Park

Main Street

Stanley

Bridge   Street

Customs

VIA Station

Great Gorge Adventure

Armory

Cleveland Ave.

Lockport Street

Oakes Park Stadium

Bus Terminal

City Hall

Road

Moses

Swimming Pool

Avenue

River Road

Niagara River

Street

Portage

Roberts Street

Parkway

Rebert

Street

Maple Leaf Village

Niagara Falls Museum

Customs

Schoellkopf Geological Museum

City Hall   Pine   Avenue

Main

Walnut   Avenue

Oaks Garden Theatre

Helicopters

Ferry   Avenue

Queen Victoria Park

Maid of the Mist

Maid of the Mist

Customs

Wax Museum

Rainbow Center

Rainbow Bridge

Convention Center

Bus Terminal

Niagara   Street

Road

Imax Theatre

Skylon Tower

Observation Tower

'The Turtle' Native American Center

Niagara Splash Water Park

American Falls

Rainbow   Blvd.

Buffalo Ave.

Cave of the Winds

Minolta Tower   Table Rock

Goat Island

Robert   Moses   Parkway

Bus Terminal

Incline Railway

Horseshoe Falls

USA
CANADA

← Niagara River

Avenue

Road

Greenhouse

750 m

© Baedeker

Queens Expressway, St. Catherines, Toronto
Lundy's Lane Historical Museum

Portage

Stanley

Avenue

Buffalo, Lake Erie

Chippawa, Fort Erie

North Bay

Dufferin Island

The southern parkway leads to Dufferin Island which has a superb park where the Niagara becomes a broad gently flowing stream. There is a fine view here of the American shore and Grand Island. At Fort Erie the Peace Bridge crosses to the huge US city of Buffalo.

Fort Erie

Fort Erie a reconstruction of the former fort which was completely destroyed. The officers' quarters, barracks, guardrooms and armouries can be visited.

★Fort George

Fort George dates from the end of the 18th c. and was erected here to protect the area against attack by the Americans in their revolt against the British. The Commander at that time was Major General Isaac Brock. During the skirmishing of the War of 1812/1813 the fort fell into the hands of the Americans who took it under fire from the lake. Abandoned in 1820, the fort was declared a National Historic Park in 1969 and has since been lovingly restored, with visitors flocking here every year to learn more about the history of the area. At the height of the tourist season there are enactments of the military drills, firing practice and cookhouse activities of the early 19th c.

★North Bay   H 15

Province: Ontario. Population: 55,000

Information

North Bay Chamber of Commerce, 1375 Seymour St, PO Box 747, North Bay, ON P1B 8J8; tel. (705) 4728480

Location

North Bay, a lively little town on the north-east shore of Lake Nipissing, in a pleasant setting about 300 km (186 mi.) from Toronto, is popular with visitors for its long sandy beach, good lake fishing, wide range of leisure facilities, and, not least, the riches and beauties of the hinterland in the north-east of the province.

Fur trade

The town was once on the fur traders' route from the Ottawa River to Georgian Bay, and still plays an important part in the trade today, staging public auctions five times a year – January, March, April, June and December – where the skins of beaver, marten and other valuable Canadian fur animals are offered for sale.

★Lake cruise

Ontario Marine Service operates a cruise that is particularly to be recommended. The "Chief Commander II" Cruise traces the route of the early "voyageurs" over Lake Nipissing along the French River to the Dokis Indian Reserve, making it possible to enjoy North Bay and the shoreland landscape from the lake.

From North Bay to Kirkland Lake

Marten River Provincial Park

Highway 11 towards Kirkland Lake, after a drive of about 60 km (37 mi.), reaches the Marten River Provincial Park where there is the first opportunity to go for a good walk or enjoy some fishing.

Trapper Museum

The Trapper Museum, which brings to life the times of the trappers and the fur trade, is open daily from mid-May to October.

Timagami Lake

One hundred kilometres (60 mi.) down the road, Timagami Lake is ideal for anyone who enjoys watery pursuits such as fishing and canoeing, with its 500 km (10 mi.) shoreline, 1600 islands and ample stocks of fish. The town of Timagami Lake is on one of the long arms of the lake. A former trading post, it owed its subsequent wealth to timber and then mining. The largest mine in the district is the Sherman Mine, which offers a chance to see iron ore mining at first hand (sightseeing tours by arrangement May–Aug., Mon.–Fri. 9am–4pm).

Provincial Forest, covering about 15,000 sq. km (5790 sq. mi.), is impressive because of its great stands of conifers.

Provincial Forest

Cobalt (140 km (87 mi.)) just off the highway, came into being in 1903 when a blacksmith, Fred LaRose, stumbled here on what turned out to be the richest silver vein in the world. Cobalt was found somewhat later, leading to a mining boom that lasted until the 1930s. The story of the town's rise to fame and its mining history are recounted in the Mining Museum.

Cobalt

Kirkland Lake (240 km (149 mi.)) is another old boom town, dating from 1912 when gold was first found here, and the supreme haunt of the prospector, achieving international fame for its legendary gold mile, a main road where gold was found at 12 spots. The Macassa Mine is the only mine still working Kirkland Lake's goldfields which are among the richest and largest in Canada.

★Kirkland Lake

Anyone wanting to be shown round should contact the Kirkland Chamber of Commerce, 65 Government Road W., PO Box 966, Kirkland Lake, ON P2N 2E9; tel. (705) 5675444.

Northwest Passage

C–E 5–18

The Northwest Passage is the waterway on about 73° of latitude north along the north coast of the American continent, passing from the Atlantic through the Canadian Arctic archipelago and the Beaufort Sea and the Bering Straits to the Pacific Ocean.

The search for the Northwest Passage was begun in the 16th c. by Dutch and English navigators hoping to find a favourable sea route for trade with the Far East and thus circumvent the Portuguese monopoly on trade round the Horn of Africa. Martin Frobisher, in 1576, made the first attempt, assuming that this could not be the legendary sea of ice but just

History

A walrus in the Northwest Passage

Helpmate and Sporting Companion

Steel blue eyes, piercing gaze and wolf-like build – these are the trade marks of the animals which for hundreds of years have been indispensable helpmates to the people of the Arctic. Huskies, which in fact belong to the Pomeranian family and originated in Siberia, are found throughout the Canadian North as house-, watch- and sledge dogs.

Tough, and blessed with immense stamina, the husky closely resembles the wolf. Full-grown the dog stands 50 to 60 cm (20 to 24 in.) at the shoulder, averages 27 kg in weight and has a thick fur coat which can be any shade between black and white. The Inuit, who call them "malamut", brought the dogs to North America from their original home in northern Asia. In the settlements of the Canadian north, husky teams were used to draw sleds for transporting supplies and mail, a task which nowadays has been taken over by motor sleds and snowmobiles.

Even so, husky numbers are far from declining, principally because the dogs are chief protagonists in a sport acquiring an ever larger following world wide. This is husky sled racing, which today can be enjoyed in places as far afield from Canada as Scotland and Germany. Husky racing first started during the time of the gold rush, at the turn of the 19th and 20th c. The first husky clubs were founded soon afterwards. As a result, husky racing has become extremely popular throughout Canada. Now even the adventure-seeking tourist can be introduced to the sport under the guidance of expert dog-drivers.

The supreme challenge for any dog-sledder is the annual "Yukon Quest", which takes place in February. This astonishing race, fiendishly demanding on human and dog alike, is run over a course of more than 1000 miles from Fairbanks in Alaska to Whitehorse in Canada's Yukon Territory. It takes the best "mushers" (dog-sled drivers) at least twelve days to complete this marathon of endurance, traversing seemingly endless snowfields, frozen tundra and dark, forbidding forests.

a frozen lake since saltwater never froze. In 1585–87 John Davis penetrated through the strait later to bear his name as far as Baffin Bay. Henry Hudson was looking for the Northwest Passage when he discovered Hudson Bay in 1609/1610. In 1616 William Baffin got as far as Lancaster Sound, but since he concluded that the Northwest Passage simply did not exist there was no more exploration for another 200 years.

It was 1818 before John Ross resumed the search at the head of an English expedition, although the motive this time was scientific rather than commercial. In 1829 he discovered the magnetic north pole on the Boothia-Felix Peninsula. The doomed expedition of John Franklin followed in 1845. After last being seen in July of that year in the Lancaster Sound, the members of the expedition were finally found dead, after numerous searches, on King Williams Island, having succeeded in exploring much of the Arctic coast of North America. McClure was the first, in 1850 to 1853, to be able to trace the passage on foot, coming over the iced up straits from the west, but the first person to manage finally to navigate the Northwest Passage from east to west was actually Roald Amundsen, the Norwegian polar explorer in 1900–03.

Since the way the ice forms in the Arctic Ocean can vary enormously from year to year and decade to decade its reconnaissance has always been of prime importance. This has improved over the years firstly with the use of planes and then, since 1960, of satellites. The first submarine, the US nuclear sub "Sea Dragon", went through the Barrow Strait in 1960, and in 1969 the special tanker "Manhattan", assisted by the Canadian icebreaker "St Laurent", succeeded in sailing through the Northwest Passage to Alaska, with the aid of satellite and aerial reconnaissance, and in the knowledge that the ice in the Arctic is at its thinnest between August and October and the Barrow Strait is largely ice-free.

The Northwest Passage has gained in importance of late with the discovery of oil in the Arctic off Alaska and Canada.

Importance

Northern Woods and Water Route

F/G 6–11

Provinces: British Columbia, Alberta, Saskatchewan

Northern Woods and Water Route, The Secretary, Box 699, Nipawin, Saskatchewan S0E 1E0

Information

The start of the 2400 km (1419 mi.) of the Northern Woods and Water Route – 300 km (186 mi.) of it over gravelled roads – is Dawson Creek, in British Columbia. It leads through virtually unpopulated territory towards Winnipeg, and there is the possibility of catching a quick fish or seeing game from the road on the way. Service stations are a day's journey apart.

Location

Highway 2, west of Athabasca, becomes part of this route, dubbed the Northern Woods and Water Route in 1974, and opening up the northern districts of Canada's four western provinces.

This route from Dawson Creek through the north of Alberta and Saskatchewan to Winnipeg in Manitoba gives access to a chain of lakes and rivers, and to delightful, but little visited, provincial parks. At the northern edge of the settlement cornfields and grazing meadows, villages and lonely farmsteads alternate with great expanses of timberland.

Northwest Territories

B–E 3–10

Geographical situation: 60°–82° latitude north/102°–142° longitude west
Area: 1,526,320 sq. km (589,159 sq. mi.)
Population: 41,000. Capital: Yellowknife

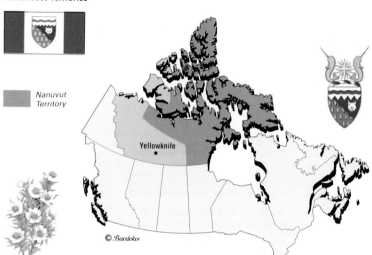

Nanuvut Territory

Yellowknife

© *Baedeker*

Information	Northwest Territories Arctic Tourism, Box 610, Suite 400, Yellowknife, NT X1A 2N5; tel. (867) 8737200, fax. (867) 8734059.

Location

Almost six times the area of the United Kingdom, the Northwest Territories cover a large tract of north-western Canada. They extend from the high Mackenzie Mountains in the west, to the tundra regions of the east Mackenzie catchment area, where today they share a border with the newly established (1999) Nunavut Territory. Their southern boundary is defined by the 60th parallel, while in the north they stretch to within a few hundred kilometres of the North Pole. The tree line, cutting right across the Northwest Territories, constitutes a striking feature which can be followed all the way from the Mackenzie delta in the extreme north-west, to Lake Dubawnt on the border with Nunavut. South-east of this line sparse forests of fir, spruce and birch predominate; to the north and north-east, in the so-called Barren Grounds and the western Canadian archipelago, there is treeless tundra with dwarf shrubs, grasses, moss and lichen.

From a topographical point of view there are three major regions. In the far west near the border with the Yukon Territory are the northern foothills of the Rockies – the Mackenzie Mountains, up to 2972 m (9754 ft) in height, and the Franklin Mountains (average height 1600 m (5250 ft)) and Richardson Mountains. To the east is a lowland region drained by the Mackenzie River, a landscape of numerous lakes including the Great Bear Lake (31,200 sq. km (12,040 sq. mi.)) and Great Slave Lake (28,44 sq. km (10,960 sq. mi.)). Off the northernmost extremity of the mainland are the generally flat islands of the Canadian archipelago, the best-known of which are Victoria Island (the greater part of which is now in Nunavut Territory) and Banks Island. The polar region north of the Arctic Circle is characterised by deep fiords and extensive glacial fields.

Climate

The area covered by the Northwest Territories has a predominately cool, sub-Arctic or Arctic climate, with very pronounced regional and local variations. Winter temperatures of −30°C (−22°F) are recorded in virtually all parts. By contrast during the short summer, which lasts only a few weeks, temperatures at the Great Slave Lake sometimes exceed

Northwest Territories: Tuktoganiuk settlement

20°C (68°F); even in the Arctic on Banks Island for instance, they can reach 12°C (53°F).

The long winter passes almost imperceptibly into the short summer. The Great Slave Lake may still be ice-covered even though the air temperature has reached 20°C (68°F) or more. North of the Arctic Circle the summer sun barely sets – hence "land of the midnight sun" – while in winter it remains dark virtually round the clock, the so-called "polar night".

Cut off by the mountains in the west from the moderating influence of the Pacific, the climate of the Northwest Territories is of an extreme continental type, manifest not least in the relatively low levels of precipitation.

About 12,000 years ago, following the recession of the last Ice Age, the ancestors of the present-day Indians migrated across the Bering Strait from Siberia to mainland North America. Several thousand years later, the Dene Indians would follow the vast herds of caribou northwards on their summer migrations to the Arctic, then back again to winter in the forest country further south.

History

In contrast to the mainland, the islands of the Canadian archipelago were settled only about 10,000 years ago, when the forebears of the present-day Inuit also crossed from northern Asia to Alaska and the coastal regions of the Beaufort Sea. They produced the pre-Dorset culture. A few thousand years later their descendants migrated to the Canadian Arctic, establishing the Dorset culture. A final great migration took place about 1000 years ago, bringing the Thule culture from Alaska to northern Canada.

In the mid 17th c. the first white men penetrated the Canadian northwest, reconnoitring on behalf of the big fur trading companies (the North West Company and the Hudson's Bay Company). Samuel Hearne travelled west from the Hudson Bay to the Great Slave Lake. In 1789 Alexander Mackenzie (see Famous People) made his way down the river which today bears his name, to its outlet in the Beaufort Sea.

Prior to the formation of the Canadian confederation in 1867, large areas of northern Canada, known collectively as Rupert's Land, were administered by the Hudson's Bay Company on behalf of the British Crown. From then until the late 19th c., the Northwest Territories comprised not only what has been the Nunavut Territory since April 1999, but also Labrador, the northern parts of the present-day provinces of Québec, Ontario and Manitoba, the whole of present-day Saskatchewan and Alberta, and the entire Yukon Territory. The boundaries of the Northwest Territories in force up to the establishment of Nunavut were drawn up in 1912. Until 1921 the region was administered by the Royal Canadian Mounted Police; since then it has had its own parliament and administration.

From the 1970s onwards a series of disputes erupted involving members of the First Nations (as the Indians and Inuit are now more generally known), who vociferously demanded recognition of their traditional rights. The most recent and crowning achievement of this movement for self-determination has been the establishment, as from April 1st 1999, of the Nunavut Territory, hived off from the rest of the Northwest Territories.

Population

The Northwest Territories have a population of approximately 41,000, a density of less that 0.03 per sq. km (0.01 per sq. mi.)! Two thirds of the population are Indians and Inuit, making the Northwest Territories the only Canadian region, apart from the newly-created Nunavut, in which the so-called First Nations form the majority. Europeans were very late arrivals. In the 1920s the white population numbered only a few hundred, a figure which has since risen to about 20,000.

Economy

Half a century ago the fur trade was still by far the most important contributor to the region's economy, now superseded by exploitation of the Territories' mineral resources. There are large reserves of copper, zinc, silver, lead, uranium and other minerals. Gold has been mined at the Great Slave Lake since 1896. Just a few decades ago rich deposits of oil and natural gas were discovered in the Far North, but these have proved difficult to exploit because of the hostile climate. Among the activities most impervious to crisis are freshwater fishing in the large rivers and lakes, forestry in the south of the Mackenzie District, and the rearing of animals for furs. Recently introduced developments include the cultivation of renewable resources and fish farming. Also expanding is the small business sector, producing goods for marketing locally. Crafts and handicrafts (leather goods, jewellery, etc.) are thriving, being particularly popular with tourists.

Transport

Principal access to the still largely unspoilt landscape of the Northwest Territories is via the Mackenzie Highway from Peace River (Alberta) to Yellowknife and/or Fort Simpson and Wrigley. The Liard Highway, opened in 1983, goes from Fort Nelson (British Columbia) or the Alaska Highway (Yukon Territory) to the Nahanni National Park and thence to Fort Simpson. The Dempster Highway runs north from Dawson City (Yukon territory) into the vast Mackenzie River delta and on to Inuvik.

Tourism

Not surprisingly given the limited infrastructure, tourism in the Northwest Territories is still in its infancy. For anglers and canoeists, however, conditions are little short of ideal. Adventure tourists can explore the northern wastes by bush aeroplane, while those who prefer their comforts can choose a Wilderness Tour with accommodation in well appointed lodges. The Northwest Territories now boast a number of National Parks, though some are difficult to reach. Only the vast Wood Buffalo National Park is easily accessible by road. It is also possible to drive to within a relatively short distance of the popular Nahanni National Park, but the final lap of the journey into the Park itself must be made by canoe.

Nova Scotia

Geographic situation: 43°–47° latitude north/58°–67° longitude west
Area: 55,000 sq. km (21,230 sq. mi.)
Population: 950,000. Capital: Halifax

Nova Scotia Department of Tourism, PO Box 456, Halifax, NS B3J 2P5; tel. (902) 4245000, fax. (902) 4242668

Information

The most important of Canada's Atlantic provinces, the Maritimes, is the only one to have a Latin name – Nova Scotia, or New Scotland.

Location

Nova Scotia is a peninsula on the eastern edge of the Canadian mainland, to which it is joined by the Chignecto isthmus, only about 30 km (19 mi.) wide. Between latitudes 43° and 47° north and stretching for 610 km (380 mi.) from north-east to south-west, the peninsula varies between 80 and 160 km (50 and 100 mi.) across. Canada's second smallest province, at around 55,000 sq. km (21,230 sq. mi.), Nova Scotia also includes Cape Breton Island to the north, from which it is separated by the narrow Canso Strait, although linked by the Canso Causeway over a dam built in the 1950s.

In broad morphological terms Nova Scotia is part of the Appalachian system, from which the peninsula is only separated by the Bay of Fundy, which itself splits into two narrow arms of the sea, Chignecto Bay and the Minas Basin. Its rocks are part palaeozoic granite and sediment, Pre-Cambrian slate and quartz, but also part magmatic.

Geology

The landscape of much of the peninsula is determined by the Atlantic uplands (150 to 300 m (492 to 985 ft)) which gradually slope down to the coast, and the Cobequid Mountains, 350 m (1149 ft) high in places, the

Nova Scotia

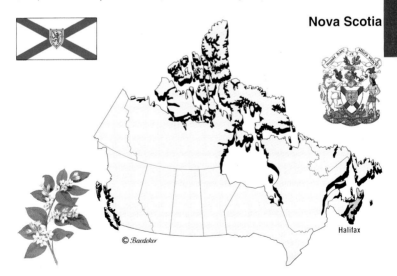

© Baedeker

Halifax

347

Pictou-Antigonish Range and the North and South Mountains. Nova Scotia's highest point, at 532 m (1746 ft), is on Cape Breton Island.

The scenery often shows the telltale signs of the last Ice Age – glacially rounded outlines to the hills, drumlins showing the direction of the flow of the ice, and over 3000 lakes completing the picture of a morainal landscape. The biggest of these is Bras d'Or Lake on Cape Breton Island, linked to the Atlantic both in the north (Great Bras d'Or, Little Bras d'Or) and the south (channel to St Peter Inlet). Nova Scotia's coastlines are very different, with the Atlantic coast an indented mass of fiords and bays, while the Bay of Fundy has saltmarsh and mudflats. Here too is Nova Scotia's most amazing natural phenomenon, the greatest tidal fall in the world which can be as much as 15 m (49 ft) in its uppermost reaches, and even 20 m (65 ft) at spring tides. With this enormous difference between high tide and low tide the surging seawater rushes in at a speed that may be only 5 kmph (3 mph) at the mouth of the bay, but can reach about 17 kmph (10.5 mph) where the estuary narrows in the Minas Basin. Owing to the braking effect exercised by the floor of the bay, as the tidal surge spills into the river estuaries in Fundy's furthest reaches, such as the Petitcodiac out of Chignecto Bay, it pushes before it an advance wave, a tidal bore sometimes up to 1 m (3 ft) high, travelling at a speed of up to 17 kmph (11 mph), with a roar like a distant express train. For visitors, it is an unforgettable sight.

Climate

In these maritime latitudes Nova Scotia has a pleasantly breezy if rather damp climate. Average temperatures in July are around 17–18°C (62–64°F), and in January around −3°C (26°F). Total rain and snowfall is generally between 1200 and 1300 mm (47 and 51 in.). Weather conditions can often cause fog in winter, and when the Arctic winds blow in from the north Nova Scotia can suffer from blizzards combined with a sharp drop in temperature.

Vegetation

A good 80 per cent of Nova Scotia is still covered with woodland, mostly deciduous and predominantly ash, alder, maple and larch, but fir and pine can also feature prominently in places. Those worth mentioning include the Kejimkujik National Park in the west and the Cape Breton Highlands National Park.

Indians

Nova Scotia's culture has largely been shaped by almost 500 years of European colonisation. Before the advent of the Europeans all of what is now Nova Scotia (including Cape Breton Island), Prince Edward Island and the north and east of New Brunswick was the hunting grounds of the Micmac Indians who, unlike the Huron, a tribe of gatherers rather than hunters, roamed the land as nomads, hunting elk, bear, beaver, porcupine and caribou in winter, and camping on the coast under their skin wickiups in spring and summer, trapping sea otters and catching fish. They had no metal tools but fashioned implements from animal bones, stone or wood. Unfortunately Nova Scotia has not retained any Indian settlement as such.

European settlement

European settlement, and the consequent inroads into Indian lands, began around 1500, although there is a theory that Leif Erikson may have also touched the coast of Nova Scotia around AD 1000, but there is still no historic confirmation of this.

The actual history of the discovery by Europeans began with John Cabot, originally Venetian Giovanni Caboto, in 1497/1498, sent by the English king to look for a shorter way to the Far East, in higher latitudes. He reached either Labrador or the northern tip of Cape Breton, but failed to leave records on the subject.

The area was explored in 1528 by Verrazano, a Florentine merchant working for the King of France, and he christened the peninsula New France. In 1604 the French, including Samuel Champlain (see Famous People), settled the Annapolis Valley, founding Port-Royal, the first last-

Nova Scotia: the lighthouse on Cap d'Or

ing European settlement north of Florida. They called it Acadia, a name that eventually came generally to refer to French settlement on Nova Scotia.

In 1621 the British succeeded in their attempt at settlement. King James I had granted landrights to Scottish noblemen led by Sir William Alexander, hoping for settlement by British colonists, on the grounds that the discovery by John Cabot duly entitled him to do so. Hence the peninsula came to be called "Nova Scotia".

Disputes between the two nations over the territory continued until finally Nova Scotia, if you were British, or Acadia, if you were French, was assigned to Great Britain in 1713 by the Treaty of Utrecht. The first large British settlement to be founded was Halifax, in 1749, as a garrison to counter the French's Vauban-type fortress of Louisbourg built on Cape Breton Island after 1719. Captured by the British in 1745, then returned to the French in 1748, Louisbourg was finally retaken by the British in 1758, and this time destroyed. Also in order to counter the French and their Catholicism the British encouraged Protestant settlers in the late 18th c., including the 2000 Germans who founded Lunenburg. Because about 10,000 French settlers refused to swear England unqualified allegiance, most of them were deported and their lands confiscated. With the ending of the American War of Independence about 7000 Loyalists came and settled here (around Shelburne, for example), and in time many of the Acadians eventually returned to their former territory.

In 1867 Nova Scotia joined Québec, Ontario and New Brunswick to form the Dominion of Canada, and became a Canadian Province.

The place names in Nova Scotia already indicated that the people living there came from England, Scotland, France, Germany and Holland. When Nova Scotia became Canadian about 350,000 people lived on the peninsula. The figures rose steadily to 883,000 in 1986, and by now they are over 900,000. At the last census 75 per cent put themselves down as originally British, 11 per cent French, 5 per cent German and 3 per cent Dutch. In terms of religion, 34 per cent were Catholic, 22 per cent United Reformed, 18 per cent Anglican, 14 per cent Baptists, and 7 per cent Presbyterian.

Three-quarters of the people live in towns. The largest of these is Halifax, which, together with Dartmouth, has a population of around 300,000.

Fisheries

The fishing industry has long been traditionally Nova Scotia's chief source of employment, apart from a modest amount of farming, which tends to be confined to local needs. About 11,000 people, 3 per cent of the workforce, earn their living from catching fish, which in the north-west Atlantic and the coastal waters of the continental shelf tend to be mainly cod and sole, but also lobster and shell-fish.

Falling catches due to overfishing forced the Canadian government to extend territorial waters to 200 sea miles in 1977. In terms of numbers of fishermen, Nova Scotia comes second in Canada after British Columbia. Much of Nova Scotia's fishing industry is centred around Yarmouth and Lunenburg, together with Halifax and its ice-free harbour. The old fishing villages on St Margaret's Bay also have a claim to fame.

Agriculture

Agriculture has been declining for decades both in terms of cultivated area (only about 4 per cent of the province) and the number of farms. Dairy farming is the main form of agriculture but fruit and vegetables are also grown quite intensively in the Annapolis Valley.

Forestry

Nova Scotia's timber industry is of supra-regional importance, but its vast woodland, covering about 80 per cent of the province, only permits an annual felling of 300,000 cubic metres, most of which is processed for the construction industry, with the rest going for paper and cellulose (in Port Hawkesbury, for example).

Mining

Mining, like agriculture, is also a declining industry. Coal was found in 1865 on Cape Breton Island and, using iron ore imported from Newfoundland, Sydney's steel industry developed near the coalmines. Also found are iron ore (Annapolis, west Westville, south New Glasgow, at Cape George and on Cape Breton Island), manganese (south-west of Windsor, together with tin, and north-west Halifax), copper (chiefly on Cape Breton Island), gypsum and antimony. Sherbrooke even experienced a brief gold rush in the 19th c. (Nova Scotia Gold District). Its decline is partly because these minerals are only found on a small scale, and partly because of anticipation of imminent closures. In value terms, Nova Scotia's mining only accounts for about 1 per cent of the total for Canada.

Manufacturing

The most important sector of the economy is manufacturing and processing (timber, engineering, etc.).

Nunavut   A–E 6–18

Geographical situation: 60°–84° latitude north/60°–122° longitude west
Area: 1,900,000 sq. km (733,400 sq. mi.)
Population: 25,000
Capital: Iqaluit

Information

Nunavut Tourism, PO Box 1450, Iqaluit, NU X0A 0H0; tel. (867) 9796551, fax. (867) 9791261

Location

The Nunavut Territory, a new administrative unit hived off from the former Northwest Territories, officially came into being on April 1st 1999. Nunavut, which in the language of the Inuit who live here means "our land", covers the whole of the eastern section of northern Canada, from the Beaufort Sea in the west to Baffin Bay and the Davis Strait opening into the north-west Atlantic, and from the eastern rim of the Mackenzie basin to Hudson Bay. With an area of 1.9 million sq. km (733,400 sq. mi.), Nunavut is almost eight times the size of the United Kingdom and comprises roughly one fifth of the total area of Canada. Its southern border is the 60th parallel, while in the north it extends to within about 800 km (500 mi.) of the North Pole. Most of the Territory is situated north of the tree line, in a region of predominantly treeless tundra with dwarf shrubs, grasses, mosses and lichens.

The greater part of mainland Nunavut consists of the Keewatin District (altitude 400–500 m (1313–1640 ft)), a vast area dotted with thousands of lakes. To the north and north-east of Hudson Bay, the huge Baffin Island and little Bylot Island form the continental rim of the North American landmass. Immediately west lie a group of generally flat islands. Typical of these Arctic regions are fiords cutting deep inland and extensive glacial fields.

Winter temperatures of below −30°C (−22°F) are recorded in all parts of Nunavut. By contrast, during the brief summer, temperatures can exceed 18°C (64°F) in the vicinity of some of the lakes. With the long winter merging almost imperceptibly into the abbreviated summer, the lakes of the Keewatin District can be frozen solid even as the air temperature reaches 20°C (68°F) or more. North of the Arctic Circle the summer sun shines almost round the clock, while in winter the region is enveloped in the seemingly endless darkness of the polar night. Because Hudson Bay remains frozen well into spring, temperatures there are comparatively low even in summer.

Climate

Although Nunavut only came into existence as a Territory on April 1st 1999, it already boasts a certain historical development. Up until the 1970s its history coincided with that of the Northwest Territories, but in the first half of the decade the Inuit laid claim for the first time to a land of their own. The Inuit organisation "Inuit Tapirisat of Canada" began pressing for the creation of a new Territory of Nunavut in 1976. In a referendum on the issue held in 1982, more than 50 per cent of the population of the Northwest Territories voted in favour, and a further plebiscite in 1992 agreed the boundaries proposed. In 1993 the Nunavut Land Claims Agreement Act was ratified in Iqaluit in the presence of Canada's Prime Minister, Brian Mulroney. That same year the Federal Parliament approved the creation of Nunavut. In 1995 the population chose Iqaluit the capital. On February 15th the first elections were held for the legislative assembly and on April 1st 1999 Canada's newest administrative Territory, Nunavut, was born.

History

Some 25,000 people live in Nunavut, a density of only 0.013 per sq. km (0.005 per sq. mi.). About one fifth describe themselves as Inuit, approximately 70 per cent of the Inuit population of Canada.

Population

Thanks to its rich but still largely untapped natural resources, the economic prospects for Nunavut are relatively good. As well as fossil fuels such as oil and natural gas, large quantities of gold, silver, copper, zinc, lead and diamonds await extraction. There is also potential for a lucrative fishing and fish farming industry. Prawn and shrimp fishing in particular promise to be highly profitable.

Craft- and handicraft-based businesses have already achieved extraordinary success. Produced mainly in small workshops, the leather goods, jewellery, ivory work etc. have great appeal for tourists throughout Canada. Hence, in addition to meeting the demand from the as yet small number of tourists who visit the Far North, there is a lively "export trade" to the major tourist centres of the Canadian South (including Québec, Toronto, Niagara Falls, Banff, Lake Louise and Vancouver).

Economy

★★Okanagan G/H 7

Province: British Columbia

Information	Okanagan Similkameen Tourism Association, 1332 Water Street, Kelowna, BC V1Y 9P4; tel. (604) 8605999, fax. (604) 8617493
Access	By air: Airports at Kelowna and Penticton. Scheduled flights to and from Vancouver/Calgary.
	By bus: Greyhound Bus Lines on Highway 97: Osoyoos, Oliver, Penticton, Summerland, Kelowna, Armstrong, Enderby.
★★Natural features	The Okanagan, the Ticino of Canada as it's often known, is a lush, sunny valley south of British Columbia's High Country, with sandy lakeside beaches, abundant orchards and excellent vineyards which make it a favourite destination for holidaymakers. Drained by the Okanagan River, a tributary of the Columbia River which rises in the US State of Montana, the valley, between 4 and 19 km (2½ and 12 mi.) wide, nestles in the rolling uplands, as high in places as 2000 m (1243 ft), of the Southern Interior Plateau, and extends for about 160 km (99 mi.) from Osoyoos, a village on the US border, to Armstrong in the north. From here it continues north of a barely perceptible watershed in valleys running more or less parallel to the main direction to Sicamous and Salmon Arm on Suswap Lake. The largest in its chain of lakes is Okanagan Lake, about 120 km (75 mi.) long, east of which, in the northern part of the valley, lie Swan Lake, Kalamaka Lake and Wood Lake still in the broad valley floor, joined by Skaha Lake, Vaseux Lake and Osoyoos Lake to the south.
Climate	Thanks to its exceptionally mild climate, with dry, hot and sunny summers (often with temperatures topping 30°C (86°F)) and relatively mild winters (average January temperature 0°C (32°F)), giving about 150 frost-free days a year – Okanagan and Skaha Lakes very seldom freeze over – the Okanagan is Canada's orchard. In season the produce of the fruit trees planted all over the valley floor and its terraced slopes can be bought from roadside stands.
★Wine producers	Eleven of the fourteen wine producers of British Columbia are now located in the Okanagan area; their wines have gained international acclaim.
Vegetation	Unlike the Okanagan Valley with its lush greenery which is mostly artificially watered, the relatively bare semi-arid plateau uplands are in the rain-shadow of the steep Coastal and Cascade Mountains, with an annual rainfall usually well below 400 mm (16 in.). Consequently the vegetation is sparser, mostly sagebrush or Ponderosa pine, cactus can often be found and, in Vaseux Lake Provincial Park Canada's only desert, stretching for about 40 km (25 mi.) from Osoyoos Lake north to Skaha Lake. Here too, early in the morning, Californian Bighorn sheep can often be seen close to the road or on the rocky slopes.
History	Before the advent of Europeans the Okanagan was the preferred territory of the Salish peoples, and it was their Indian trails that the fur traders followed in the early 19th c. In 1811 men of the North West Company set up an outpost where the Okanagan flowed into the Columbia River, from which they explored the hitherto unknown south-east of British Columbia, competing all the time with their American rivals, the Pacific Fur Company, already established at the mouth of the Columbia River. Until 1846, when it was agreed latitude 49 should be the frontier between the USA and Canada, a busy trail led through the Okanagan Valley to Kamloops. Fearing trade restrictions, this trail was abandoned and a new,

more difficult route to the coast was sought through the canyons of the Fraser and Thompson Rivers. Hard on the heels of the fur trappers now came goldminers and prospectors, stock-farmers and settlers. As artificial irrigation increased the turn of the century brought fruit farming which is now the mainstay of the economy of the Okanagan Valley.

Highway 97 runs through the Okanagan linking Osoyoos on the Crowsnest Highway (see entry) in the south with Kamloops and the TransCanada Highway in the north.

Highway 97

Surrounded by orchards and vineyards. the little township of Oliver (pop. 2000, 304 m (998 ft)) came into being after the First World War when the Canadian government gifted returning soldiers with 3000 ha (7413 acres) of irrigated land. The Oliver Heritage Society Museum (106 West 6th St). Open Jun.–Aug. 9.30am–8.30pm, and at other times Mon.–Thu. 9am–4pm. It has displays on the natural history of the Canadian desert, and on the pioneer days in and around Oliver and the old mining town of Fairview (1887 to 1906) and Camp McKinney.

Oliver

The 4 km (2½ mi.) long shores of Vaseux Lake 17 km (11 mi.) to the north are a bird sanctuary where Canada Geese nest and it is possible to see the rare Trumpeter Swan.
   Bighorn sheep can be found among the rocks, but so can rattlesnakes, so care is necessary.

Vaseux Lake Provincial Park

In a scenic setting between Lakes Skaha and Okanagan, Penticton (pop. 24,000, 351 m (1151 ft)) has miles of sandy beaches and marinas. A popular pastime in summer is rafting from here 8 km (5 mi.) down the Okaganan River Channel to Lake Skaha.

Penticton

The town gets its name from the Salish "Pen-Tak-Ton", or "place to stay", since the Indians found that the good climate and wealth of fish and game meant it was a place where they could stay all year round. Irishman Thomas Ellis was the first European to settle here when he started farming cattle on this land in 1866, then in the 1890s the ranch gradually turned into a settlement.
   Only 400 people lived here when plans were announced to build the Kettle Valley Railway in 1912, but irrigation projects, land speculation, steamboats chugging up and down the lake, and fruit farms, followed by packing and canning plants, not to mention sawmills, soon transformed the area. Today fruit and tourism are the town's two main industries.

History

Waterslides, whirlpool and miniature golf are among the attractions offered by White Water Slide (3235 Skaha Lake Rd., open: May-Labour Day) and Wonderful Waterworld (225 Yorkton Ave., open: May–Labour Day). Other amenities available include golf, ranch horseback riding, and paddle steamer trips.

Leisure amenities

Okanagan Game Farm, 8 km (5 mi.) south of the town on Highway 97 and open daily from 8am, has large paddocks holding about 130 species of animals from all over the world, most of them endangered, and including Bighorn Sheep, rhinos, bear, wolf, reptiles, etc.

Okanagan Game Farm

Penticton Museum, at 785 Main Street, has a good collection drawing on local history and Indian cultures (open Jun.–Sep. 10am–5pm, at other times Mon.–Sat. 10am–5pm).

Penticton Museum

Apex Alpine, about 30 km (19 mi.) south-west, is a modern ski station with descents of 610 m (2002 ft), ski-lifts, etc., and a season from December to April.

Apex Alpine

A good excursion out is to Munson Mountain (1680 m (5513 ft)), with a magnificent view, and along a winding road round the eastern lake shore to Naramata.

Munson Mountain

Okanagan

Summerland

Most of the township of Summerland (pop. 8000, 411 m (1349 ft)) is on terracing above the lake shore amid fruit trees and vineyards.

Giant's Head

There is a wonderful view of Okanagan Lake from Giant's Head Park (910 m (2987 ft)), reached by about half a mile of narrow mountain road.

Peachland

Peachland (pop: 3000) lives from its thriving orchards and molybdenum mining in the Brenda Mine (29 km (18 mi.) into the mountains above Highway 97).

Kelowna

On the eastern shore of the narrowing Okanagan Lake, Kelowna, a town of 65,000 people (344 m (1129 ft)), is the centre of the Okanagan Valley, and has developed into a popular resort, thanks to its sandy beaches and more than 2000 hours of sunshine a year, it has over 2000 beds and an enormous camp site for visitors.

There is good fishing in the surrounding mountains in the many lakes, most of them used to irrigate the valley, and the town also serves as an important marketing and processing centre for the fruit and vegetables produced around the valley. Other major industries are timber (Crown Forest Industries) and manufacturing (Western Star Trucks).

The town is also popular with retired people on account of its mild climate and lovely setting, plus its good social facilities and a large number of golf courses.

History

Before the arrival of the first fur trappers in the early 19th c. this was the site of one of the ten main Salish villages of the interior. Around 1859/60 Father Charles Pandosy, a Catholic missionary, with two theological students, built a mission station here where Mission Creek runs into the lake. Persuaded by the Father's farming success the first European settlers soon began moving into the valley, and in the 1890s a town started to grow up on the lakeshore. A number of the larger farms were split up into fruit orchards. Around the turn of the century Kelowna became the landing for the sternwheel steamers of the Canadian Pacific Railway which operated on Okanagan Lake, steadily bringing in new settlers. By about 1909 the thrusting new town already had a population of 1800, and it received a further boost at the end of the Second World War with the opening of the Hope-Princeton Highway in 1949 and the building of the Okanagan Lake Bridge in 1958. This replaced the ferry that was the only link between Kelowna and Westbank, and is still, at a length of 650 m (2133 ft) and carried on 60 m (196 ft) high pontoons, Canada's longest floating bridge.

International regatta

Kenowna is famous today for its annual international regatta, held every year since 1906 at the end of July, with sailing and waterskiing, plus tree-felling contests and the "Across-the-Lake Swim".

Big White Ski Village

The Big White Mountain (2319 m (7611 ft)) in the Monashee Mountains just 60 km (40 mi.) east of Kelowna, is the location of one of Canada's most spectacular ski resorts opened in recent years. The mountain is known for its snow, an average of 5.63 m (19 ft) of the glorious white stuff falling in winter. There are now 102 runs of all grades of difficulty, and ten ski lifts. Situated at 1510 m (4956 ft), the particularly family-friendly Big White Ski Village offers a range of resorts, apartment complexes and sports facilities (including an ice-rink and cross country ski runs).

Father Pandosy Mission Historical Site (Oblate Mission of Immaculate Conception

The cabins built from tree-trunks by the missionaries at the Father Pandosy Mission (2685 Benvoulin Rd/Casorso Rd; access daily from 9am) show just how hard and full of deprivation their life was. Besides the plain little church, the school and simple homes of the mission, there are also two typical pioneer cabins that have been brought here.

Kelowna Centennial Museum

This local history museum vividly recreates scenes from the town's past, including a reconstructed kekuli, the winter home of the Salish, a typical street around 1910 and a trading post from 1861. The museum is at 470 Queensway and is open Jul./Aug. Tue.–Sat. 10am–5pm, and Sun. 2–5pm.

By the Okanagan Lake ▶

Okanagan

Sun-Rype Tours

Sun-Rype Products, at 1165 Ethel Street, produces juice from about 65,000 tonnes of fruit every year in one of Canada's biggest plants, have guided tours from Jun.–Sep. 9am–2.30pm.

Flintstones Bedrock City

Flintstones Bedrock City at 990 McCurdy Road, 7 km (4 mi.) north-east on Highway 97, is a pleasure park and an imitation Stone Age village in the style of the television series, complete with Fred and Wilma and their Stone Age friends (open Apr.–Oct. 10.30am–4pm).

Wild Waters Waterslide Park

Wild Waters Waterslide Park nearby, also on McCurdy Road, has, of course, lots of waterslides, as well as miniature golf (open May–Sep. 11am–6pm, and till 7pm in peak season).

Old MacDonald's Farm

Old MacDonald's Farm (13 km (8mi.) south on Highway 97) is a children's theme park with baby animals that can be stroked.

M.V. "Fintry Queen"

The "Fintry Queen", the ferry that ran between Kelowna and Westbank from 1948–58, now takes people on pleasure trips round the lake from the town marina (refreshments on board).

The "Okanagan Princess" also leaves on excursions from Kelowna Marina at the end of Queensway.

Vernon

A little town between three lakes, Vernon (pop. 22,000, 381 m (1250 ft)) is the point where all roads meet in the northern Okanagan Valley. Its history goes back to 1864 when the Vernon brothers, after failing to strike it rich as prospectors in the Monashee Mountains, were encouraged by the valley's fine weather to turn their hand to farming, and started a cattle ranch on the site of what is now the Coldstream Ranch today. The B.X. Ranch also came into being at the same time nearby, providing horses for the Cariboo mail coaches and Barnard's Express.

This sleepy little hamlet began to thrive with the advent of the Shuswap & Okanagan Railway in the early 1890s, and irrigation projects brought fruit and vegetable farming.

Nowadays tourism is Vernon's main industry, together with the fruit processing, and visitors come for the watersports, diving, fishing, hang-gliding, golf, riding and hiking.

Vernon Museum

Vernon Museum and archives in the Civic Centre, at 3009 32nd Avenue, tells of the Canadian Pacific sternwheel steamers which used to ply the lake, and the pioneers and Indians who used to live here (open Mon.–Sat. 10am–5pm).

Atlantis World of Water

Atlantis World of Water, with waterslides, etc., is about 7 km (4 mi.) north on Highway 97A (open Jun.–Sep. 10am–8pm). Just over a mile further north there is the Okanagan Bob Slide, about 580 m (1903 ft) long (open Easter–mid-Oct. 10am–8pm).

★Silver Star Recreation Area

Silver Star Mountain Resort, 87 sq. km (34 sq. mi.) of recreation area, lies about 22 km (14 mi.) north-east along Silver Star Road – unsurfaced for the last 10 km (6 mi.). It has 35 ski runs, descents of 485 m (1591 ft), several chair-lifts and ski-tows, and at summer weekends a chair-lift takes visitors up Silver Star Mountain (1885 m (6187 ft)) where there are attractive walks and fabulous views.

O'Keefe Historic Ranch

One of the biggest ranches in the Okanagan Valley, the O'Keefe Ranch, 12 km (7 mi.) north on Highway 97, goes back to 1867, and the O'Keefe family actually lived there until 1977. Nowadays an open-air museum (open May–mid-Oct. 9am–5pm, and Jul./Aug. until 7pm) it has a dozen historic buildings, furnished according to the period, from the first blockhouse up to the pretty 1890s Victorian O'Keefe Mansion and St Ann's Church.

Armstrong

The township of Armstrong (pop. 3000, 362 m (1188 ft)) lies in the

Spallumcheen Valley, the northern continuation of the Okanagan, where the fruit trees gradually give way to fields of vegetables and dairy farms.

Armstrong's first settlers arrived around 1866, and the many wooden buildings have retained something of a Western atmosphere. Main Street is still shared by automobiles, pedestrians and Canadian Pacific's freightcars.

The little place is particularly known for its "Cheddar" cheese, which visitors can watch being made at the Armstrong Cheddar Cheese Plant on Pleasant Valley Road.

Ontario

F–J 11–16

Geographic situation: Canada's central province
Area: 1,068,580 sq. km (412,472 sq. mi.)
Population: 11.4 million. Capital: Toronto

Ontario Travel, Queen's Park, Toronto, ON M7A 2R9; tel. (416) 3140944, fax. (416) 4436818

Information

Ontario Province is the political, industrial and cultural heart of Canada and its second largest province, situated between Québec and Manitoba. An inland province, it nevertheless has 7600 km (4723 mi.) of freshwater shoreline along the Great Lakes in the south and 1200 km (746 mi.) of saltwater coast on James and Hudson Bay in the north.

Location

A fifth (200,000 sq. km (77,200 sq. mi.)) of Ontario's surface area is not land but water, and its highest point is Mt Ogidaki, at 665 m (2183 ft). The province extends for 1730 km (1075 mi.) from north to south, and 1690 km (1050 mi.) from east to west.

Apart from a few exceptions in its extreme north and the south, Ontario belongs to the world's earliest geological era, its bedrock being the Pre-Cambrian Canadian Shield, mostly slate, granite and gneiss.

Geology

Geographically the province can be divided into two parts. The northern, larger part, with some of the Hudson Bay coastal lowlands, the Patricia and Kesagami Plains and the Central Highlands and the

Ontario

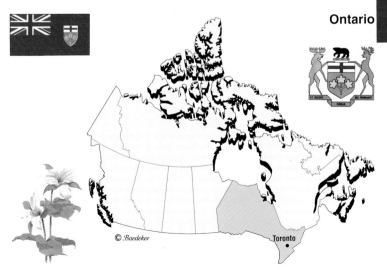

© Baedeker

Toronto

Cochrane Plain are geologically part of the Canadian Shield, but the southern part, with only 12 per cent of the total area, is formed by the Niagara Escarpment. South of Hudson Bay is a district area, of 50,000 sq. km (19,300 sq. mi.) which belonged to a much larger lake after the Ice Age, where the sediment deposited makes the land good enough for farming. The variation in sealevel is due to the land being raised several hundred feet after the melting of layers of ice that were miles thick.

Ice-ages

All life in the province was frozen out by the massive ice-sheets of the Laurentide Glacier at most 18,000 years ago. The glacier's retreat, begun in the south about 12,000 years ago, and lasting until about 7000 years past in northern Ontario, left its enduring mark on the landscape as it scooped out lakes and briefly blocked the St Lawrence, the whole of the meltwater flowing south along the Mississippi. The morainal scenery shows the direction taken by the long-gone glacial flows – particularly evident from the air – leaving a hilly landscape with many lakes and swamps.

Climate

Ontario has a distinctly continental climate, although marked differences exist between north and south. Its southern part, especially the Ontario "peninsula", has milder winters, thanks to the Great Lakes, but wetter summers than the north of the province, where the winters are long, bright and very cold and the summers are short but sunny and hot. In Toronto the average July temperature is 22°C (71.6°F) and the frost-free period lasts from early May to mid-October. In Thunder Bay the average July temperature is 17.6°C (63.7°F) and in January a frosty −13.7°C (9°F), while it is without frost only from early June to mid-September. Annual rainfall varies in the province from 650 to 1020 mm (26 to 40 in.), and is thus evenly distributed throughout the year. Three to six feet of snow is normal in winter, and from autumn until well into spring blizzards can bring heavy snowfalls and abrupt drops in temperature. In spring and early summer the weather can be very capricious.

Vegetation

Most Europeans will feel very much at home in the deciduous woodlands of the south. The transition to boreal conifers begins north of the River Severn as spruce, fir and pine come increasingly to dominate the landscape. The wildlife and vegetation of the fen and marshland is particularly interesting.

History

Before the Europeans came, the land was the home of the Eastern Woodland Indians, among them the Iroquois and Algonquin, particularly in the south. They lived mostly from cultivating maize, beans and squash; they know nothing of rotation of crops or of fertilising the land, and after ten years, when the soil was exhausted, simply moved on, taking the whole village, where large families lived in longhouses, to another place. The Huron, on the other hand, were nomadic traders in fur and other goods, and they were the first to make contact with the French on the lower reaches of the St Lawrence.

Samuel de Champlain decided in 1610 to push French influence further west and, with the Huron as allies, became the first missionary. The first Jesuit mission station was built in 1639 but Christian attempts at expansion came to an abrupt end in 1650 when the Iroquois destroyed it.

In 1673 the Hudson's Bay Company founded Moosonee, the oldest settlement in the province, on Hudson Bay in the north. Ontario itself came about as a result of the American War of Independence. After Canada became British in 1763 10,000 Loyalists moved here from America, and, led by Joseph Brant, the Six Nations Indians, who had fought on the side of the British, settled on Grand River.

Speedy settlement led to self-administration and in 1791 the old province of Québec became divided into Upper and Lower Canada, with Upper Canada becoming Ontario after 1867, at first with Niagara-on-the-Lake as its capital, and then Toronto.

In 1812 the Americans attempted to capture Canada and declared war. Since England was busy fighting Napoleon at the time the Americans

Ontario: an old fire-station   *Trillium, the flower of the province*

thought it would be an easy conquest, but they met bitter resistance on the Niagara Peninsula. Success in this struggle sharpened local self-awareness and gave Upper Canada a sense of its own identity.

After the Anglo-American war the policy of encouraging immigration with land-grants and other inducements led to a quadrupling of the population. Between 1820 and 1840 1.5 million people emigrated to Upper Canada from Europe alone, in search of a better life and bringing with them new strengths and political ideas. The successful struggle for democracy and parliamentary government in Europe made Canada appear backward, with power residing in the hands of the British Governor and a few influential groups. The armed uprising led by William Lyon Mackenzie in 1837 was soon put down but it set the struggle for independence on the move again and in 1867 Ontario and Québec headed the Confederation of provinces, set free from England.

There are 125 seats in the provincial parliament and thanks to the British first-past-the-post voting system the Conservatives have held power since 1943. Ontario, on the basis of its population, is entitled to 95 members in the Federal Parliament and 24 senators in the Senate.   Administration

Together with Québec, Ontario is one of the two Canadian provinces to have two-tier local government, with counties as well as parishes and towns. Planning committees, especially in the Toronto conurbation, have recently been set up in an attempt to control urbanisation.

Since the first census in 1871 Ontario has been the Canadian province with the largest population. From 1.6 million it reached 3.7 million in 1941. There was a new influx of immigrants after the Second World War, particularly from Europe. In recent years emigration from Asia has increased, and with the Crown Colony being handed over to China in 1997 several thousand of the newcomers are Chinese from Hong Kong.   Population

Ontario

Since the Second World War Ontario's population has risen up by about 1 million every decade. The most densely populated area is greater Toronto, with over 3 million people, tending to be concentrated in the urban areas, with over 65 per cent in townships of more than 10,000 people.

Geographically speaking, 85 per cent of the population live in the south on only 15 per cent of the surface area. The north is virtually unsettled apart from mining, timber and fishing settlements.

The largest ethnic group is the 65 per cent or so of originally British Canadians, followed by the French, Germans and Italians.

Farming and forestry

The southern part of the province has good fertile soil, and the growing period is one of the longest in the whole of Canada, yielding tobacco as well as maize, soya beans and sugarbeet. Fruit and wine can only be produced in very sheltered locations.

Furs, whether farmed or trapped, make a very important contribution to the economy in the north, and although timber does not play as great a part as in some other provinces its economic potential should not be underestimated.

Mining and energy

Sudbury Basin was discovered in 1883 when the railroad was being built. It conceals the largest nickel deposits in the world, much of the output going to the USA. The primary deposits of plutonium also contain extractable amounts of platinum, gold, silver, cobalt, copper and tellurium.

In 1903, not long after Sudbury Basin, large silver deposits were found at Cobalt, again as a result of the railroad.

During the Second World War there was an economic boom in Atikokan as its iron ore was mined, then in the 1950s and 1960s the first uranium began to be brought out.

The Canadian Shield still has many mineral resources that can be tapped in the future, and outside the Shield, in the extreme south, salt and gypsum are also to be found in abundance. The absence of fossil fuels has inevitably led to the development and generation of waterpower.

Industry

About 50 per cent of the goods that Canada produces come from Ontario. In value terms supply and vehicle manufacture are the main industrial sectors, but heavy engineering, iron and steel, rubber, paper and food and drink all make important contributions to the economy. Industry tends to be centred on Toronto, Hamilton (iron and steel), Windsor (vehicles) and Sarnia (petro-chemicals).

USA/Canada

Thanks to its common boundary with the States Ontario has closer links with the USA, and therefore greater economic interdependency, than any other Canadian Province.

Tourism

Its many lakes, National and Provincial Parks, resort areas and magnificent scenery make Ontario an unforgettable holiday destination, with canoeing, camping, hiking and fishing in such lovely places as the Haliburton Highlands, Georgian Bay, Karwatha Lakes and Thousand Islands on the St Lawrence.

Canoeing

For Ontario canoeing is the national sport, whether it be on the clear waters of a quiet lake or shooting the rapids. Probably the best known mecca for canoeists is Algonquin Park, with 1600 km (994 mi.) of water trails. Quenitico Provincial Park is on a similar scale, with 525 km (326 mi.) of fur trapper canoe route and 43 cross-country routes. Details of routes and maps can be obtained from Ontario Travel (see Information section in Practical Information).

Another exciting experience is whitewater rafting on the Ottawa River.

Walking

There are good wilderness walks along the shores of Lake Superior in Pukaskwa National Park, a chance to observe nature in all its beauty. In fact all the other parks also have walks of various lengths and degree of difficulty.

Winter sports

Like everywhere in Canada, Ontario is good for winter sports, with cross-country trails and snowmobile tracks always accessible. There is also some downhill skiing at, for example, Thunder Bay and the Blue Mountains, which have fine, challenging pistes.

The fishing will gladden any angler's heart, particularly in the rugged north. All non-residents need a licence which can be obtained at specialist stores or from the Ministry of Natural Resources (see Practical Information, Fishing).

Fishing

★Orillia

J 15

Province: Ontario
Population: 28,000

Orillia Chamber of Commerce, 150 Front Street St., Orillia, ON L3V 4S7; tel. (705) 3264424

Information

From Toronto on Highway 400 north to Barrie, then on Route 11 to Orillia.

Access

Orillia is a little town about 120 km (75 mi.) north of Toronto (see entry) on the northern end of Lake Simcoe. It is also the gateway to the Muskoka Lakes region (see entry).

Location

For centuries Orillia was at the heart of lands that were home to many Indians. Samuel de Champlain passed through here in 1615.

History

Sights

Couchiching Beach Park, with its statue of Champlain, is part of Orillia's bustling and attractive lakeshore area.

Couchiching Beach Park

The town's opera house is famous for its good acoustics.

Opera House

The town's great son was Stephen Leacock (1869–1944), Canada's famous author and humourist. A professor of political science at Montréal's McGill University, Leacock spent his summer holidays here, from where there are fine views over Brewer Bay, and he drew on the town for his book "Mariposa".

Stephen Leacock

His pretty holiday home, built in 1908, is off Highway 128 on Old Brewery Bay, and is now a museum (open mid-Jun.–end Aug. daily 9am–5pm, mid-Apr.–mid-Jun. and Sep.–mid-Dec. Mon.–Fri. 9am–noon).

Museum

Surroundings

The Mara, who have their reserve outside Orillia, belong to the Ojibwa Indians. They make and sell fine examples of their native crafts and also act as guides on hunting, fishing and canoeing trips around Orillia's scenic lakeland.

Mara Reserve

There are boat cruises from Orillia in July and August on Lake Simcoe and Lake Couchiching.

Boat cruises

Lindsay is a resort about 80 km (50 mi.) from Orillia via Highway 7, set in farmland with two big mills. It is a good place for fishing in the well-stocked local waters.

Lindsay

Lindsay is also a good base for trips to Kawartha Lakes, in their lovely setting, and the Haliburton Hills.

Kawartha Lakes

Oshawa

★**Trent & Severn Canal**

The Trent & Severn Canal is a whole system of waterways linking Lake Ontario with Georgian Bay on Lake Huron, wending its way through various river and lake systems, such as the Trent River and Lake Simcoe, in the east of Ontario Province.

The changing levels mean that it needs over 40 locks, including the world's highest hoist, built in 1905 at Peterborough (see entry), to operate a travelator covering a height of 20 m (66 ft).

In the past the Canal was mainly used for carrying grain and timber, and there were lots of mills along its banks, but these have nowadays been replaced by power stations. Visitors enjoy cruising the waterways too, and Orillia is a good place to start.

Muskoka   See entry

★Oshawa   J 15

Province: Ontario
Population: 135,000

Information

Oshawa Chamber of Commerce, McLaughlin Square, Oshawa, ON L1G 7C7; tel. (905) 7281683

South-western Ontario is the commercial centre of Canada, and this is particularly true of the "golden horseshoe" which starts at Oshawa, on the northern shore of Lake Ontario, about 50 km (31 mi.) from Toronto, and is the area between Lakes Michigan and Ontario where almost a third of Canadian industry is based and which is highly populated. The mainstay of Oshawa's business is the car industry, founded by the efforts of Robert McLaughlin, who began building automobiles here, starting with the McLaughlin Buick, in 1907 with his son, Robert Samuel McLaughlin (1871–1972). His plant eventually merged with the USA's General Motors in 1918, thus taking Oshawa from a lake port to being one of the main centres of the automobile industry in Canada.

★**Parkwood**

At 270 Simcoe Street in the north of the city, in a beautiful park stands the mansion of the industrialist, art collector and patron Robert Samuel McLaughlin. After the death of the owner the luxurious mansion was given to Oshawa in order that it might be opened to the public.

Robert McLaughlin Gallery

The Robert McLaughlin Gallery, downtown near the Civic Centre, built in 1969 and designed by Arthur Erickson, houses works of the "Painters' Eleven", a group of abstract artists founded in 1953. Open daily except Mondays the gallery has temporary exhibitions by contemporary Canadian artists as well as the permanent collection.

★**Canadian Automotive Museum**

This extremely interesting museum, charts the history of the automobile in Canada, using models, design drawings, photographs and other documents, best of all, its collection of over 80 vintage cars from between 1898 and 1930, including the 1912 McLaughlin Buick. Open daily; tel. (416) 5761222.

Cullen Garden

Whitby, on the way from Oshawa to Toronto (see entry), is definitely worth a visit to see Cullen Garden, a park of over 20 ha (49 acres) which, in addition to its masses of flowerbeds and other park features, also has painstakingly accurate miniature versions of Ontario's historic buildings, monuments, farms, etc. Cullen Garden is open every day (information: tel. (416) 6686606).

Othello-Quintette Tunnels Historic Park   H 6

Province: British Columbia

See British Columbia

Information

★Old railroad

To get to the Othello-Quintette Tunnels Historic Park, in Coquihalla Canyon Recreational Area, take the Kawkawa Lake road and the Othello road. The tunnel in the Coquihalla Canyon for the Kettle Valley Railway (closed in 1959) will give the visitor the feeling of being back in the good old days of steam, when the Canadian Pacific line was laid between 1911 and 1918 linking the Kootenays with the Pacific.

   The old railway bridges between the tunnels were replaced with hair-raising foot bridges in the 1960s. Anyone wanting to follow the tunnel trail should definitely take a good torch!

See Fraser Valley

Yale
Fraser Canyon

★★Ottawa

H 15

Province: Ontario
Population: 324,000 (Greater Ottawa 850,000)

Ottawa Tourism & Convention Authority, 130 Albert Street, Suite 1800, Ottawa, ON K1P 5G4; tel. (613) 2375150

Information

Canada's capital is more strictly bilingual than any other place in the country.

Languages

By air:
Ottawa International Airport has commuter airlines from most large Canadian cities, especially Toronto and Montréal, plus direct flights, particularly in summer, to the major European cities.

Access

By rail:
VIA Rail – Ottawa's station was relocated a few years ago from the centre to the south-east of the city. Trains run several times daily to Toronto and Montéal.

By bus:
The city is well served by the Canadian intercity bus lines.

Ottawa Transit's city buses run at short intervals on an extensive and closely integrated system of routes.

City buses

Ottawa stands at the confluence of the Ottawa and Rideau rivers, and is also the starting point of the Rideau Canal linking it to Lake Ontario.

Location

The city grew up between 1820 and 1840 from the construction base which had been set up where the Rideau Canal diverged from the Ottawa River. In charge of the project was the British Colonel John By (1779–1836) and consequently the town was known until 1853 as "Bytown". In 1854 the town changed its name to Ottawa.

History

From 1864 Ottawa was developed as the Canadian capital. The Parliament buildings were built in 1865, high above the Ottawa River, and this is where, in 1867, the first Canadian Parliament met following the founding of the Dominion of Canada.

   In the course of time Ottawa has become a busy government seat, with all the marks of the federal city, but it has some industry too, especially timber, paper and printing.

   Although the city may have been considered rather provincial in the past, it now has a very real feeling of the international metropolis, due in no small measure to the cosmopolitan nature of the many people who have come to live here.

Capital city

As Canada's capital Ottawa not only houses the national parliament but also the Supreme Court, as well as the many government departments and cultural institutions such as major museums and two universities, plus a Catholic and an Anglican bishop.

Institutions

As the seat of government of a nation that is an economic force to be reckoned with, Ottawa has also been able to develop into a top-ranking venue for conferences, many of them of worldwide significance.

Conferences

Together with Hull (see entry) in Québec Province on the other side of the Ottawa River, Ottawa has succeeded more than any other Canadian city in developing a life of lively intellect and culture. The Royal Society of Canada, University of Ottawa, Carleton University and several research institutes have all contributed to this, as have such internationally famous venues as the National Arts Centre (since 1969; opera, concerts), the National Library and Archives, the National Gallery (since 1988 in a fine new building by Moshe Safdie) and the Canadian Museum of Civilization (since 1989 in an imposing new building by Douglas Cardinal, see Hull).

Science and culture

Although Ottawa cannot be said to have the commercial importance of Montéal or Toronto (see entries), in recent years a great many major companies have made it their headquarters, particularly in the high-tech sector, and its status as a capital city and centre for the arts have also attracted bankers, stockbrokers, and insurers, together with publishers.

Business interests

Parliament Hill · Rideau Canal

The Parliament Buildings, in all their splendour of Victorian Gothic sandstone, are quite an imposing sight on their 50m/165ft high hill looking out over the Ottawa River, and, with the highrise towers that have grown up around them of late, seem to frame the city skyline.

The building of the Houses of Parliament was begun in 1860. In their Neo-Gothic style, they look as though they have been transplanted straight from Westminster. The part that was destroyed by fire in 1916 has been completely restored.

★★Houses of Parliament

The Peace Tower (glockenspiel with 53 bells), in the centre, was built in 1927 to commemorate the Canadian dead of the First World War.

Peace Tower

The two houses of Parliament, the House of Commons and the Senate, are in the buildings on either side of the Peace Tower, and can be visited, as part of a guided tour, along with Confederation Hall and the Hall of Honour (tickets can be obtained from the Information Service in the grounds, but apply in good time).

Legislative Building

The Parliamentary Library, at the back of the building opposite the entrance, is a wonderfully furnished octagon that was untouched in the 1916 fire. Its beautifully panelled interior is very reminiscent of the Reading Room of the British Museum in London.

★★Library

The east wing houses the Government offices, some of them restored to look as they did in the 1870s in the time of Lord Dufferin and Premier John Macdonald.

East wing

The MPs and Senators have their offices in the west wing, which also used to contain support services such as the printroom and the employees' quarters.

West wing

In front of the Parliament buildings extends an attractive grassed area which is patrolled in summer by members of the Canadian Mounted Police, looking very dashing in their Mountie uniform of scarlet jackets, stetson, riding breeches, and kneeboots.

★Grounds

◀ *Ottawa: Parliament*

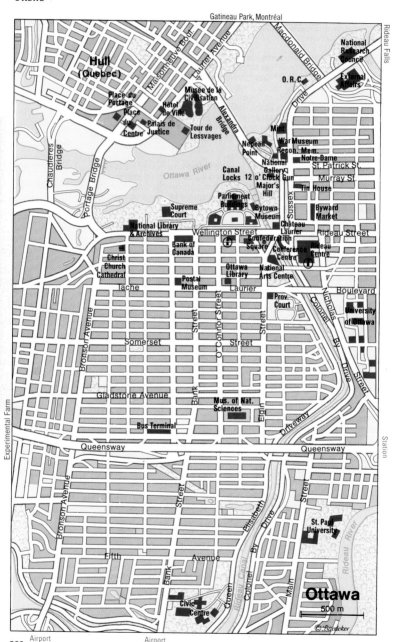

Airport

Airport
Kingston, Toronto

Houses of Parliament

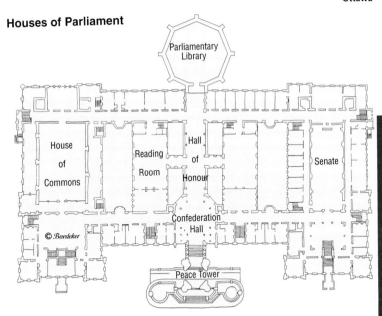

Parliamentary
Library

House
of
Commons

Reading
Room

Hall
of
Honour

Senate

© *Baedeker*

Confederation
Hall

Peace Tower

The Changing of the Guard takes place on the front lawn every morning at 10am in July and August, weather permitting.

Changing of the Guard

The Centennial Flame in front of the main building was lit in 1966 to commemorate the centenary of the Canadian Confederation.

★Centennial Flame

The sculpture in the grounds behind the Parliament building, from which there is a fine view across the Ottawa River, includes statues of Queen Victoria and several famous Canadian prime ministers. Many of them are by Philippe Hébert, a notable sculptor from Québec Province.

Sculpture garden

Below Parliament Hill there is a really lovely walk that runs alongside the Ottawa River.

★River walk

Canada's Supreme Court is to the south-east of the Parliament and has a glistening green roof. Built in 1875, it also has a good view of the Ottawa River.

Supreme Court

Colonel By's Rideau Canal starts east of the Houses of Parliament, in a gully taking it up from the Ottawa River to the Rideau valley through a system of 9 locks that bridge the difference in height between the two rivers. The War of 1812 with the young United States had shown how easily the US could threaten the St Lawrence. After the war the Duke of Wellington despatched scouts to upper Canada to see if a solution could be found to the difficult situation. Colonel John By was sent to Canada in 1826 to oversee the building of a canal that would circumvent the dangerous waters of the St Lawrence and provide an alternative route for navigation as far as Lake Ontario 200 km (124 mi.) to the south-west. The canal was finished in 1832 but never achieved its anticipated strategic or economic importance.

★★Rideau Canal

367

Ottawa

★★Locks

The locks were completely overhauled some years ago, and an interpretive trail runs alongside the canal.

Old Commissariat

Ottawa's oldest surviving stone building, the Commissariat, built in 1827 as a depot for military supplies, is now the Bytown Museum (open mid-May–mid-Oct. daily, mid-Oct.–Nov. and Apr.–mid-May weekends only), and tells of the early days of Ottawa, or Bytown as it was called at the time.

Canal

By climbing up alongside the staircase of locks the level stretch of the canal is reached. Here in summer there are boat trips and in winter, when the canal is frozen over, hundreds of skaters enjoy themselves on the ice.

Events by the canal

The canal banks provide space for all kinds of activities. Winterlude/snowballing: in February the winter festival takes place. Then the canal becomes a gigantic fair on ice. At many places professional and amateur artists try their hand at ice-sculpture.

Festival of Printemps

Festival of Spring: in mid-May this spring festival marks the ending of winter as the tulips – given by Queen Juliana of the Netherlands in gratitude for the city's hospitality during the Second World War – come into bloom all over the city. The canal banks are the scene of general festivities, full of festival-goers, including those from the nearby Arts Centre.

Fête du Canada

Ottawa Festival: this lively event takes place in July, complete with flower parade and waterborne procession and entertainment to suit every taste.

★Château Laurier

An ornate building, with the air of a medieval castle but actually built in 1912, the Château Laurier, at the upper end of the canal locks, is a prime example of the grand hotels built by the big Canadian railroad companies, which is what it still is today.

Conference Centre

The splendid conference centre in front of the Château Laurier was actually Ottawa's central station until that was transferred to the south eastern edge of the town in the 1980s.

Rideau Centre

Ottawa's latest grand mall, the Rideau Centre, is an ultra-modern complex of shopping arcades, cinemas, restaurants and conference rooms, on what was railway land behind the former station.

★National Arts Centre

Set amidst lawns, in themselves a kind of sculpture park, the National Arts Centre, the cultural "pulsating heart" of Ottawa, has three auditoria famous for their acoustics. Leading national and international orchestras, appear here, as do opera, theatre and dance companies.

Upper Town

The fashionable Upper Town extends below Parliament Hill and south-west of the Rideau Canal. The streets are laid out in a checkboard pattern. The busy thoroughfares are Wellington Street, Kent Street, O'Connor Street, Metlalfe Street and Sparks Street pedestrian precinct.

Confederation Square

The principal square of the city is Confederation Square at the upper end of the Rideau Locks staircase, below the Parliament Buildings. It is also the eastern gateway to the Upper Town. The main post office is situated here.

★Sparks Street

Canada's first pedestrian mall, Sparks Street can be said to be the Upper Town's shop window, a string of top department stores and smart boutiques, together with banks and business houses, interspersed with gourmet eating places.

★Bank of Canada

Probably the most striking architecture of the Upper Town is the Bank of

Canada building, by the famous architect Arthur Erickson. The atrium behind the twelve-storey tinted glass façade has the feeling not so much of a bank as of a great greenhouse, with works of art, plants the height of trees, and the splashing of fountains.

The Currency Museum is inside the original Bank of Canada building, and has a cross-section of coinage ranging from ancient China, Greece, Rome and Byzantium, through medieval Europe and the Renaissance, to the detailed evolution of currency in North America as it is today. This includes playing cards from "Nouvelle France" and the tokens used for payment by the Hudson's Bay Company.

★Currency Museum

Place de Ville is at the south-west end of Sparks Street.

Place de Ville

Not far from Sparks Street several ultra-modern highrise buildings, such as Minto Place, the Metropolitan Centre and the Four Seasons Hotel, thrust their way into the Ottawa skyline.

Highrise buildings

Lower Town · Major's Hill

Ottawa's busy Lower Town, the city's market place, full of food stores and market stalls, lies to the north of the Rideau Canal, with Rideau Street its main thoroughfare.

Byward Market has enjoyed a colourful existence since 1846. In summer the food stores in the main market hall are supplemented by stalls in the streets between the market buildings where fruit, flowers and vegetables are on sale. In fact around the whole market area, lovingly restored a few years ago, with lots of restaurants, smart boutiques, etc., there are delicacies on sale from all over the world, further proof of just how cosmopolitan a city this is.

★Byward Market

Just north-west of the market hall, Tin House Court with a pretty fountain is a delightful little courtyard with some of the city's oldest buildings, including the façade of a house owned by a former tinsmith, and decorated by him with examples of his work.

Tin House Court

On Sussex Drive, at St Patrick Street opposite the new national gallery, Notre Dame is the church of the Catholic bishopric. Consecrated in 1846 it contains beautiful mahogany carving by Ph. Parizeau, figures of the four evangelists, prophets and apostles by Louis-Philippe Hébert, and some particularly fine stained glass.

★Basilica of Notre Dame

Major's Hill Park, south-west of the basilica, aflame with thousands of tulips in May and June, is where the "12 O'Clock Gun" stands, an old ship's cannon that since 1869 has been fired at noon on weekdays and 10am on Sundays and public holidays.

Major's Hill Park

Protruding into the river at the southern end of Alexandra Bridge, Nepean Point has a fine view over the river, and on clear days it is sometimes possible to see as far as the Gatineau hills to the north.
   On the point stands an idealised version of a statue to Samuel de Champlain (see Famous People), who passed this way in 1613 to 1615.

Nepean Point

Also on Sussex Drive, the Canadian War Museum (open daily 10am–5pm) concerns wars fought on Canadian soil and others that Canadian forces took part in, including the fighting between the French and the Iroquois in the 16th c. and the Canadian contribution to the First and Second World Wars (e.g. diorama on the Normandy landings).

Canadian War Museum

Erected in 1994 the bronze Reconciliation Memorial near by provides a fitting monument to the dedication of Canadian Blue Caps in fulfilling a

Reconciliation Memorial

Basilique Notre-Dame

Tin House Court

12 O'Clock Gun in Major's Hill Park

peace-keeping role – in Korea (1947), Palestine (1948) and more recently the Golan Heights, the former Yugoslavia and Somalia.

The National Gallery of Canada, designed by Moshe Safdie, is an architectural masterpiece, a highly successful, ultra-modern building that, with its prism-like glass towers, echoes the lines of the nearby Parliament Buildings, and while strongly contrasting with their Neo-Gothicism and the mock medieval Château Laurier nevertheless fits very well into Ottawa's cityscape.

★★National Gallery

Open May–Sep. Tue.–Sun. 10am–6pm; Oct.–Apr. 10am–5pm

Ground Floor:
The gallery shop, auditorium, lecture rooms and cafeteria are on the ground floor, with a colonnade leading to the prism-shaped great hall.

First Floor:
The first floor traces the development of Canadian art, including early religious art from Québec and Nova Scotia (much of it 19th c.), the reconstructed late 19th c. convent chapel, works by Tom Thomson and the Group of Seven, by Paul Kane, Emily Carr and Cornelius Krieghoff, and by Jean-Paul Lemieux, the Canadian Group of Painters, and L.L. Fitzgerald, as well as such contemporary artists as Ian Carr-Harris, Yves Gaucher and Guido Molinari.

Second Floor:
The second floor covers a wider spectrum, ranging from European art of the 17th and 18th c., through Impressionism, and up to American art after 1945, in addition to 20th c. British artists, international Modernism, and art from Asia and the Far East.
    The rooms of Inuit art between the library and the great hall are particularly worth looking at.
    Print, graphics and photography are shown in temporary exhibitions.

Among the gallery's major works, those by Canadian artists include "Joseph Brant" (1805) by William Berczy, "North Shore, Lake Superior" (1926) by Lawren S. Harris, "Blunden Harbour" (1930) by Emily Carr, "Journey on Foot" (undated) by Pitseolak, and "Reason over Passion" (1968) by Joyce Wieland.

Canadian artists

From Europe come Hans Memling's "Virgin and Child with St Antony", Lucas Cranach the Elder's "Venus", and El Greco's "St Francis of Assissi", together with "The Mechanic" (1920) by Fernand Léger; also works by Gustav Klimt, Pablo Picasso, Claes Oldenbourg, George Segal and Andy Warhol.

European artists

Outskirts

Laurier House, halfway between the Rideau Canal and the Rideau River, stands on Avenue Laurier. It was the residence of a number of Canadian Prime Ministers including Sir Wilfrid Laurier, Prime Minister from 1896 to 1911, and William Mackenzie-King, Premier from 1921 to 1930 and 1935 to 1948, and also contains reminders of Nobel Peace Prizewinner Lester Pearson, Prime Minister from 1963 to 1968.

Laurier House

Since 1989 the National Museum of Natural Sciences has occupied the beautiful building that was the National Museum of Man (see Hull, Canadian Museum of Civilization), on the southern rim of downtown Ottawa. The museum traces the earth's geology and the making of seas and continents, focusing particularly on North American aspects such as meteor strikes, mineral deposits, etc. Highlights include the dinosaurs found in the Alberta Badlands, and there are wildlife dioramas showing North American and mammals such as Arctic musk oxen, moose from

★National Museum of Natural Sciences

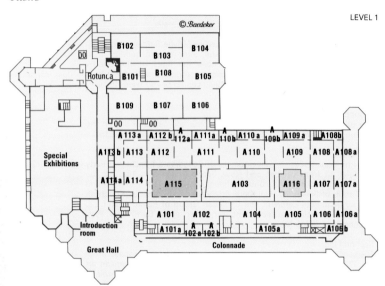

LEVEL 1

© Baedeker

B102 B103 B104

B101 B108 B105

B109 B107 B106

A113a A112b A112a A111a A110b A110a A109b A109a A108b

A113b A113 A112 A111 A110 A109 A108 A108a

A114a A114 A115 A103 A116 A107 A107a

A101 A102 A104 A105 A106 A106a

A101a A102a A102b A105a A106b

Special
Exhibitions

Rotunda

Introduction
room

Great Hall

Colonnade

National Gallery of Canada · Ottawa

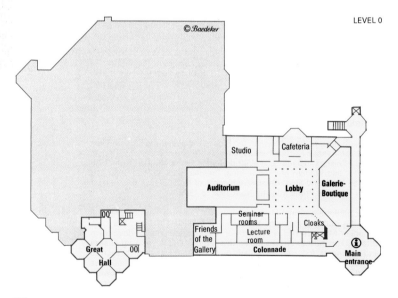

LEVEL 0

© Baedeker

Studio Cafeteria

Auditorium Lobby Galerie-
Boutique

Seminar
rooms

Friends
of the
Gallery Lecture
room Cloaks

Great
Hall Colonnade Main
entrance

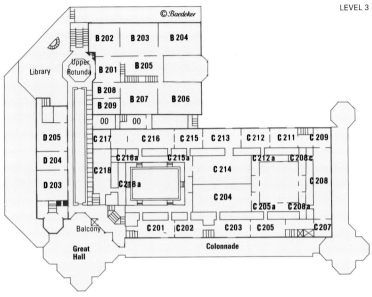

© Baedeker

Plan labels (Level 3):

B 202, B 203, B 204, B 201, B 205, B 208, B 209, B 207, B 206
Upper Rotunda, Library
00 00
D 205, C 217, C 216, C 215, C 213, C 212, C 211, C 209
D 204, C 216a, C 215a, C 212a, C 208c
C 218, C 214, C 208
D 203, C 218a, C 204, C 205a, C 208a
Balcony, C 201, C 202, C 203, C 205, C 207
Great Hall, Colonnade

CANADIAN GALLERY

A 101–A 102b	Early Quebec art
A 102a	Theme room 1
A 103	Rideau Street Monastery Chapel
A 104, A 104a	Atlantic provinces Upper Canada
A 104b	Croscup Room
A 105, A 105a	Royal Canadian Academy of Arts
A 106, A 106a	Late 19th c.
A 106b	Theme room 2
A 107, A 107a	Canadian Art Club
A 108, A 108a	Tom Thomsen Group of Seven
A 108b	Theme room 3
A 109	Group of Seven
A 109a	MacCullum Jackman Cottage
A 109b	Montréal 1920–40
A 110	Canadian Group of Painters
A 110a	British Columbia 1900–50
A 110b	David Milne L. L. Fitzgerald
A 111	Contemporary Arts Society
A 111a	Early automatists
A 112	Automatists and sculptors
A 112a	Theme room 4
A 113–A 114a	1950s and 1960s
A 115	Garden court
A 116	Fountain court

CONTEMPORARY ART (1960–80)

B 101	Dan Flavian
B 102	Claes Oldenburg, George, Segal, Andy Warhol, etc.
B 103	Nancy Graves, Richard Serra, etc.
B 104	Donald Judd
B 105	Courtyard
B 106	Paterson Ewen, Ron Martin, David and Royden Rabinowitch
B 107	Ian Carr-Harris, Michael Snow, Murray Favro, Greg Curnoe, Joyce Wieland
B 108	Charles Gagnon, Yves Gaucher, Guido Molinari

CONTEMPORARY ART

B 201–208	1975 to the present day
B 209	Video

EUROPEAN AND AMERICAN GALLERIES

C 201	Italy: 14th and 15th c.
C 201a	France: sculpture
C 202, C 202a	Northern Europe: 15th/16th c.
C 203	Italy: 16th c.
C 204, C 205a	17th c.
C 205	Northern Europe: 17th c.
C 207	Venice: 18th c.
C 208	Great Britain: 18th c.
C 208a, C 208c	Continental Europe 18th c.
C 209	Neo-Classicism
C 211, C 212	Great Britain/France 19th c.
C 212a	Great Britain: 19th c.
C 213	Impressionism Post-Impressionism
C 214	United States: after 1945
C 215	Early 20th c.
C 215a, C 216a	Great Britain 20th c.
C 216	International Modernism
C 217	Marcel Duchamp

ASIATIC ART

C 218, C 218a	Various works

INUIT ART

D 201, D 202	Various works

PRINTS, DRAWINGS, PHOTOGRAPHS

D 203–D 205	Various works

eastern Canada and grizzly bears from British Columbia, as well as birds of Canada and the distribution of the country's flora and fauna.

Billings Estate

Billings Estate, in the south of the city near the Rideau River, is one of the oldest estates still left in Ottawa, and was built by Braddish Billings in 1828. His descendants lived here until the 1970s when it was made into a museum tracing the life history of four generations of the Billings family.

★Experimental Farm

The Canadian Ministry of Agriculture's experimental farm, on the south-western edge of the town, dates back to the 1920s. Attached to it is a farming museum, showing farming as it was in the past, and also providing guided tours of the kitchen-gardens, seedbeds and arboretum.

Pearson Building

The Pearson Building, a gleaming glass tower on Sussex Drive near the Rideau Falls, houses Canada's Foreign Office, the Department of External Affairs.

★Rideau Falls

The Rideau Falls are a series of cascades, with Green Island in the middle, where the Rideau drops down into the Ottawa River. They are a particularly impressive spectacle when the torrent is swollen by the melting snows in spring.

Prime Minister's official residence

The Canadian Prime Minister's official residence is just north of the Rideau Falls.

Rideau Hall

Further east amid a green open space stands Rideau Hall, the residence of the Queen's representative in Canada, the Governor General.

★Rockcliffe Park

Rockcliffe Park, to the north, has a fine view over the Gatineau River valley (see Hull).

★National Aviation Museum

The National Aviation Museum is at Rockcliffe Airport, on the northern edge of town, and dates from 1988. Telling in detail the story of Canadian civil and military aviation, among the aircraft on display are a replica of the Silver Dart, which in 1909 made the first flight in Canada, fighter planes from the First and Second World Wars, and some of the seaplanes and other aircraft that helped open up Canada's uncharted northern wilderness. The Royal Canadian Airforce Hall of Tribute commemorates the exploits of the service.

★National Museum of Science & Technology

On the eastern edge of the town, this is another museum worth visiting. Exhibits include a Nova Scotia lighthouse, old boats and farming equipment, a whole series of vintage cars and an Atlas rocket, vintage steam engines and steam locomotives. There are also special exhibitions about communications and modern physics, and an interesting collection of timepieces. Astronomy and space exploration are also covered and the museum has an excellent observatory for stargazing on clear nights.

Portage

At the south-western end of Wellington Street lies the southern end of Portage Bridge. Here there is a little park by the rapids of the Ottawa River containing a number of panels showing the development of industry in the Ottawa area, alongside an ageing hydro-electric plant, and some unsightly industrial buildings and old mills.

★L'Outaouais H 15/16

Provinces: Québec, Ontario

Information

See Québec and Ontario

Location

The area known as "L'Outaouais" stretches along both sides of the Ottawa River between the cities of Ottawa and Montréal (see entries). North of this 300 km (186 mi.)-wide stretch of land there are the low hills where the tumbling tributaries of the Ottawa River such as the Rouge, Lièvre and Gatineau have their source.

The Ottawa River always has been of major importance. Samuel de Champlain (see Famous People) had already realised on his first expedition in 1603 that the Huron and Algonquin used it to get from the Great Lakes to the St Lawrence to barter their furs. From then on it was the crucial transport link in the Canadian fur trade. Its history is one of strife, punitive expeditions and bloody massacres, as well as treaties.

History

In the 18th c. Canadian "voyageurs", such as the fur company men, took over from the Indians, travelling in fleets of canoes, hundreds of men at a time every year, to the Great Lakes in spring, even getting as far as James Bay (see entry), and returning laden with furs in the autumn.

As the fur trade began to decline in importance in the early 19th c. the American Philemon Wright started up a new industry by commercially exploiting the forest timber, an industry that is still of considerable importance in the Québec economy today, albeit beset with problems. Wright set himself up near what is now Hull (see entry) in a beautiful country estate. He had no income to start with that would cover the vast expense that his plans involved, but finally he saw his chance. Deprived of its timber sources in Scandinavia by the Napoleonic Wars, England was desperately looking to its American colonies to meet its demand for wood. The densely forested Outaouais had plenty, and it could easily be floated down in rafts to the next port, Québec, so in the winter of 1805/1806 Wright had his men felling the pines and the other trees.

The first consignment of timber was finally despatched on June 11th 1806 down the Ottawa River from Gatineau to the St Lawrence (see entry). After this success the lumberjacks of Québec in their thousands fell upon the timber on the banks of the Ottawa River and its tributaries. In 1860 the Bishop of Ottawa estimated that there were more than 20,000 "Hommes des Bois" in his diocese alone.

In Gatineau Park, just outside Hull and Ottawa (see entries), the Outaouais has one of the province's most beautiful parks, as well as the Papineau – Labelle nature reserve.

The Papineau–Labelle nature reserve, named after the Canadian politician who had made his home there, has rivers, lakes, waterfalls, dams and his "Petite-Nation" estate.

Papineau–Labelle Reserve

There is plenty going on in the constantly expanding towns of the Outaouais. Hull, its capital (see entry), has changed a lot since the 1970s, and is now home to over 20,000 Federal government employees.

★Tour of L'Outaouais from Montréal (430 km (267 mi.))

This route is mostly along Highway 148 to Hull, and then Highway 17. Ferries can provide shortcuts – it is possible to cut 260 km (162 mi.) off the journey just by taking the ferry from Fasset to Lefaivre. From Montréal, take Autoroute 40 towards Ottawa, then after 13 km (8 mi.) Autoroute 13 towards St-Eustache.

St-Eustache (pop. 34,000), after 33 km (21 mi.), is on the eastern part of Lac des Deux-Montagnes. Its church still shows signs of the fighting in 1837 when about 250 of the "patriot" rebels, only half of them armed, made a stand in the church, the presbytery and the adjoining buildings, but were unable to withstand the English soldiers and their cannon.

St-Eustache

From St-Eustache continue on Route 344, passing Park Paul-Sauvé. This is an estate leased by Louis XV to the Siegneur of St-Sulpice, and acquired by the province in 1962. Walnut trees, oak and elm grow right down to the lakeshore. Fishing is allowed, but not hunting.

Park Paul-Sauvé

Oka

The resort of Oka (pop. 1500), almost 60 km (37 mi.) further on, is famous for its "Oka" cheese, at one time made by the Trappist monks of Notre-Dame-des-Lacs, a foundation dating from 1831. Of the pilgrimage chapels (1740–42) that used to stand on the hill near the lake, only three remain (date of pilgrimage September 14th).

Como

Como can be reached by a ferry that operates from 6.30am to 5pm or 11pm, depending on the season (tel. (514) 4584732 for information).

Sainte-Placide

The village of Sainte-Placide, on Lac des Deux-Montagnes, is the birth-place of Sir Adolphe Routhier (1839–1920), who wrote the French words to the Canadian national anthem.

Carillon

Carillon, a former trading post, was a popular base for travellers en route to the high country. A monument commemorates Adam Dollar des Ormeaux and his companions who, together with a number of Huron and Algonquin, held out behind a palisade for days against several hundred Iroquois at the Long Sault rapids.

Pointe-Fortune ferry

There is a ferry to Pointe-Fortune that operates from April to December between 7am and 9pm.

Grenville

Grenville, after 103 km (64 mi.), is an industrial town that grew up out of a trading post, founded by English settlers in 1809, where a canal was built between 1819 and 1823 to bypass the Long Sault rapids. This was replaced by a new one in 1963, leading to Carillon. A bridge over the Ottawa River makes it possible to get to Hawkesbury.

Calumet

Calumet is a timber town beyond Grenville.

Fasset ferry

Between April and December, from 6am to 10pm, Fasset has a ferry service over to Lefaivre (Ontario).

Montebello

Montebello (pop. 1500) is a pleasant village in what were the hunting grounds of the Algonquin.

Château

Montebello's Château, near the Château de Montebello Hotel, was built in 1850 by Louis Joseph Papineau. A liberal deputy to Lower Canada's legislative assembly, and subsequently leader of the rebel "Patriots" in 1837, he returned to Canada in 1845 from exile in the USA and Paris, where he had become friends with the Count of Montebello. The château was also the childhood home of Henri Bourassa (1868–1952), the liberal politician and founder of the newspaper "Le Devoir", and it was his father Napoléon Bourassa (1827–1916), an architect, artist, sculptor and writer, who was responsible for building Montebello church.

Plaisance

Plaisance is a village built on part of the Petite Nation estate, which was leased by the East India Company to the Sieur de Laval in 1674, when the company held the monopoly for the fur trade.

Thurso

The industrialised village Thurso (pop. 3000) was founded in 1886 to take out the timber from this part of the Ottawa valley. There is a ferry to Rockland from April to December between 7am and midnight (tel. (819) 4235025 for information).

Masson

Masson is mainly concerned with producing pulp for the paper industry. It has a ferry to Cumberland between April and December (on request).
  From Masson Route 309 proceeds towards Mont-Laurier and the mining town of Buckingham, and to Val-des-Bois, near an entrance to the Papineau-Labelle nature reserve.

Hull
Gatineau Park

See Hull

Peace River
F 7

Province: Alberta

See Alberta

The Peace River, which gets its name from "Peace Point" on its lower reaches, rises in the Rocky Mountains of British Columbia. Its two main tributaries are the Smoky River and the Heart River. On leaving the Rockies, it flows east through the Peace River Valley, and then turns northwards. After 1920 km (1193 mi.), just north of Lake Athabasca, it joins the Athabasca River (see entry) to form the Slave River, the largest of the rivers flowing into Great Slave Lake.

Course

The middle section of the Peace River Valley, in the eastern Rockies, with places such as Grand Prairie, Peace River and High Prairie – an area of 65,000 sq. km (25,090 sq. mi.) – is famous as fertile farmland with higher-than-average yields of grain and vegetables (potatoes, wheat, rye, etc.). Its good climate and topography meant that the valley was settled very early on, developing into an important farming region and centre for the fur trade, particularly with the coming of the railroad in 1915.

Farming

Peace River

Province: Alberta. Population: 6000

Land of the Mighty Peace Tourist Association, P.O. Box 3210, Peace River T0X 2X0

Information

The little town of Peace River, on the banks of the river of the same name, lies in the heart of the Peace River Region. Its history goes back to the early 18th c., when it was already a meeting place for traders and fur trappers. The explorer Sir Alexander Mackenzie (see Famous People) set out from here in 1742 on his expedition to the north.

History

The town has a larger-than-life wooden statue of its most famous son, the legendary Henry Fuller Davis. A spectacular gold discovery made the "little" man – his nickname was "Twelve-Foot Davis" – into a local celebrity overnight, and the town still likes to remember the kindness and generosity of its esteemed citizen.

Henry Fuller Davis

★Peterborough

J 15

Province: Ontario. Population: 70,000

Greater Peterborough Chamber of Commerce, 175 George Street N., Peterborough, ON K9J 3G6; tel. (705) 7489771

Information

Peterborough is the gateway to the Kawasthra, part of the Trent-Severn Waterway lake district and the centre of a recreational area extending from Rice Lake in the east to Lake Suncoe in the west.

Location

Peterborough was founded in 1818 when a sawmill was built on the river here. The area around it has many traces of Indian settlements.

History

The area just north of the town on Lake Story, now protected as a Provincial Park, has more Indian rock drawings than anywhere else in Canada, with about 900 which are between 500 and 1000 years old. The park is open from mid-May to mid-October between 9am and 6pm.

★Petroglyph National Park

Peterborough's locks are one of its special attractions. Uptown it has three locks regulating the waterlevel for shipping, among them the famous hydraulic lock built in 1904. One of only eight of its kind in the

★Locks

world, it enables vessels to overcome a difference in waterlevel of 20 m (66 ft).

The Interpretive Centre has exhibitions and audio visuals showing how the locks were built and how they work (open: mid-May–mid-Oct. 9am–5pm). The centre also covers the Trent-Severn Waterway, popular for boating holidays, which has another hydraulic lock and more than 36 ordinary locks.

★★Waterway cruises

In summer and autumn cruises on the waterways depart from the landing in the town centre. The various trips are particularly enjoyable when the leaves are changing colour in the autumn.

Lang Century Village Museum

It is worth taking a trip just 20 km (13 mi.) along the TransCanada Highway to Lang Century Village Museum which is a reconstruction of a 19th c. pioneer village. The old mill, dating from 1845 and in full working order, is particularly interesting. There are displays of the old craftsmen's tools in, for example, the mill, smithy, and sawmill, etc. The museum is open 1 to 5pm from mid-May to mid-October.

★★Point Pelee National Park   J 14

Province: Ontario

Information

Point Pelee National Park, The Superintendent, Leamington, ON N8H 3V4; tel. (519) 3222365

Location

Point Pelee National Park is at the southernmost point on the Canadian mainland, an almost triangular peninsula which juts out into Lake Erie. It has long been famous as a resting place on the path of many migratory birds, and for its now very rare Monarch butterflies.

Morphology

The sandy peninsula of Point Pelee came into existence about 10,000 years ago, when wind and water deposited great quantities of sand here from the slowly retreating glaciers of the last Ice Age. In places this sand is still as much as 60 m (200 ft) deep.

★Plantlife

Its favourable climate has given the peninsula lush mixed woodland, mostly deciduous, but also some evergreens. Its trees include mountain maple, walnut, mulberry, hickory (pecan), and red cedar, along with various kinds of hops, climbers and creepers. There are also plenty of prickly pears, with their lovely yellow flowers.

★★Bird reserve

Point Pelee is where two major bird migration routes meet so that in spring and autumn often over a hundred different bird species can be seen in a day, and there are more than 300 species recorded in the course of the year.

★Monarch butterfly

In September the trees of this national park are full of beautiful Monarch butterflies resting, like some of the birds, on their migration to the south.

Boardwalk

From the boardwalk with two tower hides on the edge of the marsh it is possible to see fish, turtles and musk rats as well as birds.

Lighthouse

A lighthouse off the southern tip of Point Pelee warns passing ships of the shallows around the peninsula.

Visitor Centre

The Visitor Centre, open daily, has films and slideshows about various aspects of the National Park, plus very interesting leaflets, etc. (canoe and bike rental, picnic sites, refreshments; tel. (519) 3263204 for information).

Park railway

A little train takes visitors round the park, starting from the Visitor Centre.

A rare visitor to the most southerly point of Canada

★Portage la Prairie   H 11

Province: Manitoba. Population: 7,000

Portage Chamber of Commerce, 11 2nd Street N.E., Portage 1a Prairie,   Information
MB R1N 1R8; tel. (204) 8577778

Many early French explorers passed through here on their way to Lake   History
Manitoba, in their vain search for the Northwest Passage to the Far East,
and this is where, in 1738, Sieur de la Vérendrye built Fort La Reine as
his base for exploring the prairies. The town's name dates from that
time, when it was on the portage between the Assiniboine River and
Lake Manitoba. John Sutherland Sanderson made it the first settlement
in western Canada.

Manitoba's history is vividly illustrated by the displays in Fort La Reine   ★Fort La Reine
Museum and the Pioneer Village on the outskirts of the town at the inter-   Museum, Pioneer
section of Highways 1A and 26 (open: May–mid–Sep. Mon.–Fri.   Village
8am–6pm, Sat. and Sun. 10am–6pm).

The museum complex includes a trading post, a smithy and stables, and
the Pioneer Village has an early wooden house, a trapper's cabin, the
"Farm of the Century", a country church and an 1880s schoolhouse.
Other exhibits include a reconstructed York boat and a Red River wagon,
brought here from Joliette, Québec, for Manitoba's centenary. These
carts drawn by oxen were the principal means of transport of the early
settlers. Built entirely of wood they were very noisy because their
wheels were not greased against the dust. A railway service wagon can
also be seen.

★Island Park, Crescent Lake	Island Park and Crescent Lake Nature Reserve, with its horseshoe-shaped lake, are also worth a visit to see the deer and wildfowl, including the large colony of captive Canada geese. The park also has a little zoo, a golf course, tennis courts and picnic sites, as well as canoeing and swimming facilities. The monument to Arthur Meighen commemorates this son of Portage La Prairie who was elected Canada's Prime Minister in 1920.

Prescott   J 15

Province: Ontario. Population: 5000

Information	Tourism Prescott, 360 Dibble St, Prescott, ON K0E 1T0; tel. (613) 9251861
History	Founded by Loyalists in 1784, Prescott was for a long time an important port on the St Lawrence because of the rapids downstream. These held up the grain shipments so they had to be loaded onto barges here to continue the journey, or to be ground into flour in the town.
★Fort Wellington	The main building of Fort Wellington is the restored blockhouse, but the officers' quarters and fortifications can also be seen. The fort was the scene of heavy fighting when William Lyon Mackenzie led his supporters and American allies in rebellion.
Museum	Nowadays the fort is a military museum, and stages re-enactments of the old military drill parades in the British and American uniforms of the time.
Lighthouse	East of Fort Wellington is a former windmill that was converted into a lighthouse in 1838. Mackenzie's supporters took refuge here during the uprising (open: mid-May–Sept. daily 10am–8pm; and Mon.–Fri. 9am–4pm at other times).

Prince Albert   G 9

Province: Saskatchewan. Population: 34,000

Location	Prince Albert, a lively town on the North Saskatchewan River, is an important centre for the timber and farming areas of northern Saskatchewan. It is also the gateway to the Prince Albert National Park (see entry) north of the town.
Historical Museum	The Historical Museum (open May–Aug. daily 10am–6pm, and by arrangement in winter) is housed in the Old Fire Hall (view over the river) and provides an interesting account of the history of the locality and the town (North West Rebellion, pioneers, Indians, mineral resources), with interesting photographs, documents and objects as well as staging annual photographic exhibitions.
Diefenbaker House	Diefenbaker House (open mid May–beginning of Sep. daily 10am–8pm) commemorates the close links between Canadian Premier John Diefenbaker and the town, which was his constituency, telling his life story through photographs and other memorabilia.
Grace Campbell Gallery	Art lovers will be interested in the Grace Campbell Gallery (open Sep.–Jun., Mon.–Fri. 9am–9pm, Sat. 9am–5.30pm, Sun. 1–5pm; and on Fri. and Sun. until 6pm in summer).

The John Cuelenaere Library and the Little Gallery (open all year) in the Prince Albert Art Centre show works by local, provincial and national artists (painting, photography, etc.).

The Lund Wildlife Exhibit on River Street, west of the river (open Jun.– Aug. daily 10am–10pm, Sep. and Oct. daily noon–9pm), has an outstanding collection of North American wildlife.

Lund Wildlife Exhibit

★★Prince Albert National Park

G 9

Province: Saskatchewan
Area: 3875 sq. km (1496 sq. mi.)

Prince Albert National Park, PO Box 100, Waskesiu Lake, Saskatchewan S0J 2Y0; tel. (306) 6635322

Information

Probably Saskatchewan's most attractive park, Prince Albert National Park is on the edge of the Canadian Shield as it stretches away to the north. The gently undulating landscape is a mixture of spruce swamp, large lakes and aspen-dotted uplands, the legacy of the ice that retreated from here about 10,000 years ago, but has continued to leave its mark on the park's flora and fauna. The park is in an area of transition from aspen parkland to boreal northern forest, and this is reflected not only in the park wildlife, but also in the course of this area's history.

National Park

Native Americans have lived here for thousands of years, and there is archaeological evidence that in severe winters tribes from the prairies moved north up here to its sheltered woodlands, intermingling with the people who lived here.

History

The park's creatures vary according to the habitat, with moose, wolf, black bear, fox, lynx, caribou and eagles in the northern forests, and elk, deer, badger, coyote and squirrel in the parkland in the south. The park has some species that are unique in their national significance. There are also unique resources of natural importance.

Wildlife

Lavallée Lake holds Canada's second largest colony of white pelican, and a limited area in the north-west of the park is given over to one-third of Canada's fescue grassland, once a widespread habitat, where one of the park's two herds of buffalo still roam.

★★**Lavallée Lake**

M.S. "Neo Watkin" in the Prince Albert National Park

Grey Owl

Grey Owl, the best-known, colourful and at the same time controversial naturalist of the 1930s, lived in this park for seven years in a small log cabin called "Beaver Lodge" on Ajawaan Lake. A trapper turned conservationist and author, his popular books, inspired by the woodland and wildlife of the park, tell of his love for the wilderness and the people and creatures who live there, threatened by the advance of civilisation. He returned to the lake after his triumphant lecture tour of England and the States, and died in 1938, but his message – "remember you belong to nature, not it to you" – lives on, and has even greater significance today. His cabin can be reached by boat or canoe across Kingsmere Lake, or by a 20 km (13 mi.) trail from the south end of the lake, where there is a campsite.

Waskesiu Lake

The busy little resort of Waskesiu Lake which serves the park, at the edge of its wilderness, gets its name from the Cree word for "red deer".

★Nature centre

The Prince Albert National Nature Centre (open end Jun.–beginning Sep. daily 10am–5pm) and has exhibitions on the themes of Grey Owl, the boreal wilderness, and the transition from the prairies grasslands, through parkland, to the northern boreal woodlands.

Recreation

Several hundred miles of trails and canoe routes allow the visitor the chance to see moose, wolf, fox and black bear in their natural surroundings, and well over 200 species of bird have been recorded. With one-third of the park area taken up by water, it is also possible to observe beaver, musk rat and otter. There is canoeing and boating on the many lakes, and Kingsmere, Crean and Waskesiu Lakes are all very popular with anglers. The park also boasts picnic areas, riding stables, beaches, tennis courts, good golf courses and fully serviced campsites, not to mention 150 km (93 mi.) of cross-country skiing trails.

★★Prince Edward Island   H 18

Indian name: Abegweit ("cradled on the waves")
Situation: in the Gulf of St Lawrence
Area: 5660 sq. km (2185 sq. mi.)
Population: 137,000
Capital: Charlottetown
Language: English

Information

Tourism Prince Edward Island, PO Box 940, Charlottetown, PEI C1A 7M5; tel. (902) 6292400, fax. (902) 6292428

Access

By plane:
Direct daily flights to Charlottetown from Toronto, Montréal, and Halifax.

By road:
Via the roughly 13 km (8 mi.)-long Confederation Bridge (completed 1997) over the Northumberland Strait from Cape Tormentine (New Brunswick) to Borden (Prince Edward Island).
Car ferries still operate between Caribou/Nova Scotia and Wood Islands.

By train/bus:
By train to Moncton/New Brunswick, then by bus to Cape Tormentine, and across the new bridge over the Northumberland Strait to Borden and on to Charlottetown.

Landscape

The Micmac Indian legend tells how the god Glooscap painted all of the world's beautiful places then dipped his brush in every colour and created Abegweit, his favourite island. Canada's smallest province, but one of its loveliest, Prince Edward Island's natural beauty lies in its

Prince Edward Island

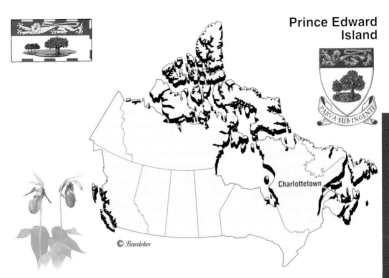

© Baedeker

gently rolling hills and scenic beaches of powdery white sand in the north, and edged with red sandstone cliffs in the south. Its pleasant climate, good beaches and rural charm make it a favourite with holiday-makers who swell its population every year to well over half a million. Unlike its neighbours, most of the island's countryside is farmland, thanks to its exceptionally fertile, brick-red soil.

The island nestles in the Gulf of St Lawrence, separated from the mainland by the Northumberland Strait, only 14 km (8½ mi.) across at its narrowest point. It extends between longitude 61° and 64° and between latitude 45° and 47°.

Location

It stretches 224 km (139 mi.) and is from 6 km (4 mi.) to 64 km (40 mi.) across. The coastline is broken up by a mass of bays and inlets, and its highest point, at 150 m (492 ft), is in Queens County.

Prince Edward Island is very young in geological terms. Its sandstone was formed by sediment deposited about 250–300 million years ago. The oldest sediments were found in the Miminegash region and the striking redness of the soil is due to the high iron oxide content. The whole island bears the imprint of the Ice Age. As the ice retreated about 15,000 years ago the sea level rose, and the three small islands that appeared in the Gulf of St Lawrence gradually grew together to form the present landmass.

Geology

The most spectacular morphological change is currently along the coastline, where the erosive forces of wind and rain, waves and frost have created long beaches and sandbanks, and vulnerable sandstone can be worn away at the rate of several inches a year.

Morphology

Thanks to its position in the Gulf of St Lawrence, Prince Edward Island has pleasantly moderate temperatures, although it can become very cold in winter. In high summer the thermometer can climb up to 30°C (86°F). The precipitation of 1090 mm (43 in.) falls on only 160 days of the year. July and August are the driest and warmest months, when the water around the island can be as warm as 21°C (70°F).

Climate

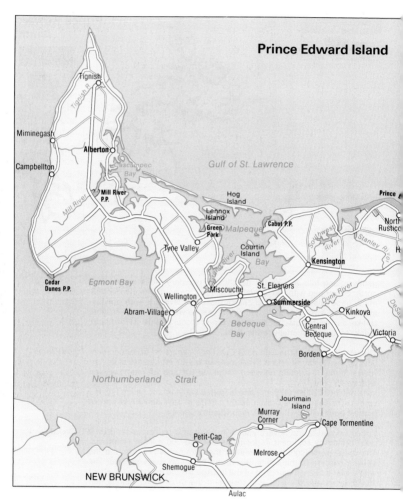

Prince Edward Island

Gulf of St. Lawrence

Tignish

Miminegash

Alberton

Campbellton

Mill River P.P.

Hog Island

Lennox Island

Green Park

Cabot P.P.

Prince

North Rustico

Tyne Valley

Courtin Island

Malpeque Bay

Kensington

Cedar Dunes P.P.

Egmont Bay

Wellington

Miscouche

St. Eleanors

Abram-Village

Summerside

Kinkova

Central Bedeque

Victoria

Bedeque Bay

Borden

Northumberland Strait

Jourimain Island

Murray Corner

Cape Tormentine

Petit-Cap

Melrose

Shemogue

NEW BRUNSWICK

Aulac

Vegetation	About 90 per cent of the land on the island is farmed. Potatoes are the main crop, but some cereals and other vegetables are grown as well. There are sizeable orchards, but no real woodland.
Wildlife	Over 300 bird species have been recorded on Prince Edward Island. These include albatross, petrels, cormorant, gannet, heron, osprey, etc.
History	The mainland Micmac Indians, who came here about 2000 years ago and named the island "Abegweit". As nomadic people they lived in small groups, fishing in summer and hunting on the mainland in winter. France laid claim to the island as early as 1523, even before Jacques Cartier sailed here in 1534. He was fascinated by the glorious beauty of

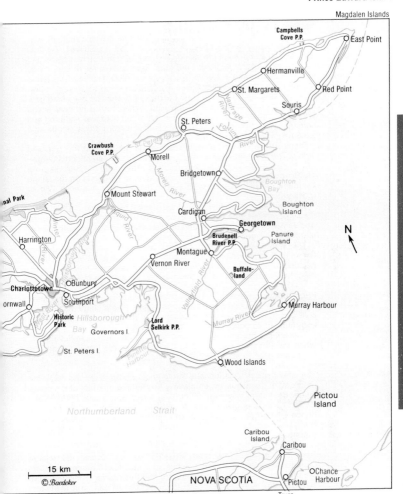

Magdalen Islands

Campbells Cove P.P.

East Point

Hermanville

St. Margarets

Red Point

Souris

St. Peters

Crawbush Cove P.P.

Morell

Bridgetown

Boughton Bay

nal Park

Mount Stewart

Cardigan

Boughton Island

Georgetown

Brudenell River P.P.

Panure Island

Harrington

Montague

Vernon River

Buffalo-land

Charlottetown

Bunbury

Southport

Murray Harbour

ornwall

Historic Park

Governors I.

Lord Selkirk P.P.

St. Peters I.

Wood Islands

Pictou Island

Northumberland Strait

Caribou Island

Caribou

15 km

© Baedeker

NOVA SCOTIA

Pictou

Chance Harbour

Truro

N

the island. The French named it Île St Jean, and the first of them arrived in 1663. In 1719 the first influx of immigrants of any size settled in Port de la Joie, now Fort Amherst. Jean-Pierre de Roma founded a settlement at Three Rivers, Brudenell Point, in 1732, and French Acadians came here in 1755, driven out of Nova Scotia by the British. Apparently the Micmac and the early French settlers managed to live in relative harmony with one another.

After the French fortress of Louisbourg on Cape Breton Island fell into British hands in 1758 many of the local French settlers fled to Prince Edward Island, prompting the British to occupy the island and deport the Acadians because of their questionable loyalty to the British crown. They were sent either to British North America, or to England to be returned to France after the war. The few who remained on the island escaped deportation by fleeing into the woods.

Under British rule, St John's Island (as the British called it) was annexed to the colony of Nova Scotia in 1763. In 1764/65, General Samuel Holland divided the island into three administrative districts and 67 lots, each of 20,000 acres, and these were drawn for in London by wealthy Englishmen at a grand lottery for the distant colony. This led to a century of struggle against absentee landlords and harsh rent collectors until finally, in 1853, the Land Purchase Act enabled the island government to buy back most of the land. When Prince Edward Island joined the confederation in 1873, the rest of the land was acquired and sold. In 1769 the island won independence from Nova Scotia and became a British colony in its own right.

Many British settlers, mostly Scots, came here during the 18th and 19th c. The Montgomerys arrived around 1770, and early Scottish immigrants settled in Scotchfort and Tracadie. After 1803 the Selkirks from the Scottish Highlands settled around Eldon, to be joined on the island by many loyalists who moved north following the American War of Independence.

The legislative assembly named the island Prince Edward in 1798 after the Duke of Kent who was later to become the father of Queen Victoria, and who was commander of the English troops in Halifax at that time, and the island got its own government in 1851.

The Conference of Charlottetown was held in 1864 to discuss Canadian Confederation, but it was 1873 before the islanders reluctantly decided to join the Union, after the still relatively new federal government had promised to set up communications with the mainland.

Population

Prince Edward Island is Canada's smallest but most densely populated province. Its population is 80 per cent British, 17 per cent French, 2 per cent Dutch, and 4 per cent descendants of the original Indians. About two-thirds of its people live outside the towns.

There was a big increase in population after the American Revolution, when the British loyalists fled to Canada. Over the last ten years the figure has risen to about 137,000.

Agriculture

The island soil is exceptionally fertile and farming is far and away the mainstay of the economy, employing about three quarters of the population. Each farm is around 63 ha (156 acres), and a total of 70,000 ha (172,970 acres) is given over to potatoes, the island's main product. Prince Edward produces all its own cereals, as well as a good deal of fruit and vegetables such as apples, strawberries, broccoli and tomatoes.

Fishing

Fishing is another important industry, earning almost 180 million Canadian dollars a year, with catches totalling 100,000 tonnes. Lobsters are the most profitable, accounting for half this source of income. Cod, sole, herring, salmon, trout and tuna are also landed, and Malpeque oysters, originally from Malpeque Bay in Prince County, are famous the world over.

Industry

Prince Edward Island has little manufacturing, and what there is is mostly associated with processing its fish and farm products, but there is some printing, glass fibre, farm machinery and paint production. In terms of employment, services make up the largest and fastest growing sector. Timber processing plays a subordinate role.

Tourism

Tourism is the island's second biggest earner, with over 700,000 visitors a year and bringing in more than 110 million Canadian dollars. The season is from May to October, but is at its peak in the summer months, although the number of year-round visitors is growing.

Many of the farmers supplement their income by providing accommodation for tourists, and there are actually more tourist flats, cottages and rooms in farms than there are hotel and motel rooms.

See entry   Charlottetown

Suggested routes

The province has three sightseeing routes, Lady Slipper Drive, Blue Heron Drive and Kings Byway Drive, all of them scenic routes around the island's beautiful coast which also take in other major attractions. They are clearly marked and can be followed by car or bicycle.

Although varying in length from 190 km (118 mi.) to 375 km (233 mi.), each of them can be done in a day by car. There are other attractions not actually on the route, but because distances on the island are surprisingly short none of them are much of a detour.

Although these routes are signposted clockwise along the highways they are, for convenience described here in an anti-clockwise direction.

Named after the Lady Slipper orchid, Prince Edward Island's floral emblem which grows in its shady woodland, the drive is signed by a red orchid in a red frame on a square white background. The drive (about 300 km (186 mi.)) follows the coastline in the western part of the island, with its red sandstone cliffs, silvery sands and lush green meadows, passing through peaceful farmland growing mostly potatoes.

★**Lady Slipper Drive**

This part of Prince County has lots of little villages, many of them quite old and still following a traditional way of life. Here live the descendants of the French-speaking Acadians who since 1884 have had their own flag as a symbol of their cultural unity.

The Acadian Pioneer Village (open in summer daily 10am–7pm) at Cape Egmont, 5 km (3 mi.) west of Mont Carmel on the Acadian Shore, is a recreation of an authentic early 19th c. village, with a church, village hall, store, school, a well and smithy. The houses have objets d'art and restored furniture of the period.

★**Acadian Pioneer Village**

Further north along the coast, at the island's westernmost point, the 2 km (1 mi.) white-sand beach of Cedar Dunes Provincial Park is overlooked by the West Point Lighthouse, an old wooden lighthouse from 1874 that had its own keeper until thirty years ago. It was restored a few years ago and now contains a little museum a shop for craftwork and rooms for visitors.

★**Cedar Dunes Provincial Park**

Early this century Alberton was a centre for silver fox farming for the fur trade, which had started up here in 1894 and flourished for four decades until it was badly hit by the depression of the 1930s. The treelined streets and fine big houses are a reminder of these prosperous times.

Alberton

Nowadays Alberton is one of the home ports for Canada's deep-sea fisheries, and it is possible to make long-shore fishing trips from here.

Alberton Museum is in the town's first courthouse, built in 1878 on the corner of Church Street and Howlan Street. It is a local history museum, with special emphasis on the silver-fox farming, as well as displays of Indian items, farm tools, books and photographs as well as other memorabilia (including furniture) of the early European settlers (open Jul./Aug. Mon.–Sat., 10am–5pm).

★**Alberton Museum**

Lennox Island is the biggest Indian reserve in the province, and home to many descendants of the Micmac, whose history is recounted in its little museum.

Lennox Island

Prince Edward Island

★Malpeque Bay

Malpeque Bay is where Prince Edward Island's world-famous oysters have their main beds. It is the centre of Canada's oyster-farming, yielding about 5 million oysters a year. In the west of Malpeque Bay numerous branches of the fishing industry have their bases.

★Green Provincial Park

The road to Green Provincial Park winds its way through woodland groves and open fields. At the centre of the park is the elegant villa of shipbuilding magnate James Yeo Jr. Built in 1865, the villa has been restored and filled with period furniture. The history of shipbuilding on Prince Edward Island is told in a modern exhibition building and a 19th c. shipyard at the water's edge shows how a wooden ship was built. The park has what are probably the finest campsites on the island.

★Blue Heron Drive

Blue Heron Drive (about 200 km (124 mi.)), in the central part of the island, has as its main attraction the long silvery beaches of the North Shore – the best are in Prince Edward Island National Park (entrance fee only if by car). The drive passes through many little holiday resorts and many of the island's tourist attractions and leisure parks, the most interesting being places connected with that famous book "Anne of Green Gables".

From Charlottetown Blue Heron Drive follows the North Shore, with its fine beaches and red sandstone cliffs, then at New London Bay, further west, it comes to the home of the blue heron after which it is named (the sign is a blue heron on a blue-framed square white background). From here it turns south to the South Shore, with several Provincial Parks and their beaches, campsites and picnic areas, ending up back at Charlottetown.

York

From Charlottetown take Highway 2 to Marshfield then Highway 25 to York. Jewells Gardens & Pioneer Village is a restored early 19th c. village surrounded by gardens, with a shop, smithy, school and chapel. There is also a glass museum.

★Prince Edward Island National Park

Take Highway 25 out of York, then turn right onto Highway 220 to Grand Tracadie, then left to Prince Edward Island National Park. This extends from Tracadie Bay in the east to Cavendish Bay in the west, a long line of lovely white-sand beaches. Over 200 species of birds can be seen here, including the superb blue heron. Despite the enormous influx of tourists in summer, the park has surprisingly managed to maintain its ecological balance.

★Cavendish

Cavendish has one of Canada's most popular beaches. Its Rainbow Valley amusement park of about 9 ha (22 acres) has pleasant gardens, a boating lake and a barn (open Jun.–Sep. Mon.–Sat. from 9am and Sun. from 11.30am until dusk; admission fee).

★Green Gables Farmhouse

The countryside around Cavendish was the setting for Avonlea, Lucy Maud Montgomery's fictional farming community of her famous novel "Anne of Green Gables". The Green Gables Farmhouse, about 2 km (1 mi.) west of the town on Highway 6 near the Cavendish entrance to the national park, is an enduring reminder of this popular children's classic (open mid-Jun.–mid-Aug. 9am–8pm, otherwise 9am–5pm).

★Anne of Green Gables Museum

The "Anne of Green Gables Museum" is in the house built in 1872 where Lucy Maud Montgomery lived from time to time, and is packed with Montgomery memorabilia including signed copies of the first edition of the famous novel (open daily, 9am–9pm).

★Malpeque

Malpeque is one of Prince Edward Island's historic sites. A home to the Micmac, it was settled by the French in the early 18th c. Captain Samuel Holland, sent here by the British in 1765, named the place "Princeton", but it later reverted to its old Indian name. Much of the later immigration was from Scotland, and many of their descendants still live here today.

One of the finest gardens in eastern Canada, Malpeque has several hundreds of different kinds of flowers, including dahlias and roses, and contains such interesting features as an old windmill and a showcase beehive.

Port de la Joie, was the first place on the island to be settled by the French in 1720. The British built Fort Amherst here in 1758 after they captured the settlement, but today only the earthworks remain. The whole site has been declared a National Historic Park. The museum is open daily.

Micmac Indian Village, near Rocky Point, is the reconstruction of a 16th c. village showing how the Micmac lived before the Europeans came; contains wigwams and canoes, hand-made hunting and fishing implements, and life-sized sculpture. The museum showing how the island's first inhabitants used their weapons and tools is particularly interesting.

Kings Byway Drive (about 380 km (236 mi.)), signed by a purple crown on a square white background with a purple border, is mostly in Kings County, hence its name, and takes the visitor through the most interesting parts of the island. The people who live here are predominantly the descendants of early Scottish settlers. Its special attractions include red and white sandbanks, photogenic lighthouses, and North Lake Harbour, which prides itself on being "the tuna fishing capital of the world". Anyone wanting to cover the whole drive should plan for two overnight stops on the way.

The drive starts from Charlottetown in the strawberry fields above the Hillsborough River, then runs south to Elden, and cuts across the hilly tobacco-growing district to the east coast. The provincial parks along the route provide plenty of opportunities for swimming and camping. The drive then follows the east coast up to North Lake Harbour then turns along the rugged north coast, passing through several little fishing villages before coming full circle in Charlottetown.

Prince George

Province: British Columbia
Population: 75,000. Height: 570 m (1871 ft)

Tourism Prince George, 1198 Victoria Street, Prince George, BC V2L 2L2; tel. (250) 5623700

Prince George, often referred to as the "Gateway to the North", is situated at the confluence of the Nechako and Fraser rivers in the north of British Columbia. It is the chief town of an extensive surrounding area in which some 170,000 people live. Above all, though, it is an important road and rail junction, where the east–west Yellowhead Highway (TransCanada Hwy 16) intersects the north–south John Hart Highway–Cariboo Highway (Hwy 97), and where C.N. trains en route between Prince Rupert and Vancouver both make stops. Prince George is also an important centre for the west Canadian cellulose and paper industry.

During his first expedition Alexander Mackenzie (see Famous People) camped briefly at the confluence of the two rivers in 1793, and thought it a suitable place for later settlement. He was followed in 1806 by Simon Fraser of the North West Company, who founded Fort George here a year later as, so to speak, an outpost of Fort St James.

Despite its strategic position for the fur trade and the 1858 Cariboo gold-rush largely passed Fort George by. Only with the opening of the Grand Trunk Pacific Railway, bringing hordes of hopeful settlers, adventurers and tradespeople, did the Fort George area experience its own economic boom. In addition to the existing settlement at Fort George, a rival settlement, South Fort George, grew up on the south side of the Fraser River. In 1915 they merged to form the new township of Prince George. Thereafter the population continued to expand and at the outbreak of the Second World War, Prince George boasted more than 4000 inhabitants. Already by then timber was the mainstay of the town's economy. When three big paper and cellulose factories were built here in the 1960s, the population shot up to over 60,000. The advent of more industry resulted in Prince George becoming one of Canada's highest per capita income areas in the 1970s.

★Fort George Park

This pretty park on the bank of the Fraser River holds a replica of the old Fort George, complete with palisades. The Fort George Regional Museum (20th Avenue; open: May–Sept. 10am–5pm) outlines the history and the background of the region (timber, ethnography, temporary exhibitions). There is also an Indian burial ground that can be visited.

Other buildings

There are several other older buildings worth seeing, including the schoolhouse and the station, with a steam train that runs at weekends in summer.

Prince George Railway Museum

The Prince George Railway Museum in Cottonwood Island Park was opened in 1986 (River Road; open May–Sep. Thu.–Mon. 10am–5pm).

★Prince Rupert   G 4

Province: British Columbia. Population: 17,000

Information

Prince Rupert Visitor Information Centre, 100 1st Avenue, PO Box 69, Prince Rupert, BC V8J 3S1; tel. (250) 6243207

The port

The port of Prince Rupert is scenically located on Kaien Island among the fiords of Canada's often rain-shrouded Pacific coast just 60 km (37 mi.) from the southern tip of Alaska. Its large ice-free natural harbour near the mouth of the Skeena soon made Prince Rupert one of Canada's prime fishing ports, but it is also important as the terminus of the Grand Trunk Pacific Railway, now Canada National Railway. Grain, coal and timber are shipped out through the port, which is also the main destination of B.C. ferries, sailing between here and Vancouver Island (see Inside Passage) and the Queen Charlotte Islands (see entry), and along the Alaska Marine Highway. The town and its fisheries expanded considerably after the Second World War, adding paper and cellulose to its other industries, and more recently tourism as well.

History

The town was founded in 1906 by Charles Hays, the ambitious General Manager of the Grand Trunk Pacific Railway, as a northern rival to Vancouver, and the railway line was completed in 1914. During the Second World War it served as a base for the Canadian and American forces.

Sights

Downtown

Downtown Prince Rupert still retains many of the buildings from its earliest years.

★Totem poles

Haida and Tsimshian beautifully carved totem poles can be found throughout the town as a reminder of the peoples who originally lived here. There are some particularly fine examples at Harbour Viewpoint, at Summit Avenue on the edge of Roosevelt Park, from where there is also a good view over the bay and the harbour, especially at sunset.

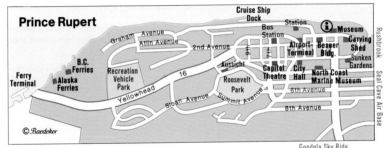

Gondola Sky Ride,
Terrace, Yellowhead

The Museum of Northern British Columbia (1st Ave./McBride St; open mid-May–Labour Day, Mon.–Sat. 9am–9pm, Sun. 9am–5pm; at other times Mon.–Sat. 10am–5pm) is devoted primarily to the Indian culture of the Pacific coast. Outside the building is a brakeman's cabin of 1917, a former Skeena fishing boat; native carvers can be watched at work in the adjoining carving shed.

★Museum of Northern British Columbia

Near the museum stands the B.C. Court House, a building of 1921 in Neo-Classic style.

Court House

Behind the museum lie the so-called "Sunken Gardens" which attract many visitors. They were laid out after the Second World War on the site of a munitions dump.

Sunken Gardens

Next to the modern VIA rail station stands the former Kwinitsa Station. Built originally in 1915 and moved here in 1985, it contains a little museum on the subject of the building of the Grand Trunk Pacific Railway.

Kwinitsa Railway Museum

The Indian Cultural Days are in June every year and feature traditional Indian dances and crafts.

Indian Cultural Days

Surroundings

From the summit of Mount Hays (732 m (2402 ft)) there is a magnificent panoramic view of the Pacific coast. On a clear day it is possible to see as far as the Queen Charlotte Islands (see entry) and the Alaska Panhandle. The cable railway from Prince Rupert (Wantage Road) takes four hours to reach the summit and operates in July and August (timetable available from the Tourist Information Centre, good skiing in winter).

Mount Hays

Hovercraft trips lasting several hours operate from Prince Rupert to Port Simpson, a remote Indian village about 30 km (19 mi.) to the north. Set up as an outpost of the Hudson's Bay Company in 1834, Port Simpson is also served by a twice-weekly ferry or by hydroplanes from of the Seal Cove hydroplane terminal.

Port Simpson

Pukaskwa National Park

H 13

Province: Ontario

Pukaskwa National Park, Bag Service No. 5, Marathon, Ontario P0T 2E0; tel. (807) 2290801

Information

Pukwaskwa National Park is 24 km (15 mi.) south-east of Marathon on Highway 627.

A vast park of 1900 sq. km (733 sq. mi.) on the shores of Lake Superior on the south-west edge of the Canadian Shield, with typical boreal pine forest.

Recreational facilities

The park centre is Hattie Cove, where the visitor centre has various displays and can provide information on the park's campsites, canoe routes and wilderness trails. The scenery is particularly pleasant along the shores of Lake Superior on the 64 km (40 mi.) Coastal Trail where there are walks lasting one or several days.

Qu'Appelle Valley   G 10

Province: Saskatchewan

Legend

The Qu'Appelle Valley gets its name from the Indian legend about a young brave who is going on a journey in his canoe, but soon after setting out the beautiful young maiden he loves falls ill, and calls his name. Although some miles away, he hears her voice and turns around with the cry "qu'appelle?" – who's calling? When he gets back home the maiden is dead, and it is said that ever since his cry can be heard echoing through the valley.

Pauline Johnson, the well-known Indian writer at the turn of the century, enshrined the valley in several of her poems.

Location

The beautiful Qu'Appelle Valley, north of Regina between the TransCanada and Yellowhead Highways, extends along the Qu'Appelle River which rises in Lake Diefenbaker to the west of the province. In the floor of this steep-sided valley, carved out of the gently undulating prairie by the glacial waters following the Ice Age, there is a rich garden-style landscape.

With good timber for both fuel and building it became a staging post for the fur traders before later attracting the pioneers. Eight lakes are strung out along the valley, from Buffalo Pound in the west to Round and Crooked Lake in the east, as well as several scenic parks and little townships.

Katepwa Provincial Park

Katepwa – which is Cree for "calling river" – is a pretty little provincial park (8 ha (20 acres)) on the shores of Katepwa Lake, and has a lovely beach, particularly suitable for families with children.

Lebret

In 1865 Lebret's Sacred Heart Church, also known as Fieldstone Cathedral, was the first church to be built in this district. The present building dates from 1925.

Fort Qu'Appelle

Fort Qu'Appelle museum (open mid-May–Labour Day 10am–noon and 1–5pm, at other times by arrangement) is worth seeing. It is linked to an original Hudson's Bay Company trading post, and has displays covering the Indians, the pioneers and the North West Mounted Police.

★Echo Valley Provincial Park

Echo Valley Provincial Park, west of Fort Qu'Appelle, is in the heart of the Qu'Appelle Valley, and extends over 650 ha (1606 acres) between Lakes Pasque and Echo. It has scenic trails and good swimming in the lakes, as well as particularly fine fishing.

The Saskatchewan Fish Culture Station in the eastern part of the park, on Highway 210, is the only fish farm in North America that breeds fish for both cold and warm waters, raising about half a million trout and 20 million walleye and whitefish every year. The information centre is open to visitors May–Aug. 9am-noon and 1–4pm. There are guided tours throughout the year, by arrangement, and the best time for a visit is between January and July.

The 1900 ha (4695-acre) Buffalo Pound Provincial Park (open all year), west of Regina in Qu'Appelle Valley, is where the Indians used to round up the wild buffalo herds, and there are still buffalo herds in the park today.

Buffalo Pound Provincial Park

Buffalo Pound Lake within the park is ideal for all kinds of watersports, and the park has a big swimming pool, tennis courts, riding stables, campsites, a beach and trails, as well as downhill and cross-country skiing and ice-fishing in winter.

Québec (Province)

E–H 15–18

Area: 1.54 million sq. km (594,440 sq. mi.)
Population: 7.5 million
Capital: Québec. Language: French

Tourisme Québec, C.P. 979, Montréal, PQ H3C 2W3; tel. (514) 8732015, fax. (514) 8643838

Information

Québec reaches almost to the Arctic Circle in the north, and borders on Labrador, Newfoundland and New Brunswick in the east, the American States of Vermont and New York in the south and south-east, and Ontario Province and Hudson Bay in the west. It encompasses the east Canadian land mass north of the Ottawa and St Lawrence Rivers, while south of the St Lawrence it takes in the lowlands as far as the US border, as well as the Gaspé Peninsula projecting out into the Gulf of St Lawrence. In the west an artificial line divides Québec from Ontario, and in the east the border with Labrador is still a matter of dispute.

Location

A vast province about one-sixth of the whole of Canada, Québec could accommodate the United Kingdom five times over, but has a population of only 7.5 million people representing a population density of just 5 per sq. km (10.4 per sq. mi.). Most Québécois live in the two large conurbations of Montréal (about 3.3 million) and the provincial capital Québec (about 600,000). The province's lifeline is the St Lawrence, almost 1200 km (750 mi.) long, which, with the St Lawrence Seaway, has since 1959 been the direct link between the Atlantic and the Great Lakes.

Québec

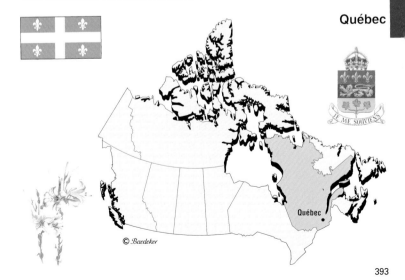

Québec

© Baedeker

The Gaspésie

Natural features

Québec Province can be divided into three major physical regions. Firstly, the north belongs to the primeval Laurentian mountains, and is part of the Canadian Shield. These rounded uplands, dotted with lakes, rise up to about 1000 m (3,300 ft), then slope gently down towards Hudson Bay and James Bay in the north. The Torngat Mountains in the north-east are the highest part of the Canadian Shield, reaching over 1500 m (4900 ft), while the densely wooded Laurentians form the southern edge of the Shield. The extreme south of the province and the Gaspé Peninsula, are considered part of the Appalachians, which extend as far as Newfoundland, and rise to between 970 m (3184 ft) and 1270 m (4168 ft). The third region, the St Lawrence Lowlands between the Laurentians and the foothills of the Appalachians, was the first part of the province to be settled, and is today where 90 per cent of the population live, on the rich land along both banks of the great river.

Climate

Québec's climate is influenced by its northerly position (45°–74°N) and the cold Labrador current. The north, and particularly the north-west, is sub-Arctic with bitterly cold, dry winters and cool summers, while the south of the province is subject to strong seasonal variation. With no high mountains to contend with, the air masses can circulate freely. Spring begins in April/May, and often lasts for only two weeks before the onset of the often humid heat of summer. Average temperatures are around 20°C (68°F), but records of 35°C (95°F) are not unusual. Although it may have started abruptly, summer is slow to fade and there can still be a few warm, autumn days in late October, and sometimes even early November, those days of Indian summer when the bright autumn colours permeate the leaves of the mighty forests. Winters are cold, with a great deal of of snow. The average January temperature in Montréal is −8.9°C (16°F), and further north up the St Lawrence River is even colder, with more and more snow. The average January temperature in Québec City is (−11.6°C) (11.1°F), and while Montréal gets 2.5 m (8 ft) of snow,

Québec gets over 3 m (10 ft), and Sept-Îles, still farther east, has more than 4 m (13 ft). It is thanks to this cold winter that the Canadians can rely on getting ideal conditions for their national game of ice-hockey.

As the climate varies from one zone to another, so does the vegetation, with fruit and vegetables being intensively farmed around the St Lawrence and then, on the poor soil stretching far to the north, come the vast tracts of mixed timber (maple, birch and pine) which cover two-thirds of the province. Then as these woods peter out in the far north, the mosses and lichens take over.

Vegetation

In 1534 the Breton Jacques Cartier reached the mouth of the St Lawrence on his quest for a Northwest Passage, and on the shore of the Gaspé Peninsula he claimed the land on behalf of the King of France. The Algonquin and the Iroquois Indians lived at that time in large villages along the St Lawrence. On his second journey a year later Cartier got as far as the Indian settlements of Stadacona (now Québec) and Hochelaga (Montréal). However, when he returned to Paris from his third voyage in 1542 bringing only "worthless" minerals, interest in this far land waned for a while. This was to change in 1600 when Canada's wealth of furs, especially beaver, prompted Pierre Chauvin to set up a first trading post at Tadoussac. Samuel de Champlain set out to explore the St Lawrence, founding the settlement of Québec in 1608. He immediately began establishing links with the local Indians, and bartering for furs. Conflict with the Iroquois, who were allied with the British, began soon after, inhibiting further settlement, and the few colonists that there were lived in daily fear of attack.

History

It was Louis XIV who made the region the crown colony of "Nouvelle (New) France". Wanting to increase France's fame and prestige, he sent over troops and settlers, appointing the Comte de Frontenac, Louis de Buade, its governor. The province owed its stability to three factors: the absolutist government, the strong Catholic Church, and the seigneurial system, based on the French feudal system, whereby the landed gentry (seigneurs) rented out land to settlers (habitants) who paid their rents in kind.

Between 1641 and 1760 the French-speaking population grew from 500 to over 80,000. In the 18th c., however, the conflicts between the British and the French intensified, but the Seven Years' War (1756–63) put an end to France's colonial aspirations and "New France" was ceded to Britain by the Peace of Paris in 1763.

In the Québec Act of 1774 the British Parliament guaranteed the French Canadians a say in their government and the right to their own language, religion and culture. When many English Loyalists moved up here after the American War of Independence, and the two differently structured national groupings fell out, it was decided, by the Constitutional Act of 1791, to divide the territory into Upper Canada (more or less present-day Ontario) and Lower Canada (Québec). The limitations on the rights of the elected parliament, which had no authority over the British Governor, led to unrest in both colonies. This was put down and well over half a million Québécois subsequently emigrated to the USA.

In 1840 Upper and Lower Canada joined together to become the "Province of Canada", and in 1867 the British North America Act made Québec a province in its own right in the Dominion of Canada, together with the other three provinces of Ontario, New Brunswick and Nova Scotia.

Little changed in the decades that followed in this province of farmers and lumberjacks, where the exploitation of its raw material resources was mainly in the hands of Anglo-Canadian and US business.

The end of the 1940s saw Québec's French-speaking majority starting to take up the cudgels against the overbearing role of the Anglo Canadians. The movement gathered strength in the 1960s and the "Parti

Québécois" went as far as to demand full independence from the state of Canada. In 1974 French was declared the sole official language, and two years later the "Parti Québécois" won the provincial elections. However, a provincial referendum held in 1980 produced a majority against secession, a result which was repeated in October 1995 in a second referendum held following the separatists' election victory of 1994. A further ballot on the issue is under consideration (see Baedeker Special, p. 398).

Iroquois

In the 17th c. the powerful Iroquois Nations represented a great threat to the settlers of New France. In 1657 they even besieged Québec. Armed with muskets and tomahawks by the Dutch and the British, the war-like Iroquois were greatly feared, often luring soldiers and traders into ambushes or falling unexpectedly on homesteads. Their great rivals were the Huron, but they managed to eliminate them in the mid-17th c. This was despite the arrival of the Carignan-Salières Regiment and the bounties offered by the French – 20 crowns for every Iroquois captured, and 10 crowns for every Iroquois scalp.

The Iroquois settled around Lake Erie and Lake Ontario, living in large families in the longhouses of their little villages. They grew some crops but lived mainly from hunting, fishing, and fur trading, and usually wore garments of deer-skin. They also held great religious festivals every winter, and celebrated harvest with ritual dances by masked men swinging axes and spears.

Population

Québec is the French province of Canada – about three-quarters of its 7.5 million people are of French origin. Those of British ancestry, about an eighth of the total, live mostly in and around Montréal. The rest are mainly descendants of Italian, Jewish, Greek and German settlers, and in recent years there has been an influx of Vietnamese and Hispanics. The Indians and Inuit, who live in smallish settlements in the north of the province, are becoming an ever diminishing group.

Québec's present-day French-speaking population can actually be traced back to a very small group of immigrants. These were the 10,000 or so French people who came here between 1608 and 1759. It was their birthrate of 10–15 children per family that led to the present population figure. In the recent past, however, as in other industrialised countries, the birthrate has declined sharply.

Economy

The three mainstays of the Québec economy can be summed up as wood, minerals and water.

Over half the province's vast forests are used commercially for timber, of which about three-quarters is softwood which is turned into cellulose and paper. Québec supplies one-fifth of the world's newsprint, and has no fewer than 60 paper mills producing over 8 million tonnes of paper a year.

Mining

The province's mineral resources are concentrated in the rocks of the Canadian Shield, which abound in various ores. The large deposits in the Abitibi and Témiscamingue region in the west account for one-fifth of Canada's copper and gold; silver, zinc, lead and nickel are also there in smaller amounts. Iron ore has begun to be mined on the Ungava Peninsula in Labrador (see entry) relatively recently. Québec is also the world's largest producer of asbestos, with what is reckoned to be over one-third of all the asbestos in the world in the south-east of the province, in the foothills of the Appalachians at Estrie (see entry).

Farming

In the late 19th c. 70 per cent of the people of Québec were still engaged in farming but today that proportion is down to less than 30 per cent, and agriculture's contribution to total production has dropped to about 4 per cent. Very little of the land actually lends itself to farming, yet the regions around Montréal, the St Lawrence lowlands, parts of southern

Tapping maple syrup

Québec and the Lac St Jean district (see entry) produce fruit and vegetables, meat and dairy products in sufficient quantities to feed the people of the province.

Richly endowed with waterpower, the province has enormous hydro-electric power stations on the Rivers St Lawrence, St Maurice and Manicouagan, but the largest and most modern is on the Grande Rivière (see Baie James) and produces over 10 million kW. Much of Québec's energy is exported to the USA. Its power sources have also led to Québec becoming one of the world's top aluminium producers. The services sector makes another considerable contribution to the prosperity of the province.

Energy

In recent years a number of high-tec companies based in Québec province have made names for themselves, in electronics and telecommunications in particular.

New technology

As far as transport is concerned, the St Lawrence River is the backbone of the province; Québec City, Montréal, Trois Rivières and Rimouski all have important freight and container ports.

St Lawrence River

Tourism also plays a large part in Québec's economy, with many of Canada's visitors arriving at Montréal's two international airports, Dorval and Mirabel, probably the most important airports in the east of the country for both domestic and international air traffic.

Tourism

★★Québec (City)

H 16

Province: Québec. Population: 168,000 (Greater Québec: 600,000)

Vive le Québec – libre...

Charles de Gaulle's rallying call during a visit to Montréal in the summer of 1967 was deeply ambiguous: was he simply applauding the achievements of the largest francophone community in the western hemisphere; or was he expressing his support for the separatist vision of a free (i.e. independent) Québec? Certainly his remarks caused deep offence to some members of the federal government of the day.

The seed sown by the French president quickly took root. A great many French Canadians, especially Québécois, considered themselves, as still today, imposed upon in numerous aspects of their lives by the English-speaking majority. In the 1960s and 1970s the Québécois independence movement grew significantly, eventually forcing a referendum on the issue in Québec Province in 1980 and 1995; more than 40 per cent voted in favour of secession from federal Canada.

Although a majority of the electorate in Québec Province, in which approximately a quarter of all Canadians reside, have long demanded greater, more far-reaching powers of self-government, a nationwide referendum in 1992 voted against granting special status to the province with its distinctive language and culture.

That the dissatisfaction of French Canadians had diminished not a whit in the intervening year was made abundantly clear by the parliamentary election of autumn 1993 from which the francophone separatist Bloc Québécois emerged the second most powerful political force in Canada. French-speaking members of parliament from Québec Province, whose declared aim is secession from the Canadian federation, now form the strongest opposition group in the Lower House in Ottawa.

Québec Province itself was led until recently by a committed federalist and Liberal, Robert Bourassa. In elections which took place in 1994 the Québécois Separatist Party emerged the victors. This gave fresh impetus to the movement fuelled by the deep economic recession.

Office de Tourisme et des Congrès de la Région de Québec, 835 Av. Wilfrid-Laurier, Ville de Québec, PQ G1R 2L3; tel. (418) 69224 71

By plane: Québec has an international airport which foreign airlines and charter companies make use of mainly in the summer months. There are good connections with Canadian domestic flights, particularly to Montréal and Toronto (the hub of Canada's air network) as well as to New York (USA).

By rail: Several trains a day run between Montréal and Québec.

By coach: Being one of the most popular tourist destinations in North America Québec enjoys the benefit of excellent long-distance coach services. These include services to the big east coast cities of the USA.

Québec City (the name derives from the Indian word "kebek" meaning "at the meeting of the waters") is situated at the mouth of the Rivière St-Charles which flows into the St Lawrence River at the head of the St Lawrence Estuary. The city, built on a rocky spur reaching a height of 100 m (330 ft), considers itself the "cradle of North America" and still retains something of a European air. Ever since its foundation in 1608 by Samuel de Champlain (see Famous People) Québec has been the political, spiritual and intellectual heart of "la Nouvelle France" (New France). As well as being the capital of Québec Province it is a university city and the seat of both Roman Catholic and Anglican archbishoprics.

Québec is also an important commercial and industrial centre (e.g. for the food and brewing industries, leather goods, textiles, wood and metal processing, engineering, shipbuilding and the printing trade). Its port handles more than seven million tonnes/tons of merchandise a year.

95 per cent of Québécois are French speaking. Wherever the visitor goes – be it to a shop, a restaurant or the theatre – the French way of life is

The idyllic situation of the City of Quebec

Chûtes Montmorency, Ste-Anne-de-Beaupré, Île d'Orléans

Parc de la Jeunesse

Nouvel Palais de Justice

Gare du Palais

CHARLESBOURG, BEAUPORT

Rue Prince Edouard

Rue Prince Edouard

Rue de la Reine

Rue St-Paul

St-François

Rue des Prairies

Barre

Samson

Centre d'Achat

Rue Ste-Marguerite

Rue de la Couronne

Rue Colbert

Fleurie

Rue St-Jean

Artille

Sœurs Grise

Rue Côte

Avenue Dufferin-Montmorency

Patronage St-Vincent de Paul

Sœurs de la Charité

Old Foun

Aquarium, Airport

Rue Dorchester

Rue Côte d'Abraham

Richelieu

St-Olivier

Rue Ste-Genevieve

Rue St-Joachim

Pa Monte

St-Mathieu

Centre Municipal des Congrès

Rue Sutherland

St-Jean Baptiste

Rue St-Gabriel

Boulevard St-Cyrille Ouest

Hôtel d Parleme

Rue St-Jean

Rue Lockwell

Rue Claire Fontaine

Parc de l'Amérique-Française

Marie-Guyart

St-Amable

Manège Militaire

Bon-Pasteur

Grand Théâtre

Grande Ouest Allée

Avenue Laurier

Synagogue

Boulevard St-Cyrille Ouest

Rue Turnbull

St-Cœur-de-Marie

Avenue Cartier

La Laurentienne

Grande Ouest Allée

Avenue Cartier

Avenue Georges Vi

Avenue Laurier

Parc des

Champs de Bataille

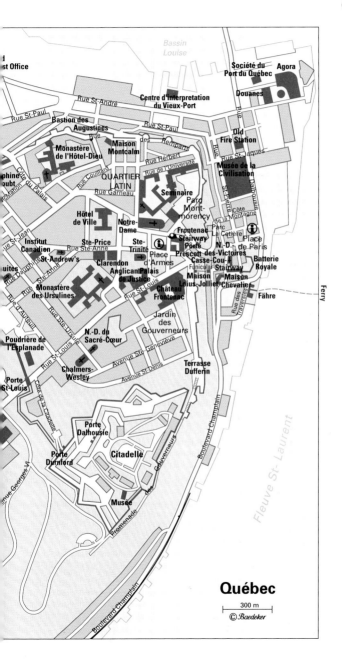

Québec

300 m

© Baedeker

always in evidence. Québec Old City has been designated a historical monument and is listed by UNESCO as a World Heritage Site.

There are four reasonably large ski resorts and 20 golf courses all within a radius of 40 km (25 mi.) of the city. Hunting, fishing, tennis and watersports (including white-water rafting on the Rivière St-Charles and sailing on the St Lawrence) are among other leisure activities also well catered for.

History

In 1608, having penetrated as far as this stretch of the St Lawrence River, Samuel de Champlain (see Famous People) established a small settlement on the northern bank close to the confluence with the Rivière St-Charles. Initially a centre for the trade in furs, within a few years the arrival from Paris of Louis Hébert, an apothecary, saw the infant colony developing a thriving agriculture. The soils of the nearby Île d'Orléans were found to be extremely fertile, as were those of the north bank of the St Lawrence below the Montmorency Falls where climatic conditions also proved especially favourable. The colony grew rapidly to become the administrative centre of French America. From Québec expeditions pushed upstream into what is now the province of Ontario, as well as southwards to the foothills of the north-east Appalachians and beyond to where the city of New York would later be founded.

Despite its defensively strategic position on a rocky spur protected on two sides by rivers, Québec fell to the British in 1629, only to be returned to France in the Treaty of St-Germain. In the autumn of 1690 a British fleet of some three dozen ships commanded by Admiral Sir William Phipps appeared off the town, carrying more than 2000 troops. Bad weather intervened however to thwart their assault.

The British under General Wolfe again laid siege to Québec in the summer of 1759. This time the fleet of more than 40 ships carried 2000 cannon and an army 10,000 strong. Wolfe stationed his troops on the Île d'Orléans – abreast of Lévis on the southern bank of the St Lawrence – and also near the Montmorency Falls. Québec was subjected to heavy bombardment. In September 1759 a force of 5000 led by Wolfe made a landing on the north bank of the St Lawrence and a bloody battle ensued on the Plains of Abraham between the British and the French under Montcalm. Both Wolfe and Montcalm lost their lives in the carnage. A few days later the British entered Québec. The French, having retreated to their winter quarters near Montréal, returned the following April to defeat the British at the Battle of Ste-Foy. Little was gained by the victory however, New France being finally ceded to Britain in the Treaty of Paris of 1763.

In 1774 the "Québec Act" was passed by the British Parliament guaranteeing religious freedom for the French population and ensuring the survival of the French Civil Code.

In the winter of 1775/76 troops from Britain's rebellious American colonies tried to enlist the aid of their northern neighbours in the struggle for independence, laying siege unsuccessfully to Québec. When in the following spring the British frigate "Surprise" appeared in the river the Americans withdrew.

Between 1820 and 1850 Québec's citadel was strengthened at huge expense, mainly to counter any further attempts at encroachment by the now independent United States. Large numbers of cannon were mounted on the cliffs of the Old City, trained to fire on the opposite bank or any hostile ships in the St Lawrence River.

The first meeting of the "Conseil Général de la Nouvelle Québec" was held in the city in 1648. Laval University – now the foremost institution of its kind in Canada – was founded four years later. Within another fifteen years the erstwhile proud capital of New France had also become the administrative centre of a new French speaking province of Québec. Over the next hundred years or so the city acquired its very Parisian parliament building, its City Hall and, in 1892, its most famous landmark, Château Frontenac, a luxury hotel in the style of a medieval château.

In the first half of the 20th c. Québec endured a period of stagnation. During the Second World War the city was the venue for some major conferences and it was here in 1943 that the Allies planned the D-Day invasion of Normandy. In 1945 delegates from 31 countries gathered in Québec to sign the charter setting up the World Food Organisation (WFO), an agency of the United Nations which had itself been founded only a short time before.

Since the 1960s the city, one of the most beautiful in North America, has enjoyed something of a renaissance as the administrative and economic capital of its region and the focal point of French culture in North America.

Québec's Lower Town, site of the original settlement, is built on the low-lying ground bordering the St Lawrence. The Upper Town, atop the 100 m (330 ft) cliffs, grew up to accommodate the government of New France as well as being the location of the military barracks.

Lower Town

Place Royale, the nucleus from which the city developed, has undergone exceptionally sensitive restoration in recent years. It stands on the site of Québec's actual foundation, the spot where, in 1608, Samuel de Champlain erected his first "habitation", a farm and storage shed. Named in honour of Louis XIV whose bust adorns it, Place Royale is the largest surviving ensemble of 17th and 18th c. buildings in North America.

★★Place Royale

One of the most lovingly restored buildings on the Place Royale is the little church of Notre-Dame des Victoires (1688), a name which evokes so much in the city's history.

★★Notre-Dame des Victoires

With its tall chimneys and red tiled roof this fine stone house the wings of which form three sides of a square was built in 1752 for Jean-Baptiste Chevalier, a wealthy merchant. Completely renovated in 1959 it is now used for exhibitions on ethnography.

★Maison Chevalier

Adjacent to the Place Royale, facing out over the river and encircled by stout walls and palisades, the little Batterie Royale was constructed in 1691. Having been threatened with destruction on a number of occasions over the years by the St Lawrence in spate, a way has now been found of safeguarding what remains.

★Batterie Royale

The Place Royale was once the commercial heart of old Québec and a merchant's shop has been re-created in the Maison Nicolas Jérémie as a reminder of those earlier days.

Maison Nicolas Jérémie

An exhibition devoted to the city's history is housed in the restored Maison Soumande (Rue Notre-Dame 29). Among the displays is a model of Québec at the time of its foundation.

Maison Soumande

The delightful Quartier Petit-Champlain at the foot of the steps leading to the Upper Town is nowadays much favoured by artists and crafts people, many of whom have set up business there. Indian leather goods and furs in particular, also examples of Inuit art, are among the many items offered for sale.

Quartier Petit-Champlain

Built to designs by the well-known architect Moshe Safdie the new Musée de la Civilisation (Rue Dalhousie 85; open: Tues.–Sun. 10am–5pm, Wed. 10am–9pm) is of great architectural interest in its own right. In addition to its permanent collection the museum mounts a variety of temporary exhibitions on different aspects of human civilisation. Among its prize exhibits are what is thought to be the earliest barque built in America (in Québec soon after 1608), vaulting from the Maison Pagé-Quercy, remains of the old town wharf and items of modern sculpture. Old furniture and various articles of everyday life contribute to a thoroughly fascinating re-creation of the early days of Québec.

★Musée de la Civilisation

The Batterie Royale   *In the Upper Town*

Every bit as interesting are the special exhibitions, many sponsored by business and industry, on the theme of technical innovation and its effect on people's lives.

★Vieux Port

In the last few years the area around the 19th c. Old Port (Vieux Port) has been turned into a National Monument. What was once a hive of commercial activity centred on the Bassin Louise now has more the air of a leisure park. But the 19th c. is brought vividly to life again in the new Centre d'Interprétation (open May–Aug. Tue.–Sun. 11am–6pm) where visitors are treated to an excellent audio-visual presentation on the shipbuilding industry, the lumber trade, and Québec's commerce. Fine views of the picturesque Old City, the St Lawrence River, and the Laurentian Mountains can be enjoyed from the special observation platform in the Centre.

★★Château Frontenac

Built in 1894 for the Canadian Pacific Railway the majestic Château Frontenac, visible for miles around, is Québec's most famous landmark. The palatial hotel, standing on the site once occupied by Fort St-Louis, the governor's residence in colonial times, is named after the Comte de Frontenac, a French nobleman who was a leading figure in "la Nouvelle France".

From the moment the huge building was completed it became adopted as a fitting emblem for Québec City. Still the provincial capital's foremost hotel, it was here at the Québec Conference in August 1943 that the Allied Powers in the persons of Winston Churchill, Franklin D. Roosevelt, William L. M. King, Vice-Admiral Lord Mountbatten and the US Chief of Staff, General George C. Marshall, and others, laid preparations for the D-Day landings in Normandy (June 6th 1944).

Jardins du Gouverneur

Adjoining the Château on its southern side are the pretty Jardins du Gouverneur. Here Generals Montcalm and Wolfe, adversaries in life but united in death, are honoured by a single monument (see History).

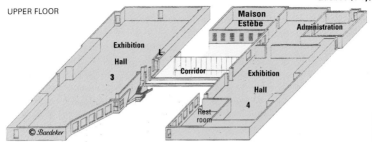

UPPER FLOOR

Maison Estèbe

Administration

Exhibition Hall 3

Corridor

Exhibition Hall 4

Rest room

© *Baedeker*

Musée de la Civilisation   Québec

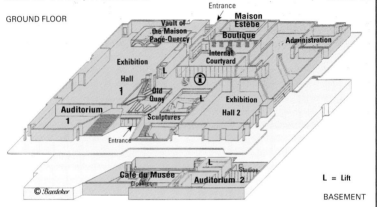

GROUND FLOOR

Entrance

Maison Estèbe

Vault of the Maison Pagé-Quercy

Boutique

Administration

Internal Courtyard

Exhibition Hall 1

Old Quay

Exhibition Hall 2

Auditorium 1

Sculptures

Entrance

Café du Musée

Cloakroom

Studios

Auditorium 2

L = Lift

BASEMENT

© *Baedeker*

The Terrasse Dufferin with its oriental-style baldachins (also the entire length of the Promenade des Gouverneurs) affords stunning views northwards to the Laurentians (see entry) and south-eastwards where, in good visibility, it is possible to make out the foothills of the Appalachian Mountains in the north-east USA.

★Terrasse Dufferin

From Dufferin Terrace the Promenade des Gouverneurs – a footway high (about 90 m (300 ft)) above the St Lawrence in places – leads southwards from the Château Frontenac, past the Citadel and then along the cliffs of Cap Diamant to the Plains of Abraham.

★★Promenade des Gouverneurs

The Place d'Armes (Arms Square) in the Upper Town is Old Québec's busy main square.

Place d'Armes

The little Musée du Fort in the Place d'Armes is well worth a visit by anyone with an interest in history. The story of the city and the various battles for Québec are vividly recounted with the aid of a son et lumière show.

Musée du Fort

The Catholic cathedral with its lovely façade was designed by the architect Baillairgé and completed in 1844.

Cathédrale Notre-Dame

In the basement of Québec's venerable old city hall (directly opposite the cathedral) there is an interesting exhibition on urban life and history. A statue of Cardinal Taschereau (1820–98) stands in the hotel forecourt,

Hôtel de Ville

The world-famous Château Frontenac

which once served as a marketplace. Taschereau, a former rector of Laval University, was the first Canadian to be made a cardinal.

★Séminaire

Established by Bishop Laval in 1663 to provide training for the priesthood Québec's Jesuit Seminary quickly became, under the guidance of its founder, the leading institution of learning in New France and the nucleus from which the Université Laval was formed. With upwards of 22,000 students the university now has its own campus in the southwestern suburb of Ste-Foy.

A number of university faculties (e.g. architecture) still occupy some of the Seminary's historic old buildings.

The Seminary's Briand Chapel was built in 1785 and its 18th c. interior remains unchanged. Many of the wood carvings are masterpieces of their kind.

Musée du Séminaire

In addition to notable works by local artists the Seminary museum has a collection of European religious and secular art, including a portrait by Joshua Reynolds of the British General Wolfe, killed in battle on the Plains of Abraham. The skill and artistry of Québec's goldsmiths are specially featured in the museum, which also has an interesting collection of scientific instruments.

★Rue du Trésor

The Place d'Armes leads into the colourful Rue du Trésor, Québec's equivalent of Montmartre. Like its Parisian counterpart the street is usually crowded with artists exhibiting their work. Paintings and prints in particular are among the many items offered for sale.

Musée du Cire

The Musée du Cire, its waxwork scenes illustrating the history of Québec City, is housed in a 17th c. building at the southern end of the Rue de Trésor facing the Cathédrale Notre-Dame.

The exterior of Québec's Anglican cathedral is very similar to London's St Martin's in the Fields. It was the first Anglican cathedral to be consecrated outside the United Kingdom (in 1804). The interior has a very fine choir installed in honour of the British monarch, with beautiful choir stalls.

★Cathédrale Anglicane

The Rue St-Louis, main thoroughfare of the Upper Town, extends south-westward as far as the old Porte St-Louis. Along it are found some of the city's oldest stone buildings including the Maison Kent, Maison Maillou and Maison Jacquet.

Rue St-Louis

Just off the Rue St-Louis stands the old Ursuline convent. Founded in 1639 by Madame de la Peltrie it provided an education for young girls, Indian as well as French.

★★Vieux Monastère des Ursulines

The convent's first Mother Superior was Marie de l'Incarnation who came from Tours in France. She made great efforts to get to know the Algonquin and Iroquois Indians, compiling the first ever dictionaries in their two languages. Surrounded by an aura of mystery during her lifetime and already revered as a saint in the 17th c. she was beatified in 1980.

The convent church is exceptional, being adorned with beautiful early 18th c. altars and statues by Levasseur, an artist very well known in his day. A small chapel next to the church contains the tomb of Marie de l'Incarnation. This has become an occasional place of pilgrimage.

Also full of interest is the convent museum, vividly conveying to 20th c. visitors the realities of convent life in earlier days. The lives of the convent's foundress and its first Mother Superior are thoroughly documented too. Among items of interest preserved in the museum is the skull of the French Général Montcalm who died in battle on the Plains of Abraham.

Visitors to the old powder magazine near the Porte St-Louis can see a film tracing the various stages in the development of the city's defences.

La Poudrière

Proceeding northwards from La Poudrière leads in the first instance to the partly restored Porte St-Jean. Beyond the old gate lies the Parc de l'Artillerie (open May to Oct. Mon. 1–5pm, Tues.–Sat. 10am–5pm) into

★Parc Historique de l'Artillerie

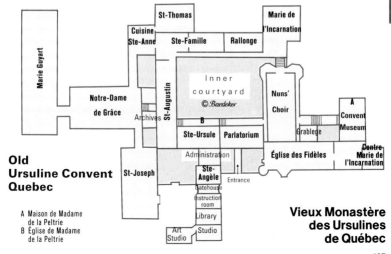

Old Ursuline Convent Quebec

A Maison de Madame de la Peltrie
B Église de Madame de la Peltrie

Vieux Monastère des Ursulines de Québec

which a number of ancient buildings have been incorporated (part of a military complex including barracks which was constructed here in the 17th and 18th c.). The Logis d'Officiers (officers' quarters) and the neighbouring Redoute Dauphine with its mighty walls have been excellently restored. In 1879 an arsenal was established on the site, and afterwards a factory making munitions and other military equipment. The latter closed in 1964. The factory building now houses an information centre devoted to the city's history (with an enthralling model of 19th c. Québec).

★City fortifications

In the more than 300 years of its history Québec has come to possess a variety of fortifications, all of which can be explored on a (fairly long) circular walk. The bastions, walls, towers, gates and countless old cannon leave no doubt as to the thoroughness with which the former French colony was protected.

Completed in 1832 the 4.5 km (2¾ mi.) of defensive ramparts on the west flank of the Old City were constructed of granite and sand, the only fortifications of this kind in North America.

The numerous pieces of weaponry positioned along the ancient parapets and terraces encircling the Upper Town are a constant reminder of Québec's troubled past.

Hôtel Dieu

A short distance north-east of the Parc de l'Artillerie stands the Hôtel Dieu, an Augustinian hospital built in the 1640s. The small museum contains some handsome pieces of old furniture and a variety of domestic items from days gone by. There are also displays of old surgical instruments and a collection of religious art.

The hospital's well preserved vaults were used as workshops and stores and also as places of refuge.

Voûtes du Palais

The Voûtes du Palais, to the north-west and a little way down from the Hôtel Dieu, were once the cellars of the Intendant's Palace. They now house exhibitions on the city's history.

★★Citadel

Thrusting upwards from the west towards the St Lawrence, Cap Diamant reaches a height of 100 m (330 ft) and commands an extensive and varied panorama. On it stands Québec's Citadel, completed in 1832, a massive fortress with hardly an equal anywhere in the world. Within the protection of its thick walls, ramparts and ditches (laid out roughly in the shape of a star) are military quarters for generals, officers and men. One of the excellently restored buildings is now the summer residence of the Governor General of Canada while the mid-18th c. powder magazine in the southern corner of the Citadel has been converted into a military museum.

Today the Citadel is the headquarters of the 22nd Canadian Regiment which, formed at the beginning of the First World War, boasts a distinguished record including action at the Battle of the Somme and – much later – in the Korean War.

Guided Tours mid-May to mid-Oct. daily (tickets need to be obtained in plenty of time). Colourful "Changing of the Guard" ceremony daily 10am.

★Plains of Abraham

To the west of the Citadel stretches the green expanse known as the Plains of Abraham (Champs de Bataille) where in 1759 the British led by General Wolfe fought the French under Montcalm.

Information boards are provided, making it possible to trace the course of events. Also to be seen are the remains of two Martello towers, later additions to Québec's fortifications.

Musée de Québec

There is an excellent collection of work by Canadian artists in the Musée de Québec (in the Parc des Champs Bataille on the former battlefield).

"Living history" on the Plains of Abraham

In front of the museum stands an imposing monument to General Wolfe.

Monument de Wolfe

South-west of the museum Terrasse Grey provides a lovely view of the wide St Lawrence River valley.

Terrasse Grey

The spaciously laid out district immediately south-west of the old Upper Town is the seat of Québec's provincial government. The Parliament, completed in 1877 but later extended, could have been modelled on any number of Parisian public buildings. The Salle de l'Assemblée Nationale (National Assembly) and Salle du Conseil Législatif (Legislative Council) are open to the public (tickets should again be obtained in plenty of time). Both are fine old chambers, sumptuously furnished.

★Parliament Hill

Still on Parliament Hill but a little further down, the Palais des Congrès is a large hotel/shopping/entertainment complex. It includes a 3800 sq. m (41,000 sq. ft) congress centre capable of accommodating up to 5000 people.

Palais des Congrès

As well as plays the Grand Théâtre de Québec (along the Boulevard St-Cyrille Est) also stages concerts by the Conservatoire and the Québec Symphony Orchestra, the latter being the oldest orchestra of its kind in Canada.

Grand Théâtre

Northern part of the Lower Town

The vast Centre Commercial on the northern side of Parliament Hill is Québec's answer to the Underground City in Montréal (see entry). The completely roofed over and centrally heated complex with its many arcades is an ideal place for shopping or just walking around, even in the harshest winter weather.

Centre Commercial

The Provincial Parliament of Québec

Palais de Justice	Further north again, on the lower ground bordering the Rivière St-Charles, is the eye-catching, shimmering green outline of the ultra-modern Palais de Justice.
Gare du Palais	Québec's main railway station near the Palais de Justice was rebuilt a few years ago. The former station building next to it has been converted into an old people's home.
Sillery	South-west of the Plains of Abraham lies Sillery, a suburb with attractive villas. Pleasant views can be had from a number of vantage points on the elevated ground sloping down to the St Lawrence.
Aquarium	Québec's well-stocked aquarium is situated overlooking the Boulevard Champlain at the northern end of the Pont de Québec, the older of the two bridges over the St Lawrence.
★Pont de Québec	Spanning the St Lawrence River at a slight narrows the massive iron frame of the Pont de Québec, built between 1899 and 1917, became familiar to the world even before its completion. During construction two serious accidents occurred in which more than 80 workmen lost their lives.
Pont Pierre-Laporte	The Pierre-Laporte Bridge was opened just a few years ago. Its span of 1040 m (3400 ft) and the height at which it crossed the river (40 m (130 ft)) made it one of the most ambitious bridge-building projects ever undertaken in North America.
Chûtes de la Chaudière	Not far from the southern end of the two bridges a pleasant picnic area has been created at the Chûtes de la Chaudière where the Rivière Chaudière plunges over an escarpment into the St Lawrence.

West of Sillery is the modern residential and commercial suburb of Sainte-Foy.

Sainte-Foy

Having outgrown Québec's Old City the tradition-rich Université Laval now occupies a large modern campus in Ste-Foy. About 25,000 students attend what is the oldest French speaking university in America.

Université Laval

Situated on Québec's northern side, across the Rivière St-Charles, Charlesbourg is an industrial suburb and the site of a large timber processing factory.

Charlesbourg

The open-air Cartier-Brébeuf Museum (open May–Sep. Mon. 1–5pm, Tue.–Sun. 9am–5pm) stands on the banks of the St-Charles River in the city's Limoilou district, an evocative monument to events in the very early history of colonial New France. It was here, on his second voyage to Canada, that Jacques Cartier and his men passed the winter of 1535/36 aboard their ship "La Grande Hermine". There is a reconstruction of the vessel which can be visited. Another pioneer to spend a winter here was the missionary Jean de Brébeuf, later destined to enter ecclesiastical history as Canada's first martyr (he was killed by the Iroquois at Ste Marie among the Hurons). A palisaded long-house provides some insight into the life of the indigenous peoples at that time. The influential role of the Jesuits during the early days of French colonisation is one of the themes explored in the museum's information centre.

★Parc Historique Cartier-Brébeuf

Not far from one another in the suburb of Vannier are a sizeable Centre Commercial and the Parc de l'Exposition, an exhibition site which is also the location of the city's racecourse (known as the Hippodrome).

Parc de l'Exposition

Québec's very fine zoo is situated to the north-west of the city, on the outskirts of Charlesbourg.

Jardin Zoologique

Also on Québec's north-western periphery is an Indian settlement called Village Huron where traditional art and craftwork is found on sale.

Village Huron

A few kilometres downstream from Québec the Île d'Orléans splits the St Lawrence waterway into two. 35 km (22 mi.) long and 9 km (6 mi.) wide the island has kept its rural character almost intact. Despite a recent influx of prosperous Québécois in search of their own small haven of peace, life on the island still evokes something of the pioneering spirit of the earliest colonists of New France.

★Île d'Orléans

Jacques Cartier originally christened the island the "Isle of Bacchus" (having found wild grapes there, so the story goes). Later it was renamed in honour of the Duke of Orléans. The Marquis de Roberval visited the island in 1542, and Samuel de Champlain in 1608, but the first settlement by Europeans only began after 1648. Colonisation was completed under Bishop Laval.

In 1759 the British General Wolfe attempted to mount his assault on Québec from the island but was repulsed by Montcalm's French.

A steel suspension bridge linking the island to the mainland was built in 1935.

There are six delightful villages on the Île d'Orléans well worth visiting.

In the early days of French colonisation Huron Indians, converted to Christianity by Jesuit missionaries, established a retreat on the island, building a chapel at the south-western end in 1651. It was from here that the island was settled by French colonists.

Ste-Pétronille

St-Laurent, on the east side, was founded in 1675, though the present church dates only from 1862. This is where General Wolfe came ashore in 1759 to set up his headquarters.

St-Laurent

St-Jean

Further to the north-east stands the village of St-Jean, its church dating from 1732. The village's major attraction however is the Manoir Mauvide-Genest, a 1735 manor house complete with valuable period furniture.

St-François

The parish of St-François occupies the north-east tip of the island, from where the much smaller Île Madame and Île-aux-Réaux are plainly visible lying a little way offshore. In 1759 the village church, built in 1734, was used as a hospital for the wounded. The church was damaged by fire in 1988. There are fine carvings to admire in the interior.

Ste-Famille

Ste-Famille, on the north-west side, is almost certainly the oldest European settlement on the island.

St-Pierre

On the way back to the mainland the road passes through the village of St-Pierre. The church was built in 1717. Wood carvings by the artist Vézina on the altar and pulpit also date from the 18th c.

Québec to Ste-Anne de Beaupré-Avenue Royale

Heading north-east from Québec towards Ste-Anne de Beaupré both the newer (and faster) Highway 138 and the older more leisurely Highway 360 follow the direction of North America's first paved road, the Avenue Royale, constructed in the early 18th c.

★★Chûtes Montmorency

A bare 10 km (6 mi.) north of Québec the Montmorency River plunges over an 84 m (275 ft) high escarpment. Despite being 30 m (98 ft) higher than the Niagara Falls (see entry) the Chûtes Montmorency are not nearly so spectacular.

Québec City: a cellar in the Avenue Royale

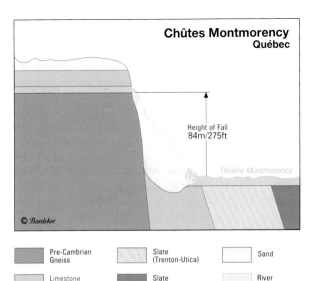

Chûtes Montmorency
Québec

Height of Fall
84m/275ft

Rivière Montmorency

© *Baedeker*

Pre-Cambrian Gneiss	Slate (Trenton-Utica)	Sand
Limestone (Trenton)	Slate (Lorraine)	River Montmorency

Trails with many fine views and attractive picnic places have been marked out in the vicinity of the Falls.

In the 1790s Maison Montmorency (also known as "Kent House") to the left of the Falls was a great favourite of the Duke of Kent (father of the Victoria who later became Queen). From the house there are particularly fine views.

Beyond Montmorency the road passes through the agricultural "garden" of Québec Province, an area of countryside blessed with a particularly favourable local climate and dotted with old mills, farmsteads and unusual cellars half-buried in the valley sides. At some of the attractive old farmhouses and country inns travellers stopping for a welcome rest can savour the local produce (especially the bread, butter and maple syrup). This is a part of Québec also popular with artists; their work, religious and non-religious, is to be seen displayed in a number of places.

★**Côte de Beaupré**

Where the little Petit-Pré flows into the St Lawrence there is an old mill open to visitors during the tourist season.

Petit-Pré

A small exhibition in the village of Château-Richer (population 4000) is devoted to local agriculture and the local economy.

Château-Richer

★Ste-Anne de Beaupré

The little monastery town of Ste-Anne de Beaupré (pop. 3000) is situated on the banks of the St Lawrence only 40 km (25 mi.) north-east of Québec.

Location

The first chapel dedicated to St Anne was built here in the 17th c., quickly becoming a place of pilgrimage following reports of miraculous events. The original wooden building fell victim to a flood however, and in 1661 a new stone-built chapel was erected on the valley side. Fifteen years later it too was replaced.

★Church

413

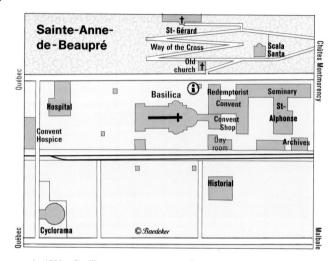

In 1872 a basilica was constructed at St-Anne, only to be destroyed soon afterwards in a fire. The present massive neo-Romanesque church, designed by the Parisian architect Maxime Roisin and completed in 1923, was the work of Louis Audet, a master-builder from Sherbrooke. Among the most pleasing features of the spaciously proportioned interior are the mosaics and colourful stained glass windows. However there are also fine sculptures and paintings by European and Canadian artists. Some services are held in the basement of the church.

Stations of the Cross

On the way up to the chapel on the hillside (this one built in 1878) the Stations of the Cross are marked by beautifully executed life-size metal figures. The altar dates from the 18th c. while the clock tower, designed by Claude Baillif, was already there in 1678.

Scala Santa

The nearby Scala Santa Chapel (Chapel of the Holy Steps) was built in 1871. The steps are a replica of those which Christ mounted to be taken before Pontius Pilate.

Historial

Located on the large car park in front of the basilica the waxworks museum known as the Historial is dedicated to the cult of St Anne in North America and the history of the shrine at Beaupré.

Cyclorama

Painted in the 1880s this intriguing oddity consists of a huge 360° panorama of Jerusalem on the day of the Crucifixion. It shows the places where Christ paused on the way to Golgotha.

Around Ste-Anne de Beaupré

Cap Tourmente

About 10 km (6 mi.) east of Ste-Anne, at Cap Tourmente, a wildlife reserve has been established on the northern shore of the St Lawrence Estuary. Here each spring and autumn thousands upon thousands of migrating snow geese break their long northward or southward journey.

★Chûtes Ste-Anne

Some 7 km (4 mi.) north of Ste-Anne de Beaupré the Ste-Anne River has carved a romantically wild gorge through the foothills of the Laurentians (see entry) on its way down to the St Lawrence Estuary. Although certainly impressive the Ste-Anne's Falls scarcely deserve the accolade of "Grand Canyon of Québec".

A few kilometres beyond the Chûtes Ste-Anne on Highway 360 are the equally impressive Sept-Chûtes (access from mid-June to mid-Sept). There are a number of fine viewpoints and an ecology trail. A large hydro-electric station has been built to harness the energy of the falls.

★ Sept-Chûtes

Also to the north of Ste-Anne de Beaupré lies Mont-Ste-Anne, the slopes and surrounding areas of which have been turned into a provincial park (one of many popular leisure areas in the Laurentians close to Québec). There is good walking and in winter excellent skiing. There are a number of establishments offering accommodation and also restaurants. Facilities include ski-lifts on the slopes of Mont-Ste-Anne where snow is guaranteed and several restaurants. An emergency rescue service operates in the Park.

★ Parc du Mont-Ste-Anne

Lévis, situated on the east side of the St Lawrence opposite Québec, is today a heavily industrialised suburb of the city. In earlier times its fortifications stood guard over the waterway.

Lévis

Foremost among the sights around Lévis is Fort No. 1 (open mid-May to Aug. daily 10am–5pm), constructed by British troops between 1865 and 1872. Built on Pointe-Lévis (115 m (375 ft)) just across the river from Québec's Citadel, the fort was one of three defence works erected on the south shore of the St Lawrence for the protection of Québec City.

Fort No. 1

Also situated on the east side of the river, a little lower down abreast the southern tip of the Île d'Orléans, Lauzon has a number of dry-docks.

Lauzon

★Queen Charlotte Islands

G 4

Province: British Columbia
Location: Between 52° and 54°N
Population: 5000

Queen Charlotte Visitor Information Centre, 3220 Wharf St, P.O. Box 819, Queen Charlotte City, BC V0T 1S9; tel. (250) 559–83 16

Information

By plane:
Daily flights operate between Vancouver International Airport and Sandspit (Moresby Island), also between Prince Rupert and Sandspit and between Prince Rupert and Masset (seaplane).

Access

By ferry:
Three to five sailings a week from Prince Rupert to Skidegate Landing. Several sailings a day between Graham Island and Moresby Island.

By bus:
Buses run between Masset, Port Clemens, Tiell and Sandspit Airport; also between Queen Charlotte City and Sandspit Airport.

The Queen Charlotte (Haida Gwaii) Islands are an isolated group of more than 150 islands lying out in the Pacific at the western edge of the continental shelf. The two main islands, Graham and Moresby, are about 50 km (30 mi.) and 150 km (90 mi.) respectively off the coast of British Columbia. The Queen Charlottes are often called "the Misty Islands", partly because the sky is usually overcast and the deeply indented cliffs on their western sides frequently enveloped in mist, partly on account of the enigma of their native inhabitants, the Haida Indians. The Haida,

Islands

thought to have lived on these islands for at least 8000 years, were known and feared as proud warriors and daring navigators. With their awesome 20 m (65 ft) long war-canoes they traversed the length of the Inside Passage as far south as Puget Sound. Nowadays they are rather more famous for the skill and artistry of their carving. Their totem poles and wonderfully elaborate argillite carvings (argillite is a black slate-like but soft stone found only at Slatechuck Mountain in south Graham Island, which only the Indians are allowed to work) occupy pride of place in every ethnographic museum on the Canadian Pacific coast. The Haida were also notorious for their lavish potlatches – ceremonial feasts at which the distribution of gifts served not only to display the wealth and status of the tribe but also to consolidate the often extremely complex systems of kinship and allegiance.

History

Canada's western isles were discovered in 1774 by the Spaniard Juan Pérez. In the 19th c. skilled Haida hunters kept white traders supplied with sea-otter pelts, which at that time fetched particularly high prices in China. But the white man also brought European diseases and epidemics soon decimated the native population. Several Haida coastal settlements were abandoned and numbers fell from an estimated 8000 or more to just 588 in 1915. Today most of the 1300 surviving Haida Indians live on reservations at Skidegate Mission and Haida on Graham Island, the largest island in the group. A permit issued by the Indians themselves is required for visiting the reservations or abandoned Haida villages (for south Graham Island apply to the Skidegate Band office in Skidegate Mission, tel. 559–4496; for north Graham Island and Langara Island apply to the Masset Band office in Haida, tel. 626–3337).

White settlement of the isolated Queen Charlotte Islands began relatively late at the beginning of the 20th c. A number of homesteads and small self-sufficient rural communities were set up, mainly on the flatter eastern side of Graham Island. Most however soon failed. Today four fifths of the islands' population live in twelve villages and logging camps on Graham Island, generally close to the Yellowhead Highway (Hwy. 16). Since 1980 when the new, non-tidal ferry terminal was completed near Skidegate, there have been several sailings a week to and from Prince Rupert (6–8 hours, depending on the weather).

Climate

Owing to the influence of the warm Japanese current the climate stays relatively mild throughout the year. Precipitation though is high, averaging 1260 mm (50 in.) per annum. May and April – the driest months – are best for travelling. Mean daily temperatures in August are around 17°C (63°F) and in January 4°C (39°F). Cool, wet and windy or misty weather must be expected at any time of year.

Sights

Masset

This fishing port and Canadian army base in sheltered Masset Inlet is the Queen Charlotte Islands' largest settlement (population about 2000).

★Haida

An Indian reserve of some 600 inhabitants situated 3 km (2 mi.) north of Masset near the abandoned Haida (Old Masset) village of Ka-Yung. Numerous fairly recent totem poles celebrating important events and people. Ed Jones Haida Museum in the old school house. Sale of typical Indian handwork. Beaches strewn with agate, cornelian, large shells and "sand dollars" (a type of sea urchin).

Naikoon Provincial Park

This stunningly beautiful 726 sq. km (280 sq. mi.) Provincial Park on the north-eastern tip of Graham Island is accessible either from Masset or from Tiell on the island's east coast. From Masset a spit of sand 26 km

(16 mi.) long runs along the northern coast as far as the basalt Tow Hill (109 m (360 ft); splendid views). Old planking, still visible in places, is all that remains of the original road which once served a remote settlement. The present vehicle track ends at Agate Beach (campground). Some of the beaches around McIntyre Bay are more than 300 m (330 yd) wide, superb for walking on in fine weather. Metres-high piles of driftwood thrown up by the sea fringe the sand dunes behind the beach. A very pleasant 10 km (6 mi.) walk (the Cape Fife Trail) crosses "Argonaut Plain" – which Ice Age glaciers have left dotted with small lakes, bogs and meandering streams – to Fife Point on the east coast.

The 5 km (3 mi.) Rose Spit after which the park is named ("naikoon" means "long nose") can only be reached on foot. This ecologically fragile area of dunes is now a reserve and an ideal place to watch waterfowl.

The Park Headquarters (brochures, cards, etc.) are at the southern entrance near Tiell, set amongst massive sand dunes. From the entrance a 10 km (6 mi.) circular trail winds through typical lichen-rich rainforest to the Tiell River estuary, then north for a short distance to the wooden wreck of the "Pesuta" which ran aground here in 1928. This marks the start of the 64 km (40 mi.) trail along East Beach to Tow Hill (for the experienced only; 4–6 days; good equipment, up-to-date guide and tide tables essential).

The Queen Charlotte Islands regional museum, a modern glass and native cedarwood building located right by the sea at the western end of the Skidegate Mission reserve (Second Beach; open: May–Sept. 9am–5pm, at other times from 1–5pm) is devoted chiefly to the history and culture of the Haida Indians (totem poles, carvings, wickerwork). It also has a fine collection of old photographs from pioneering days as well as displays on natural history. The old photos show numerous totem poles standing in front of traditional long-houses. Today though only one pole survives. About 350 Haida Indians live on the Skidegate Mission reserve. The most striking building houses the new tribal administration offices. Built in the style of a long-house it has a totem pole by the celebrated carver Bill Reid towering in front of it.

Regional museum

Every year on the first Saturday in June a festival is held to mark the building of the long-house (traditional Indian dancing).

Indian dancing

Moresby Island

The large south island is for the most part accessible only to people with their own boats or travelling on foot. The only public roads (32 km (20 mi.) in all) run between the ferry landing and Sandspit – though at weekends it is also possible to drive on the privately-owned forestry roads (guides and cards from the Crown Forest Industries office in Sandspit).

South Moresby Island

Boat trips and bus tours are a good way of getting to know the islands, even some of the remoter parts (details from the information centres in Queen Charlotte City, Masset and Sandspit).

Tours

Plant and animal species now scarcely found anywhere else in the world survive on South Moresby, which was made a National Park in 1989 to protect the remaining rainforest and the alpine-like mountain meadows. Some of the best preserved remains of the extraordinarily rich Haida Indian culture are also to be seen on the island.

★★South Moresby National Park

The ruins of the long abandoned Haida village of Ninstints are included on UNESCO's list of the world's most important cultural heritage sites.

Ninstints

South Moresby

★★Regina G 10

Province: Saskatchewan. Population: 192,000

Information
Regina Conventions & Visitors Bureau, Victoria Avenue E., PO Box 3355, Regina, SK S4P 3H1; tel. (306) 7895099

Economy
Regina is a cosmopolitan commercial, cultural, industrial and tourist centre which, in addition to being the agrarian capital of Canada, boasts a major oil refinery, the country's biggest steelworks, numerous other factories and a number of research establishments. As the seat of the Saskatchewan provincial government and also of several federal government departments, a high percentage of Regina's citizens are employed in the public sector. This economic diversity has enabled the city to prosper, making it a desirable place to live.

Culture
A rich programme of drama, music and dance (including performances by ethnic groups) and the presence of the Saskatchewan Centre of Arts, one of the best concert halls in North America, testify to the city's long-established cultural tradition. The Regina Symphony Hall prides itself on being the home of Canada's oldest permanent symphony orchestra founded in 1908.

History
Regina's history can be traced back to a time when the locality was known as "Pile o'Bones" on account of the huge quantities of buffalo bones to be found here. It would seem that, in yet earlier days, native hunters drove these animals down to Wascana Creek for slaughter.
    A settlement first grew up on the site with the building of the railway. When in 1882 the little township became capital of the Northwest

Territories it was rechristened Regina in honour of Queen Victoria. Having been granted city status in 1903 just two years later it was pronounced capital of the newly created province of Saskatchewan.

Towards the end of the 19th c. Regina was the headquarters of the North West Mounted Police – later to become the Royal Canadian Mounted Police (RCMP). In 1920 RCMP headquarters were moved to Ottawa but the RCMP Academy, the sole training centre for the "Mounties", remains located in Regina. In the early 20th c. immigrants from all over the world flocked to Regina helping to transform the region into a highly productive wheat growing area.

The Royal Canadian Mounted Police Museum (open Jun. to mid-Sep. daily 8am–8.45pm; mid-Sep. to May daily 8am–4.45pm) is located in the west of the city at the RCMP Academy in Dewdney Ave. W. Both the Sergeant Major's Parade (Mon.–Fri. 12.45pm; venue: Parade Square or, in winter or bad weather, the Drill Hall) and the Sunset Retreat (Jul. to mid-Aug. Tue. 7pm) attract large crowds. The latter, a colourful lowering the flag ceremony involving a parade of recruits and a marching band, was re-introduced to mark the centenary of the force. It harks back to the tattoos of the 18th c. and to 19th c. British military tradition. ★★Royal Canadian Mounted Police (RCMP)

The museum, which attracts over 250,000 visitors a year, is Canada's largest devoted to the Mounties and includes items of equipment, weaponry, uniforms, photographs, archive material, personal effects and memorabilia. One theme of the museum is the history of the force from its foundation to the present day, setting it in the context of Canada's development as a nation. Another theme is the celluloid image of the RCMP as portrayed in innumerable Hollywood films about the Mounties. Famous personalities and historic events are also featured in the museum, among them Chief Sitting Bull who took refuge in Saskatchewan after the massacre of Custer and his men at the Little Big Horn. A substantial part of the museum is given over to the North West Rebellion of 1885 and its leader Louis Riel.

Other items on display include Red Indian artefacts and clothing. The large, painted buffalo skin on which an entire history is recorded in pictographs is one of the most valuable of its kind in Canada.

The historic RCMP chapel, one of the oldest buildings in Regina, is also well worth a visit. It began life in 1883 as a casino before being partly destroyed by fire in 1895. Following restoration it was turned into a chapel, made particularly attractive by the contrast between the richness and variety of its splendid stained glass windows and the simplicity of the basic structure and original pews. Finest of all are the two superbly coloured windows behind the altar depicting red-uniformed Mounties. One is dedicated to the many police wives who played such an important role in their husbands' absence on duty, manning telephones and taking care of prisoners.

Laid out on the shores of an artificial lake in the middle of Regina the 930 ha (2300 acres) of the Wascana Centre form one of the largest city parks anywhere in the world. The park is the setting for Saskatchewan's Legislative Building, the Museum of Natural History, the Saskatchewan Science Centre, the Diefenbaker Homestead, the Saskatchewan Centre of Arts and the University of Regina. ★Wascana Centre

Wascana Lake is also a bird sanctuary, its islands and reedbeds providing refuge for ducks, geese, swans, pelicans and a variety of other birds. Picturesque Willow Island at the northern end of the lake makes an ideal spot for picnicking (open Mon.–Fri. noon–4pm; reached by ferry).

Located just to the west of Broad St. the Diefenbaker Homestead (open daily 10am–5pm) was the childhood home of J. G. Diefenbaker, Prime Minister of Canada from 1957 to 1963 and Saskatchewan's most famous son. It was brought to Regina in 1967 from Borden and contains some personal possessions and memorabilia of the Diefenbaker family. Diefenbaker Homestead

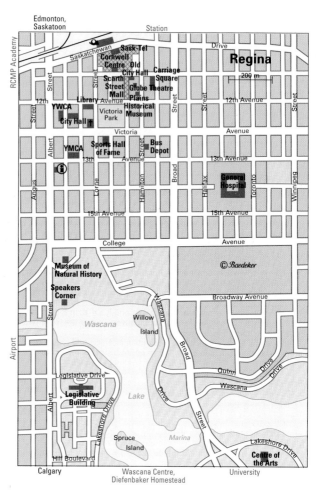

★Legislative
Building

The Legislative Building (open end of May–beginning of Sep. daily
8am–5pm) was built between 1908 and 1912. Shaped like a cross it
shows the influence of both the English Renaissance and the Age of
Louis XVI. In addition to the local Tyndall limestone 34 kinds of rare
marble were used in its construction. The building has a total area of
about 19,000 sq. m (205,000 sq. ft).

Included among the 265 rooms are the Prime Minister's Office and
Cabinet Chamber. The Legislative Building also houses various items of
historical interest and a number of works of art.

One wing is occupied by the Canadian Native Gallery. It has displays
of native Indian art and a photographic collection.

★Mackenzie Art
Gallerie

The Mackenzie Art Gallery in the south-west corner of the Wascana
Centre (open Tue.–Sun. noon–6pm, Wed. noon–10pm) possesses an

Regina: the Legislative Building

excellent collection with exhibits ranging from the art of ancient Mesopotamia to contemporary Canadian works. The Gallery also puts on important temporary exhibitions.

Regina's newest tourist attraction, the 464 sq. m (5000 sq. ft) Saskatchewan Science Centre, opened in 1989. Occupying a converted former power station on the north bank of Wascana Lake the Centre is rather special in encouraging "hands on" involvement with the sciences (e.g. geology and astronomy). Visitors are able to handle the exhibits, perform experiments and ask questions as well as experiencing simulated space travel and "seeing" their voices reproduced on a computer screen.

★Saskatchewan Science Centre

Visitors to the Museum of Natural History on the corner of College Ave and Albert St. (open May 1st–Labour Day daily 9am–8.30pm; Sep.–Apr. daily 9am–4.30pm) find themselves taken back 2 billion years in time. There are over 100 glass display cabinets devoted to geology, palaeontology, archaeology and anthropology. The new Earth Sciences Gallery is quite exceptional with its fascinating series of extremely lifelike dioramas showing mastodons, dinosaurs, etc. (also contemporary wildlife) in their natural environment.

Museum of Natural History

The Regina Plains Museum (open Mon.–Fri. 11.30am–5pm, Sat., Sun. 1–5pm, winter Wed.–Fri. 11.30am–5pm, Sat., Sun. 1–5pm) occupies the former Post Office in Scarth St. It recalls the lives of the plainsfolk, Indians, Metis and early pioneers and there are reconstructions of a typical turf hut, schoolroom, church, saloon and Red River cart as well as displays of old photographs and artefacts.

★Plains Museum

The Dunlop Art Gallery (open Mon.–Fri. 9.30am–9pm, Sat. 9.30am–6pm, Sun. 1.30–5pm) in the Central Library on 12th Ave. is used for exhibitions of one sort or another – art, crafts or theme-related.

Library

Also in the Library the Prairie History Room (open Mon.–Wed. 9.30am–9pm, Thu., Fri. 9.30am–5pm., Sat. noon–5pm, Sun. 1.30–5pm) contains a large collection of items relating to the history of the prairies and the prairie provinces (including photographs and newspaper cuttings).

Goverment House

Goverment House in Dewdney Ave. (open Sep.–Jun. Tue.–Sat. 1–4pm, Sun. 1–5pm, Jul., Aug. Tue.–Sun. 1–5pm) was built in 1891 and until 1945 was the official residence of the Lieutenant Governor. Now all the elegance of the turn of the century is again reflected in its restored rooms.

Every summer Government House is the setting for "The Trial of Louis Riel", a dramatic reconstruction based on documents from the original trial.

Saskatchewan Sports Hall of Fame

The Sports Hall of Fame (open Mon.–Fri. 9am–5pm, Sat., Sun. noon–4pm) in Victoria Ave celebrates the province's sporting achievements. Exhibits include portraits and a variety of memorabilia.

IPSCO Wildlife Park

The IPSCO Wildlife Park (open mid-May–Sep. 1–6pm, Jun., Aug. 11am–8pm) about 4 km (2½ mi.) north of Regina is home to a variety of animals including buffalo, elk, deer and pheasant.

Repulse Bay   D 13

Administrative unit: Nunavut

Information

Nunavut Tourism, PO Box 1450, Iqaluit, NV X0A 0H0; tel. (867) 9796551, fax. (867) 9791261.

Access

By plane: From Winnipeg via Churchill or Eskimo Point and Rankin Inlet to Repulse Bay (Naujaat).

Location

Forming the most north-easterly point of mainland Nunavut (designated an independent territory in 1999), is the Melville Peninsula, over an isthmus just 70 km (43 mi.) wide separating Hudson Bay from the Gulf of Boothia. Repulse Bay (Naufaat) lies on the south side of the isthmus exactly on the Arctic Circle (marked by an arc of stones at the airfield).

History

The "European" chapter of this part of Canada's history opened in 1741 when Captain Middleton sailed into the deep bay – known to the Inuit as "Naujaat" (= gulls' nesting place) – in search of the Northwest Passage. In his disappointment Middleton christened the bay Repulse. In the mid-19th c., Roses Welcome Sound, with Repulse Bay at its northern end, was a much frequented British and American whaling ground, many Inuit (called "Avilingmiut") being employed as "scouts" on the whale boats. Their local knowledge proved to be of inestimable value. When the American explorer Hall arrived here around 1864 an Inuit from Repulse Bay was able to draw him an astonishingly accurate map of Foxe Basin (between the Melville Peninsula and Baffin Island) which was of inestimable value. The same traditional experience, handed down from generation to generation, is still made use of today by Inuit tourist guides. Until 1954 Repulse Bay was simply a Hudson's Bay Company (H.B.C.) settlement (H.B.C. standing, so it is said, for "Here before Christ"!) and a Catholic mission.

Economy

Now there are about 500 inhabitants, virtually all of them Inuit. While a subsistence economy based on hunting still survives, Arctic tourism has also brought new opportunities for employment. Thus the wealth of flora and fauna on land and sea continues to support the Inuit way of life, albeit in a rather novel manner.

★★Réservoir Manicouagan

Province: Québec

Highway 389 from Baie-Comeau (on the north shore of the St Lawrence Estuary). Distance: 430 km (270 mi.).

Access

Association touristique régionale de Manicouagan, Rue de Puyjalon 871, Baie-Comeau, Québec, tel. (418) 5895319.

Information

About 210 million years ago a meteorite struck the Canadian Shield north of the St Lawrence Estuary to the north-east of the Laurentians (see entry). Its highly destructive impact resulted in the formation of a crater some 100 km (62 mi.) across. So much energy was released that part of the meteorite itself and some of the surface rock evaporated, the tremendous pressure causing an explosion in which vast quantities of rock were hurled into the air and scattered over the surrounding countryside. At the same time metamorphosis of the rock produced mineral concentrations which today form important raw material deposits (including iron ore).

History

Taking advantage of the valleys and depressions produced in the vicinity of the meteorite crater by erosion and glaciation, a huge reservoir was constructed to exploit the electricity generating potential of the area. The 214 m (700 ft) high Daniel-Johnson Dam, built in the 1960s by the Hydro-Québec Company, resulted in an artificial lake covering some 2000 sq. km (770 sq. mi.).

Daniel-Johnson Dam

The gigantic barrage was inaugurated in 1968 by Canada's then Prime Minister Daniel Johnson.

Manicouagan: the huge Daniel-Johnson Dam

Revelstoke

<table>
<tr><td>Complexe Manic-
Outardes</td><td>Ever since 1958 work has also been in progress to harness the hydro-
electric potential of the Manicouagan and Outardes rivers, which flow
parallel to one another from the north-east Laurentians.
Over this period two Hydro-Québec Co. generating plants known as
Manic 5 and Manic 2 have come into operation.</td></tr>
<tr><td>Manic 5</td><td>This ultra modern power generating plant started producing electricity
in 1990. With a capacity of 1064 megawatts it is one of the biggest of its
kind anywhere in the world.</td></tr>
<tr><td>Centre
d'Interprétation</td><td>Visitors to Hydro-Québec's Centre d'Interprétation can learn anything
and everything about power generation. Bus tours are arranged from
mid-Jun. to the beginning of Sept.
Departure: daily 9 and 11am, 1.30 and 3.30pm.
Information: tel. (418) 2943923.</td></tr>
<tr><td>Manic 2</td><td>The 70 m (230 ft) dam powering Hydro-Québec's Manic 2 generating
station is situated on the lower reaches of the Rivière Manicouagan
about 20 km (12 mi.) north of Baie-Comeau. Tours are arranged from
mid-Jun. to beginning of Sep. daily 9 and 11am, 1 and 3pm.
Information: tel. (419) 2943923.</td></tr>
</table>

★Revelstoke   G 7

Province: British Columbia
Population: 9000

Location

The town of Revelstoke lies between the snow-clad ranges of the Selkirk and Monashee Mountains, where the Illecillewaet flows into the Columbia River (see entry). It marks the western end of Rogers Pass through the Glacier National Park (see entry), which posed so many problems to the road builders and railway engineers. Both upstream and downstream of Revelstoke the once raging waters of the Columbia River have been tamed to form a string of sizeable lakes extending for more than 300 km (186 mi.). Lakes Revelstoke and Kinbasket (north) and Arrow (south) offer good facilities for watersports.

History

First settled in 1883, Second Crossing/Farwell (as it was originally called) was renamed in honour of Lord Revelstoke whose bank contributed substantially to the financing and completion of the Canadian Pacific Railway. As early as the beginning of the 19th c. however, fur trappers had already penetrated this far up the Columbia River – the great 2000 km (1250 mi.) waterway of the Canadian West – followed soon afterwards by traders, missionaries, gold prospectors and the earliest settlers.

Revelstoke today

Revelstoke is a popular summer and winter holiday resort for hill walking, heli-skiing, white-water rafting, fishing, etc. (see also Mount Revelstoke and Glacier National Park).

Architecture

A redevelopment project in the early 1980s saw a number of the town's early 20th c. buildings restored, including the Court-House (1912), the King Edward Hotel, the McKinnon Building and the Roxy Theatre. At the same time parts of the town centre were pedestrianised and greened.

Revelstoke Museum

The former Post Office at 315 West 1st St, built in 1926, now houses the Revelstoke Museum (open Jun. to Sep. Mon.–Sat. 2–9pm). Old photographs, etc. are used to document local history, mainly the building of the railway and the era of river navigation.

The Mount Mackenzie Ski Area (610 m (2000 ft) vertical drop, 20 ski runs, 2 chair lifts, T-bar), 6 km (4 mi.) from the town centre, is well known for its abundant snow (3–5 m (10–16 ft) a year). Heli-skiing; cross-country skiing and ski touring (mainly in the Mount Revelstoke National Park); snowmobile trails.

★Mount Mackenzie

About 5 km (3 mi.) north of the town on Highway 23 the Revelstoke Canyon Dam, a 175 m (570 ft) high concrete barrier completed in the early 1980s, controls a stretch of the Columbia River extending as far as the Mica Dam 144 km (90 mi.) to the north. B.C. Hydro's new hydroelectric station will eventually produce 2.7 million kilowatt hours of electricity a year making it one of the biggest in the province.

★Revelstoke Canyon Dam

Even today scars inflicted on the Mount Revelstoke landscape during the building of the dam are clearly visible. A modern Visitors Centre opened in 1985 (open Jun.–Aug. 8am–8pm, at other times 10am–6pm) explains technical aspects of the barrage and generating plant and the operation of the Columbia River system. An elevator takes visitors up to a view point on top of the dam.

Highway 23 North continues along the east side of the reservoir to Mica Dam.

Heading in the other direction from Revelstoke towards Nakusp (altitude: 415 m (1360 ft); population: 2000) Highway 23 South skirts Upper Arrow Lake through a densely forested, sparsely inhabited area.

Nakusp

Nakusp, which in recent years has acquired a reputation as a base for winter sports, is known throughout the country as a spa. The thermal baths and other amenities at Nakusp Hot Springs (3 km (2 mi.)) have recently undergone modernisation and expansion and today attract visitors from around the globe. The healing waters of the thermes can be enjoyed daily from 9.30am to 10pm.

Highway 23 South links up with Highway 6 at Nakusp, leading in one direction to Okanagan (see entry) and in the other to Kootenay Lake and then on to Crowsnest Highway 3, the main east-west route in the south.

Ferries run across Arrow Lake between Shelter Bay and Galena Bay and between Fauquier and Needles.

Ferries

At Halcyon and St Leon there are more hot springs. Being as yet undeveloped however, they are accessibly only via poorly signposted minor roads.

Halcyon

Tourist facilities at Albert Canyon Hot Springs (35 km (22 mi.) east of Revelstoke on the TransCanada Highway) include a thermal pool, camping ground, cafeteria and souvenir shop.

Albert Canyon Hot Springs

Rogers Pass (1327 m (4350 ft)) cuts through the high mountains and breathtaking, glacial scenery of the Glacier National Park (see entry).

★Rogers Pass

Rideau Canal

H/J 15

Province: Ontario

The 200 km (124 mi.) long Rideau Canal, only 1.6 m (5¼ ft) deep, connects Ottawa with Kingston on Lake Ontario. It was originally intended as a second strategic route between Montréal and Lake Ontario, the military need for which was demonstrated during the war with the United States in 1812.

History

At the time of building (1826–32) the canal was a triumph of constructional engineering. More than four dozen dams were required to control the water levels, and the 83 m (272 ft) ascent to the summit between Ottawa and Lake Ontario meant that boats had to pass through numerous locks.

Although steamers plied the canal for over a hundred years it never came to have any major economic significance. Today the waterway with its 24 operational locks is used mainly by pleasure boats and for tourism.

Ottawa

It is one of history's curiosities that a camp for 2000 construction workers employed on building a branch of the canal from the Ottawa River should eventually become the capital of Canada.

The staircase of eight locks on Parliament Hill is highly photogenic. Ottawa's first stone building was on a site next to the canal.

Jones Falls

Among the many interesting features on the canal is Stone Arch Dam at Jones Falls.

Kingston Mills

As well as the Visitors Centre the Block House (museum) at Kingston Mills is also worth visiting.

Boating season

Mid-May to mid-October. Information: 12 Maple Avenue N., Smiths Falls, Ontario, K7A 1Z5; tel. (613) 2835170.

★★Riding Mountain National Park

G 10

Province: Manitoba
Area: about 3000 sq. km (1158 sq. mi.)

Information

Superintendent, Riding Mountain National Park, Wasagaming, Manitoba, R0J 2H0; tel. (204) 8482811

Nature park

Riding Mountain National Park is located 310 km (190 mi.) north-west of Winnipeg (see entry) on Highway 10. Accessible throughout the year this scenic park is a combination of recreation area and nature reserve, a varied landscape of prairie, aspen parkland, fir and deciduous forest and wonderfully clear lakes and streams. The park extends over part of the glacially formed Manitoba Escarpment where a series of plateaux rising to heights of about 340 m (1100 ft) overlook the surrounding prairie with its gentle hills, meadows, lakes and watercourses.

Fauna

The cold deep lakes such as Clear Lake, Lake Katherine and Deep Lake are rich in pike, whitefish, walleye and trout (good angling). Beavers live in the shallow, marshy bays.

Near Lake Audy a herd of buffalo roam freely about a 552 ha (1360 acre) enclosure. There is a special look-out from which the animals can be observed in their natural environment, and an informative display about bison – now virtually extinct except for this one remaining species. Bears, wolves, elk and deer also inhabit the park ("The Duke", the largest brown bear ever reported in Canada, was killed by poachers here in the autumn of 1991).

Flora

Yellow potentilla and violet gaillardia are among the flowering plants which grow on the prairies of the Canadian West.

Leisure activities

The park has innumerable trails for use by walkers, cyclists and riders. One trail leads to the log cabin formerly belonging to the English naturalist Grey Owl who, in the early 1920s, wrote books about the wildlife of the area.

There are winter sports facilities for downhill and cross-country skiing (Mt Agassiz).

Wasagaming

Wasagaming (Indian for "clear water") at the southern entrance to the park is a leisure resort on the shores of Clear Lake (18-hole golf course, tennis, badminton, roller-skating rink and camping).

Housed in a fine 1930s wooden building at Wasagaming the Interpretive Centre focuses on Riding Mountain's rich natural history. **Interpretive Centre**

Clear Lake, 33 m (108 ft) deep and largest in the park, has facilities for swimming, angling (pike, walleye, trout, whitefish), boating, wind surfing and sailing. **Clear Lake**

Saguenay H 16/17

Province: Québec

The Saguenay is the major tributary of the St Lawrence River. Tremendously deep in places (up to 275 m (900 ft)), all sorts of marine life including whales and salmon are found in its tidal, salt water reaches. **Topography**
The countryside through which the Saguenay Fiord twists and turns (sometimes between cliffs 180–300 m (590–980 ft) high) presents three quite different faces, dense forest giving way in turn to agricultural land and industrial development.
By far the best – and in some parts the only – way to see the Saguenay is by water. There are cruises daily from Chicoutimi between June and September.

The Saguenay Fiord was discovered by Jacques Cartier on his second expedition up the St Lawrence in 1535/36. Having largely escaped colonisation by Europeans until the mid-19th c. the sunken valley underwent its most dramatic transformation following the Second World War. Exploitation of the Saguenay for hydro-electric power led to the construction of one of the world's largest aluminium plants at Jonquière. Meat processing and paper are other industries which now play an important role in the local economy. **History**

Saguenay Fiord

Saguenay

Whale-watching

Every year between the end of July and October hundreds of whales congregate where the Saguenay flows into the St Lawrence. The result is a unique spectacle – and an unmatched opportunity to observe these magnificent creatures at close quarters from aboard one of "whale-watching" boats from Baie Ste-Catherine, Tadoussac or Rivière-du-Loup. As many as ten different species of whale have been identified among those which gather here, including the huge fin whales and white whales. Plans are afoot to create a special reserve to protect these splendid mammals, now threatened with extinction.

Sights

Rivière-Eternité

From Rivière-Eternité a 9 km (5½ mi.) footpath leads to the 457 m (1560 ft) high Cap-Trinité with its statue of the Virgin Mary erected in 1881. Of interest in Rivière-Eternité itself is the Parc national du Saguenay Interpretation Centre (open mid-May–mid-Oct. daily 9am–5pm).

La Baie

Primarily an industrial town, La Baie nevertheless boasts the Musée du Fiord (3346, bd. de la Grande-Baie S.) with worthwhile collections of ethnography and regional art treasures (open end of Jul.–beginning of Sep. Mon.–Fri. 8.30am–5pm, Sat. and Sun. 1–5pm. Tue.–Sat. also 7.30–9pm; Sep.–Jun. Mon.–Fri. 8.30am–noon and 1.30–5pm, Sat. and Sun. 1–5pm).

Chicoutimi

Attractively situated on a hill in heavily wooded country on the south bank of the Saguenay, the town of Chicoutimi more than lives up to its sobriquet of "Queen of the North".

Musée du Saguenay, Centre Culturel

Among Chicoutimi's attractions is the Musée du Saguenay-Lac St-Jean in the Cultural Centre (534 rue Jacques-Cartier). There are comprehensive ethnological and archaeological displays of Indian artefacts, etc. as

Chicoutimi

well as a collection of early 20th c. furniture (open end of Jun.-beginning of Sep. Mon.–Fri. 8.30am–5pm, Tue. and Thu. also 7–9pm, Sat. and Sun. 1–5pm; Sep.–Jun. Mon.–Fri. 8.30am–noon and 1–5pm, Sat. and Sun. 1–5pm).

Built in 1921 and dedicated to St-François-Xavier the cathedral has a lovely painting in the transept vaulting.   **Cathedral**
    A magnificent view along the southern shore of the sunken valley is obtained from the Pont Dubuc which crosses the Saguenay.

Jonquière, another industrial town, has a most unusual church, Notre-Dame-de-Fatima, shaped like a wigwam.   **Jonquière**

Also worth seeing is the Musée de la Nature (open daily 8.30am–9pm) in picturesque little Ste-Rose-du-Nord. It has extensive collections of stuffed animals and wooden artefacts (magnifying glasses, witches broomsticks).   **Ste-Rose-du-Nord**

See entry   Tadoussac

★Saint John   H 17

Province: New Brunswick. Population: 73,000

Saint John Conventions & Visitors Bureau, PO Box 1971, Saint John, NB E2L 4l1; tel. (506) 6582990   Information

Saint John (the name is always written in full and without an apostrophe "s" to distinguish it from St John's which, as the locals are quick to point out, is in Newfoundland), New Brunswick's largest town, is also the province's major industrial centre and a thriving port. It stands on a rocky estuarine spur at the point where the Saint John River disgorges into the Bay of Fundy. Known affectionately to the people of the province as "fog city" (on account of the sea fogs which from time to time roll in off the Bay), the peculiarities of its site mean that Saint John has few straight roads, and a great many cul-de-sacs instead.   Location
    On a clear summer's day, with a wind to blow the smell of wood pulp (emanating from the big, riverside paper mills) away from the town, Saint John is really rather attractive.

Samuel de Champlain and Sieur de Monts set foot ashore in the Saint John Estuary in 1604. They were followed a few years later by their compatriot, Charles de la Tour, who established a trading post. In 1645 Sieur de Menou d'Aulney, a fellow Frenchman from Port Royal, destroyed the post, initiating a period of intense internecine rivalry among the French in Acadia (see entry) – at a time also of almost continuous Anglo-French hostilities.   History
    Eventually the area was ceded to Britain at the Treaty of Paris in 1763 and a new trading post was set up.
    The town of Saint John is regarded as having itself been founded in 1783. On May 18th of that year the sails of a huge fleet were sighted in the mouth of the river. Aboard the ships were 3000 Loyalists fleeing the American War of Independence and with their arrival the little settlement was transformed almost overnight into a boom town. By the end of the year the number of newcomers had risen to 4200, many of whom made their way north along the river to settle at Fredericton. Most of the new arrivals were well-to-do people who had lost nearly everything during the revolution. Few came equipped with the necessary pioneering skills for wresting a home from the wilderness. But somehow they survived and in due course built up a prosperous maritime city known in addition for its lively social life.

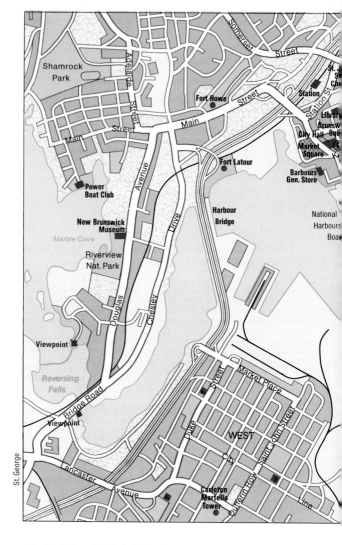

In the 19th c. the city's flourishing shipbuilding industry and many trading links earned Saint John the reputation of being North America's Liverpool.

In 1877 more than half the town was burned down in a catastrophic fire. When some years later the era of wooden ships came to an end, Saint John fell into decline, a fate shared with other communities on the Atlantic seaboard. Although the port continued in operation it was

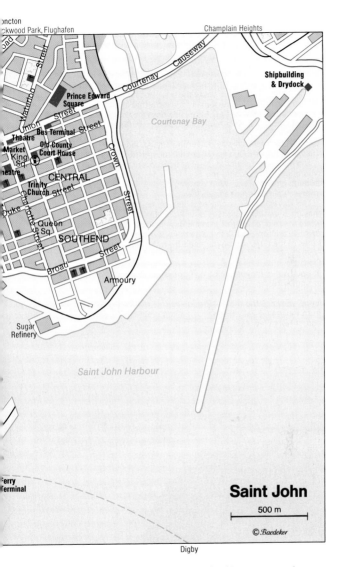

Saint John

500 m

© Baedeker

Digby

only in the 1960s that prosperity returned, with vast sums of money being invested in the paper industry and sugar and oil refineries. Harbour facilities were improved by the construction of a container terminal and deep water berths (for supertankers) and Saint John experienced both a resurgence of its shipyards and the growth of a number of newly diversified industries responsive to the needs of its port.

Saint John

Events

In July each year the founding of the city is celebrated in style with a re-enactment of the Loyalist landing. Everyone dresses up in 18th c. costume and there is a big parade. Wining, dining and dancing in the street complete the festivities.

★★Reversing Falls Rapids

The Saint John River flows south-east through New Brunswick from its source in the US state of Maine, spilling out into the Bay of Fundy (see Fundy Bay) at Saint John where the tidal range is 8.5 m (29 ft). At low tide the sea level is more than 4 m (13 ft) below that of the river, and a torrent of water pours into the Bay. As the tide rises the flow of the river slackens, then becomes still as a mill pond before eventually being reversed. At high water the level in the Bay rises more than 4 m (13 ft) above the river and the sea forces its way powerfully inland, the effects of the incoming tide being felt as much as 130 km (80 mi.) upstream at Fredericton.

The most spectacular reversal of flow occurs at Reversing Falls Rapids where, prior to reaching the Bay of Fundy, the river narrows, plunging through a deep gorge. With a strong current flowing (in either direction) impressive rapids and eddies form.

The Reversing Falls can best be appreciated in all their variety by making a number of visits at different states of the tide (e.g. at low water when the river pours towards the Bay, at slack water to observe the flow reverse, and on the full flood as the water surges upstream). The exact times of the tides can be obtained from the Tourist Office.

Reversing Falls bridge

From the bridge craft can be seen making their way up and down river at slack water, movement being impossible at other times because of the strong currents.

Falls View park

Good views of the rapids (though not nearly as dramatic as the views from Reversing Falls Bridge) can also be obtained from the park at the end of Falls View Ave.

Reversing Falls Rapids

There are two places from which, on a fine clear day, attractive views can be had over the attractively situated town. One is Fort Howe Lookout (reached from Main St. via Metcalfe St. and Magazine St.). From the site of this wooden blockhouse perched high on its rocky cliff a magnificent panorama unfolds of the shipyards, harbour, river and town.

Fort Howe Lookout

The Carleton Martello Tower (open mid-May–mid-Oct. daily 10am–7pm) stands in what is now a National Historic Park. The tower was built in 1813 to protect the port against possible attack by the United States. It had various uses from time to time in the 19th c. and again during the two World Wars. In the Second World War it served as area headquarters for the anti-aircraft defence and fire fighting services, a two-storey steel and concrete structure being added for the purpose.

Carleton Martello Tower

Today the tower houses an exhibition of military life in the 18th c. with guides in historical costume. The general history of the region is also the subject of several displays.

Rising high above its surroundings the tower is the second vantage point from which fine views can be enjoyed over the town, the harbour and far out to sea across the Bay of Fundy.

Founded more than a century ago the museum is devoted to the natural history, life and art of the province. The "golden age" of New Brunswick's shipbuilding industry in the 19th c. is especially well represented, with collections of model ships, paintings and other items of interest. Various exhibits pay tribute to the city's role as a major trading centre during that period, quite apart from its shipbuilding. A vivid picture emerges of the huge quantity of goods of all kinds which passed through the port.

★New Brunswick Museum

There is an interesting section on the indigenous Indian culture of New Brunswick including artefacts made from birchbark, quill and bead work, traditional furnishings and clothes, etc.

In addition the museum possesses an outstanding collection of watercolours, drawings and photographs of Saint John, New Brunswick and other parts of Canada. The collection is used to mount a series of temporary exhibitions based on different themes.

The natural history section concentrates on flora and fauna native to New Brunswick (especially birds, insects, fish and mammals) as well as the geology of the province.

Open May–Sep. daily 10am–5pm, Oct.–Apr. 2–5pm.

In recent years new life has been breathed into the city centre making it a particularly pleasant place to explore on foot. Various tourist "trails" have been marked out (information from the Tourist Office).

Downtown

Opened in 1983 the Market Place is actually an attractive multi-level shopping centre with atrium-like inner courtyard, part of a complex which also includes a hotel, conference centre, a number of flats. A street of 19th c. warehouses incorporated into the complex now faces a pretty "plaza" around Market Slip (where in 1783 the Loyalists came ashore from their ships).

Market Place

Today Market Slip provides a berth for an elderly deep sea tug "Ocean Hawk II". In summer the plaza is a lively place, with street cafés and musical entertainment.

"Ocean Hawk II"

On the south side of the plaza Barbour's General Store (open: daily except mid-Apr.–mid-May) occupies a red and cream coloured building erected in 1867. On display is a wide range of merchandise typical of the times.

Barbour's General Store

An elevated walkway crossing over Dock St. links Market Square with the Saint John City Hall and Brunswick Square (a complex of shops, offices and hotels). There is an observation gallery in the City Hall (open on weekdays).

Dock Street, City Hall, Brunswick Square

Loyalist House	Built in 1817 by David Merrit, a Loyalist who fled New York in 1783, the house was among the few to survive the great fire of 1877 and is thus one of the oldest buildings in Saint John. The plain, partly shingle-clad façade conceals a spacious and elegant Georgian interior. Notice especially the arches between the rooms, and the curved staircase. The solid rock foundations on which the house is built, visible on the Germain St. side, are typical of houses in Saint John. (Guided tours daily Jun. to Sep. from 9am.)
★King Square	Generally regarded as the centre of Saint John, King Square with its two-storey bandstand is planted with trees and flowerbeds in the form of a Union flag. Almost any product of New Brunswick – including the edible seaweed known as dulse – can be found at the old City Market off one corner of the square.
Burial Ground	Situated off the side of the square opposite the market is the old Loyalist Burial Ground.

★Saint John River Valley   H 17

Province: New Brunswick

Information	New Brunswick Tourism & Heritage, PO Box 12345, Fredericton, NB E3B 5C3; tel. (800) 5610123
Course	The Saint John River, 660 km (410 mi.) long with a catchment area of more than 67,000 sq. km (25,800 sq. mi.), rises in the US state of Maine before flowing south-eastwards through the Canadian province of New Brunswick. For some 100 km (62 mi.) of its length it forms the frontier between the two countries. It enters the sea at Saint John on the Bay of Fundy (see entries).
★Geography	After emerging from the northern-most foothills of the Appalachians the river traverses New Brunswick's agriculturally rich "potato belt", reaching the relatively flat coastal region near Fredericton.
History	Throughout its history the valley of the Saint John River has served as an important highway. European immigrants, arriving in numbers from the 17th c. onwards, settled in the valley, at the heart of the region which came to be known as Acadia (see entry). The river itself was christened by Samuel de Champlain, who landed in the estuary on St John's Day (June 24th) 1604.
	The natural route represented by the valley is still followed today by two major links in Canada's modern transport system, the TransCanada Highway and the railway.
Hydro-electric power	Several big dams have been constructed on the Saint John River, producing between them enough hydro-electric power to meet a large part of New Brunswick's needs.

Suggested route

The route described follows the Saint John River downstream from the provincial boundary between New Brunswick and Québec.

Edmundston	Set in an otherwise largely rural area the small industrial town of Edmundston (population 12,000) lies at the centre of the mainly French-speaking and Catholic "République de Madawaska", a relic of the old Acadia dating back to the end of the 18th c.
	The twin spires of Edmundston's Catholic cathedral are a striking land-

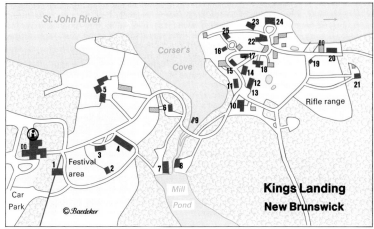

Kings Landing
New Brunswick

© Baedeker

1 Agricultural Hall	10 Kings Head Inn (1855)	18 Perley House (1870)
2 Print Shop (1890)	11 Lint House (1830)	19 Parish School (1840)
3 Hagerman House (1850)	12 Horsepower & Dragsaw (1890)	20 Snack Bar
4 Carriage Shop	13 Lint Barn	21 Killeen Cabin (1830)
5 Joslin House (1860)	14 Blacksmith Shop (1870)	22 Morehouse House (1820)
6 Jones House (1830)	15 Long House (1845)	23 Kings Theatre
7 Gristmill (1880)	16 Heustis House (1850)	24 Ingraham House (1840)
8 Sawmill (1830)	17 St. Mark's Church (1890)	25 Fisher House (1820)
9 Brunswick Lion		

mark, visible for miles around. Also worth seeing is the Musée Madawaska (Bd. Hébert; open: mid-May–mid-Sept. Tues.–Sun.) which traces the history of the area.

★Grand Falls

An hour's drive beyond Edmundston, at the little town of Grand Falls (Grand Sault), the Saint John River is transformed into a thundering cascade as it squeezes through a picturesquely wild gorge. A large hydroelectric power station harnesses the water's energy.

The most interesting section of the gorge is now a Provincial Park and a Visitors Centre (open mid-May-mid-Sep.) has been built beside the falls.

Florenceville

South of Grand Falls Highway 105 offers a pleasant alternative to the TransCanada Highway, passing through an attractive agricultural landscape with many lovely views down into the valley.

Hartland

Potato fields dominate the scenery around the village of Hartland (population 1000). McCain's is one of the potato processing companies to have a factory here, products such as frozen potatoes being exported all over the world.

Covered bridge

Hartland used to be better known for its covered bridge, built over the Saint John River in 1897. At 391 m (1280 ft) it is the longest of its kind in the world. The bridge has suffered serious damage on a number of occasions in its lifetime and requires almost continual repair.

Woodstock

Next stop downstream is the attractive township of Woodstock, not far from the Canada-US frontier.

★King's Landing

The King's Landing outdoor museum south of Woodstock (open daily, end of May to mid-Oct.) vividly re-creates village life in 19th c. New

Brunswick. The houses of the restored village, in an attractive setting at the mouth of a little creek, were originally built by King's American Dragoons who settled along the river after the American War of Independence. When the river was dammed some years ago all the buildings had to be moved to a more elevated site.

The working sawmill and King's Head Inn (restaurant, refreshments) are particularly enthralling, the latter the epitome of a 19th c. country coaching inn. Various scenes of "Living History" are enacted during the main tourist season.

**Mactaquac
Provincial Park**

About half an hour's drive from the New Brunswick capital of Fredericton (see entry), Mactaquac Provincial Park (boating, walking and a variety of other leisure facilities) provides opportunities for relaxation in delightful surroundings.

★★Saint John's   H 20

Province: Newfoundland. Population: 102,000

Information

The City of St John's Tourism Division, PO Box 908, St John's, NF A1C 5M2; tel. (709) 5768106

Location

The capital of Newfoundland, undisputedly the oldest "European" town in North America, occupies a spectacular site on one of the finest natural harbours in the world. Entered through "the Narrows", a 200 m (660 ft) wide passage flanked by cliffs 150 m (490 ft) high, the harbour widens out into a basin some 800 m (2625 ft) across, surrounded by steep rocky slopes on which St John's is built.

Typical of St John's are the traditional square, flat-roofed, wooden houses painted in different colours. Many date bak to Victorian times; sadly however, because of the many fires to engulf the town in the 18th and 19th c., few have survived from earlier years.

Name

The city was named after St John the Baptist, John Cabot having reputedly discovered Newfoundland on June 24th (sic!) 1497.

History

Whatever uncertainty surrounds the exact date of its discovery, there is no doubt that, from about 1500, the harbour was used as a base by fishing vessels from various European countries, leading to Britain's claiming official possession in 1583 in the reign of Elizabeth I.

There followed a long period during which, having developed into a thriving fishery and trading post, St John's was "governed" by a succession of ruthless "Fishing Admirals".

In subsequent centuries British possession was disputed with the Dutch, Portuguese, Spaniards and particularly the French. In addition St John's was attacked on a number of occasions by pirates. British sovereignty was finally confirmed in 1762 following a short period of French occupation.

In the 19th c. under British rule the city developed rapidly as a centre of commerce, despite being devastated several times by fire – in 1892 it was almost completely rebuilt. Its prosperity continued into the early 20th c. and was revived during the Second World War when St John's became the departure point for North Atlantic convoys. In 1949 Newfoundland joined the Canadian Confederation, a development which resulted in the city's decline. But recent years have seen the capital revitalised, especially following the discovery of oil reserves offshore.

Transatlantic
communication

The city played an historic part in the development of transport and communications. It was in St John's that the first transatlantic wireless signal was received in 1901 and it was also from St John's that John

The centre of St John's, capital of Newfoundland

Alcock and Arthur Brown took off on the first successful non-stop flight across the Atlantic.

Signal Hill, the steep cliffs of which make up the north side of the harbour entrance, was the scene of the final engagement of the Seven Years' War between Britain and France. During the annual Military Tattoo, held here mid-July–end of Aug. (Tue., Thu., Sat. and Sun. 3 and 7pm), the battle is commemorated by the sounding of the last post.

★★Signal Hill National Historic Park

Despite its strategic position Signal Hill remained unfortified following the Seven Years' War until the present defences were built during the hostilities of 1812. The hill traditionally served as a marine look-out however, which is how it acquired its name.

The thump of cannon can still be heard each midday, echoing round the Signal Hill National Historic Park (open: mid-June–beginning Sept. daily 9am–8pm, at other times daily 8.30am–4.30pm). The Park is one of the largest of its kind in Canada and, being situated 152 m (500 ft) above the sea, affords superb views day and night over the city, the harbour and the adjacent coast.

The Visitor Centre has several interesting displays illustrating the history of Newfoundland, especially the development of St John's.

Visitor Centre

Cabot Tower (open daily) was built in 1897 to mark the four hundredth anniversary of the discovery of Newfoundland. It also now commemorates Guglielmo Marconi's reception here in 1901 of the first transatlantic radio telegraphy signal, transmitted over a distance of 2700 km (1700 mi.) from Poldhu in England. In the tower are exhibitions on the history of Signal Hill and the history of communications (with a special section on Marconi). From the top there is a panoramic view of the city and the coast as far as Cape Spear – the most easterly point of North America.

Cabot Tower

Saint John's

Queen's Battery	An excellent view of the harbour can be had from the 18th c. Queen's Battery overlooking the Narrows. The lighthouse on the other side of the Narrows stands among the remains of an old fort – Fort Amherst.
★Quidi Vidi	Quidi Vidi, a delightful little fishing community which forms part of St John's, is situated on a small cliff-enclosed inlet on the north side of Signal Hill. A narrow channel links the inlet with Quidi Vidi Lake, where the oldest sporting event in North America, the annual St John's Regatta, is held. The now restored Quidi Vidi Battery (open daily in summer) overlooking the inlet was built during the French occupation of St John's. In 1780, after the British regained control, the battery was strengthened and used as a garrison by British troops until their withdrawal from Newfoundland in 1870. What is possibly the oldest house in British Canada, built in 1740, survives within the fort (it was used by the British as a dressing post during the Battle of Signal Hill). In 1967 the Battery was restored for the centenary celebrations.
Commissariat House	Standing next to one another in King's Bridge Road Commissariat House and the little Anglican Church of St Thomas make an attractive ensemble. The house (built between 1819 and 1821) and the church (1836) are among the few buildings to have escaped the devastating fires in the 19th c. The restored Georgian-style house (open: daily in summer; in winter by appointment only) was the headquarters of a Commissariat responsible for keeping the St John's military post supplied. An Interpretive Centre in the adjoining reconstructed coach house illustrates how the house was restored.
Colonial Building	Built in 1850 of white Irish limestone and embellished with a Classical portico, the Colonial Building in Military Road was until 1960 the seat of the Newfoundland government (afterwards the provincial parliament moved into the newly erected Confederation Building). The old building now houses the provincial archives (open in summer Mon.–Fri. 9am–4.15pm, in winter Mon.–Fri. 9am–5pm).
★★Basilica of St John the Baptist	Also in Military Road, on the highest point of the ridge above the city (fine view over the Narrows), stands Newfoundland's architecturally most important building, the Basilica of St John the Baptist (1842–92). Built in the form of a Latin cross and graced by slender twin towers 42 m (138 ft) high, the Basilica is noted for some fine statues and its beautiful ornate gold leaf ceiling. The statue of Our Lady of Fatima in one of the transepts was a gift from Portuguese sailors who were fortunate enough to survive being shipwrecked on the Banks. The basilica is now a National Historic Site.
★Anglican Cathedral of St John the Baptist	Also dedicated to St John the Baptist, the Anglican cathedral on Church Hill (a short distance south of the basilica) is likewise a National Historic Site. The cathedral, the foundation stone of which was laid in 1849, was designed by Gilbert Scott and ranks among the finest examples of pure neo-Gothic architecture in North America. It also has fine interior furnishings. After suffering serious damage in two major 19th c. fires the cathedral was not restored until 1905. Among other valuable treasures kept in the chapter-house is a gold communion vessel presented by William IV.
★Newfoundland Museum	The Newfoundland Museum, just across the road from the Anglican cathedral, traces the history of Newfoundland and Labrador back 9000 years, with exhibits dating from prehistoric as well as colonial times (open Mon.–Wed., Fri. 9am–5pm, Thu. 9am–9pm, Sun. and holidays 10am– 5pm). One section includes an excellent collection of Indian art

while another is devoted to the lives of the European pioneers who settled the province – from the hardships of the fisherfolk to the elegant drawing rooms of the prosperous city dwellers.

The War Memorial (1924) in Water Street E. stands on the spot where in 1583 Sir Humphrey Gilbert claimed possession of the colony in the name of Queen Elizabeth I.

War Memorial

The harbourside Murray Premises are restored mercantile buildings dating from 1847, now converted into shops, restaurants and offices and containing a branch of the Newfoundland Museum. Opened in 1983 the branch is devoted to the natural, military and maritime history of the province, including the development of maritime trade, underwater archaeology, navigation, cartography and shipwrecks (open Mon.–Fri. 9am–5pm, Sat. and Sun. 10am–6pm).

★Murray
Premises

With its many bars and restaurants George Street is a popular city centre rendezvous.

George Street

For more than 400 years Water Street, one of the oldest streets in North America, was the commercial centre of St John's. It is still the meeting place for sailors from all over the world, with a host of inviting shops, restaurants and bars.

Water Street

Occupying a site high above the rest of the city the Confederation Building (guided tours Mon.–Fri.) is the seat of Newfoundland's provincial govenment. It is also the location of a permanent exhibition which includes some of the best of the province's art both traditional and experimental.

Confederation
Building

Strikingly modern in its architecture the Arts and Culture Centre in Prince Philip Drive was built in 1967 for the centenary celebrations. It plays a leading part in the province's cultural life and incorporates a quite exceptional theatre, two art galleries, a museum of the sea, three libraries and a commercial art school.

★Arts and Culture
Centre

The Centre is the venue for the Summer Festival of the Arts (theatre, concerts, etc., including some open air performances).

Summer Festival
of the Arts

The Longshoremen's Protective Union Hall at the bottom of Victoria St. (referred to simply as the LSPU) is home to the highly successful Newfoundland Theatre. The company stages a wide variety of modern and classical plays, including works by Newfoundland authors. Interesting art exhibitions are mounted in the gallery of this lively cultural and social centre. It is also a centre for municipal activities.

Longshoremen's
Protective Union
Hall

Situated on the northern perimeter of St John's, C.A. Pippy Park (opened in 1968) extends over nearly 1400 ha (3460 acres). There are walkers' trails, picnic places, a golf course and a children's animal farm.

C.A. Pippy Park

C.A. Pippy Park is also the location of a botanical garden belonging to St John's Memorial University. The garden (open May to Nov. Wed.–Sat. 1.30–5.30pm, Sun. 10am–5.30pm) occupies some 42 ha (100 acres) of undulating ground and incorporates the about 6 ha (15 acre) Ox Pond. Spruce and fir, bog, heath and alder intersperse with rocky outcrops and natural landscape.

Botanical gardens

St Lawrence Waterway

H/J 12–17

The St Lawrence River is Canada's main transport corridor, along which lies the country's major axis of development. The river is a highway

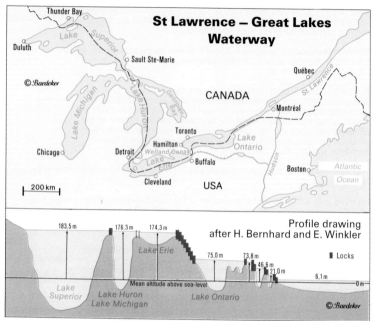

St Lawrence – Great Lakes Waterway

Thunder Bay
Lake Superior
Duluth
Sault Ste-Marie
© Baedeker
Lake Michigan
Lake Huron
Georgian Bay
CANADA
Québec
St Lawrence
Montréal
Toronto
Lake Ontario
Chicago
Detroit
Hamilton
Welland Canal
Lake Erie
Buffalo
Cleveland
USA
Boston
Hudson
Atlantic Ocean
├ 200 km ┤

Profile drawing
after H. Bernhard and E. Winkler

183.5 m   176.3 m   174.3 m   ■ Locks
Lake Erie   75.0 m   73.8 m
46.6 m
21.0 m   6.1 m
Mean altitude above sea-level   0 m
Lake Superior
Lake Huron
Lake Michigan   Lake Ontario
© Baedeker

serving all the regions most favoured in terms of climate, soil and raw materials, areas incalculably rich in timber, mineral resources and agricultural potential. No wonder then that Canada's oldest and most densely populated areas of settlement lie in a ribbon along its banks. Aptly referred to as the "Main Street" of this vast country, 60 per cent of all Canadians live within this belt. Just as importantly the St Lawrence is the gateway to Canada, and running east–west links several of the country's differing geographical regions. In this it contrasts strikingly with what also purports to be a "natural" route to the heart of North America, Hudson Bay, which in fact leads only into a cul-de-sac of inhospitable and largely unexploitable wastes. The importance of the St Lawrence even extends beyond the frontiers of Canada. On the one hand it forms a continuation of major transatlantic routes and thus a direct link with Europe; on the other it opens the way to the Mississippi river system, completing a line of communication used by the French as early as the 17th c. to maintain their colonial empire.

This draws attention to another factor – the significance of the St Lawrence to the neighbouring USA. Around the Great Lakes is concentrated one of the largest agglomerations of population and industry in the whole North American continent. As well as Chicago and Detroit with their millions of inhabitants and cities such as Milwaukee, Cleveland and Buffalo with populations of around half a million each, the industrial centres of the Prairies and the Mississippi basin all lie within the river's reach.

Even this is not yet the whole story. The great US east coast megalopolis with its more than 40 million inhabitants, seemingly cut off from the lowlands of the St Lawrence by the barrier of the Appalachians, is in practice easily accessible thanks to the Hudson–Champlain and Hudson–Mohawk depressions. The important New York–Montréal–Toronto transport triangle created by these natural routeways brings together the two largest concentrations of population and economic activity in the USA and Canada (Boston–New York–Philadelphia–Baltimore–Washington and the Québec–Windsor corridor i.e. "Main Street"). This same valley system also provides traffic on the St Lawrence with access to ice-free Atlantic ports (as does the St John River Valley in New Brunswick). Last but not least, not only does the St Lawrence form with Lake Superior by far the most important waterway in North America, the course of the river is also followed by Canadian Pacific (CP) and Canadian National (CN) Railways' busiest lines, by most VIA Rail routes, by the major highways (including the Trans-Canada Highway) and the busiest air corridors.

Traffic travelling up and down the St Lawrence Seaway maintains an almost perfect balance. Shipped east from the ports on Lake Superior (Duluth and Thunder Bay) are bulk cargoes of iron ore and grain, the latter carried the length of the St Lawrence on its way to ports abroad, the former, from the Mesabi Range, bound for the centres of US heavy industry (Sault Ste-Marie, Chicago–Gary and Detroit–Toledo).

In the opposite direction comes Pennsylvanian coal, heading west from ports on Lake Erie towards those self-same blast-furnaces or destined for the industrial cities on Lakes Erie (Cleveland, Ashtabula, Buffalo) and Ontario (Hamilton). These latter are in turn supplied, not with American iron ore from Lake Superior (Duluth) but with Canadian ore from further east (from the deposits in Labrador, opened up after the Second World War). This pattern of shipment means that upstream of the Niagara Falls (bypassed by the Welland Canal) most of the tonnage carried is of lowland origin whereas on the St Lawrence itself about half the tonnage comes from mountain areas.

The winter freeze-up poses a great problem for shipping – in the Toronto area for instance it lasts for 90 days.

Winter freeze-up

Topography throws down other sorts of challenges to navigation, the first being met with as the St Lawrence crosses the foothills of the Canadian Shield – a landscape of rocks worn smooth by glaciers – in the vicinity of the Thousand Islands. The second is faced on the middle section of the waterway where, at Niagara Falls and the adjacent Niagara Gorge, a difference in height of 100 m (330 ft) between Lakes Ontario and Erie has to be overcome. Without the removal of these two barriers – not to mention the 7 m (23 ft) height difference at the Sault Ste Marie Rapids between Lakes Superior and Huron – no truly efficient through route would be possible.

Topography

The existence of these three natural obstacles determined the character of the eventual waterway, involving the bypassing of Niagara Falls and construction of lock staircases at Sault Ste Marie and below Kingston.

Lock staircases

Although the Niagara escarpment with its massive Falls represented a seemingly insurmountable obstacle, it was precisely at this point (between Lakes Erie and Ontario) that the need for an efficient transport link was most acute. As a result no less than four successive canal and lock systems were constructed, not all being on the same route.

Niagara escarpment

The present Welland Canal (see entry) overcomes the 100 m (330 ft) difference in level by means of a staircase of seven huge locks. The result is one of the most prodigous feats of structural engineering to be seen on any transport system in the world.

Welland Canal

The locks on the St Mary's River at Sault Ste Marie are the hub of navigation on the Great Lakes, neutralising the 7.2 m (23 ft) drop from Lake Superior to Lake Huron. The first canal to be built at this strategic point was constructed by the North West Company in 1798, but was destroyed in the 1812 war. Next came a lock in 1855, followed in 1895 by a canal on

St Mary's River

the Canadian side and lock staircase on the American, circumventing the rapids. Today there are five parallel locks of which the 9 m (29 ft) deep McArthur Lock (on the USA side) is the largest.

Lake Ontario–
Montreal section

The most difficult problem on the whole St Lawrence Waterway was posed by a 300 m (984 ft) section between Lake Ontario and Montréal. Here the river crosses the Canadian Shield, dropping a total of 75 m (246 ft) and forming a series of rapids. The idea of building a canal to circumvent the Lachine Rapids above Montréal was first canvassed as long ago as 1680, but only came to fruition in the 19th c. The original 5 km (3 mi.) long Lachine Canal was 1.50 m (5 ft) deep and ascended 13 m (43 ft) with the aid of seven locks. In subsequent years more canals and locks were built until, by about 1900, a system of shallow water canals was in operation all the way from Lake Superior to Montréal.

Creation of the
Seaway

In 1954, after initial resistance from the USA (which feared the effects of competition on other American shipping routes), the long awaited construction of the St Lawrence Seaway began. The Seaway was completed and officially opened in 1959. The installations on this major waterway comprise efficient technologically advanced canals navigable by vessels of 8.2 m (26 ft) draught, with locks 233.5 m (766 ft) long, 24.4 m (80 ft) wide and 9.1 m (30 ft) deep, together with several large hydro-electric stations (some new, some enlarged).

The 22 old locks formerly needed to surmount the 75 m (246 ft) rise on this section of the river are today replaced by just seven large ones, with lifts of between 1.8 and 15.2 m (6 and 50 ft). But the massive engineering project inevitably had a profound effect on the local environment; traffic routes had to be relocated, bridges built, and industrial plant and harbour installations constructed or enlarged. In many places what had previously been cultivated land was flooded, and a total of 500 buildings and 6500 people were moved to new sites on higher ground.

The benefits which this has brought in terms of improved transport efficiency have been felt over a wide geographical area. Before the Seaway opened, ocean-going vessels would off load their cargoes at Montréal onto small "canallères" with a capacity of 2000–3000 tonnes. At Lake Ontario the freight would be transferred for a second time, aboard the big "lakers". Today this three-stage operation is no longer necessary and ocean-going ships and "lakers" of more than 25,000 tonnes ply the whole length of the St Lawrence. As a result many ports and industrial areas have seen their economies expand. Total shipments increased from 12.5 million tonnes in 1956 to 20 million tonnes by 1959; by 1984 they had more than doubled again to some 48 million tonnes. In that same year, on the Montréal–Lake Ontario section of the Seaway, wheat accounted for 15.9 million tonnes (33.5 per cent), iron ore 11.4 million tonnes (24 per cent) and iron and steel 4.5 million tonnes (9.5 per cent).

Of all the freight carried on the Seaway, almost half was transported within Canada, one sixth went from Canada to the USA, and one tenth from the USA to Canada. Exports from Canada to countries other than the USA accounted for 5 per cent, imports for 3 per cent. Non-Canadian imports to the USA amounted to one sixth, exports from the USA just under a tenth. These figures are eloquent testimony to the huge national and international importance of the St Lawrence Seaway.

Saskatchewan F–H 9/10

Geographical location: 49° to 60°N 102° to 110°W.
Area: 652,330 sq. km (251,799 sq. mi.)
Population: 1,024,000. Capital: Regina

Information

Tourism Saskatchewan 500–1900 Albert Street, Regina, SK S4P 4L9; tel. (306) 7872300

Saskatchewan

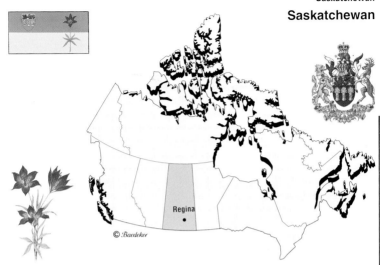

© Baedeker

Saskatchewan, "province of 100,000 lakes", has shared borders with Manitoba in the east, Alberta in the west and the two US states of Montana and North Dakota in the south.

Location

Two-thirds of the province belong to the Interior Plains of Canada, the remaining (northern) third being part of the Canadian Shield. As a result Saskatchewan reveals two very different topographical faces. The north, shaped long ago by glaciation, is a landscape of extensive bogs with litterally thousands of lakes. In the south gently rising prairies of fertile brown and black earth merge into the hill country further west. The province's highest point (1392 m (4570 ft)) is found in the Cypress Hills, the lowest at Lake Athabasca (65 m (213 ft)). Half the province is wooded, a third is arable land, and one eighth (totalling 80,000 sq. km (30,880 sq. mi.)) is covered with freshwater. The vast majority of the almost 100,000 lakes, relics of Ice Age glaciation, are found in north Saskatchewan.

Topography

Of the major river systems three, the Assiniboine, the North and South Saskatchewan and the Churchill, all flow into Hudson Bay; the Frenchman River (in the far south-west) flows into the Mississippi.

Name

To the Cree Indians living on the Great Plains centuries ago the biggest of these waterways was "the river that flows swiftly" or "Saskatchewan". It was from this that the province later took its name.

Saskatchewan has a distinctly dry continental climate with temperatures that increase progressively from north to south. The long cold winter begins in October, average temperatures being below freezing point (January temperatures in the north range from about −20° to −25°C (−4° to −13°F)). But the sun alleviates the cold even when the thermometer falls to −30°C (−22°F), and the warm chinook wind can lift the temperature within hours by up to 25°C (77°F). The north averages 130 cm (51 in.) of snow, the south 76 cm (30 in.).

Climate

Spring generally arrives in April. In the very short but extremely hot summer temperatures of up to 38°C (100°F) can be reached, though from May through to August they most often hover between 20°C (68°F) and 35°C (95°F). Saskatchewan is Canada's sunniest province and

Saskatchewan

Estevan the country's "Sunshine Capital" (averaging 2540 hours of sun-shine a year). Nights are usually quite cool. Rain accompanied by violent thunderstorms is a quite frequent feature of the late afternoon or evening. Annual rainfall ranges between 250 and 600 mm (10 and 24 in.).

Vegetation

Influenced by the climate the vegetation also varies progressively from north to south. The sub-Arctic coniferous forests of north Saskatchewan give way to mixed coniferous forests (spruce, aspen, poplar and birch), these latter yielding in turn to the prairie grasslands of the south.

History

The history of the area now comprising Saskatchewan can be traced back at least 30,000 years, to the time when nomadic hunting tribes crossed from Asia into North America over the land bridge which then connected the two. These first inhabitants of North America migrated with the seasons, moving between the prairies and the forests and river valleys. They lived primarily by hunting buffalo. Few vestiges of their presence now remain though archaeological excavations near Saskatoon have revealed some evidence of Indian tribal culture from 8000 years ago.

Saskatchewan's more recent history reflects the complex interplay of differing ethnic groups. Its opening chapters were written centuries ago when the native Assiniboine, Blackfoot, Chipewyan and Cree Indians, living on the Great Plains, came into contact with the first European adventurers pushing west into the interior from the shores of Hudson Bay.

The earliest recorded arrival (1690) was that of Henry Kelsey, com-missioned to reconnoitre the area on behalf of the British Hudson's Bay fur trading company. Soon other explorers followed, also making their way inland from Hudson Bay or from the Great Lakes, men such as La Vérendrye, Hearne and Pond, who helped map out Canada and in doing so opened the hinterland to the growing trade in furs. Rupert's Land, as it was then called, remained in the possession of the Hudson's Bay Company for 200 years, before recognition of the vast mineral wealth led to its purchase by the Canadian government in 1870. This was fol-lowed by large-scale settlement of the prairies where plots of arable land were sold to pioneer farmers for just a registration fee.

In 1873 the Canadian government appointed a provisional adminis-tration for the region (renamed the Northwest Territories and incorpo-rating the bulk of western Canada). Battleford became the territorial capital in 1876.

It was also at this time that the police force known today as the Royal Canadian Mounted Police came into existence. It was formed in 1874 when 300 police recruits, charged with establishing the rule of law in the North-West, set out on an incredible 1300 km (800 mi.) trek from Fort Dufferin in Manitoba.

In 1885 simmering unrest in the new frontier region boiled over into armed conflict between the Metis and the Canadian government. The root cause of the North West Rebellion (as the conflict became known) was the failure of the federal authorities to concern themselves with the problems of the frontier folk. Several clashes took place between gov-ernment troops and the insurgents led by Louis Riel before the rebellion was finally quashed. Riel was found guilty of treason and hanged the same year.

The population of Saskatchewan and Alberta increased rapidly in the first decades of the 20th c. with the arrival, in wave after wave, of 700,000 new settlers. Attracted to the prairies by cheap land they quickly established agriculture as a major sector of the country's economy.

Saskatchewan only became a province in 1905 and has the reputation of being the most politically radical in the Canadian federation.

The 1930s were a turning-point for the economy. First came the stock market crash of 1929 and the worldwide Great Depression which fol-lowed. Then drought and failed harvests brought the country to the edge of ruin. Within a short time, however, Saskatchewan had recovered and today enjoys the benefits of a stable economy based on a wealth of natural resources.

In 1944 the people of the province elected the first socialist government in North America, keeping it in power until 1967. A series of measures were introduced to improve living conditions. These included the creation of state enterprises, modernisation of schools and expansion of electricity supplies throughout the region.

Many of the more than one million Saskatchewans trace their roots back to Europe, to Russia, Scandinavia and the British Isles.

Population

About 55 per cent of the population are urban dwellers, of whom a third live in Regina and Saskatoon. Most people are concentrated in the south of the province, 40 per cent of them in farming communities.

Saskatchewans have the highest life expectancy in Canada – 78.6 years for women, 71.1 years for men.

The Saskatchewan economy reflects the richness of its natural resources, particularly the mineral deposits, energy reserves (mineral oil, natural gas) and huge supplies of timber.

Economy

Between 1982 and 1987 skilful management of the economy saw Saskatchewan's GNP rise from $14.7 billion to $18.4 billion. 40 per cent of goods produced in the province are exported, three quarters of them beyond Canada. Almost half (45.2 per cent, mainly oil, potash and uranium) go to the USA.

The second most important market (24.7 per cent) is in Asia and the countries of the Pacific basin, which between them import $1.4 billion worth of produce, primarily cereals, potash and uranium. Exports to western Europe account for 8.8 per cent.

Saskatchewan is a major source of potash, oil, gold and uranium. It is the world's leading supplier of potash possessing almost two-thirds of the planet's known reserves. 25 per cent of world demand is met by ten mines.

The richest deposits of heavy oil in Canada are also found in the province, a total of 662.7 million barrels (1988). Production in 1987 was 76.2 million barrels.

Saskatchewan is the world's largest exporter of uranium, more than 300 million kg (661 million lb) of uranium bearing ore (about 80 per cent of the earth's total) having been discovered in the Athabasca basin. Annual production is presently running at 8.2 million kg (18 million lb).

In its first year the Star Lake mine, one of a number of gold mines opened in 1987, produced 1056 kg (2328 lb) of gold valued at $20 million.

Saskatchewan also exports increasingly large quantities of natural gas. Reserves are estimated at more than 69 billion cu.m.

Lignite deposits totalling 7.6 billion tonnes/tons supply almost 75 per cent of the province's electricity requirements.

Mining of all kinds contributes 9 per cent of the province's GNP.

Saskatchewan's largest renewable resource is its forests, barely half of which are exploited commercially. The most important woods are spruce, aspen, poplar and birch. In 1987/88 timber production was worth $258 million.

As a result of deliberate economic diversificiation into new technologies the province is today a world leader in the fields of biotechnology, fibre optics and satellite communications. SaskTel developed and installed the world's first commercial fibre optics telephone, television and data communications system (still one of the largest) and, with telecommunications playing an increasingly important role, runs a worldwide service network (video conferences, data and teleprinter communications, etc.)

Agriculture, cereal production in particular, continues to be a major source of income for Saskatchewan, possessing as it does 44 per cent (20 million hectares) of the federation's agricultural land. Canada's

445

"Echo Valley Farm" in Saskatchewan

"bread basket" produces 60 per cent of the country's wheat and meets 12 per cent of total world demand.

Livestock represent another important branch of agriculture, with more than 25 per cent of the country's cattle and 20 per cent of its sheep, pigs and poultry being reared in the province.

The food processing industry also contributes substantially to the economy (meat and potato products, pasta, etc.)

Leisure

In its still largely unspoilt landscape Saskatchewan has a further resource, particularly attractive to anyone with a love of the great outdoors and the untouched, tranquil beauty of the land. While canoeing, angling and swimming can all be enjoyed on the numerous lakes, many visitors want nothing more than the opportunity to observe wild creatures in their natural environment. But for those keen to participate in any of the various sports and leisure activities excellent facilities are provided by the National and Provincial Parks (walkers' trails, swimming and a wide range of other pursuits).

Suggested route

TransCanada Highway (600 km (370 mi.))

A substantial part of the province can be seen by following the TransCanada Highway as it runs across the prairies and wheatfields of southern Saskatchewan. It is best to start from the province's south-east border with Manitoba (see entry) and drive east–west along the Highway (which passes through the capital Regina and the town of Swift Current). Detours can then be made either north or south to visit the many places of interest (Moose Mountain Provincial Park, Qu'Appelle Valley (see entry), Cypress Hills Provincial Park (see entry), etc.). Plenty of opportunities for swimming, fishing and hunting will be found along the way.

★Saskatoon

Province: Saskatchewan. Population: 194,000

Tourism Saskatoon, 6–305 Idylwyld Dr. N., Saskatoon, SK S7K 0Z1; tel. (306) 242–12 06

Information

Saskatoon, the province's biggest city and a melting pot of different cultures, lies on the banks of the South Saskatchewan River. Known as "the city of bridges" it has wide tree-lined streets and 1620 ha (4000 acres) of parks and green spaces. It is the acknowledged "mining capital" of Canada and is often referred to as a mini Silicon Valley because of its leading role in Canada's high-tec and mining industries. It is the home of the highly respected University of Saskatchewan with some 17,000 students.

Location

Before the arrival of Europeans this area was inhabited by Cree Indians, the dominant prairie tribe. Each spring and summer they hunted buffalo on the Great Plains, setting up camp in the vicinity of Saskatoon.

The town itself was founded in 1882 by Methodists from Ontario who, led by John Lake, intended to establish a temperance colony. In due course the settlement was named Saskatoon (from "misakwatomin", the Indian word for the red berries which grew locally). Already by this time the great buffalo herds had disappeared and the days of the Indians' nomadic existence were numbered. For the new arrivals life was far from easy. Floods, blizzards, prairie fires and mosquitoes exacerbated the normal hardships of the daily round, instilling into the early pioneers a stubborn determination to overcome adversity.

The temperance ideal attracted few settlers however, and 20 years on the township could still only claim 113 inhabitants. This soon changed, partly because by 1901 agricultural production was on the increase, and partly because, with the opening of the railway in 1908, the entire region saw an influx of new immigrants. The result was that people of many different nationalities – Germans, Scandinavians, Ukrainians and Britons – have all contributed to the development of the town. By 1911 Saskatoon had a population of more than 11,000. In the years that followed both population and economy continued to grow, slowly but steadily.

History

Highly recommended is a visit to this, the largest of Saskatchewan's four Western Development Museums (open in summer daily 9am–9pm, reduced opening in winter) which authentically recreates and documents the history of the Canadian west. "Boomtown 1910", the reconstructed main street of a typical prairie town (the longest such street anywhere in North America), is lined with old-style shops – including a Chinese laundry and a barber's shop – as well as a church, fire-station, railway station, and other period buildings. There is also a collection of vintage cars (priceless today) and ancient tractors.

★Western Development Museum

The John Diefenbaker Centre (open Mon.–Fri. 9.30am–4.30pm, Sat., Sun. and holidays 12.30–5pm) on the University campus is a combined archive and museum devoted to the life and times of Canada's 13th Prime Minister. In addition to its permanent displays, among which are replicas of the Cabinet Chamber and Prime Minister's office in Ottawa, the Centre is used for temporary exhibitions on history, politics, science and art. Diefenbaker and his wife are buried nearby.

John Diefenbaker Centre

Also located on the University campus is a restored school dating from 1905 (open May–Sep. Mon.–Fri. 9.30am–noon and 12.30–4.30pm, Sat.,

Little Stone School House

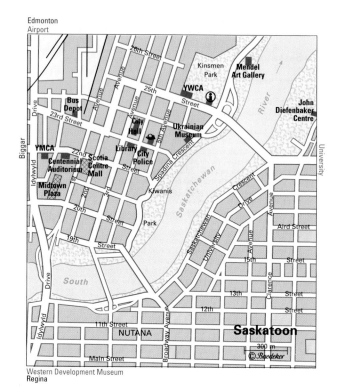

Sun. and holidays 12.30–5pm). Victoria School was Saskatoon's very first school and is its oldest surviving public building.

★Ukrainian
Museum of
Canada

The Ukrainian Museum of Canada (open mid-Sep.–mid-Jun. Tue.–Fri., Sun. 1–4.30pm, mid-Jun.–Labour Day Mon.–Fri. 10am–4.30pm, Sat., Sun. 1–8pm) is dedicated to the many settlers who came here from the Ukraine and who contributed in such large measure to the country's development. Craftwork on display includes embroidered fabrics, wood carvings, traditional items of a religious kind (such as decorated Easter eggs) and ceramics.

★Museum of
Ukrainian Culture

Other Ukrainian memorabilia, some dating from the 18th and 19th c., are collected together in the Museum of Ukrainian Culture (open Jun., Jul., Aug. Mon.–Sat. 11am–5pm, Sun 1–8pm, winter Sat., Sun. 2–5pm) in Ave. "M" S. This ethnographic museum, founded by the Ukrainian Catholic Church, has various collections devoted to the religious, secular and folk heritage of Ukrainian immigrants.

Memorial Art
Gallery

The Memorial Art Gallery in 11th St. (open Mon.–Fri. 8am–noon and 1–4pm) commemorates students who lost their lives in the First World War. On display are paintings and wood cuts by 20th c. Canadian artists.

Mendel Art
Gallery

The Mendel Art Gallery (open daily 10am–10pm) in Spadina Cres. East has temporary as well as permanent exhibitions of international, national and regional art.

Adjoining the gallery is a conservatory filled with colourful tropical plants.

Located about 3 km (2 mi.) north of Saskatoon the Wanuskewin Heritage Park – from the Cree word "Wanuskewin" meaning "living together in harmony" – aims to encourage a better understanding of the indigenous peoples who inhabited the region in earlier times.

★★**Wanuskewin Heritage Park**

The park, spread over land purchased in 1983 from the Meewasin Valley Authority (the body responsible for the river valleys around Saskatoon) is the site of some exciting archaeological discoveries, research into which has established that Plains Indians lived in the area at least 6000 to 7000 years ago.

Among the major archaeological finds is a "medicine wheel", estimated to be about 1500 years old, consisting of a central cairn enclosed in a ring marked by three smaller cairns. Other cairns have been found marking the trail along which buffalo were herded before being driven over a precipice to their deaths. The animals were butchered in the valley below, the meat being preserved and the hides, bones, etc. processed for making into clothing, tools and tepees.

★Sault Ste Marie

H 14

Province: Ontario
Population: 80,000

Sault Ste Marie Chamber of Commerce, 334 Bay St, Sault Ste Marie, ON P6A 1X1; tel. (705) 9497152

Information

The Canadian border city of Sault Ste Marie, principal town of Algoma County, is situated on the delightful St Mary's River which joins Lake Superior to Lake Huron.

Location

Long before the arrival of Europeans the significance of this particular location was appreciated by the native Indians for whom it was a place to meet and trade. As early as the first half of the 17th c. French "voyageurs", fur traders and timber raftsmen had already formed close links with local tribes. In 1667 the Ste Marie Mission was founded by French Jesuit missionaries and in 1671 possession was taken of the land in the name of the French king, Louis XIV.

History

Increasing numbers of settlers, the majority British but also some French, came to Sault Ste Marie after 1797/98 when a canal was dug to by-pass the rapids. In 1861 the town became a free port, and 26 years later was granted civic status. A second canal built on the Canadian side in 1895 and a rail-link to the Canadian Pacific Railway further quickened the pace of settlement. In 1899 the (iron and steel producing) Algoma Steel Company was established, to be followed in later years by numerous other industries (including timber processing, paper and chemicals). The city is also well known for its long established and highly regarded forestry and land research institute.

The waterway connecting Lakes Superior and Huron forms the frontier between the USA and Canada. Like Sault St Marie ("The Soo"), Ontario, to which it is joined by a bridge, Sault Ste Marie, Michigan, has a number of major industries (timber, leather and food processing, ship building, rail repair shop, etc.).

Sault Ste Marie (USA)

Navigable only from mid-April to mid-December the 2 km (1¼ mi.) long canals on the US and Canadian sides of the frontier at Sault Ste Marie together make up the world's busiest waterway. Well over 100 million tonnes/tons of freight (mainly mineral ore and grain) pass through the locks en route from the industrial centres, mining and wheat growing

★Soo Locks

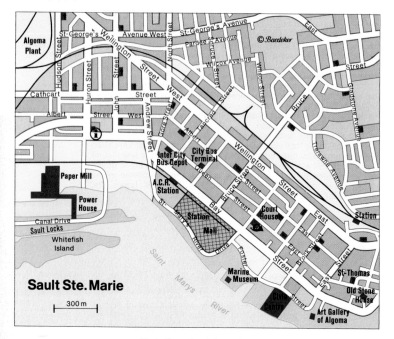

© Baedeker

Sault Ste. Marie

| 300 m |

areas around Lake Superior. A boat trip through the "Soo Locks" – those on the Canadian side of the St Mary's Rapids were completed in 1895 – is an experience not to be missed. Boats leave from Norgoma Dock (near Foster Drive) daily between the end of May and mid-October.

Sights

Art Gallery of Algoma	An eye-catching modern building on the St Mary's embankment houses the Art Gallery of Algoma (10 East St.; open Mon.–Sat. 9am–5pm, Sun. 1–5pm) where the County's extensive art collection is on display. Temporary exhibitions.
★Ermatinger House	This attractive solid 1814 stone-built house (831 Queen St. E.; open: Apr.–Nov. every afternoon) originally belonged to a fur trader whose wife came from the local Ojibwa tribe. Now restored it provides a graphic insight into what life was like here almost 200 years ago.
Bellevue Park	Queen Street East is the location of the lovely Bellevue Park with its conservatories, small zoo, lighthouse and marina.
Sault Ste Marie Museum	The Sault Ste Marie Museum occupies a listed building in East Street (no. 107). Use is made of temporary exhibitions to illustrate 10,000 years of the area's history. Open daily.
M.S. "Norgoma"	The M.S. "Norgoma" was the last passenger ship built for service on the Great Lakes. Now on permanent moorings and converted into a museum the 24 m (79 ft) vessel can be visited daily from June to mid-October.

Surroundings

Reached via Highway 565 the Forest Ecology Trail ("Deer Run" and "Windfall" trails) is open to walkers from the end of June until August. Guided walks.

The Great Lakes Forestry Centre (1219 Queen St. E.; guided tours mid-Jun.–Aug. Mon.–Fri. 10am–2pm) provides a feast of interesting information about forestry in the Great Lakes region.

Searchmont, a winter sports resort, is situated about 50 km (31 mi.) north of Sault Ste Marie on Highway 556. It is open from mid-December to mid-April.

★★Agawa Canyon

Between June and mid-October the Algoma Central Railway (ACR) runs a particularly delightful excursion from Sault Ste Marie to the Agawa Canyon (dep. 9am daily). The train winds its way along the 183 km (114 mi.) of track amidst the mountainous Algoma scenery, taking about 2½ hours to reach the impressive gorge through which wild, amber-coloured water rages and roars (the most striking views are obtained by walking up to the Bridal Veil and the Black Beaver Falls). The journey is at its loveliest in autumn when the leaves are on the turn.

The ACR also runs excursions to the Agawa Canyon in winter (Jan.–Mar., Sat., Sun.; 8 hour round trip), continuing beyond Agawa as far as Eton. This is an opportunity for nature-lovers and photographers alike to revel in the entrancing winter landscape – the trees with their thick caps of snow, the streams and lakes covered with ice, the waterfalls frozen into the strangest shapes. Information: Algoma Central Railway, Sault Ste Marie, Ontario; tel. (705) 254–433.

★St Joseph Island

St Joseph Island lies in the channel leading from Lake Huron to Lake Superior, at the western end of the Manitoulin chain of islands in Lake Huron. It is of some geological interest on account of its jasper conglomerate or "pudding stone".

Still very rural in character the island is becoming increasingly popular as a leisure area, with good angling and swimming.

On the south-west side of the island stands the ruined Fort St Joseph (1796–1812), now designated a historical monument. The Visitors Centre (open May–Oct. daily) explains the one time military and economic significance of the fort (the fur trade, European-Indian relations, etc.). Nearby is an extensive animal reserve and bird sanctuary.

About 6 km (4 mi.) south of the bridge linking the island to the mainland there is a museum of local history (open daily Jul.–beginning Sep.) with an interesting collection of memorabilia from pioneer days.

★Thessalon

The old lumber town of Thessalon (population 1500), north of Sault Ste Marie, occupies a pleasant river-mouth site at the head of Lake Huron. During the warmer months it is busy with holidaymakers, one of the attractions being its marina.

These falls are situated just off Highway 129 between Thessalon and Chapleau. The now dammed Mississagi River plummets over a distinctive 39 m (128 ft) escarpment, carving a path for itself through a gorge.

★Selkirk

Province: Manitoba
Population: 10,000

Information

Manitoba Fun Belt, 356 Main Street, Selkirk, MB R1A 1T6; tel. (204) 4822022

General

A 9 m (30 ft) high sculpture on Selkirk's Main Street underlines this agreeable east Manitoban town's claim to be North America's Mecca for anglers in pursuit of catfish. Indeed, so many catfish have been caught between Selkirk and Lockport that restrictions on fishing have had to be introduced. There is a well appointed yacht marina on Lake Winnipeg.

Marine Museum

Several historic ships have been brought together in a park to form this interesting Marine Museum (Eveline/Queen St.; open mid-May–Jun. Mon.–Sat. 9am–6pm, Sun. 10am–7pm, Jul., Aug. daily 9am–8pm). The main attraction is an old steamship, the S.S. "Keenora", which operated cruises on Lake Winnipeg from 1923 to 1965. Other vessels on show are the icebreaker "C. G. S. Bradbury", the passenger and cargo carrying "Chickama", and an elderly fishing cutter, the "Lady Canadian".

City Park

A reproduction Red River cart has been placed in the City Park to commemorate the early pioneers. Carts such as this were the sole means of transport in those days for goods of every kind.

★Fort Gary National Historic Park

The Fort Gary National Historic Park outside Selkirk has as its centrepiece the only stone fort from the fur trading era to survive intact anywhere in North America (the park itself is open throughout the year; the buildings mid-May to beginning of Sep. daily 9.30am–6pm, Sep. Sat., Sun. 9.30am–6pm.). Lower Fort Gary was erected by the Hudson's Bay Company in the 1830s, becoming an important centre for the fur trade and serving as a base for the exploration of the Northwest Territories. It was built to replace an earlier fort which originally stood at the confluence of the Red and Assiniboine Rivers in what is now the centre of Winnipeg. This old fort was destroyed by floods in 1826, after which George Simpson, Governor of Rupert's Land, ordered the construction of the Lower Fort on a more elevated (but more isolated) site at some distance from the existing busy settlement.

In later years the fort was used successively as a training camp for the Royal Canadian Mounted Police, a prison, a mental institution, and a company headquarters, before eventually being leased to the Manitoba Motor & Country Club in 1911. It was handed over to the Crown by the Hudson's Bay Company in 1951. In 1964 Parks Canada began a programme of restoration.

The fort has been equipped with period furniture, crockery, pictures, etc. painstakingly gathered together over a period of years not only from within Canada but also from Britain and the USA.

Costumed Parks Canada employees act out the roles of the fort's earlier inhabitants, e.g. smiths, labourers, servants and "voyageurs" (i.e. traders who travelled by canoe bringing back pelts from the territories further north). Visitors are able to talk to the "Governor" and his wife and to various employees and domestic staff, as well as enjoying oatmeal biscuits in the basement kitchen. The result is a vivid impression of the complexities of life in a fur trading community.

Displayed in the building where the furs were stored are samples of pelts of every kind – lynx, fox, beaver, racoon, mink and wolf. On the ground floor, a Hudson's Bay Company shop has been re-created, stocked with everything from clothing and household goods to beads, horse bells, traps, brooms, boots and blankets. The settlers were entirely dependent upon such shops to keep their needs supplied.

Standing beside the storehouse is an example of a "York Boat".

Hundreds of these solidly built craft (capable of carrying up to 2 tonnes/tons) plied the lakes and rivers all the way from Hudson Bay to the Rocky Mountains and from Red River to the Arctic.

An audio-visual presentation on the history of the fort greets visitors arriving at the Reception Centre (opened in 1980) which also has excellent displays on the fur trade and the lives of the early settlers, illustrated with the aid of a variety of artefacts, pictures and models.

After visiting the Fort continue on Highway 9 via Petersfield to Netley Marsh.

The 36,000 ha (89,000 acre) Netley Marsh is one of the largest waterfowl breeding grounds in North America, the permanent home of 18 varieties of duck as well as of geese, herons, pelicans, terns and various kinds of diver. In spring the population is swollen by thousands of migratory birds. *Netley Marsh

The best way to see the marsh is by canoeing along its narrow waterways, the alternative being to follow the footpath which runs through the wetland reserve. Between 4am and 6am in the morning there is a good chance of spotting more than a hundred different species of bird.

★Sudbury   H 14

Province: Ontario
Population: 92,000 (160,000 if the environs are included)

Sudbury Welcome Centre, 1984 Region Street S., Sudbury, ON P3E 5S1; tel. (705) 5220104 | Information

Sudbury, often referred to as the mining capital of the world, is situated beside Ramsey Lake in northern Ontario, about five hours' drive north of Toronto (see entry). | Location

Iron bearing lodes of mineral ore were first noticed here in 1883 during construction of the Canadian Pacific Railway. Before long other minerals were discovered, massive deposits of sulphurous nickel in particular. The latter have been mined on a large scale ever since and today more than three quarters of the world's output of nickel comes from the Sudbury Basin. Platinum, gold, silver, copper, cobalt, lead, zinc and iron are among the other metals found in the area. | Minerals

The huge smokestacks towering above the copper and nickel processing plants are among the town's many landmarks. Sudbury also possesses a first-class technical university. As for the surrounding landscape, it is reminiscent of the surface of the moon.

Up-to-date research into the geology of the region suggests that the depression or "basin" in which Sudbury lies is a massive crater formed by a meteorite striking this south-western part of the Canadian Shield with enormous velocity many millions of years ago. Particles of material from the impact were condensed into the existing rock or transformed by metamorphosis into new rocks, minerals and ores. The shock waves of the collision scattered debris over a wide area. This cataclysmic event is believed to have been responsible for the formation of the sulphurous nickel deposits which lie in extensive fields about 60 km (37 mi.) long, and of other ores. | Geology

The latest theory has superceded an earlier one which sought to explain the origin of the crater together with the presence of large quantities of minerals as the product of a violent volcanic eruption in Palaeozoic times.

Until just a few years ago toxic gas emissions were allowed into the atmosphere at a rate of 3600 tonnes per day, resulting in acid rain which | Environmental problems

453

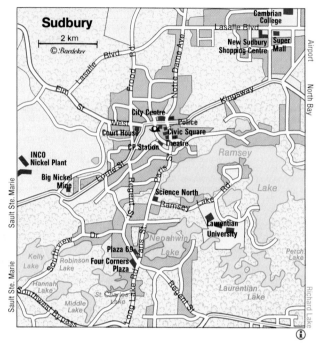

attacked and destroyed vast tracts of vegetation over a wide area. Damage was even caused to forests as far afield as the Labrador Peninsula, 1200 to 1500 km (750 to 930 mi.) to the east. Nowadays, thanks to the installation of efficient desulphurising systems, the gas plumes issuing from the tall chimneys (up to 350 m (1150 ft) high) are much less toxic and dangerous to the environment. Both local industry and the government (provincial as well as federal) are committed to further reductions in pollution levels.

Sights

★Copper Cliff Museum

Copper Cliff Museum (open Jun.–beginning Sep. Mon.–Fri. 10am–4.30pm) is a rich source of interesting information about copper mining in and around Sudbury.

Mine

The Big Nickel Mine (open: mid-May–mid-Oct.; tel. (705) 522–3701) is operated by Science North. Visitors are able to descend more than 300 m (985 ft) to the workface.

Big Nickel

The Big Nickel itself is a massive (about 10 m (33 ft) high) replica of the Canadian commemorative coin minted in 1951.

Giant Stacks

The mining and industrial area around Sudbury boasts the highest smokestacks in the world (350 m (1150 ft)), built in the hope of preventing toxic gases emitted by local industries from laying waste the entire surrounding countryside. It soon became clear however that the poisonous fumes from the new chimneys were simply being carried fur-

The celebrated "Big Nickel" of Sudbury

ther afield (as far as Labrador for example) before wreaking similar havoc there. Now waste-gas purification plants have been installed to reduce the damaging effects of the emissions.

The Flour Mill Heritage Museum (a former mill; St Charles St.; open mid-Jun.–beginning Sep. Mon.–Fri. and Sun. afternoons) contains old furniture, domestic equipment, tools and weaponry.

Flour Mill Heritage Museum

The Galerie du Nouvel Ontario (No. 20, Rue St Anne) provides an opportunity to see works by French Canadian painters, sculptors and potters and is well worth the visit.

Galerie du Nouvel Ontario

The bilingual Laurentian University specialises in science and technology. There are guided tours of the super-modern campus beside Ramsey Lake and of the Doran Planetarium adjoining it.
    The University Museum in the W.J. Bell House (built 1906; corner of John St. and Nelson St.; open Tue.–Sun. afternoons) is also full of interest.

Laurentian University

Accommodated in a striking modern building designed to resemble a snowflake this extraordinary Science Centre (Ramsey Lake Rd./Paris St.; open daily) vividly conveys a wealth of information about the geology and landscape of North Ontario and the Canadian Arctic. There are also various fascinating presentations (e.g. films and demonstrations) on the history of the universe and the development of communications. Visitors are invited to conduct scientific experiments for themselves, with the assistance of the staff.

★★Science North

Everything from classical drama to the most recent plays is performed in the very modern Sudbury Theatre (near City Hall).

Sudbury Theatre

Bell Park	Attractively laid out on the shores of Ramsey Lake, Bell Park is Sudbury's most popular recreation area. It has an outdoor theatre where various festivals and open-air concerts are held.
Lake Ramsey	Some very pleasant boat trips can be enjoyed on Lake Ramsey (mid-May to Sep. daily from the Science North pier).
★★Path of Discovery	The "Path of Discovery" bus tour (taking several hours) is highly recommended for anyone visiting Sudbury in the summer months. Starting at the Big Nickel Mine this mini geological field-trip makes a circuit of the Sudbury meteorite crater. There are various stops en route for guides to point out traces of the meteorite's impact on the earth's surface and to explain its consequences in terms of the geological composition and present day topography of the area and the formation of the mineral fields.

Surroundings

★French River	French River, the 112 km (70 mi.) long waterway between Lake Nipissing and Georgian Bay (see entry), is about an hour's drive south of Sudbury. A group of French "voyageurs" and missionaries, Samuel de Champlain among them (see Famous People), set off into the interior from here in 1620. Nowadays the river is very popular with canoeists, anglers, and outdoor enthusiasts generally.
★Killarney Provincial Park	Also about an hour's drive from Sudbury, but to the south-west, lies the 363 sq. km (140 sq. mi.) Killarney Provincial Park. This area bordering on Georgian Bay (see entry) is still a part of the Canadian Shield, and includes the La Cloche mountains – sometimes snow capped even in early autumn. The Park is another much favoured haunt of canoeists.

★Tadoussac   H 17

Province: Québec. Population: 1000

Access	Highway 138
History	Tadoussac lies surrounded by the most delightful scenery north of the junction of the Saguenay Fiord and St Lawrence River. Jacques Cartier made a stop here in 1535 and before long the burgeoning trade in furs saw it develop into something of a centre. It was the site of the first trading post established in New France (built by Pierre Chauvin in about 1600) and fifteen years later of the first mission station. Tadoussac's importance diminished following colonisation of the upper Saguenay.

Sights

★Riverside walk	A very pretty walk runs along the banks of the St Lawrence, from where in summer boat trips depart for the Saguenay Fiord (for whale-spotting in particular). There is an interesting reconstruction of Pierre Chauvin's trading post from 1600 (open during the summer tourist season only). Also worth seeing is the mid-18th c. wooden fisherman's chapel nearby.

Surroundings

Le Désert	About 3 km (2 mi.) outside Tadoussac sand has been blown by the wind into great dunes over 100 m (330 ft) high. Known locally as "Le Désert", sand ski races are held here in summer.

The harbour at Les Escoumines, just 35 km (22 mi.) north of Tadoussac on the St Lawrence River, has been a port of call for Basque fishermen since the 17th c. From the middle of the last century it has also been an increasingly important outlet for the timber trade.

Les Escoumines is one of Canada's most popular centres for underwater sports.

Les Escoumines

★Terra Nova National Park

H 20

Province: Newfoundland
Area: about 400 sq. km (154 sq. mi.)

Terra Nova National Park, Superintendent, Glovertown, NF A0G 2L0; tel. (709) 5332801

Information

The Terra Nova National Park on the shores of Bonavista Bay south-east of Gander is a heavily glaciated region of wooded hills and indented coastline, with deep, narrow fiords extending far inland. In spring the coastal waters are dotted with icebergs carried down by the Labrador current. The beaches in the Park are extremely beautiful but the coldness of the water makes them unsuitable for bathing.

Topography

The Park supports a rich and varied wildlife. While animals such as black bear and moose can often be seen from the road others including beaver, red fox, lynx and Canada geese are best observed by taking to the 80 km (50 mi.) of hiking trails.

Fauna

Bluehill Pond Lookout is situated some 9 km (5½ mi.) from the northern entrance of the Park (turn off for the fire tower after about 7 km (4 mi.), continuing for a further 2 km (1¼ mi.)). There are superb panoramic views over the whole Park, with Newman Sound, the Southwest Arm and Alexander Bay all clearly visible.

Bluehill Pond Lookout

To reach Newman Sound head for the Information Office which is about 12 km (7½ mi.) from the Park's northern entrance. The Sound is a deep inlet with low cliffs rising directly from the water. A short walking trail leads along the shore.

Newman Sound

About 23 km (14 mi.) from the north entrance a road branches off to the Ochre Lookout Tower (3 km (2 mi.)). From here there are more panoramic views to be enjoyed over Clode and Newman Sounds. A display at the tower explains how Newfoundland was shaped by Ice Age glaciation.

Ochre Lookout Tower

The Park offers a host of leisure facilities including canoeing, cycling, angling, cross-country skiing, and a 9-hole golf course by the sea. It also boasts some very attractive camp sites.

Leisure facilities

★Thunder Bay

H 13

Province: Ontario
Population: 114,000

Tourism: Thunder Bay, Terry Fox Information Centre, Hwy 11/17 E., Thunder Bay, ON P7C 1M9; tel. (807) 9832041

Information

Thunder Bay, on the north-east shore near the head of Lake Superior, is the furthermost port on the St Lawrence Seaway/Lake Superior accessible to sea-going vessels. It is the primary outlet for grain exported from the Canadian Prairies. Grouped around the docks are a whole series of

Location

gigantic grain elevators and storage silos with a total capacity of about 4 million cu. m. (141 million cu. ft).

History	The city came into being in 1970 with the amalgamation of two existing communities, Port Arthur and Fort William. The latter began life as a trading post in the second half of the 17th c., the former being founded some 200 years later.
★Fort William	Fort William (open mid-May–Sep. daily 10am–4pm) is the reconstruction of an old British fort originally erected in 1816. Situated on the banks of the Kaminiskwia River in south Thunder Bay it comprises some 40 buildings enclosed within exceedingly substantial palisades. Long before the fort was built the site was occupied by a French trading post, and it was from here that Pierre de Varennes set off in 1731 to explore the American West. When possession of Canada passed to the British the post was handed over to the North West Company, serving as the company's headquarters from 1803. Throughout the summer months European and Indian trappers would converge on Fort William to trade their pelts and furs with the "voyageurs" from Montréal (who brought with them all sorts of goods to barter in return).
★Centennial Park	Among the attractions of the spacious Centennial Park in north Thunder Bay (open end of May–beginning Sep. daily 10am–7pm) is the re-creation of a logging camp, complete with log huts, smithy and a canteen serving "loggers' steaks" and other equally "hearty" meals. There is plenty in the park to keep children amused.
Centennial Conservatory	The Centennial Conservatory (Balmoral St./Dease St.; open every afternoon) boasts an incredible variety of plants.
Hillcrest Park	From Hillcrest Park excellent views are obtained over Thunder Bay, the port, and across to the Sleeping Giant (see below).
International Friendship Gardens	The different ethnic groups who have made a new home for themselves in Thunder Bay each find recognition among the flowerbeds of the International Friendship Gardens (Victoria Avenue).
★Art Gallery	Thunder Bay Art Gallery (Confederation College Campus; open Tue.–Sun. afternoons) is mainly devoted to Red Indian art. The impressive collection of pictures, weaving, sculptures and pottery by Indian artists is the equal of any in the country.
Auditorium	Opened in 1985 and acknowledged as one of the best equipped theatres in Canada, the Auditorium (Beverly St./Winnipeg Ave.) stands as a tribute to the city's prosperity.
Canada Games Complex	Thunder Bay's "state of the art" sports complex on Winnipeg Ave. (open every day) includes an Olympic swimming pool and huge water slide.
Historical Museum	Among items of interest in the town's Historical Museum (219 S. May St.; open Tue.–Sun. daily) are examples of Indian art pre-dating the arrival of Europeans. The museum also focuses on the history of navigation and the military history of this central part of Canada.
★★Harbour tour	The opportunity to see at close quarters the impressive installations of the largest grain-handling port in the world (enormous silos, grain elevators, loading bridges, 30,000 grt grain ships, etc.) turns this tour of the harbour into a thoroughly fascinating experience.
Chippewa Park	Chippewa Park on the shores of Lake Superior south of the town (Highway 61B; open end Jun.–beginning Sep.) has a sandy beach as well as a whole range of recreational and pleasure facilities.

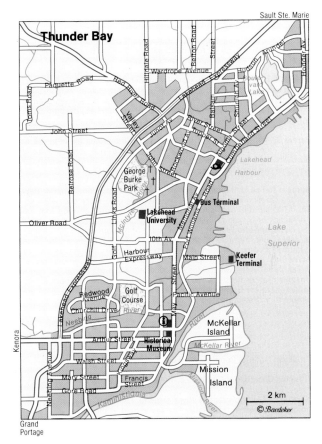

Sault Ste. Marie

Thunder Bay

Wardrope Avenue

Paquette Road

John Street

Lakehead
Harbour

George
Burke
Park

Bus Terminal

Oliver Road

**Lakehead
University**

Lake
Superior

10th Av

Harbour
Expressway

Main Street

**Keefer
Terminal**

Redwood
Avenue

Golf
Course

Pacific Avenue

Churchill Drive

Neebing

McKellar
Island

Arthur Street

**Historical
Museum**

McKellar River

Walsh Street

Mary Street

Francis
Street

**Mission
Island**

Gore Road

Kaministiquia

2 km

© *Baedeker*

Grand
Portage

Kenora

From 183 m (600 ft) up the slopes of Mount Mckay (part of an Ojibwa
Indian reservation on the south side of Thunder Bay) more fine views
are gained over the town.

Mount McKay

The Paipoonge Museum (on the Rosslyn road on the western edge of
the town; open: mid-Apr.–beginning Sept. daily) has memorabilia from
the pioneering days and interesting material relating to the growth of
industry in and around Thunder Bay.

Paipoonge
Museum

There are four excellent ski areas close to Thunder Bay (also two large
ski jumps).

Ski resorts

The 250 sq. km (96 sq. mi.) Sibley Provincial Park occupies most of the
Sibley Peninsula, which juts out into Lake Superior on the east side of
Thunder Bay. Large numbers of black bear, deer, lynx, fox and beaver
still inhabit the heavily ravined and scenically delightful outliers of the
Canadian Shield, the extremities of which lie hidden beneath the waters
of the Lake. The Park is also home to more than 200 species of bird.

★**Sibley
Provincial Park**

Timmins

Sleeping Giant

At the tip of the peninsula the land rises to form the 304 m (1000 ft) hill known as the Sleeping Giant.

★Amethyst mines

A number of open-cast amethyst mines are found in the area between 55 and 75 km (34 and 47 mi.) north-east of Thunder Bay. Local dealers usually have some fine quality stones for sale.

★Ouimet River

About 80 km (50 mi.) north-east of Thunder Bay the Ouimet River has carved a canyon 5 km (3 mi.) long and up to 150 m (490 ft) deep through solid rock. Even in the height of summer snow and ice lingers on in nooks and crannies where sunlight scarcely penetrates, despite which the canyon still manages to support an interesting plantlife.

★Kakabeka Falls

Barely 30 km (19 mi.) west of Thunder Bay the wildly beautiful 33 m (108 ft) high Kakabeka Falls are the show-piece of a small provincial park. The falls form the entrance to a narrow gorge through which the Kaminiskwia River thunders between dark rock walls.

★Quetico Provincial Park

Some distance further west (about 160 km (100 mi.) from Thunder Bay) lies the Quetico Provincial Park. This extends over more than 4500 sq. km (1740 sq. mi.) and is for the most part accessible only on foot, on horseback or by canoe. Belonging geologically to the Canadian Shield the landscape shows all the familiar signs of glaciation with a multitude of lakes and hummocks sculpted by ice from the crystalline Pre-Cambrian bedrock. There are still some black bears around, as well as numerous animals such as otters and beavers (also some ospreys) which thrive in the water-filled environment. Although a stranger might imagine him- or herself transported to a truly primeval northern forest, in fact there are traces of lengthy human occupation. Among them are simple rock drawings of a hunting people and their animal quarry.

Timmins   H 14

Province: Ontario. Population: 48,000

Information

Timmins Chamber of Commerce, Timmins; tel. (705) 3601900

Economy

North-east Ontario's largest town owes its rise more than anything to gold, discovered in the nearby Porcupine field at the beginning of the present century. Not only does output exceed that of all but a few gold producing countries in the world, in addition Timmins boasts one of the world's richest silver and zinc mines. The population, which grew rapidly as a result of the gold strikes, is largely made up of central European, Italian, British, Finnish and Ukrainian immigrants who have helped foster other industries apart from mining, the timber and brewing industries in particular.

Porcupine Outdoor Mining Museum

The Porcupine Outdoor Mining Museum offers an intriguing insight into the daily operations of a mine, and an understanding of mining technology. All kinds of equipment and tools are on display including mine cars and steam-powered track vehicles.

Timmins Gold Mine Tour

This very informative three-hour tour is of an old gold mine about 2 km (14 mi.) off Park Road, together with the old mining settlement of Hollinger Townsite. Guided tours: Jun.–Sep. daily 9.30 and 10.30am and 1.30 and 3pm.

Kettle Lakes Provincial Park

This nature reserve with its many little lakes just 32 km (20 mi.) from Timmins on Highway 101 is an open invitation to anyone keen on canoeing and fishing.

★★Toronto

Province: Ontario
Population: 654,000 (city), 4 million (metropolitan area)

Metropolitan Toronto Convention & Visitors Association, 207 Queen's Quay W., Suite 509, Toronto, ON, M5J 1A7; tel. (416) 2032500.
Free telephone information: tel. 18003631990.
Information kiosks at the Queen's Quay Terminal and the corner of Yonge St. and Dundas St.

Information

Toronto (Indian for "meeting place"), capital of the Canadian province of Ontario (see entry) and the country's leading industrial metropolis, stands on the north-west shore of Lake Ontario (see entry) bordering Toronto Bay. For quite some time now the city has found itself being swept along by a tidal wave of dynamic development, evidenced by the construction of not only numerous hyper-modern skyscrapers but also the highest television tower in the world and the huge sports arena known as the Skydome. In the last two decades the already highly industrialised conurbation has expanded deeper and deeper into what was once its hinterland. The original relatively small city centre is today ringed by a succession of interconnecting fast roads and highways, and one after another new communities spring up along the big main roads leading from the town.

Development

In 1793 the then Governor of Ontario John Graves Simcoe selected the north side of Toronto Bay for the site of a new settlement, to be laid out on the model of a European city. Christened York and made the capital of Upper Canada, the town was subjected to military attack on a number of occasions in the decades which followed.

History

One such occasion was in the spring of 1813 when a fleet belonging to the now independent United States of America bombarded the town. A number of important buildings were destroyed by fire. In retaliation the British burned down part of the US federal capital Washington.

By 1834 the population had risen to almost 10,000 and the burgeoning community on the shores of Lake Ontario was granted civic status. At the same time its name was changed from the English "York" to the Indian "Toronto".

The combination of a good road system and its status as provincial capital soon led to a further rapid increase in the city's population and, in particular, economic growth. The harbour was enlarged and numerous industries established. A second wave of industrialisation starting at the end of the 19th c. gave a particularly strong boost to the economy. By the turn of the century the population had passed the 200,000 mark.

The two World Wars were a further stimulus to Toronto's prosperity. Statistics from the end of the 1950s show as many as 3000 companies with in excess of 120,000 employees. By then the port was handling more than 3500 ships annually, with freight totalling 4 million tonnes/tons.

This present century has also seen Toronto develop into a major cultural centre. The city has two universities, some excellent colleges and a number of leading theatre companies and orchestras. It is justifiably proud of its fine museums and galleries. Its cultural standing is further reflected in its religious life, Toronto being a Catholic archbishopric and seat of the United Ruthenian Church's apostolic exarch for eastern Canada.

Toronto's continuing development has already transformed it economically speaking into by far the most important city in Canada, wielding immense financial influence through its concentration of banks and insurance companies and its stock exchange (the fourth largest in North

Economy

America). Modern industrial plants and factory units representing a wide range of industries (construction, machine and vehicle manufacture, electronics, chemicals, food processing, brewing, textiles, paper manufacture and printing) can be seen all over the city, but especially around the harbour and the airport. The Toronto trade fairs attracts several million visitors every year.

Both Toronto's airport and its seaport are of major economic significance, the latter benefiting from its position on the St Lawrence Seaway, the former from being located at an important junction of routes.

Few cities have a skyline to rival Toronto's – particularly impressive given a bird's eye view and even more striking when seen from the offshore islands which encircle the harbour. The tallest skyscrapers, mostly financed through investment by banks and insurance companies, cluster together in the old city centre, constantly augmented by new ultramodern structures sheathed in aluminium, eloxal and glass. The 553 m (1815 ft) high CN Tower completed in 1976 points skywards like a gigantic antenna, with at its foot the huge arched canopy of the 1989 Skydome (the roof of which can be opened in fine weather).

Skyline

The old city centre, relatively small and rectangular in shape, is laid out on a "grid-iron" pattern. Now known as the "Central Business District" it is bounded by Yonge St. or Church St. (east), Spadina St. (west), Front St. (south) and Bloor St. (north). Two large thoroughfares – Yonge St. and University Ave. (beneath which the city's subway runs) – bisect the CBD from north to south. These are crossed at right angles by several streets and lead to Toronto's main railway station and the harbour. With street by street redevelopment being carried out apace, very few old buildings now remain. The original two-storey stone and timber houses, dating from the settlement's earliest days, have almost entirely disappeared. Even the first generation of skyscrapers are today being replaced by taller, more up-to-date blocks. The only old buildings to have survived this apparently insatiable urge for modernisation are some of the larger, more splendid and historic edifices such as the railway station, the old City Hall, parts of the old University, one or two venerable buildings housing the provincial government, and a few palatial dynastic family mansions. Many of these lovely old buildings are of course almost submerged in the sea of glass and reinforced concrete, as are numerous ageing churches the survival of which is becoming a major cause for concern.

Cityscape

The residential area of Mount Pleasant (Richmond Hill) (pop. 20,000), about 20 km (12 mi.) north of the city centre, is the site of the University of Toronto's David Dunlab Observatory (interesting and worth a visit). The district is also known as Richmond Hill, having been named after the Duke of Richmond in 1819.

Mount Pleasant

Toronto's old waterfront, which until a few years ago was dominated by storage sheds and wholesale warehouses, is now transformed into the 38 ha (94 acre) multipurpose Harbourfront Park. This incorporates everything from hotels to luxury apartments, offices, art galleries, a range of boutiques, shops, restaurants and cafés, theatres, a French cultural centre, a yacht marina (with a sailing school) and the railway museum.

Harbourfront Park

Toronto's huge main railway station belonging to the Canadian National Railway Company was opened in 1927 by the Prince of Wales (later King Edward VIII). Today it stands as a reminder of the vigour of the Canadian economy in the 1920s when vast quantities of rail freight in the form of wheat, timber, cellulose and non-ferrous metals passed through

Union Station

◀ *Toronto: Central Business District*

Toronto Downtown

Prince Arthur Avenue

Charles Street

Gloucester Street

Bloor Street West

Charles Street W.

Royal Ontario Museum

Gardiner Museum

Planetarium

University of Toronto

St. Joseph

Queen's Park

Ontario Houses of Parliament

University of Toronto

Wellesley Street

Maitland Street

YMCA

Maple Leaf Gardens

Allan Gardens

Carlton Street

College Street

YWCA

Ryerson Institute

Gerrard Street

Toronto General Hospital

Board of Education

Mt. Sinai Hospital

CHINA-TOWN

Kensington Market

Dundas Street

Bus Terminal

Trinity Church

Eaton Centre

Mus. for Church Textiles

Moss Park

Swimming Pool

Armouries

Art Gallery of Ontario

Grange

City Hall

Old City Hall

Osgoode Hall

Campbell House

Hudson's Bay Co.

Queen Street

The Arcade

St. James Cathedral

Richmond Street

Adelaide Centre

First Canadian Plaza

Scotia Plaza

St. Lawrence Market

Stock Exchange

Toronto Dominion Centre

Commercial Centre

Royal Alexandra Theatre

St. Andrew

BCE Place

O'Keefe Centre

Canadian Broadcasting Centre

Roy Thomsen Hall

Royal Bank Plaza

Union Station

King Street West

Metro Hall

Convention Centre

Skyway

World Trade Centre

Wellington Street

Front Street

Skydome

CN-Tower

Conference Centre

Westin Harbour Castle

Ferry Terminal

The Esplanade

Lake Shore Boulevard

Harbourfront Park

Queen's Quay

Fort York

Antique Market

Pier 4

York Quay

York Quay Centre

Maple Leaf Quay

John Quay

Inner Harbour

Gardiner Expressway

Lake Shore

Spadina Quay

Bathurst Quay

Alexandra Yacht Club

Toronto Island Air Terminal

Lake Ontario

Wards Island

Gardiner Expressway

Queen's Quay

500 m

© Baedeker

Hanlan's Point   Olympic Island
TORONTO ISLANDS

—○— U-Bahn   ·········· Tramway

Toronto. Passenger traffic, especially holidaymakers travelling by rail, also provided important business until well into the 1950s. Nowadays the station is the terminus for fast inter-city trains from Montréal, Ottawa and New York (via Niagara Falls), as well as express services to the Canadian West and northern Ontario. Recently Union Station became the hub of a local fast transport system serving Toronto and its suburbs.

The declining importance of rail transport in the Toronto area forced the Canadian National Railway Company to find new uses for its growing stock of surplus property. Today the tallest television tower in the world is just one of the buildings which have been erected on what was formerly railway land. A new amusement and shopping area with restaurants has recently opened.

Railway redevelopment

The 553 m (1815 ft) high CN Tower, constructed between 1972 and 1976, can claim to be the tallest building ever. This modern landmark beside Lake Ontario is more than two and half times the height of Stuttgart's television tower (which, built just 20 years earlier, was the prototype of all such towers). About two-thirds of the way up the Tower (335 m (1100 ft)) the seven-story "Skypod" houses the biggest revolving restaurant in the world, and observation platforms from which, in clear weather, views extend for 120 km (75 mi.). On occasions it is even possible to make out the cloud of mist and spray which hangs above the Niagara Falls. Anyone so inclined can take the lift even further up, to the 447 m (1470 ft) high Space Deck, above which rises the Tower's enormous aerial.

★★CN Tower

Being in the Tower during a thunderstorm is particularly dramatic. The view from above as lightning flashes and wind and driving rain rage below, is quite simply awe-inspiring.

Strobe lighting has been installed on the Tower to warn not only approaching aircraft but also birds, especially the many which fly past on migration in spring and autumn.

The Tower also carries a rich assortment of aerials belonging to a host of television, radio and telephone companies.

At the foot of the tower is an amusement park with an interactive multimedia centre. Here visitors can learn about the construction of the tower, try out a flight simulator, watch the film "Cosmic Pinball" in a 360° cinema, and immerse themselves in a variety of virtual reality computer games. Open daily 9am–10pm (Fri. to 11pm).

The Tour of the Universe at the foot of the Tower is very popular with visitors. It simulates a journey into space aboard a replica of the Hermes Space Shuttle.

Tour of the Universe

Immediately adjacent to the CN Tower is Skydome, a massive domed sports arena the roof of which slides back allowing it to be opened in favourable weather. This mega-structure, completed in 1989, is Toronto's answer to the ambitious Olympic Stadium built by its arch rival, Montréal. Skydome can accommodate many thousands of spectators and is a venue for every kind of sport – baseball and football in particular – as well as for rock and pop concerts.

★Skydome

The ultra modern Convention Centre immediately north of the CN Tower was completed within the last three years. This, too, is built on former railway land.

Convention Centre

North again is the new and equally modern Toronto Opera House.

Opera House

Beyond the Opera House the circular Roy Thomson Hall was designed by the famous architect Arthur Erickson. The concert hall is known throughout Canada for the excellence of its acoustics.

Roy Thomson Hall

CN Tower

TECHNICAL DATA

Building begun
1972

Inauguration
1976

Height
553.35m/1816ft
(tallest building in the world)

Weight
143,299 tonnes

Volume of mast
48463 cu.m/1,711,713 cu.ft

Lifting capacity
68,343 tonnes

Viewing platforms
Space Deck (446.5m/
1465ft)
Sky Pad (335.3m/1100ft)

**Range of View (in good
weather)**
south to the Niagara Falls in
the area of Rochester and
New York (USA), north to
Lake Simcoe

Transmitters
6 TV and 8 radio

Stairs
1760 steps

Revolving restaurant
Diameter: 45.75m/150ft
Radius: 137.15m/444ft
Rotation cycle: 90 minutes

Speed of lift
365.75m/1200ft per minute

Frequency of storms
60–80 per annum

Movement in strong winds
Top of tower: 2.5m/8ft
Shaft of tower: 0.25m/
9 inches

© Baedeker

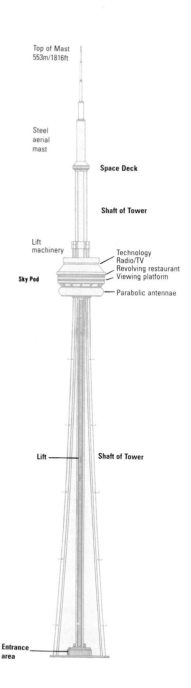

Skydome

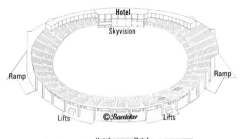

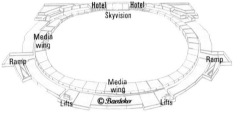

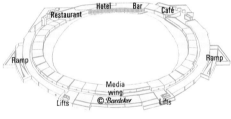

SKYDECK
Level 500
17,506 seats

UPPER SKYBOXES
Level 400
100 suites (2238 seats)

LOWER SKYBOXES
Level 300
61 suites (1180 seats)

SKYCLUB
Level 200
5800 seats

ESPLANADE
Level 100
21,295 seats

Toronto

★Central
Business District

A vast number of commercial, financial and professional institutions and services together with several government agencies are concentrated in the Central Business District (CBD), easily recognised by its towering skyscrapers. Every weekday a multitude of bankers, stockbrokers, insurance and property agents, lawyers and business people join with an army of civil servants to squeeze themselves into this relatively small downtown area. Their reinforced concrete office blocks, encased – some attractively, some rather less so – in glass and eloxal, bear fine sounding names such as the Sun Life Centre (28 storeys), Commerce Court (57 storeys), the Toronto Dominion Centre (designed by Mies van der Rohe and others) and First Canadian Plaza (consisting of the 72-storey Bank of Montréal, the 36-storey Stock Exchange and the massive Sheraton Hotel). Also prominent is the 70-storey Nova Scotia Bank. The majority of these modern high-rise developments have shopping levels with supermarkets selling food and household goods, fashion boutiques, banks, medical practitioners, hairdressers, hi-fi and camera shops and a variety of similar facilities including, of course, cafés, bistros and restaurants.

★Underground

The high-rise office blocks in the CBD are virtually all connected to one another by underground walkways and shopping concourses. Whatever the weather – rain or snow, strong winds or bitter cold – shoppers can make their way dry shod along the 1½ km (1 mi.) from Union St. to Dundas St. (north). Outlets selling all the daily necessities stay open till well into the evening. The large Toronto department stores are also linked into this system of subterranean precincts, and at various points there is access to the big city centre car parks and the subway.

Old City Hall

The Old City Hall (as it is called) stands on the corner of Bay St. and Queen St., a magnificent stone building dating from the end of the 19th c. Following the completion of the new City Hall near by, various

Toronto: Old City Hall ...   *... and New City Hall*

468

branches of the Justice Department (including the Law-Courts) were transferred to the old building.

Dominating the spacious Nathan Philips Square with its bronze sculpture "The Archer" by Henry Moore is the still highly acclaimed new City Hall, designed by the gifted Finnish architect Viljo Revell and built in 1965. It consists of two arc-shaped high-rise blocks (20 and 27 storeys high respectively), wrapped around a lower central building topped by a flattened cupola (housing the chamber in which meetings of the Toronto and Greater Toronto councils are held).

★New City Hall

Anyone taking a car into the city centre for some shopping should make for the huge Eaton Centre at the north end of the CBD. With its own subway station and indoor parking for several hundred cars this ultra-modern shopping complex extends over several blocks and is continually being renovated and enlarged. Strangers can quite easily lose their way in the bewildering maze of department stores, specialist shops, boutiques, restaurants, caféterias and snack bars which crowd the different levels above and below ground. There is hardly a speciality from anywhere in the world which cannot be found for sale here. The original Eaton department store opened in Toronto in 1869. Since then it has grown into an enormous retail business, with branches in all the larger Canadian towns and cities and as well as abroad.

★Eaton Centre

Yonge Street was one of the original streets built by Toronto's founder Governor John Simcoe at the end of the 18th c. Running north to south it is now the city's primary thoroughfare and stays busy day and night. The 2½ km (1½ mi.) section between Bloor St. (north) and the main railway station (south) is a sort of microcosm of the city as a whole, epitomising its dynamism and the unceasing cycle of renewal. Yesterday's "small town" shops and businesses housed in modest old-fashioned premises have today given way to the glitzy shop fronts of the latest in fashionable boutiques, each intent on seducing eager shoppers with plenty of money to spend. By tomorrow these too will probably have been swept away to make room for the next generation of ultra-modern skyscrapers. A huge and immensely varied selection of food and entertainment is available along Yonge St., ranging from the most luxurious of restaurants to the seediest of dives.

Yonge Street

The five-storey red brick and glass encased Metro Toronto Library was completed in 1979, one of architect Raymond Moriyama's acknowledged masterpieces. Mounting a wide-ranging programme of cultural events the library has become a popular focus for the activities of Toronto's middle class intelligentsia.

★Metro Toronto Library

Osgoode Hall (1835–55), a former law-courts situated immediately west of the new City Hall, was named after Upper Canada's first High Court Judge. Its gardens, bounded by heavy iron railings, have a special charm, especially in the spring.

Osgoode Hall

Campbell House (guided tours Mon.–Fri.) once belonged to Sir William Campbell, chief justice of Upper Canada from 1825 to 1829. It was moved to its present site on the west side of University Ave. in 1972. The house is well worth a visit for its 19th c. furnishings and displays on local history.

Campbell House

The renowned Art Gallery of Ontario (AGO) occupies a pleasing modern building on the west side of the city centre.
   The handsome old building in the garden (known as "The Grange", and in which the Art Gallery was formerly housed) was built in 1816/17 by a prosperous New England family. For a time it was a meeting place for the political opponents of William Lyon Mackenzie. The house was restored to its 1830s elegance some years ago.

★Art Gallery of Ontario

Open Tue.–Sun. 11am–5.30pm

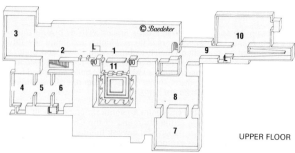

UPPER FLOOR

1 Exhibition Gallery
  (modern art)
2 Walter Trier Gallery
  (temporary exhibitions)
3 Signy Eaton Gallery
  (contemporary collection)

4 J. S. McLean Gallery
  (historical collection)
5 John Ridley Gallery
  (historical collection)
6 Georgia Ridley Gallery
  (historical collection)

7 Zacks Gallery South
8 Zacks Gallery North
9 Irina Moore Gallery
10 Moore Sculpture Centre
11 Members' Lounge
L Lift   00 Toilets

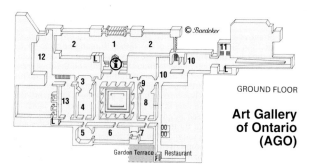

GROUND FLOOR

Art Gallery
of Ontario
(AGO)

1 Main Lobby
2 Gallerie-Boutique
3 Fudger Rotunda
4 Fudger Gallery
  (old masters)
5 F. P. Wood Gallery
6 E. R. Wood Gallery
  (old masters)

7 Laidlaw Gallery
8 Leonard Gallery
  (19th and 20th c.
  modern art)
9 Leonard
  Rotunda
10 Gallery of
   Contemporary Art

11 Moore Atrium
12 Edward P. Taylor
   Audio-Visual Centre
13 Margaret Eaton Gallery
   (prints and drawings)

L Lift
00 Toilets

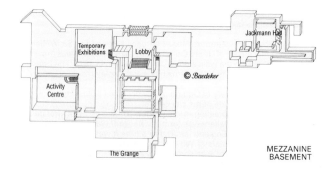

MEZZANINE
BASEMENT

A whole series of temporary exhibitions are mounted throughout the year by this exceptionally well endowed gallery. There are three main collections – Canadian art, European art and sculptures by Henry Moore.

Collections

The collection of Canadian paintings is particularly impressive. The work of the early Québécois painters is well represented, as is that of Cornelius Krieghoff, Tom Thomson and the Group of Seven, Emily Carr, David Milne and Paul Peele. Contemporary Canadian artists are accorded special attention.

Paintings by old and modern masters alike feature in the European collection. Included are works by Pieter Brueghel the Younger, Tintoretto, Rembrandt, Frans Hals, Gainsborough, Van Gogh, Monet, Gauguin, Dégas, Renoir and Picasso.

European

The Gallery has a complete wing devoted to the English sculptor Henry Moore, more than a dozen of whose large bronzes are on display. Sketches, lithographs and miniatures offer illuminating insight into the creative genesis of his work.

Henry Moore

Toronto's Chinatown occupies the district immediately north and west of the Art Gallery of Ontario, extending along Dundas St. and into some of the adjacent side streets. Crowding together into this small area are people from every part of East and South-east Asia, some of whom are the descendents of Chinese contract workers but many others being more recent arrivals from Hongkong and Vietnam. At all hours the place buzzes with commercial activity, the selection of goods in the innumerable shops being correspondingly wide. All the delicious aromas of the orient waft from the restaurants and snack bars.

Chinatown

Kensington Market is situated on the far side of the Dundas St./Spadina Ave. intersection in a district peopled at one time by newly arrived Jewish and other European immigrants, the latter mainly from southern Europe and the Balkans. Later they were joined by members of Toronto's Portuguese community and today the area between Spadina Ave. and Augusta St. is home to immigrants and "tourists" from every corner of the globe. From the very beginning this formerly residential suburb seems to have evolved a lifestyle of its own, with a motley selection of colourful little shops, flower stands, pleasant bars, cafés and snack bars. During the year the Asian community holds a number of lively celebrations.

★Kensington Market

The market itself, some of whose traders seem to deal in a highly exotic assortment of wares, is open Mon.–Sat. 7am–7pm.

Running north–south along the west side of the CBD parallel to Yonge St., University Ave. passes through Toronto's university quarter and the district which houses Ontario's provincial parliament.

University Avenue

In addition to a great many government buildings the Avenue is also the site of several scientific institutions and clinics. North of Queen's Park are a number of important museums.

The Royal Ontario Museum (open daily 10am–6pm) on the corner of University Ave. and Bloor St. W. ranks high on the list of places of interest in Toronto. Unusually for such a museum it brings together a series of outstanding collections in the fields of both science and the arts.

★★Royal Ontario Museum

The opening section "Mankind Discovering" is an imaginatively presented introduction to the work of a museum. It traces in a clear and informative way all the stages from the moment a "find" is uncovered to the time it is labelled and then eventually goes on display.

Collections

The natural history section concentrates primarily on the evolution of life on earth. Among its highlights are a superb display of dinosaur

Royal Ontario Museum (ROM)

GROUND FLOOR

G Cloakroom
R Escalator
W Temporary exhibitions
00 Toilets

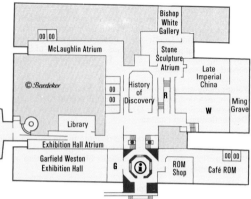

FIRST BELOW

1 ROM Theatre
2 Creative Arts Studio
3 European musical instruments
4 Portraits
5 Canadiana
6 Pre-history of Ontario
7 Toy Boutique

G Cloakroom
R Escalator
00 Toilets

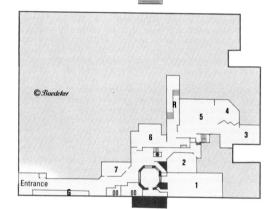

SECOND BELOW

1, 2, 3, 4 Instruction rooms

Discovery Gallery
Here items from the museumn
can be examined. Minimum
age for visitors 7 years

00 Toilets

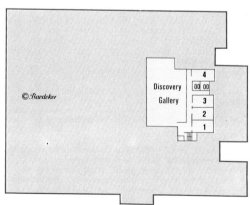

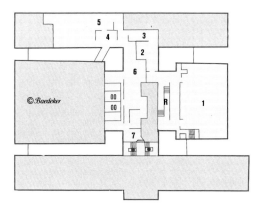

1 Caravans and Clipper Ships
   (History of East–West trade)
2 Egypt and Mesopotamia
3 Near East
4 Etruscans
5 Greeks
6 Romans
7 Islamic civilisation

R Escalator
00 Toilets

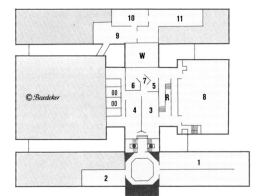

SECOND FLOOR

1 Dinosaurs
2 Fossils
3 Evolution
4 Reptiles
5 Botany
6 Arthropods
7 Living invertebrates
8 Interdisciplinary Gallery
9 Forest
10 Bat cave
11 Mammals

R Escalator
W Temporary exhibitions
00 Toilets

skeletons and a series of fascinating wildlife dioramas (including some featuring mammals native to Ontario).

Also of great interest are the museum's gem collection and the sections devoted to the pre- and early history of Ontario (with e.g. Indian rock drawings) and the period since the arrival of the first Europeans. Then there are the exhibitions on the Mediterranean World (including the civilisations of ancient Egypt, Greece and Rome) and European decorative crafts since the 17th c., each occupying several rooms. Many rewarding hours could be spent just looking round the wonderfully comprehensive textiles section and the small collection of musical instruments!

The Royal Ontario Museum is known throughout the world for its magnificent Far East collection of Chinese art covering four millennia – from the Shang Dynasty (c. 1500 BC), through the Tang Dynasty (7th to 10th c. AD) and Ming Dynasty (14th to 17th c.) right up to the period of the Manchu Emperors (early 20th c.). Wonderful examples of religious (temple) art are displayed alongside exquisite ceramic figures and superb vases. Normally the centre of attention in this section of the museum is the arresting ceramic figure of "Yen Lo Wang", King of the Underworld. Also quite exceptional however is the Ming tomb (17th c.).

★★ Far Eastern
Collection

The special exhibition on Imperial China since the 10th c. succeeds brilliantly in bringing its subject to life.

★Bishop White Gallery

On display in the Bishop White Gallery are some huge Chinese temple paintings. The largest, a Buddhist work, dates from about 1320.

McLaughlin Planetarium

Adjoining the main museum on its south side is the McLaughlin Planetarium and Astrocentre.

★Gardiner Museum of Ceramic Art

Situated opposite the Royal Ontario Museum and definitely worth a visit, the Museum of Ceramic Art (open Tue.–Sun. 10am–6pm) owes its existence to a pair of private collectors, Mr and Mrs George Gardiner. On exhibition are objets d'art representing over four thousand years of mankind's creativity, including American pottery from the Pre-Columbian period (e.g Nazca, Peru and Mexico), European porcelain (e.g. Delft, Meissen, Vienna, Sèvres and various British manufacturers) and Italian Majolica. Also rather special is a delightful series of "Commedia dell'arte" figurines.

Queen's Park

A short distance south of the Royal Ontario Museum lies the spacious and beautifully maintained Queen's Park, dominated by the Neo-Gothic outline of the Ontario Parliament buildings (1885–92). Guided tours are organised during the summer recess and at other times by arrangement.

Government buildings

East of the Parliament are more provincial government buildings.

Canadian decorative arts collection

Housed in a building just to the west of the Ontario Parliament this quite exceptional collection of "Canadiana" (open daily 10am–5pm) includes splendid items of Colonial period furnishings and furniture brought together from all over eastern Canada. There are also some very fine works by Canadian artists (e.g. portraits of Generals Montcalm and Wolfe, adversaries in that famous battle fought on Québec's Plains of Abraham in 1759).

Yorkville

The tastefully redeveloped district of Yorkville with its many high-class boutiques, galleries and elegant restaurants extends northwards from Bloor St. Hazelton Lanes and the nearby Cumberland Court represent luxury shopping at its most stylish.

Spadina Avenue

Spadina Ave. runs north-south along the western side of the city centre.

★Spadina Mansion

Dating from the 1880s and restored only a few years ago the splendid old Spadina Mansion (Spadina Ave. 285; at the north-western extremity of the city centre) now belongs to the Toronto Historical Society. There are guided tours daily.

★Casa Loma

Standing in beautifully kept grounds just across the Avenue from Spadina Mansion, Casa Loma is an extraordinary building somewhat reminiscent of a medieval castle. It was originally constructed for Sir Henry Pellatt, an eccentric Canadian multi-millionaire who was among the first to recognise and exploit the money-making potential of the Niagara Falls.
With close to 100 rooms (including three dozen bathrooms) the house is now a museum (open daily).

★Old Fort York

Located at the south-western end of what used to be a huge block of CNR-owned land, Old Fort York now finds itself penned in between the railway line and the Gardiner Expressway. The original fort, built by Governor Simcoe in 1793, was destroyed by US forces in 1813. It was quickly rebuilt but soon lost any strategic importance.

Inside the fort (open: end May–Sept.) is a small museum devoted to its history. During the main tourist season military parades are held in period uniform.

Beyond the Gardiner Expressway lies Toronto's exhibition site.

The Marine Museum of Upper Canada in the surviving part of the old Stanley Barracks is an interesting source of information about navigation on the Great Lakes and the St Lawrence River.

Ontario Place (open: Victoria Day–Labour Day) is a large and inviting pleasure park and recreation area. It occupies a number of man-made islands close offshore to the south-west of the Exhibition Grounds. As well as a wide range of amusements for youngsters the facilities include a marina, various restaurants and shops, neat gardens, a large open-air theatre (where e.g. pop concerts are held), a six-storey Cinesphere and a captivating Children's Village.

Now permanently berthed at Ontario Place and always a popular attraction with visitors is the destroyer HMCS "Haida" which saw service in the Second World War and Korean War.

What few traces remain of Toronto's predecessor York are largely to be found in the area just to the east of the Central Business District. In addition to one or two elderly churches, and the St Lawrence covered market, the "Old Town" has some rather pleasant places at which to eat.

The O'Keefe Centre (close to Union Station) is a theatre with a long established reputation for the performing arts.

Also worth visiting in the Old Town is the modest Bond Street home of William Lyon Mackenzie, Toronto's first mayor and leader of the "Upper Canada Rebellion". Open daily.

The ferry trip from Queen's Quay Terminal to the Toronto Islands (about a kilometre offshore) is the prelude to a thoroughly enjoyable outing. There are lovely walks on the islands, and the opportunity for rowing, sailing, swimming, etc. or simply to relax. One or two marinas and the odd cluster of weekend homes bring a touch of variety to the scene. In summer the islands are the venue for numerous open-air events, including the occasional Indian pow-wow.
In favourable visibility there is a stunning view of the Toronto skyline.

The Ontario Science Centre (open daily) occupies a site overlooking the Don Valley, about 10 km (6 mi.) north-east of the city centre. Designed by the virtuoso architect Raymond Moriyama this extremely modern building was completed in 1969. Visitors to the Centre are brought face to face with the latest developments in e.g. laser technology, telecommunications, optics, biology, atomic physics, space travel and meteorology, all presented in an absorbing and imaginative way. The emphasis is very much on visitor participation, with many inter-active displays and widespread use of suitably installed computing and other equipment.

Toronto's huge zoo with its collection of several thousand animals is situated on the Red River some 40 km (25 mi.) north-east of the city centre. In concept the zoo is similar to Munich Zoo (though on a very much larger scale) and is divided into four sections, each representing a major region of the globe. The North American section is unique, enthralling the visitor with its spacious grizzly bear enclosure, vast bison park and impressive polarium, etc.

Toronto

Skyline of Toronto

★Black Creek Pioneer Village

The farm making up the nucleus of Black Creek Pioneer Village (about 30 km (19 mi.) north-west of the city centre and well worth a visit) originally belonged to a Dutch Pennsylvanian of German extraction who settled here in the early 19th c. The village consists of more than two dozen homesteads and other buildings (including a mill, cartwrights shop and smithy). Some are original, some rebuilt and some are replicas. Together they provide a fascinating glimpse of pioneer life during the last century, with costumed museum staff demonstrating the old crafts and re-enacting everyday scenes from those far-off times. Visitors can even sample some of the exceptionally tasty food enjoyed by the early pioneers.

Canada's Wonderland

Also about 30 km (19 mi.) north-west of the city centre is Canada's Wonderland. The theme park's many attractions make for an enjoyable family day out.

Kleinburg

Kleinburg is a small town situated about 40 km (25 mi.) north-west of the city centre in the wooded Humber Valley.

★★McMichael Collection

Anyone with an interest in art will certainly wish to see the McMichael Collection which is located here. Although started only a few decades ago, the collection encompasses a wide range of works by Canadian artists, including Tom Thomson and the Group of Seven, Emily Carr, David Milne, Lawren Harris and Clarence Gagnon. Also noteworthy are sculptures by North-west Coast Indians, and Inuit carvings and lithographs.

★Ontario Agricultural Museum

Ontario's Agricultural Museum (open mid-May–Sep.) is to be found a few kilometres/miles south of the international airport.

Mississauga

Devotees of contemporary architecture make pilgrimages to Mississauga (15 km (9 mi.) south-west of the city centre) from all over the world, drawn by its striking post-modernist City Hall. Constructed a few years ago, the distinctive complex with its clock tower, rotunda, large hall and office wing was designed by architects Jones & Kirkland and is now considered the finest expression of modern Canadian architecture.

★City Hall

Trois-Rivières

H 16

Province: Québec. Population: 115,000

See Québec (Province)

Information

Trois-Rivières was founded in 1634 when Sieur de Laviolette built a fort to regulate the fur trade in the Saint-Maurice Valley and protect the local Indians from raids by the Iroquois. The settlement flourished and was the home of some famous pioneer explorers, including, for example, La Vérendrye. When first established the iron smelting works here (see below) was the only industry in the whole colony. Exploitation of the great forests to the north of town began this century, transforming the economic outlook of the area.

Trois-Rivières takes its name from the once wild Saint-Maurice River, which divides into three island-separated channels before flowing into the St Lawrence. The delta still survives today, but hydro-electric schemes have tamed the river's rapids and falls. With water and timber both in plentiful supply, paper manufacturing has prospered on a vast scale and the town is often referred to as the "newsprint capital of the world".

Quite apart from its thriving modern industries Trois-Rivières has also managed to preserve something of its past, particularly in the "old" quarter near the river. The beautifully restored Manoir Boucher de Niverville, built in 1729, was originally the residence of the town's first seigneur. Now, in addition to a couple of rooms of old French-Canadian spruce furniture and works of art, it houses the local tourist office (168 rue Bonaventure, tel. (819) 375–9628).

Standing next to the Manoir is a statue of the town's most illustrious citizen, Maurice Duplessis, Prime Minister of Québec from 1936 to 1939 and again from 1944 to 1959.

The archaeological museum belonging to the University of Québec is also worth visiting (3351 Blvd. des Forges).

Truro

H 18

Province: Nova Scotia. Population: 12,000

Truro Tourist Office; tel. (902) 8956328

Information

Situated near the mouth of the Salmon River at the extreme head of the funnel-shaped Bay of Fundy, the small town of Truro experiences the highest tides in the world (normally around 15 m (49 ft) but reaching heights of up to 21 m (69 ft) at spring tides!).

Today Truro is a highly industrialised town with agricultural and teacher training colleges.

Truro, or "Cobéquid" as its Acadian inhabitants called it, was first settled in the 17th c. When the Acadians were deported in the mid-18th c. they were replaced by incoming settlers from Northern Ireland. These were later joined by Loyalists from New Hampshire (in the US) and new immigrants from Scotland.

History

The several hundred hectare (acre) Victoria Park is a favourite place to relax, retaining something of the wild with its delightful little streams and romantic ravines. People also come to swim, jog and picnic.

Victoria Park

Upper Canada Village

★★Tidal bore
The twice daily tidal bore on the River Salmon makes a marvellous natural spectacle. The river level can rise a metre in just five minutes and reaches high water mark (15 m (49 ft)) within an hour. The phenomenon is particularly dramatic at spring tides when the water can rise as high as 21 m (69 ft). These huge tides are responsible for some very striking coastal scenery in the Truro area.

Suggested route

Minas Basin
From Truro it is possible to combine drives by car to the Northumberland Strait and the Minas Basin (coal mining district) in a very pleasant circular tour.

Parrsboro
From Truro follow Highway 2 westwards for about 100 km (60 mi.). The road runs along the north side of the Minas Basin, crossing the slopes of the Cobequid Mountains to Parrsboro (population 2000). Here, in addition to the impressive tides which characterise this arm of the Bay of Fundy (see entry), agates and amethysts can also be found.

Springhill
From Parrsboro the route heads north for 35 km (22 mi.) to the former mining town of Springhill (population 5000). Set in the midst of delightful scenery the town is nevertheless the centre of what was once a coal mining district, the history of which is recorded in Springhill's mining museum (open May–Oct. 10am–6pm).

Amherst
30 km (19 mi.) or so beyond Springhill the pleasantly green city of Amherst (pop. 10,000) stands at the "gateway" to Nova Scotia. Amherst evolved from a former Acadian settlement founded in the 17th c. beside a Micmac Indian village. When English-speaking colonists took over in 1760 it was renamed after Baron Amherst, the British general who captured Montréal in that year and later became Governor of the US state of Virginia.

Today Amherst is a lively industrial town (e.g agricultural machinery, railway).

★★Upper Canada Village   J 15

Province: Ontario

Access
Hwy. 2 (eastbound) from Morrisburg, exit to Hwy. 401 at Upper Canada Road for Cryslers Farm Battlefield Park.

"Living history" is a speciality of the Canadian museum service and Upper Canada Village near Morrisburg is one of the most outstanding and fascinating examples of the technique which involves faithfully reproducing a period from the past in every living detail. Many of the buildings in the village came from sites in the old St Lawrence Valley condemned to extinction by the great new inland waterway. Now re-erected here they convey all the appearance and atmosphere of a real 19th c. community, a community which has progressed over the years between 1780 and 1867 through the efforts of its white settler inhabitants.

Upper Canada Village very vividly re-creates the everyday lives of people in the St Lawrence Valley from the beginnings of settlement and the initial cultivation of the land to the first phase of industrialisation.

Tour

Entrance
A bridge and a gate lead into the museum village.

The village has 35 houses in all. These range from simple timber shacks built by fur trappers and pioneer settlers to homely farmsteads, brick-built houses exuding solid middle-class comfort, and the refined elegance of a Greek Revival villa.

Everything a 19th c. community would have possessed in the way of public buildings is reproduced here – schools, an Anglican church, shops, bar and even a doctor's surgery; likewise tradesmen's premises – bakery, smithy and sawmill.

A great bustle of activity prevails in the streets and houses of Upper Canada Village. Dressed of course in the costumes of the day, the "villagers" go about their routine daily business (visitors are welcome to join in if they feel so inclined).

The Asselstine Factory is a reconstruction of a textile mill. Regular demonstrations are given showing how cloth was manufactured in the early days of industrialisation.

Life on a 19th c. North American farm is portrayed in detail, all kinds of authentic farmyard activities being carried out for real.

In Willard's Hotel the meals as well as the architecture are in the style of the 1850s.

Anyone wanting to try out the transport of the time can venture on a boat trip or take a drive in a horse-drawn carriage.

Daily from mid-May to mid-Oct. 9.30am to 5pm. Admission fee.

Vallée Richelieu   H 16

Province: Québec

From its source in Lac Champlain, south-east of Montréal, the Rivière Richelieu winds its way northwards to enter the St Lawrence at Sorel. The 130 km (80 mi.) long river played a significant role in the history of both New France and New England, but even before the arrival of Europeans it was a busy trade route and communications corridor for the Indians. During the period of Anglo-French conflict, especially the years between 1754 and 1763, the Richelieu gave the warring nations and their Indian allies two-way access to the area east of Montréal. Only a few information boards along the river's course now recall those troubled times; today the quite delightful Richelieu Valley is the preserve of tourists and others in search of relaxation.

Sights

Boucherville still has a large number of 18th c. houses, among which are La Chaumière (416 rue Ste-Famille; built 1741), the Manoir Pierre-Boucher (468–470 Bd. Marie-Victorin) and the Maison Lafontaine (1780). In addition the church of St-Famille possesses some of the finest wood carvings in the whole of Canada, including side altars (dated 1808) by Louis Amable Quévillon and a 1745 tabernacle by Gilles Bolvin.

The small industrial town of Sorel is situated at the confluence of the Richelieu and the St Lawrence. It owes its name to an officer of the Carignan-Salières Regiment engaged in the 1665–66 campaign against the Iroquois. At that time Sorel was an important forward post for the French. Between 1781 and 1830 the Manoir des Gouverneurs (rue du

Roi) served as a summer residence for a succession of governors of Canada.

St-Ours   St-Ours, founded in 1672, is the region's oldest parish after Sorel.

Mont-St-Hilaire   Mont-St-Hilaire nestles at the foot of a hill bearing the same name. The town is best known for its orchards while the hill, 411 m (1350 ft) high and volcanic in origin, offers splendid views across to Lake Champlain and the US states of New York and Vermont.

Chambly   Chambly, another industrial town, lies on the edge of the Montréal plain. Its principal tourist attraction is the well-preserved Fort St-Louis, steeped in 18th c. French colonial history. The stone fort was built in 1709, replacing the wooden fortifications constructed earlier by Jacques de Chambly in 1655. In 1760 the fort fell to the British, and in 1775 to the Americans. It was used to hold American prisoners of war during the 1812–14 conflict and in 1837–38 Québécois "Patriotes" were also interned here. Open May–Sep. Tue.–Sun. 10am–5.30pm.

★★Vancouver   H 6

Province: British Columbia
Altitude: 0–12 m (40 ft)
Population: 450,000 (Vancouver City), 1.8 million (Vancouver Metropolitan Area).

Information   Vancouver Travel Information Centre, Suite Pavilion, Four Bentall Centre, 1055 Dunsmuir Street, PO Box 49296, Vancouver B.C. V7X 1L3; tel. (604) 6832000.

Access   By plane:
Most of the major airlines fly to Vancouver. The International Airport is on Sea Island (Richmond), about 11 km (7 mi.) south of the city centre.
    Airport buses depart for the city centre from Level 2.
    There are regular flights by seaplane between Vancouver (city centre: Seaplane Terminal in Coal Harbour) and Victoria (Inner Harbour).

By rail:
VIA Rail: Vancouver–Banff–Calgary–Winnipeg or Vancouver–Jasper–Edmonton–Winnipeg (CN Station, 1150 Station St., at the eastern end of False Creek).

BC Rail: North Vancouver–Whistler–Lillooet–Prince George (BC Rail Terminal, 1131 W. 1st St.). From Prince George there are connections to Prince Rupert and Edmonton.

By coach:
Inter-City Bus Depot (150 Dunsmuir St.), Greyhound, Pacific Coach Lines (Vancouver–Victoria), Maverick Coach Lines (Vancouver–Seattle Int. Airport; Vancouver–Nanaimo; Vancouver–Whistler; Vancouver–Sunshine Coast).

City transport:
Vancouver Regional Transit System: buses to all suburbs.
    SkyTrain: (ALRT=Advanced Light Rapid Transit), a fully automated urban rail system covering the 22 km (14 mi.) between Waterfront Station (downtown Vancouver) and New Westminster. (The track runs underground in the inner city area.)
    SeaBus: (passenger ferry) across Burrard Inlet to North Vancouver.

Vancouver, the commercial (though not the administrative) capital of British Columbia, lies in Canada's extreme south-west corner, only 40 km (25 mi.) from the US border. It has the reputation of being one of the most beautiful cities in the world. Downtown Vancouver is superbly situated on a peninsula in the Strait of Georgia, bounded to the north by Burrard Inlet, a deep fiord reaching far inland, and to the south by the delta of the Fraser River. Curbing any westward expansion are the sandy beaches of the Pacific coast and the Strait of Georgia, to the west of which rise the mountains of Vancouver Island and the Olympic Peninsula. Further to the north, beyond Burrard Inlet, gleam the often snow-covered ranges of the Coast Mountains.

Location

With its relatively equable climate keeping temperatures mild throughout the year and its delightful surroundings, extensive parks, green spaces and busy cultural life, Vancouver is a paradise for leisure activities.

Vancouver today

In the last 20 years increasing numbers of skyscrapers, bank and insurance company offices, apartment blocks and hotels have sprung up in the city centre, many of them incorporating modern shopping precincts – the clearest possible sign of the city's economic vitality.

Vancouver today is Canada's gateway west (i.e. to the Far East), the country's access route to the markets of Asia. As such it is the premier port on Canada's Pacific coast, in addition to being a financial, industrial and cultural centre. Even so Vancouver remains a thoroughly attractive city, with a downtown area easily explored on foot. The city also reflects the diverse origins of its inhabitants with many an echo of other parts of Canada and of Europe, Asia and the USA (Vancouver's Chinatown is the second largest of any west coast city in America). Concealed among the gleaming tower blocks and modern building complexes are some delightful shopping streets (Robson St., Granville St., Denman St.), while Gastown, the oldest district, has recently been carefully restored and turned into a major tourist attraction.

Opposite downtown Vancouver, across Burrard Inlet, stretch the extensive residential suburbs of North and West Vancouver. Immediately beyond them, just a few minutes by car from the bustling city centre, British Columbia's untamed wilderness begins – a vast area of forest untouched by all but the timber companies. There are good, properly surfaced roads only along the coast (Hwy. 101) and along the shores of Howe Sound (Hwy. 99) to Whistler, an increasingly popular holiday resort.

Research suggests that the Vancouver area was already inhabited thousands of years before the start of the Christian era. Archaeologists now believe that the Fraser Estuary was a centre of the Pacific Coast Indian fishing culture.

History

Prior to the coming of Europeans the land on the southern shores of the Strait of Georgia was occupied by the Salish tribe of Coast Indians. The first recorded arrival of a white man was in 1791 when the Spaniard José Navéz sailed into and explored English Bay. A year later he was followed by an Englishman, Captain George Vancouver, seeking the elusive Northwest Passage. For a time after that only fur hunters and trappers penetrated to these western shores, but in 1808 Simon Fraser, travelling overland, reached the Fraser Estuary, having followed the river all the way from the Rocky Mountains. Even then, when gold diggers passed through on their way to the Cariboo Mountains in 1858, there was still no permanent settlement in the area. It was only later in the 1860s that, first lumberjacks and other frontiersmen, and then settlers, finally established themselves on the peninsula. In 1886, by which time the population was still barely 2000, Vancouver was officially declared a town – only to be destroyed by fire the same year.

Boom time came when the Canadian Pacific railway reached Burrard Inlet, eventually transforming Vancouver into North America's principal

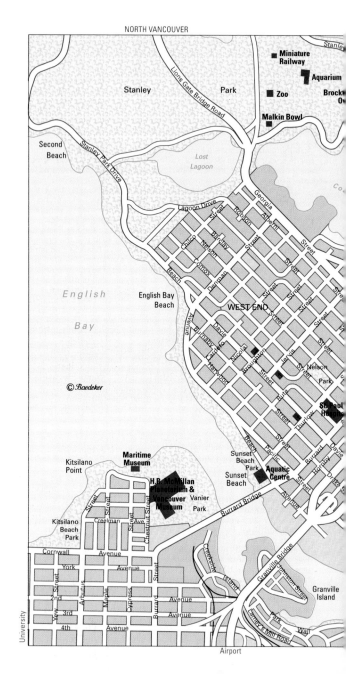

NORTH VANCOUVER

Stanley

Lions Gate Bridge Road

Stanley   Park

Miniature
Railway

Aquarium

Zoo

Brock
Ov

Malkin Bowl

Second
Beach

Stanley Park Drive

Lost
Lagoon

Co

Lagoon Drive

Georgia
Street

Robson
Street

Alberni
Street

Street

Chilco

Nelson
Barclay

Comox

Denman

English
Bay

English Bay
Beach

WEST END

Street

Street

Street

Beach Avenue

Davie

Cardero

Harwood

Nicola

Broughton

Jervis

St.
Street

Nelson
Park

© Baedeker

Bute
Street

Thurlow

St. Paul
Hospita

Maritime
Museum

Kitsilano
Point

Sunset
Beach
Park

Beach

Pacific

Burrard

Sunset
Beach

Aquatic
Centre

Highway

Drake

H.R. McMillan
Planetarium &
Vancouver
Museum

Vanier
Park

Street

Avenue

Kitsilano
Beach
Park

Creelman
Ave

Chestnut Street

Burrard Bridge

Cornwall   Avenue

York   Avenue

Creekside

Granville Bridge

Johnston Street

Granville
Island

Arbutus

1st
Street

Maple

Cypress

Burrard

Avenue

Johnston Street

2nd

3rd

Avenue

Burrard's Mill Road

Park

Wall

University

Vine
Street

4th   Avenue

Airport

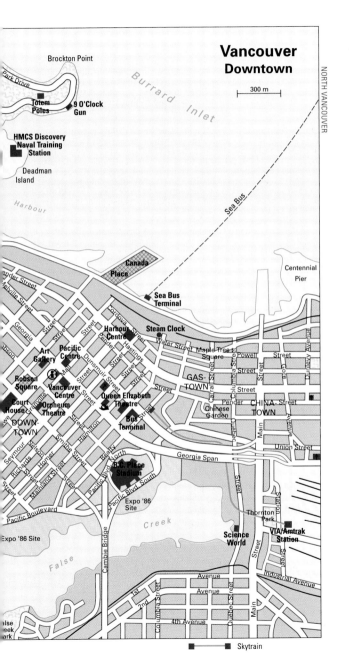

Vancouver
Downtown

300 m

NORTH VANCOUVER

Brockton Point

Burrard Inlet

Park Drive

Totem Poles

9 O'Clock Gun

HMCS Discovery Naval Training Station

Deadman Island

Harbour

Sea Bus

Canada Place

Centennial Pier

Sea Bus Terminal

ander Street

Melville Street

Georgia

Robson

Street

Street

Street

Cordova Street

Harbour Centre

Steam Clock

Water Street

Maple Tree Square

Powell Street

Street

Art Gallery

Pacific Centre

Pender Street

Hastings Street

Dunsmuir Street

Street

GAS-TOWN

Cambie Street

Columbia Street

Carrall Street

Street

Dunlevy Avenue

Robson Square

Vancouver Centre

Street

Street

Pender Street

CHINA-TOWN

Court House

Orpheum Theatre

Granville

Queen Elizabeth Theatre

Chinese Garden

Main

Avenue

Union Street

DOWN-TOWN

Seymour

Richards

Howe

Hornby

Smithe Street

Hamilton

Beatty

Bus Terminal

Georgia Span

Street

Street

Street

Street

Mainland Street

Street

Pacific Blvd North

B.C. Place Stadium

Quebec Street

Richards

Street

Pacific Boulevard

Pacific Blvd South

Expo '86 Site

Creek

Thornton Park

Science World

VIA/Amtrak Station

Street

Industrial Avenue

Expo '86 Site

Cambie Bridge

False

Creek

1st

2nd

Columbia Street

Avenue

Avenue

Quebec Street

Main

4th Avenue

alse reek ark

Skytrain

483

Vancouver

Pacific coast port (today handling 50 million tonnes/tons a year). The major exports are mineral ore, cellulose, and timber, mainly bound for Asia. Long freight trains also bring wheat from Canada's prairie provinces to Vancouver for onward shipment.

In just 100 years Vancouver has grown to become the third largest metropolitan area in Canada, a conurbation whose inhabitants number 1.4 million. Almost half the population of British Columbia now live here at the mouth of the Fraser River. In addition to overseas trade and the service industries, wood processing and fishing are also economically important.

★★Stanley Park

Situated on a small peninsula immediately west of the city centre Stanley Park is a 405 ha (1000 acre) park-cum-nature reserve with a host of sights and leisure facilities including a zoo and an aquarium. Particularly on the western side of the peninsula there are numerous huge, centuries-old, red cedar and Douglas fir trees. Being earmarked for use if repairs were needed to sailing ships of the British navy, they escaped the woodcutter's axe and saw. The park, now criss-crossed by more than 80 km (50 mi.) of trails and roads, was handed over to the then new town of Vancouver in 1888 by the Governor General of Canada, Lord Stanley.

Seawall promenade

Coal Harbour (where a small coal seam was discovered in the 19th c.) is the start of an 11 km (7 mi.) walk/cycle ride along the top of the low sea wall encircling the peninsula. One splendid view follows another – of Vancouver's towering skyline, of Burrard Inlet with shipping inward and outward bound, and across First Narrows to North Vancouver and the mountains beyond.

Scenic Drive

The one-way, about 10 km (6 mi.) Scenic Drive round the park begins from Georgia St., branching off past Coal Harbour with its view of the Vancouver Rowing and Yacht Club.

View from Stanley Park of the skyline of Vancouver

"Discovery", the ship in which Captain George Vancouver surveyed the waters around Vancouver Island in 1792, is now permanently berthed at Deadman's Island (naval base). | Deadman's Island

From Halleluja Point there is a very fine view of downtown Vancouver.

Standing almost opposite are the famous Stanley Park totem poles, the work of various North-west Coast Indian tribes. The oldest erected herewere acquired by the city in 1912. Also worth seeing is the more than 100 year-old Nootka canoe. | Totem poles

Every day without fail an old cannon known as the 9 O'Clock Gun is fired from its position near the tip of Brockton Point. Manufactured in England in 1815 it was brought to Vancouver in the late 19th c. and used to be fired at 6pm to signal the end of the fishing day. | Brockton Point

From Brockton Point (lighthouse) there are fine views of the Lions Gate Bridge and the port of Vancouver. The cross commemorates the victims of a 1906 shipwreck.

Adding a touch of history at another viewpoint is a replica of a figurehead from the Canadian Pacific Line's "Empress of Japan". The ship plied the Pacific Ocean between Vancouver and east Asian ports from 1891 to 1922. A rock at the water's edge in front of the figurehead provides the setting for Vancouver's equivalent of the Copenhagen Mermaid, although Elek Imredy's Canadian girl, sports a wet suit. | "Empress of Japan"

The walk to attractive Beaver Lake (so-called because it was once home to a beaver colony) is well worth the effort. In summer the lake, the only natural freshwater lake in the park and haunt of herons and trumpeter swans, is a mass of variously coloured waterlilies. | Beaver Lake

Only a few metres from Prospect Point (at the north-western tip of the peninsula) the Lions Gate Bridge spans First Narrows, linking North Vancouver to the city centre. Both the bridge and the nearby totem pole date from 1939. The pole was carved by Chief Joe Capilano and commemorates George Vancouver's original meeting with the Salish Indians in 1792. | Prospect Point

From the "Hollow Tree", a partly hollow red cedar estimated to be between 800 and 1000 years old (about 1 km (½ mi.) beyond Prospect Point) walking trails lead to Third Beach (very popular in summer) and Shiwash Rock lying close offshore. | Hollow Tree

As recently as 1945 Ferguson Point, another "look-out", was the site of some important military installations. The Teahouse restaurant, formerly the CO's quarters, is a great favourite on account of its views. | Ferguson Point

Second Beach is a much frequented part of Vancouver. In 1912 sand dredged from False Creek was used to build up the beach and bathing huts were erected. Today the large swimming pool and wide range of leisure facilities draw crowds of visitors. | Second Beach

Prior to construction of the road and causeway the marshy Lost Lagoon was part of Coal Harbour and virtually dried out at low water. In 1936 an electrically lit fountain was installed. Despite so much human intervention large numbers of waterfowl continue to gather here; the Canada geese, swans and ducks clearly enjoy being fed. | Lost Lagoon

This small zoo with its unusually interesting bear enclosure is located off one of the side roads in Stanley Park. | Stanley Park Zoo

There is a children's zoo in the north-west corner where youngsters can hold and feed the animals and have pony rides, etc. | Children's Zoo

Vancouver

Miniature Railway   The Miniature Railway (open daily 11am–5pm) is just one more of Stanley Park's many attractions.

Dining Pavilion   When it was built in 1911 the wooden Dining Pavilion housed the park administration. Today it is used as a restaurant.

Rose garden   Next to the Pavilion there is a pretty rose garden, first laid out in the 1920s.

★Vancouver Aquarium   Also situated in Stanley Park is the internationally renowned Vancouver Aquarium (open May–Aug. 9.30am–9pm, at other times daily 10am–5pm). In the Max Bell Marine Mammal Centre performing dolphins, white and killer whales, captivating otters and powerful sea-lions attract large audiences. In addition however the aquarium provides a fascinating introduction to the marine life of the North Pacific (Sandwell North Pacific Gallery) while salmon and other freshwater fish can be seen in the nearby R. Gibbs Hall.

Robson Square   Right in the centre of Vancouver the Robson Square complex extends across three blocks between the old court-house (now the Vancouver Art Gallery) and the seven-storeyed glass pyramid housing the new court-house (designed by the Vancouver-born architect Arthur Erickson and built in 1979). Various government departments occupy the different levels in the complex. With roof garden terraces, small waterfall, pond and well-designed foyer the Square lends itself to open-air events in summer.

Off Robson St. there is a wide shopping concourse with restaurants, outdoor cafés and roller skating rink (ice skating in winter).

Vancouver Art Gallery   The excellent collection of paintings by Emily Carr (1871–1945) ranks high among the attractions of the Vancouver Art Gallery at the northern end of Robson Square (750 Hornby St.; open: Tues.–Sun. and holidays 10am–6pm). One of the best-known of all Canadian artists, much of her work depicts scenes of British Columbia and reflects her fascination with the art and culture of Canada's North-west Coast Indians. The Gallery also mounts temporary exhibitions.

Robson Street   Robson St. always seems to be busy, attracting the crowds with its high-class boutiques and galleries (Indian arts and crafts) and huge range of restaurants and shops selling goods from all over the world. The two blocks between Burrard St. and Bute St. are known locally as "Robsonstrasse" because many of the shops were at one time German-owned.

Robson Public Market   This covered market on the corner of Robson St. and Cardero St. was obviously influenced by London's Crystal Palace. A variety of nationalities are represented among the several small restaurants serving fast food on the first floor.

Denman Street   There are more little shops and restaurants in Denman St. (city centre west). At its northern end is the wharf used by the harbour ferries.

Train/boat excursion   In summer the excursion to Squamish (Wed.–Sun.) aboard the MV "Britannia" or the "Royal Hudson" (an old steam train) is immensely popular. It takes the same time (7½ hours) by ship or train and passengers can sample both forms of transport by switching for the return journey.

Harbour tour   Harbour tours on the paddle steamer "Constitution" are a delight. (Wed.–Sun. 1½ hours)

Granville Mall   Since 1976 Granville Mall between Nelson St. and Hastings St. has been Vancouver's main shopping street (closed to all private traffic). The Pacific Centre and the Vancouver Centre (at the Georgia St./Granville St.

intersection) are two big shopping complexes with numerous shops and cinemas above and below ground. The Orpheum Theatre (865 Seymour St., off the Mall) used to be the Variété Théatre of Vancouver. Today the lovingly restored building is the concert hall home of the famous Vancouver Symphony Orchestra.

Further along the Mall a number of large Canadian department stores have branches.

Granville Mall is also the location of Vancouver's museum of technology (600 Granville St.; open Mon.–Sat. 10am–5pm, Sun. 1–5pm or later in summer). Visitors are able to handle or operate most of the exhibits on the museum's three floors and are encouraged to try out some experiments for themselves. In addition the museum has a programme of science lectures and films.

Arts, Science and Technology Centre

At the north end of Granville St. the CP Waterfront Station (the old Canadian Pacific Railway terminal) is now the point of departure for the city's "SkyTrain" and "SeaBus" services.

CP Waterfront Station

The 15 minute passenger ferry crossing to North Vancouver gives superb views of the city skyline.

British Columbia pier just to the west of Waterfront Station is the site of one of Vancouver's newest landmarks, "Canada Place". The unusual roof of this architecturally remarkable structure creates the impression of a huge sailing vessel. Built for Expo '86 the complex houses a convention centre with a hotel, restaurants, a number of exclusive shops and an ultra-modern IMAX film theatre. Cruise liners can berth at the pier alongside the centre, which itself has a series of "promenade decks" on different levels like those of a ship. These make excellent vantage points for viewing the activities in the harbour, including the Air B.C. seaplanes as they take off and land.

★Canada Place

Vancouver: Canada Place

Vancouver

Harbour Centre — A few steps in the opposite direction from the north end of Granville Mall is all that is needed to reach the Harbour Centre (555 W. Hastings St.), a modern highrise development incorporating a large shopping precinct. The topmost storey (167 m (550 ft) up) has a revolving restaurant and viewing platform, both of which are served by "Skylift" – a pair of glass enclosed external lifts operating daily 10am–10pm (Fri. and Sat. 10am–midnight). On clear days the view extends to Vancouver Island and Victoria (in the south-west) and south-east as far as the snow-covered peak of Mt Baker.

Vancouver Discovery Show — The "Vancouver Discovery Show", a rousing, 25 minute, multi-media presentation, tells the story of Vancouver throughout its 100-year history.

★Gastown — The old part of Vancouver known as "Gastown" begins just beyond the Harbour Centre, at the eastern end of the city's main shopping and banking quarter. It occupies the area bounded by Richard St., Columbia St., Hastings St. and Water St. Carefully restored Victorian buildings and old warehouses put to new uses (full of restaurants, bars, boutiques, art galleries and souvenir shops) give the district its distinctive atmosphere.

History — Gastown came into existence in 1867 when a man called John Deighton (1830–75) arrived on the scene with a barrel of whisky and set up a saloon for the benefit of the thirsty employees of a nearby sawmill (the nearest bar at the time was some 20 km (12 mi.) away in New Westminster). Deighton had a habit of launching into lengthy, bragging monologues and soon acquired the nickname "Gassy Jack". As a result the vicinity of the saloon (on the corner of Water St. and Carrall St.) became known as "Gassy's Town" or "Gastown".

As Vancouver grew the city centre gradually expanded in the direction of Gastown, as well as further to the west.

In the 1960s the charm of this old district came to be appreciated anew and renovation of the run-down buildings began. In 1972 Gastown was declared a historical monument.

With its cobblestones and gaslights Water St. is particularly attractive.

★Steam Clock — Standing on the corner of Cambie St. and Water St. is a steam operated clock which toots every quarter hour. Made in the 1870s it is today linked to the district heating system.

Gassy Jack and his whisky barrel are commemorated by a statue in Maple Tree Square at the end of Water St.

Chinatown — Vancouver's exotic and interesting Chinatown, the largest in North America apart from San Francisco's, extends east of Carrall St. as far as Gore Ave. Set among the modern functional buildings are many older ones dating from Victorian times, some with typically Chinese features. E. Pender St. and Keefer St. (the main shopping streets) are crowded with restaurants. At lunchtime these serve "dim sum", a sort of Chinese brunch which can sometimes include less familiar Chinese dishes. Many of the shops describe their wares only in Chinese and some of the foodstuffs on display are to say the least unusual to European eyes. Vegetables and fruit are sold on the streets. Even the telephone kiosks are shaped like pagodas. Running between the streets proper are narrow alleyways such as the Truance or "Blood" Alley. These are used for deliveries to the shops and also give access to the flats and habitations. Every year the Chinese New Year festival is celebrated with a procession and fireworks.

History — The first Chinese came to western Canada in the 19th c. during the gold-rush and most of the labourers hired in the 1880s to build the railway were also Chinese coolies. Those who survived the rigours of such a hard life settled mainly in the Vancouver area. With their alien ways the

Chinese were generally looked down upon and their preparedness to work for low rates of pay led to friction with white workers. As a result they suffered numerous attacks. With its opium cellars and secret societies the Chinese quarter used to be regarded with the utmost suspicion and was long considered a place to be avoided. Not only were the Chinese population denied Canadian citizenship, they were also made to pay additional taxes and had special conditions of employment imposed. They were only granted the right to vote in 1949.

Today there are about 100,000 inhabitants of Vancouver who are of Chinese origin, only a few of whom live in Chinatown.

Look out for the newly renovated Sam Kee Building (8 W. Pender St.) which being barely 2 m (6½ ft) wide claims to be the narrowest office building in the world.

Sam Kee Building

Artisans and landscape gardeners from the city of Suzhou (China) laid out this classical Chinese garden (in Carrall St. on the edge of Chinatown) for Expo '86.

Dr Sun Yat Sen Garden

The Chinese Cultural Centre (housed in a modern building at 50 E. Pender St.) provides visitors with an opportunity to learn about the history and cultural life of Vancouver's Chinatown. Temporary art exhibitions.

Chinese Cultural Centre

A harbour tour (1hr) aboard the little "Tymac" leaves from the wharf at the northern end of Main St.

Tymac

The Queen Elizabeth Theatre & Playhouse (Cambie St./Dunsmuir St.) is Vancouver's largest theatre. It stages opera, ballet and musicals as well as drama.

Queen Elizabeth Theatre & Playhouse

The B.C. Stadium on the north side of False Creek is a huge multi-purpose amphitheatre capable of accommodating up to 60,000 spectators for large sporting and other cultural events.

B.C. Place Stadium

The once mainly industrial Granville Island (beneath Granville Street Bridge, Hwy. 99) has recently undergone transformation – part of a major redevelopment scheme encompassing the entire False Creek basin. The result is a thriving new centre of activity with a relaxed and distinctive atmosphere. Artists and art students have moved into the converted warehouses beside the houseboats and theatres, shops, galleries and restaurants have all been opened (together with a marina and a number of greened areas). Granville Island Public Market is one of the most popular attractions, selling fruit and vegetables, seafood and a great variety of other specialities. The island is linked to the residential suburbs on the south bank of False Creek by road and foot bridges. Ferry from Burrard Bridge.

Granville Island

Located in Vanier Park on the south side of False Creek (cross via Burrard Bridge) the Vancouver Museum (1100 Chestnut St.; open Tue.–Sun. and holidays 10am–5pm) is the biggest municipal museum in Canada and definitely worth visiting. It has sections devoted to the history of the city and the Pacific coast as well as collections on natural history and ethnography (the culture of the North-west Coast Indians in particular). Also housed in the modern domed building, completed in 1968, is the H.R. MacMillan Planetarium (several programmes, laser show) while adjacent to it stands the Gordon Southam Observatory (with a 15 cm (6 in.) Zeiss telescope). Instructive audio-visual presentations accompany the displays. From the museum splendid views can be enjoyed over English Bay and Sunset Beach to the city and the North Shore mountains beyond.

★Vancouver Museum

Vancouver Maritime Museum	The nearby Maritime Museum (1905 Ogden St.; open daily 10am–5pm) covers various aspects of the maritime history of the area (from the exploration of British Columbian waters to the development of navigation, the fishing industry and the port of Vancouver).

A number of old vessels are moored in the Heritage Harbour. Most interesting of all however is the "St Roch", lying in the dry dock. Built in 1928 for use by the Royal Canadian Mounted Police (RCMP) as an Arctic patrol and supply ship, this wooden two-master successfully negotiated the Northwest Passage to Halifax and back in a single year (1944). She was taken out of service in 1954. |
| Kitsilano Beach Park | The main attraction at the Kitsilano Beach Park is a heated seawater swimming pool. |
| Old Hastings Mill Store Museum | Of Vancouver's first sawmill only the store and post office survived the 1886 fire and the later rapid development of the city. Built in 1865 the Old Hastings Mill Store is today a museum (1575 Alma Rd.; open Jun.–Sep. daily 10am–4pm, at other times Sat. and Sun. 1–4pm) housing items from pioneering days and the period of Indian settlement. |
| ★University of British Columbia | From the end of 4th Ave. North West Marine Drive continues past delightful stretches of beach along the south side of English Bay to the University of British Columbia at Point Grey. The extensive 2470 ha (6100 acre) campus is also the site of the university's renowned Anthropological Museum, housed in a quite exceptional building designed by Arthur Erickson (6393 North West Marine Drive; open Tue. noon–9pm, Wed.–Sun. 11am–5pm).

The many items of Indian culture on display include totem poles, carved wooden posts from long-houses, and sculptures by the Haida woodcarver Bill Reid. These are augmented by glass cabinets filled with eye-catching masks, textiles, jewellery and smaller objects of wood, bone, horn, ivory and argillite – eloquent testimony to the highly developed skills and artistry of Indian craftsmen. Completing the collection are anthropological exhibits from all over the world. Visitors are recommended to join one of the theme-related guided tours.

More Indian totem poles and long-houses, etc. can be seen in the museum grounds. |

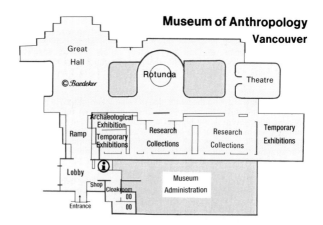

Museum of Anthropology
Vancouver

Totem pole ...   *... in the Anthropological Museum*

Also on North West Marine Drive is the University of British Columbia's botanical garden, divided into sections to facilitate teaching and research. Among the highlights are the austere, contemplative Nitobe Japanese Garden (with pretty tea-house) and a gem of a herb garden established more than a century ago.

UBC botanical garden

Of considerable interest too are the Van Dusen Botanical Gardens (5251 Oak St., east of Granville St. between 34th St. and 37th St.). Each of the 40 or so plots is given over to a different geographical region or botanical species and the collection includes a number of exotic plants from around the world.

Van Dusen Botanical Gardens

Canada's biggest timber company has an information centre in MacMillan Bloedel Place (Oak St./37th St.) where it is possible to learn all about the forests of British Columbia and their economic significance.

MacMillan Bloedel Place

Just to the east the 53 ha (130 acre) Queen Elizabeth Park (W. 33rd and Cambie Sts.) extends up the slopes of Little Mountain – at 150 m (500 ft) the highest point in the Vancouver municipal area. There are excellent views of the city centre and the mountains to the north. The park's major attraction however is the Bloedel Conservatory, a 15 m (49 ft) high dome made up of 1490 triangular plexiglas panels.

Queen Elizabeth Park

At the northern end of Clark Drive, east of the city centre, there is public access to part of Vancouver's port (Vanterm) where container ships can be watched loading and unloading. (Guided tours Sun.–Thu. 9am–noon and 1–3pm; reservations tel. 666–6129; diashow and information on port.)

Vanterm

One block further east the B.C. Sugar Company museum at the end of Rogers St. (open Mon.–Fri. 9am–3.30pm) is full of interesting information

B.C. Sugar Terminal

491

on beet and cane sugar production. Old equipment and machinery can be seen displayed next to it.

Surroundings

Port Moody

Port Moody (population 17,000), now a suburb of Vancouver, lies at the head of Burrard Inlet some 20 km (12 mi.) east of the city centre. For just one year it was the terminus of the Trans-Canadian Railroad – hence the Golden Spike Festival held annually at the end of July/beginning of August. Built in 1907 the restored CPR station has now been converted into the Station Museum (2734 Murray St.; open Jul./Aug. daily 1–8pm, at other times Sat. and Sun. 1–4pm) recalling the early days of the railway era on Canada's west coast.

Burnaby

Now just a continuation of Vancouver Burnaby (population 145,000) is the home of Simon Fraser University. The university campus, another of Vancouver architect Arthur Erickson's striking designs, occupies a beautiful site in Burnaby Mountain Park – atop Burnaby Mountain from which magnificent panoramic views unfold over the south-west mainland of British Columbia. The Museum of Archaeology & Ethnology displays the results of research into the about 10,000 years of Indian settlement in the province. There are also a number of totem poles and everyday items of contemporary North-west Coast Indian culture, together with a small ethnographic collection (open Mon.–Fri. 10am–4.30pm, Sat. and Sun. noon–3pm). In addition to mounting special exhibitions of contemporary art the Simon Fraser Gallery owns some 900 works by Inuit artists.

Burnaby Village Museum

With its 30 or so replica buildings the open-air Burnaby Village Museum on the north side of Deer Lake (4900 Deer Lake Ave.; open Mar.–Oct. daily 11am–4.30pm, at other times limited opening hours) offers an insight into British Columbian life in the years between 1890 and 1925.

New Westminster

Situated on the Fraser River about 25 km (15 mi.) south-east of Vancouver, adjoining Burnaby to the south-east, New Westminster (present population about 40,000) is the oldest town on mainland British Columbia. Founded in the 1850s it was a boom town during the goldrushes and by 1868 had been elevated to provincial capital. In the town centre are many Victorian buildings which, having survived a major fire in 1898, have now been carefully preserved. Particularly worth seeing are Irving House (302 Royal Ave. open May–Sep. 11am–5pm, at other times Sat. and Sun. 1–5pm), the impressive home of a riverboat captain, and (beyond it) New Westminster's Museum.

New Westminster Waterfront

New Westminster Waterfront, a recent development on the banks of the Fraser River, features a small promenade and modern shopping centre. Westminster Quay Public Market aims to create all the colour and atmosphere of a weekly market.

Richmond

Richmond (23 km (14 mi.) south of Vancouver; population 96,000) was founded in 1879 on a large island in the Fraser River delta. On its southwest side (and now incorporated into the town) is the picturesque former fishing village of Steveston with delightfully restored old timber houses, boatsheds and landing stages. Scores of fishing craft still bring their catch ashore here. Located in Moncton Street is the Steveston Museum.

Buddhist temple

Built in traditional Chinese style the Buddhist temple at 9160 Steveston Hwy. (open 10am–5pm) has some valuable interior furnishings. As well

Log transportation in the Burrard Inlet, Vancouver ▶

as religious ceremonies, lectures and tea ceremonies are also held. Attached to the temple are a small museum and library.

North Vancouver

From downtown Vancouver North Vancouver is just a few minutes drive on Highway 99, crossing First Narrows by the Lions Gate Bridge. The latter was constructed in 1939 to give the Guinness brewery convenient access to company property on the north side of the inlet. Adorned with twin lions the bridge is named after "The Lions" (two peaks a little way up the coast which from a distance resemble a pair of lions).

Horseshoe Bay

For an outing with numerous superb views follow Marine Drive through West Vancouver (a prosperous satellite of Vancouver with 40,000 inhabitants), past Lighthouse Park (excellent for walking), to the very attractive Horseshoe Bay (and Whytecliff Park). From the north side of the Bay ferries depart for Nanaimo (Vancouver Island), Bowen Island and Langdale.

Cypress Provincial Park

About 12 km (7 mi.) from downtown Vancouver a winding 8 km (5 m.) long access road branches off TransCanada Highway 1 in West Vancouver to the Cypress Provincial Park. At the heart of the park Hollyburn Ridge (Mt Hollyburn 1325 m (4350 ft), Mt Strachan 1454 m (4772 ft)) offers more magnificent views and splendid walking.

Lonsdale Quay

North Vancouver's Lonsdale Quay can be reached in 15 minutes by SeaBus. In the course of redevelopment over the last ten years it too has acquired a public market – also a small shopping centre (boutiques), street musicians, open-air waterside cafés and weekly market atmosphere. From the Observation Tower there is a fine view of Vancouver city centre opposite.

North Shore Museum and Archives

North Shore Museum (209 W. 4th St.; open Wed.–Sun. 1–4pm) is mainly devoted to the history of the area since the arrival of Europeans though some Salish Indian artefacts are to be seen as well. Changing exhibitions.

Capilano Suspension Bridge

Since 1899 people with a good head for heights have been able to cross the 70 m (230 ft) deep Capilano Canyon on foot by suspension bridge (3735 Capilano Rd.; access daily from 8am). The 140 m (460 ft) long bridge is now something of a tourist attraction in its own right. On the far side are a number of massive old red cedar and Douglas fir trees.

Capilano Salmon Hatchery

Just beyond the suspension bridge Capilano Park Rd. branches off left and descends to the Capilano Salmon Hatchery (4500 Capilano Park Rd.) in the Capilano River Regional Park. When the impressive Cleveland Dam was constructed to secure Vancouver's water supply, salmon returning from the Pacific to spawn found themselves cut off from their traditional breeding grounds. The hatchery was created in an effort to maintain stocks. The spawning cycle of the salmon is explained in informative detail and from July to October fish can be observed ascending the salmon-ladder.

★Grouse Mountain

From the 1250 m (4100 ft) high Grouse Mountain – Vancouver's "private" peak – an unmatched panorama can be enjoyed in clear weather, especially in the evenings when the city lights are on. A cable car (Skyride; operating daily 10am–10pm) runs from the end of Nancy Greene Way to the summit restaurant (at 1128 m (3700 ft)) from where a chair-lift continues to the summit itself. In winter Grouse Mountain is a popular skiing area. (Hang-gliding and helicopter tours.)

★Royal Hudson Steam Train

The Royal Hudson Steam Train leaves from the foot of Pemberton St. on a 60 km (37 mi.) excursion to the small town of Squamish. Hauling the train on its approximately two hour journey through the delightful scenery beside Howe Sound is CP Rail's legendary steam locomotive No. 2860, the engine which in 1939 hauled a train carrying King George VI from Québec to Vancouver (hence the title "Royal Hudson").

Departure times May, Jun., Sep. Wed. and Sun., Jul., Aug. Wed.–Sun. 10.30am.

Information: tel. 6879558.

The return journey can if desired be made by boat (M.V. "Britannia").

Lynn Canyon Park on the east side of North Vancouver is a good place for short hikes and walks. Here too a suspension bridge spans the 83 m (270 ft) deep gorge (waterfalls). The Lynn Canyon Ecology Centre (3663 Park Rd.; open Mar.–Nov. daily 10am–5pm, at other times weekends only) has all sorts of interesting displays on the ecology of the area.

Lynn Canyon Park

Extending around the 1453 m (4768 ft) Mount Seymour and almost on Vancouver's doorstep (8 km (5 mi.) north-east of North Vancouver; 15 km (9 mi.) north-east of the city centre by Second Narrows Bridge), the 35 sq. km (13 sq. mi.) Mount Seymour Provincial Park is a popular skiing and recreation area criss-crossed by several trails. A winding but good road with frequent impressive views climbs to about 1000 m (3282 ft), from which point hiking trails continue to the summit and to some small karst lakes (more views). While racoons, eagles and other birds of prey are relatively common the park's black bears are generally only encountered in remoter areas. The 42 km (26 mi.) "Baden Powell Centennial Trail", starting at Deep Cove on Indian Arm and continuing west through the Cypress Provincial Park to Horseshoe Bay on Howe Sound, is much favoured. In summer the Mystery Peak chair-lift takes visitors up to an altitude of 1200 m (3938 ft).

This particular provincial park was established in 1936. Although the first recorded ascent of Mount Seymour was in 1908, it, like other peaks in the Coast Mountains, was largely neglected until the end of the 1920s. In 1929/30 however the Alpine Club of Canada began to take an interest and the first skiing facilities were installed shortly afterwards.

★Mount Seymour Provincial Park

Tucked away on the west shore of Indian Arm at the foot of Mount Seymour lies the picturesque little village of Deep Cove, a good place for boat trips and also for diving.

Deep Cove

Nugget Route (circular drive)

Leave Vancouver via Georgia St. (Hwy. 99) and the Lions Gate Bridge heading for Horseshoe Bay (21 km (13 mi.)) where the B.C. Ferries terminal is situated.

From Horseshoe Bay Hwy. 99 runs along the east side of Howe Sound, its route blasted directly out of the rock in places. The scenery here is exceptional.

★Howe Sound

56 km (35 mi.): When in production between 1930 and 1935 the Britannia Beach copper mine was the largest in the British Empire. Today there is an interesting mining museum (open May–Labour Day daily 10am–5pm) with collections of old photographs, equipment, machinery and minerals. Visitors are taken by mine railway to a specially laid out gallery underground.

Britannia Beach B.C. Museum of Mining

66 km (41 mi.): In its spectacular setting at the head of Howe Sound the old logging town of Squamish (population 10,000) is the destination for excursions aboard the Royal Hudson Steam Train and the M.V. "Britannia". The trunks of trees felled in the Squamish Valley are rafted together here before being towed down to Vancouver.

The first Europeans to arrive (in 1888) were quick to appreciate the

Squamish

value of the sheltered harbour, and consequently founded a settlement around it. Until 1956 when the line was extended as far as Vancouver, Squamish was the southern end of the Pacific Great Eastern Railway from Prince George (operated today by B.C. Rail). There is a small museum devoted to the Squamish Valley in old Brightbill House (2nd Ave.; open Wed.–Sun. 10am–4pm).

Shannon Falls

The Shannon Falls are located about 3 km (2 mi.) south of Squamish.

Stawanus Chief

A popular challenge for rock climbers, the "Stawanus Chief" is a 510 m (1673 ft) high granite monolith.

Guided treks on horseback into the still largely undeveloped interior are another much indulged form of recreation.

Flights over the ice-fields and glaciers of the Coast Mountains can be arranged from Squamish Airport (with a landing on the remote glaciers one of the highlights).

The town's annual Squamish Days (at the end of July/beginning of August) are to all intents and purposes a full-scale international lumber-jacks' championship. Teams come from all over the world to compete in the traditional logging contests.

Garibaldi Provincial Park

Squamish is also a starting point for visits to the southern part of the 1950 sq. km (750 sq. mi.) Garibaldi Provincial Park, including a trip to one of the most popular areas – Diamond Head. One or two alpine refuges and a few basic campsites are provided in this magnificent and still largely untouched mountain wilderness centred on the majestic, glacier-clad Mt Garibaldi (2678 m (8790 ft)).

Signs of relatively recent volcanic activity abound in the park, many of the peaks, especially in the vicinity of Garibaldi Lake, being volcanic in origin. The waters of the lake itself are contained by a about 300 m (985 ft) high lava wall known as "The Barrier". This is believed to have been formed about 12,000 years ago when lava flowing from Mt Price cooled rapidly on contact with a glacier. The present physiognomy of the mountains is also partly the result of a landslip, probably caused by an earthquake in 1855.

About 4 km (2½ mi.) north of Squamish a 16 km (10 mi.) long access road (mainly unsurfaced) branches off Hwy. 99 to Diamond Head from where there are marvellous views over the Squamish Valley and Howe Sound. The Elfin Lakes refuge (trails to Mamquam Lake and Little Diamond Head) can be reached in about four hours from the car park.

Rubble Creek

Access to the Black Tusk area (at the heart of Garibaldi Park; highest summit 2316 m (7600 ft)) and also to the delightful Garibaldi Lake is from the car park at Rubble Creek (37 km (23 mi.) north of Squamish).

Whistler

123 km (76 mi.): Whistler (see entry).

Pemberton

157 km (97 mi.): Leaving the asphalted Hwy. 99 at the scattered settle-ment of Pemberton (90 m (295 ft) above sea level; population 350) follow instead the well-surfaced Duffy Lake Road which crosses the 100 km (62 mi.) or so of virtually uninhabited country to Lillooet on the Fraser River.

Lillooet

260 km (161 mi.): Lillooet (population 2000) owes its existence to the so-called "Cariboo Gold-Rush" of 1858. It stood at the end of the Harrison trail, a canoe route up the Fraser River bypassing the Fraser Canyon.

It was here that the gold hunters exchanged their canoes for ox-carts before setting off up the "Cariboo Road", and to cater for them a settle-ment quickly became established on the Cayoosh Flats. By 1860 the shanty town of log huts and tents was at times filled to overflowing with as many as 16,000 inhabitants. The Pacific Great Eastern Railway line reached Lillooet in 1912.

Be sure to visit the Lillooet Museum in the former Anglican Church (Main St.; open Jul./Aug. 9.30am–5.30pm, May/Jun. and Sep./Oct. 1–4pm). It is full of memorabilia from the gold-rush days. Also interesting are the "0" milestone on the old Cariboo Road and the "Hanging Tree" where rough frontier justice was meted out to law-breakers. In 1980 the name of the old Fraser Bridge was changed to the "Bridge of the 23 Camels", commemorating the animals imported from Asia in 1862 by an enterprising entrepreneur who intended to introduce them into the mines as beasts of burden. Having frightened the life out of the local people and their horses the camels were eventually set free. Mineral collectors will enjoy sifting through the gravel for jade and semi-precious stones.

330 km (205 mi.): From Lillooet take Hwy. 12 to Lytton (population 400) at the confluence of the Fraser and Thompson rivers. From here TransCanada Highway 1 offers a quick route back to the Vancouver area. | **Lytton**
670 km (416 mi.): Vancouver

Fraser River Valley

37 km (23 mi.) east: From Port Coquitlam (population 30,000) the 30 km (19 mi.) Poco Trail provides splendid walking upstream along the Pitt River to Widgeon Creek Lodge and the large Pitt Lake (where the effect of the tides is still felt). Canoes can be hired at the Pitt River Bridge. | **Pitt River**

42 km (26 mi.) east: Maple Ridge (15 m (49 ft) above sea level; population 38,000) has an interesting local museum (22535 River Rd.; open May–Aug. Tue.–Sat. 9am–5pm, Sun. 1–4pm, at other times Wed. and Sun. 1–4pm) in a former private house dating from 1907. There are also fine views of the Fraser River and the historic part of Port Haney. | **Maple Ridge**

Trips are run from Maple Ridge to the Golden Ears Provincial Park in the Coast Mountains (close to the southern extension of the Garibaldi Provincial Park (see Vancouver, Nugget Route) which is only about 10 km (6 mi.) to the north). Most of the park's leisure activities are centred on Alouette Lake (dam); these include watersports, horse riding, hiking and nature trails. The approximately ten hour hike to Alouette Mountain (1371 m (4500 ft)) where the views are quite outstanding, and the one hour walk to the Lower Falls can both be thoroughly recommended. | **Golden Ears Provincial Park**

5 km (3 mi.) further east at Albion the Fort Langley ferry crosses the Fraser River. | Fort Langley ferry

The recently established Fraser River Heritage Park in East Mission (5th Ave.; see entry) occupies the site of the original St Mary's Mission. The park contains a museum and a small arts centre and there are delightful views of the river. | **Fraser River Heritage Park**

100 km (62 mi.) east: The highlight of Kilby Provincial Historic Park, on the Harrison River 1 km (2/3 of a mile) south of TransCanada Highway 1, is a General Store from the 1920s. The accommodation at the rear and the "hotel" rooms on the first floor say much about living conditions in the first half of this century. Settlement of the area took place as early as 1870, by which time the first sawmills had also been built. In the latter part of the 19th c. many pioneers and gold diggers took the Harrison River route north in order to avoid the treacherous Fraser Canyon. | **Kilby Provincial Historic Park**

From the 1880s freight brought by rail was loaded onto sternwheel paddle-steamers at Harrison Mills (on the opposite bank) for onward shipment by river. It was in 1904 that Thomas Kilby opened the "Th. | **Harrison Mills**

Kilby Hotel & General Store", a two-storey building supported on piles. His son was still running the business in 1976.

Agassiz

120 km (75 mi.) east: Standing in the grounds of the agricultural research station at Agassiz (18 m (59 ft) above sea level; population 4000), the old CPR building (1893; renovated) now houses the Agassiz-Harrison Historical Museum (6947 Hyw. 7; open May–Labour Day daily 10am–3pm). The telegraph office and waiting room have been restored to their original state.

Harrison Hot Springs

Situated on the exceptionally attractive Harrison Lake some 6 km (4 mi.) north of Agassiz, Harrison Hot Springs (13 m (43 ft) above sea level; population 700) has a public thermal pool and a 3 km (2 mi.) long sandy beach (excellent for sunbathing in summer).

Boats run trips to Port Douglas at the northern end of the 70 km (43 mi.) lake.

The Sasquatch Provincial Park, 10 km (6 mi.) further north, is a favourite leisure area for local people (sailing, windsurfing, waterskiing, canoeing, etc.). Canoes and pedalos can be hired.

From Harrison Hot Springs follow the Fraser River eastwards for another 33 km (20 mi.), rejoining TransCanada Highway 1 about 3 km (2 mi.) north of Hope.

145 km (90 mi.): Deer Park exit, Burnaby Village Museum: see Vancouver

152 km (94 mi.): New Westminster: see Vancouver

170 km (105 mi.): see Fort Langley

Vancouver Game Farm

185 km (115 mi.): The roomy enclosures of the Vancouver Game Farm (open daily from 8am) are home to more than 100 species of large animal from all over the world. Access to the farm, located 1 km (2/3 of a mile) south of TransCanada Highway 1 near Aldergrove (pop. 10,000), is via Hwy. 13.

Clearbrook Abbotsford

220 km (137 mi.): see entry

★★Vancouver Island   G/H 5/6

Province: British Columbia
Population: 450,000

Access

By plane:
Seaplane from Vancouver (see entry) (Coal Harbour) to Victoria, Nanaimo and Port Hardy. Several of the major North American airlines fly to Victoria International Airport situated on the Saanich Peninsula. There are regional airports at Campbell River and Comox. Numerous connections by seaplane to out-of-the-way places or camps.

Ferries:
Swartz Bay–Tsawwassen (–Vancouver); Swartz Bay–Gulf Islands; Victoria–Port Angeles/Washington State (USA); Victoria–Seattle (passengers only); Sidney–Anacortez/Wash; Departure Bay–Horseshoe Bay (–Vancouver); Courtenay/Comox–Powell River; Port Hardy–Prince Rupert; numerous local ferry and boat services.

Location

Some 450 km (280 mi.) long, and 100 km (60 mi.) across at its widest, Vancouver island is the largest island on the Pacific coast of North America. It extends parallel to the coast of mainland British Columbia, separated from it by the Georgia and Queen Charlotte Straits. The island is densely wooded and mountainous, rising at its centre to its highest point, the 2200 m (7220 ft) Golden Hinde, the summit zone at least being

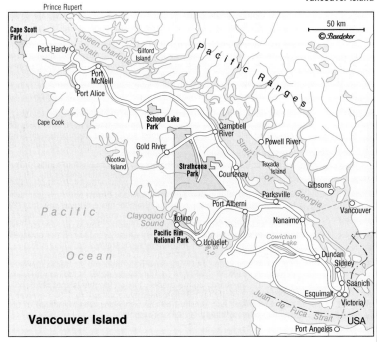

Prince Rupert

50 km

© *Baedeker*

Cape Scott
Park

Port Hardy

Queen Charlotte Strait

Gilford
Island

Pacific Ranges

Port
McNeill

Port Alice

Cape Cook

Schoen Lake
Park

Campbell
River

Powell River

Gold River

Strait

Nootka
Island

Strathcona
Park

Courtenay

Texada
Island

Gibsons

of Georgia

Parksville

Vancouver

Pacific

*Clayoquot
Sound*

Port Alberni

Tofino

Nanaimo

Pacific Rim
National Park

Ucluelet

*Cowichan
Lake*

Ocean

Duncan

Sidney

Saanich

Esquimalt

Victoria

Vancouver Island

Juan de Fuca Strait

USA

Port Angeles

snow covered. The extremely rugged and still largely virgin western coast is deeply indented, with numerous inlets and Bays extending far inland. The particularly beautiful southern section was turned some years ago into the Pacific Rim National Park. Lying in the rain shadow, the gently rolling hill country on the east and south coasts is relatively sunny; here agriculture and horticulture thrive. The likewise flat but deeply indented northern tip of the island is by contrast covered with ancient forest and scarcely opened to the outside world,

Rain forests

Frequent precipitation on the west coast favours the growth of dense rain forest, with giant trees overgrown with moss and ferns. These ancient forests are an indispensable resource for the island's thriving timber, cellulose and paper industry (see Baedeker Special, page 000). Following bitter clashes with the indigenous Indians as well as conservationists, for example at Clayoquot Sound, the provincial government and logging companies operating on Vancouver Island have agreed a more cautious and environmentally friendly approach to the "timber harvest".

Fauna

Particularly in the Provincial Park and areas little touched by human settlement or industry, wapiti, deer (especially black deer), black bears and wolves are often to be seen. There are also, reportedly, still some cougars here; visitors should be extremely wary of them.

Settlement

Vancouver Island has long been settled by north-west coast Indians belonging to three different language groups. Descendants of the Nootka live on the west coast, some Kwakiutl groups in the north, and in the south-east the coast Salish. The majority of the mainly small Indian communities can only be reached by boat or seaplane.

The east and south coasts are relatively densely populated. Victoria, in the extreme south, is the capital of both island and province (British Columbia). Further north, almost directly across the strait from Vancouver, are the port of Nanaimo and the popular residential area and resort of Qualicum Beach. In the extreme north of the island. ferries calling in or their way through the Inside Passage (see entry) to Prince Rupert (see entry) and beyond have helped Port Hardy to prosper.

History

At the time of the first contacts with Europeans three different West Coast Indian language groups were represented among the tribes of Vancouver Island. The Nootka hunted and fished from settlements on the island's west coast while the north was inhabited by bands of Kwakiutl and the south-east by the coast Salish.

The first European to reach the area was probably Sir Francis Drake. Voyaging along the Pacific coast of America at the end of the 16th c. Drake reached as far as present day Vancouver. It was not however until the end of the 18th c. that Spanish, Russian, British and American seafarers explored the west coast of Canada more extensively. In 1778 Captain James Cook, sailing up the west coast of Vancouver Island, landed at a small Indian settlement on Nootka Sound, presumably the first white person to do so. Cook very quickly recognised the possibilities for the fur trade and the potential for trade with China and soon British and American ships were making regular visits to the west coast Indians to exchange pelts. This growing British and American presence in territory to which Spain had formal claim quickly led to disputes, and in 1790 the Spaniards built a modest fort on Nootka Island, at Friendly Cove. Subsequently four British ships were seized. In 1795 however a new agreement was reached by the two sides which resulted in the Spanish relinquishing their remote outpost.

Pacific Coast, Vancouver Island

The Interior ...   *... of Vancouver Island*

It was at the close of the 18th c. that Captain George Vancouver, successfully negotiating the Johnstone Strait, established that the territory he took possession of for Britain and to which he gave his name was indeed an island. Later Vancouver Island came under the control of the Hudson's Bay Company which dominated the fur trade and in 1843 the company founded the first European settlement – at Fort Victoria – to which, in 1846, its western headquarters were transferred. The island would probably have long remained the exclusive domain of fur traders had not the discovery of gold in the Cariboo Mountains brought thousands of gold prospectors and settlers to Victoria.

Timber is still the island's primary industry. In consequence large tracts   Economy
of ancient forest, much of it many hundreds of years old, have already
been destroyed. The larger tree trunks are shipped away elsewhere
while the smaller ones end up at the cellulose factories and paper mills
of Duncan, Nanaimo, Campbell River, Port Alberni and Port Alice. The
rest of the tree is burned. The timber companies are nowadays required
to replant deforested areas, which they do mainly with fast-growing
Douglas firs to yield another "harvest" in 50 to 70 years time. Estimates
suggest that with the exception of protected areas Vancouver Island will
have lost all its ancient forests by the middle of the 21st century. But it
would be difficult to overestimate the importance of the timber trade to
the economy, particularly the contribution made by the logging
companies and related industries to the island's infrastructure. Outside
working hours private cars are able to use most of the unsurfaced
forestry roads. Fishing and tourism are Vancouver Island's other major
activities.

Fish provide the livelihood of many islanders. Until a few years ago the
coastal waters were fished, but recently so-called aqua farming has
become established. Salmon and trout principally, but also other good

Brazil of the North

In 1993 the Canadian economy earned in excess of 21 billion Can.$ from the export of timber and derivative products. Forestry has always been one of the pillars of the Canadian economy and about a million people are estimated to be employed in timber-related industries.

Today about half of Canada's "timber harvest" comes from British Columbia. Every year in this "Brazil of the North", one per cent of the currently 6.5 million ha (16 million acres) of virgin forest disappears. On the abundantly wet Pacific coast of Vancouver Island grow the largest, oldest and most valuable trees in the world; giant moss- and lichen-covered arbores vitae, Sitka spruces and hemlock firs several hundred years old, and red cedars not far short of a thousand years old. The coastal areas of British Columbia with their year-round comparatively mild and very wet climate, are one of the few regions on earth where temperate coastal rain forest still flourishes. This unique eco-system, not unlike tropical rain forest in its organic richness and diversity, has in the course of time evolved more than 120 different species of tree and no less than 48,000 species of animal. Now it is endangered. The provincial government proposes to open up to forestry Canada's largest remaining continuous and as yet virtually untouched area of virgin rain forest, around Clayoquot Sound. Only a third of the existing forest would be protected, the rest being available for exploitation, for which reason, in the summer of 1993, a massive campaign was mounted against the plan by environmental groups and conservationists.

The fear is that even greater damage will result here than is already evident elsewhere on Vancouver Island, where forest clearance has caused irreparable harm, leaving mountaintops denuded of trees, soil erosion and nutrient loss on a large scale, and natural freshwater fish stocks under threat.

The temperate coastal rain forest is capable of absorbing seven times the quantity of carbon-dioxide as the same area of tropical rain forest and is therefore of inestimable importance from the point of view of the dynamics of global climatic change. Yet as long as, for example, a tenth of all the paper used by the German printing industry is manufactured from Canadian cellulose and annual per capita paper and cardboard consumption in German-speaking countries remains at 200 kg, what hope is there for the "Brazil of the North"?

Rain forest around Clayoquot Sound

quality fish, are "produced" in huge fish-rearing tanks. Tourism is growing in economic importance, with increasing numbers of tourists, including many from Europe, captivated by the island's lovely scenery.

The little town of Duncan (population 5000) lies 60 km (37 mi.) north of **Duncan**
Victoria on TransCanada Highway 1, and is the hub of the island's timber
processing industry. The first settlement of the Cowichan Valley took
place in 1887. The town itself came into existence in 1912 when greater
numbers of settlers were attracted to the area by the discovery of what
turned out to be limited copper and coal deposits at nearby Mt Sicker.
Today only abandoned mines and the remains of buildings and camps
bear witness to the short lived "boom". From Mt Prevost there are
splendid views.

Large numbers of Cowichan Indians, a coast Salish tribe, still live in and **Cowichan Indian**
around Duncan. They grey and white sweaters they craft from home- **sweaters**
spun wool make very sought-after presents.

The open-air, 40 ha (99 acre), British Columbia Forest Museum (about **British Columbia**
2 km (1¼ mi.) north of Duncan; open May–Sep. daily 10am–5.30pm) pro- **Forest Museum**
vides a vivid introduction to the history and development of the timber
industry – from the first primitive logging camps, a 100 year old
sawmills and old steam engines of yesteryear to the cellulose factories
and paper mills of today. There is even an old narrow-gauge railway.

The Native Heritage Centre (open mid-May–mid-Oct. daily 9.30am– ★Native Heritage
5.30pm) on the western outskirts of Duncan is well worth visiting. You **Centre**
can see totem poles being carved and baskets being woven, and sometimes traditional north-west coast Indian dancing.

Duncan to Parksville

From near Duncan, Hwy. 18 heads westwards to Cowichan Lake (31 km **Cowichan Lake**
(19 mi.)), the largest freshwater lake on the island. Posted at various
viewpoints along the way are boards with information about the local
forestry. Cowichan Lake Village is a good place from which to set out on
the 75 km (47 mi.) drive round the lake.

From Duncan follow TransCanada Highway 1 north for 16 km (10 mi.) to ★**Chemainus**
Chemainus (population 2500). Here many of the houses are adorned
with larger-than-life size murals illustrating the history of the town,
painted by well-known artists. A "Festival of Murals" is held every year
in July. Restored Victorian buildings have been turned into restaurants
and shops. The big waterwheel in the town centre is a relic of the first
sawmill, constructed here in 1862.

From Chemainus there are boat trips to the scenically delightful Thetis **Thetis Island**
Island near by.

9 km (6 mi.) north-west of Chemainus at Ladysmith (population 4500) **Ladysmith**
the TransCanada Highway crosses the 49th Parallel. In addition to its
various species of tree Ladysmith's Canada Crown Zellerbach Forest
Arboretum also has a collection of vintage locomotives and steam
engines.

The Vancouver Island section of the TransCanada Highway terminates at **Nanaimo**
Nanaimo (population 51,000; the island's second largest town) where
ferries leave Departure Bay on the 67 km (42 mi.) crossing to Horseshoe
Bay (Vancouver). Nanaimo evolved from a Hudson's Bay Company
settlement called Colville Town, which owed its existence to the alert-
ness of Company agents who saw the potential in the coal deposits they

were shown by local Indians. The first settlers, mainly English and Scottish miners, arrived in 1851 and for the next 75 years coal dominated Nanaimo's economy. Demand fell sharply after the Second World War however and in 1953 production ceased at the town's last remaining mine. Today Nanaimo makes its living from the timber and fishing industries, from its harbour, and to an ever increasing extent from tourism. The offshore islands in the Strait of Georgia, and the surrounding mountains and lakes, all offer good opportunities for recreation. Indisputably the highpoint of Nanaimo's year is the "Great International Bathtub Race" in mid-July. Nothing daunted the participants in this now classic event set out to cross the 55 km (34 mi.) Georgia Strait to Vancouver in a flotilla of variously modified, outboard-engined bathtubs.

Nanaimo Centennial Museum

Nanaimo Centennial Museum (100 Cameron St. open May–Sep. Mon.–Sat. 10am–6pm, at other times Mon.–Fri. 10am–4pm) concentrates on the area's local history. Among the well-presented displays are a re-created coal mine, an old miners' hut and a diorama on the coastal Salish. The museum also has an interesting collection of coast Salish masks, basketwork and carvings. Tourist information available.

Bastion

Standing on Front St. is a small wooden tower known as the Bastion. The only remaining one of its kind it was built by the Hudson's Bay Company in 1853 as protection for the settlement's pioneer miners in the event of Indian attack. Inside today is a little museum. Every noon throughout July and August soldiers in period uniform fire one of the two cannon with appropriate ceremony. The old town centre overlooking the picturesque little smallcraft harbour (also the seaplane terminal) has been rejuvenated with many restored old buildings, re-cobbled streets and sidewalks, and open-air cafés in which to sit and relax. The walk along Waterfront Promenade, past Georgia Park with its display of authentic Indian canoes and totem poles, to Swy-A-Lana Lagoon is really delightful.

Newcastle Island Park

Popular with trippers (passenger ferry in summer) the 300 ha (740 acre) Newcastle Island which directly faces the harbour provides fine views of the coast and the mountains (Nares Point). The Pavilion, built in 1931, contains a Visitors Centre (information about walks, coastal flora and fauna, and the island's interesting history). Boat hire and beach.

Harmac Pulp & Lumber Mill

Definitely to be recommended is the tour of MacMillan Bloedel Ltd.'s fascinating Harmac Pulp & Lumber Mill (a sawmill and cellulose factory, open Mon., Wed., Fri. 1pm).

Gabriola

20 minutes away by ferry Gabriola (population about 3000), the northernmost of the Gulf Islands, is a quiet holiday retreat with little chalets and holiday homes, enchanting bays and eye-catching viewpoints. Scuba diving.

Petroglyph Park

Rather than the work of the coast Salish living in the area at the time of their discovery, the Indian rock drawings preserved in Petroglyph Park (3 km (2 mi.) south of Nanaimo) are believed to be more than 1000 years old.

Nanoose Bay

26 km (16 mi.) north-west of Nanaimo, Nanoose Bay has some well-frequented bathing beaches and a large, sheltered yacht harbour (sailing school, boat hire, Naval submarine training establishment).

Parksville

With its long sandy beaches on tranquil Georgia Strait, Parksville (population 6000) is a favourite summer holiday resort. Be sure to visit the Craig Heritage Park, a small local museum with a number of historic buildings (open: Sun. noon–4pm).

Among its many attractions this much-visited Provincial Park, about 3 km (2 mi.) south of Parksville, has a level sandy beach over 2 km (1¼ mi.) long. At the Park office information can be obtained about guided tours of the "Horne Lake Caves" situated some 20 km (12 mi.) to the north (there are many more caves than those so far open to the public).

Rathtrevor Beach Provincial Park

West coast detour to the Pacific Rim National Park

About 4 km (2½ mi.) south of Parksville, Hwy. 4 branches off at the start of a thoroughly rewarding 185 km (115 mi.) detour to Tofino on the west coast.

Just 20 km (12 mi.) west of Parksville Little Qualicum Falls is one of Vancouver Island's loveliest Provincial Parks, a forested upland area with numerous little ravines and waterfalls and glorious sparkling blue-green pools irresistably inviting for a swim.

Little Qualicum Falls Provincial Park

In the MacMillan Provincial Park some 15 km (9 mi.) further on, a stand of towering Douglas firs known as "Cathedral Grove" (which somehow managed to escape a forest fire about 300 years ago) includes several specimens between 600 and 800 years old. A forest walk winds through the grove past trees up to 75 m (245 ft) tall with trunks as much as an impressive 3 m (10 ft) across. Beyond the Park the road continues westwards across the Beaufort Range, where Mount Arrowsmith (1806 m (5930 ft)) is a popular ski area (Dec.–Apr.).

MacMillan Provincial Park

With a population of 20,000 Port Alberni (16 km (10 mi.)) is the largest town on the west coast of Vancouver Island as well as a major port; despite its length Alberni Inlet, which penetrates 50 km (31 mi.) inland, is deep enough for ocean-going ships. Fishing vessels operating out of Port Alberni account for about 20 per cent of all the salmon caught in British Columbian waters. Huge cellulose factories, paper mills and sawmills (the earliest of which was built in 1864), process the region's wealth of timber. From Port Alberni a 69 km (43 mi.) unsurfaced road goes to Bamfield at the northern end of the West Coast Trail (a six to eight day hike).

Port Alberni

In summer the little M.V. "Lady Rose", built in Scotland in 1937, makes her way along the Barkley Sound to Bamfield or (on alternate days) north through Broken Group Islands (part of the Pacific Rim National Park) to Ucluelet, delivering passengers, post and freight to outlying communities en route.

"Lady Rose"

The Alberni Valley Museum in the Echo Recreation Centre (4255 Wallace St., open daily 10am–5pm, Thu. till 9pm) has among other things displays of pioneer artefacts and baskets and tools made by west coast Indians. It is also a mine of information about fishing.

Alberni Valley Museum

Seaplane, boat or 100 km (62 mi.) of gravel road from Port Alberni (thrice-weekly bus service) are the only ways of reaching the picturesque little fishing community of Bamfield (population 240), snugly situated in the shelter of Bamfield Inlet on the eastern side of Barkley Sound. Here instead of a village street there is just open water and a boardwalk over a kilometre long. Bamfield is also the start of the 72 km (45 mi.) West Coast Trail to Port Renfrew (see Pacific Rim National Park). There are a couple of reasonably short and entirely delightful walks, one to Keeha Bay on the Pacific, the other to the lighthouse at Cape Beale. Boat hire; scuba diving on sunken wrecks off the deeply indented coastline; excursions by boat to the Broken Group Islands, part of the National Park.
  See Pacific Rim National Park (91 km (56 mi.) from Port Alberni).

Bamfield

Vancouver Island

Ucluelet

Situated on a promontory right on the Pacific coast, the small fishing village of Ucluelet (Indian = "safe harbour"; population 1600) is a convenient gateway to the northern section of the Pacific Rim National Park (see entry). Near Ucluelet itself Amphitrite Point with its lighthouse and Marine Tracking Station is exceptionally scenic. In years past the tortuous, often storm-battered and mist-shrouded coastline brought disaster to many ships.

Trips to the Broken Group Islands, big game fishing, scuba diving and whale-watching are also possible from Ucluelet. In April and again in late autumn Pacific grey whales pass by on their long migration.

Tofino

Also at the end of a promontory, some 42 km (26 mi.) north of Ucluelet, Tofino (population 1000) is another very attractive little fishing village and one of the oldest settlements on the west coast, a trading post supplying local settlers having first been established on Stubbs Island in 1875. There are boat trips to Hot Springs Cove (Maquinna Marine Park, 30 km (19 mi.) north) where the water temperature reaches almost 50°C (122°F), and to Meares Island. Whale-watching trips and scuba diving can also be arranged. West Coast Maritime Museum (open: June–Aug., Mon.–Sat. 10am–5pm). Scenic flights by seaplane.

Long Beach

Around Tofino there are magnificent beaches of fine sand, Long Beach included, where in summer it is possible to bathe.

Clayoquot Sound

Clayoquot Sound, which with its deep fiords and countless little islands opens out north-west of Tofino, is one of the last surviving areas of temperate rain forest. A recent decision by the provincial government to allow clearance of half the remaining 3500 sq. km (1350 sq. mi.) of virgin wilderness has met with increasingly fierce opposition (see Baedeker Special, page 502).

Tofino, Vancouver Island

Detour to Strathcona Provincial Park

About 10 km (6 mi.) north-west of Campbell River there are more gigantic Douglas firs to be marvelled at in the Elk Falls Provincial Park, as well
as several waterfalls plummeting as much as 25 m (80 ft). Nowadays
these latter can only really be appreciated in the Spring, when the flow
of water from the nearby dam is increased following the melting of the
snow.

**Elk Falls
Provincial Park**

When the Quinsam River was dammed in 1974 a hatchery was established in an attempt to counteract the effect of the dam on salmon
stocks. Although in 1976 only 2000 fish returned to spawn, by 1986 the
numbers had recovered to several hundreds of thousands. The Visitor
Centre at the hatchery (variable opening hours) provides imaginatively
presented and comprehensive information on the life cycle of the
Canadian salmon.

Quinsam River
salmon hatchery

Created in 1911 in a mountainous area of exceptional scenic beauty to the
west of the Campbell River, the Strathcona Provincial Park can claim to be
the oldest in British Columbia. Included in its more than 2300 sq. km (900
sq. mi.) are over 100 km (62 mi.) of hiking and nature trails, good water-
sports facilities on Upper Campbell and Buttle Lakes (accommodation,
campsites) and three Nature Conservancy Areas, virgin wilderness
accessible only on longer hiking tours. Strathcona is a magnificent landscape of clear mountain lakes, waterfalls, exceptionally rugged peaks
snow-covered throughout the year, small glaciers and karst country
(caves). The "Canadian Outdoor Leadership Training School" (Strathcona
Lodge) organises various courses (mountaineering, canoeing and kayaking, survival in the wilde, etc.). Information about the Park can be obtained
from the Park headquarters at Buttle Lake. A good 40 km (25 mi.) road runs
alongside the lake to the Westmin Resources Mines (mining and logging
co-exist in the Park together with nature conservancy). In summer there
are free guided tours of the mine (zinc, copper, lead).

**Strathcona
Provincial Park**

Northern Vancouver Island

Alert Bay, on the small, crescent-shaped Cormorant Island (45 minutes
by ferry from Port McNeill via Sointula), is the site of one of the earliest
Nimpkish Indian (Kwakiutl) coastal settlements. At the end of the 18th c.
Indians were encouraged to move to the island to make up a workforce
for salmon curing during the fishing season. This in turn led to the establishment of a mission station (Church Mission). Today the inhabitants of
the delightful little fishing village and the Nimpkish Indian Reserve total
about 1100. Twelve elaborately carved totem poles adorn the Indian
cemetery while in nearby Fir St. a small local museum has been set up.
A short distance along is the Village Office (information). Sunday services at the charming Anglican church (on the waterfront; built in 1879)
are in Kwakiutl.

Alert Bay

As well as displays of the typical Indian masks and everyday artefacts
the U'Mista Cultural Centre (open May–Sep. Mon.–Fri. 9am–5pm, Sat.
1–5pm), about 2 km (1¼ mi.) west of the ferry terminal, houses a collection of potlatch gifts confiscated in 1921 when potlatch ceremonies were
banned. Guided tours of the centre (Mon., Tues., Sat.) sometimes also
feature dancing, films, or demonstrations of traditional food preparation
(reservations required, P.O. Box 253, Alert Bay, B.C. V0N 1A0; tel. (604)
974–5403).

U'Mista Cultural
Centre

Not far from the Centre stand a traditional long-house (used as a community centre) and the "world's tallest totem pole" 73 m (240 ft) high.
Made by Indian craftsmen in 1971 it is carved from top to bottom.

Totem pole

Totem poles in Alert Bay

Tallest totem pole in the world

Port Hardy

500 km (310 mi.) after leaving Victoria the Island Highway terminates at Port Hardy (population 5300) on Vancouver Island's northern end. From here ferries make the trip through the Inside Passage (see entry) to Prince Rupert, departing from the new Bear Cove ferry terminal on the east side of Hardy Bay. In addition to the income generated by tourism and the ferry services, the economy of this increasingly prosperous, sprawling little town is dominated by the fishing and timber industries and more especially by the big copper mine at nearby Rupert Inlet. Utah Mines Ltd. is the largest employer in the area and responsible for 10 per cent of Canada's entire copper production. The original settlement at Port Hardy, founded in 1904, was on the east side of the bay. When the government decided to locate the new harbour installations on the west side, the inhabitants had either to cross the bay or drive round. Beyond Port Hardy the extreme north of Vancouver Island remains virtually untouched, just as it was when the earliest settlers first saw it.

Fort Rupert

Not far from the airport a chimney stack is now all that remains of the Hudson's Bay Company's old fort, erected in 1849 to serve as an Indian trading post as well as a base for workers at the Beaver Harbour colliery. It was destroyed by fire in 1890. In 1912 the Indians of the Kwakiutl village at Beaver Harbour were the subject of an early documentary film "In the Land of the Canoes" (of which there are showings at the Provincial Museum in Victoria). The Port Hardy Museum (Market/Shipley St.; open in summer daily 10am–4pm, in winter Tue.–Sat. noon–4pm) has exhibitions devoted to the history of the region as well as an excellent collection of Kwakiutl artefacts. Nature trails.

Cape Scott Provincial Park

Created in 1973 the 151 sq. km (58 sq. mi.) Cape Scott Provincial Park on the north-west tip of the island is virgin countryside, accessible only on foot and completely unexploited even from a tourist point of view. Almost permanently drenched in rain throughout the year this inhospitable coast is pounded by mighty Pacific rollers which surge in over vast tracts of sand. The Park is about 60 km (37 mi.) from Port Hardy. After 37 km (23 mi.) the more than adequate gravel surface gives way to a good forestry road, which continues as far as Holberg (since the Second World War a Canadian military base/radar station; small motel, pub, small shop and filling station). Anyone intending to make the trip on a working day is advised to call in at the Western Forest Products (WFP) Ltd. office first, to enquire about road conditions. This is also where the drivers of the huge timber transporters operating in the area get their information from.

★★Pacific Rim National Park

Central west coast of Vancouver Island
Area: 5110 sq. km (2000 sq. mi.)
Established: 1970

The Superintendent, Pacific Rim National Park, PO Box 280, Ucluelet, B.C. V0R 3A0; tel. (604) 7627721.

Information

From Victoria: Hwys. 1 and 19 to Parksville, then Hwy. 4 westwards via Port Alberni to Tofino or Ucluelet. (Beyond Port Alberni the road deteriorates.)

Access

The best known part of the Park is the Long Beach section which begins a few kilometres/miles south-east of Tofino. Here on the superb long sandy beaches massive piles of driftwood testify to the violence of the ocean waves. Away from the beach are areas of moss- and fern-covered rain forest typical of the Pacific north-west, and also stretches of swamp and

Long Beach

Tree trunks washed ashore on the coast of the Pacific Rim National Park

bog. Various hiking and nature trails cross the Park. Beach combing is a more popular pastime than bathing on the magnificent beaches – even in high summer the water is cold (6 to 15°C (43 to 59°F)) and the currents strong. All kinds of flotsam comes ashore (the glass floats from Japanese fishing nets being much sought after) and sea creatures and flora abound. Whales can often be spotted, especially in spring and autumn.

Although the maritime climate is relatively mild it tends to be very changeable and damp. Blanketing mist and lengthy rain showers can be expected at any time even in summer.

Wickaninnish Centre

The Wickaninnish Centre is worth visiting (information, natural history displays, films, Park Ranger programmes, restaurant, terrace with telescope for sea-lion and whale-watching). North-west of the Centre the beach extends for 16 km (10 mi.).

Broken Group Islands

The Broken Group Islands lie a short distance south-east of Ucluelet in the Barkley Sound, a multitude of characteristically densely wooded small islands and islets separated by a labyrinth of narrow channels. For the most part completely undeveloped they can be reached only by boat. There are eight campsites, all without facilities of any kind, and a Park Ranger on Nettle Island. This section of the Park is popular mainly with canoeists and the more adventurous outdoor enthusiasts who enjoy camping in the wildest of the wilds. Ospreys are a common sight. Access from Port Alberni, Bamfield and Ucluelet.

West Coast Trail

Until the beginning of this century Canada's stormy Pacific coast with its treacherous shallows and rocky headlands was known to sailors as the "graveyard of the Pacific"; a great many ships were lost in storms and fog. To give survivors a means of escape from this otherwise impassably rocky coastline backed by impenetrable rain forest, a primitive trail was opened in 1906, following the route of the telegraph lines laid in 1890 between the various lighthouses. About 40 years ago, having lost its raison d'àtre with the advent of modern navigational aids, communications and aircraft, the trail was allowed to lapse. In the 1960s however, the 6 to 10 day hike along the West Coast Trail was discovered by backpackers, and when the National Park was created the authorities set about restoring and extending the route. Throughout the summer Park Rangers now regularly patrol the 72 km (45 mi.) trail, a richly rewarding but extremely arduous hike across challenging terrain. The trail is still only roughly marked out and the very basic campsites along the way have no sanitary facilities. Nor can any supplies be obtained. In the season Indians will ferry hikers across the Nitinat Narrows for a small fee; other rivers have to be waded or crossed by simple bridge or (in some cases) primitive cable-car. Good equipment and waterproof clothing are essential – it can be soaking wet or foggy and cool even in July and August. At Pachena Bay, 5 km (3 mi.) south of Bamfield at the northern end of trail, there is an Information Centre where maps are available. Most people begin the hike from there.

★★Victoria   H 6

Province: British Columbia. Altitude: 17 m (56 ft)
Population: 70,000 (Greater Victoria 263,000)

Information

Tourism Victoria, 812 Wharf Street, Victoria, B.C. V8W 1T3; tel. (604) 382 2127.

Access

By plane:
Victoria International Airport near Sidney, 20 km (12 mi.) to the north on Hwy. 17; regular scheduled flights from Vancouver and Seattle (USA), regional Vancouver Island services.
Airport bus to/from the Empress Hotel.

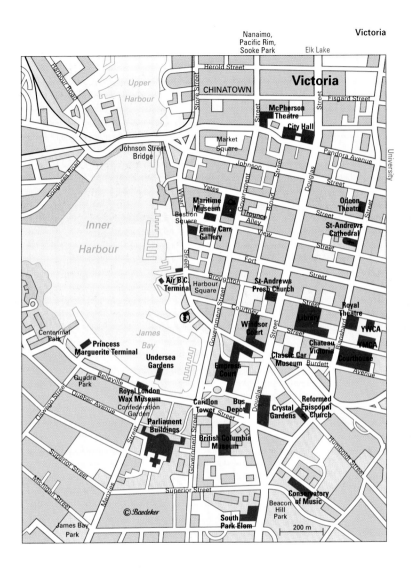

By rail:
VIA Rail station, 450 Pandora St.: daily service between Victoria and
Courtenay (Vancouver Island).

By bus:
Pacific Coach Lines: Victoria–Vancouver, as well as regional Vancouver
Island services.
Island Coachline: Victoria–Port Hardy.

Empress Hotel and Harbour

City transport:
Vancouver Island Transit System: buses from downtown Victoria to Sooke and Sidney.

Ferries:
Victoria–Port Angeles/Wash. (Olympic Peninsula).
Sidney–Anacortez/Wash.
Swartz Bay (29 km (18 mi.) north)–Tsawwassen (Vancouver).
Victoria–Seattle/Wash. (only in summer).
Nanaimo (111 km (69 mi.) north-west)–Horseshoe Bay (West Vancouver).
Victoria Clipper (passengers only) Victoria–Seattle.

Victoria, provincial capital of British Columbia since 1871, lies at the southern tip of Vancouver Island (see entry), the largest island on the Pacific coast of North America. Only the narrow Juan de Fuca Strait separates it from the USA's Olympic Peninsula with its often snow-covered peaks. Sheltered in the lee of mountains and influenced by the warm North Pacific current the city enjoys the mildest climate in the whole of Canada. Even in January the temperature averages 5°C (41°F) (August 17°C (63°F)) as a result of which Victoria's parks and gardens are festooned with foliage and flowers throughout the year. In comparison with Vancouver (the province's commercial capital on the nearby mainland) Victoria is quiet, skyscraper-free and largely administrative and residential. To these charms is added a downtown area around the snug Inner Harbour which retains its Victorian buildings and atmosphere. Well-tended parks, flower baskets hanging from bright blue lamp standards, red double-decker buses and a leisurely rhythm to life, all help to foster the impression of a typically English colonial town. In the Empress Hotel people still gather for afternoon tea at five. Victoria today is more British than the UK and has been a favourite destination for American tourists since the early part of this century.

Victoria was founded in 1843 as a Hudson's Bay Company fort. Faced by the impending loss of its Oregon territories to the USA, the Company abandoned its western headquarters at the mouth of the Columbia River and moved to Vancouver Island, christening the new trading post Victoria in honour of the British Queen. Six years later the island became a British Crown Colony. When in 1858 there was a gold strike in the Cariboo Mountains, being the southernmost harbour on the west coast of Canada Victoria and its 800 inhabitants experienced turbulent times. More than 20,000 gold hunters and adventurers flocked to the province from California (among them a great many Chinese, and for a time Victoria had the largest Chinatown north of San Francisco). Overnight the little port became the base and supply depot for the prospectors. A town of tents sprang up around the harbour, the surrounding forest was cleared and a frantic building boom got under way. In next to no time new arrivals from America made up the vast majority of its residents and the sleepy pioneer settlement had become a typical gold-rush town with all the trappings of saloons, bars and dives. Even so Victoria's founding Governor James Douglas managed to maintain some semblance of law and order and in less than ten years the gold fever had subsided. In 1866 Vancouver Island and mainland British Columbia were united into a single Crown Colony with Victoria as its capital, joining the Canadian Confederation five years later in 1871. With the arrival in Vancouver in 1887 of the trans-continental railroad Victoria gradually yielded economic supremacy to its mainland rival while itself remaining the seat of provincial government. Even as long ago as the turn of the century Victoria's peaceful ambience and mild maritime climate attracted more and more visitors, and the south-east coast of Vancouver Island quickly found favour among wealthy Canadians for holiday, second or retirement homes. Together with the provincial government and the tourist industry the Canadian armed services are today among the area's major employers, in particular the naval base at Esquimalt. Fishing, timber and horticulture play a subsidiary role.

★Inner Harbour Visitor Centre

Situated on the Inner Harbour, Victoria's city centre is easily explored without transport. Maps and leaflets detailing circular walks (e.g. "Victoria on foot"), are available from the Information Centre on the harbour's east side. Daily guided tours are arranged in summer.

Parliament Buildings

Dominating the south side of the Inner Harbour is the imposing seat of British Columbia's provincial government, the Parliament Buildings, designed by the Yorkshire architect Francis M. Rattenbury and erected in 1897. Set in neat, orderly gardens, the complex of buildings, of heavy stone construction, is very attractive in appearance, and especially so in the evening when lit by festoons of lights. Perched high above the massive dome is a gilded statue of Captain George Vancouver (1757–98) who accomplished the first circumnavigation of Vancouver Island.

Figures of famous personalities from the province embellish the façade. (Guided tours of the buildings Mon.–Fri. from 10am.) A large statue of Queen Victoria surveys the Inner Harbour from the terrace. Tours of the town centre by horse-drawn carriage leave from near by.

Royal London Wax Museum

On the harbourside north of the Parliament Buildings stands the grandiose former Canadian Pacific terminal, likewise designed by Rattenbury and built in 1924. It now houses the Royal London Wax Museum (open daily 9am–9pm), a collection of more than 200 highly authentic wax models of famous people.

★Pacific Undersea Gardens

A myriad creatures native to the Pacific, including seals, salmon, sharks and – most fascinating of all – a really scary octopus, can be observed at close quarters through the large underwater viewing window of the Pacific Undersea Gardens. Open May–Sep. daily 9am–6pm, Oct.–Apr. daily 10 am–5pm.

Victoria: Parliament Buildings

★Empress Court Hotel	Built in 1908 for Canadian Pacific, the Empress Court Hotel on the Inner Harbour is one of Victoria's best-loved landmarks. Like the Château Frontenac in Québec (see entry), of which it might be said to be the West Coast counterpart, the Empress Court was designed by architect Francis M. Rattenbury. Entering the vast lobby of this luxurious hotel is like journeying back in the time to before the First World War. "Five o'clock tea", served with great style, is an experience for any visitor,
Miniature World	An extension on the north side of the hotel houses a collection of several dozen *scenes en miniature*, among the most pleasing of which are the World of Charles Dickens, scenes from old London, and a miniature circus. Young and old alike are captivated by the model of the Canadian Pacific Railway. Open daily 9am–4pm.
Old Town	Immediately north of the Empress Court are the principal thoroughfares of Victoria Old Town – Wharf Street, Government Street and Douglas Street running north-south, Johnson Street, Yates Street and Fort Street crossing them. Painstakingly renovated and restored over recent years, the Old Town boasts some historic buildings and old-fashioned shops such as Roger's Chocolate and the tobacconist E.A. Morris. Bastion Square, with its pretty shops and restaurants, occupies the site of the original Fort Victoria, constructed in 1843. Market Square and the hidden away Trounce Alley, a redevelopment of old warehouses, are also charming. More old buildings between Government Street and Douglas Street house the Victorian Eaton Centre, a shoppers' paradise, The Harbour Walkway, which starts at the light blue painted Johnson Street Bridge (a restored suspension bridge) and continues round the busy harbour with its colourful boats to Laurel Point and Fisherman's Wharf, makes a delightful waterfront promenade.
★Emily Carr Gallery	This gallery at 1107 Wharf St. features the work of Victoria's most famous daughter, the outstanding and internationally renowned artist

Emily Carr (1871–1945). Canadian landscapes and the life of the north-west coast Indians provide the dominant themes. An instructive and well put together audio–visual programme documents the artist's life and work. Open Tue.–Sun. 10am–5pm.

The former Court House (1869) in Bastion Square is now the Maritime Museum of British Columbia, displaying a host of items from the age of sail. Centerpiece of the exhibition is the "Tilikum", a large Indian canoe in which, at the beginning of the century, some fearless souls voyaged to England. Also commemorated – appropriately enough in the old Court House – is the legendary Richard Matthew Begbie whose administration of justice at the end of the 19th c. led to his being christened "the Hanging Judge". Open daily from 9.30am–4.30pm.

Maritime Museum of British Columbia

Adjoining the Old Town to the north is Victoria's small but nevertheless charming Chinatown. Entered through a conspicuous red gate it occupies just two blocks close to Government Street and Fishgard Street. A century ago, when 8000 people lived in the Chinese quarter, it was notorious for its brothels, gambling and opium dens.

Chinatown

British Columbia's provincial museum is situated in Heritage Court, midway between the Parliament Building and the empress Court Hotel. Open daily from 9.30am to 5pm, it is by far the best museum of natural and cultural history in Canada.

★★Royal British Columbian Museum

On the first floor a series of dioramas recreate the varies landscapes and wildlife of the province (including a life-size mammoth featured to particular effect). On the second floor visitors are taken on a journey through time; reconstructions of an old sawmill, a gold mine, a fish processing factory and a turn-of-the-century street bringing to life days long past. The museum's Indian History Gallery houses what is almost certainly the finest and most comprehensive exhibition of any on the history, culture and art of the north-west coast Indians (including canoes, wooden masks, a variety of textiles, a Salish earth house and a traditional Kwakiutl Big House). Haunting Indian songs are played through loudspeakers. Be sure also to visit Thunderbird Park located behind the museum. Here, in addition to some marvellously carved totem poles, a typical Haida Long House has been erected, in which Indian craftsmen can be seen at work. The museum's newest attraction is the National Geographic Theatre (opened 1998), turning the spotlight on a range of natural phenomena and traces of long forgotten cultures.

In front of the museum stands the 30 m (98 ft)-high Carillon, a bell tower paid for in earlier times by Canadians of Netherlands extraction.

Open to visitors to the south of the museum is the mid-19thc., Helmcken House, J.S. Helmcken, a practising doctor, was also a leading local politician. He campaigned vigorously for the then British colony of Victoria and British Columbia to join the newly established confederation of Canada.

Helmcken House

The Crystal Garden, situated diagonally opposite Helmcken House, is certainly worth a visit. Constructed in 1925 (modelled on London's Crystal Palace), the glass building is today a kind of tropical conservatory filled with fragrant plants. Flamingoes, parrots and monkeys add a further exotic touch. Open daily 8am–5.30pm.

Crystal Garden

Green and well-tended, Beacon Hill Park, south-east of the Royal British Columbian Museum, is a favourite recreation area close to the town centre. From its highest point there are lovely views across the Juan de Fuca Strait to the snowy peaks of the Olympic Peninsula (Washington/USA). A milestone on the south-west edge of the park marks the western end of the TransCanada Highway (see Nature, Culture, History; Suggested Routes).

Beacon Hill Park

British Columbia Provincial Museum

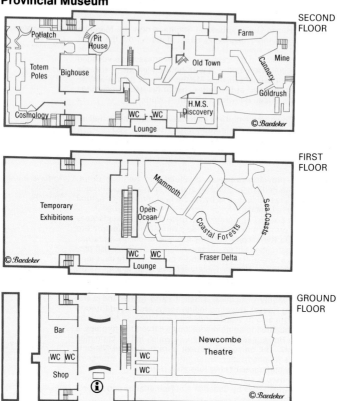

SECOND FLOOR

Potlatch · Pit House · Farm · Mine · Old Town · Totem Poles · Bighouse · Cannery · Goldrush · H.M.S. Discovery · Cosmology · WC · WC · Lounge · © Baedeker

FIRST FLOOR

Temporary Exhibitions · Mammoth · Open Ocean · Coastal Forests · Sea Coasts · WC · WC · Fraser Delta · Lounge · © Baedeker

GROUND FLOOR

Bar · WC · WC · Shop · WC · WC · Newcombe Theatre · © Baedeker

★Carr House

A few minutes walk west of Beacon Hill Park stands the Carr family's handsome old timber house (207 Government St.), dating from 1864. Richard Carr's wealth was acquired through his extremely profitable real estate business. His daughter Emily achieved international recognition as an artist. Viewing mid-May–mid-Oct. daily 10am–5pm.

Rockland

The elegant Rockland area extends south-east of the town centre. Government House, in its beautifully kept gardens (1401 Rockland Ave.), is the official residence of Her Majesty's representative in British Columbia. The house itself is closed to the public but the gardens are a delight.

Craigdarroch Castle

A short walk north leads to the striking Craigdarroch Castle (1050 Joan Crescent). This fairy-tale mansion, considered a gem of Victorian archi-tecture, was built in the 1880s by an immigrant Scottish entrepreneur Robert Dunsmuir for his wife. Dunsmuir made his fortune when coal mining started on Vancouver Island. Open daily 10am–5pm, certain days in summer until 9pm.

Further west, near Fort Street, stands the celebrated Gallery of Greater Victoria (1040 Moss St), occupying a most beautiful Victorian building. In addition to contemporary western Canadian art, there is an impressive display of Indian artefacts and archaeological finds of art-historical interest. The gallery also possesses what must certainly be one of the best collections of Far-Eastern art anywhere in the world. Among its treasures is the only Shinto shrine outside Japan. Open Mon.–Sat. 10am–5pm, Sun. 1–5pm.

★Art Gallery of Greater Victoria

The Scenic Marine Drive is a 13 km (8 mi.) panoramic route along the south and south-east coast of Vancouver Island as far as Cattle Point on Oak Bay (leaving Victoria proceed along Dallas Rd., Hollywood Cres., Crescent Rd. and Beach Dr.). One superb view follows another of the bays on the Juan de Fuca Strait.

Scenic Marine Drive

For a visit to one of the area's premier attractions follow Highway 17A north for 22 km (14 mi.) to the magical Butchart Gardens at Brentwood Bay on the Saanich Peninsula. Here in 1904 Jenny Butchart, wife of a wealthy quarry owner, started to lay out a fragrant garden in abandoned limestone workings. Flourishing, not least because of the mild climate, the gardens have since been developed into a 20 ha (50-acre) horticultural tour de force without rival in Canada. The Italian garden, rose garden, Japanese garden and sunken garden are among the loveliest. Open spaces among the pools, fountains and the many exotic plants are used for artistic and musical performances. Open Jul.–Aug. daily 9am–11pm, May, Jun., Sep. daily 9am–9pm, Mar., Apr., Oct. daily 9am–5pm, Nov.–Feb. daily 9am-4pm. Fireworks every Saturday evening in high summer.

★Butchart Gardens

The gun batteries at Fort Rodd in the Hill National Historic Park, about 13 km (8 mi.) west of Victoria, used to guard the sheltered waters of Esquimalt Harbour, once a British naval base. The guns were in service from 1895 to 1956. Today the well-preserved fortress can be visited; in summer expert guides are on hand to explain about the defence works and ordnance.

Hill National Historic Park

Victoria Island

C/D 7–10

Administrative units: Northwest Territories, Nunavut
Area: 21,000 sq. km (8106 sq. mi.)
Altitude: 0–655 m (0–2150 ft)
Population: about 2000

Situated directly off the northern coast of mainland Canada Victoria Island is the third largest in the Canadian Archipelago. Over 550 km (340 mi.) from north to south and 650 km (400 mi.) from east to west it lies well north of the Arctic Circle (the latitude of its southernmost point being 68°30′N). Ice-Age glaciers were responsible for the monotonous, mainly flat terrain and moraines, drumlins and glacial lakes dominate the landscape. The greatest heights are found on the Wollaston Peninsula in the south-west (up to 518 m (1700 ft) and in the north where the Shaler Mountains reach 655 m (2150 ft) above sea level.

Location

Victoria Island was discovered in 1826 by Sir John Franklin (1786–1847) but was never properly mapped until quite recently. The creation of the new Territory of Nunavut in 1999 divided the island administratively into two.

History

Canada's central Arctic region is administered and supplied from Iqaluktuutiak (Cambridge Bay) on the island's south-east coast. European seafarers searching for the Northwest Passage, missionaries

Iqaluktuutiak

517

and fur traders were among the earliest to call in at this remote spot which, in 1839, was named after the Duke of Cambridge by a pair of English traders. Until the 1950s the area was used chiefly by the Copper Inuit as a summer camp; "Iqaluktuutiak" it was called in Inuktitut, meaning "good place to fish". After the Second World War a US military Early Warning station was established here, bringing a corresponding boost to the economy. Iqaluktuutiak's main features are its stone-built Catholic church and modern wind-generation plant. There is a fish canning factory processing mostly arctic char, a relative of the salmon with exceptionally good red meat. Other sources of income are handicrafts and servicing expeditions (fishing, trekking and birdwatching). During the short Arctic summer there is an abundance of animals and in particular birds to be observed.

Holman

The second place of any significance on Victoria Island is Holman on the west coast. Located at the tip of the Diamond Jenness Peninsula this small community of 300 is already quite well prepared for the burgeoning numbers of tourists attracted to the North. There is even a golf course.

"Qiviut"

This is an appropriate point at which to mention one of the area's more unusual tourist enterprises – courses on the preparation and use of "qiviut" i.e. musk ox hair (softer than camelhair, though not quite as soft as genuine cashmere). Those taking part learn to make dyes from lichen and to spin, weave, or knit the yarn.

★★Waterton–Glacier International Peace Park   H 8

Province: Alberta. US State: Montana
Area: 4630 sq. km (1787 sq. mi.)
Established: Waterton Lakes National Park 1895; Glacier National Park 1910.

Information

Waterton Lakes Information Center in Waterton Townsite.
Entrance Rd./Prince of Wales Rd. (open mid-May–mid-Sep. 8am–6pm, in the summer months until 10pm).
Glacier National Park: St Mary Visitor Center (open May–Oct.)
Logan Pass Visitor Center (open Jun.–Sep.).
Apgar Visitor Center (open May–mid-Dec.).

Location

The Waterton–Glacier International Peace Park in the Rocky Mountains straddles the border between the Canadian province of Alberta and the US state of Montana. It is about three hours drive from Calgary (see entry). Of the two National Parks making up this relatively unspoilt area of the Rockies close to the Continental Divide (watershed), Canada's Waterton Lakes National Park is the smaller. It was amalgamated with the adjoining US Glacier National Park in 1932. Though bisected by the frontier, the two form a single geographic unit. The Waterton–Glacier International Peace Park was designated a UNESCO Biosphere Reserve in 1979.

Topography

To the Indians the Waterton–Glacier area was "the land of the shining mountains"; to the American journalist and naturalist George Bird Grinnell it was "the crown of the continent". The magnificent high mountain scenery with precipitous rock faces, more than four dozen glaciers and over 200 lakes is to a large extent untapped wilderness traversed by a network of just under 1500 km (930 mi.) of hiking trails and mountain tracks. A number of strikingly scenic roads, generally closed in winter, make this mountain fastness accessible to anyone touring by car. There are excursions by boat on the larger lakes such as Waterton Lake and McDonald Lake.

In the shape of their central mountain chain consisting of the Lewis and Livingston Ranges the two National Parks comprise a distinctly alpine section of the Rockies. The north-west/south-east orientated continental watershed forms the western border of the Waterton Lakes National Park and splits the Glacier National Park in two. From the east, the mountains appear like a huge wall rising abruptly out of the Great Plains. On the western side on the other hand they slope up more gradually.

Geology

The landscape here was fashioned by dramatic movement of the earth's crust over a period stretching from 200 million to 40 million years ago. During the formation of this segment of the Rocky Mountains, relatively hard Palaeozoic sedimentaries were displaced eastwards some 70 km (43 mi.) and upward at an inclination of some 10°, coming in the process to overlie more recent chalk strata. Geologists believe that the resulting mountains originally reached heights of about 5000 m (16,400 ft). Mt Cleveland (3190 m (10,469 ft)) is the highest mountain in the Park today.

During the last glacial periods a vast ice sheet covered the mountain range, which was shaped by slow-moving glaciers. Ice Age glaciation was at its most severe during the Wisconsin icing about 12,000 years ago, when only the highest peaks protruded.

The principal features of the landscape are U-shaped valleys with high vertical rock faces, lateral hanging valleys from which countless waterfalls cascade into the main valley below, narrow sharp-edged ridges and crests, and more than 200 smallish karst lakes in addition to larger lakes in the terminal basins. All are testimony to the heavy glaciation occurring during the Pleistocene period. The 50 or so glaciers in the Park at the present time are not however relics of the great continental ice sheets, having formed more recently and after the intervening warm period. In contrast to the usual type of valley glacier they are mostly wide and relatively short. They are found on slopes exposed to the north-east wind, which piles the snow up in great accumulations below the normal snow-line

The prevailing winds are southerlies and south-westerlies, bringing with them moist air from the Pacific. The resulting precipitation mainly affects the western parts of the Park; on the eastern side the winds are felt as a "chinook" (a warm, dry wind occurring in the lee of mountains). Thanks to the chinook, winter in Waterton is normally milder than elsewhere in Alberta. Not only do these warm winds speedily melt any snow lying in the valleys, they also swiftly dispel the incursions of cold air from the Arctic which hold the rest of the province in their wintry grip. The onset of a strong chinook in January 1966 saw the temperature near Pincher Creek rise by 21°C (70°F) in only four minutes, and though the average winter minimum temperature at Waterton Lake is −32°C (−26°F), the average maximum temperature is as high as 10°C (50°F). While in mild winters the lake only freezes for a few days, in severe ones it can be covered by a thick sheet of ice from January to April, making it possible to skate the 6½ km (4 mi.) to the lake-end in Montana.

Climate

Summers are generally pleasantly warm and dry but unfortunately also short (mid-June to the end of August). In the relatively windless months of July and August maximum daily temperatures range between 23°C (73°F) and 35°C (95°F).

Precipitation varies considerably within the Park. The prairie section near the eastern entrance averages only 760 mm (30 in.); below the ridge of mountains at Cameron Lake on the other hand, twice that amount is recorded (1520 mm (60 in.)). As a result, while hemlock spruce, fir and red cedar forests (Lake McDonald Valley) clothe the valleys and slopes to the west of the watershed and thrive in the wetter, warmer Pacific air, on the drier eastern side the tree-line is considerably lower and the sub-alpine fir cover much less dense. Where to the east the mountains give way to prairie there are some open stands of aspen.

Flora

In the short snowfree summer months the mountain meadows of the

Arctic sub-alpine vegetation zone are transformed into a gloriously colourful sea of wild flowers, vast in number and some being rare. Beargrass (*Xerophyllum tenax*) is typical of the species found on the mountain slopes, a cyclical flowering plant which in many years carpets great tracts with its creamy-white petals on tall stalks and in other years is nowhere to be seen.

Fauna

Botanists divide the Park into six bio-climatic zones. First comes a wet zone of many lakes and areas of swamp, populated by sedges, birch and willow (e.g. Maskinonge Lake and the beaver ponds at Blakiston Creek) and offering food and shelter to beaver, musk rat, mink, duck, geese and also moose. Second is a narrow prairie zone – the furthest western extremity of the Canadian Great Plains – intruding into the Park from the east and providing a habitat for coyote and bison (since 1952 the Park has once again come to support a small herd of bison in the special Bison Paddock near the entrance on Hwy. 5). Next there is a parkland zone bordering the prairie, with open aspen stands and groves (e.g. Belly River, Vimy Peak Trail), followed by the "montane zone" of mountain valleys and lower slopes, where the pine and Douglas fir forests are the haunt of red deer, cougar and black bear. The fifth, sub-alpine, zone extends to the tree-line (Cameron Lake, Summit Lake Trail); here spruce, Englemann fir, larch and silver pine flourish along with bear-grass, gentian and – among other fauna – grizzly bears. Finally comes the alpine zone (above the tree-line; dwarf-pine) merging into alpine meadows, the home of marmot, Rocky Mountain goats and bighorn sheep (which make their way down to the valleys in the autumn).

234 different species of bird, 57 species of mammal and 17 species of fish have been recorded in the Park, emphasising its importance as a refuge for increasingly threatened wildlife. In autumn the lakes are a stopping place for countless migratory birds. None of the three types of snake found in the Park is poisonous. Since the 1980s there has again been a pack of grey wolves roaming the Park. These keep mainly to the more remote valleys of the North Fork Flathead River in the north-west together with the adjacent parts of British Columbia. Unlike bears, wolves pose no danger to visitors hiking in the Park.

Far more likely to be seen are bighorn sheep, white Rocky Mountain goats, wapiti, moose, whitetail and mule deer, beaver and marmot. One of the largest attractions though is the little herd of bison grazing its prairie pasture. With luck it is also possible to catch a glimpse of the white-headed osprey, sadly now facing extinction. In autumn kokanee salmon congregate to spawn in lower McDonald Creek.

Sights

★Bison Paddock

A road circuits the large buffalo enclosure situated north of the Park entrance (Hwy. 5). The little herd is kept as a reminder of the vast numbers of bison which once roamed the Prairies.

★Red Rock
Canyon Parkway

About 5 km (3 mi.) beyond the Park entrance a narrow road branches off Hwy. 5 towards Red Rock Canyon, following Blakiston Creek which has here created a massive alluvial fan between Lower and Middle Waterton Lake. The road passes through successive bio-climatic zones between the prairie and Mt Blakiston (2940 m (9650 ft)), highest peak in the Waterton Lakes National Park. The very attractive Red Rock Canyon, reached after 15 km (9 mi.), was formed by a small tributary cutting deep into the red sedimentary rocks (from the Pre-Cambrian Grinell Formation). The canyon's distinctive colouring is due to the high iron content of the rock, set off by patches of bluish green algae.

Waterton Lakes

From its superb site above the narrow "Bosporus" which flows between Upper and Middle Waterton Lakes, the majestic Prince of Wales Hotel, designed by a Swiss architect and completed in 1927, enjoys magnificent views of the two lakes and the surrounding mountains. In the 1920s the President of the American Great Northern Railway hit upon the idea of offering coach tours from Glacier National Park to Jasper and Waterton Lakes was judged the ideal stop-over. With a depth of 152 m (498 ft) Upper Waterton Lake (1279 m (4197 ft) above sea level) is the deepest in the Canadian Rockies. Walkers can take advantage here of the water-taxi to Crypt Lake. All year round in Emerald Bay sub-aqua enthusiasts are to be seen diving to the wreck of a steamer which sank there in 1918. The vessel, built in 1907, was used to ship logs to a sawmill on the Waterton River.

The twin Canadian and US National Parks are linked by the Chief Mountain International Highway (Hwy. 6/SR 17), passable from mid-May to mid-September. Built in 1935 and running partly through the Park and partly through the Blackfoot Indian Reserve, the road initially provides exceptionally fine views of the Waterton Valley. Then follows a long stretch when Chief Mountain (2763 m (9068 ft)) is plainly visible, an isolated limestone relic of the Pre-Cambrian period which erosion has separated from the main mountain range. This furthermost manifestation of the Lewis overthrust towers above the rolling hills of the prairie, a sacred mountain to the Indians and a once important point of orientation. Crossing the US frontier after a drive of 22 km (14 mi.) (the highest peak in the Glacier National Park, the 3190 m (10,469 ft) Mt Cleveland, can be seen to the south-west), the road continues for a further 24 km (15 mi.) before meeting US 89. Following this south for another 21 km (13 mi.) leads to St Mary and the eastern entrance to the Glacier National Park. Outside the summer months access to the two National Parks is via US 89 and Hwys. 2 and 5 via Cardston (Alberta). This route also provides superlative views.

★ Chief Mountain International Highway

At Babb, about 14 km (8½ mi.) from St Mary, a 20 km (12 mi.) side road (closed in winter) branches off to Many Glacier, an area of exceptional scenic beauty. Rocky Mountain goats and black bears can often be spotted from the road. Built in 1914 the Many Glacier Hotel on the shores of Swiftcurrent Lake is the Park's principal resort, conjuring up an image of Switzerland with staff dressed in lederhosen and dirndls. From here there are various walks and mountain hikes to e.g. the Grinnell Glacier, the Granite Park area, Iceberg Lake (where even in high summer ice-floes dot the sparkling emerald water) and Red Rock Falls. By following the 4 km (2½ mi.) Swiftcurrent Lake Nature Trail starting from the hotel much of interest can be learned about beavers, geology and the forested mountain sides. Boat excursions are also run from the hotel on Swiftcurrent and Josephine Lakes. Boat rental, trail riding.

★ Many Glacier

Opened in 1932 the 80 km (50 mi.) road from St Mary over the Logan Pass (2026 m (6650 ft)) to West Glacier is considered one the loveliest mountain roads in North America, offering some of the very finest views. The narrow winding route is generally only passable from the second week in June to mid-September and is closed to vehicles over 2.5 m (8 ft) wide or 9 m (29 ft) in length. From St Mary it first skirts the northern shore of St Mary Lake (look out for the information board after about 6 km (3½ mi.) giving details of the "Triple Divide" just to the south – the watershed of three drainage systems flowing into the Pacific, North Atlantic and Gulf of Mexico respectively). The view of St Mary Lake and the encircling peaks from the big bend beyond Rising Sun must be one of the most photographed in the entire Park. From the lake the road climbs steeply up to Logan Pass and Logan Pass Visitor Center, above which tower the imposing Reynolds (2782 m (9130 ft)) and Clements Mountain (2674 m (8776 ft)). From the Visitor Center a 2 km (1¼ mi.) Nature Trail leads through the Hanging Gardens. The brilliant display of colour from the wild flowers blooming in the short summer season is a

★ Going-to-the-Sun Road

never-to-be-forgotten sight. There is also a good chance of seeing some of the inhabitants of this alpine ecosystem, the marmots and Rocky Mountain goats. Two of the mountain walks here deserve particular mention, one to the crescent shaped Hidden Lake and the other to the Granite Park Chalet (along the steep sided Garden Wall with its sharp ridge). Beyond Logan Pass the road down into the McDonald Valley is a marvel of highway engineering, snaking daringly through various curves and a big, sharp bend to the valley below.

From Avalanche Creek campsite in the McDonald Valley a popular walk along the "Cedar Trail" goes to Avalanche Lake, fed by five waterfalls. Built as a private house in 1913 the historic Lake McDonald Lodge, right on the lakeside, retains much of the atmosphere of the old West and acts a base for mountain hikes to Sperry Chalet and the Sperry Glacier (backpackers can carry on over Gunsight Pass to St Mary Lake). Boat trips on the lake are run from the Lodge. Boat rental, trail riding. From July to the beginning of September hikers can use the cabins at Sperry Chalet and Granite Park Chalet for overnight stops provided they book in advance (Belton Chalets, P.O. Box 188, West Glacier, MT 59936).

★Welland Canal   J 14

Information	Welland Canal Society, St Catharines, Ontario; tel. (416) 6841135.
Location	The 42 km (26 mi.) Welland Canal joins Lake Ontario (75 m (246 ft) above sea level) and Lake Erie (at 174 m (571 ft) above sea level almost 100 m (330 ft) higher). The canal is situated not far from the world famous Niagara Falls and close to the Canadian-US frontier. It takes eight massive locks to surmount the so-called "Niagara Escarpment" separating the two large lakes.
Canal craft	Every year more than 1000 ocean-going ships and about 3000 other sea-going vessels pass through the locks, as well as "lakers" and other inland craft mostly sailing under the Canadian flag. In 1990 freight carried totalled about 48 million tonnes, wheat, iron ore and coal being the principal commodities.
History	The first Welland Canal was opened in 1829. A second was built between 1845 and 1915, and a third between 1887 and 1930. Even this was unable to meet the demands of ever increasing traffic and larger ships however, and on August 6th 1932 the Governor General of Canada inaugurated a route designed for modern needs. Between 1967 and 1973 a 13 km (8 mi.) stretch near the little town of Welland was re-aligned and straightened and the opportunity simultaneously taken to rebuild an important road and rail underpass. The old canal which leads directly through Welland is now used by pleasure craft and water-skiers.
Welland route	The eight locks are each 261.8 m (860 ft) long, 24.4 m (80 ft) wide and 9.1 m (30 ft) deep. Ships using the seven lifting locks and the single containing lock which make up the canal staircase are restricted to a maximum length of 222.5 m (730 ft) and 23 m (75 ft) beam. The maximum permitted draught is 7.9 m (26 ft) and the maximum air draught 35.5 m (116 ft). To raise or lower a ship 14.2 m (46 ft) in one of the seven chamber locks involves sluicing 94.5 million litres (20 million gallons) of water into or out of the lock, a procedure which normally takes about ten minutes.
Lock 1	Lock 1 is located right at the Lake Ontario entrance to the canal. Close by are the Port Weller dry-docks.
Lock 2	The second lifting lock is at St Catharines a short distance inland. Picnic place nearby.

An observation platform at Lock 3 (south of St Catharines) gives an excellent view of the lock in operation. Information centre.	Lock 3
The three twin-flight locks (4, 5 and 6) are the most interesting part of the canal. They can handle two ships simultaneously, one going up and the other in a parallel lock going down.	Locks 4, 5, 6
Situated at the small town of Thorold Lock 7 is the final lifting lock on the Niagara Escarpment section of the canal.	Lock 7
The Thorold Tunnel (Hwy. 58), the first to pass under the canal, was opened in 1968.	Thorold Tunnel
In August 1974 the M.V. "Steelton" rammed Bridge No. 12 at Port Robinson, destroying it.	Port Robinson
The length of old canal made redundant by the new stretch completed in 1974 is now used for watersports and by pleasure craft. Leisure and sports facilities are provided on Merritt Island, which lies cut off between the two canals. Information board (history of the canal).	Merritt Island
Main Street Tunnel (road) under the canal at Welland was opened in 1972.	Main Street Tunnel
The Townline Tunnel (road and rail) was built under the canal in 1973.	Townline Tunnel
The regulating system at Lock 8 (at the Lake Erie end of the canal at Port Colborne) is one of the largest in the world. Interested spectators can watch from the viewing tower in the adjacent park.	Lock 8
The interesting Merritt Trail takes in various old and modern sections illustrating different phases in the enlargement of the canal.	Merritt Trail

An ocean-going freighter in the flight of locks on the Welland Canal

Whistler

G 6

Province: British Columbia. Population: 7000

Resort

The famous ski resort of Whistler at the foot of the Whistler and Black Comb massifs is the centre of the biggest winter sports area in North America.

Two cable cars and 30 chair- and T-bar lifts give access to the two massifs. Downhill skiers can choose between about 200 pistes (the longest having a drop of 1600 m (5250 ft)). Snowmobile trips, heli-skiing and ski marathons are all popular with visitors. The newest attraction is "7th Heaven", a summer ski area on the Horstman and Black Comb Glaciers.

Whistler has more than 1300 units of tourist accommodation ranging from apartment blocks to hotels. Activities such as tennis, golf and riding, as well as white-water rafting and kayaking on the area's untamed rivers, attract growing summer tourism, as do canoeing, rambling and backpacking in the peaceful isolation of the magnificent highland wildernesses (including the Garibaldi Provincial Park, Cheakamus Lake, Singing Pass Region).

★Whitehorse

E 3

Administrative unit: Yukon Territory
Population: 20,000

Location

Whitehorse, capital of the Yukon Territory (see entry) since 1953, stands at the intersection of the Alaska and Klondike Highways (see Klondike), about 80 km (50 mi.) north of the provincial border with British Columbia (see entry). Home to half the population of the Yukon Territory, in recent years Whitehorse has become a major centre for the opening up of the Canadian north-west.

Tourism

Tourism is of increasing importance to the town, a starting point for tours of the Northland. Today, with scheduled flights augmented by charter planes bringing in several thousands of Europeans for adventure holidays, Whitehorse offers all the necessary facilities. Among the items in the shops especially typical of the area are gold nuggets and Indian and Inuit craftwork, carvings in wood, ivory and soapstone, drawings and paintings, and the Inuit boots called mukluks, all being very popular.

History

Whitehorse, like Dawson, owes its existence to the Klondike gold-rush which began in 1897. Having survived the arduous journey from Skagway over White Pass (in the course of which many lost their lives) the gold prospectors then had to negotiate the Miles Canyon and Whitehorse rapids before descending the Yukon River to Dawson (see entry). Almost from the first a small settlement grew up on the river's right bank opposite the present town. The seething, foaming waters of the rapids, rearing like white steeds, gave the settlement its name – White Horse. Although nothing remains to be seen of the rapids (the Sunwapta Lakes having since been dammed), driving through the canyon today still conveys a vivid impression of the hardship which this stretch of the river must have represented in those early days.

When in 1898–1900 the White Pass/Yukon Railway from Skagway was constructed, its northern terminus was on the western bank and so the present town was born. From Whitehorse the legendary Yukon River sternwheelers pounded their way downstream to Dawson (see entry). One of the largest, the S.S. "Klondike", is now permanently berthed in Whitehorse and forms one of the town's major landmarks. When the gold-rush subsided the population of Whitehorse fell dramatically. For a time copper mining kept the town alive but when this too halted in the

1920s numbers sank to fewer than 400 inhabitants. In 1942 however the building of the Alaska Highway (see entry) and with it an influx of more than 20,000 newcomers, provided a fresh impetus comparable to the first arrival of the railway. At the same time Dawson (see entry) was experiencing an ever deepening crisis which led eventually to its relinquishing its role as capital of the Territory to Whitehorse in 1953.

Sights

The sternwheelers on the Yukon River remained the region's most important mode of transport for decades after the gold-rush. It was not until 1955 that the S.S. "Klondike", built in 1937, gave up carrying ore from the silver mines in Mayo (see Klondike, Klondike Highway, Silver Trail) to Whitehorse for onward shipment by road. Today the restored and refitted paddle steamer welcomes visitors on the Yukon embankment in the town centre.

★S.S. "Klondike"

The McBride Museum in First Ave. has a large collection of relics and photographs from the gold-rush days. These include the log cabin belonging to Sam McGee about whom Robert Service, "Bard of the Yukon", wrote a famous ballad. There are also numerous bits of old machinery and implements and an interesting display on the wildlife of the Yukon (open mid-May to Sep.).

McBride Museum

The "Frantic Follies", a nightly revue (June–Sept.) in the Sheffield Hotel is hugely popular. Can-can girls and honky-tonk piano naturally feature in this 1890s-style vaudeville show. Book in advance: tel. (403) 668–7377.

★Frantic Follies

On weekdays there are guided tours of the Territorial Government Building in 2nd Ave.

Government Building

On the way from Skagway to Whitehorse

It is decorated with tapestries and paintings produced in the Yukon (particularly worth seeing).

Works by local (as well as other Canadian) artists can also be seen in the Art Gallery, housed in the building next to the city library.

Art Gallery

Standing on the corner of 3rd Ave. and Elliot St. the old wooden Anglican cathedral, built for the Rev. R. J. Bowen and completed in October 1900, has a collection of documents and photographs recording early missionary work in the Yukon Territory (see entry).

Old Log Church Museum

A visit to Whitehorse's 9 ha (22 acre) botanical garden is the best possible introduction to the region's trees and other flora.

Yukon Gardens

Free history tours of Whitehorse are arranged by the Yukon Historical & Museums Association (tel. (403) 667–4704).

Town tour

Once the ice has begun to break up in the spring, king salmon hurry upstream from the Pacific to their Yukon River spawning grounds. Some even journey as far as Whitehorse, taking about 60 days over the about 3000 km (1860 mi.) trek. To watch as these magnificent fish climb the fish ladder provided for them is a unique and very moving experience.

★Ascent of the king salmon

Surroundings

Members of the Conservation Society lead nature walks through the pleasant environs of the town (tel. (403) 668–5678). Local travel agents also lay on a variety of tours e.g. by bus, horse-drawn carriage or aboard the M.V. "Schwatka" to Miles Canyon and Schwatka Lake.

Tours

The twin-decked M.V. "Anna Maria" makes the traditional trip down the Yukon River to Dawson (see entry). Highly recommended: tel. (403) 667–4155.

Yukon River trip

See Klondike, Klondike Highway.

Takhini Hotsprings

Visitors are made welcome at the Yukon's solitary reindeer farm near Lake Laberge (Shallow Bay Road, 30-minute drive from Whitehorse).

Reindeer farm

The museum at Black Mike's Gold Mine, 37 km (23 mi.) south of Whitehorse, brings to life gold mining in the old Klondike days.

Black Mike's Gold Mine

Windsor

J 14

Province: Ontario. Population: 250,000

The industrial city of Windsor is situated on the south (Canadian) side of the Detroit River, linked to the US city of Detroit by bridge and tunnel. Strategically positioned on the Great Lakes waterway Windsor's port comes second only to its car industry which, like Detroit's, is the main pillar of the local economy. The good neighbourly relations between the two cities are clear for all to see when they annually join forces to celebrate Canada's National Day (July 1st) and America's Fourth of July.

Location

Windsor (founded in the 1830s) and Detroit lie in an area first settled by the French at the turn of the 18th c. A trading post established by Antoine de Lamothe de Cadillac in 1701 on the north side of the Detroit River quickly became the regional centre for the French fur trade before

History

◀ S.S. "Klondike", Yukon sternwheeler

being captured by the British in 1760 and later handed over to the Americans after the War of Independence. Except for a short interval during the 1812 Canadian-American War the river has formed the frontier between the two countries ever since

Sights

Hiram Walker
Museum

This historical and ethnological museum which traces Windsor's development since the earliest days of colonisation, occupies the oldest house in the city, overlooking the river. The section on North American Indian culture is especially interesting. Open Tue.–Sat. 9am–5pm, Sun. 2–5pm.

Gardens

The Jackson Park Sunken Gardens (Tecumseh Rd.) and the Dieppe Gardens (Quellette St.) are particularly worth seeing for their roses (500 varieties in all totalling some 11,000 bushes).

Surroundings

Fort Malden

Fort Malden (30 km (19 mi.) from Windsor) was built between 1797 and 1799 by the British, after they were forced to abandon Detroit to the Americans. Only the base of some ramparts remain and a barracks restored to its 1840 state. The site commands a magnificent view of the Seaway. It was here that the Shawnee Chief Tecumseh met General Brock to negotiate peace. In the small museum in the grounds a slide show illustrates the fort's history and its role during the 1812 war and the Mackenzie Rebellion of 1837 to 1838.

**Jack Minor
Sanctuary**

The Jack Minor Bird Sanctuary, 47 km (29 mi.) away in Kingsville, was established in 1904 by the naturalist Jack Minor. It is at its best during the spring and autumn migrations (Mar./Apr. and Oct./Nov.) when huge flocks of Canada geese and wild duck call in on their flight north or south. Open Mon.–Sat. 9am–6pm.

★★Winnipeg   H 11

Province: Manitoba. Population: 650,000

Winnipeg, the "Prairie capital", is situated equidistant from the Atlantic and Pacific at the confluence of the Red and Assiniboine rivers. Within a period of 260 years it has evolved from little more than a muddy pool (Indian, "win nipi" = "murky water") to become the capital of Manitoba and the fourth largest city in Canada. In addition to its excellent economic structure Winnipeg enjoys a very active cultural life. It has six professional performing arts companies offering everything from drama and ballet to concert and opera, some of which e.g. the Royal Winnipeg Ballet and the Manitoba Theatre Centre, have won international acclaim.

Ethnic diversity is one of the hallmarks of the city, Britons, Germans and Ukrainians heading the list of more than 40 ethnic groups. St Boniface, the French quarter, has the largest Franophone community west of Québec.

Winnipeg is also a city of trees, an estimated 2 million. Mostly planted before 1920 various species are represented including some 250,000 elms alone.

History

In 1738 Sieur de La Vérendrye chose the site for his Fort Rouge which later became the nerve centre of a flourishing fur trade marked by increasingly bitter rivalry between the North West and Hudson's Bay

Seven Oaks House

Lockport

Winnipeg

Highway

Nairn. Ave.

Rue

Thunder Bay

Logan

Avenue

Higgins

Henderson

Avenue

CHINATOWN

Oak Point

Ukrainian
Cultural Centre

Manitoba Museum
of Man and Nature

Planetarium

Centennial
Centre

Civic Centre

Whitler
Park

Archibald

Notre Dame Ave.

Winnipeg
Square

Provencher

Thunder Bay

Portage
Place

Portage

Main

Ave.

Smith

Boulevard

College
St-Boniface

Cathedrale
St. Mary's

St. Boniface
Cathedral

Convention
Centre

Union
Station

Civic
Auditorium

Street

The Forks

St. Boniface
Museum

Upper Fort
Garry Gate

Tache Avenue

Government
House

Legislative
Buildings

River

Street

Airport

Winnipeg Gallery University

Western Canada Aviation Museum

Fort
Rouge
Park

Assiniboine

Marion

Street

OSBORNE
VILLAGE

Eugenie Street

Osborne

Red River

St. Mary's

Dubuc Street

Donald

Assiniboine Park

Highfield Street

Lyndale Drive

Street

Churchill Drive

Winnipeg

500 m

© Baedeker

Pembina

Bartlett Avenue

USA

Zoo

The Mint

Companies. In 1821–22 the Hudson's Bay Company established its own Red River trading post, christened Upper Fort Garry. The settlement which grew up outside the fort took its name from the Cree word "winnipi" meaning "murky water".

It was still a small community of only 215 inhabitants when the province of Manitoba was created in 1870. But by the time of its incorporation in 1874 the figure had grown to 1,879, and ever since then Winnipeg has been the premier manufacturing and marketing centre in western Canada. In 1882 it became an important stop on the first Canadian east-west railroad, soon developing into the financial, industrial and retailing capital for the entire West. At the same time, agriculture became a major factor in the province's economy. Following the first shipment of wheat from Manitoba in 1876 a multitude of grain trading businesses sprang up in the city and the Winnipeg Grain Exchange, now the Winnipeg Commodity Exchange, was founded.

The greatest period of expansion however occurred between 1901 and 1914. The population increased to 100,000 as immigrants from Europe and America poured into the prairies, among them large numbers of Ukrainians, French-Canadians, Germans, Poles and Scandinavians, producing the city's characteristic mix of ethnic groups each of which preserves its language and traditions.

This was the time also when the city centre began to take shape, the insatiable demand for housing, offices and business premises brought about by the influx of immigrants giving rise to a building boom.

Winnipeg was hard hit financially in 1914 by the opening of the Panama Canal which proved to offer a cheaper route for freight to British Columbia and Alberta. The set-back proved temporary, being overcome in time by the city's transformation into the major manufacturing centre in the prairies with, amongst others, extensive clothing, food processing, furniture, farm machinery, machine tool and electronic components industries. It is this diversification which largely accounts for the city's enviable economic stability.

In the 1920s Winnipeg began to present a more outward-looking and cosmopolitan face, as well as acquiring a symphony orchestra, ballet company and professional theatre (it already had a university, the University of Manitoba founded in 1877). In the early 1970s the city enjoyed another building boom. Old and dilapidated downtown buildings were replaced and the centre was revitalised with numerous high-rise blocks. Following a period of recession at the start of the 1980s the pace of new building quickened again in 1983.

Sights

Main Street

Main Street is the heart of Winnipeg, a principal thoroughfare giving access to all parts of the city, and for over a century the throbbing artery of its business and commerce. At one time the houses were concentrated together and everything could be bought here. Today the street is a kaleidoscope of Winnipeg's past, present and future.

★Exchange District

Turn-of-the-century Victorian and Edwardian commercial architecture is most in evidence in the vicinity of the old market place neighbouring the present Civic Centre. This area is known as the Exchange District, its name a reflection of the many financial and commodity dealing houses which sprang up in Winnipeg between the 1880s and 1920s when the city was the undisputed centre of expansion in western Canada. Thanks to the Hudson's Bay Company's fur trade, the Stock Exchange, and the Winnipeg Grain and Produce Exchange, vast quantities of goods and money changed hands in the town.

More recently the Exchange District has seen a revival of its earlier role as the hub of local commerce, with old warehouses, bank and business premises being converted into fashion boutiques, up-market shops, art galleries, bureaux and restaurants.

The area is also a focus for the city's cultural life with an impressive selection of venues including the Pantages Playhouse Theatre, the Manitoba Theatre Centre, the Prairie Theatre Exchange, the Manitoba Centennial Centre, the MTC Warehouse Theatre and the Artspace. Shoppers too will find plenty to interest them (fashions, art and furniture).

A weekend market is held in summer in the Exchange District's Market Square, a showplace for the city's wide range of ethnic products. On sale is a vast variety of traditional home cooking as well as work by local artists and craftsmen. Street musicians add their own distinctive flavour to the market atmosphere.

Old Market Square

The Manitoba Centennial Centre with its lovely terraced gardens embellished with attractive fountains and appealing sculptures, was built for the Canadian centennial celebrations in 1967. Other features to date include a concert hall and planetarium. The province's own centenary was celebrated in 1970 when the Manitoba Museum of Man and Nature and the Manitoba Theatre Centre were opened.

★Manitoba Centennial Centre

While the outstanding and highly informative Museum of Man and Nature (Rupert Ave.; open Mon.–Sat. 10am–5pm, Sun. and holidays noon–6pm) is primarily devoted to the human and natural history of Manitoba province, it also has sections covering the formation of the earth and universe, early human history, and the regional environment, past, present and future. All are entertainingly and instructively presented with the aid of dioramas, reconstructions, original exhibits, graphics and audio-visual material. Among other things visitors can see the first sailing craft to cross the Hudson Bay in 1668, "journey" from the

★★Manitoba Museum of Man and Nature

View of Winnipeg

531

Winnipeg

Arctic to the Prairies, and enjoy the experience of 1920s vaudeville theatre. They can also examine pieces of the most ancient rock on earth from the Canadian Shield, formed some 3.75 million years ago during the Pre-Cambrian era.

Planetarium

The excellent Planetarium has programmes illustrating the wonders of the universe as well as shows and films on topics such as the exploration of space. The superb "Touch the Universe" science gallery with more than 60 multi-dimensional exhibits and hands-on activities for all ages engenders a unique appreciation of the universe as we know it today.

★Ukrainian Cultural & Educational Centre

The important Ukrainian Centre (Alexander Ave.; open Tue.–Sat. 10am–4pm, Sun. 2–5pm (not the library); closed holidays, including Ukrainian ones) comprises a historical and ethnographic museum, art gallery (temporary exhibitions) and library. The folk art collection includes embroideries, weaving, pysanky (Ukrainian Easter eggs), wood carvings, ceramics and traditional costume.

The Centre also possesses stamp, coin and map collections.

City Hall

Standing on a site occupied by two generations of its predecessors, City Hall was completed in 1974. It consists of two buildings joined by an underground link. (Guided tours arranged by the Mayor's office.)

Winnipeg Square

Situated at the Main Street/Portage Avenue intersection, Winnipeg Square is an attractive modern shopping precinct.

★Portage Place

A few blocks further west on Portage Avenue stands the complex of ultra-modern buildings known as Portage Place. Located in this architecturally striking development are numerous shops and offices, several restaurants, three cinemas and an IMAX theatre with a vast screen on which action movies in particular show to spectacular effect.

University of Winnipeg

Founded in 1867 the University of Winnipeg (guided tours) enjoys something of a liberal reputation. The oldest building on campus dates from 1894. Also noteworthy are the Western Canada Pictorial Index, an archive of some 45,000 old photographs, and the splendid new Athletics Centre, a facility used by top athletes.

Fort Garry Place

This site on south Main Street near Union Station was where Upper Fort Garry formerly stood, close to the confluence of the Assiniboine and Red Rivers. Only the north gate survives from what was one of the Hudson's Bay Company's foremost trading posts in the Canadian West. Opposite, on the south-east side, stands the modern headquarters of the now almost completely restructured fur trading company.

The Forks

A few years ago the large open space adjoining to the east was successfully developed as "The Forks", a popular entertainment and shopping centre – a kind of vast multi-purpose indoor market.

Winnipeg Commodity Exchange

The Winnipeg Commodity Exchange (Main St.; open Mon.–Fri. 9.30am–1.15pm) is the most important institution of its kind in Canada. There is a gallery from which visitors can watch trading.

Knox United Church

For all its modern appearance Knox United Church in Qu'Appelle Street (city centre) is one of Winnipeg's oldest places of worship. It was built during the First World War.

Seven Oaks House

Seven Oaks House (Rupertsland Ave., not far from Main St.; open mid-May–mid-Jun. Sat., Sun. 10am–5pm, Jul.–Labour Day daily 10am–5pm) has the distinction of being the oldest habitable house in

Manitoba. Built in 1851 the large two-storey dwelling was constructed entirely of wood without using a single nail. It is decorated and furnished in period style.

Winnipeg has had a Chinese population for about 100 years, the earliest arrivals having migrated to Canada to work on the trans-continental railroad. The at first small and rather isolated Chinese community only really started to expand in the 1920s. From then on more and more businesses of every conceivable sort started to appear, ranging from exotic spice shops and porcelain and silk emporia to laundries and restaurants (some of which count among the city's best).

★Chinatown

Although a big tourist attraction Winnipeg's Chinatown still manages to preserve its distinctive oriental atmosphere.

Dedicated to the preservation and promotion of Chinese culture the Dynasty Building was part of a programme of redevelopment undertaken in the Chinese quarter. The Chinese gate between Logan Ave. and James Ave. was also erected as part of the same programme.

Dynasty Building

The St Boniface Museum (Tache Ave.; open Mon.–Fri. 9am–5pm, Sat., Sun. and holidays noon–5pm), the oldest building in Winnipeg, was constructed in 1846 for the Grey Nuns and was the first convent, hospital, girls' school and orphanage in the Canadian West. After restoration in 1967 it became a museum. On display are 2300 items, pictures, photographs, etc. documenting the history of Manitoba's French minority; also an extensive collection of Canadian and Metis artefacts. There are reconstructions of a workshop, Metis hunting camp, spinning room, shop, dining, working and sleeping quarters and a kitchen. The display of religious objects and vestments in the chapel off the foyer includes a small bell, the first in western Canada, originally presented to the convent by Lord Selkirk.

★St Boniface Museum

St Boniface Cathedral (Ave. de la Cathédrale) is the oldest cathedral in western Canada. Founded in 1818 fire caused it to be rebuilt on several occasions since. The façade and parts of the walls survived however and are incorporated in the latest (1970) building. The interior has modern furnishings. The grave of Louis Riel, born in St Boniface, can be seen in the churchyard.

★St Boniface Cathedral

St. Boniface Cathedral   Winnipeg

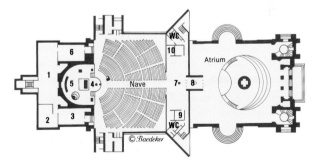

1 Catechism Room	4 Altar	7 Narthex
2 Workshop	5 Organ	8 Vestibule
3 Sacristy	6 Discussion Room	9 Cloakroom
		10 Vestry

Orthodox Church, Winnipeg

St Boniface

On Tache Ave., facing St Boniface Hospital, a monument salutes Pierre Gautier de La Vérendrye, the first white man to sail west on the lakes and reach the confluence of the Red and Assiniboine Rivers.

La Vérendrye Monument

No expense or modern comfort was spared when the now beautifully restored Victorian home of Hugh John MacDonald, former Prime Minister of Manitoba, was first built and furnished in 1895. Staff dressed in period costume escort visitors through the rooms (Carlton St.; open Jun.–Aug. daily 10am–6pm, Sep.–Dec., Mar.–May daily noon–5pm, Jan., Feb. Sat., Sun. noon–5pm; closed Mon., Fri. and holidays).

Dalnavert-MacDonald House

Riel House (National Historic Park in River Rd.) belonged to Louis Riel's family. It has been restored to reflect the social, economic and cultural realities of life for the Lagimodière and Riel families in the 1890s.

★Riel House

Built of local Tyndall stone and Italian marble the magnificent Neo-Classical Legislative Building (Broadway/Osborne St.; open daily 9am–8pm, guided tours mid-May–beginning Sep.) was completed in 1919. It contains the provincial legislative chambers, Prime Minister's and other ministerial offices and some government departments.

★Legislative Building

Surmounting the 72 m (236 ft) dome is a statue known as the Golden Boy, a 4 m (13 ft) high bronze weighing 5 tonnes and plated with 23.5 carat gold. A torch in his right hand and sheaf of wheat on his left arm symbolise Manitoba's enduring agriculturally based prosperity.

The building is set in 12 ha (30 acre) grounds adorned with statues of Queen Victoria and various influential statesmen. A monument to Louis Riel stands by the riverside.

Housed in its very modern building shaped like the bow of a ship, the Art Gallery (Memorial Blvd.; open Tue., Fri., Sat. 11am–5pm, Wed., Thu. 11am–9pm, Sun. noon–5pm) not only possesses a fine collection of old and contemporary art by Canadian, American and European artists but also one of the world's best collections of Inuit art.

★Art Gallery

The Living Prairie Museum (Ness Ave.; open Jul., Aug. 10am–6pm, at other times Mon.–Fri. 9am–1pm, Sat., Sun. noon–5pm) is an opportunity to visit one of the few remaining vestiges of natural prairieland. The 16 ha (40 acre) former conservation area harbours 200 species of native plants, including some now rare. Audio-visual and other explanatory material is provided in the reception area.

Living Prairie Museum

The University of Manitoba founded in 1877 is the oldest university in western Canada. It has its own art gallery, zoological museum, geological mineral collection, planetarium, greenhouses and many different displays.

University of Manitoba

Regional history and the pioneering days are the subject of this small historical museum (Portage Ave.; open daily mid-May–Labour Day, at other times workdays only).

The Historical Museum of St James Assiniboia

The Naval Museum in Smith St. (open by appointment only) has an assortment of items of interest relating to the British and Canadian Navies from the First World War to the present day. Naval personnel from the prairies and naval vessels named after prairie towns are two of the principal themes.

Naval Museum

The watermill known as Grant's Old Mill (in Portage Ave., near Grace Hospital; open Jun.–Aug. daily; May, Sep., Oct. weekends only) occupies the site of the Red River Settlement's first mill built in 1829.

Grant's Old Mill

Dating from 1853 St James Church (Portage Ave., by Tylehurst St.) is western Canada's oldest timber church.

St James Church

Winnipeg

Royal Canadian Mint

The Royal Canadian Mint (Lagimodière Blvd.; open Mon.–Fri. 9am–3pm) produces coins not just for Canada but for a number of other countries as well. Anyone interested can follow the whole minting process.

The ultra-modern building also contains a tropical garden, fountain and museum.

Manitoba Children's Museum

The Children's Museum (Pacific Ave.; open Tue.–Sat. 10am–5pm, Sun. and holidays 1–5pm) is a sort of activity centre for the young. In The Big Top, for example, they are able to re-create the world of the circus for themselves by dressing up, etc.

Winnipeg Police Museum

The museum at the Winnipeg Police Training Division in Vermilion Rd. brings together pictures, items of equipment and other memorabilia of the Winnipeg Police Department from its foundation to the present day.

Kildonan Presbyterian Church

Completed in 1854 Kildonan Presbyterian Church in John Black Ave. was the first of this particular denomination in western Canada.

Ross House

Ross House (in the Joe Zuken Heritage Park in Meade St.) was the Red River Settlement's first post office and is one of the area's earliest examples of a half-timbered building.

★Western Canada Aviation Museum

The Aviation Museum at the airport (open Mon.–Sat. 10am–4pm, Sun. and holidays 1–4pm) is the second largest of its kind in Canada. As well as several vintage aircraft (including a Tiger Moth, a Junkers JU 52, and a Bristol Freighter) the museum traces the signifance of aviation in Canada's history. One section is dedicated to Canadian Women in Aviation.

★Assiniboine Park

Assiniboine, Winnipeg's oldest park (Corydon Ave.; open daily 10am till dusk) encompasses 150 ha (370 acres) of grass together with superb trees and an English garden.

Zoo

The zoo is one of Canada's best, a collection of 1250 animals belonging to 300 species, many now threatened with extinction. Special emphasis is given to creatures of the northern latitudes (many of which are indigenous to Canada though there are also some rare exotic species such as the European bison, Siberian tiger and North Chinese leopard).

The zoo's internationally renowned tropical house is home to hundreds of free-flying birds, monkeys and reptiles. Also of interest are the Monkey House and the Native Bird Building. For children there are young animals at Aunt Sally's Farm.

The Winter Garden contains tropical plants and flower displays. Shows are held every month.

Assiniboine Forest

Adjoining Assiniboine Park on its southern side Assiniboine Forest (open 8am–10pm) is a large, 280 ha (692 acre) nature reserve. Various wild creatures and plants can be seen and there is an observation area beside the pond for birdwatching.

Kildonan Park

Some of the province's most ancient trees are to be found in the delightful Kildonan Park (open daily). There are also splendid flower gardens, a Hänsel and Gretel Witch's Hut, and an open-air theatre – the Rainbow Stage – where plays are performed in summer. Other attractions include a swimming pool and boat trips on the Red River.

Fort Whyte Centre

The Fort Whyte Centre (McCreary Rd.; open Mon.–Fri. 9am–5pm, Sat. and Sun. 11am till sundown) is known for its four lakes, grass and aspen parkland and areas of bog (accessible via boardwalks) where waterfowl and other wildlife can be observed. Walking trail. Information from the Interpretive Building.

Uniforms, weaponry and a variety of other items illustrating the history of western Canada's oldest military unit are displayed in the Royal Winnipeg Rifles Museum in St Matthews Ave.

The Pan Am Pool (Poseidon Bay) was built for the Pan American Games held in Winnipeg in 1967. The 65 m (213 ft) by 25 m (82 ft) pool is one of the largest in Canada. The generously proportioned Hall of Fame houses a collection of watersports memorabilia including a large array of stamps with designs reflecting sporting themes.

Exhibited in the Red River House Museum are items belonging to a former Hudson's Bay Company fur trader and explorer.

★Wood Buffalo National Park

Administrative units: Northwest Territories/Alberta
Area: 44,802 sq. km (17,294 sq. mi.)
Altitude: 183–945 m (600–3100 ft)
Established: 1922

On the Mackenzie Highway (AS Hwy 35; NT Hwy 1) through northern Alberta and the adjoining Northwest Territories to Enterprise. Thereafter NT Hwy 2 to Hay River and from there NT Hwy 5 south through the National Park to Forth Smith, from where the centre of the huge conservation area can be reached.

With a total area of about 45,000 sq. km (17,370 sq. mi.) Wood Buffalo National Park to the south of Great Slave Lake is one of the biggest national parks in Canada. Two-thirds of the Park lie in the province of Alberta, one-third in the Northwest Territories. The Slave River marks the eastern boundary of the Park.

Now listed as a World Heritage Site this vast conservation area extends across one of the world's largest inland deltas (the Athabasca-Peace River Delta), an immense wilderness of dried-out salt plains and wild landscape, dotted with lakes and swamps and traversed by rivers, the habitat of numerous now rare species of wildlife.

The Park was established in 1922 with the purpose of saving from extinction the last free-roaming herds of wood buffalo. Today more than 3000 of these animals graze the Park, together with moose, black bear, cariboo, beaver and a great variety of smaller mammals.

Every year whooping cranes arrive from Texas to breed and rear their young. Wood Buffalo National Park is one of the last, if not the very last, refuge for this extremely rare species of crane, now in desperate need of protection.

White pelicans breed beside the Slave River rapids, feeding from the Park's many lakes. The steep river banks afford good views of the nesting grounds.

Huge flocks of migratory birds visit the Athabasca-Peace River Delta on their annual pilgrimmage south.

Fort Smith evolved from a one-time fur trading post on the Mackenzie River route to the far north of Canada. From 1911 to 1967 it was the administrative capital of the Northwest Territories, a role which was then assumed by Yellowknife (see entry). A number of NWT government departments are still located in Fort Smith and the town's schools and training colleges have a national reputation.

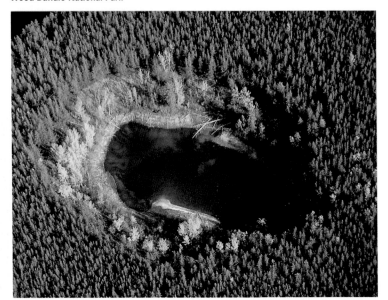

Sink hole

Salt plains in Wood Buffalo National Park

Apart from various prehistoric finds such as mammoth remains, etc. the Northern Life Museum (110 King St.) concentrates on the human history of the region. Exhibits include everyday Inuit artefacts and handwork, photographs and other documents relating to the pioneering days and early settlers, and Indian craftwork.

Open May–Labour Day, Tue.–Sun. (excl. Sat.), Tue. and Thu. 7–9pm.

★Yellowhead Highway

G/H 4–11

Route:
Prince Rupert–Prince George–Mount Robson PP–Jasper–Edmonton–Saskatoon–Winnipeg

The modern Yellowhead Highway (TransCanada Highway 16), the most northerly road link to Canada's Pacific coast, extends for almost 3000 km (1864 mi.) from Prince Rupert (see entry) on the west coast of British Columbia to Winnipeg. For the most part the well-surfaced road follows the traditional routes taken by fur trappers, prospectors and the early settlers. Roadside information boards (mileposts) detail important chapters in the opening up of western Canada.

A few miles west of Mount Robson Provincial Park a southern branch of the Yellowhead Highway (BC Hwy 5) turns off towards Kamloops where it joins TransCanada Highway 1.

The highway takes its name from Pierre Hatsination, a fair-haired Iroquois trapper who worked for the Hudson's Bay Company and was nicknamed "Tête Jaune" i.e "Yellowhead".

Name

Several roads branch off the Yellowhead Highway penetrating sparsely populated areas still very much in their wild state. Anyone embarking on one of the longer detours should recognise the element of risk involved and go properly equipped with adequate supplies of fuel, food and maps.

Detours

See entry

Prince Rupert

Called "kaien" (meaning "frothing water") by local Indians, the Butze Rapids are an interesting tidal phenomenon produced by the strong currents at the edge of the Morse Basin. Viewpoint on Hwy. 16 (5 km (3 mi.) east of Prince Rupert).

Butze Rapids

Another short detour leads to Port Edward (about 10 km (6 mi.) south of Hwy. 16) where in 1987 a museum (open: summer daily 10am–5pm) was created in the remnants of the old North Pacific Cannery, shut down in 1981. The cannery, established in 1889, was one of nineteen which used to operate on the Skeena River. It employed as many as 400 people in its heyday and a small, still very picturesque settlement grew up around the isolated factory with its warehouses and wharves. Like the factory itself a number of the simple log cabins are supported on stilts and linked by boardwalks. Some are now used for selling souvenirs and refreshments.

Port Edward

A few kilometres further on are the remains of the Inverness Cannery, burned down in 1973.

Inverness Cannery

The mighty fast-flowing Skeena River (called "K-shian" or "water from the clouds" by the Indians), about 500 km (310 mi.) long, played an important role in opening up the Canadian north-west. In the second half of the 19th c. this ancient Indian trade route became much used by European settlers as well, and from 1889 onwards sternwheelers plied its waters until the coming of the railway. Huge quantities of wood were needed to fuel the steamers on their way upriver, leading to a string of

★Skeena River

little settlements with jetties where stockpiles were kept. Most of these were gradually abandoned after the railway was built.

The stretch of railroad across the Coast Mountains posed serious problems for the engineers, vast amounts of explosives being used to blast a route through the granite of the Skeena valley. The 150 km (93 mi.) from Prince Rupert to Terrace cost $100,000 per mile, an enormous sum in 1910.

The Skeena River and its tributaries teemed with salmon, as a result of which canneries sprang up along its lower course. Fleets of fishing boats, generally two-man cutters, followed the shoals upstream. In the first half of the 20th c. depletion of salmon stocks caused by overfishing forced many plants to close.

Port Essington

40 km (25 mi.): An information board, some foundations, and a number of decayed wharves are a sad reminder of Port Essington, for 50 years the most important harbour on the Skeena River. It first came into existence in the 1870s during the Omineca gold-rush, quickly developing into a centre of river navigation and fishing. The arrival of the railway and the disappearance of the salmon led to its decline. By the 1950s only a few Indians and one or two fishermen remained. The bulk of the town was destroyed by a big fire in 1961.

Terrace

149 km (92 mi.): The small town of Terrace (67 m (220 ft) above sea level; population 11,000) lies on the eastern edge of the Coast Mountains which rise here to more than 2000 m (6500 ft). Until the 1960s life in Terrace was shaped entirely by the timber trade, but gradually the town has developed into a commercial and cultural centre serving the some 40,000 inhabitants of the lower Skeena River. Being fairly low down and in the lee of mountains it enjoys a relatively mild climate for its northerly latitude.

For a number of years now Terrace has been a popular base from which to venture into the surrounding wilderness on hunting, fishing, white-water rafting or "survival" expeditions. Other possibilities include floatplane and helicopter flights over the snow and ice covered Coast Mountains, "flightseeing" tours (taking several hours) to Ketchikan in Alaska, and holidays at a very remote but exceptionally well-equipped lodge complete with its own lake and hunting-grounds. For those in search of even more excitement there is hiking in the mountains and exploring the river in an inflatable boat.

Climbing Thornhill Mountain (1500 m (4923 ft)) brings rewards in the shape of marvellous views of the Skeena, Kalum and Kitimat valleys. The trip to the Sleeping Beauty Ridge area (Nass River) is equally full of delights.

Heritage Park

The fascinating Heritage Park outdoor museum (Kalum St./Kerby St.: open mid-May to Aug. daily 10am–6pm) features a number of log cabins and other interesting timber buildings dating from between 1910 and 1935. Some, furnished in the style of the period, evoke life in the pioneering days; others house various displays illustrating the region's history.

Lakelse Lake Provincial Park

Across the new Skeena River bridge (completed in 1976) Hwy. 37 South branches off Hwy. 16 to Kitimat, a small town 60 km (37 mi.) distant, at the head of a fiord penetrating deep inland. Some 26 km (16 mi.) along the road lies Lakelse Lake (pronounced "La-kelse", Tsimshian for "fresh-water mussel") where large quantities of mussels can be found even today.

From an ecological point of view the Lakelse Provincial Park (campground, etc.) remains largely intact – hemlock fir, gigantic Sitka spruce and, not least, red cedar all being found in the area. There is good swimming and excellent walking.

In August thousands of sockeye and blueback salmon arrive to spawn in Williams Creek. Black bears are common in the Park and trumpeter swans, otherwise threatened with extinction, winter on the lake.

At the Lakelse Hot Springs, 6 km (4 mi.) to the south, mineral water without taste or smell gushes out at a temperature of 42–72°C (108–162°F). The first albeit modest hotel was built here as long ago as 1910, but with Prince Rupert rather than Kitimat being chosen for the terminus of the trans-continental railway the spa was never fully developed.

Lakelse Hot Springs

The small town of Kitimat (altitude 35 m (115 ft); population 13,000) has been in existence only since the 1950s. In 1951 Alcan (the Aluminium Company of Canada) began constructing a huge aluminium smelter, now the second largest in the western world. The project came just at the right moment to exploit the area's enormous hydro-electric potential. Today the foundry employs more than 2000 workers and produces about 300,000 tonnes/tons of aluminium a year, 90 per cent of which is exported.

Kitimat

Extending 100 km (62 mi.) inland the deep Douglas Channel gives giant ocean-going freighters access to Kitimat's ice-free harbour.

Other companies besides Alcan have located here to take advantage of the cheap energy.

It is possible to see round the Alcan plant by joining one of the company's 90 minute "Alcan Smelter Tours" (Jun.–Aug. Mon.–Fri. 12.45 and 1.30pm, Sep.–May Tue. and Thu. by appointment only, tel. (604) 639–8259).

Tours

The Eurocan Pulp and Paper Complex, which came into operation in 1967, and the chemical firm Ocelot (1981; petro-chemicals, natural gas conversion to methanol and ammonia) provide interesting guided tours as well.

Also worth seeing in and around Kitimat are the Moore Creek Falls, the massive 500-year-old Sitka spruce (diameter of trunk: 3.5 m (12 ft)) in Radley Park, the Kitimat Centennial Museum (town history, pioneer period, Haisla Indian culture), the Moore Creek Falls, and Kitimat Village (on the east bank of the Douglas, 13 km (8 mi.) south of Kitimat; traditional Haisla community, Indian crafts).

Sights

From Terrace the exceptionally scenic Kitsumkalum (Kalum) Lake Road. heads north into a largely undeveloped hinterland. Viewpoint after viewpoint reveals extensive views over the valley and west to the glacial peaks. The road is surfaced only as far as Rosswood (51 km (32 mi.)), a small settlement at the northern end of Kitsumkalum Lake.

Kitsumkalum Lake Road

At Rosswood the Kalum Lake Rd. meets the Nass Rd., a gravelled logging road belonging to the Skeena Cellulose Company. The road is open to private vehicles but the big timber trucks, usually travelling at speed, always have right of way (keep headlights on and take avoiding action!). Black bear, moose, deer, Rocky Mountain goats and beaver are a common sight in this area. Look out also for the rare and seldom seen kermodei bear.

Nass Road

64 km (40 mi.) along the road Lava Lake lies contained by the Tseax lava stream. When the volcano (8 km (5 mi.) further east) erupted sometime in the 18th c., lava poured into the Nass River Valley, diverting the river northwards. Since then there have been no more eruptions.

Lava Lake

The actual lava stream is another 14 km (8½ mi.) beyond the lake itself. This area, known as the Tseax Lava Beds, remains largely denuded of vegetation, colonised only by lichens. As the lava cooled innumerable fissures, hollows and little lakes appeared. The expert eye can identify various different kinds of lava formation.

Tseax Lava Beds

By the Skeena River

Lava on the Nass Road

After 94 km (58 mi.) Greenville Rd. branches off left to Canyon City (8 km (5 mi.)). Here the Nass River has cut deeply into the lava and the settlement can only be entered on foot across a swaying suspension bridge.

The side road ends at the remote Nishga Indian village of Greenville (population 1000).

98 km (61 mi.): New Aiyansh is now the main Nishga settlement, dating back only to 1958 when the road was laid. Note the richly decorated Tribal Council Hall and ornate totem poles. Permission can be obtained from the Band office to wander down to the river bank for a glimpse of the abandoned village of Old Aiyansh on the further side. It was founded by an Anglican missionary in 1885.

Continuing past the Nass Camp logging station the road eventually meets (after 138 km (86 mi.)) the now tarmacked Stewart Cassiar Highway (Hwy. 37), principal route from British Columbia to Alaska. – A map of the Nass River region is available from the Terrace Chamber of Commerce (Terrace, 4511 Keith Ave.).

From the road-end the detour can be extended by taking the Stewart Cassiar Hwy. north over Bear Pass to Stewart (147 km (91 mi.)). Alternatively follow Hwy. 37 south again for 86 km (53 mi.), passing the Indian villages of Kitwancool and Kitwanga, to rejoin the Yellowhead Highway (Hwy. 16) north-east of Terrace.

168 km (104 mi.): North-east of Terrace the Skeena River divides into three narrow rock-girt channels, only two of which were navigable by sternwheelers. Even then the boats lacked the power to fight their way upriver under their own steam and had to be hauled through the Kitselas Canyon using strong hawsers. These were secured to massive iron rings cemented into the rock walls. A number of steamers came to grief and sank, including the "Mount Royal" in 1907. She reputedly carried a large shipment of gold which was never recovered.

A trail runs down to the river and along to Ringbolt Island (1hr) where some of the old iron rings can still be seen.

243 km (151 mi.): From a junction here on the Yellowhead Highway the Stewart Cassiar Highway (Hwy. 37/37A) runs north to Stewart (231 km (143 mi.)), eventually (after 735 km (457 mi.)) joining the Alaska Highway about 25 km (15 mi.) west of Watson Lake. This route offers anyone making for the Yukon and Alaska a rewarding alternative to the Alaska Highway itself. The Stewart Cassiar Highway is also popular with tourists heading west from Prince George to explore northern British Columbia.

Formerly made up of private roads owned by logging companies, the highway evolved in stages from about 1926 onwards, being passable throughout its entire length only since 1976 (the surface is still mainly gravel, so it is essential to drive slowly). It traverses an extremely sparsely populated region in the north-west of British Columbia, with very few tourist facilities, shops or filling stations along the way. What there is however is a magnificent, largely undisturbed landscape of mountain ranges, glaciers, volcanoes (e.g. in the Mt Edziza Provincial Park), untamed rivers, lovely lakes and – perhaps the greatest attraction of all – an exceptionally varied plant and wildlife.

4 km (2½ mi.): Just north of the mouth of the Kitwanga River lie the settlement of Kitwanga and the neighbouring Gitksan ('Ksan) Indian reserve. Gitwanga – which acts as a centre for the about 1500 inhabitants of the Kitwanga Valley (timber and modest farming), encircled by high, mostly snow-capped mountain peaks – boasts a number of very fine, typical 'Ksan totem poles some of which are more than 100 years old (look particularly for those in School Rd.). Also interesting is the

Anglican church, built in 1893 and one of the oldest surviving wooden churches in British Columbia.

Kitwanga Fort

A short footpath leads up from Kitwanga Valley Rd. to Battle Hill, once the site of a palisaded Gitksan stronghold known as Kitwanga Fort where early in the 19th c. a battle took place between rival Indian tribes. – Kitwanga Fort is the first purely Indian "National Historic Site" in western Canada.

Kitwancool

19 km (12 mi.): Also famous for its totem poles is another Indian village in the Kitwanga Valley – Kitwancool. Many of the twenty poles date back to the 19th c. and are still in their original positions. One of the oldest is the "Hole in the Ice" totem, erected in about 1850. It symbolises the resourcefulness of a man who saved the people of his village from starvation one winter by catching fish through a hole hacked in the ice. A small local history museum (open: daily 10.30am–4.30pm but closed Tues. and Wed. in winter) is currently being expanded.

Cranberry Junction

86 km (53 mi.): Known as Cranberry Junction this is where the still largely unsurfaced Nass Rd. (see above) branches off south-west to Terrace (138 km (86 mi.); see entry).

Meziadin Lake

172 km (107 mi.): At Meziadin Junction Hwy. 37A forks off to the left for Stewart (60 km (37 mi.)). Meziadin Lake has a superb setting and, being popular with anglers, some modest tourist facilities as well. The road to Stewart is not only good but exceptionally attractive from a scenic point of view, passing a number of wild, roaring waterfalls and as many as ten magnificent glaciers cascading down from the peaks of the Cambria Range (up to 2700 m (8860 ft) high).

Mountain goats

The scenery around Bear Pass and the Bear Glacier is incomparable. Keep a look-out for Rocky Mountain goats scaling the steep rock-faces – quite a common sight here.

Stewart

From Bear Pass the road follows the narrow, deeply incised valley of the Bear River to Stewart (population 1300), situated at the head of a 145 km (90 mi.) long fiord known as the Portland Canal down the centre of which runs the Canadian-Alaskan (US) frontier. The harbour here, the most northerly on the Pacific coast of Canada, remains ice-free throughout the year and is a ferry stop for the "Alaska Marine Highway".

With worthwhile deposits of gold, silver and copper in the surrounding, over 2000 m (6550 ft) high mountains, Stewart started life at the beginning of the century as a mining town, its fortunes being closely linked to raw materials prices. In its short heyday around 1910 the population grew to over 10,000, but after the Second World War fell to below 20.

The town's chequered history is recorded in the old Fire Station. Quite a number of films have been made on location in Stewart, and in the exceptionally attractive country around it.

Hyder

Hyder, only 3 km (2 mi.) west of Stewart (Canada) but already in Alaska (USA), can be reached from Stewart either by road or across the Portland Canal. This must be one of the few places where the US frontier can be crossed without strict controls (the border post is nailed up!) Once a prosperous mining town like its neighbour but now with a population of barely 80, Hyder is to all intents and purposes a ghost town. There are three bars (which stay open virtually 24 hours a day), a souvenir shop and a post office.

Grizzly Bear Lodge

Grizzly Bear Lodge is full of atmosphere. Gigantic moose heads bedeck the restaurant walls and there is also a fully-grown grizzly (an awesome sight even when stuffed). The saloon walls are covered with dollar bills

Yellowhead Highway: the Bear Glacier

– in the old days prospectors and miners would leave a signed dollar bill nailed to the wall as insurance against being broke when they next returned!

The one or two remaining wharves are a reminder that the town was once a busy little port shipping out ore.

Wharves

Be sure to make the 8 km (5 mi.) drive to Fish Creek. This is a favourite spot with anglers and wildlife enthusiasts, where from August to October thousands of rare chum (or dog) salmon arrive to spawn. Since the 1960s the spawning grounds have been increasingly threatened by floods – from a glacial lake which periodically bursts its banks – so special channels have been built to protect the fish. Whiteheaded eagles and a relatively large number of bears also inhabit the area.

Fish Creek

The unsurfaced mountain road which continues over the 960 m (3150 ft) high "Summit" to the Tide Lake Flats and the abandoned Granduc Copper Mine (58 km (36 mi.); back into British Columbian territory) is not recommended for private motorists. In summer however Seaport Limousine (tel. 636–2622) run trips there. Lasting several hours they provide some majestic views – on Salmon Glacier for example.

287 km (178 mi.): see 'Ksan

The Hazeltons

Gitanmaks was an Indian village where in 1866 a Hudson's Bay Company outpost was established, only for it to be abandoned shortly afterwards. White settlers arriving in the 1870s christened the place "Hazelton" on account of its numerous hazelnut bushes, and from 1898 the settlement was the start of the so-called "poor folk's route" along the

Gitanmaks

Telegraph Trail to the Yukon goldfields. With its many pioneer-age buildings and its location on the edge of the untapped wilderness, Hazelton still has very much the feel of a frontier town.

Kispiox Village

From Hazelton a road follows the valley of the Kispiox River for 14 km (8½ mi.) to the small Indian village of Kispiox. Here permission should be sought from the Band office to visit the splendid group of carved red cedar totem poles standing at the junction of the Skeena and Kispiox Rivers. Originally these poles stood in front of the long-houses belonging to the individual clans whose status and family history they depict. The very popular Kispiox Rodeo is held here every year in June.

Moricetown Canyon

323 km (200 mi.): At Moricetown Canyon the Bulkley River suddenly narrows from almost 500 m (1640 ft) to a mere 15 m (49 ft), becoming a seething rapids in the process. During the salmon season Carrier Indians can be seen fishing its waters in their traditional way.

Smithers

355 km (220 mi.): The little town of Smithers (altitude 496 m (1639 ft); population 5000) started life in 1913 as a rail depot. Surrounded by fertile farmland and meadows it lies in the shadow of Hudson Bay Mountain (2576 m (8454 ft); a favourite winter ski resort) with its Kathlyn Glacier and Twin Falls.

The best vantage point from which to view the glacier and falls is on Kathlyn Lake Rd. which branches off about 10 km (6 mi.) north-west of the town.

Much effort has gone into giving the town a Bavarian atmosphere with Bavarian-style architecture.

The Bulkley Valley Museum (Central Park Building on Hwy. 16/Main St.; open: in summer daily 10am–5pm, winter Tue.–Sat. 1–5pm) is devoted mainly to the history of settlement in the Bulkley Valley and to local Indian culture.

★ Tweedsmuir Provincial Park

The 9810 sq. km (3788 sq. mi.) Tweedsmuir Provincial Park is the biggest in British Columbia, the northern part in particular being still largely undisturbed wilderness. Ootsa, Whitesail and Tetachuck Lakes have however been dammed and a pipeline runs through the Hazelton Mountains to Kemano (generating electricity for the huge aluminium smelter at Kitimat). Moose, deer, bear and also beaver are a relatively common sight along roads in the vicinity of the Park. A number of resorts catering for anglers offer accommodation (rustic cottages, little log cabins) and there are also boats for rental on the lakes.

Fraser Lake

570 km (354 mi.): For many years Fraser Lake (altitude 786 m (2580 ft); population 1500) consisted of just a railway halt and sawmill. Today most of the inhabitants are employed at the Endako Mine, 22 km (14 mi.) to the south-west (the biggest molybdenum mine in Canada; viewing by appointment only).

Highway 5

782 km (486 mi.): At Tête Jaune Cache Hwy. 5 – also known (confusingly) as the Yellowhead Highway – branches south off Hwy. 16 and makes a good route through to Kamloops and the TransCanada Highway (338 km (210 mi.); see entry).

★ Clearwater

On Hwy. 5, about 250 km (155 mi.) south of Tête Jaune Cache, the little town of Clearwater (altitude 406 m (1332 ft); population 6000) on the North Thompson River is the gateway to Wells Gray Provincial Park, established in 1939. The northern section of this 5,200 sq. km (2000 sq. mi.) conservation area ranges over part of the heavily glaciated Cariboo Mountains and Wells Gray is renowned for its breathtaking waterfalls and picturesque lakes. Few tourist facilities exist in the Park.

From Clearwater a 40 km (25 mi.) long minor road with many spectacular views follows the Clearwater Valley past Spahats Creek

Provincial Park (15 km (9 mi.); Spahats Creek Canyon, 122 m (400 ft) deep with a 61 m (200 ft) waterfall – at its most attractive against a background of autumn foliage) to the main entrance at Hemp Creek (Park office, information; recreation area at Helmcken Falls Lodge with boat and canoe hire). From here a gravel road continues north to Clearwater Lake providing access to several superb hiking trails (e.g. Placid Lake Trail, Whitehorse escarpment) and some awe-inspiring waterfalls.

At Dawson Falls, 5 km (3 mi.) beyond Hemp Creek, the waters of the 91 m (300 ft) wide Murtle River plunge 18 m (60 ft) into the depths. A small side road leads to a rugged gorge on the Murtle known as the Mush Bowls (Devil's Punchbowl).

From the end of the Mush Bowls road a path leads to the marvellously spectacular Helmcken Falls.

★★ **Helmcken Falls**

The many volcanic features found in Wells Gray Park (e.g. cooled lava beds, volcanic cones and craters – the youngest between 4000 and 400 years old) point to almost continuous volcanic activity during the last 500,000 years. About 7000 to 8000 years ago, a 15 km (9 mi.) long lava flow issuing from the now inactive volcanic cone east of Ray Lake blocked the valley of the Clearwater River and led to the creation of the present Clearwater Lake.

Wells Gray Park can also be entered by a road branching off Hwy. 5 just north of Blue River (altitude 680 m (2231 ft); population 1000), about 100 km (62 mi.) north of Clearwater.

This south-eastern section of the Park, which includes the Murtle Lake, is a Nature Conservancy Area enjoying total protection. Vehicles must be left at the entrance (24 km (15 mi.) down the gravel access road) from where a 2½ km (1½ mi.) footpath leads to a bay on the lake – considered one of the loveliest in the whole of Canada. For the experienced canoeist this is the start of some superb canoe routes.

786 km (488 mi.): Rejoining the main Yellowhead Highway we come to Tête Jaune Cache, a short distance beyond which the Rearguard Falls can be seen from a vantage point barely fifteen minutes walk from the Highway. Although some 1200 km (745 mi.) from the river mouth near Vancouver, these upper reaches of the Fraser nevertheless carry a considerable volume of water which here cascades down a low escarpment. In August leaping salmon can be seen tackling this final obstacle on the long journey to their spawning grounds.

Rearguard Falls

The Yellowhead Highway now makes its way along the upper course of the Fraser River and deep into the Rocky Mountains, crossing as it does so the Mt Robson Provincial Park (2200 sq. km (850 sq. mi.); west entrance, information centre and campground 10 km (6 mi.) east of Tête Jaune Cache), another area of breathtaking scenery close to the border with Alberta and a favourite with hikers, climbers and outdoor enthusiasts generally.

★ **Mount Robson Provincial Park**

Adjoined by the Jasper National Park (see entry) to the east of Yellowhead Pass (77 km (48 mi.)), the Park takes its name from the highest peak in the Canadian Rockies, Mt Robson (3954 m (12977 ft)). This magnificent mountain landscape with its waterfalls, lonely tarns and glacier-capped peaks (including one of the few still advancing glaciers in the Canadian Rockies) was designated a provincial park as long ago as 1913. Even in those days mountaineers and tourists were drawn to the area undeterred by the distances involved.

One of the most popular hikes here is the 25 km (16 mi.) trail through the "Valley of the Thousand Falls" (Robson River Valley) to the lovely turquoise lake which nestles at the foot of the glacier-clad Mt Robson.

Other beauty spots along the Highway before it begins its climb to Yellowhead Pass are the Overlander Falls, Moose Lake (moose can often be seen on the swampy east shore) and Yellowhead Lake.

Mount Robson, the highest mountain in the Canadian Rockies

Yellowhead Pass   859 km (534 mi.): The 1131 m (3712 ft) Yellowhead Pass is one of the lowest to cross the Rocky Mountains. It forms the divide between British Columbia and Alberta and also between two time zones (Pacific Time/Mountain Time). A centuries old Indian trade route went over this easily traversed pass; sometime around 1810 the first white North West Company trappers probably found their way over it too.

A group of Hudson's Bay Company trappers certainly used the pass to cross the Rockies in 1820, making their way down the Fraser River to what is now the little town of Prince George. Among them was a fair-haired Iroquois nicknamed "Tête Jaune" i.e. "Yellowhead", who in the 1820s set up a cache near the Fraser River (though not at the site of the present settlement known as Tête Jaune Cache). Subsequently employed by the Company as a guide, he and his family were killed by Beaver Indians in 1827.

For a time the pass was used by fur traders supplying much needed leather to the forts in New Caledonia, which led to its being called "Leather Pass". From the 1830s onwards however they favoured the alternative route along the Peace River, and until the building of the two railways (the Canadian Northern (1905) to Vancouver and the Grand Trunk Pacific (1910) to Prince George) the Yellowhead Pass was rarely used.

Then, having started out as rivals, the two railway companies merged. The abandoned track came to serve as a primitive road. After upgrading it became the Yellowhead Highway, officially opened in 1970. Particularly in winter the Yellowhead has considerable advantages over the shorter (by 177 km (110 mi.)) TransCanada Highway further south, on which latter the Rogers Pass is frequently closed by heavy snowfalls and the risk of avalanches. East of Yellowhead Pass the Highway follows the narrow, thickly forested valley of the Miette River down to Jasper on its 74 km (46 mi.) journey through the Jasper National Park (see entry).

Yellowhead Highway in Saskatchewan

This section of the Yellowhead Highway (700 km (435 mi.)) is described from east to west; it begins near Langenburg and at Churchbridge there is a detour to Duck Mountain Park.

The Park caters for a wide range of leisure activities, particularly in the area around the lake. Near the Ministik Beaches, in addition to an 18-hole golf course, there are facilities for riding, tennis, cycling, boating and mini-golf, also angling on both Madge and Batka Lakes. In winter the possibilities include cross-country skiing and snowmobile trekking.

Duck Mountain Provincial Park

As the route heads west again along Hwy. 5, the Ukrainian origins of many of the inhabitants of this part of Saskatchewan are everywhere evident, most noticeably the Ukrainian Orthodox churches with their silver domes.

21 km (13 mi.) along the road in Veregin (population 128) an interesting stop can be made at the Doukhobour Heritage Village (open mid-May to mid-Sep. daily 10am–6pm, mid-Sep. to mid-May Mon.–Fri. 9am–5pm, Sat. and Sun. by appointment only). Among the nine buildings are a completely original turn-of-the-century gentleman's residence and older houses reflecting the lifestyle and customs of the Doukhobour pioneers. The career of their leader Peter Veregin is also charted in considerable detail. Other things to see include a brick oven, bath house, prayer house, museum, administration buildings, barns, a blacksmith's forge and farming implements.

Veregin

Canora (population 2569; 25 km (16 mi.) further on) has a Ukrainian Orthodox Church which is well worth visiting (Main St.; open by appointment only summer Mon.–Fri. during the day). Built in 1928 and later restored the church with its paintings and coloured glass might almost have been brought here straight from Kiev.

Canora

On the south side of Canora stands the Ukrainian Welcome Statue, designed by the inhabitants themselves. The 7.6 m (25 ft) high "Lesia", decked out in traditional Slav costume, is intended to symbolise the Ukrainian heritage.

The route now follows Hwy. 9 southwards allowing an additional worthwhile detour via Hwy. 229 to Good Spirit Lake Park.

"Good Spirit Lake" is a translation of the Indian word "Kitchimanitou", a Hudson's Bay Company trading post of that name (established in 1880) being incorporated into the Provincial Park when it was created in 1931. The 1900 ha (4695 acre) Park extends along the shores of Good Spirit Lake with its inviting sandy beaches and warm, shallow water. Planted with poplars the Park is also well known for its fine dunes of beautifully clean sand up to 5 m (16 ft) high which surround the lake. Being ecologically very sensitive these are out of bounds for walking.

Good Spirit Lake Provincial Park

Continue south on Hwys. 229 and 9 to rejoin the main route (Hwy. 16) at Yorkton.

An important east Saskatchewan centre for local commerce Yorkton (population 16,000) is also characterised by ethnic diversity. In particular the Ukrainian heritage of many of the inhabitants of the area is manifest in its architecture, exhibitions, craftwork and fine European cooking.

Yorkton

The town is also known for its internationally acclaimed Short Film and Video Festival.

Yorkton's Western Development Museum – Story of the People (open Apr.–Oct.) is full of interest, vividly illustrating the history and traditions of Canada's immigrant population.

Also rewarding is a visit to the remarkable St Mary's Ukrainian Catholic Church (Catherine St.; open in summer daily, at other times only by appointment), the first brick-built Ukrainian church in Canada.

The 21 m (69 ft) high dome is decorated with outstanding paintings (1939 and 1941) by Steven Meush.

The Yorkton Arts Council (in the Godfrey Dean Cultural Centre, Smith St.; open daily 2–5pm) exhibits work by local artists.

Parkland Village (open: mid-May–mid-Oct. daily 1–8pm), about 10 km (6 mi.) south-east of Yorkton on Hwy. 16 near Rokeby, has buildings and other exhibits dating from the early days of settlement in Saskatchewan.

From here the Yellowhead Highway makes its way westwards to Foam Lake across vast wheat-covered plains.

Foam Lake

Visits to the interesting Foam Lake Museum Association in Foam Lake (population 1443) are by arrangement only.

Foam Lake Heritage Marsh, a 1620 ha (4000 acre) area of wetland surrounded by hills about 7 km (4½ mi.) to the north-west, is an excellent place for observing waterbirds.

Wynyard

Wynyard (population 2187) is another small place with something to see – in this case the Frank Cameron Museum (open May, Jun. daily 9am–5pm, Jul., Aug. 8am–8pm).

Only a short drive away to the north are the Quill Lakes.

Quill Lakes

Lying on a major bird migration route Quill Lakes are a resting place and breeding ground for many waterbirds.

At Plunkett a detour via Hwy. 365 leads to Little Manitou Lake.

Little Manitou Lake

The medicinal properties of the mineral rich, 19 km (12 mi.) long Little Manitou Lake were well known to the early Indians, to whom it was the "Place of the Healing Waters". In its heyday the lake was called the "Karlsbad of Canada", the mineral content of the water being similar to that of the famous German spa. A new attraction has recently been added in the shape of the Manitou Springs Mineral Spa at Manitou Beach. Opened in 1988 this is now the largest indoor mineral bath in Canada.

Saskatoon

Return on Hwy. 365 to the Yellowhead Highway, continuing to Saskatoon (see entry) from where a day trip can be made to Pike Lake Park situated 30 km (18 mi.) south-west (Hwys. 7 and 60).

Pike Lake Provincial Park

A long sandy beach and lush expanses of grass with aspen, ash and birch make Pike Lake Provincial Park (open all year) a pleasant place to relax. For the more energetic there are tennis courts and a new swimming-pool.

West of Saskatoon Hwy. 16 threads its way across farming country for 138 km (86 mi.) to North Battleford.

North Battleford

See Battleford

Detour

By taking Hwy. 4 northwards from North Battleford, then branching off on Hwy. 26, a detour can be made to the lake district in north-west Saskatchewan.

Edam

The Washbrook Museum (open May–Sep. Mon.–Fri. 10am–6pm, evenings by appointment) in Edam (population 463) provides an insight into Sakatchewan rural life.

St Walburg

St Walburg (population 731) also has an interesting museum, the St Walburg & District Museum (open Jul.–Aug. Mon.–Sat. 10am–noon and 2–5pm, Sun. noon–5pm) housed in the Old Church of the Assumption in Main St. Exhibits come from the village and its surroundings pre-1945 and include paintings by Imhoff. The church organ, made in 1885, still plays.

Loon Lake's Big Bear's Trail Museum (open Jul., Aug. Mon.–Fri. 10am– **Loon Lake**
8pm, otherwise by appointment only) stands on the highway in this
small community (population 401).

★★Yellowknife E 8

Administrative unit: Northwest Territories
Population: 18,000

By plane: Daily flights from Edmonton. **Access**
By car: From Edmonton (quickest route), Highway 43, then, from near
Peace River, north on the Mackenzie Highway to Great Slave Lake.

Although situated south of the tree limit, on the shores of Great Slave
Lake, the modern town of Yellowknife still lies in the transitional zone
between northern fir forest and treeless tundra. The largest community
in the Mackenzie district, it has been the capital of the Northwest
Territories since 1967. It was founded only in 1935 after gold was discovered there, the first such strike in the cold north (average temperature: −6°C (21°F)!). A second gold-rush occurred in 1944 since when the
community, set in a landscape of dwarf firs, birch and poplar, has developed steadily into the nerve centre of northern Canada.
   The gold mines at Yellowknife are among the biggest in Canada and
gold has unquestionably been the spur to the town's growth. The population figures tell the story: in 1961 Yellowknife had 3250 inhabitants,
today that total has increased almost sixfold..
   Indians have hunted in the Yellowknife area for thousands of years.
Europeans on the other hand made their first appearance in the third to
last decade of the 18th c., and settled permanently only after the gold-
rush of 1934.

Yellowknife, the chief town in the Northwest Territories

Yellowknife

Name

The name "Yellowknife" derives from the copper knives long used by the local Indians.

Sights

★The Prince of Wales Northern Heritage Centre

The Prince of Wales Northern Heritage Centre (open Tue.–Sun. 10.30am–5pm) is exceptionally interesting.

As well as displaying its large mineral collection and finds from the Centre's archaeological research, the museum explores in depth the culture of the Dene Indians and traces the pervasive influence of the fur trade, in operation here since at least the 18th c.

Northwest Territories State Archive

Well-known local artists and craftsmen also exhibit their work in the Centre and visitors can view the extensive collection of photographs and old documents in the Northwest Territories State Archive.

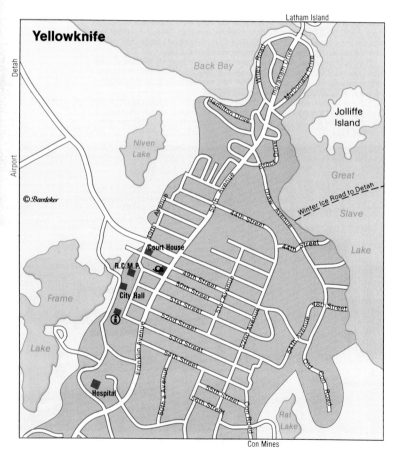

The gold mines are situated in an area about 4 km (2½ mi.) north of the town. Tours of the Giant Yellowknife Mine can be arranged (summer only), tel. 8736301.

★★Giant Yellowknife Mine

In the peak holiday season excursions are run on Great Slave Lake (from the Yellowknife Trading Post dock). These usually include a visit to the Indian village at Detah.

Boat trips

There are interesting drives around Yellowknife, one being eastwards along the Ingraham Trail (Hwy. 4) to Tibbet Lake, continuing to the Yellowknife Preserve (conservation area). Another follows Hwy. 3 north-west through the unspoiled country beside Great Slave Lake to Edzo. The same road goes to the Mackenzie bison reserve.

Excursions

The major event in Yellowknife's calendar is the annual Caribou Carnival and dogsled race in March. The Canadian Flying Clubs' "Midnight Sun Golf Tournament" also takes place here every year on June 21st.

Events

★★Yoho National Park

G 7

Province: British Columbia.
Area: 1313 sq. km (507 sq. mi.)
Altitude: 1098–3562 m (3604–11,690 ft)
Established: 1930

Road:
TransCanada Highway 1 (Calgary–Banff–Lake Louise–Kicking Horse Pass–Golden–Kamloops–Vancouver).

Access

Rail: Canadian Pacific Railway; Rocky Mountaineer (Calgary–Banff–Lake Louise–Golden–Kamloops–Vancouver)
Station for the National Park at Field.

The Yoho National Park extends over part of the western flank of the Rocky Mountains, adjoining both the Banff and Kootenay National Parks. As the fourth largest nature reserve in the Canadian Rockies it encompasses some magnificent and extremely varied mountain scenery, with snow-covered peaks, thundering rivers, majestic waterfalls and delightful mountain lakes (especially in the eastern section of the Park in the vicinity of the main range). The Park's two chief areas of interest are the valley of the Kicking Horse River and the over 20 km (13 mi.) Yoho Valley ("yoho" is Cree for "awe").

In 1985 all four National Parks in the Rocky Mountains were adopted by UNESCO's World Heritage Programme on account of their great scenic beauty and the extent to which they have preserved their natural environments.

The TransCanada Highway passes through the Park making access very easy. There are viewpoints at three particularly scenic spots. Side roads branch off the Highway to major places of interest.

The history of the Yoho National Park is closely linked to the building of the trans-continental railway. The first white man to reach the area was almost certainly the geologist Sir James Hector, a member of the Palliser Expedition charged with reconnoitring road and rail routes through the Rocky Mountains. Hector made his way over the Vermilion Pass and into the Kootenay Valley which he followed northwards. Crossing another little pass he arrived at Beaverfoot Creek, a tributary of the Kicking Horse River. Near the Wapta Falls he was kicked so badly by his horse that his companions at first took him for dead. With great difficulty the little

History

Mount Hungabee

expedition struggled back to the valley of the Bow River by way of a pass they christened "Kicking Horse" on account of the incident.

1884 saw the construction of the Kicking Horse Pass section of the Canadian Pacific Railway. Initially the gradient at some places on the descent to Field was as great as 4.5 per cent (1 in 3½) and several serious accidents occurred when brakes failed on the downward run. In 1909 two spiral tunnels were built, reducing the gradient to 2.2 per cent.

Following completion of the railway, Canadian Pacific also built the first tourist accommodation in the area. A stretch of road laid along the disused section of the original track in 1927 eventually became part of the Trans-Canada Highway. In 1886 some 26 sq. km (10 sq. mi.) in the vicinity of Mt Stephen (3199 m (10,500 ft); near Field) were declared a protected area and named Dominion Park. This modest beginning was eventually to lead to the creation of the Yoho National Park in 1930.

Kicking Horse Pass	The climb up to Kicking Horse Pass from the east (see above: "History", for the origin of the name) begins at the border between the two provinces of Alberta and British Columbia.
Avalanche Path	A broad scar down the nearby mountainside marks the track of an avalanche which some years ago thundered down the slope sweeping away an entire forest in its path.
Great Divide	A sign about 3 km (2 mi.) east of the TransCanada Highway marks the continental watershed (Hudson Bay/Pacific Ocean).
Wapta Lake	Wapta Lake (1586 m (5205 ft)), a pretty little mountain lake, is the haunt of some rare species of waterbird as well as being the source of

the Kicking Horse River which flows west alongside the TransCanada Highway.

From Wapta Lake a road follows Cataract Creek southwards to Lake O'Hara (camp site), set against an impressive backdrop of high mountains – to the east Mt Huber (3368 m (11,053 ft)), Mt Victoria (3364 m (11,040 ft); glacier) and Yukness Mountain (2847 m (9343 ft)), to the south Mt Schaffer (2693 m (8838 ft)), on the south side of Lake McArthur), and to the north-west Catherine Mountain (3189 m (10,466 ft); mountain trail) and Mt Vanguard (2469 m (8103 ft)).

★★Lake O'Hara

The old bridge on the "Big Hill" (the notorious steep section where the height difference is 400 (1300 ft)) was once part of the original CPR track over Kicking Horse Pass.

Old Bridge, Big Hill

An observation tower about 9 km (5½ mi.) west of the 1625 m (5333 ft) summit of Kicking Horse Pass provides a good view of the daringly engineered later section of track with its two spiral tunnels (modelled on the St Gotthard rail tunnels in Switzerland).

Lower Spiral Tunnel viewpoint

This is a fine vantage point from which to admire the hanging glacier on Mt Stephen (3199 m (10,500 ft)). Below and to the right of the glacier the entrance to the now abandoned Monarch Mine is clearly visible. Lead, zinc and small amounts of silver were extracted until the mine was closed in 1952.

Mount Stephen viewpoint

The best place from which to admire the upper of the two railway tunnels.

Upper Spiral Tunnel viewpoint

The supremely attractive, ice-field framed Yoho Valley has a 360 km (224 mi.) network of hiking trails which make for some outstanding walking (details from the information centre at the Park office). A memorial near the information centre honours Edouard Gaston DeVille, Canada's Surveyor-General in 1885. A narrow 13 km (8 mi.) long road (dead-end; closed to campervans) winds its way tortuously up the valley.

★★Yoho Valley

The Yoho Valley Rd. ends at the stupendous Takakkaw Falls (camp site), among the highest in North America. The main fall, where melt-water from the Daly Glacier (tip of the Waputik Ice-field) plunges 254 m (834 ft) over a rock-face, is a magnificent spectacle.
The ice-fields of Mts Yoho (2760 m (9058 ft)), Gordon (3153 m (10,348 ft); Wapta Ice-field), Daly (3152 m (10,345 ft); Waputik Ice-field) and Niles (2972 m (9754 ft)) ring the valley. West of the falls rises the glacier-covered Vice-President Massiv (3066 m (10,062 ft)).

★★Takakkaw Falls

During the age of steam when extra locomotives were needed to push or pull trains up or down Big Hill, Field (altitude 1224 m (4017 ft); population 400) was a busy railway town. Nowadays it is the peaceful home of the Parks Administration (round-the-year information available at the side of the Highway). Fossil-rich Palaeozoic shales and sedimentaries are found on the slopes of Mts Field and Stephen nearby.

Field

The Burgess Shale fossil beds to the east of Field have proved of supreme importance to palaeontology. Fossils more than 530 million years old (Cambrian; esp. trilobites) recovered from these unique, undisturbed beds, have yielded major insights into the development of life on earth.

★★Burgess Shale fossil beds

About 2 km (1¼ mi.) south of Field an 8 km (5 mi.) long road (dead-end) crosses the Kicking Horse River to Emerald Lake. A little way along the road is a remarkable natural bridge, beneath which the river squeezes

★Emerald Lake

A natural bridge on the Emerald Lake   *Takakkaw Falls*

through extremely resistant rock. An information board explains how this geological curiosity was formed. The lovely, shimmering, turquoise-blue Emerald Lake nestles at the foot of the over 3000 m (9800 ft) glacier-capped President Range.

Hikes	Several splendid hikes begin at Emerald Lake, among the most attractive being the Lake Circuit, the climbs to Yoho and Burgess passes, and the Hamilton Lake trail (to a small lake hidden in a hanging valley, a feature typical of the Rocky Mountains). North of Emerald Lake the 2696 m (8848 ft) summit of Michael Peak beckons competent mountaineers, while to the south rises the 2583 m (8477 ft) Mount Burgess.
Ottertail viewpoint	An information board at Ottertail Viewpoint gives details of the rock formations exposed by the Ottertail and Kicking Horse rivers. In the valley below there used to be a sawmill owned by the Canadian Pacific Railway.
Misko viewpoint	From this vantage point good views are obtained of Mts Hunter and King. The information board explains the effects of glaciation in high mountains.
Avalanche Nature Trail	This mountain trail leads to a huge avalanche slide on the 3320 m (10,896 ft) Mt Vaux.
★★Hoodoo Creek	A well marked and scenically very attractive trail, Deerlodge Trail follows Hoodoo Creek to the Park's first wardens' cabin, built in 1904. The pyramid-shaped "hoodoos" of hardened sand and clay with a capping of relatively hard rock are real oddities of nature.
Leanchoil Marsh	Given a little luck a visit to Leanchoil Marsh will be rewarded with sightings of some of Canada's high mountain fauna (including beaver).

On the way to the Chancellor Peak camp site (a few kilometres off the TransCanada Highway), a beautiful view unfolds across the valley of the Kicking Horse River to Mt Vaux (3320 m (10,896 ft)), Chancellor Peak (3280 m (10,765 ft)) and Mt Ennis (3132 m (10,279 ft); large glacier).

Chancellor Peak campground

Before the western entrance to the Park is reached a side road branches off, terminating after 5 km (3 mi.) in a dead-end. A trail then leads to the Wapta Falls where Sir James Hector suffered his near fatal accident (see above) and where, at a bend in its course, the Kicking Horse River cascades down over a wide rock-step.

Wapta Falls

★★Yukon Circle Route

E 2/3

Administrative units: Yukon Territory/Alaska

The approximately 1500 km (930 mi.) long Yukon Circle Route makes use of three highways, the Klondike Highway (see Klondike), the Top of the World Highway (see Dawson City, Surroundings) and the Alaska Highway (see entry), each a heady mixture of exciting scenery and historical fascination.

The circuit is best begun at the Yukon capital, Whitehorse (see entry), following the Klondike Highway (see Klondike) to the famous gold-rush town of Dawson (see entry), situated where the Klondike joins the Yukon River. Those who prefer to retrace the actual route taken by prospectors at the turn of the century can book a river passage from Whitehorse to Dawson instead.

★**Klondike Highway**

From Dawson, having been sure to visit the legendary Klondike goldfields, head west through the majestic scenery of the Top of the World Highway (see Dawson, Surroundings) across the US/Canadian frontier to Tetlin Junction in Alaska.

★**Top of the World Highway**

Joining up with the Alaska Highway in Tetlin Junction, drive southeastwards into Canada again, continuing through Beaver Creek to the snow-covered peaks of the St Elias Mountains in the Kluane National Park (see entry). From there return via Haines Junction to Whitehorse (see entry).

★★**Alaska Highway**

Yukon Territory

D–E 2–6

Location: 60°–69°N 124°–141°W
Area: 483,450 sq. km (186,612 sq. mi.)
Population: 32,000. Capital: Whitehorse

Tourism Yukon, PO Box 2703
Whitehorse, YT Y1A 26C; tel. (867) 6675340, fax. (867) 6673546

Information

The name Yukon comes from the Indian "diuke-on" meaning "clean water". The Yukon Territory is almost twice the size of the United Kingdom. Situated in the far north-west of Canada, it shares its western border in the Coast Mountains with the US state of Alaska. Mount Logan (5951 m (19,531 ft)) in the heavily glaciated Kluane National Park (see entry) is the highest in Canada. To the north the Territory has a short stretch of coastline on the Beaufort Sea, while in the east the Mackenzie Mountains form the border with the Northwest Territories (see entry).

Location

Yukon Territory

Yukon

The 60th Parallel divides the Yukon from the Pacific province of British Columbia to the south.

Yukon Plateau

Encircled by high mountain ranges the Yukon Plateau forms a middle- to high-altitude upland region (mean altitude: 1000 m (3282 ft)), mainly composed of lava-covered, mineral-rich, crystalline rock.

Yukon River

Dominating influence over the entire Territory is the Yukon River, 3185 km (1979 mi.) from source to mouth and disgorging into the Bering Sea via an immense 30,000 sq. km (11,580 sq. mi.) delta in Alaska. Having its headwaters in the southern Yukon (Pelly River, Lewes River) the great waterway has a total catchment area of 855,000 sq. km (330,000 sq. mi.). It begins by flowing north through Whitehorse (see entry) and Dawson City (see entry), then along the American Cordillera until, having reached the Arctic Circle, it makes its "big bend" to the west.

The Yukon is a gently flowing river, ice-covered from October to May. In summer melting snow causes it to flood. Made famous by the gold-rush at the end of the last century its best-known tributary the Klondike (see entry) joins the Yukon River at Dawson (see entry).

Climate

The climate of the Yukon is principally determined by the north–south alignment of its mountain ranges, as a consequence of which polar air is able to flow unhindered from the north in winter. This results in bitter winter cold and the lowest recorded temperatures on the North American continent (about −60°C (−76°F)).

Owing however to the continental-type climate, summers (June to mid-September) tend to be dry and relatively warm, and 20 hours of sunshine a day are not uncommon in these high northern latitudes. The frost period extends from October to April, the transition to summer being comparatively short. In Whitehorse (see entry) the average minimum temperature in January is −25°C (−13°F), the maximum only −16°C (3°F); in summer the corresponding values are 8°C (46°F) and 21°C (70°F) respectively.

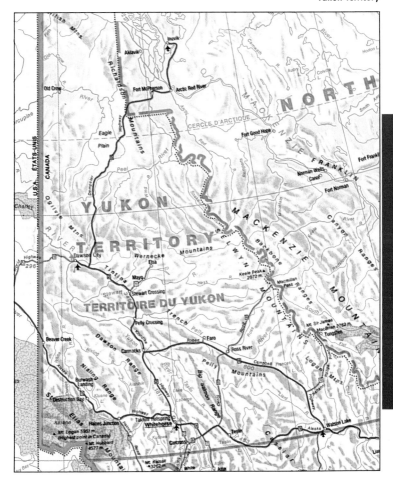

The Territory is divided into two regions as far as vegetation is con- Flora
cerned, boreal coniferous forest predominating in the south and
coniferous tundra in the north. Altitude likewise produces distinct vegetation zones, coniferous and birch forests in the valleys, tundra on the
heights. Owing to the permafrost numbers of plant species are relatvely
low. The few which are adapted to the conditions have also had to battle
hard to re-establish themselves following the retreat of the last
(Wisconsin) Ice Age about 13,000 years ago.

Prior to the 17th c. any settlement of the Yukon was by the indigenous History
peoples only. Initial European exploration of the region – later part of the
Northwest Territories (see entry) – was mainly by the Hudson's Bay
Company following its foundation in 1670. Around 1850 the demand for
furs increased, and not long afterwards, in 1880, the first gold prospec-

tors arrived in the Yukon as yields from the claims in British Columbia (see entry) began to fall. In 1887 Dawson reconnoitred for the first time the area around the town which now bears his name. These developments led to the Yukon being made a separate district of the Northwest Territories in 1895. When on August 17th 1896 George Carmack discovered fist-sized nuggets of gold in a tributary of the Klondike (Bonanza Creek) the find triggered a gold-rush of unbelievable proportions. Within a few months the population of Dawson City soared to 25,000 (some sources even suggest more than 50,000), and in the boom year of 1898 the Yukon proclaimed itself a Territory in its own right on the strength of its gold finds. Between 1897 and 1904 gold valued at almost 100 million dollars was extracted. From 1905 onwards a decline set in until the building of the Alaska Highway (see entry) in 1942 gave a fresh impetus to development. In 1952 Whitehorse (see entry) became the Yukon's administrative centre, replacing Dawson as Territorial capital. 1978 saw the opening of North America's only public road north of the Arctic Circle, Dempster Highway (see entry), named after Corporal Dempster who led an expedition there in 1911.

Population

With scarcely 30,000 inhabitants the population density in the Territory is a mere 0.05 per sq. km (0.02 per sq. mi.). Before the influx of white settlers lured by the discovery of gold in the latter part of 1880, those living in the Yukon were mainly Athapaskan Indians who supported themselves by hunting and fishing (the Athapaskans are members of the large Na-Dené language family to which the Navajos and Apaches in the south also belong). Otherwise the only inhabitants were a very small number of Inuit settled on the coast. Although today about 21.4 per cent of the people living in the Yukon are Indians, they constitute just 0.7 per cent of Canada's indigenous population as a whole. Among the Yukon's white population 48 per cent are of British extraction. Today the biggest towns in the Yukon Territory are Whitehorse (see entry) with about 19.000 inhabitants and Dawson (see entry) with fewer than 2000.

Transport

Transport in the Territory relies on four major highways: the Alaska Highway (see entry) through Whitehorse, the Campbell Highway, the Klondike Highway (Whitehorse–Dawson; see Klondike) and the Dempster Highway (Dawson–Inuvik, NWT).

Economy

The bitterly cold climate and consequent permafrost mean that agriculture, normally the prime requirement for permanent settlement, is possible only to a very limited degree. Instead mining heads the list of economic activities. Of the ten minerals extracted, silver, lead, wolfram and antimony deserve special mention (the wolfram deposits, worked since 1961, are thought to be the biggest in America). Tourism has now overtaken forestry in second place.

Activities

The endless expanses of unspoilt wilderness are a paradise for the more adventure-minded. Canoeists in particular find conditions in the Territory ideal.

Of the Yukon's two national parks, the Kluane National Park (see entry) enjoys comparatively easy access via the Alaska Highway (see entry). As well as boasting Canada's highest mountains it is an area of huge icefields and calf glaciers – challenging country for experienced mountaineers. The Northern Yukon National Park on the other hand lies off the beaten track on the shores of the Beaufort Sea.

Dawson (see entry), reached via the Klondike Highway (see Klondike) or the Top of the World Highway from Alaska (see Dawson, Surroundings), has developed into quite a tourist centre. Something of the atmosphere of the old gold digging days can still be recaptured in the saloons, dance halls and houses of the now restored town.

"Discovery Day" (August 17th) is celebrated annually with colourful cavalcades and a legion of other events. Anyone wanting to try their hand at gold panning will find plenty of opportunity on the special gold field tours.

**Practical
Information
from A–Z**

For Canada the standards to apply beforehand to such matters as distance, travelling time, comfort, etc., are quite different in many respects from those for Europe. There is no problem so far as the relatively densely populated south of the country is concerned, but anyone planning to journey to the north or far from human habitation in the timberland would be well advised to take the proper precautions both in terms of equipment and personal fitness. Canadians are always willing to lend a hand in an emergency, but there can be times when travellers are thrown back entirely on their own resources, making it vital to acquire some knowledge of survival techniques before setting out – such as how to get through a blizzard or a tornado, or what to do when faced with a bear!

A certain degree of caution is also called for in urban Canada, especially at night. Although social strife here has not reached the extremes of New York or Los Angeles in neighbouring America, visitors should be on their guard against street crime, since attacks on the person do happen. And the same applies, albeit to a lesser degree, to places further off the beaten track.

Care and consideration should also be the watchword in dealings with Canada's native peoples, the Indians and the Inuit, as they increasingly assert their own identity. They are a dignified people who should be treated with respect, and the word "eskimo" should be avoided at all costs, since it is an insult.

Air Travel

In Canada travel by air is obviously the first choice for anyone whose time is limited and who has to cover long distances. Canada's air network is surprisingly closeknit for a country of its size, and it is possible to penetrate to the remotest corner through the gateways of the main cities.

Airports

The major airports which provide international services in Canada are Calgary, Edmonton, Halifax, Montréal (Dorval), Ottawa, Toronto, Vancouver and Winnipeg. Gander in Newfoundland, Goose Bay in Labrador, and Québec City airports are in a rather special position serving as transatlantic staging posts, military bases and tourist destinations respectively. Saskatoon and Regina, both in Saskatchewan, and Victoria, on Vancouver Island, are also international destinations but not by direct flights.

Most of Canada's international airports also connect with America's main cities, including New York and Chicago.

The services provided by Canada's larger airports are well up to international standards.

Airlines

Air Canada, Canadian Airlines International

The two biggest Canadian airlines are Air Canada (now completely privatised) and Canadian Airlines International, serving over 100 destinations in Canada, as well as connecting with other major airports throughout the world.

Smaller Canadian airlines

Besides the two national airlines there are a number of smaller carriers who often only operate on a regional or provincial basis. Many of them also provide charter flights on smaller planes – including hydroplanes – to remoter places.

Air France, British Airways, Lufthansa, KLM and Swissair all have direct or connecting scheduled services from Europe to Canada. British Airways has up to 23 services each week, serving Montréal and Vancouver daily, including nine flights a week to Toronto. For addresses, see Getting to Canada.

Non-Canadian airlines

Air travel in Canada is relatively cheap compared with Europe. Air Canada and Canadian Airlines International link up with smaller internal airlines to provide cut-rate multiple ticketing. There are special rates for young people, students and senior citizens. In fact, there is a wide range of fares, varying from the regular economy, business and first-class, to the value-for-money Maple Leaf fares, the Pond-Hopper fares, Airpass, Go Canadian Travel Pass and Flexipass, providing two, four, six or eight flight coupons for travel in Canada and the USA (supplementary coupons available also for flights to the Caribbean).

Air fares

Information on these and other special deals can be obtained from travel agents and airline offices.

Airline offices in the UK

7–8 Conduit Street, London W1R 9TG;
tel. (0181) 7592636, fax (0181) 5728727

Air Canada

23–59 Staines Road, Hounslow, Greater London TW3 3HE;
tel. (0181) 5777722 (London Area), (0345) 616767 (other areas)

Canadian Airlines International

Private pilots

Holders of a pilot's licence and an English radio-operator certificate can rent planes in Canada after taking a test. Further information from:

Pilot's licence

Aeronautical Information Service, Department of Transport, Place de Ville, Tower C, Ottawa, Ont., Canada K1A 0N5

Bears

Where Canada is concerned, no animal is more fascinating to humans than the bear. The embodiment of the primeval wilderness, bears play an important role in myth and legend, but are also seen as a threatening danger in the wild. Basically, bears will eat anything, and are very much like humans in this respect. Although they live mainly on fruits and various plants they occasionally kill live prey. They turn up in larger numbers in places such as National Park picnic sites, for example, where people leave food, scraps or rubbish around.

Black bears have a wide distribution in Canada, and there are estimated to be about 300,000 of them between the Atlantic, Pacific and Arctic Oceans. Their preferred habitat should be more or less primeval forest, but they also enjoy tracking down the haunts of campers, tourists, etc.

Black bears

Grizzlies are bigger, stronger and more determined, tending to occur in the Rockies and the Yukon. If attacked by a grizzly, get into a tree – they are poor climbers!

Grizzly bears

The few polar bears still roaming free can be found in the cold and remote fastnesses of Canada's uninhabited North. They can be very

Polar bears

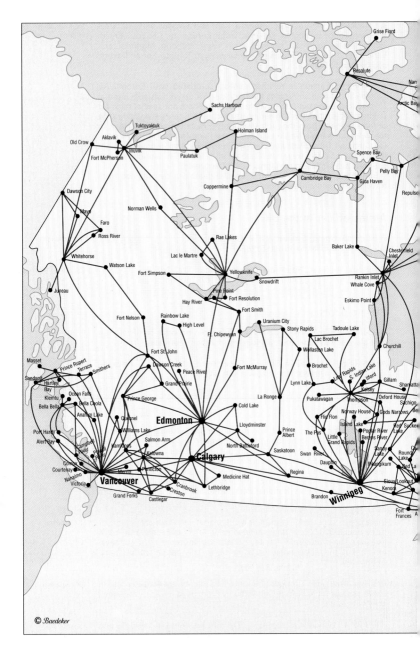

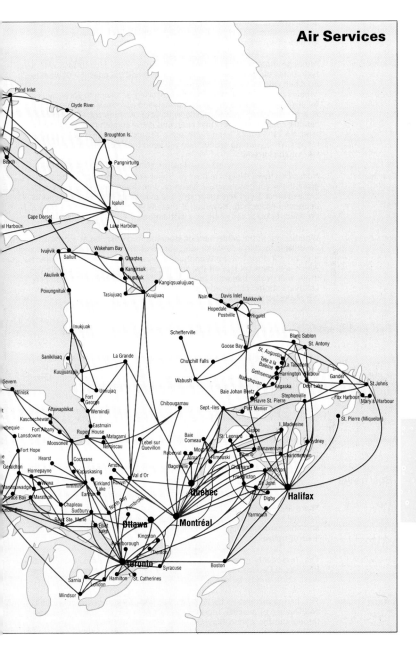

Air Services

Pond Inlet
Clyde River
Broughton Is.
Pangnirtung
Iqaluit
Cape Dorset
Lake Harbour
al Harbour
Ivujivik
Wakeham Bay
Salluit
Oraqtaq
Kangirsuk
Akulivik
Aupaluk
Kangiqsualujjuaq
Povungnituk
Tasiujaq
Kuujjuaq
Nain
Davis Inlet
Makkovik
Hopedale
Postville
Rigolet
Inukjuak
Scheff;erville
Blanc Sablon
St. Antony
Sanikiluaq
La Grande
Goose Bay
St. Augustin
Kuujjuarapik
Chushill Falls
Tete a la
Baleine
La Tabatier
Gethseman
Harrington Harbour
Gander
Severn
Umiujaq
Wabush
Natashquan
Kegaska
Deer Lake
St John's
Winisk
Fort
George
Baie Johan Beetz
Stephenville
Fox Harbour
Attawapiskat
Wemindji
Chibougamau
Havre St. Pierre
Mary's Harbour
Kaschechewan
Eastmain
Sept.-Iles
Fort Menier
St. Pierre (Miquelon)
bebeque
Fort Albany
Rupert House
Matagami
Lansdowne
Moosonee
Nemiscau
Lebel sur
Quevillon
Baie
Comeau
I. Madeleine
Fort Hope
Hearst
Reberval
St. Leonard
Bonaventure
Geraldton
Hornepayne
Cocrane
Amos
Bagotville
Almo
Rimouski
Charlo
Chatham
Sydney
antouwadge
Kapuskasing
Val d'Or
Chaliem
Charlottetown
Terrace Bay
Wawa
Timmins
Kirkland Lake
Fredericton
Moncton
Marathon
Chapleau
Sudbury
North Bay
Earlton
Rouyn
Québec
St. John
Digby
Halifax
Sault Ste. Marie
Pembroke
Montréal
Yarmouth
Elliot
Lake
Ottawa
Kingston
Peterborough
Trenton
Toronto
Boston
Sarnia
Hamilton
St. Catherines
Syracuse
London
Windsor

567

aggressive, and at certain times of year they gather in a few places in great numbers. One of these is Churchill, in Manitoba, where they congregate in autumn, making life quite difficult for the locals.

Bear country

Although most visitors to Canada will never come face to face with a bear, polar, black, brown, or grizzly, there is still the question of what to do if and when.

Bears can be kept at bay when backpacking or having to carry canoes for stretches overland by the occasional loud call, clapping or whistle (it is a good idea to take a whistle with you). Anyone travelling in bear country should take particular care, and know something about how to read tracks. Female bears with cubs should be treated with special respect. With warning grunts they will send their cub to safety and then take on the intruder.

Bear attacks

No looking them straight in the eye. Speak softly, soothingly, drop to the ground on your stomach, protecting your head and shoulders with crossed arms. Don't scream or yell, just play dead. A rucksack can act as additional protection. However, if there is a chance to climb a tree, a dropped rucksack can serve as a distraction.

Precautions

Whether out in the wilderness or stopping in civilisation at a campsite, never keep food in a canoe or tent, but do as the Canadians do and keep it in airtight drums or watertight containers and hang it from a branch which is at least six feet off the ground, placed so that it is no less than three foot from the trunk and hangs 18 inches below the branch. Leftovers should be buried deep in the ground as far away from sleeping places as possible.

Bed and Breakfast

Bed and Breakfast accommodation is widely available in Canada, and can be a real bargain. Local tourist offices keep lists of B & B providers, while some regions and provinces handle reservations and sell directories of homes taking part in bed and breakfast schemes.

Toronto

Bed & Breakfast Homes of Toronto, PO Box 46093, College Park Post Office, 444 Yonge Street, Toronto, Ontario M5B 2L8; tel. (416) 3636362

Montréal

Bed & Breakfast à Montréal, 422 Cherries, Montréal, Québec H2L 1G9; tel. (514) 7389410

Bus Travel

There are bus services linking almost every town and city not on the national rail network. Buses are very comfortable, with air conditioning and on-board toilet, and the leg and head room are comparable to airlines or trains.

Canada Pass

The reasonably priced Canada Pass is available from Greyhound Buslines of Canada. Valid for a period of 15 days, it covers travel in the west, north and Ontario.

Voyager Tourpass

The Tourpasses issued by Voyager Bus, a provincial operator (Ontario and Québec provinces), represent excellent value for money. Available throughout the period May–Oct. they can be purchased in Canada as well as abroad.

Bus companies (selection)

Acadian Lines, 6040 Almon Street, Halifax, Nova Scotia B3K 5M1   Canada
Brewster Transport Co. Ltd. 100 Gopher Street, Banff, Alberta T0L 0C0
Frontier Coach Lines, 16–102 Street, Hay River, Northwest Territories
   X0E 0R9
Greyhound Lines of Canada Ltd., 877 Greyhound Way SW, Calgary,
   Alberta T3C 3V8
Ontario Northland Railway, 65 Front Street West, Toronto, Ontario M5J
   1E6
Pacific Coach Lines Ltd., 1150 Station Street, Vancouver, British
   Columbia V6A 4C7
Pacific Western Transportation Ltd., 1857 Centre Avenue SE, Calgary,
   Alberta T2E 6L3
Saskatchewan Transportation Co., 2041 Hamilton Street, Regina,
   Saskatchewan S4P 2E2
VIA Rail Canada Inc., 2, place Ville-Marie, Montréal, Québec H3B 2C9
Voyageur Inc., 505 Boul. de Maisonneuve est, Québec, H2L 1Y4

Greyhound World Travel Ltd., Sussex House, London Road, East   United Kingdom
Grinstead, West Sussex RH19 1LD; tel. (0342) 317317

Camping

Canada has over 2000 campsites, some private, some official, located
along the main highways – about every 160 km (100 mi.) on the
TransCanada Highway – and in almost all the national and provincial
parks. They are very well equipped, usually with a table, benches and
fireplace for every camper. The facilities provided vary according to the
price, which ranges between 20 and 30 dollars a night.

Private campsites are more expensive and less spacious.

Many sites have places for buying camping equipment.

The Canadian Automobile Association (1145 Hunt Club Road, Ottawa,
Ontario, Canada K1V 0Y3; tel. (613) 2470117, fax (613) 2470118 and the
provincial tourist offices have information on the most appropriate
campsites.

Some provinces publish annually updated campsite directories, which   Directories
can be obtained from the relevant tourism office (see Information).

Advance reservation is not possible for many campsites, and this can   Reservations
cause considerable problems, especially at peak holiday times in the
summer. It is advisable therefore to arrive at a campsite as early as
possible.

Camping outside an official site close to towns is not encouraged, and   Unauthorised
camping in parks in forbidden.   camping

Campers and Motorhomes

Many holidaymakers explore Canada in motorhomes and campers.
They can be rented in all the big cities and at all international airports.
They differ considerably from their European counterparts, so it pays to
familiarise yourself with how they handle. It also pays to book campers
and motorhomes before departure with a reputable hire firm or a
specialist travel agency, since this can be much cheaper than renting
them on the spot.

Caravan Abroad Ltd., 56 Middle Street., Brockham, Surrey RH3 7HW;
tel. (01737) 842735
Cruise Canada, The Old House, High Street, Balcombe Forest, West
Sussex; tel. (01444) 811991

Be sure to read the small print of the contract. Find out what the pro-
cedure is in the event of an accident (repair costs, towing fees, extra
hotel charges, etc.), and precisely what the insurance covers.

When taking over, record the state of the vehicle and put down any
recognisable defects and damage. Check whether everything on the
inventory is there, and that you also have the operating instructions and
the address and telephone number of the rental company.

For most rented vehicles it is necessary to use a credit card as
security.

Take care when loading a mobilehome or camper to store heavy items
as low down as possible in front of the back axle. Fuel consumption is
likely to rise by 1 to 2 per cent per additional 100 kg (220 lbs). Empty the
watertank before starting out then fill up with fresh water on arrival.
Mobilehomes hold between 25 and 40 litres (5½ and 9 gallons) of fuel,
depending on the make. The most economic driving speed is between
70 and 80 k.p.h (43 and 50 m.p.h).

When renting a camper, besides Sales Tax – the equivalent of Europe's
value added tax – the hirer also has to pay Goods and Services Tax, and
additional insurance in the form of collision damage waiver (CDW) and
vacation interruption protection (VIP).

Canoeing and Rafting

Canoeing in Canada in summer is as much a way of life as skiing in the
Alps is in winter. Over thousands of years the Canadian canoe has been
shaped and refined to suit the geography and materials found in North
America to such good purpose that it has become the ideal craft, as
regards weight, seaworthiness, carrying capacity, etc., for the job it has
to do.

Canada was opened up by the canoe and the voyageurs and coureurs
de bois who paddled it up and down the country's three million or so
lakes, and countless other waterways. Nowadays, even though no
longer of birchbark, but more likely polyester or aluminium, the canoe is
still "the" way to explore the country. No one who has "discovered"
Canada by canoe can say they have simply "been there".

The method of propulsion is simple enough – the paddlepower generated by a person's own biceps which, apart from the sheer exhilaration
of the experience, gives the canoeist the kind of freedom and independence that enables him or her, preferably a crew of two anyway, to get
to places quite different from the camper in his mobilehome. To where
cruisers and sailing boats simply cannot pass, and where it is too rocky
or shallow for small motorboats, or where the ground cannot take a
heavy vehicle. With a canoe, one person picks up the canoe, the other
the baggage, and in next to no time there's a whole different environment opening up – with no engine fumes, no traffic sounds, no mech-
anical breakdowns, but a world without noise, something quite new to
many Europeans.

This freedom need not only be exercised on the rushing waters of a
mighty river. It could be on a little chain of lakes, of which Canada has
many thousands, or even just exploring one lone stretch of water in
splendid isolation.

Equipment Canoes and equipment can be rented from "outfitters" in Canada, or
experienced canoeists from abroad will probably bring with them their
own lifejackets, watertight bags for food and clothing, even, possibly,

Rafting on the Ottawa River

their own inflatable canoe. Besides light footwear, a tent, good maps and insect repellent, another essential requirement is sturdy rubber shoes with soles that have a good grip, since in the event of capsizing keeping a firm footing can be a matter of life or death.

Various watertight bags will protect foodstuff against an involuntary ducking. Main stocks of sugar, flour, pasta, etc. are best kept in sealed muslin or linen bags packed in sturdy watertight plastic. Pepper, salt, jam, etc. can be kept in wide-necked plastic containers obtainable in Europe from camping shops and chemists. In Canada they are only available at specialist shops in big cities, and finding them can be time consuming and costly.

For emergency rations take good European chocolate (rather than American candy bars) and dried egg, plus dried fruit mixtures. Do not take bacon and salami since they will immediately be confiscated by Canadian customs.

Rafting, which has become increasingly popular over the past twenty years, is more of a group activity, an organised thrill, and consequently a safer if no less exciting way of riding the white water of the bigger rivers. These are not as spectacular as the Colorado in America's Grand Canyon, but the Thompson, Fraser and Chilcotin Rivers in British Columbia have plenty of rock walls and rapids, while in the Northwest Territories there are tours on the Slave River, and even from the skyscrapers of Ottawa it is a relatively short step to the calmer waters of the Ottawa River at Beachburg, Ontario. Here the crew of eight or ten have to paddle themselves, whereas over in the West the heavyweight pontoons are propelled from behind by outboard motors. Early reservation is necessary in high summer. The equipment, i.e. wetsuits, life jackets, etc., comes as part of the package.

Guides to the rivers in particular provinces can be had from the local

Rafting

provincial offices, while newspaper kiosks, general stores, etc. also sell guides to the smaller rivers for certain areas.

Car Rental

Car rental in Canada is relatively cheap by European standards but it can get expensive if a car is hired in one place and returned to another. The different rates of taxation in the individual provinces can also impact on the cost. The minimum age for drivers hiring a car is 21, and for campers it is 25. A national driving licence is sufficient. The highest insurance premiums are those that have to be paid by young drivers.

It is cheaper and easier when hiring a car or camper in Canada to book in good time before leaving home.

As a general rule a deposit is required to hire a car, although cash and cheques will hardly ever be accepted as security. In fact the vast majority of firms will only hire a car on a credit card.

Rates

To hire a vehicle in the lower middle range a daily rate of 45 to 70 Canadian dollars is usual. In addition to that are taxes and extra mileage over that included in the price (usually 125 miles a day).

Hire firms

International hire firms such as Avis, Budget, Hertz, National-Tilden, etc. are in all the major towns and cities. There are also many reputable firms that specialise in hiring out campers and motor homes, and there are even agencies who specialise in supplying motor bikes.

Some main booking exchanges

Avis; tel. (800) 8792847 (freephone)
Budget; tel. (800) 2688900 (freephone)
Hertz; tel. (800) 2630600 (freephone)
National-Tilden; tel. (800) 3284567 (freephone)

Currency

Canadian dollar

The Canadian dollar (1 Can.$ = 100 cents) has notes in denominations of 5, 10, 20, 50, 100, 500 and 1,000 dollars, printed in English and French. The coins have a value of 1 cent (penny, sou), 5 cents (nickel, cinq sous), 10 cents (dime, dix sous) and 25 cents (quarter, vingt-cinq sous) as well as 1 and 2 dollars. The rate of exchange for the Canadian dollar can fluctuate considerably, and it is possible to make quite a loss when changing notes upon returning home.

Traveller's cheques

European visitors to Canada should take traveller's cheques in Canadian dollars, since these can be used like cash and there are very few places for cashing cheques in European currencies. Banks can often prove difficult, too, and will charge a fee. Always carry a driver's licence or passport for purposes of identification.

Eurocheques

Eurocheques will not generally be accepted in Canada.

Credit cards

The major international credit cards, especially American Express, Mastercard/Eurocard, Visa and Diner's Card, are accepted almost everywhere in Canada. Many top car-rental companies and hotel chains will only deal with credit card holders.

The relevant company should be informed immediately a credit card is lost.

Banks

Canadian banks are usually open Monday to Friday between 10am and 4pm, although opening times can vary. For business transactions a letter of credit should be obtained from the visitor's own bank before leaving home.

Foreign banknotes, traveller's cheques, etc., can be converted into Can. $ at many banks and special bureaux de change.

Currency exchange

There is no limit on the amount of Canadian dollars or foreign currency that can be taken in or out of the country.

Currency import/ export

Customs Regulations

Customs regulations on both sides of the Atlantic are currently under review. Up-to-date information should be sought from Revenue Canada (Customs and Excise), Ottawa K1A 0L5 or the nearest Canadian Embassy or Consulate prior to setting out.
  Visitors can take in personal items – including sporting equipment, cycles, cameras, portable radios and TVs – free of duty, but must be at least 18 or 19, depending on the province, to be able to do so in their own right.
  The duty-free allowances for import and export to and from Canada are 200 cigarettes or 50 cigars or 400 grams of tobacco (persons aged 16 or over), 1.1 litre of spirits or wine (persons over 18 years of age entering Alberta, Manitoba or Quebec; 19 years other provinces), and 24 regular sized cans or bottles of beer. There are strict regulations concerning the importation of plants, flowers and other vegetation. It is advisable not to bring any such into Canada, and absolutely no narcotics may be imported.
  Cars and motorcycles licensed abroad can be imported into Canada for periods of up to a year on issue of a Temporary Permit.

Cycling

Cycling has become very popular in Canada, as it has in Europe. The big cities in particular, but many of the provincial and national parks as well, have also recognised the signs of the times, and established some fine trails for use as cycletracks.
  Mountain bikes are also popular, but their use in Canada's great outdoors is very much subject to restrictions.

The network of cyclists' routes in the "Green Corridor" between the New England states of the north-east USA and Canada's Québec Province is currently being improved. Already there is a well-signposted cycleway traversing the 800 km (500 mi.) from Connecticut, USA to Montréal, Canada.

"Green Corridor"

Diplomatic Representation

British High Commission, 80 Elgin Street
Ottawa, Ontario K1P 5K7. Tel. (613) 237 1530

United Kingdom

US Embassy, 490 Sussex Drive, PO Box 866, Station B,
Ottawa, Ontario K1P 5T1. Tel. (613) 2385335

United States

There are British and American consulates in the principal cities of Canada.

Electricity

In Canada the electricity supply is 110 volts (60Hz) AC, as in the United States. Europeans should get a plug adaptor in advance if they want to use their own electrical appliances, since plugs in Canada are the standard two-flat-prong American type.

Emergencies

For medical emergencies, accidents, or situations requiring the police or fire services, use the emergency 911 telephone number in most of Canada (see below). Simply dial 911 and describe your emergency, the operator will then contact the appropriate service.

Provinces or areas using the 911 emergency number: Nova Scotia, New Brunswick, Manitoba and British Columbia; most of Ontario; major cities in Newfoundland, Québec, Saskatchewan and Yukon.

In the Northwest Territories, Nunavut and Prince Edward Island, dial 0 and ask the operator to put you through to the relevant emergency service (police, fire, ambulance, etc). Note: Prince Edward Island plans to have implemented the 911 number across the province by the year 2000.

For highway accidents, emergency telephones are provided along all the major divided highways of Canada.

Events

La Pérade (Québec): ice fishing

Québec (Québec): International Curling Tournament

Winter

January

February

Carleton (Québec): Grand Prix Baie-des-Chaleurs (snowcat racing)
Chetwynd (B.C.): Chinook Daze (winter carnival)
Chibougamau (Québec): Festival des Folifrets (ice and snow chase)
Chicoutimi (Québec): carnival
Courtenay (B.C.): winter carnival
Dawson Creek (B.C.): winter carnival
Golden (B.C.): snow festival
Hazelton (B.C.): ice carnival
Hull (Québec): marathon de ski de fond (ski marathon)
Jonquière (Québec): Jonquière en neige
Lac-la-Hache (B.C.): winter carnival
Prince Albert (Saska.): winter festival
Québec (Québec): ★Carnaval d'Hiver (winter carnival), world's biggest ice-sculpture competition
St Boniface (Man.): Festival du Voyageur
The Pas (Man.): Trappers' festival

March

Whitehorse (N.W.T.): Sourdorough Rendezvous

Baddeck (N.S.): S.A.N.S. tour
Elmira (Ont.): maple syrup festival
Hull (Québec): Salon du Livre (book fair)
Yellowknife (Yukon): Caribou Carnival

Easter

Inuvik (N.W.T.): top of the world ski meeting

March/April

Eastern Canada: maple sugar season, "sugaring off" parties
Snow geese northern migration, throughout Canada

April/May

Guelph (Ont.): Spring arts festival

May to October

Stratford (Ont.): Shakespeare festival
Niagara-on-the-Lake, Shaw festival

May

Campbell River (B.C.): Ishikari festival
Chilliwack (B.C.): festival (including races)
Creston (B.C.): flower festival
Fort St John (B.C.): stampede
Golden (B.C.): Columbia rafting

Ladysmith (B.C.): festival
Niagara Falls (Ont.): blossom festival
New Hamburg (Ont.): Mennonite auction
New Westminster (B.C.): Hyack festival, Fraser River canoe marathon
Ottawa (Ont.): ★Canadian Tullip Festival
Victoria (B.C.): Victorian Days

Digby (N.S.): Annapolis Valley apple blossom festival — Late May/early June

Banff (Alta.): arts festival
Williams Lake (B.C.): stampede — Early June to mid-August

Charlottetown (P.E.I.): "Anne of Green Gables" summer festival (theatre) — Mid-June to mid-September

Chetwynd (B.C.): rodeo — June
Chilliwack (B.C.): Indian festival
Cranbrook (B.C.): Sam Steele Day
Forestville (Québec): Festival de la Pêche (fishing festival)
Gaspé (Québec): international regatta
Grande Prairie (Alta.): stampede
Hazelton (B.C.): Kispiox rodeo
Hope (B.C.): bluegrass festival
Regina (Saska.): Western Canada Farm Progress Show
Shelburne County (N.S.): Lobster Festival (regatta)
Toronto (Ont.): international caravan show
Yellowknife (Yukon): midnight golf tournament, Folk on the Rocks

Bridgewater (N.S.): bluegrass maritime festival — Late June
Cabano (Québec): Festival de Touladi (including angling contests)
Chicoutimi (Québec): Jours de la Culture; regatta
Québec (Québec): fête nationale (Québec Province national day festival)

Campbellton (N.B.): salmon festival — June/July
Duncan (B.C.): Duncan-Cowichan summer festival
Grand Falls (N.B.): potato festival
Windsor (Ont.): freedom festival
Winnipeg (Man.): Red River exhibition and fair

July 1st, National Day celebrations throughout Canada — July
Antigonish (N.S.): Highland Games
Austin (Man.): Manitoba Threshermen's Reunion
Bella Coola (B.C.): rodeo
Belleville (Ont.): agricultural exhibition
Bridgetown (N.S.): American visitors' party
Calgary (Alta.): ★stampede and exhibition
Campbell River (B.C.): salmon festival
Campbellton (N.B.): Festival du Saumon
Drummondville (Québec): Festival de Folklore
Edmonton (Alta.): international jazz festival; Klondike Gold Rush Commemoration
Flin Flon (Man.): Flin Flon Trout Festival
Fort St. John (B.C.): stampede
Gaspé (Québec): Festival Jacques Cartier
Grand-Pré (N.S.): Acadian Days
Halifax (N.S.): Scottish games
Howe Sound (B.C.): Salmon Derby
Îles de la Madeleine (Québec): Festival du Homard (lobster festival); Festival du Pêcheur
Jonquière (Québec): Jonquière en fête
Kamloops (B.C.): rodeo
Kelowna (B.C.): international regatta

Events

Montréal (Québec): Festival international du Jazz; Bell just for laughs festival
Ottawa (Ont.): Ottawa Festival
Pugwash (N.S.): Gathering of the Clans
Québec (Québec): ★Festival d'Été (summer festival with music, dance, folklore)
Saskatoon (Saska.): Pioneer Days
Selkirk (Man.): Manitoba Highland Gathering
Shediac (N.B.): lobster festival
Shippagan (N.B.): fisheries festival
Saint John (N.B.): Loyalist Day
Ste-Anne-de-Beaupré: international pilgrimage to Ste-Anne-de-Beaupré
Thunderbay (Ont.): Rendezvous Pageant
Valleyfield (Québec): international regatta
Vancouver (B.C.): sea festival, Nanaimo-Vancouver bathtub race
Windsor (Newfoundland): Exploits Valley Salmon Festival
Winnipeg (Man.): folk festival
Yorkton (Saska.): Saskatchewan stampede and exhibition

Late July

Alma (Québec): Festirama
Carleton (Québec): Festivoile
Granby (Québec): Granby National (including classic car show)
Mahone Bay (N.S.): Mahone Bay Wooden Boat Festival, street parties
Roberval-Péribonka (Québec): Traverse du Lac St-Jean (trans-lake swim)

July/August

Whalewatching on east and west coasts
Annapolis Royal (N.S.): King's Festival
Baddeck (N.S.): Festival of the Arts
Cheticamp (N.S.): Festival de l'Escauette (Acadian festival)
Dauphin (Man.): National Ukrainian Festival
Edmundston (N.B.): Foire Brayonne
Lennoxville (Québec): English Theatre
Magog (Québec): Orford Festival
Penticton (B.C.): peach festival
Regina (Saska.): Buffalo Days
Steinbach (Man.): Pioneer Days
Toronto (Ont.): Caribana (Caribbean festival)

August

Abbotsford (B.C.): air show
Brandon (Man.): Manitoba Exhibition
Brantford (Ont.): Six Nations Indian Pageant
Bromont (Québec): Festival de la Musique Classique
Campbell River (B.C.): arts festival
Coaticook (Québec): Festival du Lait
Courtenay (B.C.): Elks Rodeo
Dawson (Yukon): Discovery Day
Dawson Creek (B.C.): rodeo
Fernie (B.C.): Rangler Valley rodeo
Gimli (Man.): Icelandic Festival
Grande-Prairie (Alta.): Muskoseepi Sunday
Halifax (N.S.): Natal Day (1st Mon.); arts festival
Havre-St-Pierre (Québec): Festival de la Minganie
Hazelton (B.C.): Pioneer Days
Hull (Québec): Festival de la Chanson, Musique de l'Outaouais
Kamloops (B.C.): international aerial meeting
Lake Cowichan (B.C.): Youbou Regatta
La Malbaie (Québec): les 95km de Charlevoix (cycle race)
Liverpool (N.S.): Musique Royale
Lethbridge (Alta.): Whoop Up and rodeo
Manitoulin Island (Ont.): Wikwemikong Pow-Wow
Maxville (Ont.): Glengarry Highland Games

Ottawa (Ont.): Canada Exhibition
Québec (Québec): air show, craft fair, Québec province fair
Saskatoon (Saska.): folk festival
Squamish (B.C.): loggers' sports day
St Ann's (N.S.): Gaelic Mod
St Catherines (Ont.): Royal Canadian Henley Regatta
St John's (Newfoundland): Royal St John's Regatta
Sudbury (Ont.): Rockhound Festival
Winnipeg (Man.): Folklorama

Campbellton and Caraquet (N.B.): ★Fête Nationale des Acadiens	August 15th

Natal Day: anniversary of establishment of city in 1749. 1st Monday in August — Mid-August
Bridgetown (N.S.): Black Power Rendezvous
Les Becquets (Québec): Festival de la Tomate
Lunenburg (N.S.): Folk Harbour (festival)

Chester (N.S.): Nova Scotia crafts market — August/September
Louisberg (N.S.): Louisberg Crab Festival
Toronto (Ont.): Canadian national exhibition
Trois-Rivières (Québec): Classique de canot de la Mauricie (canoe classic) Labour Day weekend
Vancouver (B.C.): Pacific national exhibition

Blanc Sablon (Québec): Festival de la Morue (cod festival) — September
Courtenay (B.C.): Comox Valley exhibition
Golden (B.C.): rodeo
Granby (Québec): Festival de la Chanson
Grand Forks (B.C.): Western Week, rodeo
Halifax (N.S.): Joseph Howe Festival
La Malbaie (Québec): Charlevoix open golf tournament
Lunenburg (N.S.): Nova Scotia fisheries exhibition and fishermen's reunion
Montréal (Québec): Montréal Marathon
St Catherines (Ont.): Niagara grape and wine festival
Trois-Rivières (Québec): Molson Grand Prix
Victoria (B.C.): Fall flower show

Throughout Canada: spectacular Fall colours; snow geese fly south — September/October
Muskoka Lakes (Ont.): Cavalcade of Colour
Penticton (B.C.): harvest and grape fiesta

Granby (Québec): Festival Gastronomique — October
Kitchener-Waterloo (Ont.): Octoberfest
Rimouski (Québec): Festival d'Automne

Québec (Québec): Beaujolais nouveau festival — November
Regina (Saska.): Canadian Western Agribition
Toronto (Ont.): Agricultural Winter Fair

Chilliwack (B.C.): Santa Claus Parade — December
Duncan (B.C.): Santa Claus Parade

Ferries

Along the Atlantic seaboard, the St Lawrence River and the Pacific Coast of British Columbia there are numerous medium- and short-distance ferry services, use of which can often avoid a much longer journey by road, particularly in the peak summer season. Detailed information and timetables are available from regional and provincial tourist offices.

Principal ferry routes

Bay of Fundy	Saint John (New Brunswick) – Digby (Nova Scotia)
Northumberland Strait	Caribou (Nova Scotia) – Wood Islands (Prince Edward Island)
Îles de la Madeleine	Souris (Prince Edward Island) – Havre-Aubert & Grande-Entrée (Îles de la Madeleine, Québec)
Newfoundland	North Sydney (Nova Scotia) – Argentia (Newfoundland) North Sydney (Nova Scotia) – Channel – Port-aux-Basques (Newfoundland) Lewisporte – Goose Bay (Labrador)
USA/Nova Scotia	Portland or Bar Harbour (Maine) – Yarmouth (Nova Scotia). Early booking essential!
Québec	Several ferry services on the St Lawrence River
British Columbia	B.C. Ferries run services to no less than 42 ports on the Pacific coast and Vancouver Island, including the exceptionally busy Port Hardy – Prince Rupert route (early booking essential). Further information from: B.C. Ferries, 1112 Fort Street, Victoria, B.C. V8V 4V2, tel. (604) 3863431; alternatively in Vancouver, B.C., tel. (604) 4442890 Main UK agent; tel. (0181) 3930127 The MV "Queen of the North" runs regular passenger and vehicular services (cars, campers and motorhomes) from Port Hardy on Vancouver Island to Prince Rupert, connecting with the Alaska Marine Highway ferry service.
Alaska	Alaska Marine Highway System, PO Box R, Juneau, Alaska 99811; tel. (907) 4653941 Juneau Regular passenger and vehicular services (cars, campers and motorhomes) from Seattle (restrictions apply) and Prince Rupert to Ketchikan, Wrangell, Juneau, Petersburg, Sitka, Haines and Skagway.

Filming and Photography

Filming and photography in Canada pose no problems whatsoever. Processing is up to European standards and film, with DIN or ASA values, is easily available just about everywhere. The largest towns and cities have rapid processing labs, where colour prints can be ready in a few hours.

Filling Stations

In the more densely populated areas and along the main highways Canada has plenty of filling stations (gas stations), but away from the main roads they are few and far between. Anyone travelling in the far North should take spare petrol supplies. In British Columbia, Yukon and the Northwest Territories it is possible to drive for hundreds of miles without finding a single filling station.

Fishing

With three oceans – the Atlantic, Arctic and Pacific – and countless lakes, streams and rivers, in fact half the world's stock of freshwater, Canada has everything to make the keen angler's heart rejoice.

Canada's inland waters hold fish to suit every angling taste, from superb salmon, fighting their way upriver every year, to perch, pike, all kinds of trout, bass, and the like, distributed virtually throughout the country's lakes and waterways, where, compared with Europe, they grow to a most impressive size. Among the many other species commonly caught are Dolly Varden, whitefish, barbel and eel. There is good deep sea angling off Canada's Atlantic seaboard and in the Pacific off the coast of British Columbia.

Many of Canada's best places for the sport can easily be reached by rail, road or plane, and are often close to campsites, hotels, lodges and other accommodation.

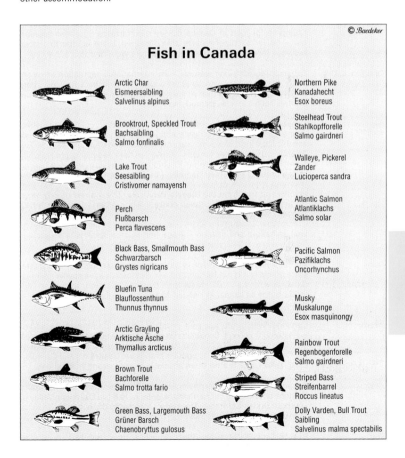

© Baedeker

Fish in Canada

Arctic Char
Eismeersaibling
Salvelinus alpinus

Northern Pike
Kanadahecht
Esox boreus

Brooktrout, Speckled Trout
Bachsaibling
Salmo fonfinalis

Steelhead Trout
Stahlkopfforelle
Salmo gairdneri

Lake Trout
Seesaibling
Cristivomer namayensh

Walleye, Pickerel
Zander
Lucioperca sandra

Perch
Flußbarsch
Perca flavescens

Atlantic Salmon
Atlantiklachs
Salmo solar

Black Bass, Smallmouth Bass
Schwarzbarsch
Grystes nigricans

Pacific Salmon
Pazifiklachs
Oncorhynchus

Bluefin Tuna
Blauflossenthun
Thunnus thynnus

Musky
Muskalunge
Esox masquinongy

Arctic Grayling
Arktische Äsche
Thymallus arcticus

Rainbow Trout
Regenbogenforelle
Salmo gairdneri

Brown Trout
Bachforelle
Salmo trotta fario

Striped Bass
Streifenbarrel
Roccus lineatus

Green Bass, Largemouth Bass
Grüner Barsch
Chaenobryttus gulosus

Dolly Varden, Bull Trout
Saibling
Salvelinus malma spectabilis

Food and Drink

Import of fishing
tackle

No special permit is needed to take in fishing tackle for personal use.

Fishing licences

Fishing is governed by federal, provincial and territorial laws, and anglers must have non-resident licences for the provinces or territories where they plan to fish. Fishing permits can be bought at stores and lodges and cost between 10 and 30 dollars.

A special permit is required to fish in all national parks. These can be obtained at any national park site for a nominal fee and are valid in all the national parks across Canada. In addition, tidal-waters sports fishing licences are required in some areas.

Information

Dept. of Fisheries and Oceans, Communications Branch, 200 Kent Street, Station 13228 Ottawa, Ontario K1A 0E6; tel. (613) 9931516.

Food and Drink

Shopping for food in Canada is very much like its European counterparts. So far as supermarkets are concerned, there is little to choose between them, and it is possible to eat very well for about $30 a day.

Canadian cooking

Canadian cooking has won itself an international reputation in recent years, thanks to the richness of the country's ethnic backgrounds. There is actually no national dish as such, but there are several Canadian specialities such as steak, salmon and lobster.

Regional
specialities

Canada's culinary highpoint is the French-Canadian cuisine of Québec, where the sturdy old French traditions are augmented by the use of specific local ingredients such as maple syrup and Canadian cheese. The Atlantic provinces are famous mostly for their lobster suppers, while Nova Scotia is also known for its solomon gundy, a marinaded herring recipe brought from their homeland by immigrant Scots. Ontario's lake pike and trout are deliciously complemented by the wine, fresh vegetables and fruit from the Niagara Peninsula. The prairies mostly serve up fare that is simple but well cooked, while Alberta is known for its peerless steaks.

The West Coast menu again features top quality shrimp and crab, as well as halibut and salmon – a poached salmon steak with vegetables from the Fraser Valley is a very special Canadian delicacy.

Game

Although Canada is so rich in game it seldom appears on the menu, since officially it is not for sale and few restaurants have special permits. Canadians hunt exclusively for their own consumption, so that an invitation home to dinner is needed to sample the best of Canada's wild game.

Whisky

Canadian whisky, 40 per cent proof, is usually drunk with ice and/or water, or with mixers. Canadian rye, a spirit made by distilling fermented cereals, matured and often blended, is reckoned to be one of the best of the Canadian whiskies. The popular brands are Seagram's and Canadian Club. Yukon Jack is a northern speciality, a very strong malt whisky.

Wine

Canadian wine can be surprisingly good. The main wineries are around Niagara-on-the-Lake, in the south of Ontario, and the Okanagan valley in southern British Columbia. The grapes are chiefly Chardonnay, Riesling, Sylvaner and Gewürztraminer.

Beer

Beer is Canada's favourite drink, usually as lager, pils and ale, as well as the stronger porter and stout, with Carling Black Label leading the field. Canada's top brewers are Molson, Labatt's, Carling-O'Keefe and Moosehead.

Getting to Canada

Flights from Europe

From London, Heathrow, to Calgary, Edmonton, Halifax/Dartmouth, Montréal, Ottawa, St John's (Newfoundland), Toronto and Vancouver (see Air Travel).
From Manchester to Toronto.
From Glasgow to Toronto.
Connections can easily be made to other Canadian cities.

Air Canada

From London to Montréal, Toronto and Vancouver.
156 Regent Street, London W1R 5TA; tel. (0181) 8974000 (London Area), (0345) 222111 (other areas).

British Airways

From London to Calgary, Montréal, Ottawa, Toronto and Vancouver (for UK address see Air Travel).

Canadian Airlines International

Flying from Manchester requires a change of aircraft at Heathrow.

By road from the USA

The main road routes into Canada are, in the east, US Highways 87, 89 or 91 for Montréal, and Queen Elizabeth Way or Highway 401 for Toronto, and, in the west, Interstate 5 and then Canadian Highway 99 to Vancouver.

Golf

Golfers will be in their element in Canada. There are more than 400 golf courses in the Province of Ontario alone. Clearly the list that follows is only a selection and for more detailed information write to the individual golf associations.

Banff Springs Golf Course
Banff, Alberta; tel. (403) 762680
18-hole, open April–October

Alberta

Kananaskis Country Golf Club
Lake Kananaskis, Alberta; tel. (403) 5917070
18-hole, open April–October

Mayfair Golf & Country Club
Edmonton, Alberta; tel. (780) 4397544
18-hole

Jasper Golf Course
18-hole; tel (780) 8526090

Royal Colwood Golf & Country Club
Victoria, B.C.; tel. (250) 4788331
18-hole, open all year

British Columbia

Uplands Golf Course (Oak Bay)
Victoria; tel. (250) 5927313
18-hole, open all year

Golf

Whistler Golf Club
Whistler; tel. (1800) 9447853
18-hole, open May–October

Chateau Whistler Golf Club
Whistler, B.C.; tel. (604) 9382092
18-hole

Manitoba

Hecla Island Golf Course (Gull Harbour)
Riverton; tel. (1800) 2676700
18-hole

Falcon Beach Golf Course
Falcon Lake; tel. (204) 3492554
18-hole

Wasagaming Golf Course (Clear Lake)
Wasagaming; tel. (204) 8484653
18-hole

New Brunswick

Mactaquac Provincial Park Golf Course
Fredericton; tel. (506) 3634925
18-hole, open March–October

Algonquin Golf Course
St Andrews; tel. (506) 5297142
18 and 9 hole, open April–October

Nova Scotia

Ashburn Golf Course
Halifax; tel. (902) 4439415
2 × 18-hole, open May–October

Ontario

Glen Abbey Golf Course
Oakville; tel. (905) 8441811
18-hole, open April–October

Niagara Parks Whirlpool Golf Course
Niagara Falls; tel. (877) 6427275
18-hole, open April–October

Knollwood Golf Club
Ancaster; tel. (905) 6486687
18-hole, open April–November

Prince Edward Island

Mill River Provincial Park Golf Course
Woodstock; tel. (1800) 3778339
6, 12 and 18-hole, open May–October

Québec

The Royal Montreal Golf Club
Montréal; tel. (514) 6263977
18, 18 and 9-hole, open March–November

Chateau Montebello Golf Course
Montebello; tel. (819) 4236341
18-hole

Gray Rocks Golf Course
St Jovite; tel. (819) 4252771
18-hole

Mont Ste-Marie Golf Course
Lac Ste-Marie; tel. (819) 4673111
18-hole

Waskesiu Golf Course
Waskesiu Lake; tel. (306) 6635301
18-hole, open June–October

Saskatchewan

Royal Canadian Golf Association
c/o Glen Abbey Golf Club
RR2, Oakville, Ontario L6J 4Z3; tel. (905) 8499700

Golf associations
in Canada

Alberta Golf Association
104–4116 Sixty Fourth Avenue S, Calgary, Alberta T2C 2B3; tel. (403)
2364616

Hotels and Motels

Throughout Canada, countless hotels and motels of all categories offer
accommodation of a generally high standard. Although many of these
are in private ownership, including fine old establishments and delightful country guest houses, most hotels belong to large chains (such as
Canadian Pacific, Best Western, Hilton, Holiday Inn, Hyatt, Meridien,
Novotel, Westin, York Hanover, TraveLodge, Trust House Forte, Ramada
and Sheraton) for which reservations can be made from Europe in
advance.

Some chains, e.g. Canadian Pacific, Four Seasons, Hilton International or
Westin Hotels, have very luxuriously appointed rooms, and all the larger
establishments have bars, restaurants and coffee shops. In some cases
the services offered include laundry, hairdressing and newspaper kiosks.
Resort hotels with spacious buildings, first-class sports facilities and a
high degree of comfort are quite expensive, but Canada has two inexpensive hotel chains, Journey's End and Relax Inn, and other attractive, clean and inexpensive accommodation can be found throughout the
country. Car-borne tourists are best accommodated in the better-class
motels, usually found along the main highways. During the summer the
large universities and colleges provide overnight accommodation for
visitors at reasonable prices, and farms and ranches offer inexpensive
bed and breakfast accommodation in informal surroundings.

Categories

In the big cities it is best to make a hotel reservation even out of season,
since some cities have convention centres, and when a big convention
is taking place the hotels are usually full. Accommodation in farms and
hotels near popular holidays areas should be booked as early as possible, as less overnight accommodation is available here than in the
cities, although a last-minute cancellation can mean a room becoming
available at short notice.

Reservations

Almost all provinces levy sales taxes on hotels, motels and restaurants.
In Alberta the hotel "room tax" is currently 5 per cent.

Taxes

The following is a guide only to the cost per night of a double room
(Spring 1999):

Room rates

Luxury hotels (L): over Can.$200
Higher standard hotels (M/L): Can.$150–300
Medium standard hotels and motels (M): Can.$100–250
Good cheaper hotels (M/B): Can.$70–160
Budget accommodation (B; mostly motels): from Can.$30

Alberta

Banff National Park	★★Banff Springs Hotel (L); tel. (403) 7622211, fax (403) 7625755 770 rooms and suites, thermal mineral baths, fitness centre with sauna, 11 restaurants, 5 bars, disco, shops, convention centre, library, 5 tennis courts, 27-hole golf course, riding stables. This traditional super de luxe château hotel and spa dates as far back as 1888, and is nowadays one of the great landmarks of Alberta Province. Buffalo Mountain Lodge (M); tel. (403) 7622400, fax (403) 7624495 108 units, restaurant, café, thermal and steam bath. This enormous log-cabin style lodge about a mile west of town, on Tunnel Mountain, currently has probably the best restaurant in Banff.
Calgary	Calgary Airport Hotel (L), 2001 Airport Road N.E.; tel. (403) 2912600, fax (403) 2508722 296 rooms, 2 restaurants, several meeting rooms. This is a comfortable staging post for the start of a trip round western Canada or as the last port of call before the journey home. Elbow River Inn (B), 1919 Macleod Trail S.E.; tel. (403) 2696771, fax (403) 2375181. 75 rooms, restaurant. Cheap but very well run hotel in Wild West territory. ★The Palliser (L), 133, 9th Avenue S.W.; tel. (403) 2621234, fax (403) 2601260 406 rooms and suites, restaurant, coffee shop, bar, fitness centre with sauna. The top hotel in town, the Palliser was opened in 1914 and totally renovated for the Olympic winter games in 1988. Close to the Calgary Tower, its VIP patrons have included Queen Elizabeth II in 1990. ★Westin Hotel (L), 320 4th Avenue S.W.; tel. (403) 2661611, fax (403) 2337471 520 rooms and suites, 7 restaurants, swimming pool, sauna. Recently renovated, the Westin's new "mission style" interior decor imaginatively harks back to Calgary's good old days as a boom town.
Edmonton	Fantasyland (L), West Edmonton Mall, 17700 87th Avenue; tel. (780) 4443000, fax (780) 4443294 360 rooms and suites, restaurant. This hotel in an ultra-modern shopping mall features fantasy-themed rooms. Crowne Plaza (M), 10111 Bellamy Hill N.W.; tel. (780) 4286611, fax (780) 4256564. 340 rooms and suites, revolving restaurant. Contemporary hotel for tourists and business travellers, with great views of the North Saskatchewan River valley. ★Macdonald (L), 10065 100 Street; tel. (780) 4245181, fax (780) 4248017 198 rooms and suites, restaurant, bar, health club & fitness centre, swimming pool and sauna, tennis, squash, lovely park. A traditional luxury hotel in the city centre, the Macdonald was built overlooking the river in 1915 by the Grand Trunk Railway Company in the then fashionable Loire Valley château style. It was extensively renovated and modernised in 1988 when taken over by Canadian Pacific. West Harvest Inn (B), 17803 Stony Plain Road; tel. (780) 4848000, fax (780) 4866060 160 rooms. Budget motel close to West Edmonton Mall.
Jasper National Park	Athabasca Hotel (B), Patricia Street, Jasper; tel. (780) 8523386 60 rooms, restaurant, coffee shop. Friendly family hotel, rather like a hunting lodge.

Château Jasper (L), 96 Geikie Street, Jasper; tel. (780) 8525644, fax (780) 8524860
120 rooms and suites, restaurant, lounge, swimming pool, thermal bath, sun terrace. Modern top class hotel with very good service and outstanding restaurant.

★Jasper Park Lodge (L); tel. (780) 8523301, fax (780) 8525107
420 rooms and suites in log cabins, 4 restaurants, café, 2 bars, night club, swimming pools, fitness centre with sauna, trails, cross-country ski-runs, golf course, various winter sports facilities. The famous Jasper Park Lodge, built in 1922, is on beautiful Lac Beauvert, and its log cabins have every comfort, often including open fires. Here visitors can walk, ride and play golf in summer and enjoy the Marmot Basin's first-class winter sports facilities in winter.

Becker's Chalets (M), on Highway 93, about 2 miles south of Jasper; tel. (780) 8523779, fax (780) 8527202
70 log cabins, restaurant.
This popular holiday resort on the Athabasca River dates from the Forties.

★Kananaskis Lodge & Hotel (L); tel. (403) 5917711, fax (403) 5917770
250 rooms and suites, 6 restaurants, 2 lounges, swimming pools, sauna, gym hall. Comfortable sports hotel in 1988 Olympic ski area where in summer visitors can play golf or simply go riding or walking.

Kananaskis Village

Best Western Kananaskis Inn (M); tel./fax (403) 5917500
100 units, swimming pool, steam bath. Modern hotel with good service and spacious rooms good for families with children.

★★Château Lake Louise (L); tel. (403) 5223511, fax (403) 5223834
513 rooms and suites, 5 restaurants, 2 bars, coffee shop, indoor pool, fitness centre with sauna, boutiques. Recently renovated, this fairy-tale castle hotel dates from 1890 and is in a breathtakingly beautiful setting amidst mountain scenery on the "emerald" Lake Louise.

Lake Louise

★Posthotel; tel. (403) 5223989, fax (403) 5223966
100 rooms and suites, restaurant, swimming pool, steam bath, conference facilities. This outstanding Swiss-run lodge-hotel began as a grand log-cabin complex in the Forties.

Prince of Wales Lodge (M/L); tel. (403) 8592231
90 rooms, garden restaurant, lobby. This lovely and expensively renovated mountain hotel was built by the Great Northern Railway Company in 1927.

Waterton Lakes National Park

British Columbia

Penticton Lakeside Resort (M/L), 21 West Lakeshore Drive; tel. (250) 4938221
200 rooms and suites, 2 restaurants, 2 swimming pools, fitness centre with sauna, tennis, golf, ski-runs. Well-appointed holiday resort for sporting guests.

Okanagan Valley
Penticton

The Grand Okanagan (M/L), 1310 Water Street; tel. (250) 7634500
202 rooms and suites, restaurant, lounge, swimming pool, fitness centre with sauna, beauty salon, boutiques, marina, beach. Fairly new and very smart complex with all modern facilities.

Kelowna

Totem Lodge (B), 1335 Park Avenue; tel. (250) 6246761
30 rooms. Simple but quite well appointed motel.

Prince Rupert

Hotels and Motels

Best Western Capilano Inn (M), North Vancouver, 1634 Capilano Road; tel. (604) 9878185, fax (604) 9875153
Modern, well-appointed medium class hotel by Capilano Bridge, quite close to the city centre and the totem poles in famous Stanley Park.

★Four Seasons Hotel (L), 791 W. Georgia Street; tel. (604) 6899333, fax (604) 8446744
385 rooms, 3 restaurants, bar, swimming pool, fitness centre with sauna. Centrally located grand hotel, famed for its elegance, and one of the top places in town.

Kingston Hotel (B), 757 Richard Street; tel. (604) 6849024, fax (604) 6849917
58 rooms, sauna, breakfast room. Friendly B & B style hotel.

Empire Landmark (M), 1400 Robson Street; tel. (604) 6870511, fax (604) 6872801
360 rooms, revolving restaurant, coffee shop, bar, sauna. There is a superb view of Vancouver from the revolving restaurant of this comfortable hotel in a 42-storey skyscraper.

Pacific Palisades (M/L), 1277 Robson Street; tel. (604) 6880461, fax (604) 8915130
233 rooms and suites, restaurant, swimming pool, fitness centre with sauna. This recently renovated first-class hotel is popular with tourists, not least for the views from the top floors.

Riviera Motor Inn (M), 1431 Robson Street; tel. (604) 6851301, fax (604) 6851335.
40 rooms and apartments. Apartment hotel in Vancouver's picturesque West End.

★Vancouver (L), 900 W. Georgia Street; tel. (604) 6843131, fax (604) 6621901
550 rooms and suites, 3 restaurants, bar, swimming pool, fitness centre with sauna. This city-centre château-style luxury hotel, complete with marble and mahagony in the guest suites, dates from 1939 and is run by Canadian Pacific with faultless standards of customer care.

★Waterfront Centre (L), 900 Canada Place Way; tel. (604) 6911991, fax (604) 6911828
460 rooms and 29 suites, 2 restaurants, lounge, bar, business centre, boutiques, health & fitness centre with swimming pool and sauna. In a 1991 high-rise block on Canada Place this striking CP waterfront hotel has a great view over the harbour.

Westin Bayshore Inn (L), 1601 W. Georgia Street; tel. (604) 6823377, fax (604) 6873102
515 rooms and suites, restaurant, swimming pool, sauna. A modern hotel close to Stanley Park with its famous totem poles, the Bayshore Inn has lovely views of both the waterfront and the mountains from its spacious rooms.

★★The Empress (L), 721 Government Road; tel. (250) 3848111, fax (250) 3814334
480 rooms and suites. One of the sights of the waterfront, this venerable Tudor-style grand hotel has recently been fully renovated and is without equal on the North American Pacific coast for its luxury and elegance.

Abigail's Hotel (M), 906 McClure Street; tel. (250) 3885363, fax (250) 3887787.

15 rooms. Romantic and very luxuriously appointed accommodation in a good peaceful location.

James Bay Inn (M/B), 270 Government Street; tel. (250) 3847151, fax (250) 3852311
50 rooms, restaurant. Recently renovated, this smart 1907 inn, home in her last years to author and artist Emily Carr, is a good alternative to the city's expensive grand hotels.

★Château Whistler Resort (L); tel. (604) 9388000, fax (604) 9382020   Whistler
343 rooms and suites, 2 restaurants, bar, convention centre, boutiques, swimming pools, fitness studio, golf course. Opened in 1989, this is very reminiscent of the traditional CP Banff and Lake Louise hotels. It is located in one of North America's top winter sports areas, but also offers golf, riding and walking in summer.

Manitoba

Wellman Lake Lodge (M/B), Minitonas; tel. (204) 5254422   Duck Mountain
7 units. The lodge is particularly popular with the hunting and fishing   Prov. Park
fraternity, and has well-appointed units on a lovely lake with a beach.

Gull Harbour Resort (M); tel. (204) 2792041, fax (204) 2792000   Lake Winnipeg
90 rooms and suites, swimming pool, sauna, golf, tennis, water sports,   Riverton
beach. Very family-friendly holiday complex, and highly favoured by a sporty clientele.

Elkhorn Lodge (M/B); tel. (204) 8482802, fax (204) 8482109   Riding Mountain
60 rooms and suites, restaurant, swimming pool, golf, riding. Friendly   National Park
and very rural accommodation, ideal for families with children and a   Clear Lake
good base for exploring the Riding Mountains with their abundant wildlife.

Charterhouse (M/B), 330 York Avenue; tel. (204) 9420101, fax (204)   Winnipeg
9560665
90 rooms, restaurant, coffee shop, swimming pool. Good cheap hotel close to the Convention Centre with locally acclaimed restaurant (prime ribs a speciality).

Radisson Winnipeg (L/M), 288 Portage Avenue; tel. (204) 9560410, fax (204) 9471129
270 rooms and suites, 2 restaurants, business lounge, swimming pool, sauna, gym, cinema, kindergarten. Comfortable city hotel, good for families with children, and for taking walks, weather permitting, to the shopping and business centres of Eaton Place and Portage Place.

Gordon Downtowner (B), 330 Kennedy Street; tel. (204) 9435581, fax (204) 9473041
40 rooms, restaurant, pub. Recently renovated, this budget hotel is in the busy shopping district of Portage Place.

Holiday Inn Crowne Plaza (M), 350 St. Mary's Avenue; tel. (204) 9420551, fax (204) 9438702
380 rooms, 2 restaurants, piano bar, lounge. Family-friendly hotel with the chain's usual comfort and a choice of Far Eastern, Mexican, French and local Canadian cuisine.

Place Louis Riel (M), 190 Smith Street; tel. (204) 9476961, fax (204) 9473029.

280 suites, restaurant, lounge. A well-run city centre hotel in a skyscraper offering particularly good value at weekends.

The Lombard (M), 2 Lombard Place; tel. (204) 9571350, fax (204) 9561791
350 rooms and suites, gourmet restaurant, coffee shop, fitness centre with swimming pool and sauna. Gleaming white post-modern highrise hotel close to Manitoba Centennial Centre.

New Brunswick

Campobello Island	Friar's Bay Motor Lodge (B), on Route 774; tel. (506) 7522056 10 rooms, good restaurant. Family hotel close to the villa of former US President Roosevelt.
Caraquet	Maison Dugas (B), 683 Boulevard St-Pierre Ouest; tel. (506) 7273195 12 rooms and 5 chalets. Friendly holiday accommodation in delightful countryside.
	Paulin (M/B), 143 Boulevard St-Pierre Ouest; tel. (506) 7279981 10 rooms, very good cuisine. Small but very comfy and charming, with views of the Gaspé peninsula from the mansard windows.
Fredericton	Lord Beaverbrook Hotel (L/M), 659 Queen Street; tel. (506) 4553371, fax (506) 4551441 160 rooms and suites, restaurant, swimming pool, sauna. The top hotel in town, next to the gallery of the same name and also close to Parliament and the theatre.
	Sheraton Inn (L/M), 225 Woodstock Road; tel. (506) 4577000, fax (506) 4574000 220 rooms, restaurant, bar, swimming pool, sauna, gym. Well located and popular with business travellers and tourists, the big attraction is the hotel's own pool in the riverside park.
Moncton	Beauséjour (L), 750 Main Street; tel. (506) 8544344, fax (506) 8580957 310 rooms and suites, 3 restaurants, café, piano bar, meeting and banqueting rooms, swimming pool. The best place in town, this is primarily a convention hotel, but also a haven for tourists en route to the famous Bay of Fundy and Cape Hopewell.
	Canadiana (M), 46 Archibald Street; tel. (506) 3821054 16 rooms, dining room. Very friendly little hotel in a Victorian mansion.
St Andrew's-by-the-Sea	★Algonquin (L); 184 Adolphus Street; tel. (506) 5298823, fax (506) 5297162 240 rooms and suites, pub, piano bar, night club, several dining rooms, meeting rooms, 2 golf courses, fitness centre. Recently renovated, the Algonquin is a very popular complex for rest and relaxation, plus sports activity, but only open from mid-May to mid-October; also renowned for its cuisine.
Saint John	Dufferin Inn (M), 357 Dufferin Row; tel. (506) 6355968, fax (506) 6742396 6 rooms, restaurant (Martello Dining Room), bar. Family hotel with lavish breakfasts; close to the ferry terminal.
	Saint John Hilton (L), 1 Market Square; tel. (506) 6938484, fax (506) 6576610 195 rooms and suites, very good restaurant, lounge, swimming pool, sauna, gym. Beautifully located and well-run hotel with particularly friendly service.

Newfoundland

Atlantica Inn, St Bride's, on Route 100; tel. (709) 3372860
5 rooms, dining room. Friendly clean accommodation, with a proprietor who is an excellent cook.

Cape St Mary's

Deer Lake Motel (M/B); tel. (709) 6352108, fax (709) 6353842
55 rooms, dining room. Modern tourist inn with friendly service.

Deer Lake

Hotel Gander (M), 100 Trans-Canada Highway; tel. (709) 2563931, fax (709) 6512641
150 rooms, restaurant, swimming pool, gym. Long famous among flyers although since renovated, the Hotel Gander's decor harks back to the great days when this was one of the greatest outposts for civilian and military air travel.

Gander

Gros Morne Cabins (M), Rocky Harbour; tel. (709) 4582020, fax (709) 4582882
22 log cabins. Rustic but reasonably comfortable accommodation in the north of the national park.

Gros Morne National Park

Best Western Traveller's Inn (M/B), 199 Kenmount Road; tel. (709) 7225540, fax (709) 7221025
90 rooms, restaurant, swimming pool. Recently renovated well-run hotel; very popular with tourists.

St. John's

Journey's End Quality Inn (M/B), 2 Hill O'Chips; tel. (709) 7547788, fax (709) 7545209
160 rooms. Modern urban hotel with lovely view of the harbour.

★Hotel Newfoundland (L), Cavendish Square; tel. (709) 7264980, fax (709) 7262025
300 rooms and suites, 2 restaurants, 12 conference and banqueting rooms, indoor pool, squash, fitness centre with sauna. All the main sights of Newfoundland's capital are easy to reach on foot from this city centre modern luxury hotel, managed by Canadian Pacific.

Terra Nova Park Lodge (M), Port Blanford; tel. (709) 5432525
80 rooms and suites, pub, snackbar, swimming pool, ski shop, golf course. Modern hotel "at the end of the world", particularly suited for sporting and nature enthusiasts, with very spacious family rooms.

Terra Nova National Park

Campbell House (M); tel. (709) 4643377
4 rooms. Pretty and very well run-haven for the keen hiker.

Trinity

Northwest Territories

Finto Inn (M); tel. (867) 7772647, fax (867) 7773442
40 rooms, restaurant. Very new hotel with comfortable rooms mainly patronised by visiting civil servants.

Inuvik

Mackenzie Hotel (M); tel. (867) 7772861, fax (867) 7773317
30 rooms, restaurant, coffee shop, bar, dancing. The oldest hotel in the town is also the main meeting place in Inuvik; very noisy here at weekends.

Nunavut

Discovery Lodge; tel. (867) 9794433, fax (867) 9796591·
53 rooms, restaurant. Modern, well appointed accommodation in the Arctic.

Baffin Island
Iqaluit

Hotels and Motels

Yellowknife

Explorer (L), 48th Street; tel. (867) 8733531, fax (867) 8732789
125 rooms and suites, dining lounge, lobby. The top hotel in town –
Queen Elizabeth II stayed here – the 8-storey snow-white Explorer continues to be Yellowknife's main meeting place.

Igloo Inn (M), 4701 Franklin Avenue; tel. (867) 8738511, fax (867) 8735547
40 rooms. Small but super inn in an architecturally stunning timber
structure.

Nova Scotia

Annapolis Royal

Queen Anne Inn (M), 494 Upper St George Street; tel. (902) 5327850
10 rooms. Very elegant and romantic small hotel in Victorian building
with antique furnishings.

Antigonish

Greenway Claymore Inn (M), Church Street; tel. (902) 8631050
75 rooms, swimming pool. Friendly hotel in the place above St George's
Bay where the Scottish Highland Games are held in July.

Maritime Inn Antigonish (M), 158 Main Street, tel. (902) 8634001, fax
(902) 8632672
33 rooms. Family-run hotel with pretty rooms and a Scottish feel about it.

Baddeck

Auberge Giselle (M), 387 Shore Road; tel. (902) 2952849, fax (902)
2952033
65 rooms and suites, restaurant. This hotel in Baddeck, where Graham
Bell, inventor of the telephone, came to relax, offers peace and quiet,
plus a superb restaurant that is famed far and wide.

Chéticamp

Laurie's Motor Inn (M), on Route 19; tel. (902) 2242400, fax (902) 2242069
54 rooms, "Acadien" restaurant. Friendly motel where the Acadian tradition is lovingly preserved.

Digby

Harbourview Inn (M), Smith's Cove; tel. (902) 2455686
9 bungalows, restaurant, tennis. Friendly family hotel on the Bay of
Fundy famed for its tides; the restaurant is one of Nova Scotia's best.

Halifax

★Hotel Halifax (L), 1990 Barrington Street; tel. (902) 4256700, fax (902)
4256214
300 rooms, conference and banqueting rooms, restaurant and lounge,
indoor pool, sauna, sightseeing tours. This ultra-modern luxurious
Canadian Pacific hotel is part of the renovated Scotia Square complex.

Westin Nova Scotia (L), 1181 Hollis Street; tel. (888) 6793784
300 rooms and suites, convention centre, swimming pool, restaurant.
On the north-east edge of the city centre (by the station), this is a very
comfortable hotel mainly used by business travellers.

Halliburton House Inn (M), 5184 Morris Street; tel. (902) 4200658
30 rooms, restaurant. Very agreeable family hotel with well-appointed
rooms and a restaurant which is recommended among Halifax's visitors.

Prince George (L), 1725 Market Street; tel. (902) 4251986, fax (902)
4296048
205 rooms and 10 suites, swimming pool. A grand hotel with very attentive service and extremely attractive rooms, the Prince George is not far
from the Clock Tower and the Citadel; it has a tunnel leading directly to
the city centre.

★Sheraton Halifax (L), 1919 Upper Water Street; tel. (902) 4211700
350 rooms and suites, restaurant. This elegant and very well-run hotel

with its excellent restaurant is right next to the lovingly restored waterfront with its many fine boutiques and restaurants.

★Keltic Lodge (L); tel. (902) 2852880, fax (902) 2852859
70 rooms and a number of bungalows, golf, tennis, beach. Cape Breton's best hotel, standing in the grand scenery of the rocky Atlantic coast, is close to the imposing Herman Falls with bathing in summer at Ingonish Beach.

Ingonish

★Liscomb Lodge (L), on Marine Drive (Hwy. 7); tel. (902) 7792307
65 units, swimming pool, tennis, boats, water sports, game fishing. Exclusive lodge on the wild Atlantic coast, where the joys of nature and pleasant solitude can be experienced.

Liscomb Mills

Bluenose Lodge (M), Falkland Avenue & Dufferin Street; tel. (902) 6348851
9 rooms, restaurant. The guest rooms in this small hotel in a Victorian villa have every modern comfort and yet are redolent of the good old times.

Lunenburg

Cranberry Cove Inn (M), 17 Wolfe Street; tel. (902) 7332171
7 rooms, dining room (for non-residents too). Small but attractive hotel in a recently lovingly restored Victorian building.

Louisbourg

Normaway Inn & Cabins (M), Egypt Road (about a couple of miles off the Cabot Trail); tel. (902) 2482987
9 rooms and 19 bungalows, restaurant, riding stables, fishing waters. The Normaway Inn is tucked away in beautiful upland scenery on Cape Breton Island and, particularly on account of its excellent restaurant, is one of those places highly recommended in the lifestyle magazines.

Margaree Valley

The Walker Inn (B), 34 Coleraine Street; tel. (902) 4851433
10 rooms. The Walkers bought a listed 19th c. mansion when they arrived here from Switzerland some years ago, and turned it into a smart, small family-oriented hotel.

Pictou

★White Point Beach Lodge Resort (M); tel. (902) 4211569, tel. (local) (902) 3542711 (Halifax)
47 rooms and 46 bungalows, conference facilities, swimming pool, restaurant, boutiques, golf course, riding stables, beach, water sports facilities. The luxurious holiday resort is on a spur extenting out into the Atlantic south of Liverpool, and is a very good place for rest and relaxation in wild natural surroundings.

White Point

Ontario

Arowhon Pines (L/M), about 8 miles off Highway 60; tel. (705) 6335661, fax (705) 6335795
50 rooms, dining room, tennis, sauna. Romantic buccolic retreat, and very comfortable despite not having television or telephones in the rooms; in an idyllic setting of pinewoods by a quiet lake.

Algonquin Park

Blue Mountain Inn (M/B), Collingwood; tel. (705) 4450231
100 rooms, dining room, swimming pool, tennis. Hotel particularly suitable for weekenders and tourists interested in nature and sports activities.

Blue Mountain

Belvedere (M), 141 King Street E; tel. (613) 5481565, fax (613) 5464692
20 rooms This loving maintained hotel with its mansard roof has very tastefully furnished rooms (partly Art Deco).

Kingston

Hotels and Motels

Kitchener

Four Points Hotel by Sheraton (M), 105 King Street E; tel. (519) 7444141, fax (519) 7441314
200 rooms, restaurant, swimming pool, squash, bowling. Well-run hotel that successfully blends English colonial with German heritage.

Muskoka
Huntsville

Deerhurst Resort (M), 1235 Deerhurst Drive; tel. (705) 7896411, fax (705) 7892431
121 rooms, 3 restaurants, pub, lounge, bar, 2 indoor pools, health & fitness centre with steam bath, 2 golf courses, several tennis courts, trails, winter sports (cross-country runs, Alpine skiing in Hidden Valley, ice skating). This comfortable holiday resort is in the scenic Muskoka lake district on Peninsula Lake and not far from Algonquin Provincial Park.

Windermere

Windermere House (M), off Muskoka Route 4; tel. (705) 7693611, fax (705) 7692168
68 rooms, restaurant, lounge, swimming pool, golf, tennis, fishing, water sports. Pleasant hotel built in 1864 close to Lake Rousseau, and recently renovated at great expense.

Niagara
Niagara Falls

Americana (M/B), 8444 Lundy's Lane; tel. (905) 3568444, fax (905) 3568576
90 rooms, restaurant, coffee shop, lounge, 2 swimming pools, sauna, tennis, gym. Delightful hotel, off the beaten track, with very good rates.

Nelson Motel (B), 10655 Niagara River Parkway; tel. (905) 2954754
24 rooms, swimming pool. Pretty, very friendly, good value accommodation in quiet location.

★Renaissance Fallsview Hotel (L), 6455 Buchanan Avenue; tel. (905) 3575200, fax (905) 3573422
260 rooms and suites, panorama café-restaurant, health club with swimming pool, fitness centre and sauna. Exclusive hotel with fine view of the famous falls.

Skyline Foxhead (M), 5875 Falls Avenue; tel. (905) 3744444, fax (905) 3574804
400 rooms and suites, penthouse restaurant, swimming pool. A recently expensively renovated hotel in the best situation.

Niagara-on-the-lake

Prince of Wales (L/M), 6 Picton Street; tel. (905) 4683246, fax (905) 4685521
100 rooms, restaurant, swimming pool, sauna, gym, tennis. Anyone who yearns for the elegance of Victorian days will be at home here – the oldest part dates from 1846.

Queen's Landing (L/M), 155 Byron Street; tel. (905) 4682195, fax (905) 4682227
130 rooms, dining room, lounge, swimming pool, gym. Smart hotel on the marina with equally smart clientele.

Ottawa

The Albert at Bay Suite Hotel (L/M), 435 Albert Street; tel. (613) 2388858, fax (613) 2381433
200 suites, gym with whirlpool. Luxurious apartment hotel for business travellers and conference visitors, but with much reduced weekend rates to suit the ordinary tourist.

★Château Laurier (L), 1 Rideau Street; tel. (613) 2411414, fax (613) 5627031
425 rooms, 2 restaurants, bar, swimming pool, fitness centre. The top place in town and within a few minutes on foot of all its main attractions, the "Château" dates from 1912; this imposing grand hotel's first guests included Canada's then premier, Sir Wilfrid Laurier.

Lord Elgin (M), 100 Elgin Street; tel. (613) 2353333, fax (613) 2353223
310 rooms, dining room, bar. Well-run medium category hotel opposite
the National Arts Centre.

Minto Place Suite Hotel, 433 Laurier Avenue W.; tel. (613) 2322200, fax
(613) 2326962
412 suites and studios, restaurant, shopping arcade, swimming pool, fitness centre with sauna. Very well appointed apartment hotel, with magnificent view of Ottawa from the top floors.

Westin (L/M), 11 Colonel Dr.; tel. (613) 5607000, fax (613) 2345396
484 rooms, restaurant, atrium lobby, dancing, swimming pool, health
club with sauna. Smart modern hotel in the city centre between Rideau
Centre and the Convention centre.

Bentley's Inn (M), 99 Ontario Street; tel. (519) 2711121, fax (519) 2721853   Stratford
13 suites. Friendly hotel with utterly English atmosphere.

Airlane Hotel (B), 698 W. Arthur Street; tel. (807) 5771181   Thunder Bay
154 rooms, restaurant, dancing, swimming pool, fitness centre.
Recently modernised well-appointed hotel.

Crown Plaza Toronto Centre (L/M), 225 Front Street W; tel. (416) 5971400,   Toronto
fax (416) 5978128
587 rooms and suites, restaurant, bistro, lounge, garden, swimming
pool, fitness centre with sauna and solarium. The very comfortable 25-
storey hotel is near the Skydome, CN Tower, Roy Thomson Hall and the
ultra-modern Metro Toronto Convention Centre.

Delta Chelsea Inn (M), 33 Gerrard Street W.; tel. (416) 5951975, fax (416)
5854302
1580 rooms and suites, several restaurants and bars, "Market Garden"
with cafeteria jazz club, business centre, kindergarten, 2 swimming
pools, fitness centre with sauna and solarium. Enormous modern hotel
with every facility, equally popular with foreign groups and business
travellers; very good special weekend rates for families with children.

★Four Seasons (L), 21 Avenue Road; tel. (416) 9640411
375 rooms, restaurant, café, bar, swimming pool, fitness centre.
Exceedingly well furnished luxury hotel in Yorkville, the fashionable part
of Toronto, and one of the city's best.

Inn on the Park (L/M), 1100 Eglington Avenue E.; tel. (416) 4442561, fax
(416) 4463308
269 rooms and suites, 2 restaurants, terrace lounge, piano bar, business
centre, kindergardten 3 swimming pools, tennis. On a hill close to the
Ontario Science Center, the very well appointed Inn on the Park is suitable for business travellers and families with children.

★King Edward (L), 37 King Street; tel. (416) 8639700, fax (416) 3675515
295 rooms and suites, 2 restaurants, café, bar lobby, ballroom, health
club with sauna. Beautifully restored 1903 luxury hotel, with Corinthian
columns, crystal chandeliers and precious wood antiques which give it
an aristocratic glitter.

★Royal York (L), 100 Front Street W.; tel. (416) 3682511, fax (416) 3682884
1174 rooms and suites, 12 restaurants, several bars, health club with spa,
swimming pool and fitness centre, conference rooms and boutiques.
One of Toronto's finest hotels, the Royal York, opened in 1929 and
recently renovated, is something of an echo from the past among

today's plate-glass skyscrapers; it was for many years the tallest building in the city.

Sky Dome Hotel (M), 1 Blue Jays Way; tel. (416) 3417100, fax (416)
3415091
278 rooms and suites, restaurant and lounge, Hard Rock Café, conference facilities, fitness centre, swimming pool and squash courts. From
70 of the hotel's rooms there is a view directly into the vast futuristic
sports arena with its swivel roof that forms part of the whole recently
opened Sky Dome complex.

The Strathcona (M/B), 60 York Street; tel. (416) 3633321, fax (416)
3634679
190 rooms, fitness centre. Medium category hotel, well fitted out, opposite Union Station.

Westin Harbour Castle (L/M), 1 Harbour Square; tel. (416) 8691600, fax
(416) 3610573
980 rooms, 2 restaurants (including a revolving restaurant on the 37th
floor), swimming pool, fitness centre with sauna, steam bath and
massage, tennis. Massive luxuriously appointed hotel in a favoured
location on the waterfront.

Prince Edward Island

Cavendish	★Shaw's Hotel (L/M), on Brackley Beach; tel. (902) 6722022, fax (902) 6723000 18 rooms and 20 cottages, dining room. Smart holiday hotel (only open May to October) with a wonderful Victorian main building: the Sunday supper buffet is quite an experience. Shining Waters (M), on Route 13; tel./fax (902) 9632251 10 rooms and 20 cottages. Popular holiday hotel on Gulf of St Lawrence, and a particular favourite with young families.
Charlottetown	★Prince Edward (L), 18 Queen Street; tel. (902) 5662222, fax (902) 5662282 210 rooms and suites, restaurant, café, ballroom, 14 presentation rooms, fitness club with spa, indoor pool and sauna, yacht club, golf, tennis, park. This first-class hotel on Charlottetown's waterfront is one of the town's landmarks. Popular with business travellers and tourists alike, it is reputed to serve some of the best food in the Atlantic Provinces. Best Western Maclauchlan's Motor Inn (M), 238 Grafton Street; tel. (902) 8922461, fax (902) 5662979 143 rooms, restaurant, swimming pool, sauna. Recently renovated and well-run hotel for tourists and business travellers.
Prince Edward Island National Park	Dalvay-by-the-Sea (L/M), Little York; tel. (902) 6722048 25 rooms. Small but smart hotel in an Edwarian country house on the north coast.
Summerside	Garden of the Gulf Quality Inn, 618 Water Street E; tel. (902) 4362295, fax (902) 4366277 92 rooms, coffee shop, lounge, swimming pool. Large family-friendly holiday complex which can act as a base for all kinds of outdoor activities.
Souris	The Inn at Bay Fortune, on Route 310; tel. (902) 6873745, fax (902) 6873540 10 rooms, dining room. This pleasant little hotel in the former summer home of a New York actress dishes up some wonderful delicacies from its kitchen.

★Matthew House Inn, 15 Breakwater Street; tel. (902) 6873461
8 rooms, dining room. One of the finest of the small, very comfortable
guest houses on the island; its heritage architecture has long made it a
favourite with photographers.

Lighthouse (M), on Route 14 (near Cedar Dunes Prov. Park); tel. (902)   West Point
8593605, fax (902) 8591510
9 rooms, dining room. Unusual little hotel with good cuisine and a
chance to spend the night in the 1875 lighthouse.

Meadow Lodge (B), on Trans-Canada Highway; tel. (902) 4612022   Wood Islands
20 rooms, restaurant. Simple and really friendly motel for families with
children.

Quebec

L'Estérel (L), Boul. Fridolin-Simard, Ville d'Estérel; tel. (450) 2282571, fax   L'Estérel
(450) 2284977
130 rooms, restaurant, golf, riding, water sports, sailing, winter sports
(esp. cross country). Comfortable hotel complex for sporting holiday
guests.

Château Bromont (M), 90 Rue Stanstead; tel. (450) 5343433, fax (450)   Estrie
5340514   Bromont
150 rooms, restaurant, swimming pools, spa with sauna and health
treatments. Comfortable accommodation in charming scenery where
guests can relax happily in summer and winter.

Baie Bleue (M/B), 482 Boulevard Perron; tel. (418) 3643355, fax (418)   Gaspé
3646165   Carleton
100 rooms, restaurant, swimming pool, tennis. Well-appointed motel
with friendly service and good cooking, that makes a good base for
exploring the peninsula.

La Normandie (M); tel. (418) 7822112, fax (418) 7822337   Percé
44 rooms, restaurant (excellent fish cuisine). Well-run tourist hotel.

Château Cartier (M), 1170 Aylmer Road; tel. (819) 7771088, fax (819)   Gatineau
7777161   Aylmer
133 rooms and suites, restaurant, bar, dancing, swimming pool, fitness
centre with sauna, golf, tennis. This hotel in the scenic Gatineau hill
country is popular with tourists and business travellers alike.

La Goéliche, 22 Av. du Quai; tel. (418) 8282248, fax (418)8282745   Île d'Orléans
20 rooms, restaurant, swimming pool. The restaurant of this hotel, beau-   Pétronille
tifully located on the western tip of the island in the St Lawrence
Seaway, is a popular destination for days out.

Auberge Mont-Gabriel (M), Mont Rolland; tel. (450) 2293547, fax (450)   Laurentides
2297034   Mont-Gabriel
125 rooms, restaurant, dancing, swimming pools, sauna, gym, golf, tennis.
Highly traditional holiday inn consisting of several timbered buildings in
the mountains north of Montreal.

Auberge du Lac des Sables (M), 230 St-Venant; tel. (819) 3263994, fax   Ste-Agathe
(819) 3269159
20 rooms. Well-run hotel in delightful mountain scenery.

Riôtel Mature (M/B), 250 Av. du Phare Est; tel. (418) 5662651, fax (418)   Matane
5627365
70 rooms, restaurant, bar, swimming pool, sauna, tennis (on request).
Right by the sea, family hotel.

Hotels and Motels

Montebello

★Le Château Montebello (L); tel. (819) 4236341, fax (819) 4235283
210 rooms, 2 restaurants, 2 bars, indoor pool, fitness centre with sauna, boutiques, golf course, winter sports facilities. This extremely luxurious holiday complex in the scenic Outaouais is barely two hours by car from both Ottawa and Montreal. In a lovely setting on the Ottawa River it also has one of the finest golf courses in eastern Canada. The Château's many VIP guests have included famous leaders and politicians, plus Hollywood Greats such as Cary Grant and Grace Kelly.

Montréal

Auberge de la Fontaine (M), 1301 Rue Rachel Est; tel. (514) 5970166, fax (514) 5970496
20 rooms and suites. Just outside the bustling city centre beside Parc Lafontaine (Plateau Mont-Royal), this pretty hotel is a delightful alternative to the inner-city hotels, especially in summer.

★Le Marriott Château Champlain (L), 1 Place du Canada; tel. (514) 8789000, fax (514) 8786761
616 rooms and suites, 4 restaurants, café, ballroom, conference and banqueting rooms, fitness centre with pool and sauna. This central luxury hotel, with its striking tall arched panoramic windows, though used mostly by business travellers, also makes an excellent base for exploring the city; its restaurants and café are well worth a visit.

Holiday Inn Montréal-Midtown (M), 420 Rue Sherbrooke Ouest, tel. (514) 8426111, fax (514) 8429381
480 rooms, restaurant, swimming pool, fitness centre with sauna and whirlpool. A modern, well-appointed large hotel, it offers relatively cheap packages for families with children all year round.

Hôtel de la Montagne (M), 1430 Rue de la Montagne; tel. (514) 2885656, fax (514) 2889658
140 rooms, gourmet restaurant, lounge, disco, swimming pool. This wonderfully appointed hotel suits tourists and business travellers alike.

★Inter-Continental (L), 360 Rue St-Antoine Ouest, tel. (514) 9879900, fax (514) 8478730
330 rooms and 20 suites, several restaurants, piano bar, business centre, swimming pool, sauna, steam bath, gym. The "Inter-Cont" in the old town near Notre-Dame Basilica is one of Montréal's leading hotels and is mainly used by business people and wealthy socialites.

Le Jardin d'Antoine (B/M), 2024 Rue St-Dénis; tel. (514) 8434506, fax (514) 2811491
25 rooms and suites, courtyard. Friendly small hotel with tastefully furnished rooms.

★The Queen Elizabeth (L), 900 Boul. René Lévesque Ouest; tel. (514) 8613511, fax (514) 9542256
1020 rooms, 4 restaurants, 3 bars, fitness centre with sauna. Right next to Montréal's large train stations the CP hotel, which has recently been renovated, draws most of its guests from the business community. It has direct access to Underground City and its miles of underground shopping arcades.

★Ritz-Carlton (L), 1228 Rue Sherbrooke Ouest; tel. (514) 8424212, fax (514) 8423383
180 rooms and 44 suites, restaurant, café, bar, dancing, garden café. Montréal's Ritz-Carlton is a legend, a wonderfully chic city centre hotel that attracts all the best people.

★Hotel Omni (L), 1050 Rue Sherbrooke Ouest; tel. (514) 2841110
300 rooms, restaurant, piano lounge, fitness centre, swimming pool. A

very luxurious hotel in a great location which attracts both business travellers and ordinary tourists.

Château Beauvallon (B), 616 Montée Ryan; tel./fax (819) 4257275
12 rooms, restaurant. Pleasantly buccolic family hotel at Mont-Tremblant; very quiet.

★Club Tremblant (L), on Lac Tremblant; tel. (819) 4252734, fax (819) 4259960
103 suites, convention centre, fitness centre with swimming pool and sauna, golf course, marina, beach, stables, fishing waters, various sports facilities. Club Tremblant, in the lovely mountain scenery of the Laurentides, barely two hours by car north of Montreal, extends along Lac Tremblant at the foot of ski slopes; skiing in winter and all kinds of other outdoor pursuits in summer.

★★Château Frontenac (L), 1 Rue des Carrières; tel. (418) 6923861, fax
(418) 6921751
610 rooms and suites, 3 restaurants, café, bar, various banqueting rooms, boutiques. This impressive Quebec landmark , perched high above the St Lawrence River, was built in 1893 and expensively renovated on its centenary; designed and furnished like a French château, it offers every conceivable luxury. One of the world's leading hotels, this is where Winston Churchill, Franklin D. Roosevelt, and Canadian Premier MacKenzie-King planned the Normandy landings by the Allies during the Second World War.

Fleur-de-Lys (M), 115 Rue Ste-Anne; tel. (418) 6940106, fax (418) 6921959
33 rooms. Well appointed motel, very quiet but also very central.

★Hilton, 1100 Boulevard René-Lévesque Est; tel. (418) 6472411, fax (418) 6476488
565 rooms and suites, restaurant, swimming pool, health club with sauna and massage. Grand hotel in the government district with direct access to the underground shopping complex and the convention centre.

Loews Le Concorde (M), 1225 Place Montcalm; tel. (418) 6472222
400 rooms and suites, revolving restaurant, café, business centre, swimming pool, fitness club with sauna. Extremely well located and also well appointed, the hotel is famous for its rooftop revolving restaurant, but there are also wonderful views from many of the other rooms.

Radisson Gouverneurs (L/M), 690 Boul. René Lévesque Est; tel. (418) 6471717, fax (418) 6472146
377 rooms and suites, swimming pool, sauna and gym. The Radisson, like the Hilton (see above), forms part of the office and shopping complex in the government district. It mainly takes business travellers but is also suitable for tourists.

Relais Charles-Alexander (B), 91 Grande-Allée Est; tel. (418) 5231220, fax (418) 5239556
19 rooms. A romantic hideaway with prettily furnished rooms.

St-Antoine (L), 10 Rue St-Antoine; tel. (418) 6922211, fax (418) 6921177.
30 rooms and suites.
Located down by the St Lawrence River the Auberge St-Antoine is still something of a find. Housed in a charmingly restored series of historic buildings, it is rather expensive, but comfortable and friendly.

Vieux Québec (M), 1190 Rue St-Jean; tel. (418) 6921850, fax (418) 6925637

41 rooms, good restaurant.
Friendly, clean hotel within the walled city.

Beaupré   La Camarine (M), 10947 Boul. Ste-Anne; tel. (418) 8275703, fax (418) 8275430
30 rooms, good restaurant.

Saskatchewan

Regina   Chelton Suites, 1907 11th Avenue; tel. (306) 5694600, fax (306) 5693531
55 suites, restaurant, lounge. Pleasant inner city hotel with extremely friendly service.

Delta Regina (M), 1919 Saskatchewan Drive; tel. (306) 5255255, fax (306) 7817188
250 rooms and suites, 2 restaurants, lounge, swimming pool. Conventional downtown hotel near the Saskatchewan Trade & Convention Centre which primarily caters for business travellers but, with its fun-pool and giant waterslides, is very popular with families at weekends.

Regina Inn (M), 1975 Broad Street; tel. (306) 5256767, fax (306) 5253680
230 rooms, 2 restaurants, lounge, night club, health club with fitness room and solarium. Modern hotel where families can get really good cheap rates at weekends.

The Sands (M), 1818 Victoria Avenue; tel. (306) 5691666, fax (306) 5253550
250 rooms, restaurant,lounge, coffee plaza, swimming pool, solarium, kindergarten. Well-appointed, with the very latest furnishings, The Sands particularly welcomes families with children.

Saskatchewan Radisson Plaza (L/M), 2125 Victoria Avenue; tel. (306) 5227691, fax (306) 5228988
200 rooms and suites, restaurant, fitness centre with sauna. The top place in town, an old-style elegant grand hotel, built in 1927 on Georgian lines and subsequently much modernised at great expense.

Saskatoon   Delta Bessborough (M/L), 601 Spadina Crescent East; tel. (306) 2445521, fax (306) 6532458
220 rooms and suites, restaurant, coffee shop, 2 swimming pools, fitness centre with sauna. Built in the Thirties to look like a French château, this grand hotel has a fine view of the Saskatchewan River and offers relatively cheap deals for families at weekends; the two pools make this a particular favourite.

Sheraton Cavalier (M), 612 Spadina Crescent East; tel. (306) 6526770
250 rooms and suites, restaurant, business centre, 2 swimming pools. Popular with tourists and business travellers alike, this Sheraton also attracts crowds of children and their families at weekends when the main attraction is a giant 800ft waterslide.

Radisson Hotel Saskatoon (M/L), 405 20th Street; tel. (306) 6653322, fax (306) 6655531
290 rooms, restaurant, pool. This luxuriously appointed hotel, also on the Saskatchewan River, has a popular leisure pool with a large adjoining sauna complex.

Yukon Territory

Dawson City   Downtown Hotel (M), 2nd & Queen Sts.; tel. (867) 9935346, fax (867) 9935076

60 rooms, restaurant, saloon. The oldest hotel in Dawson City – though recently renovated and modernised – this still has a feel of the frontier days about it.

Bunkhouse (B), Front & Princess Sts.; tel. (867) 9936164, fax (867) 9936051
30 rooms. Here visitors can imagine they are in the old Wild West although the Bunkhouse is fairly new. The rooms are clean and comfortable and quite inexpensive.

Edgewater Hotel (M), 101 Main Street; tel. (867) 6672572, fax (867) 6683014   Whitehorse
30 rooms, restaurant, lobby. Friendly and charming hotel on the Yukon River.

Westmark Whitehorse (M), 201 Wood Street; tel. (867) 6684700, fax (867) 6682789
180 rooms, restaurant, coffee shop, cocktail lounge, shopping arcade, conference rooms, dance hall. This is one of the main meeting places for the business world on the move in the Far North.

Yukon Inn (M), 4220 4th Avenue; tel. (867) 6672527, fax (867) 6687643
90 rooms, restaurant, bar, lobby. A hotel worth recommending, which is also very popular with the locals, and which has a special Inuit meeting room.

Hunting

Hunting is governed by federal, provincial and territorial laws. Non-residents must obtain hunting licences from each province or territory in which they plan to hunt. When hunting migratory game-birds a federal migratory game-bird hunting permit is also required. This is available from most Canadian post offices.   Hunting licence

Visitors may bring a hunting rifle or shotgun and up to 200 rounds of ammunition into Canada, but they must be 16 years of age or older (19 in British Columbia) and the firearm must be for sporting or competition use. In many of Canada's provincial parks and reserves and adjacent areas, the entry of any type of weapon is forbidden. Regulations available from each province provide instructions in this regard.   Hunting firearms

As a rule, anyone wanting to go big-game or trophy hunting would be well advised to obtain the services of an outfitter (see Outfitters), who will fit them out with planes, horses, guides, etc. and also set up base camps, all of which can be costly.   Big-game and trophy hunting

In most provinces and territories export permits are required to take out unprocessed game, i.e. any part of an animal, such as hunting trophies, hides and skins, and both large and small game, that has not been properly processed. Detailed information about this can be obtained from Canadian hunting tour operators or from the relevant provincial or territorial authorities.   Taking out game

Information about hunting and fishing licences can be obtained from the following: Information

Travel Alberta, 10155 102nd Street, Edmonton, Alberta T5J 4L6   Alberta

Department of Fisheries and Oceans, 555 W. Hastings Street, Vancouver, B.C. V6B 5G3; tel. (604) 0384 (saltwater licences)   British Columbia
    Fish and Wildlife Information, Ministry of the Environment, Parliament Buildings, Victoria, British Columbia V8V 1XA

Manitoba	Travel Manitoba, Department 7020, 155 Carlton Street, 7th Floor, Winnipeg, Manitoba R3C 3H8
National parks	Canadian Heritage-Parks Canada, Hull, Québec K1A 0MS
New Brunswick	Department of Natural Resources and Energy, PO Box 6000, Fredericton, New Brunswick E3B 5H1; tel. (506) 4532440 Information about the provincial parks: Tourism New Brunswick, PO Box 12345, Woodstock, New Brunswick E0J 2B0
Newfoundland and Labrador	Tourist Services, Department of Development and Tourism, PO Box 8730, St John's, Newfoundland A1B 4K2
Northwest Territories	Arctic Tourism, PO Box 400, Yellowknife, Northwest Territories X1A 2N5
Nova Scotia	Nova Scotia Tourism, PO Box 519, Halifax, Nova Scotia B3J 2R5
Ontario	Ministry of Natural Resources, Wildlife Branch, Queen's Park, Toronto, Ontario M7A 1W3
Prince Edward Island	Tourism Prince Edward Island, PO Box 940, Charlottetown, Prince Edward Island C1A 7M5
Québec	Ministère de l'Environnemet et de la Faune Complexe "G", 675 Boulevard René-Lévesque Est Québec (Québec) G1R 5V7; tel. (418) 5213830
Saskatchewan	Tourism Saskatchewan, 500–1900 Albert Street, Regina, Saskatchewan S4P 4L9
Yukon	Tourism Yukon, PO Box 2703, Whitehorse, Yukon Y1A 2C6

Indians and Inuit

Canada's native peoples, the Inuit (the term Eskimo is considered an insult, since it means "eater of raw flesh") and the Amerindians, actually cover more of the country's vast lands, despite there being less than a million of them, than the European Canadians, who tend to be mostly in southern Canada. Anyone wanting more detailed information about such peoples as the Inuit, the Kwakiutl, the Dene Nation, the Blackfoot, and the Micmac should contact: Indian and Northern Development, Government of Canada, Ottawa, Ontario, Canada K1A 0H4.

Information

Tourist offices in the UK

Tourism Programme, Canadian High Commission, Canada House, Trafalgar Square, London SW1Y SBJ; tel. (071) 6299492
Visit Canada Centre, 62-65 Trafalgar Square, London WC2N 5DT; tel. (0891) 715000, fax (0171) 3891149
Ontario Tourism, UK Office, 21 Knightsbridge, London SW1X 7LY; tel. (0171) 2451222
Québec Tourism, Québec House, 59 Pall Mall, London SW1Y 5JH; tel. (0171) 9308314, fax (0171) 9307938

Provincial tourist offices in Canada

Travel Alberta, 10155 102nd Street, Edmonton, AB, T5J 4L6;
tel. (780) 4274321, fax (780) 4270867
Internet: www.discoveralberta.com

Alberta

Tourism British Columbia, Parliament Buildings, Victoria, BC, V8V 1XA;
tel. (604) 6602861, fax (604) 8015710
Internet: www.travel.bc.ca

British Columbia

Travel Manitoba, 155 Carlton Street, Winnipeg, MB, R3C3H8;
tel. (204) 9453777, fax (204) 9452302
Internet: www.travelmanitoba.com

Manitoba

New Brunswick Tourism, Box 12345, Woodstock, NB, EOJ 2B0;
tel. (506) 7533876, fax (506) 7892044
Internet: www.gov.nb.ca/tourism

New Brunswick

Tourism Newfoundland & Labrador, PO Box 8730, St. John's, NF, AIB 4K2;
tel. (709) 7292830, fax (709) 7290057
Internet: http://public.gov.nf.ca/tourism

Newfoundland

Northwest Territories Arctic Tourism,
PO Box 610, Suite 400, Yellowknife, NWT, X1A 2N5;
tel. (867) 8735007, fax (867) 8734059
Internet: www.nwttravel.nt.ca

Northwest Territories

Nova Scotia Department of Tourism & Culture,
PO Box 519, Halifax, NS, B3J 2R5;
tel. (902) 4244709, fax (902) 4242668
Internet: www.explore.gov.ns.ca/virtualns

Nova Scotia

Nunavut Tourism, PO Box 1450, Iqaluit, NU, X0A 0H0;
tel. (867) 9796551, fax (867) 9791261
Internet: www.nunatour.nt.ca

Nunavut

Ontario Travel, Queen's Park, Toronto, ON, M7A 2E5;
fax (416) 3147563
Internet: www.travelinx.com

Ontario

Tourism Prince Edward Island, PO Box 940, Charlottetown, PEI, C1A 7M5;
tel. (902) 6292400, fax (902) 6292428
Internet: www.peiplay.com

Prince Edward Island

Tourisme Québec, C.P. 979, Montréal, P, H3C 2W3;
tel. (514) 8732015, fax (514) 8643838
Internet: www.gouv.qc.ca/tourisme

Québec

Tourism Saskatchewan, 500–1900 Albert Street, Regina, SK, S4P 4L9;
tel. (306) 7872300, fax (306) 7875744
Internet: www.sasktourism.com

Saskatchewan

Tourism Yukon, PO Box 2703, Whitehorse, Yukon, Canada Y1A 2C6;
tel. (867) 6675340, fax (867) 6673546
Internet: www.touryukon.com

Yukon

National Parks

Canadian Heritage – Parks Canada,
25 Eddy Street, Hull, PQ, K1A 0MS;
tel. (819) 9970055
Internet www.parkscanada.pch.gc.ca

Main office

Insurance

Atlantic Region	Parks Canada, 1869 Upper Water Street, Halifax, NS, B3J 1S9; tel. (902) 4263436, fax (902) 4266881
Québec Region	Parks Canada, 3 Passage du Chien d'Or, Haute-Ville, Ville de Québec, PQ, G1R 4V7; tel. (418) 6484177, fax (418) 6496140
Ontario Region	Parks Canada, 111 Water Street E., Cornwall, ON, K6H 6S3; tel. (613) 9385879, fax (613) 9385729.
Prairie Region	Parks Canada, 220 4th Av. SE., Calgary, AB, T2G 4X3; tel. (403) 2924401, fax (403) 2926004
British Columbia	Parks Canada, 300 W. Georgia Street, Vancouver, BC, V6B 6C6; tel. (604) 6660176, fax (604) 6496140
Yukon	Parks Canada, Suite 200, 300 Main Street, Whitehorse, YT, Y1A 2B5; tel. (867) 6673910, fax (867) 3936701

Insurance

Visitors are strongly advised to ensure that they have adequate holiday insurance, including loss or damage to luggage, loss of currency and jewellery.

It is essential for visitors to take out some form of short-term health insurance providing complete cover, since medical consultations and hospital treatment can be very expensive.

See also Medical Attention.

Language

Under the 1969 Official Language Act Canada has two official languages, English and French. More than 60 per cent of the population have English as their mother tongue, while French is the language of about 25 per cent, most of whom (about 85 per cent) live in Québec.

Lodges

Located far from civilisation and often only reached by light aircraft, lodges (hunting boxes, log cabins, converted logging camps) are ideal bases for touring in the remote areas. They can usually provide guides and equipment as well.

Lodges are very much a Canadian speciality, mostly with first-rate facilities. Further information can be obtained from travel agents and tourist offices.

Measurements

Canada has recently adopted the metric system of weights and measures, exchanging miles, feet and inches for kilometres, metres and centimetres, Fahrenheit for Celsius, gallons for litres, pounds for kilos, etc. However, clothing sizes and food amounts may still be given in either the metric or the British/American system.

Medical Services

Canada has good medical services, both as regards its hospitals and its dental and medical practitioners.

Doctors, dentists, hospitals

For the European visitor the problem is one of cost, rather than quality of care. A stay in hospital will usually be very expensive, particularly since some provinces impose a surcharge on care for non-residents. It is therefore strongly recommended that visitors obtain sufficient medical insurance before leaving for Canada.

Visitors taking prescribed medication should bring a copy of the prescription in case it needs to be renewed by a doctor in Canada.

Medicines

Visitors to Canada should find out before leaving home how much cover they have from their own medical and accident insurance when in the country. It will usually pay to take out special medical insurance for the duration of the stay in Canada. "Blue Cross" can provide insurance while in Canada; tel. (416) 6261447.

Medical insurance, accident insurance

It is also wise to get travel accident insurance for the time in Canada, and this can be done, if necessary, through automatic dispensers in airports and bus and train stations.

Opening Hours

In most places stores are open Mon.–Sat. 9.30am–6pm. Town centre shops stay open until 9pm one or two evenings in the week; many open on Sundays as well.

Shops

For cinemas, concert halls, theatres, etc. enquiries can be made by telephone.

Places of entertainment

Normal banking hours in Canada are Mon.–Fri. 10am–4pm; some branches stay open later, especially in the larger cities.

Banks

See entry

Post offices

Outfitters

"Outfitters" and bush-pilots act as the go-betweens twixt civilisation and the untamed wilderness and make adventure holidays possible. They deal in goods and services, supply sailing dinghies, canoes, horses, diving equipment, food, fuel, tools and whatever else may be required for a "civilised" adventure holiday.

The bush-pilot works closely with, if not, as is often the case, in personal partnership, with the outfitter, making it possible with their (occasionally ancient) hydroplanes and helicopters to penetrate into the deepest, untouched wilderness. The passenger sits next to or behind the pilot and sees clearly what is happening outside.

Quite a few outfitters and bush-pilots operate in and out of fly-in camps and lodges – clusters of tents or cabins, often surprisingly well-appointed, and used by holiday hunters, anglers and comfort-loving adventurers as bases for their expeditions.

Fly-in camps, lodges

Parks, National and Provincial

Canada currently has more than 40 National Parks and numerous Provincial Parks. These are mostly nature reserves or particularly scenic areas, where the ecosystem is left in its natural state.

Fees are charged in many national parks to use the roads, trails, campsites, etc., while there are also such commercial recreational facilities, as hotels, swimming pools, golf courses, horseback-riding in some places (see also Information, National Parks).

These parks have reception centres for informing the visitor, usually through audio-visual presentations, of that particular park's special features, besides providing literature such as maps and trails. There are also trained guides who can impart specialist information for those with particular interests.

The best views and observation points can be reached by pathways, and there are some forms of shelter that can be used overnight, but this needs approval from the park authorities.

Many of Canada's National and Provincial Parks are open on a seasonal basis. For information on any given park contact the regional offices of Parks Canada for the National Parks and Historic Sites (for addresses, see page 603) or the provincial tourist offices for the Provincial Parks (for addresses, see pages 602–3).

A list of the major parks follows:

The principal National Parks

Aulavik National Park (Banks Island), Northwest Territories
Auyuittuq National Park (Baffin Island), Nunavut
Banff National Park (Rockies), Alberta
Bruce Peninsula National Park, Ontario
Cape Breton Highlands National Park, Nova Scotia
Dinosaur Provincial Park, Alberta
Elk Island National Park, Saskatchewan
Ellesmere National Park, Northwest Territories
Forillon National Park (Gaspé Peninsula), Québec
Fundy National Park, New Brunswick
Georgian Bay Islands National Park, Ontario
Glacier National Park, British Columbia
Grasslands National Park, Saskatchewan
Gros Morne National Park, Newfoundland
Gwaii Haanas National Park (Queen Charlotte Islands), British Columbia
Head-Smashed-In Buffalo Jump Historic Park, Alberta
Jasper National Park (Rockies), Alberta
Kejimkujik National Park, Nova Scotia
Kluane National Park, Yukon
Kootenay National Park (Rockies), British Columbia
Kouchibouguac National Park, New Brunswick
L'Anse aux Meadows National Historic Park, Newfoundland
Mauricie National Park, Québec
Mingan Archipelago National Park, Québec
Mount Revelstoke National Park, British Columbia
Nahanni National Park, Northwest Territories
Northern Yukon National Park, Yukon
Pacific Rim National Park, British Columbia
Point Pelee National Park, Ontario
Prince Albert National Park, Saskatchewan
Prince Edward Island National Park, Prince Edward Island
Pukaskwa National Park, Ontario
Québec National Historic District, Québec
Riding Mountain National Park, Manitoba
St Lawrence Islands National Park, Ontario
Terra Nova National Park, Newfoundland
Waterton Lakes National Park (Rockies), Alberta
Wood Buffalo National Park, Nortwest Territories (and Alberta)
Yoho National Park (Rockies), British Columbia

Post

Post offices

Canadian post offices are generally open Mon.–Fri. 9am–6pm. Some postal outlets are also open on Saturday.

David Walliams

THE
ICE
MONSTER

Illustrated by Tony Ross

HarperCollins *Children's Books*

First published in Great Britain by
HarperCollins *Children's Books* in 2018
Published in this edition in 2020
HarperCollins *Children's Books* is a division of HarperCollins*Publishers* Ltd,
HarperCollins Publishers
1 London Bridge Street
London SE1 9GF

The HarperCollins website address is:
www.harpercollins.co.uk

5

Text copyright © David Walliams 2018
Illustrations copyright © Tony Ross 2018
Cover lettering of author's name copyright © Quentin Blake 2010
All rights reserved.

ISBN 978–0–00–816470–6

David Walliams and Tony Ross assert the moral right to be
identified as the author and illustrator of the work respectively.

A CIP catalogue record for this title is available from the British Library.

Printed and bound in England by CPI Group (UK) Ltd, Croydon, CR0 4YY

MIX
Paper from
responsible sources
FSC™ C007454

This book is produced from independently certified FSC™ paper
to ensure responsible forest management.

For more information visit: www.harpercollins.co.uk/green

For Alfred.
You are always in my heart.
Daddy x

THANK-YOUS
I WOULD LIKE TO THANK:

EXECUTIVIS PUBLISHERARIUS
Ann-Janine Murtagh

ILLUSTRATORUS MAGNIFICUS
Tony Ross

AGENTUS LITERATI
Paul Stevens

BIGGIUS BOSSIUS
Charlie Redmayne

EDITORIUS III
Alice Blacker

MARKETUS ANDUS PR DIRECTORUM
Geraldine Stroud

NATURAL HISTORY MUSEUM

PUBLISHARUM
Rachel Denwood

PUBLISHUS DIRECTORUS
Kate Burns

PUBLISHUS DIRECTORUS
Harriet Wilson

MANAGERUM EDITORIUS
Samantha Stewart

CREATIVUS DIRECTORUS
Val Brathwaite

ARTIUS FARTIUS
Sally Griffin

DESIGNUM
Matthew Kelly

ARTIUS DIRECTORUS
David McDougall

DESIGNUM
Elorine Grant

DESIGNUM
Kate Clarke

AUDIUS BOOKIUS
Tanya Hougham

NATURAL HISTORY MUSEUM

The year is 1899

and we're in Victorian London. Meet the characters
in the story…

Elsie is a homeless orphan, who lives
on the streets of London.

Dotty is the cleaning lady at the Natural History Museum. She is as daft as her brushes.

Private Thomas is Dotty's boyfriend, the shortest soldier who ever served in the British Army. His fellow soldiers call him "Titch". He is now retired, and lives at the Royal Hospital Chelsea, making him a "Chelsea Pensioner".

Mrs Curdle is the nasty old boot who runs WORMLY HALL: Home for Unwanted Children.

Mr Clout is the brute of a security guard at the museum, infamous for his hobnailed boots.

Commissioner Barker is the fearsome head of the London Metropolitan Police, famous for his tiny moustache.

Many years ago, the **Professor** was the top scientist at the museum, until one of his experiments went catastrophically wrong.

Lady Buckshot is an aristocratic big-game hunter. Across Africa she shoots elephants, giraffes and lions and brings their bodies back to the museum to be stuffed and put on display.

The **admiral** is the only sailor to live at the hospital. He was thrown out of the old sailors' home for being drunk and disorderly.

The **colonel** and the **brigadier** are also Chelsea Pensioners.

The one-eyed **sergeant major** is in charge of everyone and everything that comes in and out of the hospital, and don't you forget it.

All the Chelsea Pensioners are overseen by the Royal Hospital's formidable **Matron**.

Queen Victoria is the ruler of
the British Empire. In 1899,
she had been on the throne for
what was the longest reign in
British history, a staggering
sixty-two years.

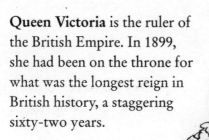

Abdul Karim is always
at the Queen's side. He
is her handsome young
Indian attendant, also
known as "Munshi".

Sir Ray Lankester is the museum's portly director.

The **sandwich-board man** roams the streets, trying to convince everyone that "THE END IS NIGH".

The **captain** is in charge of what was, in 1899, one of the Royal Navy's most modern warships, HMS *Argonaut*.

The Sticky Fingers Gang is a rough and tough band of child robbers, who are infamous for being the greatest thieves in London.

Raj the First has his own confectionery emporium – or sweet trolley.

And last, but certainly not least…

…is the **ICE MONSTER** itself, a woolly mammoth that died ten thousand years ago. The lifeless animal was discovered by Arctic explorers, perfectly preserved in the ice.

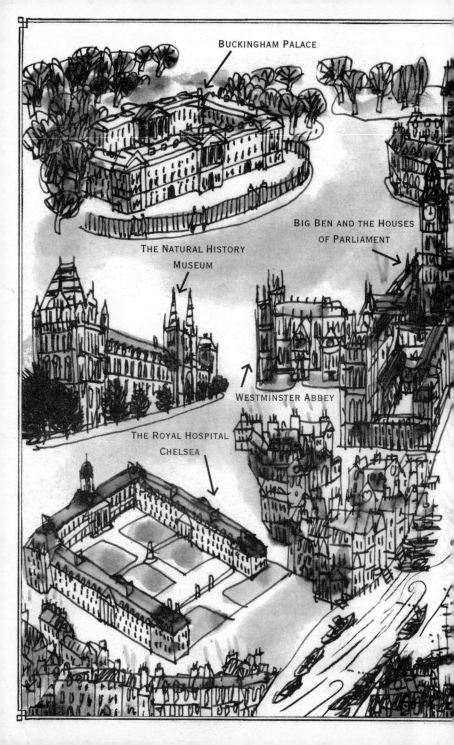

BUCKINGHAM PALACE

BIG BEN AND THE HOUSES OF PARLIAMENT

THE NATURAL HISTORY MUSEUM

WESTMINSTER ABBEY

THE ROYAL HOSPITAL CHELSEA

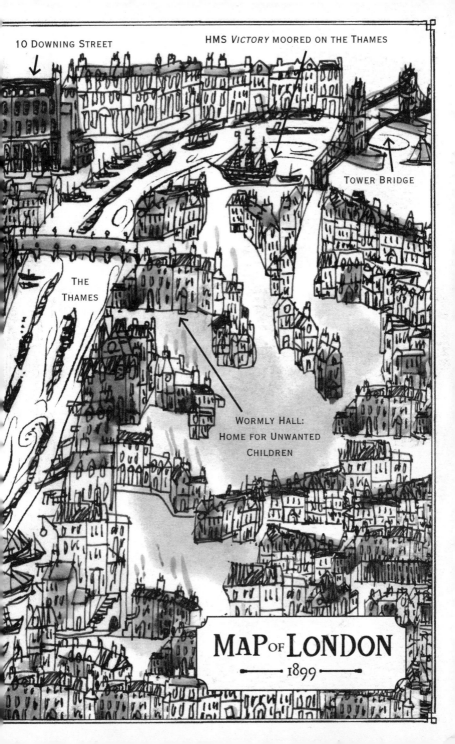

PART I

LONDON

1899

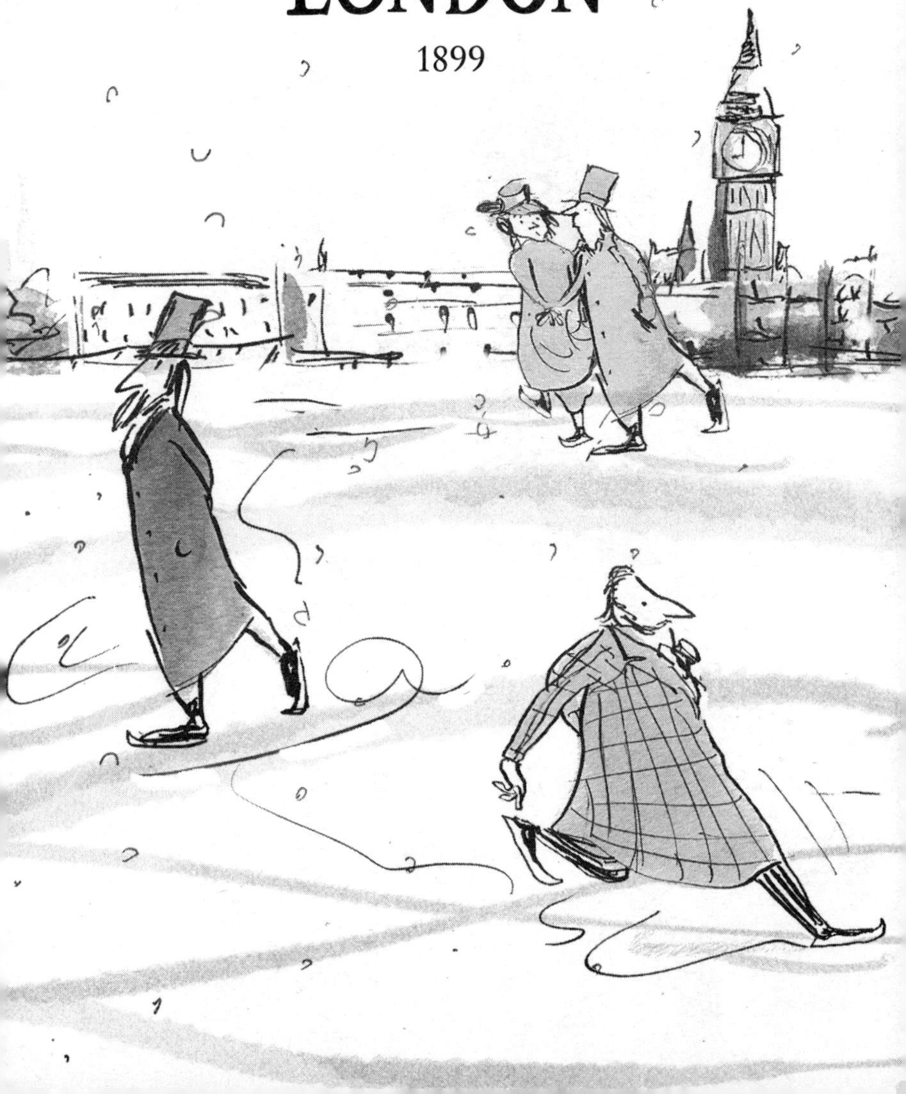

Chapter 1

COCKROACHES
<small>FOR</small> BREAKFAST

O ne bleak winter night, in the back streets of London, a tiny baby was left on the steps of an orphanage. There was no note, no name, no clue as to who this little person was. Just

the potato sack in which she was wrapped, as snow fell around her.

In Victorian times, it was not uncommon for newborn babies to be abandoned outside orphanages, hospitals or even the homes of upper-class folk. Their poor, desperate mothers hoped their children would be taken in and given a better life than their birth families could provide.

However, it was hard to imagine a **worse** start in life for this baby than at ᗯOᖇᗰᒪY ᕼᗩᒪᒪ: Home for Unwanted Children.

Twenty-six orphans lived there, all crammed into a room that should have slept eight at the absolute most. The children were locked up, starved and beaten. On top of that, they were forced to work day and night. They had to assemble gentlemen's pocket watches from tiny pieces until they went blind.

All the children were painfully thin, with filthy rags for clothes. The orphans' faces were black with soot, so all you could see in the gloom were their hopeful little eyes.

When a new baby arrived at the orphanage, all the older children would come up with a name for them. They liked to work their way through the alphabet so their names would be as different as possible. The night the baby in the potato sack was left on the steps, they had reached E. If she had been found the day before, she might have been called "Doris". A day later, she could have been a "Frank". Instead, she was named **"Elsie"**.

This prison of an orphanage was run by an evil old boot named Mrs Curdle. Her face was usually fixed in a permanent grimace, and she was covered from head to toe in warts. She had so many warts even her warts had warts. The only thing that made her smile was the sound of children sobbing.

Mrs Curdle would scoff all the food donated for the orphans, so the children in her care had to eat cockroaches for breakfast, lunch and dinner.

"Creepy-crawlies are good for you!" she would chuckle.

If any of the orphans spoke after "candles out",

she would stuff one of her pus-sodden old stockings in their mouth. They would have to keep it there for a week.

"That'll keep you quiet, windy wallet!"

When the children were sleeping on the cold stone floor, she would put wiggly worms down the backs of their shirts so they would wake up screaming.

"ARGH!"
"HO! HO! HO! HORNSWOGGLER!"

Mrs Curdle would sneeze over the orphans…

"HACHOOOOO!"

…and blow her nose on their hair.

"HOOMPH! GONGOOZLER!"

A weekly "bath" involved her dunking the orphans one by one into a barrel full of maggots. "The maggots will nibble off the dirt, you muck snipes!" Mrs Curdle would snigger.

To dry off afterwards, she would peg the children to the washing line by their ears.

TWANG!

Once, when Elsie was found with a pet rat in her pocket that she had befriended, Mrs Curdle used it as a ball in a game of cricket.

THUD!
"EEEEEK!"
WHIZZ!

"HOWZAT!"

If she felt one of the orphans had given her a funny look, Mrs Curdle would poke them in the eye with her dirty, stubby finger.

"OUCH!"

"TAKE THAT, GIBFACE!"

As a special treat at Christmas, the orphans would line up for their present, a whack on the bottom with The Bumper Book of Carols.

BASH!

"Merry Christmas, child!" Mrs Curdle would exclaim with glee on each strike.

———◆———

Elsie endured ten long, hard years at WORMLY HALL. The only thing that kept her going was the dream that one day her ma would magically appear and whisk her away. But she never did. As the girl grew up, she would invent more and more incredible stories about her.

Perhaps her ma was a jungle explorer?

Or an acrobat with a travelling circus?

Even better, a lady pirate off having adventures on the high seas?

Every night, Elsie would make up bedtime stories for her fellow orphans. Over time, the girl became a magnificent storyteller. She had all the other children in the palm of her grubby little hand.

"Then Ma found herself in a dark, dark place. It was the belly of a huge blue whale…"

"Ma escaped from the tribe of cannibals, which wasn't easy as they had already gobbled up her left leg…"

"Boom! Ma had thrown the bomb into the Thames just in time, so no one was killed. It was all in a day's work for a secret agent. The end."

When that night's story finished, the other orphans would cry out…

"Another!"

"We don't want to go to sleep yet!"

"PLEASE, ELSIE, JUST ONE MORE!"

One night, the children cheered so much at Elsie's story that they woke up Mrs Curdle.

"NO! MORE! STORIES! YOU! NASTY! LITTLE! BEAST!"

raged the woman, beating Elsie with a broomstick on every word. The pus-sodden stocking she stuffed in the girl's mouth only half muffled her screams.

"ARGH! ARGH! ARGH!"

The beating was so severe that Elsie wasn't sure she was going to survive. Her little body was black and blue with bruises, and the girl knew she had to escape or *die*.

Chapter 2

MONKEY FEET

Elsie loved all the rats and pigeons that would find their way inside **WORMLY HALL**. If she had any food, she would share it with them, and tend to any broken wings and legs. In return, they would snuggle up to her, which made her feel less lonely. In her heart, Elsie felt a deep connection to these animals that Mrs Curdle called "vermin". To her, they were little creatures all alone in the world just like her.

Elsie had noticed how the rats got into the orphanage by scuttling along a leaky pipe that came down from the ceiling.

One thing that set Elsie apart from her fellow orphans was her feet. Elsie didn't have ordinary feet. She had monkey feet.

The advantage of having long, thick toes that could grip like fingers was that it made climbing easy-peasy. So one night, when everyone else was asleep, Elsie scaled the pipe to see where the rats scrambled in. Just as she had thought, there was a small rat-sized hole at the top of the wall.

After that, every night after candles out, Elsie scaled the pipe, using her monkey feet. Once at the top, she would scrape away at the brickwork with her fingernails. Night after night she scraped and scraped, making the hole bigger and bigger.

SCRATCH! SCRATCH! SCRATCH!

Eventually, the hole was just large enough for Elsie to squeeze her tiny, underfed body through it. However, she couldn't leave **WORMLY HALL** without saying goodbye to her twenty-five friends.

"Wake up!" she called softly. Little eyes began to appear out of the dark. "I'm going to run away tonight. Who's coming with me?"

S I L E N C E .

"I said, 'Who's coming with me?'"

There were murmurs of, *"I'm too scared,"* and *"Curdle'll kill us,"* and, *"They'll catch us and beat us to death."*

The littlest little'un of the lot was named Nancy. She looked up to Elsie like she was a big sister. Nancy whispered, "Where are you going?"

"I don't know," replied the girl. "Anywhere but here."

"Please don't forget about us."

"Never!"

"Promise?"

"I promise," said Elsie. "I'll see you all again one day – I know it."

"I'm going to miss your stories," said another orphan, Felix.

"Me too," added Percival.

"Next time I see you I'll tell you the greatest story of all."

"Good luck, Elsie," said Nancy.

"You'll always be in 'ere," replied Elsie, patting her chest.

The girl gave one last shimmy up the pipe with her monkey feet. She squeezed herself through the hole in the wall, and with one final wiggle she was gone.

Chapter 3

PONG

Elsie ran and ran and ran, as fast as she possibly could. She didn't dare look back. She was free but alone, and now she had to fend for herself on the streets of London, even though she'd never been outside the orphanage before. The big city was a scary place, especially for a little girl. DANGER lurked in every corner.

Soon enough, though, Elsie taught herself how to steal food from the market stalls. As for a bed, she found an old tin bath to sleep in, and used old newspapers as sheets. In her mind, Elsie pretended that it was a grand four-poster bed fit for a queen.

With no home or family, Elsie was what was known as an "urchin". Victorian London was teeming with them.

ELSIE THE URCHIN

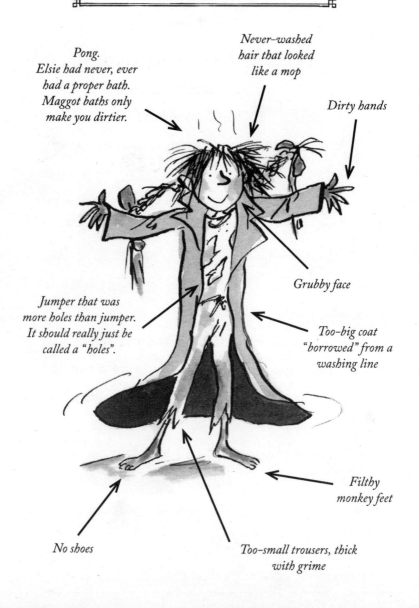

Pong.
Elsie had never, ever had a proper bath. Maggot baths only make you dirtier.

Never-washed hair that looked like a mop

Dirty hands

Grubby face

Jumper that was more holes than jumper. It should really just be called a "holes".

Too-big coat "borrowed" from a washing line

Filthy monkey feet

No shoes

Too-small trousers, thick with grime

Elsie didn't look much like a **hero.**

However, as you will soon discover,

heroes come in all

ꝒHaPeꝒ

and SiƶeS.

EXPERT THIEF

"READ ALL ABOUT IT! ICE MONSTER FOUND IN ARCTIC!"

Living on the streets of London had its advantages. You slept under the stars. You ate all the fresh fruit and vegetables you could swipe. Best of all, you were the first to know about everything. News spread fast, and this was BIG news.

Having never been to school, Elsie couldn't read or write. However, the newspaper sellers would holler the headlines to passers-by.

Could this be true?

A real-life monster?

Ten thousand years old too?

Elsie was old enough to know that monsters weren't real, and young enough to believe that they might just be.

The girl had just swiped an apple off a market stall for her breakfast. Munching contentedly, she wove her way through the march of top-hatted gentlemen

heading for work, until she reached the newspaper
stand.

"Get lost, you little thief!" shouted the
newspaper seller. He whacked the girl on the back
of her head with a rolled-up copy of *The Times*.

THWACK!

You got whacked by grown-ups every day if you were an urchin. You were the lowest of the low. At least it made a welcome change from being battered with a broomstick at WORMLY HALL.

"I only want to look!" pleaded Elsie.

"These papers is not for looking at. They is for buying. Now scram! Before I give you a kick where the sun don't shine!"

Not being a fan of a boot up the bottom, Elsie smiled at the man and ambled off down the street. She turned into an alleyway, then reached into the back of her grubby trousers and pulled out a copy of *The Times*. The girl had become an expert thief.

There were **big, bold black** letters on the front page. Elsie knew these spelled out words, but it all looked like a jumble to her. The picture underneath did speak to her, though. It was of a peculiar creature that looked like an elephant.

Once, she'd poked her head through the flap in a circus tent to get a free show, and seen an elephant performing tricks. However, *this* elephant was covered in thick hair, and its tusks were long and curved. It was encased in a huge block of ice, and a number of Arctic explorers were standing around it, looking proud. Despite the creature's bizarre appearance, Elsie found it hard to think of the poor thing as a monster. Monsters you were scared of. This animal you wanted to **hug.**

It looked a great deal smaller than the elephant she'd seen at the circus. Perhaps it was a baby. Despite having been dead for thousands of years, it still looked lost and alone.

"An orphan,"

whispered Elsie to herself.

"Just like me."

Chapter 5

UNIVERSE OF WONDER

As an urchin, Elsie was always on the outside looking in. Every day, she would see a whole other London whirling around her.

Horse-drawn carriages speeding down the street,

children in uniform marching off to school,

lords and ladies stepping over her as they left the Royal Opera House.

Elsie's brain was forever buzzing with questions.

Where was everyone going to at such a pace?

What did those scrumptious-looking cakes in the bakery window actually taste like?

And what was inside all those magnificent buildings?

One day, the girl decided to step out of her world and into **the other.**

Elsie was standing in front of the most magnificent building of all, the **NATURAL HISTORY MUSEUM**.

When she tried to walk in, she was immediately thrown out by the hobnail-booted brute of a security guard, Mr Clout.

"I don't want no trouble from **filthy beggars** like you," he shouted as he hurled her down the steps.

Elsie was not one to give up that easily, so she sneaked in behind a gaggle of top-hatted gentlemen.

At once, the girl marvelled at this
UNIVERSE OF WONDER.

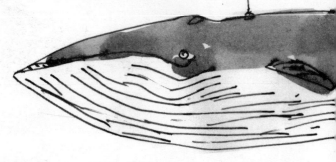

The museum was a treasure trove of life-sized models of whales…

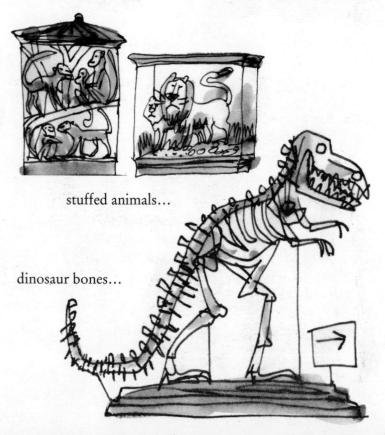

stuffed animals…

dinosaur bones…

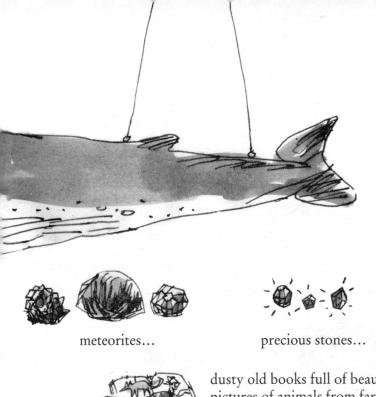

meteorites...

precious stones...

dusty old books full of beautiful pictures of animals from far-off lands...

wood carvings of prehistoric men...

and floor-to-ceiling paintings of creatures that had long since become extinct.

Soon she was sneaking into the museum every single day. Elsie couldn't read, but she earwigged in on the guides and soon became something of an expert. So, when she saw a picture of the **"ICE MONSTER"** on the front page of the newspaper, she knew instantly that it was, in fact, a woolly mammoth. Elsie had learned that these creatures had lived during the ICE AGE, when sabre-toothed tigers, GIANT bears,

sloths

and beavers stalked the Earth,

and birds like the *Teratornis,* a bird bigger than a person, darkened the skies.

Elsie was desperate to follow the story of the **ICE MONSTER**. So every morning she swiped another newspaper to search for news of the creature. Weeks passed, and then one day she spotted a jumble of letters she recognised on the front page of a newspaper.

They looked exactly like the ones she'd seen on the side of her favourite building.

Elsie knew she **had** to meet it.

Chapter 6

GIANT GHOSTS

Soon after the **ICE MONSTER** was found, London was plunged into the cruellest of winters. A bitter wind brought a flurry of snow. Before long, the entire city was hushed by a thick covering of white. The River Thames froze over.

In this kind of weather, homeless children like Elsie perished in doorways. They would go to sleep and never wake up, to be found at dawn with a dusting of frost on their faces.

Poor Elsie was HUDDLING in her tin bath under a pile of newspapers, trying to keep warm.

She looked at her hands. They were shaking with the cold, and turning blue. The girl almost missed **WORMLY HALL.** Almost, but not quite.

Elsie sneaked into the **NATURAL HISTORY MUSEUM** at closing time, behind a troupe of nuns so the security guard wouldn't see her. Once inside, she scuttled along the long corridors, past the dinosaur bones hanging on wires that looked like giant ghosts, and eventually found an unlocked cupboard. She crept inside, and closed the door. It was a cleaning cupboard and too small in which to sleep lying down, so she slept standing up, with her head nestled between some mops. She looked not unlike a mop, as skinny as a rake with a shock of tangled hair on top.

Elsie was sure no one would find her in there. But she was wrong.

Very early the next morning, before dawn, Elsie was woken by a cleaning lady opening the cupboard door. The woman yawned and grabbed the first "mop" she could find. It was actually Elsie.

"Aaahhh!" screamed the lady.

"ARGH!" screamed the girl.

Elsie was being held by the neck.

"You're not a mop!" said the lady.

"No. I'm a girl."

"What are you doing in my cleaning cupboard?"

"I was sleeping. I didn't want to *die* of the cold."

"No, you don't want to do that."

Elsie gulped. "Are you going to tell on me, missus?"

The cleaning lady did the last thing the girl was expecting.

She smiled.

Most of the time, grown-ups treated urchins like Elsie with cruelty. Not this lady. She was different.

"No! *You're* not going to tell on *me*, are you?" asked the lady.

"Tell on you?" replied the girl. Elsie was befuddled.

"I could lose me job over this."

"No, no, no. Never. I'm not a snitch."

"Thank goodness for that. Me neither. What's your name?"

"Elsie."

"I'm Dotty. Dotty by name and, I'm told, dotty by nature. Are you a child?"

The girl was confused. She thought that was obvious. "Yes."

"I only ask because you are taller than me gentleman friend."

"How tall is he?"

"Titch is shorter than you. That isn't his real name. That's the name all the other soldiers gave him."

"How old is he?"

"Seventy-three."

"Has he shrunk?"

"Nope, God made him that way."

Dotty pulled out a dog-eared photograph from her pocket. "Here's Titch."

Elsie looked at the picture. It must have been taken a while ago, as it showed a young soldier in uniform holding a gun that was taller than him.

"He is small," remarked the girl.

"He's bigger in real life than in the photograph."

"I guessed that," replied Elsie.

"He's my hero!" said Dotty as she kissed the picture, before putting it back in her pocket. "So, I bet you're hungry."

The girl nodded her head. "Ravenous!"

Elsie was always so hungry her tummy hurt. Dotty reached into another pocket.

"Here, have me packed lunch. Bread and dripping."*

Smiling, Elsie took the food. She tore a crust of bread into halves, and handed a piece back to the lady. Both were touched by the kindness of the other.

Elsie devoured her half greedily. It was only bread and dripping, but to her it was the nectar of the gods.

"Where's your mum and dad, little one?"

"Dunno. Never met them."

"Orphan, then, are you?"

"Suppose so."

"Poor thing."

---

* *Dripping is fat from cooked meat.*

"There's no point feeling sorry for meself. I gotta get on with it."

At that moment, they both heard bootsteps *CLOMPING* down the corridor. **CLICK** CLACK **CLICK** CLACK **CLICK** CLACK! The lady lifted her finger to her lips to mime *"Don't say a word"* and hurriedly shut the door.

Chapter 7

A LIKELY STORY

Elsie stayed as still and quiet as she possibly could in the cleaning cupboard. Through the door, she could hear the grown-ups arguing.

"WHO ARE YOU TALKING TO, DOTTY?" boomed a voice.

"Just me mops and brushes, Mr Clout, sir," replied Dotty.

"A likely story, Dotty!" the man scoffed. "As the museum's head of security, I order you to open that door!"

"I can't."

"What do you mean, you can't?"

"Me hands have gone all floppy."

"What do you mean your hands 'have gone all floppy'?"

"Too much mopping!"

"Well, I'll open it, then."

"I wouldn't if I was you."

"Why?"

"I just *BLEW OFF* in there."

"You did what?"

"I did a bottom burp in the cupboard so all the stuffed animals wouldn't have to smell it. It's a really stinky one. It would have peeled the paint off the walls."

"That doesn't explain why you were talking."

"I was talking to my own bottom."

"You were talking to your bottom?"

"Giving it a jolly good telling-off, Mr Clout, sir."

Elsie had to put her hand over her mouth to stop herself from laughing. This lady really was dotty.

"I have never heard so much nonsense in all my life!" thundered Clout. "Now step aside, woman, or I will be forced to use… force!"

The girl heard a slight scuffle.

"*OOF!*"

"*OUCH!*"

"GET OFF ME FOOT!"

As fast as she could, Elsie nestled herself in behind the mops and brushes.

The door swung open…

Chapter 8

◆

THE UNNATURAL HISTORY MUSEUM

Clout peered inside the dark and dingy cleaning cupboard. His hulking frame all but filled up the doorway. He had huge hobnailed boots on his feet, so polished you could eat your dinner off them. The man covered his nose.

"It don't half *REEK* in here!"

That was Elsie's pong.

"Tell it to my bottom," replied Dotty.

Just then, something caught the man's eye among the mops and brushes.

"What's this?" he said, pointing at the girl's hair poking out.

"That?" asked Dotty innocently.

"Yes, that."

"Oh, that! That is one of my new real-hair mops."

"Real-hair mops?" asked Clout.

"Yes. It's great for those areas me everyday mops can't reach. Like between the dinosaurs' toe bones."

"I don't think I can bear that $STINK$ a moment longer," said the man, his eyes watering.

"I did warn you, Mr Clout, sir. Me blow-offs are really something."

"They should have their own museum," mused Clout. "**THE UNNATURAL HISTORY MUSEUM.**"

"Very good, Mr Clout, sir," she said as she slammed the door shut. "It's always lovely talking to you, but, if you will excuse me, I need to give the dodo eggs a good spit and polish."

"Dotty?"

"Yes?"

"You need to get something for that bottom of yours."

"I'll invest in a cork."

"Then we'll all have to wear tin helmets in case you POP."

"That's a good point, Mr Clout. I'll try and think of something!"

"Get to work!"

"You get to work!"

"I can't get to work until you get to work."

"Well, you tellin' me to get to work is stopping me from getting to work."

"GET TO WORK!" thundered the man.

Dotty picked up her mop, and began cleaning the floor. On purpose, she ran the dirty mop over his highly polished hobnailed boots.

"Me boots!" he cried.

"OOPS! Sorry!"

"Stupid old hag!"

"Less of the 'old', please, Mr Clout."

"I need to get these boots sparkling for the visitors."

"Yes, that's why they all come to the **NATURAL HISTORY MUSEUM**, Mr Clout, sir. They don't come to see the dinosaur bones. They just want to see their own face reflected in your boots. You better buff 'em up, good and proper."

Clout gave the cleaning lady a filthy look before

marching off down the corridor to make someone else's life a misery.

CLICK CLACK CLICK CLACK CLICK CLACK!

After a few moments, Dotty opened the cupboard door.

"*PHEW!*" said Elsie. "That was close."

"If I know Clout, he'll be back."

"I'd better get out of here."

"Are you sure you'll be all right?"

"Don't worry. I'll find somewhere else to hide tonight."

"If you're sure?"

"I'm sure."

"Folk will be trickling in soon. Now would be a good time to make a swift exit."

"I gotta ask you something."

"Yes, dearie?"

"Why have you been so kind to me?" asked Elsie.

"Why not?" came the simple answer.

The pair shared a smile before the girl shuffled off down the long corridor.

"Take care, little one," called out the cleaning lady after her. "And please come back and see me very soon."

"I will," replied Elsie.

And she did.

Chapter 9

THE DEVIL'S WORK

Every morning, Elsie checked the newspapers for more news of the **ICE MONSTER**. Weeks passed until one day she heard the cloth-capped sellers shouting from their stands...

"ICE MONSTER
TO SAIL DOWN THE THAMES!"

"ICE MONSTER
EXPECTED IN LONDON TODAY!"

"ICE MONSTER
TO BE KEPT FROZEN IN ICE
IN MUSEUM!"

The girl's heart pounded with excitement.

Up in the Arctic, the mammoth and the huge slab of ice in which it had been found had been packed into a wooden crate full of snow and loaded on to a whaling ship. It was then transported thousands of miles from the Arctic all the way down to the mouth of the Thames.

From there it travelled upriver towards London and its ultimate destination, the **NATURAL HISTORY MUSEUM**. The whaling ship was escorted along the Thames by a formation of gleaming new boats of the British naval fleet, which broke up the ice to allow it safe passage.

The **ICE MONSTER** was being given a huge welcome as if it were a visiting king or queen. Thousands of Londoners lined the banks all along the river to catch a glimpse of the creature, and to be part of this momentous occasion.

Being little, Elsie was able to crawl under the grown-ups' legs to scramble right to the front. There she could see the whaling ship, and the huge coffin-like crate into which the animal was packed.

When the ships had passed, Elsie raced across London towards the museum. Living on the streets, the girl knew every nook and cranny of the city. She *DASHED* along back streets, across gardens, down tunnels, over rooftops and even jumped on to the back

of horse-drawn cabs to get there before the monster.

A line of policemen with linked arms formed a wall round the museum as Londoners surged forward to see the wooden box trundle by on a carriage pulled by fifty mighty horses.

"HURRAH!" cheered the crowds.

But one lone voice was shouting something different. It was an old man with a long beard, wearing a big sandwich board over his shoulders. The words "THE END IS NIGH" were emblazoned across it. He held aloft a copy of the Bible, and cried, "This is the Devil's work. The prophecy has come true. The beast has come! The end is nigh!"

Elsie tugged on his coat. "It's not a beast, sir – it's a woolly mammoth."

The old man gave her a whack on the head with his Bible.

THWACK!

"Wicked child!"

Elsie pushed past him, helping herself to a lump of mouldy cheese from his pocket as she did so. The girl had just reached the gates of the museum when she was shoved back by a policeman.

"Get back, you revolting **urchin!**" he bawled, and he shunted her aside.

"*OUCH!*" she cried as she tumbled on to her back.

"We don't want your sort here. Now clear off!"

As the lowest of the low, Elsie was used to being turned away, but, being strong in spirit, she was not going to take no for an answer. So she scrambled her way up the back of a gentleman's coat, and trod on his top hat.

SQUISH!

Before he had a chance to cry out, she leaped off his top hat and on to the branch of a nearby tree.

TWANG!

With her monkey feet, Elsie shimmied up the tree with ease, and stood on the highest branch. From there, she watched as a hundred men rolled the crate off the back of the carriage. With thick ropes, they heaved it up the stone steps.

The huge wooden front doors of the museum had been taken off their hinges. The crowd fell silent as the men began pushing the crate through the doorway. Would it fit in without taking the front of the **NATURAL HISTORY MUSEUM** with it?

A cheer went up as the crate just squeezed through.

"HURRAH!"

Soon mutterings passed around the crowd that a very important visitor would be coming to the museum today to witness the unveiling.

"She's coming here?"

"Who?"

"You know!"

"Oh, my Lord!"

"Not her?"

"Yes, her!"

"She ain't been seen in ages."

"She's so old now."

"This must really be something."

"I should have bought a new hat!"

Sure enough, barely an hour had passed before the streets echoed with the sound of trumpets.

BRUH DUH DUH DUH DUH DUH DUH

All heads turned to see a golden carriage trundling along the road. Ahead of the carriage, liveried soldiers on horseback blew trumpets to herald the arrival of the very important person seated in it.

Queen Victoria.

Chapter 10

HULLABALOO

This was a day that would go down in history, so it was only fitting that the most powerful person in the world should be there. Queen Victoria was not just the Queen of Great Britain and Ireland, but the monarch of a vast empire that spanned the globe. She had even adopted the title of "Empress of India", despite the fact that she'd never actually been there.

These were different days.

As the crowd realised that they were in the presence of their queen, a woman who'd reigned over them for more than sixty years, they erupted in wild cheers, throwing their hats into the air.

"HURRAH!"

The golden carriage turned to the right to pass through the gates of the museum, and Elsie seized her chance. While the sky was black with hats, she leaped off the branch of the tree…

WHOOSH!

…and landed on top of the Queen's carriage.

THUD!

With all the noise and commotion, no one seemed to notice this huge breach of security.

Elsie lay down flat on the roof of the carriage so she wouldn't be seen. In 1899, anyone getting this close to Her Majesty without an invitation might very well pay the price with their life.

The carriage sped into the grounds of the museum, and came to a halt at the bottom of the stone steps. Elsie lifted her head a tiny bit, and peeked over the side of the carriage.

Thousands of faces were pushed up against the metal railings, open mouths roaring their approval for their queen.

"HURRAH!"

The carriage wobbled slightly as Her Majesty stepped out. The Queen was old and frail, and tottered up the stone steps, helped by a handsome Indian attendant in a turban. She was dressed from head to toe in black and wore a solemn look on her face.

That was because she was in deep mourning for her husband, Prince Albert, even though he had died nearly forty years before. Not wanting to disappoint the crowd, the Queen slowly turned round and gave them a polite wave.

"HURRAH!"

While all eyes were on the royal guest, Elsie slid off the roof and lowered herself down the side of the carriage. There she hid behind a wheel.

The hullabaloo must have startled the horses…

"NEIGH! NEIGH!"

…as the carriage shunted backwards a little. Elsie thought she was going to be trampled to death by the horses' hooves, but the carriage driver cracked his whip…

SNAP!

…and ordered…

"WHOA!"

Elsie let out a sigh of relief as the horses came to a juddering stop.

The girl watched from her hiding place as the

Queen was greeted with a bow by the director of the museum, the portly Sir Ray Lankester, and led inside.

The huge wooden doors were closed behind her.

THUD.

Now Elsie wasn't feeling too clever. All around her she could see the legs of policemen. How was she going to get inside that museum without anyone seeing her? She was desperate to do so, but Elsie had more chance of becoming the next Archbishop of Canterbury.

As she pondered her next move on her hands and knees, the most unexpected thing happened. The carriage moved off, leaving the girl hiding behind nothing at all. She was concealed only by some air.

Air is the worst thing to find yourself hiding behind. Other bad ones include:

 A conker

A marble

A wasp   A rabbit dropping

A pea

A flea   A speck of dust

An amoeba

An amoeba dropping

The invisible man

Elsie was in deep, deep doo-doo.

. → ✳ ← .

Chapter 11

HUMAN NET

"HA! HA!" the crowd outside the **NATURAL HISTORY MUSEUM** all laughed when the little urchin was revealed hiding behind the air.

The policemen looked around in confusion.

"THERE!"

The crowd pointed at the girl, and eventually the policemen saw what was right under their noses.

They formed a circle round this uninvited guest, and began closing in on her.

Having lived on the streets, Elsie was no stranger to running away from the police, or the "rozzers"* as those who spent most of their time running away from the police called them.

The policemen crouched down and stretched out their arms, sure that she would try to escape by running through their legs.

"**We've got you!**" growled the chief of police, Commissioner Barker. He was a heavy man with a tiny postage stamp of a moustache stuck over his top lip.

The circle was closing.

The policemen linked arms to make themselves into a human net.

There was no way out.

Spotting the truncheons dangling from their belts, a daring thought crossed Elsie's mind. Just as the policemen were looming over her, she grabbed two of the truncheons with each hand, yanking them as hard as she could.

---

* "Rozzers" is a slang term for the police, loosely echoing the first name of their founder, Robert Peel.

This brought the policemen crashing towards one another.

Their heads knocked together.

BISH! BASH! BOSH!

"OW!"

"OOF!"

"ARGH!"

Dazed and confused, the policemen tumbled backwards, and collapsed on to the ground.

From above, the scene looked like a flower, with Elsie the centre and the policemen all splayed-out petals.

This brilliant move by the urchin instantly won over the crowd, and they cheered.

"HURRAH!"

No one wanted to see an army of policemen win against one little mite.

However, there was no time to lap up the attention of the crowd. Elsie darted up the steps towards the entrance to the **NATURAL HISTORY MUSEUM**. Another squad of policemen stood guard in front of the huge wooden doors. They drew their truncheons, ready to give this little creature a ruddy good bashing.

Not wanting to receive a bashing, be it a good or a bad one (neither sounded appealing), Elsie slid down the handrail. To one side of the building entrance was a drainpipe.

There was no time to think. What with her monkey feet, Elsie was soon halfway up it.

"HURRAH!" cheered the crowd once more.

One bold policeman gave chase up the drainpipe, but not being blessed with monkey feet he instantly slid back down.

W H I Z Z !

"ArGH!"

His bottom landed right on top of another policeman's face.

BOING!

"POOH!" complained the one whose nose was now stuck up the other's rear end.

Needless to say, this perfect piece of slapstick was greeted by howls of laughter from the crowd.

"HA! HA! HA!"

"AFTER HER, YOU FOOLS!"

barked Barker.

"Right away, Commissioner, sir!" said one.

"FORM A LADDER!" ordered the commissioner.

"How are we gonna do that?"

"Heaviest at the bottom."

"That's very kind of you, sir."

Barker fumed. His tiny moustache twitched. "I am not part of the ladder! I am in charge! Now, the heaviest at the bottom, then the next heaviest, then the next, and so on and so forth."

The policemen all started arguing among themselves. No one wanted to be at the bottom.

"I'm the lightest!"

"No. I'm the lightest!"

"You're the heaviest by far!"

"I've lost weight."

"You still look fat."

"I've just got a round face."

"SHE'S GETTING AWAY!"

thundered Barker.

The girl was nearing the top of the drainpipe. The commissioner took charge of his human ladder, quickly ordering who went where. Soon the policemen were reluctantly climbing on top of one another.

Needless to say, this amateur acrobatics act immediately came crashing to the ground.

"OOF!"
"OUCH!"
"ARGH!"

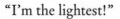

"EEK!"

"HELP! Someone's trodden on me bits!"

The crowd whooped and cheered at this brilliant piece of entertainment.

"HURRAH!"

By this time, Elsie had reached the roof of the museum. She took a moment to acknowledge her adoring audience, and gave them a little bow.

The crowd burst into wild applause.

"YES!"

"SHE'S DONE IT!"

"GO! GO! GO!"

The little girl hurried over the sloping roofs to the far side of the building, her monkey feet gripping the lead. For a moment, looking over the rooftops of London, she felt immortal. However, when a tile slipped from under her, she suddenly felt distinctly mortal.

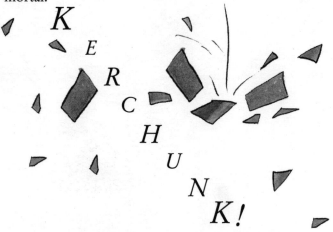

KERCHUNK!

The tile exploded on to the ground.

Instantly, Elsie slammed down on to the roof...

THUD!

...and began sliding down it at speed.

"AAAH!"

The girl rolled over in a desperate attempt to grab

on to the roof. Just as she was about to fly off, she managed to hook her fingers round the guttering. However, Elsie was going so fast she swung forward. Her fingers unhooked and she felt herself hurtling through the air.

"NOOO!"

Chapter 12

SABRE-TOOTHED TEETH

Elsie flew forward and burst through a stained-glass window.

SHATTER!

She rolled down some stone steps before landing on top of a glass cabinet that housed the skeleton of a sabre-toothed tiger.

THUD!

Elsie came down with such force that the sheet of glass on which she landed began to crack.

K E R C H U N K !

Like a shaft of lightning splintering through the sky, the crack shot across the glass.

BING!

In a split second, the glass panel at the top of the cabinet misted over as it became a thousand tiny pieces.

Elsie knew exactly what was going to happen next, but was powerless to stop it. She gulped. The glass crumbled beneath her, and Elsie fell into the cabinet, landing on the back of the sabre-toothed tiger.

CRUNCH! "OOF!"

Now the girl was trapped inside the glass cabinet, and with all the noise from the window smashing she was sure to have drawn attention to herself. If only there were some way of breaking one of the glass walls, but they were inches thick. However hard she thumped with her fists, it just wouldn't break.

BOOM! BOOM! BOOM!

Feeling that there was little chance of the sabre-toothed tiger skeleton missing it, she pulled out one of its sabre-toothed teeth. With an almighty swing of her arm, she bashed the sharp end of the tooth against the glass.

BUNK!

SMASH!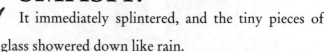

It immediately splintered, and the tiny pieces of glass showered down like rain.

PATTER!

Not needing the tooth any more, Elsie stuck it back where she'd found it, and patted the sabre-toothed tiger skeleton in thanks.

"Good boy!"

The sound of bootsteps echoed along the corridor.

CLICK CLACK CLICK CLACK CLICK CLACK!

It must be the museum's head of security, Mr Clout. Elsie knew she had to make a run for it. Having no shoes on her feet, she carefully stepped over the pieces of broken glass, and charged off down a corridor.

Staying close to the walls and keeping out of the

light – something she had learned from the rats at the orphanage – she found a balcony overlooking the main hall.

From the top floor of the museum, Elsie looked down on the historic scene.

Chapter 13

◆

A SEA OF OLD MEN

Sitting on a grand chair that made her look even smaller than her actual size (and she already looked extremely small) was Queen Victoria. Gathered behind her was a sea of old men with white beards, spectacles and stern expressions. They looked like learned men: scientists, explorers and politicians.

Mr Clout circled the room like a hungry shark, ready to attack anyone who made a lunge for Her Majesty. Commissioner Barker was doing the exact same thing. The pair kept on bumping into each other.

"OOF!"

"OUT OF THE WAY, YOU FOOL!" growled Barker.

Masked by a red velvet curtain, something the size of a house was standing in front of the tiny queen.

A portly man stepped forward and addressed the gathering. He was the director of the **NATURAL HISTORY MUSEUM**, Sir Ray Lankester.

"Your Majesty, my lords, gentlemen..." he began.

"SPEAK UP!" shouted Queen Victoria.

Elsie put her hand over her mouth to stifle a giggle. She wouldn't have had Her Majesty down as a heckler.

Poor Lankester looked aghast, as you might if the most powerful person in the world was barracking you. The man tried to carry on as best he could.

"YOUR MAJESTY, MY LORDS, LADIES AND GENTLEMEN," he began again, his voice cracking with nerves. "As director of the

NATURAL HISTORY MUSEUM, it is a huge honour to house what I am sure you will all agree is the greatest find of the century. When a group of explorers set off across the Arctic…"

"GET ON WITH IT!" shouted the Queen.

"Yes, yes, of course, Your Majesty. I am very sorry. I know you have an empire to run. Will you please do us all the honour of unveiling this creature dubbed the **'ICE MONSTER'**, which has been perfectly preserved in the ice for thousands of years?"

With some difficulty, the Queen stood up. Her handsome attendant Abdul Karim went to help her.

"I can do it, thank you very much, Munshi!"* she snapped.

"As you wish, Your Majesty," he purred.

"Actually, can you help me?" she asked, looking a little wobbly.

Abdul gracefully took her arm, and she shuffled over to the exhibit.

"It gives one great pleasure," began the Queen, "to declare this woolly mammoth open."

---

* *"Munshi" was the fond title Queen Victoria gave Abdul. It is a Persian word which means "secretary", though he was a great deal more than that to her.*

With that, she tugged on the cord, and the velvet curtain slipped to the floor.

S I L E N C E .

There it was.

In all its glory.

Housed in a huge glass tank.

Suspended in ice.

The mammoth.

Perfectly preserved.

It was impossible to believe it had been dead for ten thousand years. To all appearances, it could have died yesterday.

The creature looked like a cross between an elephant and a teddy bear. The tusks were **long** and curled, like the moustaches of many of the fusty old men gathered in the museum. Between the tusks hung a long, furry trunk. The mammoth's body was covered in coarse brown hair, with a thicker and darker tuft on its head like a wig. Its legs were as wide as tree trunks, leading down to four clumpy feet. Its eyes were open. They were small and black, and shaped like tears.

For Elsie, it was **love** at first sight.

This was the most **beautiful** thing she had ever seen. Her heart soared, and her mind began dancing with pictures.

Here she was stroking the animal's fur. There she was riding on its back. Then she was being held by its long, furry trunk.

Just as she was flying off into a land of make-believe, Elsie sensed someone standing right behind her. The girl was frozen in fear. She couldn't even turn her head to look round. Then she felt a hand come to rest on her shoulder. Elsie gasped for air to let out a cry...

"HUH!"

...but she couldn't.

A hand was covering her mouth.

. ⭐ .

Chapter 14

DEAD AS DEAD CAN BE

"Shush!" came the voice behind her. "Don't give yourself away."

Elsie knew that voice. It was the only adult voice she ever remembered speaking to her in a tone of kindness.

DOTTY'S.

Elsie turned round and whispered, "Thank goodness it's you."

"Everyone, but everyone, is looking for you, young miss."

"I know. I'm not supposed to be here."

"You don't say!" replied the cleaning lady. "Truth

110

be told, I'm not supposed to be here either. A humble cleaner isn't allowed to be in the same room as Her Queen the Majesty."

"Her Majesty the Queen?"

Dotty looked at the girl as if she were bonkers. "That's what I said. But I couldn't resist being here. I love our Queen." Dotty gazed down proudly at the lady. "Ooh, that reminds me. I must buy a stamp."

Two stories below, the Queen was looking up at the frozen creature.

"Well, well, well. So this is the famous '**ICE MONSTER**'?"

"Yes, ma'am," replied the director. "It is a huge feat of engineering for the museum to keep the animal's body conserved like this. That pipe you can see hanging down from the ceiling blows cold air into the tank through that hatch to keep the ice it is packed in frozen."

"It's a bit small for a monster."

Lankester was once again blindsided by the lady.

"Well, I, er, um," he spluttered. "I can only

apologise, Your Majesty, but this mammoth is probably only a year or so old. It's a child, really."

The Queen looked lost in thought for a moment. "Have you got any bigger ones?"

Lankester looked desperately around at the faces of the assembled great and good for help, but none came.

"Er, um, no. I am afraid not, ma'am. Finding any prehistoric creature, let alone one in such perfect condition, is extremely rare. This is the find of the century."

"Mmm. My dear departed husband, Prince Albert, would have liked it. Such a shame he isn't here with me to see this. Albert loved animals. I am more of an opera fan myself, aren't I, Munshi?"

Her elegant companion smiled weakly. "You have a unique singing voice, Your Majesty."

His wry answer made the old lady chuckle.

"HA! HA! HA!"

The chuckle turned into a cough.

"Huh, huh, huh."

A concerned Abdul steadied her.

"Thank you, Munshi. I don't know what I would do without you."

"Nor me without you, Your Majesty."

The unlikely pair shared a smile, then the Queen looked back up at the mammoth.

"Does it do anything?" she enquired.

"I am so sorry, Your Majesty, what do you mean?" replied Lankester. Sweat was now pouring off his brow.

"Like a trick?" she asked with girlish excitement.

The museum's director paused before he spoke, gathering his thoughts. "Sadly not, Your Majesty.

This creature has been dead for ten thousand years. So, as *DEAD* goes, I would say you can't get much *DEADER.* It's as *DEAD* as *DEAD* can be."

"Oh. That is a shame. I suppose it is rather pretty, if you like that sort of thing. Which I do."

Lankester shuffled awkwardly. "Do you have any other questions, Your Majesty?"

The Queen thought for a moment. "When are we having the tea and cake? I was dragged halfway across London to come here. These days I don't like to leave the palace too much. At my age, it all becomes a bit of a bother. But my eyes lit up at the promise of tea and cake, you see, and I haven't seen so much as a scone."

"I meant any questions about the *MAMMOTH,* Your Majesty."

"The what?"

"This creature here."

"No," replied the Queen with her customary bluntness.

"Shame it's $DEAD$ already," came a deep voice from the shadows of the hall. "Or I would **shoot it.**"

All heads turned to see who had so rudely interrupted Her Majesty the Queen.

Chapter 15

EXTINCTION BUSINESS

Out of the darkness stepped a figure dressed in a pith helmet, knee-high lace-up boots and a khaki coat. A plume of grey cigar smoke followed it.

"Who the blazes is that?" demanded the Queen, struggling to see.

"Oh n-no," stammered Lankester.

"Who is it?"

"Lady Buckshot the big-game hunter, Your Majesty," replied Lankester.

"Oh no!" agreed the Queen.

Disapproving murmurs echoed around the hall.

"What is she doing here?" pressed the Queen.

"Well, ma'am," replied the hunter, "I shot and killed every single stuffed animal in the museum."

"Such a shame the animals weren't armed, or they

could have fired back," hissed the Queen to Abdul, just loud enough for Buckshot to hear.

"*HA! HA!*" Abdul couldn't help but laugh.

"It's a shame this here monster is already dead," began Buckshot. "It would have been my great pleasure to shoot it, right between the eyes."

"Well, erm, um, L-L-Lady Buckshot," spluttered Lankester, "the mammoth as a species has long since been extinct."

"I am in the extinction business," replied the hunter. "I would wipe out every last creature on Earth if I could."

"How delightful for you!" said the Queen sarcastically. "Now, where is this tea and cake?"

Lankester leaped in. "Tea and cakes will now be served in the gallery. If you would follow me…"

The Queen took Abdul's arm, and she shuffled out of the hall.

The great and the good all followed, which left Buckshot alone with the mammoth. From the top of the stairs, Elsie and Dotty watched as she marched right up to the front of the tank. There she mimed taking out a shotgun, loading it and firing. *"BOOM!"* She even provided a sound effect, before miming the mammoth's brains splurging out.

"Ha! Ha! Ha!" she chuckled to herself,

before drifting back into the shadows.

Now only Elsie and Dotty were left in the main hall.

"I am trembling!" chattered Elsie, holding on to the balcony rail. The evil stench of Buckshot's cigar smoke had snaked all the way up there.

"Me too. Evil woman. She's always dragging in some poor tiger or lion she's shot, with a wicked grin on her face."

"So, now she's gone, do we dare?" asked the girl.

"Dare what?" replied the cleaning lady.

"Do we dare to go down and take a closer look?"

Dotty shook her head. "Ooh, Elsie, you'll get me into deep doo-doo."

"Let's just have a very, very, very quick look."

When the girl put it that way, it was hard to say no.

"A very quick look?" asked Dotty.

"A glance, really."

"A glimpse?"

"Less than a glimpse, a peep."

"A peek?"

"EXACTLY!" replied Elsie.

Dotty sighed heavily. "All right, then. Let's have a peek at this manmoth."

"I think it's 'mammoth'," corrected Elsie.

"Yes, 'manmoth'! That's what I said."

Elsie smiled, and pulled the lady along by her sleeve. "Dotty, come on…"

Chapter 16

CHEEKS ABLAZE

"**I** am not sliding down the banister!" protested Dotty.

"But it's the fastest way down!" replied Elsie.

Dotty was right to be reluctant. It was an awfully long way from the topmost floor of the museum to the bottommost.

"In the time we've been arguing, we could already be at the bottom," reasoned Elsie.

The girl clambered on to the banister. Dotty sighed, then hitched up her skirt and joined her.

"This is a very **extremely** bad idea," said the lady.

It was too late.

WHOOSH!

"Ouch. Me bottom cheeks are ablaze!" complained Dotty.

"HOLD ON!" called out Elsie.

Soon they ran out of banister.

The girl landed on the floor.

THUD!

Dotty landed on top of her.

THUDDER!

Mesmerised, Elsie approached the **ICE MONSTER**. All that was separating the girl from a species that had become extinct thousands of years ago were a few inches of glass and ice.

"Funny-looking thing," muttered Dotty.

"I think it's beautiful," whispered the girl. "It's like the biggest cuddly toy in the whole wide world."

Dotty chuckled. "I'm not sure it would be all that

cuddly if it was alive. Now come on. We need to get out of here before Mr Clout comes back."

The girl stood still.

"Elsie? ELSIE?"

The lady tugged at the little girl's arm. "We need to go."

"I don't want to leave it alone here," replied Elsie.

"You what?" Dotty couldn't believe what she was hearing.

"It looks sad."

"You'd look sad if you'd been dead for ten thousand years!"

"Let me climb on your shoulders."

"You what?"

"I need to take a closer look."

"Young lady, we need to get out of here now, before the Queen Her Majesty comes back."

"Quicker than a peek," implored Elsie. "A *peek-a-boo*! I promise."

"No! Now come on!" With that, Dotty tried to drag the girl out of the hall.

However, Elsie was far too quick for her. Before Dotty knew it, Elsie had climbed up her back.

"What the...?"

"Hold on to my ankles!" she ordered.

Elsie stood on the lady's shoulders as a reluctant Dotty dutifully held on to her. The girl was now at head height with the mammoth. She pressed her nose up against the cold glass, and stared deep into one of its little black eyes.

"What are you doing up there?" called Dotty.

The truth was Elsie didn't exactly know what she was doing up there. All she did know was that she was transfixed. She didn't move. It was as if she were frozen solid too.

"We need to go!" implored Dotty.

Still Elsie stared. Then the most magical thing happened. It was a moment that changed everything. A bead of water formed in the creature's eye.

"It's crying!" called down Elsie.

"Oh, my! You're imagining things, young lady. That manmoth hasn't cried since long before even I was born. Now come down!"

"Not yet."

"What do you mean, 'not yet'?"

"'Not yet' means 'not yet'."

Down the corridor, there was the sound of bootsteps.

CLICK CLACK CLICK CLACK CLICK CLACK!

Clout was on to them.

"We need to go! Now!" cried Dotty. With the girl still standing on her shoulders, she began running as fast as she could.

"WHOA!" exclaimed Elsie as she tried to stop wobbling.

CLICK CLACK CLICK CLACK CLICK CLACK!

"*WHO GOES THERE?*" Clout's shout echoed along the corridor.

Elsie toppled over and slid down Dotty's back.

Now she was riding her like a horse.

"Giddy-up!" ordered the girl as together they made their escape.

Chapter 17

CURIOUS CREATURES

In her many years of working there, Dotty had cleaned every inch of the **NATURAL HISTORY MUSEUM**. She knew all the best hiding places.

"Down here!" hissed the lady as she led Elsie down some stone steps. Ahead of them stood a huge metal door with a sign that read:

DO NOT ENTER

Dotty fished in her pocket and pulled out a jangling bunch of keys.

"It's one of these," she muttered to herself.

"But which one?" pressed Elsie.

"I know it's a metal one."

"They're all metal! They're keys! Give them here."

Elsie snatched the keys off Dotty, and after a few attempts found the right one. She unlocked the door, and ushered Dotty inside. Then, as quietly as she could, the girl closed the door behind them, and locked it.

CLUNK.

Listening through the thick metal, the pair heard the sound of bootsteps descending the stairs.

CLICK CLACK CLICK CLACK CLICK CLACK!

The door handle was turned...

RATTLE.

The pair held their breath.

There followed the sound of bootsteps ascending the stairs.

CLICK CLACK CLICK CLACK CLICK CLACK...

The pair exhaled.

"Thank goodness Clout doesn't have his keys," whispered Elsie.

"No," replied Dotty. "They're right here!" she added, holding up the set in her hand. "I lost mine so I 'borrowed' his."

"Clever Dotty!"

"I'm not just a pretty face!" said the cleaning lady.

Elsie smiled. There was no answer to that. "So, where are we?"

"The **NATURAL HISTORY MUSEUM** in London."

"Yes, I know that, Dotty! I mean *where* in the **NATURAL HISTORY MUSEUM** in London?"

"Oh, we're in the storeroom. Now stay close to me..."

. If upstairs was full of wonders, downstairs was even more so. The storeroom was full of things that were too weird to be put on show.

The pair passed a number of curious creatures pickled in tanks. There was a shark with two heads, a giant tortoise the size of a baby elephant and a snake

as long as a cricket pitch. Overlooking them were stuffed conjoined twin owls, a mighty lump of red rock that looked like it had fallen to Earth from another planet…

and an egg so big it must have belonged to a *Megalosaurus*. A prehistoric human skull squatted on a plinth. It was bizarre-looking, half human and half ape.

"What's this?" asked the girl.

Dotty ambled over. "Dunno. I wouldn't touch it if I was you. It looks spooky."

"If you think that skull looks spooky, you've never met Mrs Curdle."

"Who?"

"She ran the orphanage I escaped from. And she's got warts bigger than this!"

Elsie rested her hand on top of the skull, and it wobbled slightly. Intrigued, the girl rotated the top piece of the skull back from the jaw.

CREAK!

Suddenly, the pair realised they were spinning round!

WHIIIIIIIIIIIIIIIIZZZZZZIIIIIZZZZII!!!!!

Elsie touching the skull had opened a secret door!

Now they were plunged into total darkness.

"Argh!" they screamed.

Chapter 18

—◆—

DARKEST DARK

"Something's grabbing hold of me!" yelled Dotty.

"Something's grabbing hold of me!" yelled Elsie.

"HELP!" they screamed.

"I think we might be grabbing hold of each other," said the girl.

"Oh yes."

"Shall we let go?"

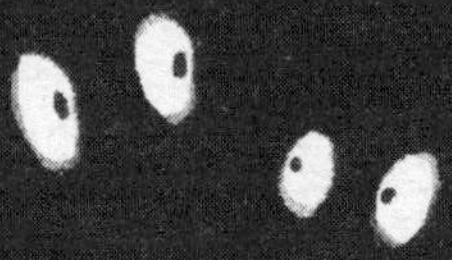

"Yes."

They did so.

"That's better," said Dotty.

"Where are we?" asked Elsie.

"Still in the **NATURAL HISTORY MUSEUM** in London."

"YES! I KNOW THAT!"

"ALL RIGHT!"

134

"I mean, where in the museum are we?"

"Dunno!" answered Dotty. "I've been cleaning this place for donkey's years and I ain't never been in here. It must be a secret room."

"A secret room! Cor blimey!" Elsie couldn't hide her excitement. "Let's explore!"

"You go first," said Dotty. "I'll be right behind you in case of an attack from the rear."

Knowing the old dear was frightened, Elsie said, "Hold my hand."

Together they made their way across the dark room towards a faint flicker of light. On closer inspection, it turned out to be a dusty old bottle, thick with cobwebs. The girl blew on the bottle to reveal its contents. A light was dancing under the glass. It was as if a ghost were trapped in there.

"It's alive," said Elsie.

"How can a bottle be alive?"

"Dunno. But look – something's inside."

Dotty peered in. "Very queer. Whatever you do, DON'T TOUCH IT!"

Like most children, Elsie had selective hearing and, on this occasion, chose **not** to listen. She reached out her hand to touch the bottle.

"Ouch!" she yelled, recoiling in pain.

"What did I tell you?"

"It's hot!"

The girl pulled down the sleeve of her coat to save her fingers from being burned.

"I wonder what's inside?" she pondered.

"Whatever you do," repeated Dotty, "DON'T OPEN IT."

Again, the child chose not to listen, and slowly she began easing the cork out of the bottle.

"I said 'don't'!" repeated Dotty.

POP!

A bolt of light shot out, illuminating the room for a split second in brilliant bright white.

Z A N G !

"ELSIE!" shouted Dotty.

It was too late.

The fizzing beam hit Elsie, and her whole body
LIT UP.

Jolts
of light
buzzed
all over her.

"AAAHHH!" she screamed. Her hair
stood on end and smoke billowed from her ears.

Was she going to explode?

Then as quickly as the light had appeared it disappeared. Elsie slumped to the floor like a sack of potatoes. THUD...

———◆———

SPLOSH!

The next thing Elsie knew was that she was wet. Soaking wet. Her eyes opened to see Dotty standing over her, holding a bucket.

SPLOSH!

Another wave of freezing-cold water drenched her.

SPLOSH!

And another!

Next the lady began slapping the girl around her face.

SLAP! SLAP! SLAP! SLAP! SLAP!

"Wake up, Elsie! WAKE UP! Please! Don't die on me!"

"ALL RIGHT! ALL RIGHT! I AM AWAKE!" she called up.

Dotty began shaking the girl just to make sure.

"STOP SHAKING ME!"

"Sorry!" said Dotty.

"What on earth was in that bottle? My reading ain't so good."

The lady read aloud what was scrawled on the label. "*Lightning.*"

"Lightning in a bottle?"

"That's what it says."

"How can you catch lightning in a bottle? That's impossible."

"**Nothing is impossible, child,**" came a voice from the shadows.

Chapter 19

LIGHTNING IN A BOTTLE

Down in the secret room, the two intruders froze in fear as a figure wheeled himself out of the darkness, holding a lantern. The man was so elderly he had the appearance of a tortoise. He was completely bald, and wore a pair of half-moon spectacles on the end of his nose. His clothes were a dirty old laboratory coat worn over a tweed suit that was falling apart at the seams. He had gnarled slippers on his feet, and fingerless gloves on his callus-encrusted hands.

"It's you!" cried Dotty. "Everyone thought you were dead!"

"No, lowly cleaning woman, I am very much alive!"

"Who is he?" said the girl.

"I am the professor!" he announced grandly.

"Professor of what?" asked Elsie.

"Exactly!" joked Dotty. "Everyone at the museum knew him. He used to be one of the top men here, until the—"

"Yes! Yes!" the professor interrupted. "We don't need to go into all that."

"What's 'all that'?" asked Elsie, intrigued.

"The professor nearly burned the whole museum down in one of his madcap experiments!" said Dotty.

The old man's face turned a furious shade of purple. "That is not what happened, you stupid, stupid woman!"

"Well then, what did happen, you not-quite-as-clever-as-you-think man?"

The girl couldn't help but smirk. Here were two grown-ups bickering like children.

The professor wheeled himself about his secret laboratory, lighting the candles around the space one by one.

Soon a room was revealed, the likes of which neither
Elsie nor Dotty had ever seen before.

There were glass tubes everywhere, chemicals in dusty old bottles and scientific equations scribbled in chalk on every inch of the walls. It was like being able to see inside the old man's brain.

Brilliant but bonkers.

"I was conducting a revolutionary experiment to harness the power of lightning," continued the professor. "Something I had been working on for many years. One stormy night ten years ago, I launched a small metal-tipped balloon into the sky. Attached to the balloon was a length of copper wire. The wire led down to that bottle that now lies smashed on the ground."

"So what happened?" asked Elsie, intrigued.

"I'll tell you what happened—" interrupted Dotty.

"Do you mind if I tell my own story, thank you

very much, you ignorant, ignorant woman?" asked the professor.

"I ain't got a clue what 'ignorant' means," scolded the woman. "But it better not be something bad!"

"My experiment was a complete success," continued the professor. "I captured lightning in a bottle. That is what gave you that little electric shock."

"Little?" exclaimed Elsie.

"Anything bigger and it would have killed you," replied the professor. "Sizzled to death in a heartbeat."

Elsie gulped. "So, if the experiment was a complete success, why did you lose your job?" she asked.

"Good question!" murmured Dotty.

"SILENCE!" ordered the professor. "The copper wire became wrapped round one of the museum's towers. Another much stronger bolt of lightning hit the balloon, and it set the tower on fire."

Dotty jumped in. "It's very lucky that it was raining cats and dogs that night or the fire would've burned the whole museum down to the ground."

The professor fell silent for a moment, then bowed

his head in sorrow. "I was hauled in front of the museum director and told in no uncertain terms that I was never to practise science again. I was thrown out! But the museum was my life – I had nowhere else to go – so I hid down here in the cellar."

"It was so long ago now, all us upstairs thought you were dead."

"I might as well be," murmured the old man. "Now I'm just rotting away in the dark, waiting for the end. My dream of becoming one of the world's most famous scientists is nothing but ashes. I have more chance of capturing lightning in a bottle!"

Elsie's face lit up. A thought had flashed across her mind. It was an idea so crazy it was brilliant, and so brilliant it was crazy. "I think there's still a chance your name could go down in history."

"How?" spluttered the old man.

"You could help bring a prehistoric creature back to life."

Chapter 20

DARK FIRE

"Not the sabre-toothed tiger!" exclaimed Dotty.

"NO!" laughed Elsie. "That's just a skeleton!"

"No. I suppose there's little help for that now. You don't mean the manmoth, do you?"

"The 'mammoth', yes."

"That's what I said," protested the lady. "Manmoth. You want to bring that manmoth upstairs back to life?"

"YES!"

"So we have a new arrival, do we?" asked the professor. "I wondered what all that noise was."

"Bringing it back to life is madness!" exclaimed Dotty.

"Good madness or bad madness?" asked Elsie.

"Is there a *good* kind?"

"YES! Listen, that creature has been perfectly

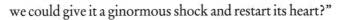

preserved for ten thousand years. It looks like it snuffed it yesterday. Right?"

Dotty nodded her head.

"So surely with the professor's lightning-catching thingummyjig we could give it a ginormous shock and restart its heart?"

Elsie and Dotty looked at the professor. He was the science expert after all, even though he had very nearly burned the **NATURAL HISTORY MUSEUM** down to the ground. His old eyes lit up with a dark fire. He stared straight ahead as the plan began to take shape in his mind.

"This is a genius idea of mine!" he whispered.

Elsie looked mightily confused. Wasn't it *her* idea?

"I can use my lightning technology to create life! The dream of all scientists since the dawn of time. To be God!"

"I think it's gone to his head a bit," murmured Dotty.

"I will go down in history as the greatest scientist

of my age. No, *of all time.* Isaac Newton? An apple fell on your head and you came up with the idea of gravity. Who cares? Nicolaus Copernicus? You discovered that the Earth revolves round the Sun rather than the

NEWTON COPERNICUS DARWIN

other way round? Big deal! Charles Darwin? So you completely changed the way we think about life on Earth with your theory of evolution? Duh! They will rip up your books, burn your paintings and tear down your statues and put up ones of ME! ME! ME! YES! IT WILL ALL BE ABOUT ME!"

There was an uncomfortable silence for a moment.

"Have you finished?" asked Elsie.

The professor paused for thought. "Yes. You two

will be my assistants. You must do everything I say, and be prepared to lay down your lives in the name of science if need be. Now come on! There's no time to lose."

Instantly, the old man started busying himself about his laboratory, handing pieces of scientific equipment to Elsie, who followed him around like an eager puppy. Dotty looked on in disbelief.

"Have you two completely lost your minds?" she asked.

"The mind is an abstract construct," replied the professor.

"What he just said," agreed the girl, not having understood a word of it.

"If you do manage to catch a bolt of lightning and somehow bring this manmoth…"

"Mammoth," corrected Elsie.

"Manmoth, that is what I said, back to life, what are you going to do with it?"

It was a good question, and stopped both of them in their tracks.

"Mmm," pondered the girl. "Well, maybe the mammoth can come and live with you?"

Dotty went dotty. "With me? I rent a tiny attic room in a boarding house. There's a **'no cats or dogs'** rule."

"What about a **'NO MAMMOTHS'** rule?" asked Elsie.

"No!"

"Well then…"

"There ain't a **'no dinosaurs'** rule either! I ain't sure the landlady thought she'd need any rules about animals that've been extinct for millions of years."

"Well, if it can't live with you, maybe it can come and live with me," said Elsie.

"You don't have a home."

"So maybe we can set it free."

Elsie noticed the professor smiling to himself. He was hiding something. But what?

"We can work on all the finer details in good time," he said. "First, we have to bring it back to life. Now, where did I put that copper wire?"

Dotty grabbed whatever bit of scientific equipment

Elsie was holding and put it down on the counter.

"Come on, Elsie, this is all going to end in tears," said the lady.

With that, Dotty grabbed the girl's hand and dragged her over to the secret door.

"Please, Dotty, I beg you," cried the professor. "I need your help too!"

"NO!"

"PLEASE!"

"NO MEANS NO!"

Just the other side of the door, bootsteps could once again be heard.

CLICK CLACK CLICK CLACK CLICK CLACK!

The pair fell silent.

"Shush!" hushed Elsie. "It's Clout."

"He doesn't know I'm here," hissed the professor. "Nobody does. If you've led him here, then—"

"Shush!" shushed the girl again.

All three kept dead still as the bootsteps came to a halt right outside the secret door.

CLICK CLACK CLICK CLACK CLICK CLACK!

There followed the sound of light tapping.

TAP TAP TAP...

Dotty held her chest. Her heart was racing.

TAP TAP TAP...

Elsie had had to hide herself countless times before. The trick was not to breathe. The girl stretched out her hand to silence the old lady. Dotty clasped her hands together and closed her eyes in prayer.

TAP TAP TAP...

Had Clout worked out there was something behind the secret door?

Not yet.

There was the sound of bootsteps again, as Clout moved off.

CLICK CLACK CLICK CLACK CLICK CLACK...

"If I know Mr Clout, he will be back," whispered the professor. "We have to move at lightning speed if we want to bring the monster back to life."

"What could possibly go wrong?" muttered Dotty.

· ⤙ ✳ ⤚ ·

Chapter 21

A THOUSAND
SILK HANDKERCHIEFS

I n his secret laboratory, the professor expounded his **madcap** plan.

"We need to make a giant hot-air balloon from silk handkerchiefs, and fly it high over the museum into a lightning storm. Elsie, you will need to steal the silk handkerchiefs. Have you ever stolen anything before?"

"Once or twice," lied the girl. "How many do you need?"

"Mmm. No more than a thousand."

"A *thousand?*"

"Give or take."

"Where am I going to get a *thousand* silk handkerchiefs from?"

"A thousand well-to-do ladies and gentlemen, of course. Now, we will also need a round piece of metal," continued the professor. "Like a soldier's tin helmet."

Suddenly Dotty jumped up and down, looking as if she desperately needed a wee, but in actual fact she was just overexcited.

"Ooh! Ooh!" she cried, waving her hand in the air.

"Yes?" asked the professor.

"I know where to get a tin helmet. Me boyfriend, Titch, will have one from his war days."

"Perfect! We will need to attach it to the top of the balloon. Let me show you…"

The professor reached into the pocket of his dirty laboratory coat. "Now where on earth is my chalk?"

Elsie looked a little sheepish. "Oh, it must have slipped out of your pocket and into my hand," she lied.

"Very good, child. Very good!" The professor was mightily impressed. "Those fingers will come in handy when you're stealing the handkerchiefs."

The old man held out his hand and she placed the stolen chalk into it. Then he began drawing his invention on the wall of the laboratory, giving a commentary as he sketched.

"So here is the balloon, with the tin helmet at the very top. The balloon will have a wicker basket attached by ropes at the bottom here. In the middle of the basket, we will place a metal drum. Inside that drum, wood will be burned. The hot air will cause the balloon to inflate and take to the skies."

"Ooh, this is all getting very involved!" muttered Dotty.

"Silence while the great professor speaks!" he

snapped. "Then the pilot of the balloon will fly up into the heart of the storm. When lightning strikes here..."

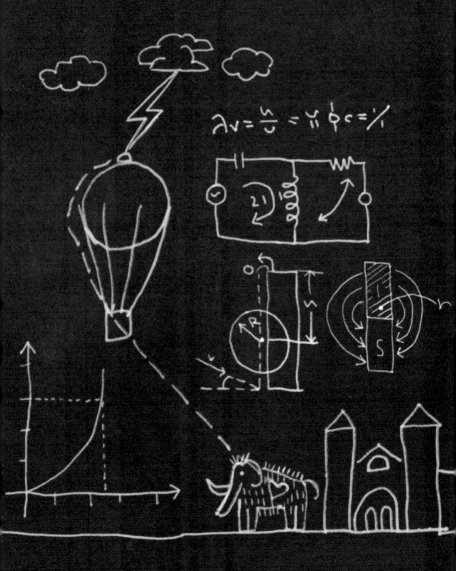

He bashed his chalk against his drawing of the metal helmet.

"...the lightning bolt will travel along this length of copper wire, all the way down through the museum itself. The end of the wire we will have embedded right into—"

But before he could finish his sentence Elsie did it for him: "The mammoth's heart."

"Exactly!" exclaimed the professor. "You're a fast learner, young lady."

Dotty put her hand in the air.

"Yes?" he asked grandly.

"Can I say something?"

"No!" he snapped.

The lady crossed her arms in a sulk.

"So you, Elsie, will steal the thousand silk handkerchiefs, then you and Dotty will sew them together to make the balloon. The tin helmet this Titch character will provide; the basket, metal drum and firewood Elsie can scavenge from the streets. Copper wire I have here from my last experiment. It couldn't be simpler!"

Dotty and Elsie stood there open-mouthed in shock. "Simple" was not the word that sprang to mind.

"So who will be going up in the balloon?" asked Elsie.

The professor grinned a wicked grin. "Not you, child."

"No?"

"No. I need a little person to squeeze through all the nooks and crannies of the museum and thread that copper wire all the way down from the roof to the main hall."

"Are you going up in the balloon, then, Professor?" asked the girl.

"HA! HA! No, child. My infirmity would prevent me from undertaking such a deadly mission."

"So who is?"

The professor's dark eyes fixed on Dotty. Elsie followed his gaze.

"Why is everyone looking at me?" Dotty asked.

"Because you, cleaning woman, will have the

honour of taking on the most dangerous – perhaps deadly – part of the mission.

Flying the hot-air balloon straight into a lightning storm!"

. → ✳ ← .

Chapter 22

THE BEAUTY
OF THE SCHEME

"ME?" exclaimed Dotty.

"YES, YOU!" replied the professor.

"But I'm scared of heights. I even feel wobbly standing on a chair to dust the ceiling."

"Listen to me, woman!" commanded the professor. "What better honour could there be in life than to *DIE* in the name of science?"

"*DIE?*"

"That would be the worst-case scenario."

"I'm too young to die."

The professor peered over his half-moon spectacles to examine the lady. "I beg to differ."

"How dare you!"

"I will go up in the balloon!" offered Elsie.

"No, no, no," began the man. "How on earth

would we get this great fat lump down a chimney?"

"Charming!" exclaimed Dotty. "Now I'm old *and* fat?"

"Don't fret, woman. There is little chance of you falling out and plunging to your death, as I can strap you to the basket."

"That's reassuring," replied the lady.

"Obviously, the real danger is being hit by lightning."

"WHAT?"

"Don't worry. It's a very quick and painless *DEATH*. You will be incinerated in a millisecond. You would barely know what hit you. That's the beauty of the scheme."

"You're nuts."

"Thank you," replied the professor.

"What about Clout?" asked Elsie.

"Yes," mused the man. "The security guard can be very troublesome. We need to somehow make sure he's otherwise engaged."

"I don't think he's engaged, or married," said Dotty.

"It's a figure of speech!" exclaimed the professor.

"Perhaps we could lock him in the cleaning cupboard," suggested the girl.

"That would be perfect," he replied.

"How are we going to get out of here without being seen?" asked Elsie. "The whole museum is swarming with police and guards right now."

"You can climb out of the coal chute, just here…"

The man wheeled himself over to the wall, and revealed a small opening hidden by a box.

Dotty examined the hole. "What about me?" she asked.

"You can try and squeeze yourself up the chute and then I can poke you through by prodding your ample bottom with this broomstick."

"That's very kind of you," replied Dotty sarcastically, "but they ain't looking for me. Just the girl. I think I'll wait a while, and then when the coast is clear go out the door and up the stairs."

"Yes, but don't wait too long, please," replied the professor. "I don't want you cluttering up the place."

"Well, excuse me!"

"Elsie?"

"Yes, Professor?"

"I want you back here at this time tomorrow night with *one thousand* silk handkerchiefs."

"Tomorrow night?"

"Yes, child. No later than nine o'clock tomorrow night. And look here, the air pressure is getting lower…" The man pointed to a barometer on the wall. "We need to be ready for a lightning storm by the end of the week."

"I'll do my best, Professor!" said the girl as she shimmied up the chute.

The professor stared at Dotty for a while.

"Are you still here?" he asked.

Meanwhile, Elsie ran away from the museum as fast as she could. Her mind raced along with her legs. How on earth was she going to steal *one thousand handkerchiefs* in just *twenty-four hours?*

Chapter 23

THE STICKY FINGERS GANG

Elsie knew there was no way she could do this all on her own. So she decided to get some help. Expert help. There was a **legendary** group of tearaways who were the best pickpockets in the whole of London. If only she could find them.

They were named the **Sticky Fingers Gang**.

They were so called because their sticky little fingers would worm their way into the coat pockets of every rich lady and gentleman in London, and then worm their way out with things stuck to them.

Sometimes, it would be nothing more than a half-sucked sweet, a snotty rag or – worst of all – a set of false teeth.

However, at other times their fingers would stick themselves to precious things. Things like **pocket watches, gold coins,** silver-rimmed spectacles, *jewels* and, of course, *silk handkerchiefs.*

The Sticky Fingers Gang

The members of the **Sticky Fingers Gang** were:

JOSEPH, or "BIG JOE", the self-appointed leader. He could pick pockets in his sleep.

ZOE, the real leader. She had been thieving since before she could walk. She was known to readers of *The Times*, who wrote often about her crimes, as the "BABY-FACED BADDY".

NELLIE was better known as "SMELLY NELLIE" as she used her bottom burps to distract her victims.

BELLA, or "LITTLE'UN", was the shortest of the gang. She could barely reach the pockets of the rich ladies and gentlemen of London, so carried a stool around with her to help.

LOTTIE was the baddest of the lot. Pickpocketing was just one of her many crimes. She was wanted by police forces all over England for "duffing up a strongman", "doing a cheesy burp in the face of a nun" and "force-feeding cheese to a nun".

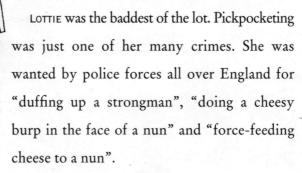

GRACE, or "DANGEROUS GRACE", was the toughest member of the gang. Nobody, but

nobody, crossed GRACE, unless they wanted a wedgie, a Chinese burn or a knuckle sandwich.

GEORGE, or "GUILTLESS GEORGE", looked innocent, but he was anything but. GEORGE disguised himself as a choirboy, which meant he could get away with absolute murder.

"LIGHT-FINGERED FREYA" could steal for England. One day at a fairground, she stole 318 silk handkerchiefs, a barrel of sugar plums and a carousel.

ASIA and ATHENA were sisters, and partners in crime. When they weren't warring with each other, they oversaw a criminal empire that included gambling, extortion and bare-knuckle boxing. They were known as the "SISTERS OF NO MERCY".

Two more sisters rounded off the gang: SANAYA and RIYANA, the "GRUESOME TWOSOME". The pair worked as a team: SANAYA would pose as a sweet flower-seller as her little sister, RIYANA, came round the back and robbed you blind.

The **Sticky Fingers Gang** were legendary figures on the streets of London. Rumours of their exploits swirled across the city. But nobody had a clue where to find them. Except Elsie.

Chapter 24

HANDPRINTS

Elsie had noticed that all over London there were small red handprints on walls and buildings. Once, in the dead of night, she had seen Dangerous Grace put one on the side of St Paul's Cathedral. Elsie was sure it was some kind of secret sign. Some way that the gang communicated with one another. So Elsie had followed Grace as she added more red handprints to the door of 10 Downing Street and even Westminster Abbey.

The handprints looked like arrows, pointing somewhere.

So the night the professor sent Elsie out on her mission she followed the trail all the way to the Houses of Parliament. The last one she found was on the clock tower of Big Ben. It pointed UPWARDS. Surely this

couldn't mean that the **Sticky Fingers Gang's** secret hideout was up there?

There was only one way to find out.

Elsie forced open a tiny door at the base, and climbed up the staircase to the very top of the tower.

"Hello?" called out Elsie as she stepped into the room, the huge clock face looming behind her like a full moon.

BONG! bonged Big Ben.

"Is there anybody there?" asked Elsie.

The girl could swear she heard

scuttling. Maybe it was a rat. Maybe it wasn't.

"Hello? I'm looking for the Sticky Fingers—"

Before she could utter the word "Gang", a cloth bag was thrown over her head.

"HELP!" she screamed.

BONG!

"Shut your face," hissed an unseen voice.

Elsie was hurled into a corner, and she took the bag off her head.

BONG!

A number of children appeared from the shadows.

"What the stink are you doing here?" demanded Big Joe.

BONG!

Zoe pushed him aside. "What are you doing here, little mite? If you want to join our gang, you better think again."

BONG!

The two sisters Sanaya and Riyana pulled Elsie to her feet, then began playing catch with her as if she were a ball.

"Think you're tough enough, do ya?" said the elder one.

"You couldn't punch your way out of a paper bag," added the younger one.

BONG!

Suddenly a shove came from behind. Elsie turned round. It was Grace. The girl yanked Elsie's ear.

"OW!"

"Crybaby!" snorted Grace.

BONG!

George, dressed in his choirboy disguise, stepped forward, wielding a hymn book.

BONK!

He **bashed** it down on the girl's head.

"OW!"

"OOPS!" he chuckled. "I dropped me hymn book!"

BONG!

Now it was Bella's turn. The little girl marched forward and plonked her stool down in front of Elsie. She climbed on it and then poked Elsie in the eye.

PLONK!

"ARGH!"

BONG!

"You ain't seen nothing, right? Or if you like I can do the other eye?"

"NO, NO, PLEASE…" pleaded Elsie.

BONG!

Then Asia and Athena took their turn, using the girl as a punchbag.

"She's about as tough as a plate of jelly."

"She'll be jelly when we're finished with her."

BONG!

Finally, Nellie stepped forward. She wore heavy boots far too big for her and stamped on the little girl's toes.

DONK!

"AAAHHH!"

BONG!

"Not so tough now, are you?" sneered Nellie. "Why don't you go running back to Mummy?"

Elsie took a deep breath and gathered her thoughts.

"Because, like you, I ain't got no mummy. And, please, I need you to help someone, or rather *something*, that don't have one neither…"

"Something?" asked Zoe.

The **Sticky Fingers Gang** all leaned forward.

Elsie grinned from ear to ear. She had them hooked.

Chapter 25

PICKPOCKETING
ON ICE

This was the best bedtime story ever. Up in the clock tower of Big Ben, Elsie told the gang of child thieves the whole tale. Just as with all the orphans at **WORMLY HALL**, the girl had the entire audience enthralled with her storytelling. She told them how the mammoth had been found, about ᴏQueen Victoria's visit and how the plan was to bring it back to life with a bolt of lightning.

"Let me get this straight," began Big Joe. "You need us to help you steal one *thousand* silk handkerchiefs?"

Elsie nodded her head.

"Well," began Zoe, "that should be all in a day's work for the **Sticky Fingers Gang**."

Indeed, it was. And, for Elsie, the most fun day ever.

London had become so cold that winter that the

River Thames had frozen over. Ladies and gentlemen had put on their skates and were spinning across the ice. The perfect setting for a ballet of pickpocketing. Elsie became part of the most infamous child gang in London for the day, as they swooped and twirled and robbed.

D I N G !

A silk handkerchief.

And another.

D I N G !

And another and another and another.

D I N G !

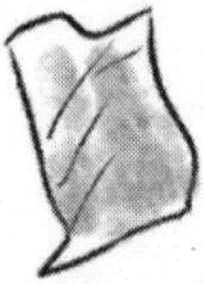

A toffee apple. Yum.

D I N G !

A box of toenail clippings.

Not so yum.

D I N G !

A silk handkerchief.

D I N G !

Another.

D I N G !

A pair of ladies' bloomers?

What were they doing in a

bishop's pocket?

D I N G !

A Scotch egg.

D I N G !

A silk handkerchief.

D I N G !

Another!

D I N G !

A glove.

D I N G !

A flask of brandy.

D I N G !

A silk handkerchief.

The day went like a

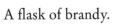

dream.

When two policemen made their way across the ice, Elsie assumed that the fun might be over. Far from it. The **Sticky Fingers Gang** were such skilled thieves they simply stole from the policemen too!

DING!

A cheese-
and-pickle
sandwich.

DING!

A pair of handcuffs.

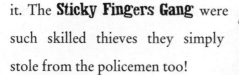

———◆———

After a long and surprisingly tiring day of robbing, the gang and Elsie retired to the clock tower to share out the spoils.

"I've lost count of how many 'kerchiefs we got," said Zoe. "But there must be over a *thousand* 'ere! The rest of the loot we'll give to the poor!"

"Yeah! Us!" snorted George.

All the gang laughed.

As for Elsie, her eyes lit up with joy. With the help of her new friends, she had achieved the impossible. Now she could return to the **NATURAL HISTORY MUSEUM** in triumph.

"Good luck, kid," said Bella.

It was strange being called "kid" by someone considerably smaller than you, but Bella was a feisty one and so Elsie let it pass.

"Goodbye," said Elsie as she threw the haul of handkerchiefs over her shoulder, and hurried out of the clock tower as the bell chimed eight times.

BONG! BONG! BONG!
BONG! BONG! BONG!
BONG! BONG!

The girl had done it.

Chapter 26

◆

A LITTLE PROBLEM

E lsie took the thousand silk handkerchiefs and one pair of ladies' bloomers to the professor. Immediately, he put her and Dotty to work sewing them all together to make something that resembled a balloon. The other bits and pieces the professor asked for were gathered together, and by the end of the week the unlikely trio were ready.

As storm clouds gathered over London, the professor decided that tonight was the night to take to the skies. Now was the moment to see if a prehistoric creature that had been *DEAD* for ten thousand years really could be brought back to life.

But, before all that, there was the little problem of Mr Clout. The security guard patrolled the **NATURAL HISTORY MUSEUM** at night and, although he wasn't the brightest spark, there was every chance he would notice a live mammoth.

CLICK CLACK CLICK CLACK CLICK CLACK!

You could hear him coming a mile off in those hobnailed boots of his.

"Good evening, Mr Clout, sir," said Dotty as she pretended to mop the corridor.

"Why are you still here?" asked the security guard. He took pleasure in treading all over the clean part of the floor, so poor Dotty would have to do it all again. It was way past closing time at the museum, and Clout was used to having the place to himself. Dotty should be long gone by now.

"Yes, Mr Clout, sir. And behold. There is a very stubborn stain on the ceiling."

"The ceiling?"

"Yes."

"How would there be a stain on the ceiling?"

"Maybe someone spilled their tea and it went upwards."

"Upwards?"

"It can happen."

Clout peered up. "I can't see anything."

"Keep looking," urged Dotty.

This was Elsie's cue. Unseen by Clout, she crawled between his legs and began untying his long bootlaces.

Dotty stole glances at the girl to check her progress.

"There is no stain," said the man.

"Keep looking!"

Then Elsie began tying his boots together.

"I think you have finally lost your marbles, madam."

"Keep looking."

Elsie nodded to Dotty. That was her cue. The cleaning lady

whisked up her bucket and slammed it down over Clout's head.

CLANG!

The man couldn't see a thing.

"Who turned the lights out?"

As his boots were tied together, he couldn't get away.

"QUICK!" shouted Elsie, and together she and Dotty bundled him into the cleaning cupboard.

"GET OFF ME!"

They slammed the door.

DONK!

And locked it.

CLICK!

BOOM! BOOM! BOOM!

Clout thumped on the door. "LET ME OUT!"

Outside the door, the pair giggled like naughty schoolchildren.

"TEE! HEE! HEE!"

"Right," said Elsie, "let's get to work."

· →✱← ·

Chapter 27

THUNDERSNOW

Standing on the top of one of the **NATURAL HISTORY MUSEUM'S** towers, Elsie ordered Dotty to listen.

After a few moments, the lady became restless and asked, "What are we listening for?"

"Silence," replied the girl.

"It's quite hard to hear that."

"Shush!" chided Elsie. "Listen, the birds in the trees have gone quiet."

"You're right," replied Dotty.

Above their heads, black clouds rolled across the sky.

"It feels too cold to rain," said the lady.

"It's not going to rain. It's going to snow. *THUNDERSNOW*. You get to know this stuff when you don't have a roof over your head."

"*THUNDERSNOW*? Sounds very dramatic. Do you think it's safe to be all the way up here during a '*THUNDERSNOW*'?"

"No."

"I thought as much. Oh well, if anything happens to me, please tell Titch I love him."

"Oh yes. Titch."

"You'll find him at the Royal Hospital. He lent us this tin helmet."

"Oh yes. I thought it was tiny."

"Good things come in small packages. Now, I want to leave all my earthly goods, my mops, my brushes and my bucket to you, Elsie."

"That's very kind. I'm touched, Dotty. Truly."

"But if I get a job as a cleaning lady in heaven I'll need them back. Understood?"

"Yes. You can have them back any time you want them, either in this world or the next. Now, let's get this fire going."

They turned their attention to their home-made hot-air balloon, which they had assembled by following the professor's instructions.

After a few attempts, they got the wood in the drum burning. Hot air began to rise. Slowly, the balloon of handkerchiefs (and one pair of bloomers) began to inflate. Miraculously, the stitches held firm.

The multicoloured globe grew and grew until it looked big enough to take Dotty's not-inconsiderable weight.

Elsie turned to Dotty. "Now, when I tug on the copper wire three times, that means the other end is stuck right in the mammoth's heart."

"The manmoth's? Yes."

There wasn't time to correct her, so Elsie ploughed on. "Then, and only then, should you launch the balloon into the air. Understand?"

"Yes. Three times." Dotty nodded.

BOOM!

Thunder echoed across the sky.

To the side of the tower was a narrow chimney pipe. It wasn't much wider than a dinner plate. Elsie breathed out all the air she had inside her, and lowered herself feet first down the chimney.

"See you at the bottom," she called up.

"Aren't you forgetting something?" asked Dotty.

Elsie looked up at the lady, confused. "The wire?"

"Oh yes. That would be useful," said Elsie.

"You're as daft as I am!" chuckled Dotty.

She held out the end of the wire and Elsie placed it in her mouth before disappearing down into the darkness. The girl's hands and feet frantically searched the sides for nooks and crevices to hold on to. Eventually, she could see a tiny square of light beneath her. It was the fireplace that opened into the museum director's office.

SQUAWK!

"Argh!" screamed the girl.

Something was attacking her.

Feathers. A beak. Talons.

A bird! It must have been nesting in the chimney stack.

The creature seemed as frightened as she was. Both were flailing around in a desperate attempt to survive.

In all the commotion, Elsie began sliding down at speed.

"AAAHHH!"

she cried.

Chapter 28

A GIANT CATAPULT

What seemed like a split second later, she was lying in a crumpled heap on the floor of Sir Ray Lankester's oak-panelled office. The girl had brought a cloud of soot with her, and she couldn't help coughing and spluttering as she tried to breathe.

"HUH! HUH! HUH!"

As the cloud passed, she found herself face to face with a horned creature.

"NOOO!"

As her hand reached out to stop it attacking her, she realised it was STUFFED. A plinth underneath read PYRENEAN IBEX (not that Elsie could read).

The girl scrambled to her feet. Although everything hurt, she hadn't broken any bones.

Elsie took the copper wire in her hand and tiptoed over to the door of the office.

She rattled the handle. It was locked!

BLAST! That wasn't part of the plan.

There must be a key somewhere in the room. Elsie opened every drawer, turned every box upside down and swept her hands over every shelf, but she couldn't find it anywhere. There was a cupboard of clothes, and she felt in every pocket, but there was no key.

Elsie looked back at the strange horned creature. It looked back at her. The stuffed Pyrenean ibex was the perfect battering ram.

She leaped on to the creature's back and, using her feet to power it along, slammed against the heavy oak door. It barely made a scratch.

BING!

Elsie had an idea. She returned to the cupboard and pulled out a pair of elasticated braces from some trousers that were hanging there. She tied the ends of the braces to the leg of the heavy desk on one side, and to the door handle on the other. Then she moved the ibex into position, with the braces behind its behind. Using all her might, the mite pulled it as far back as she possibly could.

Elsie had created a giant catapult!

When she couldn't hold it for a moment longer, she let go.

TWANG!

The braces shot the ibex across the office. It smashed through the door.

BOOM!

It sent shards of wood flying through the air.

W H I Z Z !

Elsie couldn't help but smile at the destruction she had caused.

She picked up the end of the copper wire and with a smile on her face waltzed through the hole she had made in the door.

Chapter 29

◆

DINO-LADDER

Down in the main hall, the professor was sitting in his wheelchair, staring up at the **ICE MONSTER**. Frozen air was smouldering from the glass tank. Elsie dashed down the steps to join him.

"The ice! It's melting!" she exclaimed.

"Yes, child. I turned off the cooling system," replied the professor. "Otherwise we would never get the end of that copper wire into the creature's heart."

"But what if we bring it back to life and it immediately drowns in the water?"

"I've thought of that, young lady. That's what *THIS* is for!"

From under his wheelchair, he produced a frightening tool that looked halfway between a hammer and an axe.

"A pickaxe?"

"Yes, child. This will break through the glass. Now, are you ready?"

"Ready for what?"

"To dive into the tank, of course."

"Me?"

"Yes, you."

"I can't swim. What if I drown?"

The professor thought for a moment. "Then, urchin, you will be immortalised."

"Immortalised?"

"Yes, immortalised as a short footnote* in the story of how I, the great professor, brought the **ICE MONSTER** back to life. Now climb to the top of the tank."

Elsie looked around the hall. "Have you got a ladder, Professor?" she asked.

The man's expression darkened. "Oops," he replied. "I forgot that."

"Not so great after all, are you?" mused the girl.

The professor gripped the pickaxe tightly.

"I'll find a way," said Elsie.

---

* A footnote is a short note written at the bottom of a page, like this.

She looked around the main hall for something, anything, that could be used as a ladder. Elsie realised that the answer was standing right next to her.

"The *Diplodocus*!" she exclaimed.

The ENORMOUS dinosaur skeleton was towering over her.

"You can climb that?" he asked.

"Yes! I have monkey feet! I'll think of it as a dino-ladder!"

"What a **genius idea** of mine!" announced the professor. "Then, when you reach the tank, you must swim down to the creature's heart."

"I already told you – I can't swim! But I could sink!"

"What do you mean?"

"Professor, may I borrow that pickaxe?"

"Be my guest."

The girl took it from him. It felt really heavy, but she did her best to pretend it wasn't. She marched over to a glass cabinet that housed a rock the size of a football.

CRASH!

She smashed the glass, and heaved out the rock.

"That's a meteorite!" remarked the professor.

"Here you go," she said, passing back the pickaxe. "This meteorite will make me sink."

"What a splendid idea of mine!" he mused.

Elsie placed the end of the copper wire back in her mouth, and picked up the rock. Slowly but surely, her monkey feet began stepping along the bones of the tail.

As if climbing a dinosaur skeleton holding a meteorite weren't hard enough already, it was dark in the museum. The only light was the occasional flash of lightning outside the snow-encrusted windows.

Dino-ladder

"Quickly!" ordered the professor. "We're going to lose the lightning!"

"I'm going as fast as I can," snapped back the girl.

The bones themselves were smooth, which meant it was very easy to slip on them. Elsie took it slowly, letting her toes grip as tightly as they could. In a short while she had reached the skeleton's back. This being a much wider part, she managed to speed up. Now the girl was at the base of the neck, and a very long way up.

Elsie looked down. That was a mistake. It was a very long way down. Instantly she felt dizzy. She shut her eyes. This just made her feel wobblier.

"Why on earth have you stopped, you pathetic, pathetic child?"

Elsie took a deep breath. A bolt of lightning struck just outside the window, illuminating everything for a split second. The girl knew she had to act now. Still holding the meteorite, she took a step forward, and another and another. Soon she was halfway across the skeleton's neck, and within leaping distance of the mammoth's tank.

BOOM!

A roll of thunder roared across the sky. It was so loud that the museum shook a little.

It made Elsie's heart skip a beat, and she lost her footing.

"AAH!" she screamed.

Chapter 30

THE HEART OF THE STORM

E lsie tumbled forward. But, by beautiful chance, the back of her coat hooked on to one of the *Diplodocus* bones. Without even realising quite what had happened, the girl found herself swinging in the air, still miraculously holding on to the meteorite.

"I'm alive!" she exclaimed.

"Yes, I can see that, you foolish child. Now come on, stop dilly-dallying! We haven't got all night."

The girl swung her legs forward and gripped on to the neck bones. With her legs wrapped tightly round the exhibit, she unhooked her coat and swung herself back up using the meteorite for momentum.

The skull of the *Diplodocus* was within

spitting distance of the tank. From there, she LEAPED on to the top.

DOINK!

The tank was freezing, and her toes tingled with the cold.

"Have you found the hatch?" demanded the professor.

Elsie looked ahead. "YES!"

"Unscrew the bolts round the edge."

She put down the meteorite and opened the hatch.

"Now get in, and push the end of the copper wire into the mammoth's heart just where I showed you."

Elsie nodded, picked up the meteorite and plunged down into the icy water.

SPLOSH!

"UH!" she exclaimed. The cold shocked her, and she could hardly breathe. Still holding the meteorite, she sank like a stone. Within a second, she was at the bottom of the tank.

From his wheelchair, the professor frantically pointed out to Elsie where the creature's heart was.

Elsie let go of the meteorite and floated upwards, plunging the end of the copper wire deep into the mammoth's chest. Elsie now felt completely out of breath, and let herself float back up to the top of the tank. Her head bobbing through the hatch, she gasped for air. With her entire body shaking from the cold, she hauled herself up on to the top of the tank. There she lay, soaking wet and shivering, but thankful to still be alive.

"Don't just lie there, child!" the professor called up.

"W-w-what n-n-now?"

"Look outside the window. We're in the middle of a storm. Time is of the essence. You need to tug the wire three times as a signal to Dotty to take off in the hot-air balloon!"

The girl did what she was told.

TUG! TUG! TUG!

Next, Elsie leaped off the tank back on to the *Diplodocus* skeleton. Within moments the length of wire tightened.

"PERFECT!" called out the professor.

Up on the roof of the museum, a cold and miserable Dotty finally got the signal. As fast as she could, she untied the ropes that were holding the basket down, and took to the skies.

WHOOSH!

The lady was flying straight into the *HEART* of the storm.

Soon bolts of lightning were exploding all around her.

BOOM! BOOOM! BOOOOM!

Against her better judgement, she steered the balloon into their path and…

BANG!

…a rush of electricity struck the tin helmet on top of the balloon.

TING!

The copper wire glowed as energy shot through it.

SIZZLE!

"Oh no," whispered Dotty to herself. "I think a bit of wee came out!"

The bolt of lightning sped all the way down the wire, to the tower, down the chimney, across the director's office, along the corridor, round a corner, down the steps and into the tank. The punch of electricity hit the mammoth straight in the heart.

They had done it.

Or had they?

The professor and Elsie looked on as nothing happened.

Nothing at all.

Nought.

Zero.

Zilch.

"NO! It hasn't worked!" raged the professor.

"Wait," whispered the girl. "I can sense something's changed."

Elsie put her hand up to the glass, and looked deep into the mammoth's eye.

Unless her mind was playing tricks on her, she was sure the creature was staring straight back at her.

Then the most incredible thing happened.

It blinked.

"Did you see that, Professor?" exclaimed Elsie.

"What?"

"It blinked!"

In his wheelchair, the professor began shaking with excitement. He took a deep breath, before proclaiming,

"IT'S ALIVE!"

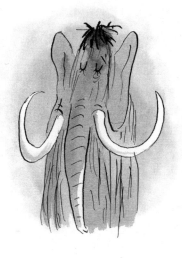

Chapter 31

——◆——

DON'T LOOK
ROUND

Elsie threw her arms round the man, and hugged him tight.

"We did it!" she exclaimed.

"Yes! I did it!" he purred. "Now release me this instant."

The celebration had come too soon, because the mammoth had started thrashing around inside the tank!

It let out a cry, muffled by the water. **"HOOO!"**

If they didn't get the creature out, and soon, it would drown.

The professor wheeled himself over and lifted the pickaxe above his head, before smashing it against the glass.

CRUNCH!

A patchwork of cracks appeared in the glass.

"**HOO!**" cried the animal under the water.

The creature lurched forward and hit the glass with its tusks.

SMASH!

All at once, the glass fell away, and icy water flooded the main hall, sweeping Elsie off her feet and the professor off his wheels.

SWISH!

"Argh!" screamed the girl as she was hurled against the stone staircase.

DOOF!

The professor had banged his head badly, and was now lying face down in the water, his wheelchair on its side a few feet away from him.

"Professor! Professor?" pleaded the girl.

Suddenly, the old man's eyes opened, and then widened.

"Whatever you do," he began, "don't look round."

Of course, there is nothing like being told not to look round to make you look round.

Slowly, the girl turned her head.

Just behind her was the mammoth, rearing up on its hind legs.

"HOO!"

The instant those legs crashed down, Elsie and the professor would be dead.

· ⟶ ✳ ⟵ ·

Chapter 32

◆

KNOCKED
AWAKE

Elsie wrenched the professor out of the way just in time before the mammoth's giant feet thumped on the floor.

SMASH!

"HOOO!" it cried.

"Why is it trying to kill us?" yelled the girl. "We just brought it back to life!"

"It's a wild beast!" replied the professor. "It's not going to say 'thank you'! Now, for goodness' sake, HELP ME!"

Elsie grabbed the old man under his armpits, and pulled him up the huge stone staircase that led upwards through the main hall. When the pair were a few steps up, the mammoth spun round and smashed into the *Diplodocus* skeleton.

CRASH!

Elsie ducked as the giant bones came thundering down all around them.

WHACK!

One struck the professor across the forehead, and knocked him out cold.

DOOF!

"PROFESSOR!" shouted Elsie. The girl slapped the old man across the face to wake him. When that didn't work, she dragged him further up the stairs to escape the animal.

The mammoth began pacing towards them. It reached the bottom of the steps just as Elsie had managed to drag the professor halfway up.

Surely the creature could not follow them up the stairs?

To Elsie's horror, it could.

"NO!" cried the girl.

Unsteadily, the mammoth rested its giant feet on the first step, then the second, then the third.

THUD! THUD! THUD!

In a rush to flee further up the steps, Elsie dropped the professor. His head hit the stone.

CLONK!

Normally, this would have been enough to knock someone out, but as he was already knocked out it actually had the opposite effect. It knocked him

awake.

"Ouch!" he cried.

"You're awake!" replied Elsie.

"Have I missed anything?"

"We're still going to die."

"Oh no."

"HOOO!"

The mammoth let out its distinctive cry again, its trunk aloft and its sharp tusks now inches from the pair's faces. The creature whisked its head back, as if getting ready to impale them.

"HELP!" cried the girl.

Just then, there was a mighty smash overhead.

KERBANG!

Dotty had crashed her hot-air balloon straight through the newly repaired stained-glass window of the main hall.

SMASH!

It descended at speed through the hall. The bottom of the wicker basket struck the mammoth hard on the head.

BOOF!

"HOOO!"

This cry sounded different. Like a cry of fear. The mammoth scuttled back down the steps and across the main hall to hide under the shadow of an archway.

Meanwhile, the basket landed with a thud and skidded across the floor, until it came to a sudden stop against the wall.

CRASH!

"OOF!" said Dotty. As the cleaning lady scrambled to her feet, she surveyed the scene. There were the scattered dinosaur bones, the shards of glass from the window and the tank, the pools of icy water, the broken basket and the hot-air balloon made of a thousand handkerchiefs and one pair of bloomers strewn across the floor.

"Naughty manmoth!" exclaimed Dotty. "Look at this mess! It will take me all night to clear this up!"

"Idiotic woman! That is the least of our troubles!" interrupted the professor. "The beast just tried to kill us. Isn't that right, Elsie? Elsie?"

The professor looked over his shoulder, but the girl had gone.

"Elsie?" he called. "ELSIE?"

Unknown to him, the girl had made her way over to the archway to take a closer look at the mammoth.

"KEEP BACK, YOU FOOLISH CHILD!" shouted the professor.

"Shush!" shushed the girl. "You're frightening it."

"Whatever you do, don't touch it!" shouted the professor.

The brave little girl ignored him, and reached out her hand to meet the creature's trunk. It was the only part of the mammoth that was not hidden in the darkness.

First, its trunk performed a little dance around the girl's hand, like a snake being charmed. Then Elsie held out her hand flat, and something magical happened. The prehistoric met the modern.

The two touched.

Chapter 33

——◆——

WHAT'S IN
A NAME?

"It's beautiful," whispered the girl.

Little by little, Elsie was gaining the creature's trust. At first, her hand only touched the end of the mammoth's trunk for a moment. The animal would retreat, before the girl would try again. Then, as gently as she could, so as not to startle it, she began stroking the fur on its trunk. The animal pressed against her a little. Elsie took this as a prompt to continue. So she started doing longer strokes, branching out to pats on its cheeks. The animal recoiled. Elsie realised her hand was too near the mammoth's eye, so moved it further away. She even tried a tickle under the chin, because stray cats always liked that. Just like the stray cats, the mammoth *PURRED* a little.

Behind Elsie, the two grown-ups were edging closer

to take a look, the professor back in his wheelchair and Dotty pushing him. Neither one could believe their eyes.

"It's extraordinary," muttered the professor. "There's a special connection between them."

"Like me and me favourite mop," added Dotty.

"I think it just misses its ma, that's all," whispered the girl. Then she spoke to the mammoth. "Don't you worry. I'll look after you. I promise."

Although the animal couldn't understand the words, it did understand the feeling. Elsie spoke in soothing tones and, with all the strokes and tickles too, the mammoth could sense the girl's kindness.

"This is history being made!" boasted the professor. "History all about me! The greatest scientist of the age. Nay! Of all time!"

Dotty rolled her eyes. "Here we go again."

"I, and I alone, have brought the dead back to life! I am the real-life Doctor Frankenstein, and this is my monster!"

The professor lifted his hand to touch the mammoth. Instantly, the creature retreated into the darkness.

"It's not a monster!" replied Elsie. She slid under the mammoth for a quick look. "It's a SHE! And she's not yours. She's not anybody's! We've set her free!"

"I don't care if this thing likes me or not!"

"It seems awful calling it a 'thing'!" chimed in Dotty. "She needs a name."

Elsie and Dotty thought for a moment.

"WOOLLY!" exclaimed the girl.

"You can't call it 'Woolly'!" replied the professor.

"Why not?" asked Dotty.

"No, no, no," scoffed the man. "It's boring! Far too obvious. It's like calling a dog 'Doggy'!"

"That's a good name for a dog," replied Dotty. "I wish I'd thought of that. I called mine 'Catty'."

"Heaven help us!" said the professor.

"Well, let's vote on it," steamed in Elsie.

"Women don't have the vote," snapped the man.

The girl grimaced. "Not yet, no, but we can vote on this."

"How?" he asked.

"Because I say so. Now, hands up if you want to name this mammoth 'Woolly'," said Elsie.

The two ladies put a hand up each.

"Looks like you're outvoted, Professor," sniggered the girl.

"DARN AND BLAST!" he thundered.

"What did you want to call her?" asked Dotty.

"I wanted to name it after me!"*

"Well, that's a surprise," mused the lady.

---

* *Many things are named after the people who made them famous. For example, the wellington boot is named after the Duke of Wellington.*

"'The professor'?" asked Elsie, her face screwed up in confusion.

"No, no, no. The Professor Osbert Bertram Cuthbert Farnaby Beverly Smith mammoth!"

"That's a mouthful," remarked Dotty. "No. It would take too long to say. She's called Woolly, and that's that."

"Not fair!" he snapped.

"And don't try and touch her, Oswald Barnaby Custard Beatrice whatever your stupid name is. She doesn't like you," said Elsie. "WOOLLY? WOOLLY?"

The girl held out her hand again, and slowly the animal's trunk uncurled out of the darkness. She touched the tip, and ran her hand down it again.

"She must be peckish!" remarked Dotty. "I'd be peckish if I'd been asleep for ten thousand years. Shall I make her a nice cheese-and-pickle sandwich?"

"Mammoths don't eat cheese-and-pickle sandwiches," snapped the professor.

---

* Sandwiches are named after the fourth Earl of Sandwich, whose idea they were.

"Ham-and-pickle?"

"NO! They don't have ham-and-pickle either. They don't have any type of sandwiches. Sandwiches* weren't invented until a hundred years ago."

"All right, brainbox. What do manmoths eat, then?" pressed Dotty.

"They are herbivores!" replied the professor.

"Herbie-who?" spluttered the lady.

"Grass! Leaves! Plants! And lots of them!"

"Well, we'd better get her to the park, then," said Elsie.

The professor shook his head. "We can't take this creature outside into the world!"

"Why ever not?" asked the girl.

"BECAUSE IT BELONGS IN A CAGE."

Chapter 34

CAGE

"A cage?" exclaimed the girl. "You can't put Woolly in a cage!"

The mammoth must have picked up on the conflict between the two humans, and hid behind Elsie. (Hid as much as a mammoth can hide behind a little girl. Which is not very much.)

"Yes, a cage. It's the safest place for a dangerous creature like this," he replied. With that, he wheeled himself over to a spot near the main entrance to the hall, and pulled a lever.

A trapdoor opened and a huge metal cage rose up out of the floor.

CLUNK! CLANK! CLINK!

The noise echoed around the hall, causing the mammoth to move further away into the darkness.

With a huge THUD, the trapdoor closed.

"Look!" said the professor proudly. "I have food and water for the beast in there." He indicated two troughs on the side of the cage.

"It's barely bigger than she is!" protested the girl.

"It will be safe in there. Trust me."

Elsie was glowing with fury. "I don't trust you one bit. That wasn't part of the plan."

"Did you really believe I would set this ten-thousand-year-old creature free to roam the streets of London?"

"But I, I, er…" For once, Elsie was lost for words.

Dotty stood by her side. "All this girl wanted to do was set Woolly free!" she exclaimed.

"The monster is free," began the professor. "**Free** from the ice. **Free** from the grave of history. **Free** to live out the rest of its days in this cage. But it won't be **free** to see her. Oh no! I'll be able to open my very own prehistoric zoo. The only one in existence. **I'll be able to charge a fortune.** A hundred pounds a view. People will come from all over the world to see **the monster.**"

"YOU'RE THE MONSTER!" seethed Elsie. "I would never have done all this if I'd known this was your plan!"

"I assumed as much, child. Which is why I thought I would keep this part of the plan a secret until you outlived your usefulness. Thank you. And goodnight. You may go."

"You can't do this to us!" yelled the girl.

"I just have," was the reply. The professor rolled himself across the hall to the cage, and pulled out a handful of grass. He shook it in his hand. *"Come on, Professor Osbert Bertram Cuthbert Farnaby Beverly Smith mammoth. Dinnertime!"*

The mammoth did not budge, and the professor's face soured. From a leather pouch on his wheelchair, he produced a pistol.

"Maybe this will persuade it," he said as he pointed it at the mammoth.

Elsie stood right in front of Woolly.

"You'll have to kill me first!" she said.

Chapter 35

❖

ETERNAL SLEEP

"Oh, and me!" added Dotty, taking up a slightly safer position right behind the girl.

"Why would you bring this beautiful creature back to life only to murder her?" demanded Elsie.

"This gun fires darts, not bullets," replied the professor. "They're tipped with a powerful sleeping drug that can knock an elephant out in seconds."

"And what about a person?" asked Elsie, feeling more than a little frightened.

The professor smirked to himself. "It would put a human being to sleep forever."

"So you're going to kill us until we're *DEAD*?" asked Dotty.

"That doesn't really make sense, but, in short, yes," he replied, now pointing his pistol straight at her.

"You evil, evil man," said the girl.

"Thank you," he replied.

"If you have to kill me, so be it," said Elsie. "Woolly can't be kept in a cage for the rest of her life."

"You can't stop me, child."

"Maybe I can," said Dotty.

The lady reached beside her for what was left of the hot-air balloon's basket. With all her might, she shoved it across the floor of the main hall towards the professor.

W H I Z Z !

He quickly spun his wheelchair out of the way, and the basket smashed against the wall.

DOOF!

"You'll have to do better than that," he purred. "Much better."

Elsie picked up one of the *Diplodocus* bones that the mammoth had helpfully rearranged across the floor.

"How about this?" she asked, wielding it in his direction.

"Goodbye forever, urchin," he said, pointing the gun at her chest.

The professor pulled the trigger.

PPPFFFTTT!

Thinking fast, Elsie whisked the bone up to defend herself. The dart stuck into it.

TWANG!

"HA HA!" said the girl.

"Don't you worry, child. I have plenty more darts. Plenty more."

Immediately, he began fumbling in his pouch for another. This bought precious time for the pair. Elsie picked up one side of the balloon.

"QUICK!" she shouted to Dotty. The lady followed suit and they ran towards the professor and threw it over him like a huge sheet.

WHOOSH!

"GET THIS THING OFF ME!"

he yelled from underneath the one thousand silk handkerchiefs and one pair of ladies' bloomers.

"NOW BASH HIM OVER THE HEAD WITH THE DINO BONE!"

shouted Dotty.

Elsie had never bashed anyone over the head before, and certainly not with a dinosaur bone, but there was a first time for everything. The girl rushed over, and then stood beside the flailing figure, unsure what to do next.

"WHACK HIM!" ordered Dotty.

Elsie did what she was told.

DONK!

"OW!" yelped the professor.

"Not hard enough!" complained the lady.

"YES, IT WAS!" came a muffled voice from under the balloon.

"HARDER!"

Another whack.

DOONNK!

"OWW!"

"Still harder!" said Dotty.

"NOOOO!" pleaded the professor.

"Third time lucky," muttered Elsie. With all her might, she whacked the man over the head with her bone.

DOOONNNKKK!

This time the professor did not cry out, but instead slumped in his wheelchair.

SLUD!

"That might have been **too** hard," remarked Dotty.

Elsie looked up at the massive hole in the stained-glass window that Dotty had crashed through. The snowstorm had passed, and night was slowly becoming day.

"We need to get Woolly out of here," said Elsie. "And fast."

They looked around, but the mammoth had gone.

"Oh no," said Dotty. "We've only gone and lost her!"

Chapter 36

MISSING MAMMOTH

Y ou might think a mammoth would be too big to lose, but that was exactly what Elsie and Dotty had done.

"WOOLLY!" called out the girl.

"I'm not sure she's going to come running like a dog," said the lady.

"She can't have gone far."

Elsie looked at the floor of the museum for any mammoth footprints. There was a trail of them that went all the way up the steps.

"She's gone upstairs!" said the girl.

"Oh no," said Dotty. "I cleaned the upper floors last night."

"Why would she have gone up there?"

The lady thought for a moment.

"Maybe she wanted to see the butterfly collections?"

Elsie shook her head. "Come on, let's go upstairs and look."

Apart from the sound of the wind, swirling in from the broken windows, the museum was eerily silent. The pair followed the footprints all the way up to the top floor, where they came to a stop outside the library.

"I didn't know manmoths could read," remarked Dotty.

Elsie shook her head in disbelief. "Where to next?"

"Well, this is the top floor of the museum. She can't have got all the way up to..."

Before Dotty could say "the roof", there was a deafening sound from above.

CRASH!

The pair looked at each other. No words were needed.

BOOM!

Debris started falling from the ceiling.

"How do we get on to the roof from here?" asked the girl.

"This is the only way. Follow me."

They scrambled up a flight of steps.

Ahead of them they could see a mammoth-sized hole in the wall.

"More mess!" muttered Dotty.

When they reached the hole, they saw the most startling sight. The mammoth was standing on the roof, looking across London's skyline as dawn was breaking.

It would have been a magnificent scene to paint, but sadly there just wasn't time right now.

"WOOLLY!" cried the girl as she stepped out on to the roof. "What are you doing up here?"

The animal chose to do the same selective hearing trick on Elsie that the girl did on grown-ups. She kept staring forward.

"What is she looking at?" asked Dotty.

Elsie followed the creature's gaze. "The Royal Albert Hall? Hyde Park? Lord's Cricket Ground?"

"Do manmoths like cricket?" asked Dotty.

"I don't imagine so."

"No. Hard to hold the bat with a trunk," she mused.

"What's beyond Lord's?" asked Elsie. She hadn't ventured too far out of central London.

"Hampstead Heath?" replied Dotty.

"Beyond that?"

"Highgate Hill."

"Beyond that?"

"I dunno. I never did History at school."

"Geography!"

"That neither!"

Elsie stood beside Woolly, and patted her side gently. "What are you looking at, my friend?" she whispered to the animal, but the mammoth just kept staring straight ahead.

She lifted her trunk to the sky and let out a
mournful cry.

"**HOO!**"

The girl wrapped her arms round the animal to give
her a hug. The mammoth leaned towards Elsie, and
wrapped her trunk round her.

"Not too close to the edge, please, Woolly," she
said, guiding the mammoth back.

Dotty took a step forward.

"It's an awfully long way down!" said the lady.

"There's the robber!" came a shout from
the ground.

Elsie looked down over the edge of the roof.

There was a whole squad of policemen looking
up at them.

———— ◆ ————

Chapter 37

BANG! BANG! BANG!

"**G**ET DOWN FROM THERE!" came a shout.

Elsie knew that voice. It was the head of the police, Commissioner Barker.

"We've had reports of a large lady in a hot-air balloon crashing through the window of the museum."

"It wasn't me!" called Dotty. "It must have been another large lady flying a hot-air balloon!"

"Pull the other one! It's got bells on it!" came the shout from below.

Elsie was shaking. "Dotty! If they catch us, they'll lock us up, and goodness knows what they'll do to Woolly."

"Oh dear. Oh dear, oh

dear. Oh dear, oh dear, oh dear."

"Please stop saying 'oh dear' over and over again. We need to find a way out of here or we're all done for!"

"Oh dear!" The poor lady couldn't help it. "Oh dear, I didn't mean to say 'oh dear'. Oh dear."

"YOU HAVE TEN SECONDS TO GIVE YOURSELVES UP OR WE WILL BE FORCED TO OPEN FIRE!"

barked Barker. Then there was the sound of rifles being cocked.

CLICK! CLICK! CLICK!

"Have you ever ridden a horse?" asked Elsie.

"No."

"A donkey?"

"No."

"TEN!"

"Ever sat on a carousel at the fair?"

"Oh no."

"Me neither. But how hard can it be?"

"NINE!"

"Are you thinking what I'm thinking?" asked Dotty.

"EIGHT!"

"What am I thinking?" replied the girl.

"SEVEN!"

"That you're going to ride on my back?"

"SIX!"

"I'm **not** thinking that," said Elsie.

"FIVE!"

"Oh dear."

"FOUR!"

"I'm thinking we're going to have to ride this mammoth out of here."

"THREE!"

"Oh dear."

"TWO!"

"Yes, I know. Oh dear. But right now we don't have much choice."

"ONE!"

"Yes!" agreed Dotty.

The pair grabbed hold of a tusk each, and with all their might forced the mammoth backwards, away from the edge of the roof.

"FIRE AT WILL!" came the bellow from down below.

Gunshots crackled in the dawn sky.

. ⇥ ✳ ⇤ .

Chapter 38

A SLAP ON THE BOTTOM

BANG! BANG! BANG! BANG! BANG! BANG! BANG! BANG! BANG! BANG! BANG! BANG!

"**HOO!**" The mammoth started wailing. Being a prehistoric creature, she had never heard gunfire before. She began flailing around in fear.

"**AH!**" cried Dotty.

"**HOLD ON!**" yelled Elsie.

The pair gripped on to the tusks as tightly as they could.

"**DON'T LET GO!**"

shouted the girl.

If they did, they would be hurled from the roof, and become human jam on the ground below.

BANG! BANG! BANG! BANG! BANG! BANG! BANG! BANG! BANG! BANG! BANG!

The mammoth retreated through the hole in the wall she had created. Now she was inside the museum, dragging her two new friends with her.

Safely inside, Elsie let go of the tusk, and fell to the floor.

DOOF!

Meanwhile, Dotty was being thrown around like a rag doll.

"HELP!" she shrieked.

"LET GO!"

"WHAT?"

"I SAID 'LET GO'!"

Finally, Dotty did so, and fell face down.

BOOF!

"This floor needs a good polish," she remarked.

"There isn't time for that!" said the girl. "We need to escape!"

BANG! BANG! BANG! BANG! BANG! BANG! BANG! BANG! BANG! BANG! BANG! BANG!

"RELOAD!" ordered Barker.

The gunfire had ended for a moment, and the mammoth stopped flailing around. The girl patted the animal, and stroked the fur on her trunk, which helped calm her down.

"Woolly, I will never let anything bad happen to you, I promise," she whispered. "But you're going to have to trust me, all right? I know you're not going to like it at first, but this is the only way out of here. Now, Dotty, give me a leg-up!"

"Are you sure this is a good idea?"

"No, but it's our only idea."

Elsie put her hand on the lady's shoulder. Dotty cupped her own hands, and the girl used them as a step to climb on to the animal's back.

"Good mammoth!" said Elsie. The girl gripped the animal's flanks with her legs, and used two handfuls of fur as reins. To her surprise, the mammoth didn't buck, or even let out a sound. In fact, she immediately seemed comfortable with this new arrangement. Elsie reached out her hand to help Dotty up.

"COME ON!" ordered the girl.

The lady was getting on a bit, and struggled to heave herself up. Once she had, Dotty couldn't swing her leg over the animal like Elsie. Instead, she lay face down on Woolly's back, her head buried in the animal's fur. It all looked rather undignified.

"Are you comfortable?" asked Elsie.

"Of course not," replied Dotty. "But I think we'd best get a move on."

"If you're sure."

The girl had seen the great and the good ride their horses through the parks of London, which had given her some idea of how it might be done. So she dug her heels into the animal's sides, tugged on her fur and ordered, *"GIDDY UP!"*

Unfortunately, the mammoth didn't move an inch.

"Oh dear," muttered Dotty unhelpfully.

"Dotty?" asked the girl.

"Yes, child?"

"Would you mind giving our prehistoric friend a little PAT on the bottom?"

"If you're sure."

"As gently as you can, just to see if we can make her move."

"Understood."

Then the lady did as she was asked. She raised her hand a touch, and brought it down on the animal's rear end.

SLAP!
"HOO!"

Instead of a nice gentle trot, the mammoth went straight into a gallop.

"WOO-HOO!" cried Elsie as they charged down the stairs.

Chapter 39

AN UNWELCOME SIGHT

Poor Dotty was thrown up and down with each step the mammoth took.

POUND! POUND! POUND!

"OOF! OOF! OOF!"

As they rode down the staircase on Woolly's back,

Elsie and Dotty were met by an unwelcome sight. The professor had come to. Now he was sitting up straight in his wheelchair at the bottom of the stairs, with the dart gun in his hand.

"You should have hit me harder," he purred.

"I wish I had now," replied Elsie.

Because of her undignified position, slumped over the back of the animal with her face buried in Woolly's fur, Dotty was struggling to keep up with what was going on.

"Oh no, not him again!" she remarked.

"Prepare to *DIE*. Both of you," said the professor. He pointed the gun straight at Dotty's bottom.

A deafening sound came from the huge wooden doors behind him.

BOOOM!

"What's that?" asked Elsie.

"That will be the policemen battering their way in," replied the professor.

BOOOM!

And another.

"There's just enough time to kill you, and claim this monster as mine!"

BOOOM!

Another!

"I'm going to enjoy this!"

BOOOOOOOMMM!

Behind the professor, the doors to the museum burst open.

SMASH!

Shards of wood flew into the air.

The battering ram, which was a huge log on wheels, was going at such a speed the policemen couldn't stop it.

WHIRR!

It sped right towards the professor, whacking the back of his wheelchair.

BOOF!

"ARGH!"

The force of the whack sent the man shooting across the floor.

WHIZZ!

He crashed straight into a glass case of stuffed apes.

BANG!

The professor was thrown up out of his wheelchair...

POW!

...and smashed through the glass.

SHATTER!

Knocked out cold, he
landed right between two
of the apes. With his mouth
wide open, he could have
passed for one of them.

All this commotion startled the mammoth, who let
out a gigantic…

"HHHHOOOO!"

Elsie patted the animal, and said, "Whoa there,
Woolly!"

It was no use; the mammoth began charging
towards the line of policemen at the door. The officers
all cried out…

"HELP!"

"NOOO!"

"I DON'T BELIEVE IT!"

"IT'S ALIVE!"

"THE ICE THINGUMMY!"

"A REAL-LIFE MONSTER!"

"I AIN'T DONE NO TRAINING FOR MONSTERS!"

"I WANT PAID OVERTIME FOR THIS!"

"MY MA SAID I HAD TO BE BACK FOR BREAKFAST!"

…as they leaped out of the way of the rampaging beast.

Elsie and Dotty held on for their lives as the mammoth galloped out of the museum.

"AFTER THEM, YOU FOOLS!" snarled Barker. "THAT MONSTER IS THE PROPERTY OF THE QUEEN! WE MUST BRING IT BACK ALIVE OR DEAD!"

Chapter 40

❖

CHOCOLATE
BALLS

Woolly was way too fast for the policemen. By the time they had scrambled to their feet, the mammoth was long gone. The creature galloped out of the grounds of the **NATURAL HISTORY MUSEUM**, and charged down the road.

"HOO!"

Try as she might, Elsie could not get the animal to slow down. Poor Dotty was thrown around on the back of the mammoth.

"OOF! OOF! OOF!"

London was waking up, and a handful of market stallholders were wheeling their produce along the snow-covered roads.

"Mind me plums!" shouted one as his barrow of fruit was trampled underfoot.

"Watch me nuts!" yelled another as his roasted chestnuts were sent flying.

"You've crushed my chocolate balls!" hollered a familiar voice.

"That must be Raj," remarked Dotty.

"Who?" asked Elsie.

"Raj! He sells sweets at the market here," replied Dotty. She called out to him. **"HELLO, RAJ!"**

The man smiled and waved. "Oh! Hello, Miss Dotty, my favourite customer! I have some half-chewed liquorice on special offer today!"

"I CAN'T STOP, RAJ!"

"And feel free to come back with that huge furry long-nosed donkey of yours for a sugar lump."

"SHE'S A MANMOTH!"

"She's very big for a moth!"

Still the mammoth galloped through the snow.

"HOOO!" she cried.

"Where's she taking us?" asked Dotty.

"I don't know!" replied Elsie. "But, wherever we're going, we're going to get there fast!"

With some difficulty, Dotty lifted her head to see for herself.

"North!" she exclaimed. "We're heading north!"

"Always north!" replied the girl.

Up ahead, Elsie saw the sandwich-board man she'd met outside the NATURAL HISTORY MUSEUM. On spotting the mammoth charging towards him, he shouted, "THE BEAST IS ALIVE! THE END IS NIGH!"

"Your end will be nigh if you don't get out of the way!" shouted Elsie.

By tugging on the mammoth's fur, the girl just

managed to make her swerve past him.

"THE END IS NOT QUITE NIGH!" he shouted as they passed.

"Woolly's going to trample someone to death if we're not careful," said Elsie. "We need to get her off the streets, hide her somewhere."

"I know the perfect place," replied Dotty.

"Where?"

"The Royal Hospital. It's not far. It's where Titch lives. He'll help us."

"How do we get there?"

"Can you steer?"

"A little bit."

"Then steer right."

The girl tugged on the fur on the mammoth's right side, and the animal veered right.

"But, Dotty, we can't just turn up there with a mammoth!"

The lady was stumped by this. "Oh yes, you're

right. I'm pretty sure they only treat old soldiers. Not animals."

"Prehistoric animals!"

"Yes. I imagine they aren't welcome."

"Someone might tell on us."

"We have to disguise her somehow!" said the girl.

"We could shave her and say she's an elephant."

"Hold on!"

"I am holding on, love! For dear life!"

"I've got an idea."

Elsie steered the mammoth down a dingy backstreet. Just ahead was a laundry where a number of sheets were hanging up to dry.

"We just need to borrow these sheets."

"Whatever for?"

"You'll see."

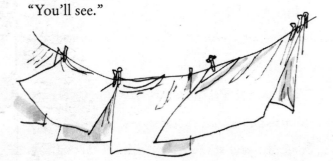

Chapter 41

GOOD EYE

"**I**T'S A WHAT?" roared the guard at the gate of the Royal Hospital. He was a fearsome old soldier, a sergeant major no less, with a chest full of medals on his scarlet coat. He sported a monocle on his left eye, and an eyepatch on his right.

"It's a brand-new top-secret tank!" replied Elsie, gesturing at the mammoth hidden under some sheets.

"BALDERDASH!"

"It's not balderdash! It's a brand-new weapon. For Private Thomas," added Dotty.

"Titch Thomas?"

"Yes, that's him! The shortish one."

"Shortish is an understatement!" chortled the sergeant major. "Titch

267

is so ᴛɪɴʏ he gets mistaken for a toy soldier! Ha! Ha!"

Dotty started to look angry. She didn't appreciate hearing the love of her life spoken about in this manner. "He may be small, but he is perfectly formed!"

"Titch is seventy-three if he's a day," replied the sergeant major. "And his feet wouldn't reach the pedals! What on earth does he need this contraption for?"

"That's top secret, isn't it?" answered Elsie. "If we told you, it wouldn't be top secret."

The old soldier did not look convinced. "Who are you, anyway?"

"That's top secret too!" replied the girl.

"Now open this gate!" ordered Dotty.

"HOO!" went the mammoth. From under the sheet, she raised her trunk. The sergeant major was becoming increasingly suspicious.

Elsie and Dotty looked at each other nervously.

"What was that?" demanded the sergeant major.

"That?" asked Dotty.

"Yes, that!"

"Erm, um, well…" began Elsie. "It was its cannon thing, just lifting up."

She pushed down on the trunk, and Woolly let out another **"HOO!"**

"It just said something!" snarled the sergeant major.

"No, it didn't!"

"Yes, it did!"

"Didn't!"

"Did!"

"It was me!" chimed in Dotty.

"I was looking at you the whole time," said the old soldier.

"From the good eye?"

"Yes! From the good eye! Your face didn't move."

"Well," began Dotty. "That's because…"

"Spit it out, woman!"

"That's because the sound came from… my botty."

"Your botty, madam?"

. ⚹ .

Chapter 42

——◆——

BACK-DOOR
BARRAGE

"It was a botty burp!" explained Dotty.

"I can't smell anything!" protested the sergeant major, pointing his nose towards the lady and sniffing the air.

"Count yourself lucky!" chimed in Elsie, continuing the lie by wafting the air in front of her screwed-up face. "POOH! IT'S A REAL STINKER."

"How utterly uncouth," huffed the old soldier. "I had no idea that ladies could even, for want of a more polite expression, unleash a gas attack."*

"Sadly, it happens," mused Dotty.

"HOO!"

"There my bottom goes again!"

---

* Other military terms for breaking wind the sergeant major could have used include: one-gun salute, bottom blast, invisible grenade, dirty bomb, back-door barrage, attack from the rear.

"HOOOOO!"

"Oops, and again!"

The sergeant major's face turned a shade of beetroot.

"Madam, do you have any control over your, for want

of a more polite expression, rear gun?"

"HOOOO!"

"It seems not," replied Dotty. "Dotty's gotty a

grotty botty."

Elsie could feel the mammoth becoming more and more restless. "Please let us through before she lets another one go!"

"Most irregular!" muttered the old soldier. He raised the gate at once, and saluted as the three unlikely visitors passed through into the grounds of the Royal Hospital.

"Thank you so much," said Elsie.

"HOOOO!"

"Naughty bottom!" called out Dotty, slapping her own rear end.

Just as they led the mammoth across the lawn, she stopped. With her trunk, she snuffled under the snow, and began to munch on the frozen grass.

"RUMPH! RUMPH! RUMPH!"

Having not eaten for ten thousand years, the animal was hungry. As much as the pair tried to keep moving, the mammoth was staying put. From under the sheets she munched and munched and munched. She must have eaten a ton of grass before she was full.

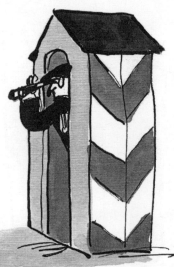

From his sentry post, the sergeant major looked on. He raised a telescope to his good eye, and spied on the strange goings-on in the grounds of the Royal Hospital.

"Just refuelling!" called out Elsie.

The old soldier shook his

head. "Ruddy strange sort of tank."

"Yes, it doubles up as a lawnmower," said Dotty.

Just as the pair thought they might have got away with it, the inevitable happened. The animal laid a mammoth poop.

PPPFFFT!
THUD!

The prehistoric poop plopped on to the snow. It was mammoth both in origin and size, large and brown and steaming.

"Just testing the brand-new weaponry," explained Elsie.

"It's a stink bomb," added Dotty.

"Don't worry!" began Elsie. "It's not explosive!" Then she added under her breath, "I think."

"Well, you can't leave it there on the lawn!" roared the sergeant major.

"What do you want us to do with it?" asked Elsie.

"Put it back in the chute."

The pair looked at the back end of the mammoth.

"I'm not sure that's going to work," said Dotty.

"I'd say it's more of an exit than an entrance."

"Well, pick it up, then!" he ordered.

"Me?" asked Dotty. She'd been a cleaning lady for forty years and had dealt with all kinds of unspeakable mess, but this was beyond beyond.

"Yes, you," said Elsie.

The lady gave the little girl a stern look.

"Don't dilly-dally, woman. Get on with it!" bellowed the sergeant major.

Reluctantly, Dotty bent down. Holding her nose as far away from the hot steaming pile as possible, the lady scooped it up in her hands. She stood up and held it away from her as far as her arms would allow.

"At last!" called out the sergeant major.

The three unlikely friends moved on. The little girl couldn't help but smile, which made the lady fume.

"Would you care to swap?" asked Dotty, already knowing the answer.

"I'm fine, thank you," said Elsie, leading the mammoth across the courtyard. She noticed an unusually short old soldier looking out at them from a tall window. He was smiling, waving and blowing kisses in the most extravagant manner.

"TITCH!" exclaimed Dotty.

Chapter 43

A GRAVE MISTAKE

"It just looks like a hairy elephant to me," remarked Titch in his musical Welsh accent.

Elsie was pleased to finally meet this man she'd heard so much about. He was indeed short. Not even taller than her. In fact, Dotty was as wide as he was tall. There was no denying that they made an unusual match. However, all that mattered was that the pair glowed in each other's presence.

The animal was drinking water from a toilet stall in the Royal Hospital, her trunk stuck down the U-bend.

"Well, she's not a hairy elephant!" replied Elsie haughtily. **"She's a woolly mammoth."**

"I've never heard of such a thing!" scoffed Titch.

"Well, that doesn't mean it doesn't exist! It's a prehistoric creature."

"I'm prehistoric myself, and I don't remember seeing those as a boy in the Welsh valleys."

"Well, that's because woolly mammoths died out thousands of years ago."

"And you just brought her back to life, did you?" said the man with a chuckle.

"Yes," replied Elsie. "Actually, we did!"

This stopped the old soldier in his tracks. He looked at Dotty for confirmation. The lady nodded her head.

"Well, what the ruddy hell is she doing here?" he demanded.

"I was rather hoping you might help us hide her!" replied Dotty.

"Me?"

"Yes."

"Here?"

"Yes."

"A great big furry elephant?"

"Well, no." Elsie jumped in to correct him. "She's a woolly mammoth."

"How long for?" he asked.

"They live for fifty years or more."

"FIFTY?"

"Yes. This is just a baby one."

"How big do they grow?"

"To about the size of a house."

"A house?"

Just then there was the sound of a flush in the stall next door.

SPLISH!

An impossibly old man shuffled out, wearing a nightshirt with a military cap, and leaning on a cane. The three looked at one another in panic. They'd had no idea the man had been in there the whole time.

"Morning, Colonel," said Titch.

"I'd leave that a minute if I were you," muttered the colonel, wafting the air and actually making the smell worse, not better. Despite the stink, the three smiled back at him, but said nothing, hoping he might shuffle on.

He didn't.

The colonel spotted the rear end of the mammoth sticking out of the stall next to his. He took a moment to admire it, before commenting. "My word, that's quite a remarkable large, furry bottom. New boy, is he?"

"It's a pet," replied Titch.

"A pet?"

"Yes! Now I would hate for you to miss your breakfast, Colonel. Let me help you to the dining hall."

The private took the colonel by the arm, but the old man was having none of it.

"You can't keep a pet in the Royal Hospital, Private! It is against regulations!"

"It won't be here for long," replied Titch, shooting a look at Dotty.

"No more than fifty years, Colonel, sir," chipped in the lady.

Elsie shook her head in disbelief at Dotty's stupidity.

"FIFTY YEARS!" spluttered the colonel. "What kind of animal is this thing, anyway?"

"She's a woolly mammoth," replied Elsie.

"A what?" asked the man.

"It's like a hairy elephant," added Dotty.

"We can't have a hairy elephant in here!" shouted the man. "Whatever is this country coming to? Get the blasted beast out!" With that, he whacked the mammoth's bottom with his stick.

THWACK!

This would prove to be a grave mistake.

Chapter 44

RIGHT UP
MY WHATSIT

"**N**O!" shouted Elsie.

"**HOOO!**" cried the animal. She began bucking from side to side.

CRUNCH!

The wooden partitions between the toilets splintered into pieces as the mammoth struggled to get out. When she lurched backwards, the colonel gave her another whack with his cane.

"**TAKE THAT,** YOU HAIRY-BOTTOMED BEAST!"

THWACK!

"**STOP!**" cried Elsie. She lurched at the colonel, and held on to his arm to stop him striking her friend again.

"Get your filthy hands off me, girl!"

The mammoth was trying to turn herself round in the cramped toilet. Her tusks bashed into the toilet bowl…

CRASH!

…smashing it to pieces.

SPLURT!

Water began gushing everywhere, soaking everybody and everything.

285

"URGH!" cried the colonel.

"Oh dearie me. More mess for me to clean up!" remarked Dotty, never one to leave her job far behind.

"I'm going to be in big trouble with Matron," said

Titch, desperately trying to sit on all the toilets at once to stop water spraying across the ceiling. All he achieved was an incredibly wet bottom.

"Ooh!" he screamed as he was propelled into the air. "The water's going right up my whatsit!"

Eventually, the mammoth managed to turn herself round, and ripped the cane out of the man's hands with her trunk. With all her might, she hurled the cane across the room.

W H I Z Z !

It hit the window…

BA**NG**!

…shattering it.

CRACK!

"Oh, cripes! Not another breakage," muttered the lady.

The water level in the room was rising rapidly. All four humans and the mammoth were soon knee-deep in it.

With all the noise, it was only a matter of time before someone came thumping on the door.

THUD!

THUD!

THUD!

"What in heaven's name is happening in there?" came a female voice.

"Matron!" hissed Titch, a flash of panic in his eyes. Then he raised his voice. "It's all right, Matron. Everything is under control. Just a minor problem with the flush."

The colonel, who had only come in for a quiet morning poo, was having no more of this nonsense.

"Matron! They've got some great hairy elephant in here!"

"Seeing things again, Colonel?" she called out.

"See for yourself, woman!" he called back.

Matron pushed open the door. A ten-thousand-year-old woolly mammoth was staring back at her. But before she had time to scream a rush of water swept her off her feet…

WHOOSH!

…and carried her down the corridor at speed.

The other five all popped their heads round the door to watch her go.

"At least that floor is getting a good clean," remarked Dotty to herself.

Chapter 45

———◆———

A LIDOLLOP

Fortunately, there were many fantastic hiding places in the Royal Hospital. With Matron flushed away, Titch led Elsie, Dotty and Woolly down to the food-storage room, and slammed the door behind them.

"It's nice and chilly in here," said Titch. "I'm sure your furry friend will feel right at home."

The mammoth did. Elsie did too, for this was where all the food for the elderly soldiers was kept. The old boys obviously ate well as there were giant jars of sweets, and tins of all sorts of goodies, like jam, honey and treacle. To a girl who had lived her entire life under the shadow of hunger, the smell of the food was like the sweetest perfume.

"I'm starving," said Elsie. "Please may I have a tiny bit of jam?"

The little girl's eyes widened, and her lip quivered. How could the grown-ups possibly say no?

"A little dollop can't hurt, can it?" said Dotty.

"No," agreed Titch. "No one would miss a dollop."

"Strawberry or raspberry?" asked Dotty.

"I've never had either," replied the girl. "What's nicer?"

"Raspberry, I think."

"**Raspberry** it is, then!"

Titch reached up, and took down a jar of raspberry jam. Slowly, he unscrewed the lid as the little girl licked her lips. However, before Elsie could dip her finger in, a huge furry trunk snaked around and slurped up the lot.

SLURP!

"What the…?" exclaimed Elsie.

"Bad manmoth!" chided Dotty, slapping Woolly's trunk away.

WHACK!

The mammoth didn't even react. She was too busy being in a state of bliss at having tasted jam for the first time.

"Maybe I should try some **strawberry,** then?" said Elsie.

But as Titch unscrewed the lid the mammoth's trunk snaked its way around and slurped up every last bit.

SLURP!

"WHAT?" exclaimed Elsie.

"BAD MANMOTH!" yelled Dotty.

"Not too loud!" hissed Titch.

"Well, she's being very naughty!"

"I know. But, if I know Matron, she'll have all the soldiers up out of their beds looking for that thing."

"She's not a thing," said Elsie. "She's a mammoth."

"Mammoth thing, then. I don't know!"

RUMBLE!

"What was that?" asked Elsie.

"Thunder?" guessed Dotty.

RUMBLE!

"There it is again!" exclaimed the girl.

"Is it the pipes?" wondered Titch.

RUMBLE!

"It is the pipes!" said Elsie. "Woolly's pipes! Listen!"

All three fell silent.

RUMBLE!

"It must be the jam," said Dotty, "not agreeing with her tum-tum. Don't let her have any more."

"I won't," replied the girl. "But I am absolutely starving. You hold her trunk while I have a tiny bit of treacle."

The treacle was in a huge tin the size of a bucket. Titch shook his head and lifted it down towards the girl as Dotty blocked the animal's view with her body, and held on tightly to its trunk. Excitedly, Elsie prised the lid off. Immediately, the sugary aroma whispered its way up her nostrils. It was so sweet that for a moment the girl felt as if she were floating. She dipped her finger in, and it felt as smooth as silk.

Just as she was about to scoop out a large dollop of treacle, she was shoved against the shelves, causing all the tins and jars to come crashing to the floor.

BANG!

CRASH!

WALLOP!

The mammoth had surged forward to slurp up every last bit of the sweet-smelling gloop. Dotty was holding on to the animal's trunk, so was shoved into Titch, who was shoved into Elsie. Now there was a cloud of sugar and flour and tea whirling around the room, causing the three non-mammoths to cough and splutter. In amongst the chaos, the mammoth's trunk searched out every last morsel of food that had been splattered on the walls, floor or ceiling – or, indeed, was still floating through the air.

The more they all tried to stop Woolly from devouring everything in sight, the faster she ate.

RUMBLE!
GURGLE!
FUZZLE!

"Oh no, listen to her tummy again!" said Dotty.

"I think we're heading for an explosion," predicted Titch.

Chapter 46

BOTTOM EXPLOSION

The girl gulped. "You don't mean a bottom explosion?" she asked.

"I do, young lady," replied Titch.

Suddenly, there was loud knocking.

BOOM! BOOM! BOOM!

"This is the military police! Open up! We know you're in there!" came a voice from the other side of the door.

"Shush!" shushed Dotty. "Nobody say a word!"

"We heard that," came a voice.

"YIKES!" exclaimed Dotty.

"We heard that too!"

"Darn!"

"And that."

"Dotty! Shush!" implored Elsie.

"We heard that as well."

"It wasn't me that time!" called back Dotty.

GRUMBLE! TRIZZLE! DURGLE!

"I fear a bottom explosion is coming," said the little old soldier, "at a terrifying speed!"

BOOM! BOOM! BOOM!

"Open this door at once!"

"Well, why don't we?" said Elsie with a smirk.

"You don't mean use its rear end as a cannon?" asked the little soldier.

"Exactly!" replied the girl. "Open the door and fire at will!"

"Just coming, officers!" called out Dotty, as she squeezed past the mammoth to get to the door.

"QUICKLY, MADAM, OR WE WILL BE FORCED TO BREAK THIS DOOR DOWN!"

"Patience is a virtue!" she called back.

TUZZER! GROOBLE! FUJOOZZLE!

"By the sound of Woolly, she's ready to blow!" said Elsie.

Dotty put her hand on the key, and began to turn it in the lock.

"Just a jiffy, officers!"

CLI<u>C</u>K! went the key.

"The door is unlocked!" Dotty called out.

CROOMADOOB! MUNTYMUNTY!

BOODADOOZLE!

The handle turned and slowly the door opened.

The three shared a mischievous look as the mammoth straightened her back and lifted her tail.

"FIRE!" shouted Titch.

Fire the creature did.

GGGRRRUUURRR!

The noise of Woolly's bottom burping sounded just like a bear growling.

It fired all over the military policemen, covering them from head to toe in hot, sticky mammoth poop. The force of the bottom blast was so strong it knocked them off their feet. The poor men were completely disorientated, as their eyes and noses were covered in the stuff.

"Let's make a run for it!" said Elsie.

"CHARGE!" cried Titch.

The three guided the animal back out of the larder, and began leading her down the corridor.

"You bring up the rear, Dotty!" ordered the old soldier.

"Not on your nelly!" snapped the lady. "I don't trust that area one bit!"

"Where are we going?" asked Elsie.

"Away from that awful smell!" replied Titch as they hurried along the corridor and up the stairs to his ward.

· ⭢ ✳ ⭠ ·

Chapter 47

A NEW COMRADE

"This is where I sleep!" announced Titch, as he opened the door to his ward.

"We should have hidden Woolly in here in the first place," muttered Elsie.

"I think he shares it with other people," replied Dotty.

"Well, I'm sure we could have told a few old soldiers to keep their **traps shut.**"

The door opened to reveal not a few, but twenty old soldiers, all poking their heads out of their berths.

"Oops!" said Elsie.

Slowly, Titch led the woolly mammoth into the ward by the tusk. He coughed and cleared his throat.

"Good morning, gentlemen. Gentlemen! If I could

have your attention, please. I would like to introduce you to a new comrade."

The old soldiers put on their spectacles, attached any wooden arms and legs, or sidled into wheelchairs. Slowly, they approached the magnificent beast.

"What in God's name is it, Titch?" piped up one.

"Does it bite, Private?" asked another.

"Is this what we're having for breakfast?" said a third, who had a long white beard that made him look like a military Father Christmas.

Elsie stepped forward. "No. This is my friend, Woolly."

"Good Lord! A female in the Royal Hospital!" remarked one old soldier.

"And another!" said another.

"The hairy elephant thingummy can stay! But they need to go!" exclaimed a third.

"HOO!" Woolly seemed to hoot in agreement.

"Three females in the Royal Hospital!" thundered another old soldier. "This is a disgrace!"

"It's worse than the Boer War!"

"This place will have to be closed down!"

"It's a scandal of **EPIC PROPORTIONS!**"

Titch raised his voice to shout over them. "Let's have some hush, men! Wait until you hear the girl's story. Elsie…"

The girl smiled, and cleared her throat.

As she told the story so far, the old soldiers were rapt. They had heard stories of **incredible bravery and derring-do**, but this tall tale topped them all.

Elsie ended with a plea. "Gentlemen! Will you help Woolly?"

"I'm in!" came one voice.

"I am too!" came another.

"Me too."

"And me."

"And me!" said another and another and another, until all but one soldier had raised his hand. All eyes turned to the one who hadn't.

"Sorry, what was the question again?" asked the one who looked like Father Christmas.

"That's the brigadier," said Titch. "He forgets

things. We'll take that as a yes."

"Who forgets what?" asked the brigadier.

The mammoth lolloped over to the window at the far end of the long ward and looked out. Elsie trailed after her friend, before following her gaze over the rooftops of London. Woolly lifted her trunk and pressed it against the windowpane, as if longing for something way out of reach. Elsie stroked the mammoth's trunk, then lifted one of her big furry ears and whispered into it.

"What are you looking at, my friend?" she whispered. "If only you could tell me."

"HOO!"

Chapter 48

◆

NORTH, NORTH, NORTH

D otty ambled down the ward to join the pair. "Do you think we could teach Woolly to talk?"

"Talk?"

"Yep. Then she could tell us what she was looking at."

"But how would we teach her to talk?"

"That would be the tricky bit," replied Dotty, looking lost in thought. "Maybe we could teach her one **HOO** for yes, and two **HOOS** for no, and three **HOOS** for maybe? Then list all the places in the world and see what she says?"

Elsie didn't want to hurt the lady's feelings. "It's a great idea, Dotty. It just might take a while to go through every single place in the world."

She turned round to address the old soldiers.

"Does anyone have a **compass?**" she asked.

"Admiral, you're never without yours!" said Titch.

"That's right, Private!" replied the admiral. He began patting his pyjama pockets. "Now, where did I put the blasted thing?"

"It's round your neck!" said Titch.

The admiral found it on the end of a chain. "It's round my neck! Why didn't you tell me?" He took it off and limped over to the girl.

DUFF! DUFF! DUFF!

Elsie noticed one of his legs was wooden.

"My leg, before you ask, was bitten off by a shark. Cheeky blighter did me a favour, really – I had gangrene anyway, so the leg had turned green. Didn't have to have it sawn off. Shark died of food poisoning. Rum old business."

The admiral passed the compass to Elsie.

"There we are, young lady. We haven't been introduced. I am the admiral. The only naval man in here."

"He was thrown out of the old sailors' home for drunkenness," remarked Titch.

"That night I'd only drunk seven bottles of rum, Private!" thundered the admiral. "It takes at least nine to get me drunk!"

A cloud of rum-smelling breath sailed right up Elsie's nose. Her eyes watered, and she sneezed. It was so strong that for a moment she herself felt drunk.

"Thank you, Admiral," replied the girl. Elsie held the compass flat in her hand. The black arrow was pointing exactly the way the mammoth was pointing too.

"NORTH!" exclaimed Elsie.

"HOO!" went the mammoth.

"See, she does talk!" added Dotty. "Every time, Woolly has been pining to go north."

"HOO!"

"She's talking again," remarked Dotty.

"So, Admiral, tell me this..." said Elsie.

"Yes, young lady?" replied the old man, with a smile.

"What is the absolute furthest north you can go?"

The admiral guided the girl over to his bedside.

"Behold my globe, child!"

Beside his bed stood a magnificent orb with a map of the world on it. "This came from my ship."

"Before it sank," chipped in Titch.

"That's quite enough of that, Private. I adore gazing at my globe. It reminds me of my glory days, all those adventures on the high seas! Look, young lady, we are here in London."

He indicated the spot on the globe. "Pop your finger there."

The girl did so.

"Now trace your finger north, north, north."

As Elsie moved her finger up, the admiral read out the places. "Scotland, Orkney Islands, Iceland, Greenland, the Arctic, the North Pole. You can't get any more north than that."

"The North Pole!" said Elsie. "Is it cold?"

The soldiers couldn't help but laugh.

"It's SO cold, young lady," began the admiral, "that the sea is **permanently frozen**. There is no land, just a huge expanse of ice."

"ICE!" she exclaimed. "Perfect for a creature from the Ice Age. That's where we must take Woolly! To the **North Pole!**"

"**HOO!**" agreed Woolly.

Elsie lifted her arms in a triumphant show of leadership. She looked around the ward. Every single old soldier stared back at her, mouth open in shock.

Chapter 49

◆

AUDACIOUS

"But how would we get to that there the North Pole?" asked Titch.

"We would sail, soldier!" announced the admiral. "This is a job for the navy."

"But surely you'll need the army for ground support, sir," replied Titch.

"You may be right there, Private. This is a job for both divisions of Her Majesty's armed forces. A joint navy and, to a lesser extent, army mission."

"Hang on, hang on, hang on!" interrupted Dotty.

"What is it, woman?" thundered the admiral.

"Don't you need a boat?"

There were murmurs from the soldiers.

"She has a point."

"She's not as daft as she looks."

"I think we're missing a chess piece."

"Yes," agreed the admiral. "If you're sailing, it's always best to make sure you have a boat, otherwise there's a strong chance you will get decidedly wet. Now, where are we going to get a boat from?"

All the old men became lost in thought, but Elsie began imagining a theft so audacious it would make the **Sticky Fingers Gang** seem like nuns.

"I know where there's a boat you can pinch!" she announced.

All eyes turned to her. There were some mocking mumbles from the old men.

"She's a mere child."

"The girl knows nothing about boats."

"This tea tastes of coffee. It is coffee!"

The admiral limped over to the girl, his wooden leg thump-thump-thumping on the floor.

DUFF! DUFF! DUFF!

"Pray tell us, young lady," he began grandly, "where is this boat you speak of?"

The girl consulted the compass to see which was east, then found a window facing in that direction.

"It's out there!" replied Elsie smugly, pointing down towards the River Thames.

The old man hurried over to the window as fast as his leg would carry him.

DUFF! DUFF! DUFF!

All the old soldiers followed. They gathered behind the admiral, eager to see where the girl was pointing.

"There!" said the girl. **"YOU CAN STEAL HMS VICTORY."**

Chapter 50

RELIC

The magnificent old sailing ship was now a museum piece and, to celebrate the coming of the new century, had been moved from Portsmouth and moored on the Thames.

"HMS *Victory*?" announced the admiral, before hooting with laughter. "HO! HO! HO!"

"*HA! HA! HA!*" chimed in the men.

Elsie was so annoyed she crossed her arms and gave them all a stern look.

"What's so funny?" she demanded.

"My dear child," began the admiral, "HMS *Victory* was Lord Nelson's flagship in the Battle of Trafalgar all the way back in 1805. She's over a hundred years old! She's a relic!"

"So are you!" snapped back the girl. "But you can still sail, can't you?"

The admiral's face soured, but there was a hint of grudging respect in his voice. "Feisty one, aren't you?"

"I have been told so, yes."

"Mmm, well, it would be quite an honour to follow in Lord Nelson's footsteps," mused the admiral. "Do you know what, men? I think this young lady might be on to something!"

Elsie beamed with pride.

"With respect, sir," interrupted Titch, "the military police may have been splattered with mammoth poop, but they will soon be on to us. We need to make a plan, and fast."

"Yes," announced the girl. "Everyone listen to me!"

The old soldiers were taken aback. Never in their long lives had they taken orders from a little girl, let alone an unwashed urchin like Elsie.

"Well, young lady," announced the admiral, "we would all dearly love to know your plan."

There were murmurs from the men.

"Yes, we would."

"A girl with a plan, whatever next?"

"Do you think we'll get a bath today?"

"We don't have much time." Elsie raised her voice.

"So, gentlemen, please listen."

The admiral sailed in. "You heard what the young lady said, men. We don't have much time, so everyone needs to stop talking and listen."

"Yes!" replied Elsie. "That includes you, Admiral."

There were snickers of laughter from the men.

"HEE! HEE! HEE!"

Nobody had ever spoken to the admiral like that, and the man's face was glowing the colour of the Chelsea Pensioners' scarlet coats.

"Right!" began the girl. "We need two divisions. The *FIRST* men need to make their way along the Thames to where HMS *Victory* is moored, and steal her. Then sail her down here to the hospital. We're just a stone's throw away from the river. The *SECOND* division needs to raid the larder, and gather as many provisions as possible. Admiral?"

"Yes, sir! I mean, madam. I mean, miss," spluttered the old sailor.

"How long will it take us to sail to the North Pole?"

The admiral limped over to his globe…

DUFF! DUFF! DUFF!

…and traced his finger along the route. "Down the Thames, into the English Channel. North Sea. Norwegian Sea. Greenland Sea. Arctic Ocean, and boom! We're there. No more than three or four weeks."

"What if I need the loo?" asked Dotty.

"You go over the side like a sailor, madam!" replied the admiral. "It's the only way to go!"

"He still plops out of the window," remarked Titch.

"It's refreshing!"

"Not for anyone standing below."

"Three to four weeks," began Elsie. "We'll need a lot of food. Not least for this one!" she added, stroking her prehistoric friend.

"**HOO!**" agreed Woolly.

"It's going to be very nippy up there at the North Pole," said Dotty.

"Good point, Dotty! So we'll need all the warm clothes you can get hold of."

The admiral put up his hand.

"Yes, Admiral?" asked Elsie.

"Please can I be in charge of the ship?" he asked meekly.

"Yes, of course you can, Admiral."

"Thank you! Thank you! Thank you! Me in charge of HMS *Victory*. This is a dream come true!"

"You pick ten men, and bring back the *Victory*."

"Right," began the admiral. "This is a dangerous mission. It could even be fatal. I need ten good men and true."

All the old soldiers puffed out their chests, and put on their most noble expressions, dying to be picked.

Chapter 51

ONE LONELY MEDAL

The admiral selected his crack team. Ten men threw their scarlet coats and black trousers on over their pyjamas, and, as their medals clinked together, they put on their tricorne hats. Elsie noticed that, unlike all the other soldiers, Titch just had the one lonely medal.

"Why has Titch only got one medal?" she whispered to Dotty.

"Ooh, don't ask!" she replied. "It's a sore point. They all tease him for it."

"Fall in!" roared the admiral.

The old soldiers organised themselves into a line. They may all have been battered by age and ill health, but they stood to attention with the same pride as the first day they signed up. Between them, they had served in the Crimean War against the Russians, battled their way across India and fought the Zulu warriors in Africa. Now, they were ready for the adventure of their lives.

The admiral approached the mammoth, and saluted her.

"We won't let you down, ma'am mammoth," he said.

"HOO!" replied Woolly, lifting her trunk as if saluting back.

"Now, men, quick march!"

With that, he led his men out of the ward.

"I need to stay here and look after Woolly," said Elsie. "You, Titch, gather up all the food you can lay your hands on. There must be something Woolly didn't eat."

"HOO!"

"I'll do my best, Elsie," replied the private.

"Thank you, Titch. And, Dotty, grab every last hat, glove and coat in here. Load them on to the ship, and then both of you come back to fetch us."

"Right you are!" Titch replied.

There were murmurs from the old soldiers.

"Not sure about Titch being put in charge."

"He's only a private!"

"Man's only got the one medal!"

"And that he got for service!"

"He's no hero!"

"This egg is repeating on me!"

Dotty put a comforting hand on her beloved's shoulder. "Don't take any notice."

"I'll show you, boys!" said Titch. "Now come on, follow me!"

With that, he led his comrades and Dotty across the ward, and left Elsie alone with her woolly friend.

"Lock this door," ordered Titch as he reached it.

"Good thought!" replied the girl.

"I'll knock twice. Then you'll know it's safe to open it."

"Understood."

"Two fast knocks or two slow knocks?" asked Dotty.

"It doesn't matter, my love!" snapped the soldier. "Just two knocks! KNOCK! KNOCK! I'll meet you back here as soon as we're ready to set sail."

Elsie rushed over to the door, and locked it behind them.

CLICK!

Then she crossed the ward to join Woolly. The girl put her arms round her.

"Don't worry, Woolly," she said. "We're going to get you home."

"HOO!" Woolly nodded her head.

Then the animal yawned, and Elsie did too. Woolly folded down on to her knees, and rolled over on to her side before letting out a long, slow sigh.

"HOOOOOOO!"

Elsie lay down next to her friend, her back nestling up against the animal's belly. The mammoth curled her trunk round the girl and held her tight. This was a world away from the cold tin bath Elsie normally slept in. Together they closed their eyes.

"Goodnight, Woolly."

"HOO."

The pair breathed in and out in time with each other, and soon both had fallen asleep. Little did they know that someone was peering in at them through the window.

· ⇀ ✳ ↼ ·

Chapter 52

RAMPAGE

Outside the window to the ward, the top of a ladder had appeared. And at the top of the ladder a pair of beady eyes, a long nose and a tiny moustache had appeared. It was Commissioner Barker. He spied the pair sleeping, and signalled to the officers below to keep quiet.

"WHAT?" one called up loudly from the ground.

"A finger on the lips means *be quiet*," he hissed back.

"RIGHTY-HO!" the constable on the ground shouted up.

"SHUSH!"

"GOT IT!"

As the snow swirled around him, Commissioner

Barker slid down the ladder, his feet landing with a crunch in the snow.

KRUNDLE!

"This time, we're not going to let them get away."

THUD!

THUD!

The noise woke up Elsie and Woolly with a start. The girl was sure she'd heard two knocks. But they were much louder than she'd anticipated.

She wanted to call out for Dotty, but her throat tightened in fear, and she couldn't make a sound.

THUD!

Another knock. Something wasn't right. It was very wrong. Elsie moved backwards, and felt Woolly wrap her trunk protectively round her.

"**HOO!**" she whimpered.

THUD!

This time the door buckled.

THUD!

Shards of wood went flying.

THUD!

328

BOOM!

The doors smashed off their hinges and fell to the floor.

DOOF! DOOF!

Framed in the doorway was Commissioner Barker, flanked by a dozen of his men holding a battering ram.

"Are you going to come quietly?" he bellowed.

"HOO!" roared the mammoth.

The sound gave Elsie strength.

"No! We're going to come really noisily!"

With that, she clambered on to the animal's back, and gave her a whack on her side.

"CHARGE!" shouted Elsie.

Woolly knew exactly what to do, and galloped towards the men.

"Hold the line!" ordered Barker.

The policemen all looked at one another nervously as they linked arms.

"HOLD THE LINE!"

The policemen gripped one another tight.

"HOLD THE LINE!"

Barker was the first to disobey his own order. He broke away from his men and leaped out of the way. His men followed suit, leaving Woolly and Elsie free to escape down the corridor.

"COWARDS!" shouted Barker. "FOOLS!"

Of course, the policemen were the exact opposite of fools, sensibly having no desire to be trampled to death by a prehistoric creature.

Seeing the flight of descending stairs ahead, the mammoth came to an abrupt halt.

"WHOA!" cried Elsie, as the force of the sudden stop hurled her through the air.

W H I Z Z !

She landed on her bottom with a THUD on the top step…

DRUMPH!

…before sliding down the remaining steps at speed.

BONK!

BONK!
BONK!

Woolly looked on with interest. Maybe this was the best way to go down stairs. She sat on her bottom and slid down too.

BONK!

BONK!
BONK!

"HOO! HOO! HOO!"

These were much bigger

BONKS. After all, the mammoth had an infinitely larger bottom. But, going by the little yelps she let out as her bottom hit each step, she seemed to enjoy it.

Soon the pair were lying in a crumpled heap at the bottom of the stairs.

Seeing the policemen arriving at the top, Elsie pulled Woolly along by her trunk.

"HOO!" cried the animal.

Spotting an open doorway, they raced in. It was a huge, grand dining room with chandeliers hanging from the ceiling and wooden panels on the walls. Table upon table was laid out neatly for breakfast. Table upon table was upturned as the mammoth charged through the room.

"HOO!"
CRASH!
BANG!
WALLOP!

A gaggle of cooks dashed out from a kitchen door to see what the rumpus was all about.

"WHAT IS THE MEANING OF THIS?" demanded one.

As soon as they saw it was a mammoth rampaging through the dining hall, they dashed back into the kitchen.

"SORRY TO DISTURB YOU! PLEASE CARRY ON!"

The policemen arrived at the doors.

"THE MONSTER IS THE PROPERTY OF HER MAJESTY THE QUEEN!" shouted Barker. "WE HAVE OUR ORDERS TO RETURN IT! ALIVE OR PREFERABLY DEAD!"

Immediately, Elsie leaped on to her friend's back, so they couldn't shoot, and raced towards the set of tall doors at the far end of the room. However, those doors swung open to reveal Matron, and a rather pooey-looking group of military policemen holding rifles.

"We have you trapped!" bawled Matron. "Now give yourselves up!"

"NEVER!" shouted the girl.

The military policemen lifted their rifles. The animal reared up on her hind legs and roared a huge roar.

"HOOO!"

Elsie's head clinked against the bottom of a chandelier. Thinking fast, she grabbed hold of it and swung backwards before launching herself at the doorway. She flew through the air and hit Matron and the military policemen like a bowling ball striking some skittles…

BASH!

…sending them flying.

"ARGH!"
THUD
THUD
THUD!

They rolled out of the way as the mammoth thundered past. Elsie sprang to her feet, and leaped back on to Woolly as she escaped through the door.

Chapter 53

◆

DANGER
EVERYWHERE

The plan was unravelling fast. Now there was no way Elsie and Woolly could wait for HMS *Victory* to reach the Royal Hospital. Danger was everywhere. They had to keep moving. The pair fled through the doors, past the columns and the statue of the hospital's much-loved founder, Charles II, and across the lawn that led down to the Thames. The river was frozen over. Would the ice take the weight of a two-ton mammoth? With policemen chasing them across the snow with rifles, there was only one way to find out.

BANG! BANG! BANG!

Shots rang out. Birds in the trees took to the sky in fear. Elsie ducked her head, and dug her heels into the animal's sides to make her gallop faster.

"HOO!"

Woolly charged across the snow and leaped off the riverbank, landing hard on the ice.

THUD!

Fortunately, the ice didn't crack, but it was slippery from all the ice skaters. The mammoth's legs slid out from under her, and she went spinning across the ice.

"HOOO!"

"NOOO!" screamed Elsie.

They'd hit the ice so fast there was no stopping them. Round and round they whirled, the mammoth's legs splayed out like a starfish.

W H I Z Z !

Woolly ploughed through some early-morning ice skaters, who were sent spinning across the ice as if they were part of some mass dance spectacular.

"ARGH!" they cried.

"SORRY!" called out Elsie, not that the apology seemed to help at all. Up ahead was a small rowing boat that must have become stuck in the ice. They were speeding right towards it.

W H I Z Z !

The girl closed her eyes.

BOOM!

The boat smashed into pieces. Wood exploded across the ice. The force of the blow caused Elsie to become separated from her friend.

"NOOO!"

They each came to a stop on opposite banks of the river. Battered and bruised, the girl rose unsteadily to her feet. She looked across the ice. The poor mammoth was having a much more difficult time of it. Every time it looked like she was back on four legs, one would slip from under her, and her belly would flop down on the ice.

DOOF!

"HOO!"

On her bare feet, Elsie skated over to help her friend. When she saw one of Woolly's legs sliding down, she would lean all her weight against it to push it up. But her little frame was no match for the mammoth's, and down they would both go.

DOOF!

"HOO!"

Finally, Elsie managed to skate round the mammoth, pushing each leg in turn, making sure they were all upright. In the distance, she could see their pursuers gathering on the riverbanks.

"Come on!" she ordered, but, as soon as she had led the mammoth one step forward, she landed flat on her belly again.

BOSH!

Elsie looked across the frozen Thames. There were

planks of wood from the boat they had destroyed scattered across the ice. These planks were long and thin, and looked a little like the things she'd seen posh folk attach to the bottoms of their shoes to race down a snow-topped Primrose Hill last winter.

Skis!

As fast as she could, Elsie skated over to them. She picked up two of the planks and a length of rope that must have been lying in the rowing boat, before skating back to her friend. Elsie laid them down in front of the mammoth. Then she skated round the back, encouraging Woolly up by pushing on her bottom.

"HOO!"

An exhausted Woolly soon got the message, and stepped forward on to the "skis".

In the distance, Barker and his men took to the ice, closely followed by Matron and the military

policemen. As quickly as she could, Elsie picked up the rope and held it out in front of the mammoth's mouth. Woolly bit into it.

"Clever girl," whispered Elsie.

"HOO!"

With all her might, Elsie pulled on the rope.

The mammoth inched forward.

Darn!

This wasn't going to work.

Darn and blast!

Elsie tried again, and really yanked this time. This created some momentum. Soon the impossible was happening.

A real-life mammoth was skiing across a frozen River Thames!

WHOOSH! WHOOSH! WHOOSH! went the skis on the ice.

"HOO!" called out Woolly joyfully, loving the feeling of speed, her fur blowing in the cold breeze!

They passed by a man roasting chestnuts on the snow.

"Lovely morning!" remarked Elsie as they slid by.

Even the orphans back at WORMLY HALL wouldn't believe this! The man stared open-mouthed in shock as the prehistoric animal let out another excited...

"HOOOOOOOOOOOOOOOOOOOOOOO!"

. ⚹ .

Chapter 54

HMS *VICTORY*

Ahead in the distance, emerging out of the fog like a ghost ship, was HMS *Victory*.

The three masts reaching up to the sky.

The tall, square stern with dozens of windows.

The magnificent crest at the top.

At the bottom, written in big proud strokes, were the letters V I C T O R Y. Elsie couldn't read, but she knew what they spelled. HMS *Victory* was the most famous ship in all the kingdom, if not the entire world.

As she and Woolly skied nearer, she could see the admiral and his men hoisting the topsail. Closer still, she could make out Dotty, Titch and their team loading boxes on to the ship. The girl couldn't help but smile. They were going to make it.

RAT TAT TAT TAT TAT!

It was the sound of a machine gun from up above!
They were being attacked from the skies!

Shots scattered across the ice, narrowly missing the
pair.

The shock caused Elsie to stumble. As she tumbled,
so did Woolly. They hit the ice hard.

BOOF! BOOF!

"AH!" screamed Elsie in pain.

"HOO!" cried the mammoth.

Elsie looked up. Through the fog, she spotted something the size of a blue whale floating in the sky. It was so large it was blotting out the sun.

It was a Zeppelin,* one of the huge state-of-the-art German airships.

In the gondola underneath, a woman with a distinctive pith helmet on her head and a murderous look on her face was positioned behind a machine gun.

It was Lady Buckshot, the big-game hunter. You could smell that foul cigar smoke for miles around.

RAT TAT TAT TAT TAT!

Another hail of bullets rained down. They went straight through the ice, blasting holes in it.

PWANG! PWANG! PWANG!

Freezing-cold river water flooded on to the ice. Slowly but surely, Elsie, who was still lying down, felt it trickle down her neck and up her sleeves. She looked over to her friend.

Woolly was sinking. And fast.

"HOOO!"

---

* Named after its pioneer, Count Ferdinand von Zeppelin. A Zeppelin consisted of a gondola under a huge envelope of hydrogen.

RAT TAT TAT TAT TAT!

More bullets. More holes. More cracks. More water. More danger.

"HOOOO!" yelled the animal in fear.

Elsie held on to her friend's trunk.

"It's going to be all right, Woolly. I'm going to get us out of this. I promise."

RAT TAT TAT TAT TAT!

"HOOOOO!?"

The ice beneath them exploded into pieces.

KABOOM!

The pair were plunged deep into the icy water.

"NOOOOO!" screamed the girl as she disappeared into the depths.

· ⚹ ·

Chapter 55

BLACK SILENCE

Everything went dark.

All Elsie could see was black.

All she could hear was silence.

All the girl could feel was a deathly chill.

At first, she didn't know what was up and what was down.

Where was Woolly?

In all the chaos and confusion, she had lost sight and sound and touch of her friend. Immediately, the cruel current of the Thames pulled her far away from the hole she had fallen through. As much as Elsie tried to paddle back to it, that proved impossible. She was being swept further and further away. In desperation, she thumped on the underside of the ice, trying to bash her way through it.

BOOM! BOOM! BOOM!

The ice was inches thick. Her tiny fists were no match for it. They couldn't even make a dent. Elsie opened her mouth and let out a scream. But underwater no one could hear her.

Just as she felt the life draining out of her, and that she was sinking down to a watery grave, she felt a surge underneath her. Something was pushing her up. It was Woolly! The girl was cradled between the mammoth's eyes as her sharp tusks smashed through the ice.

CRASH!

Elsie gasped. "AAH!"

"HOOOOO!?"

The girl was soaking wet and freezing cold but alive. Just. Elsie slid off the mammoth's face, landing on the ice with a thud.

"Oof!"

Although shivering and choking from the dirty Thames water, all Elsie could think about was her friend.

"WOOLLY!" she spluttered.

"HOOO!"

The mammoth's trunk was just poking out of the hole in the ice, as she desperately tried to breathe. With all her might, Elsie held on to it, so the animal wouldn't sink to her death.

"HOLD ON, WOOLLY! PLEASE!" she cried.

The girl knew it would be impossible for her to hoist this two-ton creature out of the river, but that didn't stop her from trying.

"HUH!"

And again.

"HUH!"

And again.

"HUH!"

"HOOO!"

All the strength in her body wasn't enough to save her friend's life. But they hadn't come this far for it to end now. There had to be a way to save her!

"SOMEBODY HELP!" screamed Elsie. Her voice echoed across the ice.

In the distance, she could see a handful of the Chelsea Pensioners in their distinctive scarlet coats and tricorne hats coming to the rescue!

Titch was leading from the front.

Under their arms the old soldiers were holding a thick rope, which snaked its way across the ice back to the ship.

Above their heads, the Zeppelin was circling for another attack.

"DIE, MONSTER, DIE!" yelled Buckshot.

RAT TAT TAT TAT TAT!

The machine gun blasted. Another hail of bullets sent shards of ice flying into the air.

KABOOM!

Slowly, the Zeppelin began coming round again to make another attack.

"THROW ME THE ROPE!" called out Elsie. The mammoth was sinking fast. Now only the tips of her tusks were bobbing out of the icy water. Elsie hooked the end of the rope round one of the tusks and tied it tight.

"HEAVE!" she ordered.

The old soldiers all gripped the rope and heaved

as hard as they could, just managing to pull the mammoth's head out of the water.

The animal spluttered, and let out a deafening **"HOO!"**

Aboard HMS *Victory* it was all hands on deck, as

the remaining pensioners took the end of the rope.

On the admiral's count…

"On three. One, two, three. Heave!"

…they all heaved, lifting the mammoth up and out of the freezing water. Woolly landed with a terrific thump on the ice.

DOOF!

"HOO!" she sighed.

"YES!" shouted Elsie. Looking behind Woolly, she saw two arcs of policemen and military policemen closing in on them. "LIFT THE SAILS!" she called out.

"Excuse me, young lady!" called back the admiral. "I am in charge of this ship!"

"All right, then! You say it!"

"LIFT THE SAILS!"

As the magnificent sails of HMS *Victory* were hoisted for the first time in years…

WHOOSH! WHOOSH! WHOOOSH!

…the gang on the ice pushed the mammoth back on to her feet.

"GO! GO! GO!" called out Elsie. She led the way across the ice to the ship, holding on to her friend so the mammoth would not slip.

In the sky, the Zeppelin was hovering round into position for yet another attack.

Behind the machine gun, Lady Buckshot had the mammoth in her sights once again.

RAT TAT TAT
TAT TAT!

"URGH!" screamed Titch as he clutched his stomach and sank to his knees.

Chapter 56

TITCH STITCH

"NOOOO!" screamed Dotty from the stern of HMS *Victory*. "TITCH!"

"Titch! No! Have you been hit?" asked Elsie.

"No. I've just got a stitch," he replied. Then in his most heroic tone he announced, "I'm not going to make it. You go on without me. Leave me here on the ice to die."

"*Die?* Titch! You've only got a stitch!"

"It's a bad one. A really bad one. But promise me one thing, young Elsie?"

"What, Titch?"

"Tell Dotty that... **I LOVE HER**. Urgh!" He clutched himself again.

Elsie shook her head. She might be the child here, but so often she felt more grown up than the grown-ups.

"You tell her, Titch!" said the girl, hooking her arm under his.

"What's happened to my darling?" called out Dotty from the ship.

"Titch has a stitch!" replied Elsie. Then the girl turned her attention back to the private. "Now stop being silly, Titch. Stitch or no stitch, we're all getting on that ship."

"I'll do my best, young miss."

The wind billowed the sails, and the ship's hull began creaking in the ice.

CRUNCH!

A huge ramp was lowered from HMS *Victory*, landing on the ice with a BOSH!

"WOOLLY FIRST!" shouted Elsie as she gathered the handful of pensioners to get behind the animal and push her up the ramp by her bottom.

As the boat rocked in the breaking ice, the ramp wobbled from side to side.

"HOOO!" hooted the mammoth.

"Nearly there, my friend!" called out Elsie, as she used all her might to make the final push over into the ship.

THUMP!

The wooden deck buckled a little under the mammoth's weight.

"HOOO!"

"HURRAH!" cried all on board, overjoyed that their large, hairy friend had made it.

Above HMS *Victory*, the Zeppelin was flying low.

"NOW I'VE GOT YOU, **ICE MONSTER!**" came a cry from the gondola.

RAT! TAT! TAT! TAT! TAT! TAT!

All the old soldiers hit the deck as HMS *Victory* was riddled with bullets.

POW! POW! POW!

"I'VE BEEN HIT!" yelled the admiral.

Dotty rushed over to him.

"Where?"

"MY LEG!"

"Which one?"

"The wooden one."

Indeed, there was a bullet lodged in there.

"Is it bleeding?" asked Dotty.

"Yes. Very badly."

"I can't see any blood!"

"No, it's just sawdust."

"Are you feeling any pain?"

"None at all. But I'm not going to let that blasted woman get away with this!"

· ⚹ ·

Chapter 57

REVENGE

With its sails in full bloom, HMS *Victory* began forcing its way through the ice.

A cold and wet Elsie looked over the stern of the ship to see who was still following. In the distance, she could see something shaped like a sail speeding along the ice, overtaking the policemen. As it came closer, she realised the sail was multicoloured. It was, in fact, the balloon they had made of handkerchiefs (and one pair of bloomers).

"What...?" she muttered to herself.

It was only when the balloon got closer that she spotted the professor underneath it! He had attached the sail to his wheelchair, and was using the power of the wind to drag himself along.

"YOU CAN'T PUT A GREAT MAN DOWN!"

he called out. With one hand, he was steering the sail. In the other, he was holding the dart gun.

"I HAVE COME TO TAKE MY MONSTER BACK!

THIS IS REVENGE!"

"Oh no!" said Dotty. "This never ends!" she called out to the admiral. "Faster! Faster!"

"It's the ice!" the man called back. "It's so thick we can't go any faster!"

"LOOK!" She pointed to the professor.

"Maybe we can kill two birds with one stone," replied the admiral, setting a course straight for the newly built Tower Bridge.

Looking across to the riverbanks, Elsie noticed that London had woken up, and crowds were beginning to line the banks of the Thames. Much to her surprise, Londoners began clapping and cheering. They were clearly delighted to see this magnificent beast, the mammoth, brought back to life. And aboard Nelson's old warship no less.

"HURRAH!"

But there was a big problem. HMS *Victory*'s masts were too tall to fit under the bridge.

"We're not going to make it, Admiral!" called out Titch from the bow of the ship.

"We need to get that bridge open!" the admiral called back.

Elsie spotted a group of a dozen children loitering on the bridge. The unmistakable figures of the **Sticky Fingers Gang**.

"ELSIE!" they shouted on seeing her.

"OPEN THE BRIDGE!" she shouted back. "UP! UP!"

Immediately, the gang began scaling the bridge to find the control room.

The Zeppelin was now just behind the ship, and gaining on them. Fast.

CLUNK! W H I R R !

Also gaining was the professor, who fired a poisoned dart.

PING!

It lodged into Buckshot's pith helmet.

"LOOK WHERE YOU'RE SHOOTING, YOU RUDDY FOOL, OR I'LL BLAST YOU TO SMITHEREENS!" she cried.

"THEN GET THAT PREPOSTEROUS CONTRAPTION OUT OF MY WAY!"

The professor fired again. This time the dart struck the Zeppelin's huge envelope of gas.

PPPFFFFFT!

There was a loud farting noise as air began escaping.

In a fury, Buckshot trained her machine gun on the professor.

RAT! TAT! TAT! TAT! TAT! TAT!!

"MISSED!" called out the professor.

"CHECK YOUR WHEELCHAIR, YOU OLD FOOL!"

He looked down. Indeed, she had blasted it out of existence. The professor was now skidding across the ice on his bottom.

In all the commotion, what neither had noticed was that Tower Bridge was beginning to rise.

The front mast of HMS *Victory* just clipped one of the sides of the bridge as it opened.

SCRAPE!

"HURRAH!" shouted the soldiers on the ship as HMS *Victory* passed under the magnificent bridge.

"HOOO!" hooted Woolly, joining in.

The admiral looked round to see not only Lady Buckshot looming right behind him in the Zeppelin, but also the professor skimming along the ice at the stern.

"Order those scallywags to lower the bridge. Quick smart!" ordered the admiral.

"DOWN! DOWN!" shouted the girl to her friends.

Right on cue, the bridge began to lower.

The machine gun blasted, once again ripping through the hull of the *Victory*.

RAT! TAT! TAT! TAT! TAT! TAT!

At the bottom of the Zeppelin, Lady Buckshot hollered her instructions to the pilot. "UP! UP!"

"Darn!" said the admiral. "She's not going to fall for it!"

A tethering cable was dangling down from the airship. Using her trunk, Woolly grabbed hold of the end.

"HOOO!"

"WOOLLY?" exclaimed Elsie in delight. This was one smart mammoth.

As the engines of the Zeppelin roared, the mammoth used all her strength to pull the flying machine down.

"HELP HER!" called out Elsie, and the old soldiers rushed to hold on to Woolly to stop her being pulled into the air.

"NOOO!" screamed Lady Buckshot, as the Zeppelin crashed straight into the bridge.

SMASH!

The envelope full of gas exploded in the air.

KABOOM!

"ARGH!" she cried as her gondola plunged right on to the professor, sending them both down into the icy waters of the Thames.

GURGLE! GURGLE! GURGLE!

PLOP! PLOP! PLOP!

GLUG! GLUG! GLUG!

"HURRAH!" shouted everyone on board the *Victory*.

"HOOO!" hooted Woolly.

The **Sticky Fingers Gang** all waved goodbye to Elsie.

"GOOD LUCK!" they shouted.

"THANK YOU!" she called back. "WE'LL NEED IT!"

The admiral addressed his crew. "Now, men, set sail for the North Pole!"

PART II

THE HIGH SEAS

Chapter 58

SLICING THROUGH THE ICE

"Which way is the North Pole, sir?" piped up Titch.

"Straight ahead, men!" commanded the admiral, pointing downriver. "Then when we reach the sea make a left!"

Just as the mammoth's arrival into the city had been a cause of great excitement, its departure was proving even more so. Word had spread fast, and soon it seemed like every Londoner was running along the

banks of the Thames, eager to be part of this awfully big adventure. The proud old admiral saluted them, which made the crowds cheer loudly.

"HURRAH!"

"**HOOOO!**" called out Woolly as she appeared to wave with her trunk.

This made the crowds go wild.

"HURRAH!"

It was a happy scene, and put joy into the hearts of all on board the *Victory*.

Titch sidled up to Dotty.

"I was very nearly a goner," he said.

"What happened, my love? I thought you'd been shot!" she replied.

"It was much, much worse than that. A stitch."

"A stitch?"

"Yes. A really bad stitch can be deadly."

"I didn't know that," replied the lady. "Maybe I need to kiss it better. Where does it hurt?"

The old soldier pointed to his lips. "Here."

They kissed. It was the shortest, sweetest kiss in the history of kisses. But the long-awaited meeting of their lips felt like fireworks to them, and they both looked light-headed as soon as they parted.

"I think I need a sit-down," said Dotty.

"I think I need a lie-down," said Titch.

"This is no time for kissing, sailors!" commanded the admiral. "We have a ship to sail!"

As he gave his orders, the men went to work. Soon HMS *Victory* picked up speed, and began slicing through the ice with ease. As the ship sailed through east London, getting nearer to the sea, the ice became thinner. HMS *Victory* began sailing faster and faster, until it passed out of the Thames Estuary and into the open sea.

"HURRAH!" cried the pensioners.

"HOOO!" cried Woolly.

"Port side!" ordered the admiral. This was the nautical term for the left side.

Waves were now hitting the ship, causing it to sway

from side to side. The mammoth had installed herself at the prow like an unofficial figurehead. Her trunk dangled down and covered the actual figurehead, which was a royal shield and a crown with a cherub on each side.

Elsie sidled up next to her friend. "Looking north again?" she said. The girl gazed out across the endless sea. The North Pole was thousands of miles away. "We'll get you home, Woolly. I promise."

With that, she stroked one of the mammoth's big furry ears. Woolly gently pushed her body against the girl as a way of saying thank you.

"HOO!" she cooed.

Chapter 59

A DIAMOND
DUST of STARS

D ays passed at sea. HMS *Victory* sailed round the furthest tip of Scotland, and found herself alone in the deepest, darkest North Sea.

Weeks passed. As the ship travelled north, the sea grew rougher and rougher. Waves as tall as trees crashed over the *Victory*.

SPLISH!
SPLASH!
SPLOSH!

Everyone had to work together to stop the ship from sinking. Even Woolly. The mammoth hosed up the pools of water on the deck with her trunk, and sprayed them back overboard.

Another night descended on the *Victory* as at last they passed into calmer waters. The pensioners worked in shifts, and slept in the bunks below deck. Woolly was too large to fit, so when it was time to sleep Elsie stayed with her. Just like at the hospital, the pair of best friends snuggled up together.

"Goodnight, Woolly," Elsie would say.

"HOO!" Woolly would reply, which if translated from mammoth language means "Goodnight, Elsie". The girl would tuck herself in under the soft fur of Woolly's belly. The mammoth would then shuffle her legs together to protect her friend from the cold. Woolly made the softest, comfiest bed, and at night, as they lay together, Elsie felt that she was home. Looking up, she could see the diamond dust of stars in the sky.

Everything seemed so perfect.

It couldn't last.

And it didn't.

· ⚡ ✳ ⚡ ·

Chapter 60

SHIPS AHOY!

"SHIPS AHOY!" came the cry one morning from the crow's nest of the *Victory*.

All the old soldiers scrambled to the stern of the ship. There they jostled, eager to glimpse what their comrade at the top of the mast had seen. The sound of footsteps had woken up Elsie and Woolly too, and they joined the line of pensioners. The admiral took out his telescope.

A fleet of metal steamships stretched out across the horizon.

"How many, Admiral?" asked Titch.

"A dozen, I would say."

"Can we outrun them?" asked Elsie.

"We can darn well try!"

"HURRAH!" shouted the men.

"HOO!" joined in Woolly.

The admiral called out his orders, to make this old ship go as fast as she possibly could.

HMS *Victory* felt as if it were taking flight as it soared across the sea.

Yet even at full speed it was no match for the modern steamships.

"They're gaining on us!" yelled Elsie.

"We're going at full speed!" replied the admiral. "Prepare the cannons!"

"With respect, Admiral, sir," piped up Titch, "we can't fire on our fellow countrymen!"

"No, you've got a point there," mused the admiral. "We'll be hanged as traitors."

"There must be something we can do!" exclaimed Elsie. "How many barrels of gunpowder have we got?"

Dotty counted them. "One, two, four, three, four, nine, three, seven, um, erm, six. A lot!" Counting was not her strong suit.

"A lot. Thank you, Dotty. I can count a dozen. A dozen barrels. What if we rolled them out to sea?"

"That's the most ridiculous idea I have ever heard, child! What a waste of jolly good gunpowder!" replied the admiral.

"I haven't finished yet!"

"OOH!" cooed the pensioners.

"I will have no 'oohing' on my ship!" thundered the admiral. "Do you understand me? Once you let sailors all 'ooh' at one another, heaven knows where it will lead!"

The old men nodded, still smirking at their own naughtiness.

"HOO!" called out Woolly.

"And less of your cheek, please," said the admiral to the mammoth.

"What I was going to say," continued Elsie, "is that we should roll out the barrels one by one. Then we wait until the ships close in. Then whoever is the best shot takes one of those muskets and shoots them."

"Shooting your own gunpowder?" thundered the admiral. "I have never heard such poppycock!"

"With respect, sir," began Titch timidly, "I think the girl is on to something. It will create a smokescreen!"

"A smokescreen?" spluttered the admiral.

"Yes! Then we will have a chance of losing the ships."

"Right, men, and erm, ladies, change tack," boomed the old sailor.

"When I give the order 'now', I want you to roll a barrel into the sea. Titch?"

"Yes, Admiral?"

"Do you know your way around a musket?"

"Well, I, er, um, the thing is..." He hesitated. The man was nervous. Only having the one medal (which was for service, the one all soldiers received), he had never thought of himself as a hero.

The last thing Titch wanted was to let everyone down.

· ⭢ ✳ ⭠ ·

Chapter 61

OPEN FIRE!

"Good!" replied the admiral. As usual, he hadn't been listening. "Titch, when I give the order 'fire' I want you to open fire on a barrel."

Poor Titch was shaking with nerves. It was clear he didn't want to be put under all this pressure.

One by one, the barrels were rolled into the sea.

ROLL
PLOP!
ROLL
PLOP!
ROLL
PLOP!

Soon there were a dozen barrels of gunpowder bobbing around in the water as the British naval fleet approached.

"Titch? Are you ready?" asked the admiral.

The poor private was struggling, trying to ram the gunpowder down the antique musket. "One moment, sir!"

Dotty tried to help by passing him the shot.

"I can do it!" he snapped.

"TITCH!" called out the admiral.

"Ready, sir!"

Titch raised the musket.

"FIRE!"

The private took a deep breath. This was his moment to prove them all wrong. To prove that he could be a hero after all. Trembling, he did something he'd never done before in all his years as a soldier. He pulled the trigger.

CLICK!

Nothing happened.

"Sorry, sir, I'm half-cocked!"

"FIRE!"

BANG!

The force of the blast threw Titch off his aim.

Instead of the shot firing across the sea towards the barrel, it skimmed over Woolly's head, parting her fur…

"HOOO!"

…before blasting a huge hole in one of HMS *Victory*'s sails.

"You ruddy fool!" raged the admiral. "I'll have you court-martialled for this!"

"I'm useless!" said Titch, bowing his head in defeat.

"Give that musket to me, Private," ordered the admiral.

"Let him have another go!" pleaded Dotty.

"Are we at the funfair?" asked the brigadier.

"I had me chance and I blew it!" Titch wailed in despair.

"No, Titch!" piped up Elsie. "You can do it. I know you can."

She turned to the admiral. "Please?"

The admiral had a soft spot for the girl.

"All right, then," he huffed. "But there are a dozen barrels and only a dozen cartridges. If he fails, that's it."

"No pressure, my love," added Dotty, somewhat unhelpfully.

The admiral let out a long sigh. "Fire at will, Private."

Titch loaded the musket, and aimed. He took a deep breath, closed his eyes and fired.

BANG!

This shot skimmed across the sea.

KABOOM!

The barrel of gunpowder exploded.

A thick cloud of black smoke appeared.

"HURRAH!" shouted the old soldiers on the deck of HMS *Victory*.

"**HOOO!**" hooted the mammoth.

"YOU DID IT, TITCH!" yelled Elsie.

"My hero!" added Dotty.

"One down. Eleven to go!" said Titch.

"FIRE!" ordered the admiral.

KABOOM!

And another.

KABOOM!

Another.

KABOOM!

KABOOM!

KABOOM!

Three in a row.

Bull's-eye!

KABOOM!

KABOOM!

YES!

KABOOM!

On a roll now.

KABOOM!

Easy.

KABOOM!

Final one…

KABOOM!

Against all the odds, Titch had hit every single barrel. Now there was a huge curtain of black smoke stretching out across the sea.

"HURRAH!" shouted the soldiers.

"HOOO!" added Woolly.

·→✳←·

Chapter 62

DOWN BUT NOT OUT

"**S**ILENCE!" ordered the admiral. "Let's listen for their ships!"

Everyone on board fell silent. Far off, they could hear the sound of horns hooting and engines grinding.

KERRANG!

There was even the sound of metal hitting metal as ships collided.

BASH!
BANG!
WALLOP!

"Oops!" said the admiral.

"We got 'em!" exclaimed Dotty.

"**HOO!**" shouted Woolly, punching her trunk into the air in triumph.

"They're the British naval fleet," began the admiral.

"The best in the world. They're down but they're not out. The smoke will lift soon. We must act fast. We need to change course if we're going to lose them. STARBOARD HO!"

All on board went to work to make the ship dramatically change course to the right. Even the mammoth was getting the hang of sailing now. Using her trunk, she grabbed hold of the wheel, spinning it hard to the right. The ship leaned the other way so fast that the old soldiers tumbled over. Woolly fell on top of the admiral.

"HOOO!"

DUMF!

"OOF!" cried the admiral. "GET THIS GIANT FUR BALL OFF ME!"

Elsie smirked as she and all available hands on deck prised the mammoth off their leader.

"Thank goodness I'm not planning on having any more children!" muttered the admiral as he clambered to his foot. He limped over to the stern of the ship.

DUFF! DUFF! DUFF!

Next, he took out his telescope and studied the sea behind them. The curtain of smoke was slowly lifting. Elsie sidled up to him and Woolly followed. The mammoth was intrigued. She plucked the telescope out of his hands with her trunk.

SWIPE!

"GET OFF THAT!"

he snapped before snatching it back. He then turned to Elsie. "Please try and control your pet mammoth."

"I'll try, sir," she replied with a grin.

"I can't see any ships," he said. "I think we've done it. My goodness, we've done it."

Just then, Elsie spotted a shape poking out of the curtain of smoke.

"THERE!" she shouted.

The admiral put the telescope back up to his eye. "BLAST! One of them has got through."

"We can't give up, Admiral," said the girl.

"NEVER! Now listen up, men! And, erm, woman, and, of course, girl…" began the admiral.

"HOOO!" added Woolly, not wanting to be left out.

"Yes, yes, apologies," replied the admiral, rolling his eyes. "And listen up, mammoth! One of the ships has got through."

"OH NO!" came a chorus of replies.

"We have to prepare for the worst. In less than an hour, they will have reached us. We must be ready to be boarded. Men, and, erm, woman, and, of course, girl…"

"HOO!" Woolly reminded him.

"…and, who can forget, mammoth. We have no more shot. The gunpowder is gone. But you must arm yourselves with whatever you can lay your hands on!"

"YES, SIR!" came a chorus of replies.

"Good luck, men, and everyone else not contained in that umbrella term!"

Immediately, the deck of HMS *Victory* was a hive of activity, as all on board went about arming themselves. There weren't enough cutlasses to go around, so most of the soldiers picked up brooms and mops.

Slowly but surely, the British naval ship that was still pursuing them came into focus. She was the mighty HMS *Argonaut.**

With four huge funnels pumping smoke from its coal engine, the *Argonaut* was powering through the waves right towards the *Victory*.

With their makeshift weapons in their hands, the old soldiers were ready for the worst. The admiral approached Elsie. "You are but a child. I think it best you go below deck."

---

* *Named after the crew of Jason's ship, the* Argo, *in ancient Greek mythology.*

"Are you kidding?" replied the girl, reaching for a long wooden sail batten. "I wouldn't miss this for the world."

"We'll make a sailor of you yet!" said the admiral. He took off his wooden leg and brandished it, ready to do battle. Forgetting he couldn't stand up on his one leg, he wobbled for a moment before hitting the deck.

THUMP!

Chapter 63

SURRENDER!

"SURRENDER!" boomed a voice over the loud-hailer from HMS *Argonaut* as it drew up alongside the *Victory*.

"NEVER!" came a chorus of voices from HMS *Victory*.

"SORRY. I DIDN'T QUITE CATCH THAT!"

"WE SAID 'NEVER'."

"DID YOU SAY 'NEVER'?"

"YES!"

"SORRY, IT'S HARD TO HEAR. YOU DON'T HAVE A LOUD-HAILER YOU COULD USE, DO YOU?"

"NO!"

"WHAT WAS THAT?"

"WE SAID 'NO'!"

"THAT'S A SHAME."

"WE KNOW."

"SORRY, WHAT WAS THAT?"

"WE SAID, 'WE KNOW'."

"THANK YOU. NOW OUR ORDERS ARE TO RETURN THE **ICE MONSTER** TO LONDON. IT IS THE PROPERTY OF HER MAJESTY THE QUEEN."

All the old soldiers looked to Elsie. She told them, "Woolly isn't the property of anyone."

"OH NO, IT'S NOT!" began the chorus from HMS *Victory*.

"OH YES, IT IS!" came the voices back.

"OH NO, IT'S NOT."

"OH YES, IT IS."

"Are we at the pantomime?" asked the brigadier.

"IF YOU RETURN THE CREATURE TO US, THEN THERE IS NO NEED FOR US TO OPEN FIRE. DO YOU SURRENDER?"

"NO!"

"I AM PRETTY SURE THAT WAS A 'NO'."

"YES!"

"SORRY, YES THAT WAS A 'NO', OR YES BECAUSE IT WAS A 'YES'?"

"IT WAS A 'NO'!"

"THANK YOU!"

"OUR PLEASURE!"

"THANK YOU."

"NOT AT ALL."

"THEN PREPARE FOR BATTLE!"

"Cor, that took 'em long enough," muttered Dotty.

HMS *Argonaut* inched closer to HMS *Victory*. The young sailors looked across at the old soldiers.

The two groups nodded to each other politely. They were all British after all. Finally, the captain of HMS *Argonaut* gave the order. "ATTACK!"

Chapter 64

A POOL OF BLOOD

The young sailors leaped from one ship to another with ease. They landed on the deck of the *Victory*, brandishing their rifles.

"CHARGE!" shouted the admiral, as he led his pensioners into battle. The old soldiers were brave, and attacked the young sailors with their cutlasses, mops and brooms.

CLUNK!

CLINK!

CLANK!

They went straight for the rifles, trying to force them to the floor.

Meanwhile, Dotty had found an old tin bucket, and was bashing the young sailors over the head with it.

BISH!
BASH!
BOSH!

Many were knocked out by the force of her blows.

"OUCH!"

THUD!

"OOF!"

THUD!

"ARGH!"

THUD!

Meanwhile, Elsie attacked the invaders by whacking them on their bottoms with her sail batten.

THWACK!

"AH!"

THWUCK!

"AAHH!!"

THWOCK!

"AAAAAHHHH!"

A smile spread across her face. This was fun.

Woolly joined in too.

"HOO!"

With her tusks, the mammoth scooped up a sailor, before dropping him in the sea.

"NOOO!"

PLOP!

As Elsie battled on, out of the corner of her eye she could see a cannon on HMS *Argonaut* swivelling round. Now it was pointing straight at the mammoth. The captain gave the order.

"FIRE AT WILL!"

"NOOOOO!" screamed Elsie as she put her hands up in the air to shield her friend. The gunner fired, and a huge net shot across the decks of the *Victory*, trapping the mammoth in its web.

"HOO!" roared Woolly. The poor thing was distressed, and began bucking and thrashing around.

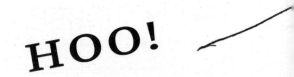

HOO!

The more she did so, the more tangled she became.

"HOO! HOO!"

"WOOLLY! WOOLLY!" cried the girl, trying to calm the creature down, to no avail.

The mammoth lurched across the deck, bashing into people and things.

"HOO!"

She swung round and knocked a sailor to the floor.

DOOF!

"ARGH!"

Another was trodden on by a giant prehistoric foot.

BOOF!

"OUCH!"

A third sailor became tangled in the net, and was dragged across the deck.

"HELP!"

Still clutching his rifle, the sailor's finger snagged on the trigger. A shot rang out.

BANG!

All was quiet and still on board the *Victory*.

Woolly was quiet and still too. She stopped thrashing around and stood motionless for a moment, before she keeled over and landed with a deafening THUD.

A pool of blood spread across the deck.

"WOOLLY! NOOOOOO!" screamed Elsie.

Chapter 65

HARD RAIN

The old soldiers and the young sailors all worked together to untangle the mammoth from the net. As soon as the captain of HMS *Argonaut* had hauled two of his sailors out of the North Sea, he stepped on board the HMS *Victory* to help.

"I'm so sorry this has happened," said the captain.

Elsie put her hands over the wound in Woolly's chest to stop the flow of blood.

"WHY DID YOU SHOOT HER?" she cried. "WHY?"

There was no answer.

"Somebody do something!" she begged.

Dotty put her ear to the animal's mouth. "I can't hear her breathing. I'm so sorry, Elsie. I know you loved her. And she loved you. But this is the end of the story."

"NOOO!" yelled Elsie.

BOOM!

Thunder rolled across the sea. Ahead, black clouds were swirling. A storm was coming.

"Sail into the storm!" ordered Elsie.

The admiral looked aghast. "No. It would be the end of us all."

"It's the only way we can save her."

"By sailing into a storm?" demanded the admiral.

"We used lightning to restart her heart before. Maybe we can do it again."

Dotty rushed over to where Elsie was trying to stop the flow of blood.

"Let me take over!" she said.

The lady pushed the end of her mop right into the wound, and the flow of blood slowed.

"We can tow you into the storm!" offered the captain of the *Argonaut*.

"No," replied the admiral. "It's too dangerous. You young sailors have got your whole lives ahead of you."

He turned to the pensioners.

"Men. Are you all with me?"

"YES, SIR!" came the reply.

"Good luck!" said the captain, and he and the admiral saluted each other. "We will make sure *Queen Victoria* is told all about your bravery."

The captain led his men back on board the *Argonaut* as the admiral called out his orders.

"Set course for the storm!"

The men went to work, and soon HMS *Victory* was flying into the darkness ahead.

"Elsie?" began Dotty. "Do you know what you're doing? We don't have a balloon or metal wire or anything."

"I know." The girl choked, fighting back a river of tears. "But there must be a way."

Her eyes searched the deck of the *Victory*. At the bow, she spotted something.

"See that metal chain, Titch?"

"Yes!" replied the old soldier. "That's for dropping the anchor."

"Put the anchor right next to Woolly's heart, and then pass me the end of the chain."

"Right-ho!"

Titch scuttled over to the bow, and with the help of his fellow pensioners he dragged the anchor and chain over to where the mammoth was lying.

Elsie took the end of the chain and wrapped it round her wrist. Then she placed a cutlass between her teeth like a pirate, and with her monkey feet began climbing the rigging.

"Where do you think you're going?" asked Dotty.

"The crow's nest, of course," Elsie replied, her speech hard to understand thanks to the cutlass in her mouth.

As the ship crashed up and down on the angry waves...

THRUMP! THRUMP! THRUMP!

...Elsie climbed up and up and up. Once at the top, she clambered into the crow's nest and looked straight ahead into the storm.

"Come on!" she whispered to the sky. *"Give me everything you've got."*

All the way up there at the tallest point of the *Victory*, the rolling of the ship in the waves became exaggerated. Elsie found herself holding on for dear life.

She looked down to see the admiral at the wheel, holding on tightly so the waves didn't hurl him into the sea. Hard rain was flying into the girl's eyes. It was a struggle to keep them open. Soon she was soaked to the skin. The wind wound around her, and the clouds skimmed her hair.

"Straight ahead, Admiral!" she ordered.

"Aye, aye, Captain Elsie!" he called back up.

BOOM!

Thunder rumbled across the black sky.

"Come on, lightning!" the girl whispered. "I know you're in there somewhere."

As if on cue, a flash of lightning illuminated the sky.

KRAZZLE!

"Are you sure you know what you're doing?" called up Dotty.

"No. This is madness!"

"Good madness or bad madness?"

"Good, I hope!"

Elsie lifted the cutlass high into the air.

"But the lightning, Elsie. It could kill you!" shouted Dotty.

"If it does, promise you'll look after Woolly for me. Make sure she gets to the North Pole? PLEASE?"

"Don't do this!"

"Why?"

"I love you, Elsie. You're like a grandma to me."

"I think you mean granddaughter, Dotty, and I love you too, but I have to save my friend. Promise you'll look after her."

"I promise!"

A bolt of lightning hit the front sail, and it burst into flames.

BOOM!

"FIRE ON BOARD!" shouted the admiral as his men struggled to put it out.

"Nearly!" whispered Elsie. She stretched her arm as high as it would go, and closed her eyes.

"COME ON!" she shouted.

A bolt of lightning struck the tip of the cutlass.

"AAH!" cried Elsie as the electricity sizzled through her.

Chapter 66

◆

A WATERY GRAVE

The bolt of lightning passed through the girl and shot down the metal chain. The anchor had been pushed against the lifeless creature's chest, and now it delivered a thump of electricity to Woolly's heart.

DUMF!

Elsie slumped to her knees at the highest point of the ship, and the mammoth's legs twitched.

One eye opened.

Then another.

"SHE'S ALIVE!" shouted Dotty. "Do you hear me, Elsie? Elsie?"

As thunder and lightning boomed around them, Dotty and Titch looked up to the crow's nest.

"NOOOO!" screamed Dotty when she saw the girl slumped over the side, lifeless.

"You look after Woolly!" cried Titch as he began climbing up the rigging.

The boat was now swinging wildly from side to side, and the higher he scrabbled, the more he felt he was going to be tossed into a watery grave.

Eventually, he reached the crow's nest. Elsie was now lying motionless on the floor.

"ELSIE? ELSIE?" he cried, but there was no response. Titch scooped her up in his arms, and put her over his shoulder. Then he made the hazardous climb down the rigging, and laid her out on the deck of the ship.

Elsie's face was blackened and, despite the rain, her hair and clothes were smoking.

It seemed that the electric bolt, which had given the mammoth life, had taken life away from the girl.

On seeing her friend laid out like this, Woolly scrambled over to her.

First, the mammoth tried to rock her friend awake with her foot.

"HOO!"

Elsie just flopped from side to side.

Next, she licked the girl's face with her tongue.

"HOO!"

A white streak appeared on her skin.

Dotty burst into floods of tears and held Elsie's lifeless body close to hers. "No! No! Please!"

Titch put his arms round her. "I think she's left us."

Chapter 67

◆

HEADS BOWED

The pensioners stood around the body with their heads bowed and their hats held close to their chests.

All was quiet and still on the deck of the *Victory*.

However, the mammoth was not giving up on her friend.

"HOO!"

To everyone's surprise, Woolly placed her trunk over the girl's nose and mouth, and blew air into her.

"What's the beast doing?" said the admiral, as he tried to keep steering the *Victory* through the storm.

"I think she's trying to recessuss... resasstate... restitiute... blow air into Elsie!" replied Dotty.

"Her chest is moving up and down!" exclaimed Titch.

"Thank the good Lord for his mercy!" cried out Dotty. "She's alive!"

Elsie's eyes opened. A huge wet furry trunk was staring back at her. At first, she didn't know where she was, or even who she was.

"What the…?"

But, as soon as she realised who was looming over her, she took the trunk in her hands and kissed it.

"Oh, thank you, thank you, thank you, Woolly! I love you!"

The mammoth wrapped her trunk round the girl, and pulled her close for a cuddle.

"HURRAH!" cried the old soldiers.

"This is all very well and good, gentlemen, and, er, lady, and, girl, and, of course, mammoth, and so on and so forth," began the admiral, "but can I politely remind you that we are still sailing through the heart of a storm? It's going to take every last man, every last person and prehistoric animal for us to survive this! Back to work at once!"

PART III

THE NORTH POLE

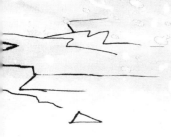

Chapter 68

❖

BATTERED AND BRUISED

Battered and bruised, HMS *Victory* eventually sailed into calmer waters.

An **icy wind** blew across the ship. They were moving closer and closer to the North Pole. A shout came down from the crow's nest.

"ICEBERG AHOY!"

Elsie whispered into the mammoth's ear. "We're getting close, Woolly."

The mammoth nodded her head up and down, and called out, **"HOO!"**

"Very close."

The admiral expertly navigated HMS *Victory* through the maze of ice.

"LAND AHOY!" came another shout from above.

"**HOOO!**" hooted Woolly. Somehow, she knew she was going home.

The ship stopped alongside the edge of the ice, causing a huddle of walruses to scatter into the water.

PLOP! PLOP! PLOP!

After weeks at sea, the mammoth was eager to step out on to solid ice. Her entire body was swaying with excitement.

"Not long now, Woolly!" said Elsie.

As soon as it was safe, she led her friend down the gangplank and on to the ice. Immediately, the mammoth rolled on to her back, rubbing herself on the snow. Elsie thought it looked like fun, so joined in too. She even fashioned a snowball, which she lobbed at Woolly.

BIFF!

In return, the mammoth hoovered up some snow with her trunk, and sprayed it at the girl.

PFFF!

Dotty and Titch looked on from the deck of the *Victory*, like proud grandparents.

When Elsie and Woolly both began to tire, the girl decided it was time to say goodbye. She gave her friend the biggest cuddle she could.

"I'm going to miss you so much," she whispered into the mammoth's ear.

Woolly shook her head.

Whatever did the animal mean?

She reached out her trunk, and took the girl by the hand, and began tugging her along.

"Woolly wants me to go with her," Elsie called out to those on the ship. "But where?"

Chapter 69

SOME KIND OF MACHINE

"We're coming too!" exclaimed Dotty, dragging Titch by the hand.

"Do we have to? I am f-f-f-freezing!" he moaned.

"Come on!"

The lady dragged her beloved off the ship, and on to the ice.

"Wait there, please!" Dotty called back to the admiral.

"We were going to go straight back to London," replied the admiral sarcastically, "but, now you ask, we'll wait."

"Thank you kindly!" said the lady.

Woolly led her three friends across the ice. Soon they had lost sight of the *Victory*.

"We'll have to try and remember which way we came," remarked Titch.

"Yes. Turn left at the mound of snow," replied Dotty unhelpfully.

Underneath the ice, there was the sound of something whirring.

RURRR!

It stopped Woolly in her tracks.

"HOOO!" she cried softly, clearly spooked.

"What's that?" said Elsie.

"What's what?" asked Dotty.

"That sound," replied the girl. She put her ear down to the ice.

"Maybe it's a killer whale," suggested Titch.

Woolly shook her head.

"No," replied the girl. "This is some kind of machine."

All four stood still and silent.

Suddenly, there was the deafening noise of something grinding through the ice.

DRERRRRR!

Ahead of them a metal nose burst out.

SMASH!

"HOOOO!" screamed Woolly.

"What's *that*?" gasped Elsie.

"It's one of them submarines," replied Titch.

"What's it doing here?" asked Elsie.

"And who's going to sweep up all the ice?" remarked Dotty.

The underwater craft forced its way up to the surface, and bobbed on the sea for a moment.

"Shall we make a run for it?" suggested Elsie.

"No. Let's stand our ground," replied Titch.

"My hero," said Dotty.

A hatch opened on top of the submarine, and a pith helmet emerged, followed by a gnarled face, which seemed to have been burned in an explosion.

"Well, well, well. Fancy meeting you here," snarled the lady.

It was Lady Buckshot. She was chomping on a cigar and wielding a shotgun.

"HOO!" cried Woolly.

"Yes, how peculiar!" replied Dotty.

"Maybe we should have made a run for it," said Titch.

"Thought you could kill me off, did you?" called out the big-game hunter, as she stepped down from her submarine on to the ice. "Thought your little stunt with Tower Bridge was clever, did you?"

"Mmm," mused Dotty. "Probably not saying the right thing here, but yes, I did, actually."

"SILENCE!"

"You asked the question!"

"It was a rhetorical question!"

"What's that?"

"You don't know what a rhetorical question is?"

"No."

"SILENCE! That was also a rhetorical question!"

"We're going round in circles now."

"Right, I'll shoot you first!"

Elsie stepped in front of Dotty.

"Never," said the girl.

Titch stepped in front of Elsie.

"NEVER!" he said.

Then Woolly swept them both aside with her trunk.

"HOOO!" she hooted at the hunter.

"I'll just stay here at the back if that's all right with everyone," announced Dotty.

"Oh, for goodness' sake!" thundered Buckshot, spitting out her cigar and pointing her shotgun at each of them in turn. "I WILL KILL YOU ALL!"

· ⥲ ✳ ⥶ ·

Chapter 70

———◆———

BEHIND YOU!

Buckshot cocked her shotgun.

CLICK!

"Don't you fools see how good all your heads would look on my wall?" she called out.

"I rather like my head attached to my body," Elsie called back. "And so does Woolly!"

"HOO!" The mammoth nodded in agreement.

"Woolly?" mocked Buckshot. "The monster has a name!"

"She's not a monster; she's a manmoth," said Dotty.

"A what?" asked Buckshot.

"A MANMOTH! ARE YOU DEAF?"

"It'll take too long to explain," said Elsie.

"Fine. I don't have the time anyway. Prepare to die…"

Titch put his hand up in the air. "Excuse me, lady?"

"What now?"

"There's a polar bear behind you," he lied.

"No, there isn't," said Dotty.

"Shut up!" he hissed.

"Yes, there is!" Elsie continued the lie. "A really big one."

"I'm not falling for that old chestnut!" thundered Buckshot.

"HOO!" hooted Woolly, pointing with her trunk at the spot where this imaginary bear might be.

"Oh, I get it," said Dotty. "There's a really big brown bear…"

"White bear!" hissed Titch.

"…white bear behind you!"

"It would look great on your wall," added Elsie. Behind her, she could sense the mammoth was straining.

"What are you doing, Woolly?" whispered Elsie.

The mammoth had shut her eyes tight in concentration.

Finally, it came.

A bottom burp.

GGGGGGGRRRRRUUUUURRRRR!

A bottom burp that sounded exactly like the growl of a bear.

The noise made Buckshot turn round and look.

It gave the gang of four just enough time to rush at her. Titch rugby-tackled her, and she fell to the ice.

THUMP!

"ARGH!"

Dotty sat on her, so she was trapped.

"GET ORFF ME, YOU PEASANT!"

Next, Elsie snatched the shotgun from her, and threw it as far away as she could, so that it landed in deep snow.

"GIVE ME THAT BACK!"

Last, Woolly lolloped forward, and with her trunk grabbed the lady by her ankle.

"WHAT ARE YOU DOING, YOU BEAST?"

Guessing what was to come, Elsie helped Dotty off Buckshot.

Then Woolly dangled her would-be killer in the air.

"HELP!" she cried.

"Not on your nelly!" said Dotty.

The mammoth lifted the hunter high in the air and began swinging her in circles.

"AAARRRGGGHHH!!!"

yelled Buckshot.

The circles became faster and faster.

WHIRR!

Soon Buckshot became nothing more than a blur.

"AAAAARRRRGGGGGHHHHH!!!!!"

"Now let go!" said Elsie.

The mammoth did what she was told.

"NNNNNNNOOOOOOOOOO!"

cried Buckshot as she spun through the air like a boomerang. W H I Z Z !

Unlike a boomerang, she didn't come back.

Buckshot flew across the Arctic, before landing far out of sight with a THUD!

"Thank you, manmoth," said Dotty. "That woman was beginning to get on my nerves."

Chapter 71

◆

SMOTHERING
to DEATH

Woolly led the three humans for many more miles across the ice. North. North. North. As night fell, the entire sky lit up red and green and purple.

"Wow! This is beautiful!" said Elsie as she stopped still and looked up in wonder.

"The Northern Lights, they're called," replied Titch. "You can only see them if you travel really far north."

"Well, I went to Yorkshire to visit my aunt Maud and I never saw 'em," said Dotty.

Titch shook his head. "I mean *really* far north."

"As far as I'm concerned, Yorkshire *is* really far north. It took me hours on the train. Now, where's the manmoth taking us?"

"North!" replied Elsie. "North, north, north!"

"Are there going to be any shops?" asked Dotty.

"I don't think so," said Titch.

"I don't need nothing fancy, just a cup of tea, some sandwiches or cakes."

"No. Just more ice."

"Shame!" Dotty said. "I'm getting rather peckish."

They climbed to the top of a tall snowdrift and looked down into a valley.

"How much longer?" moaned Dotty.

"HOOO!" hooted Woolly. She pointed ahead with her trunk, before galloping down the drift.

"Something tells me we're nearly there!" replied the girl as she chased after her friend.

"HOOO!"

"Hoooo!" joined in Elsie.

"Nearly where?" asked Dotty.

"I don't know," replied Titch. He took her hand and led her down the drift.

Ahead, Elsie could see something was sticking out of the snow. On closer inspection, she realised it was a flag. A British flag. Next to it were a series of pegs, marking out a large rectangular shape in the ice. It looked almost like a grave.

"This must be where they found Woolly!" exclaimed Elsie.

"HOOO!" hooted the mammoth, miming digging with her foot.

"Why the blazes has the manmoth brought us all the way here?" grumbled Dotty.

"There must be a reason, Dotty. Trust me," replied the girl.

As if on cue, the coloured lights that were shooting across the sky descended to the ground. The wind

whipped up the snow, and soon it swirled all around them. The four were in the centre of a spiralling snowstorm. It soon became impossible for Elsie, Dotty and Titch to keep their eyes open, and they could hardly breathe. All they could do was huddle close to the mammoth in fear.

"This is the end, Dotty!" spluttered Titch as snow swirled into his mouth. "I need to tell you that I…"

"Tell me what?" asked the lady.

"If you would just let me finish!"

"Woolly wouldn't have brought us all out here to die!" shouted Elsie. "There must be a good reason."

The mammoth wrapped her trunk round the girl.

"HOO!" she cried.

"Hold me close," said Elsie. "Please."

This felt like the end.

The storm moved in. The blizzard was smothering them. They could no longer see, or feel, or hear.

Elsie just managed to prise her eyes open for a moment.

Huge shapes were appearing out of the snowstorm.

"LOOK!" cried Elsie.

They were not alone.

Chapter 72

A PERFECT CIRCLE

A dozen figures were emerging from the storm, as tall and wide as ships.

Dotty and Titch struggled to open their eyes. When they did, the most magical sight greeted them.

A herd of mammoths.

"I wouldn't want to have to clean up after all that lot," mused Dotty.

"Is this real?" asked Titch.

"I don't know," replied Elsie. **"But it's beautiful!"**

"HOO!" cried Woolly.

As if by magic, the snowstorm moved outwards from where the gang of four were huddled. They found themselves standing in a perfect circle of calm as a wall of swirling snow surrounded them.

Slowly, Woolly broke away from the humans, and approached the herd. One of the mammoths stepped

forward and reached out its trunk. Woolly did the same, and the two trunks curled round each other in the most loving way.

All the other mammoths lifted up their trunks and let out a chorus of **HOOs.**

HOO! HOO! HOO!

HOO! HOO! HOO!

HOO! HOO!

HOO! HOO! HOO!

HOO! HOO!

HOO! HOO!

Teardrops ran down Elsie's face. They were happy tears. They were sad tears. Happy because she knew her friend was finally home. Sad because she knew this was goodbye.

Woolly turned round, and with her trunk beckoned Elsie over.

"HOO!"

The girl took a deep breath, and paced through the deep snow. Woolly wrapped her trunk round her friend, and pushed her close to the much bigger mammoth in front of them. Elsie was scared at first, but the giant mammoth wrapped her trunk lovingly round the girl. The three of them embraced. Immediately, the girl knew exactly who this was.

"Woolly. It's so great to finally meet your ma," said Elsie, choking back tears.

Both animals nodded their heads, and let out tender sighs.

"HOO!" sounded the largest animal behind them. It was time to go. The herd turned to leave.

The mother mammoth gently pushed her offspring towards the girl. There was just time for one last embrace. Elsie buried her head in her friend's fur, and wrapped her arms round her. In return, Woolly licked the girl's face with her rough tongue. It was a sweet, if slobbery, kiss.

Elsie whispered into the mammoth's ear, "I love you, Woolly. I'm never going to forget you. You won't ever forget me, will you?"

"**HOO!**" Woolly sighed.

"Hoo!" replied Elsie.

The girl reached out her hand and stroked Woolly's fur as the animal started to move away. This was the very last touch. Elsie watched as one by one the herd faded into the wall of snow. Woolly looked back one last time, and waved with her trunk, and then she too disappeared.

Tears rolled down Elsie's face again, as Dotty and Titch put their arms round the girl and held her tight. The storm passed as quickly as it had appeared, leaving the three alone on the Arctic wasteland.

· ⤙ ✳ ⤚ ·

PART IV

HOME

Chapter 73

HEADLINES
ACROSS THE WORLD

If the long sail back to London was sombre, the journey up the Thames was anything but. All of London turned out to watch HMS *Victory*, which had seen off the entire British naval fleet, make its way along the river. The news of the mammoth's adventures had made headlines all across the world.

ORPHAN GIRL
BRINGS
MAMMOTH
BACK TO
LIFE!

MONSTER
ON THE
LOOSE!

GANG'S
DARING
ESCAPE
FROM LONDON

The London Chronicle
HMS VICTORY
STOLEN!

The Evening Standard

CHELSEA PENSIONERS
BREAK OUT
OF ROYAL
HOSPITAL

Folk lined the banks to wave and cheer, and this lifted Elsie's mood a little. During the long voyage, the girl missed her friend terribly. She had grown accustomed to the mammoth's smell and sound and touch. She yearned for her trunk to be wrapped round her again. It was like a part of her was missing.

A month or more had gone by since they'd left London. The ice over the Thames had melted away, and HMS *Victory* made fast progress towards the centre of London.

Despite seeing the obvious delight of the crowds, all on board were nervous as the ship came into dock. A pack of policemen, led by Commissioner Barker, of course, were waiting on the riverbank for them.

"Don't you worry, officers. We only, ahem, borrowed the *Victory*. Took her for a quick spin," the admiral called over.

Barker's face soured. His lip quivered in barely disguised rage, causing his tiny moustache to twitch.

"Our orders are to take you straight to Buckingham Palace," he announced. "Her Majesty the Queen wants a word with you!"

The pensioners all gulped. By the sound of it, they were all in deep,

deep

trouble.

. ➤ ✳ ➤ .

Chapter 74

A FLEET OF CARRIAGES

A fleet of horse-drawn carriages raced across London to Buckingham Palace. Elsie sat between Dotty and Titch in the first one. Both grown-ups looked sick with nerves.

Dotty pulled out a handkerchief and spat on it. "Elsie, I just need to give you a quick wash." She then proceeded to furiously polish the girl's face.

"GET OFF ME!" yelled Elsie.

"You're meeting the Queen! When was the last time you had a bath?"

"A what?"

"That's what I thought!"

The fleet of carriages passed through the tall iron gates into the grounds of Buckingham Palace. Elsie, Dotty and Titch all pressed their faces up against the window to get a better look.

"WOW!" exclaimed the girl.

"It's magnificent," added Titch.

"It could be fit for royalty," remarked Dotty.

"It is fit for royalty!" said Titch. "The royals live here."

"They must have come from a very rich family," observed the lady.

The carriage stopped outside the entrance to the palace itself. A footman opened the carriage door, and the three stepped out on to the red carpet. All the old soldiers put on their tricorne hats and white gloves,

and straightened their scarlet coats. They formed a neat line, and marched into Buckingham Palace.

Elsie's eyes were dazzled by the riches. Never in her wildest dreams could she have believed anyone lived like this. Gold and marble and velvet spread across every space. Oil paintings, sculptures and ornaments lined the hallways. She wanted to stop and marvel at every last one, but there wasn't time. Her Majesty the Queen was waiting.

"Needs a good dust," remarked Dotty. "I've counted three cobwebs."

"**Shush!**" shushed Titch.

Eventually, a tall pair of wooden doors was opened by the Queen's attendant Abdul.

"Her Majesty has been expecting you," he announced.

At the far end of the room was a little old lady, sitting alone on a chair with a blanket over her knees. Her skin was as white as snow, her dress was black, and her white hair crouched on top of her head in a tidy bun.

It was ᴼQueen Victoria. Unsmiling, she looked Elsie straight in the eye.

"So, you must be the urchin who stole my mammoth?"

Chapter 75

◆

AN AUDIENCE
WITH THE QUEEN

For the first time in her life Elsie was too shy to speak, so she just nodded.

"It weren't just her that stole the manmoth!" said Dotty. "I done it an' all."

"Don't forget your manners," hissed the admiral. "It's 'I done it and all, ma'am'. 'Ma'am' not 'Marm'. It rhymes with 'ham' or 'jam'."

"I done it an' all, ham," said Dotty.

Titch shook his head in despair.

"And what gave you the right to break into my **NATURAL HISTORY MUSEUM**, bring a long-extinct prehistoric animal back to life and then set it free?"

Elsie looked down at her feet.

"Well?" pressed the Queen.

"I don't know, ma'am," she replied.

"Well, you must have some sort of idea!"

The girl looked over to Dotty and Titch, who gave her nods of encouragement.

"Well, I, erm, I suppose…"

"Spit it out, child."

"Well, I, erm, I looked at Woolly…"

"I beg your pardon, who is Woolly?"

"Oh, that's the name I gave the mammoth, ma'am."

Queen Victoria gestured for the girl to continue. "Do carry on!"

"You see, Your Majesty, everyone was calling the mammoth a monster. But I looked on Woolly as a friend."

"A *friend*?" asked the Queen, incredulous.

"Yes. A friend, and like me she seemed lost without her mother and father. So I wanted to help her. Help her find her way home."

The Queen listened and nodded her head. "Looking at you, child, I take it you are an orphan?"

"Yes, ma'am," replied the girl. "I was left on the steps of an orphanage when I was a baby. I never knew me ma or pa."

The Queen leaned in. "Do you know if they're out there somewhere?"

"No, ma'am. I don't know if they're alive or dead."

This hit Queen Victoria like a thunderbolt. She was overcome with emotion. Her eyes closed, and she struggled for breath.

"Are you all right, Your Majesty?" asked Elsie. The little girl broke strict royal protocol and stepped forward to hold the old lady's hand.

Queen Victoria looked down at the grubby little hand holding hers. This simple act of kindness made a tear well in the old lady's eye.

"Here. Use my sleeve," said Elsie, offering up her arm to wipe the lady's face. This made the Queen smile.

"You, child, are a very special young lady," said Queen Victoria.

The little girl was rather taken aback. No one had ever told her that before.

Queen Victoria opened her arms, and folded Elsie into them. For a moment, these two people, separated by oceans of age, class and wealth, held each other tight.

It felt like all the world stopped.

"Thank you, child," said Queen Victoria. "I needed that."

"We both did."

"It's been so long since anyone has given this old lady a jolly good hug. Being the Queen, no one ever gives you one."

"Any time, Your Majesty."

The pair broke away from each other.

"Well…" began the Queen. "The whole world has been following this story in the newspapers. Myself included. Little did I know what was behind this extraordinary adventure. A deep and special friendship between an orphan girl and an innocent creature who just needed to find her way home."

Elsie nodded. "That's right, Your Majesty."

"This story has moved me. Not least because of all

your incredible bravery. So I declare that some prize-giving is in order. Munshi!"

"Yes, Your Majesty?" replied Abdul.

"Be a dear and bring me my box of medals…"

Chapter 76

◆

THE BRAVEST

The Chelsea Pensioners all stood proudly to attention.

"Now, I have something here for all of you," began the Queen, opening the shiny wooden box. "For my brave soldiers."

"And sailor!" prompted the admiral.

"Oh, and sailor. My apologies, Captain."

"Admiral!" corrected the old man grandly.

"Well, I asked my commander-in-chief to look into all of you. And I was told *you* never rose above the rank of captain."

The old soldiers all stared at him.

"Well, I, erm…" the man spluttered. "I think there was some sort of mix-up, Your Majesty."

"Really?" asked the brigadier. "I'm the confused one, not you!"

"Yes. I think when I was asked to leave the old sailors' home, and arrived at the Royal Hospital, all the old soldiers just started calling me 'Admiral'. Heaven knows why!"

There were murmurs of…

"You told us to call you that!"

"Big fat liar."

"I would love to stick that leg of yours where the sun don't shine!"

"Shark should have swallowed you whole!"

"Does this pub serve any food?"

"Did they, indeed?" The Queen was not convinced. "Well, Captain, approach and collect your medal."

Nervously, the man limped over to the Queen. DUFF! DUFF! DUFF!

As he saluted, Queen Victoria pinned the medal to his chest. "As head of the British armed forces, I hereby promote you to the rank of admiral, retired."

The newly appointed admiral turned round and looked at the others smugly.

"Thank you, Your Majesty."

"Now get back to your place before I change my mind."

"Yes, of course, Your Majesty," he replied, limping as fast as his leg would carry him.

DUFF! DUFF! DUFF! DUFF! DUFF! DUFF!

One by one, she called all the old soldiers up, and pinned medals to their chests. Finally, it was Titch's turn. The soldier with just one lonely medal. The medal every soldier receives for service.

"Well, Private Thomas," began the Queen, "I have learned that your time in the military has not been distinguished. Despite serving in my army for over fifty years, you never rose beyond the rank of private. Somehow, despite being in some of the greatest battles in history, you've failed to fire even a single shot."

"I don't like loud bangs, Your Majesty."

"Over the years, Private Thomas, you have been mocked for your stature, but this extraordinary adventure has shown that you are a giant among men.

Do you know what this is?" she asked, dangling a cross-shaped medal.

Titch's eyes lit up. "Of course, ma'am. That is the highest honour a soldier can receive. The Victoria Cross."

"I rarely give these out. They only go to the bravest of soldiers. The Victoria Cross goes to you, Private 'Titch' Thomas, and you shall henceforth be known as Private 'Towering' Thomas."

The Queen bent down to pin the Victoria Cross to his chest. Titch looked at it, his eyes welling with tears.

"Thank you, Your Majesty."

As he turned round to face his comrades, they gave him an almighty "HURRAH!".

"This just proves, if ever there were any doubt, that heroes come in all shapes and sizes," said the Queen.

Private Thomas smiled proudly.

Then the Queen turned her attention to Elsie and Dotty. "Of course, heroism isn't something reserved for men only. Look at some of the great heroes of my reign. So many of them are women. Florence Nightingale,* Elizabeth Garrett Anderson** or Millicent Fawcett*** to name but a few. So I would like to award medals to you both as well. Dotty?"

The lady didn't move.

"DOTTY!"

"Me?" asked Dotty.

"Yes, you are called Dotty, aren't you?"

"Yes."

"Well, approach me, then, please."

"Now?"

"Yes. Now."

The lady curtsied with every step she took.

"Get a move on!" ordered the Queen.

"Apologies, jam."

Queen Victoria rolled her eyes, and went to pin the medal to Dotty's chest.

---

* *The founder of modern nursing, known as the Lady of the Lamp, who tended to wounded soldiers.*
** *The first woman to gain a licence to practise medicine.*
*** *She led the suffragist movement that campaigned for women's right to vote.*

"Let me help, Your Queen the Majesty," she said. All fingers and thumbs because of nerves, Dotty managed to stab herself with the pin.

"OW!"

"Are you all right?" asked the Queen.

"Yes. I'm fine. OUCH!"

"Are you sure?"

"I've just stabbed meself. But I'm fine. Really. I'm fine. OWEEE!"

Dotty then retreated, curtsying again with every step.

"Now, last but not least, Elsie!" said the Queen.

The girl curtsied respectfully, and she once again approached the old lady.

"Elsie, you have been the bravest of all. Living on the streets of London is brave enough, but you have been the driving force behind this extraordinary adventure. You did all this, not for yourself, not for personal gain, but to help, in your words, 'a friend'.

Elsie, you have shown uncommon valour."

Queen Victoria reached into her box for the final medal.

Then the girl spoke up.

"I'm sorry. I don't want to be rude and that. But I don't want a medal, ma'am."

A gasp echoed around the room.

Chapter 77

NEVER FORGET

"You don't want a medal?" spluttered the Queen. "Everyone, but everyone, likes medals."

"All I want is for you to help orphans like me," replied Elsie.

The Queen thought for a moment. "Well, after all that's happened, I can hardly hurl you back out on to the streets of London, can I?"

Then a smile spread across the old lady's face. "All right. Young Elsie, why don't you come and live with me here at Buckingham Palace? You can keep me company in my old age."

"A splendid idea, Your Majesty!" remarked Abdul.

All eyes turned to the girl.

"I've got twenty-five friends," she replied.

"TWENTY-FIVE?" spluttered the Queen.

"Yes, they're all from the same orphanage as me. When I ran away, I promised I'd never forget them. And I haven't."

"What is the name of this orphanage?"

"**WORMLY HALL**: Home for Unwanted Children."

"Sounds frightful!"

"It is."

"And you ran away, Elsie?"

"I had to, Your Majesty. The lady who ran it used to beat me black and blue. I had to get out, or she would have killed me."

The Queen took a deep breath. She could barely believe what she was hearing, but she knew this girl was sincere.

"What is the name of this 'lady', if indeed the creature can be called that?"

"Mrs Curdle, Your Majesty."

"Hm. Munshi?"

"Yes, Your Majesty?" replied Abdul.

"Have this Mrs Curdle locked up in the Tower of London."

"With great pleasure, ma'am."

A huge smile spread over Elsie's face. This story did have a happy ending after all.

"Sometimes it's wonderful being Queen!" said the Queen. "And, Munshi?"

"Yes, Your Majesty?"

"Send a fleet of my carriages to collect those poor orphans, and bring them here to Buckingham Palace."

"All twenty-five of them, ma'am?"

The Queen gulped. "Yes. All twenty-five of them. We have the room!"

"At once, Your Majesty." With that, Abdul bowed and left.

"Of course, child, tonight is a very special night…" began the Queen.

"Is it?" asked Elsie. After being at sea for weeks, the girl had completely lost track of the date.

"Yes, my child. It's New Year's Eve. At midnight,

we welcome in a new century, as the year becomes 1900. Perhaps you and your twenty-five friends would like to join me for a midnight feast as we watch the fireworks?"

"Yes, please, Your Majesty."

"Splendid. I'll have my team of cooks lay on the feast!"

"I can't wait to see them all again, and tell them this incredible tale."

"I'm sure they've missed you, young lady."

Elsie smiled and turned to look at Dotty, before addressing the Queen again.

"Your Majesty?"

"Yes, Elsie?"

"Please can my friend Dotty come to the party tonight too? She's really looked after me. She has been like a grandma, actually. I would love to see in the new century with her."

The Queen took a deep breath. "Yes, all right. Dotty, you can come too, but please refrain from calling me 'ham'!"

"Ooh, thank you, jam!" replied the lady. "OOPS!"

Private Thomas was trying to catch Dotty's eye, to no avail. When that didn't work, he gave her a sharp poke with his elbow.

"What do you want? I'm talking to Queen Majesty herself, the ruler of everybody and everything!"

"Well, shouldn't the love of your life come too?"

"Who's that?"

"ME!"

"I'll ask," replied Dotty. She put her hand in the air. "Victoria the Majesty?"

"Yes?" replied the Queen uncertainly.

"Please could Towering Thomas come to the party?" she asked proudly.

"I won't take up too much space. You'll barely know I am there, Your Majesty," added the man.

Queen Victoria sighed loudly. "Well, I suppose there's always room for one more," she said.

"THANK YOU, MA'AM!" he replied.

Just then, the admiral popped his hand in the air.

"YES?" asked the Queen.

"Ma'am, if I could be so bold, I have been an extremely close friend of Private Thomas's for many a year…"

"No, you haven't!" he corrected.

"SHUT UP!" hissed the admiral. "And I would miss him terribly if I couldn't share this momentous night with him."

The old queen sighed. "All right!"

"Should I bring my own rum?"

"I am sure we have a barrel or two."

"Splendid! But what will everyone else drink?"

"Anyone else want to come to the party?" she asked.

All the old soldiers started nodding their heads enthusiastically and murmuring in agreement.

"Oh yes."

"Is it a buffet or a sit-down thing?"

"I can't stay too late. I really need to be back at the hospital before midnight."

"Yes, yes, yes, you can all come!" exclaimed the Queen. "Now, please, everyone leave immediately before I change my mind!"

You've never seen people exit a room so quickly.

· ✳ ·

Chapter 78

NOT A DAY
GOES BY

BOOM! WHIZZ! KABOOM!

Fireworks danced in the sky over London. Those lucky enough to be on the top floor of Buckingham Palace had the best view.

The elderly Queen was hosting quite a party. There were the twenty-five **WORMLY HALL** orphans, all the Chelsea Pensioners, Abdul, Dotty and, of course, the guest of honour, Elsie.

Fittingly, a huge Victoria sponge cake was served. It was so big you could have dived into it, but it was demolished by the starving orphans in seconds.

By the fireplace, Private Thomas got down on one knee, to propose to his beloved.

"Dotty, will you marry me?"

"Where are you?" asked the lady.

"Here!"

Dotty looked down and spotted him. "Sorry, I didn't see you all the way down there."

"Dotty, will you marry me?"

"Ooh, I forgot to rinse me mops out!"

"DOTTY!" The little man was becoming irate now. *"WILL YOU MARRY ME?"*

"There's no need to shout, dear. YES!"

The pair kissed as everyone around them clapped and cheered.

"HURRAH!"

BONG! BONG! BONG! BONG! BONG!
BONG! BONG! BONG!
BONG! BONG! BONG!
BONG!

Twelve bongs from Big Ben meant it was midnight.

1899 had ended, and 1900 had begun.

Everyone crossed arms, and Queen Victoria led the singing of "Auld Lang Syne".

♪ "SHOULD AULD ACQUAINTANCE BE FORGOT,
AND NEVER BROUGHT TO MIND?
SHOULD AULD ACQUAINTANCE BE FORGOT,
AND AULD LANG SYNE?
FOR AULD LANG SYNE, MY JO,
FOR AULD LANG SYNE.
WE'LL TAK' A CUP O' KINDNESS YET,
FOR AULD LANG SYNE."

Robert Burns's words, and the mournful tune, made Elsie think about Woolly. She missed her friend terribly. As she sang, a tear rolled down her cheek, and she stole away to the far side of the room so nobody would see her. Elsie didn't want to spoil the celebration for everyone else.

Only the Queen saw that the girl was upset, and she broke away from the rest. The unlikely pair of friends found themselves alone in a corner, as fireworks illuminated them from the window.

"What's the matter, child?" asked the Queen softly as she placed her hand in Elsie's.

"The song. It just got me thinking about how much I miss Woolly."

"If truth be told, 'Auld Lang Syne' always makes me a little tearful too," replied Queen Victoria, her old eyes becoming misty. "It always makes me think of my darling husband, Prince Albert. I lost him thirty-eight years ago, but not a day goes by, not an hour, not a minute, when I don't think about him."

"It sounds like he was a very special man."

"Oh, he was, child, he was. The most perfect gentleman in all the world."

Elsie reached out her other hand to the old lady, who held it tight.

"See those fireworks, Elsie?"

"Yes, ma'am."

"That is how it felt in my heart every time my darling Albert entered the room."

PRINCE ALBERT

"That's beautiful," murmured the girl.

"It was real. In the end, we've both loved, child – and been given love in return. What more can you ask of life?"

"I suppose so," replied the girl.

"I know so. Elsie, you may look around this palace of mine, this country of mine, this empire of mine, which stretches to the four corners of the globe, and think I have everything. But believe me, child, you have nothing without love."

The Queen picked up a glass of champagne for herself, and handed a glass of lemonade to Elsie.

"To Albert," said Elsie.

"To Woolly," said the Queen.

CLINK!

The End

AFTERWORD

Learn More About Woolly Mammoths

The woolly mammoth roamed Asia, Europe and North America, and first appeared more than 400,000 years ago. They wouldn't have liked the Arctic much, because it consists entirely of ice so there is no food for them there. Even so, mammoths lived during the Ice Age and survived very harsh wintry conditions.

They were not unlike today's elephants, but with some differences – mainly their huge coat of thick, brown, woolly hair that kept them warm in the cold. They had two long pointy tusks, which they used to fend off hunters and predators. They also used their tusks to dig through the snowy ground as they searched for food and water.

Scientists believe woolly mammoths died out due to humans hunting them, or because of climate change at the end of the Ice Age, or both. The last known mammoths lived on Wrangel Island in the Arctic Ocean, around the same time that the Great Pyramid of Giza was built in Egypt about 4,000 years ago.

1. Woolly mammoths grew up to three metres tall, which is the height of two people standing on top of each other.

2. A fully grown male mammoth weighed around six tonnes. This is the weight of five Mini cars!

3. Their tusks could grow up to four metres long.

4. They were herbivores, which means they didn't eat meat. Their diet consisted of leaves, moss, berries, grass and twigs.

5. Woolly mammoths lived and travelled in large female-led family groups. This is also true of their relative, the modern elephant.

6. The average lifespan of a woolly mammoth is thought to be sixty years.

7. The best way to determine the age at which a mammoth died is by looking at its tusks. Age is shown by the number of rings on a cross-section of the tusk, but the early years wouldn't be accounted for, however, as these would show on the tip of the tusk, which usually wore away.

8. The tail and ears of woolly mammoths were actually quite small. This was to prevent heat loss from their bodies, and also stopped them from getting frostbite.

9. The first fully documented remains of a complete woolly mammoth skeleton were discovered in 1799 by a Siberian hunter, and were brought to a museum in Russia in 1806. Wilhelm Gottlieb Tilesius, using the skeleton of an Indian elephant as a guide, successfully reconstructed the mammoth except for one mistake – he put each tusk in the wrong socket, so that they turned outwards instead of inwards.

10. The youngest person to discover a woolly mammoth was an eleven-year-old Russian boy, Yevgeny Salinder. He came across the remains while out for a walk near his home in 2012. The mammoth was named "Zhenya" after Yevgeny's own nickname, but its official name is the "Sopkarginsky mammoth".

NOTES ON THE REAL VICTORIAN WORLD

The Ice Monster is a story imagined by David Walliams so some of the extraordinary things you have just enjoyed reading might never have happened in real life. But the author has set his story in 1899 so you might be interested in learning some more facts about the real Victorian London!

THE NATURAL HISTORY MUSEUM

The Natural History Museum took seven years to build – and eventually opened in 1881. In 1899, when *The Ice Monster* is set, its official name was the British Museum (Natural History) although it was commonly known as the Natural History Museum. When the museum first opened its doors, you could find animal and human skeletons there, as well as collections of minerals and dried plants originally belonging to a scientist called Sir Hans Sloane. Sloane was also famous for having invented hot chocolate. The famous replica of the *Diplodocus* skeleton – or Dippy as you might know it – wasn't actually donated to the Natural History Museum until 1905! There were no life-sized models of whales on display in 1899, though there was a blue whale skeleton, and dioramas were later painted on to curved backgrounds.

THE ROYAL HOSPITAL CHELSEA

The Royal Hospital Chelsea is a retirement and nursing home for about 300 veterans of the British Army. It was founded in 1682 at a site by the Thames in Chelsea by King Charles II as a retreat for those who had served in the British Army. For special occasions and ceremonies, the residents, known as Chelsea Pensioners, wear distinctive scarlet coats and tricorne hats.

TANKS

The mammoth is cleverly disguised as a tank by Elsie and Dotty. In fact, tanks were actually not invented until 1915 and were first used in 1916 on the Western Front during the First World War.

THE ZEPPELIN

Zeppelins were a type of airship named after Count Ferdinand von Zeppelin, who came up with the idea in 1874. They had a fabric-covered, cigar-shaped rigid metal frame filled with bags of hydrogen gas and a cabin, called a gondola, hanging underneath. The first prototype flight did not, in fact, happen until 1900 in Germany, and it was only in 1910 that airships were flown commercially.

HMS *VICTORY*

HMS *Victory* was launched in 1765 and served in the American War of Independence and the French Revolutionary War. She is perhaps best known for her role as Lord Nelson's flagship at the Battle of Trafalgar in 1805. In 1899, when the story of *The Ice Monster* is set, HMS *Victory* was actually docked at Portsmouth, where she remains today.

HMS *ARGONAUT*

HMS *Argonaut* was an armoured cruiser in the British Royal Navy. Launched in 1898, she was commissioned for service in China in 1900. During the First World War, she was used as a hospital ship. She was sold and broken up in 1920.

Queen Victoria

Victoria became queen when she was just eighteen years old on 20 June 1837 and reigned for sixty-four years until she died in January 1901 at the age of eighty-one. At the time, this was the longest reign of any British queen or king. Victoria married Prince Albert of Saxe-Coburg and Gotha in 1840, and when he died she missed him very much and felt so sad that she rarely went out in public.

Abdul Karim

Queen Victoria was also the Empress of India. She asked that two Indian people be chosen to help prepare for celebrations of her Golden Jubilee, and in 1887 Mohammed Abdul Karim arrived at Windsor Castle. He taught Queen Victoria the Urdu language and became the first Indian clerk to attend to her personally.

London Weather

Although the winter of 1899 was snowy, the River Thames did not freeze over. In fact, it had not actually frozen over since 1814, and since then has only frozen once, partially, in the winter of 1963.